Also by Pamela Belle in Pan Books

THE SILVER CITY

Pamela Belle lives in Wiltshire with her husband, Steve, and two sons, Hugh and Patrick. She is the author of eight historical novels including *Wintercombe*, *Herald of Joy*, *A Falling Star* and *Treason's Gift*. *The Wolf Within* is the second part of a fantasy trilogy begun with *The Silver City*.

THE
WOLF
WITHIN

PAMELA BELLE

PAN BOOKS

First published 1995 by Pan Books

This edition published 1996 by Pan Books
an imprint of Macmillan General Books
25 Eccleston Place, London SW1W 9NF
and Basingstoke

Associated companies throughout the world

ISBN 0 330 34788 8

1 3 5 7 9 8 6 4 2

A CIP catalogue record for this book is available from
the British Library

Phototypeset by Intype London Ltd
Printed and bound in Great Britain

For Steve

PART ONE

ZITHIRIAN

CHAPTER
ONE

'They're coming!'

'There they are, see? At the edge of the lake!'

The voices rippled up in the still, warm evening air as the people of the citadel gathered in the courtyard, jostling for the best positions by the entrance gate. And far above them, on the ramparts of the tall central tower, a boy lurked unseen, and gazed as they did, southwards, to see his father come to Sar D'yenyi.

Beyond the gate the lake lay as flat and gleaming as a sheet of liquid silver, until it touched the rocky southern shore, a mile away. In the water's sleek surface lay the mountains reflected, the perfection of the image hardly marred by wind or wave. But there was movement where land joined lake, bright colours, banners, horses. The King of Zithirian had brought half his court, it seemed, to celebrate the imminent marriage of his favourite cousin, Kefiri, the Lady of Sar D'Yenyi.

Her voice echoed suddenly up from the tower below him. 'Bron? Bron, where are you? Your father's almost here!'

The boy glanced round. A high spired roof rose from the centre of the tower, surrounded by a narrow walkway and a waist-high, battlemented parapet. Anyone emerging from below would soon see him. And for reasons of his own, he did not want Kefiri to find him.

With a swift, agile grace he swung himself over the rampart. Just below it a decorative corbelled ledge surrounded the tower. It was dangerously narrow, but there was just enough space for an undersized thirteen-year-old to crouch. He would be safely hidden from the woman hunting him, unless she actually looked over the parapet.

He heard her running up the stairs, her voice again, more urgent this time, an exclamation of annoyance as she found the tower roof apparently empty, and then the sound of her retreating footsteps. She would be anxious to welcome her cousin the

King, as well as his General, the man whom she was to marry. Knowing Kefiri, she probably hadn't even changed into her best clothes yet.

The ledge was still warm from the sun, though it had now set behind the sharp peak of Mount Estray at the south-west edge of the lake. Bron, unaffected by the dizzying drop beneath him, hugged his bare legs and rested his chin on his knees. He was still wearing his ordinary cotton summer tunic, dyed in a costly shade of rich blue. He didn't want to see his father, or his stepmother, or anyone else from Zithirian: in particular, he didn't want to encounter General Invan. If he'd had the courage, he would have stolen a boat, or swum across the ice-cold waters to the Estray shore, or hidden in the underground chambers carved through the rock on which Sar D'yenyi was built – anything, rather than face the resolution of all the problems and questions surrounding his future.

But even if he ran away from Sar D'yenyi, he could not for ever hide from what lay within him.

On the shore, the Court was embarking. The pretty lake boats were small and brightly painted, with an eye to ward off evil on either side of each sharp prow, and rigged with curved triangular sails. They put off one by one and glided slowly and gracefully across the calm water, catching the last remnants of the south-easterly breeze that had ruffled the lake all day until an hour before sunset.

Unwillingly, Bron's gaze was drawn to the joyous spectacle. Ansaryon, King of Zithirian, visited Sar D'yenyi two or three times a year, and was always given a splendid welcome. High above the boy, as from the top of every tower, hung a ceremonial banner, hardly moving in the cooling air. It was white silk, the colour of the silver city, and embroidered with the blue Aiyan, the sky-flower, symbol of hope and promise for the future, that was the King's own personal device. Garlands of mountain flowers decorated the walls of the citadel, inside and out, and the spacious kitchen had been busy all day, roasting lambs, preparing lake-caught fish so fresh they were almost still flapping, and making ready to feast Ansaryon, his court, and the man who would soon become Lord of Sar D'yenyi on his marriage to the Lady Kefiri.

And the King's bastard son, whom everyone assumed would be looking forward eagerly to his father's arrival, had been dreading it for weeks.

Below Bron the trumpets blew, keen and rather too shrill. The sound set his teeth on edge and he winced. He loved music more than anything else, and if allowed would have spent all day, every day, practising on the Sith, the national instrument of Zithirian, which he had been learning for more than two years.

The people began to cheer with joyful enthusiasm. He tried to shut his mind away from the sound, but the welcome was much too loud to be ignored. And the worst of it was that some small, bright kernel of his heart longed to pretend that all was well, longed to leap down the winding stairs of the tower, and run to greet his father as if he wanted the future that had been chosen for him just as much as everyone else did.

Unwillingly, he looked down. The first boats had tied up at the jetty below the gate. Although his view was blocked by towers and walls and the eager surge of the crowd, he could follow his father's progress as if seeing him with his own eyes. The smile on his face; the narrow silver band of kingship around his head; the sumptuous elegance of his clothes, heavy with the exquisite embroidery for which Zithiriani craftsmen and women were famous throughout the known world. And beside him, tall and slender, wearing the tunic and trousers of her own people as she always did when away from the city, walked his barbarian Queen, her red-gold hair plaited into six intricate braids.

The Lady Kefiri stood waiting for them in the exact centre of the citadel's courtyard. It was paved in a spiral pattern of subtly coloured stones, designed to be seen to best advantage from above. She wore yellow, the colour of sunlight and of joy, and Bron knew she must be smiling. *And why shouldn't she?* he told himself, trying to squash his sullen and jealous resentment. *She's glad to see them – and Invan, of course.*

The man whose love for Kefiri, recently flowered, was the cause of this visit, the origin of Bron's troubles, the reason why he was hiding here on this ledge instead of standing at Kef's side to welcome his father, followed his King and Queen under the gateway and on to the spiral, to face his affianced bride. Invan was Ansaryon's General, and had followed him into exile when his younger brother Tsenit usurped the throne. He had returned with his master to drive Tsenit and his evil accomplices, the barbarian tribe called the Ska'i, out of Zithirian. To win the kingship, Ansaryon had defeated his younger brother in single combat: and the Ska'i, fleeing his diverse but united army, had come to a gruesome end, their camp destroyed in a furnace of witchfire and sorcery. The only survivor, out of six thousand savage barbarian warriors, had been a nine-year-old captive called Bron . . .

However much he tried to forget that terrible scene of slaughter, he still dreamed about it almost every night, and woke screaming. The flames rose up now in his mind, white and gold, flickering with a hideous, greedy yet seductive beauty. He thrust the memories back to the depths of his soul, and concentrated on Invan.

The General's sturdy reliable figure seemed even more substantial and ominous from above, when only his red-plumed ceremonial helmet and the broad expanse of his armoured shoulders were clearly visible. Kefiri's glad clear voice, granting him welcome, came strongly up to Bron's eyrie, and the boy clenched his fists. Why was he marrying Kefiri, who had once been betrothed to the traitor Tsenit, and had taken years to overcome her consequent sense of shame and betrayal, when Bron knew that the General loved Queen Halthris, and always would? And Invan could not be allowed to learn the truth about him because he hated sorcery, and thought only that his King's bastard son was here for his education.

The urge to hurt Invan was suddenly and overwhelmingly so strong that Bron's head reeled from the force of it. He felt as if he could reach out to pluck the General from the courtyard and smash his head against the mighty stones of the gate tower. Temptation surged through him, beckoning invitingly, offering a solution to his predicament. *Kill him, and you can stay at Sar D'yenyi with Kefiri for always. Stay here, and be happy, and no one need ever know about the Wolf within you.*

No! he cried in his mind to the insinuating, lupine voice. *No, no, NO!*

Why not? demanded his tempter.

Bron stared at the ledge in front of him, seeing him crouched there, the Death God, Ayak, with his bloody fangs and greedy red eyes, to whom he had been dedicated at birth.

You can do it, said the Wolf in his mind. *You can kill without even a snap of your fingers. You have done it before – why not do it now, and put an end to all your troubles?*

'NO!' Bron cried aloud, in despair. Forgetting where he was, he leapt up, intent only on flight from his tormenter. He turned to run from the voice pouring evil into his heart, and stepped out into the free air.

White faces looked up as he fell. Someone screamed. The Wolf howled as he saw his quarry escape – *Save yourself, boy, save yourself!* And, most dreadful and final of all, he knew that in a few brief seconds all the terror and the pain, the anguished nightmare of his short life would end, and he would no longer be a menace to everyone and everything he loved.

He could save himself. He had the power. But he would not, for Kefiri's sake, and his father's, and his own.

'Bron! BRON!'

Kefiri was screaming in horror and disbelief. And at the last instant he could not let himself smash into the unyielding stones. Power flooded through his clutching hands, slowing his descent, bringing him to a comparatively gentle landing on the courtyard below the tower. A jarring pain shot through his feet and ankles, but it was no worse than if he had jumped from a head-high wall. He fell to his knees, his mind reeling with the full force of the sorcery within him and buzzing and crackling around him.

There was utter silence, save only for a whimper of fear from a woman in the crowd. Several hundred faces, gaping with shock and incredulous amazement, stared at him blankly. Involuntarily, Bron glanced up at the ledge from which he had fallen. It was ten times the height of a man above the ground. And there was no Wolf crouched upon it.

'Bron – '

It was his father's voice, sharp with fear, and concern, and anger. The sound was curiously remote. He saw Ansaryon begin to run towards him, but the King's figure seemed to be blurring into a dark mist. He heard himself saying faintly, 'Sorry – I'm sorry – ' And then the mist enveloped him entirely, and brought welcome oblivion.

Ansaryon was the first to reach the small, huddled figure of his son, crumpled on the stones of the courtyard. As the wild buzz of horrified comment broke out around him, he knelt to examine the boy, hardly daring to hope that he had even survived such a terrible fall, let alone unscathed. Surely he had imagined that last moment when, a heartbeat or two from certain death, Bron's hurtling descent had slowed as abruptly as if invisible wings had taken hold of him and lowered him softly to the ground.

But there was not a mark on his son, and he was breathing strongly and regularly, although he was very pale beneath the feathery strands of fair hair. Sick with relief and also with fear,

Ansaryon sat back on his heels and brushed the cold sweat from his face.

His eldest child was alive – but he had displayed the terrifying extent of his power not only to the people of Sar D'yenyi, most of whom probably suspected something already, but also to the Court of Zithirian. Up until now they had known only that Bron was their ruler's bastard son by an unknown mother, reared here in decent obscurity with the generous consent of the Lady Kefiri. For four years, the sinister truth about him had been successfully concealed. And now, through a moment of stupidity or carelessness, Bron's dreadful gift of sorcery had been revealed in a manner so brutally dramatic that it could not possibly be hidden any longer.

Halthris knelt down beside him. Once, fearing Bron's capacity to destroy, she had offered to kill him. Now, the anxiety on her freckled face showed how her attitude to her stepson had changed. 'Oh, Ansary – is he all right?'

'I think he's only fainted,' her husband said aloud, for the benefit of all the people crowding round with varying degrees of concern, curiosity and fear. And silently he added, in the thought-linked speech they shared, *We shall have to talk about this with Kef, as soon as possible. He can't be passed off now as just an ordinary child.*

Hardly, said her dry voice in his mind. *But what can we do with him, in a city which still hates and fears all sorcerers? You excepted, of course.*

I don't know. We'll think of something, between the three of us. Ansaryon slid his hands under Bron's slight, frail body. The child's physique had never recovered from early neglect and the near starvation he had endured during the dreadful year when the Ska'i had occupied Zithirian, and he could lift his son with ease. Bron muttered something, stirred briefly in his arms, and then was still.

No one else could have heard it, but Ansaryon's face twisted fleetingly with pain and foreboding. For the boy had whispered the forbidden name of Ayak, Lord of Death, in whose honour his devotees sacrificed men, women and children. Bron had been dedicated to the Devourer by the evil priestess, D'thliss, who had bred him for his power in the same way that others bred dogs or horses, and who had cared for him, if her callous and brutal neglect could be called that, for the first nine years of his life.

The King walked through the crowd of people, sensing with his own, more limited powers their shock and fear, seeing the averted eyes, the glances full of horror and furtive curiosity, the swift gestures that traditionally warded off evil. Whatever he decided to do about Bron, one thing was starkly clear: the child's abilities could no longer be ignored.

After supper, the adults who were most concerned with Bron's future gathered in Kefiri's chamber, high in the central tower. Reluctantly, Ansaryon had invited Invan to attend the discussion, and he studied his handsome, rather heavy face with some wariness. His General's loyalty was absolute, but it had taken him some time to overcome his instinctive mistrust of sorcery. The powers that were accepted as commonplace elsewhere in the known world – particularly in the Empire of Toktel'yi, far to the south – had always been forbidden to all Zithiriani, except for the priests of Tayo, Divine Ancestor of the Royal Family. The Tayan Temple had been destroyed by the Ska'i nearly four years ago, along with every man and woman inside it, so magic was rare, these days, in the Silver City. And since the priests and priestesses of Tayo had employed their exclusive powers to spy on the people and to enforce their hated authority, most of the citizens loathed and feared the use of sorcery. They had accepted the fact that their new King was a mage with surprising ease: after all, better him than the murdering, treacherous usurper Tsenit, from whose tyranny Ansaryon had liberated Zithirian. But the apparently boundless magical gifts of his bastard son Bron, reared and nurtured by the High Priestess of Tayo, would be much harder to stomach.

What they would say, or do, if it ever became known that the small, blond, dark-eyed boy had used his powers to incinerate six thousand Ska'i warriors, Ansaryon dreaded to think.

But Invan would have to be told everything. After all, he was about to marry Kefiri, so he was almost one of the family. But Ansaryon had hoped to avoid any detailed explanation about Bron, and had already informed his General that the boy would return to Zithirian with his father after the wedding, to continue his education at Court. After all, he could hardly reveal his fear that Invan might discover what the child's true capabilities were.

Well, there was no hiding them now. But at least Invan

wouldn't have to live in close proximity to Bron. It had been one of the conditions of his marriage, that he make his home in this remote and lovely place. Kefiri had lived here almost all her life, and would not consider leaving it, despite a most tempting offer from the son and heir of King Temiltan of Minassa.

Invan, very earnest and twenty years her senior, was not the man that Ansaryon would have chosen for his favourite cousin, but he was kind, honest and reliable, and he would treat her well. And as far as Kef was concerned, he possessed one overwhelmingly attractive quality. If she married him, she wouldn't have to leave Sar D'yenyi.

'Wine?'

The lady of the citadel stood before him. She was small, hardly coming up to his shoulder, and her chief beauty lay in her mass of dark curling hair, and blue eyes. Despite her youth – she was only twenty-two – Kefiri was an energetic and efficient chatelaine, and her people loved her dearly.

So did Bron, for she had rescued him from an abyss of grief and guilt and despair that would have tested an adult's sanity, never mind a child's. And Ansaryon wished that his son could have been left in obscurity here for a little longer. If he had not saved himself from death in such a dramatic and spectacular fashion, it might have been possible. But Invan, loyal though he was, would be unlikely to tolerate the boy's disturbing presence in his new household, and it was hardly fair to force him to do so.

They all took wine, and sat down on the cushioned chairs in the centre of the semi-circular chamber. A menacing silence hung as heavily as a thundercloud. Then Kefiri, her voice resolute, said, 'We're here to talk about Bron, aren't we? Then let's talk.'

Invan's blue eyes spoke eloquently of his unease. 'What *is* he, Ansaryon? Is he really your son?'

'Yes, he is my son,' said the King of Zithirian. 'He is not a demon, nor is he a sorcerer. His powers are innate, and untrained – he was born with them.'

'But I thought – I thought it was impossible to practise sorcery without that drug.'

'Without Annatal? Yes, that was what everyone believed, certainly – but it isn't true. I took Annatal for many years, until the Ska'i captured Zithirian. If you remember, I fled here after the attack, and I had no supplies of the drug with me. I should have died – indeed, as far as I know, I am the only person ever to have survived the effects of withdrawal. And when I recovered, I found that I was still in full possession of my powers. In fact, I think they were probably enhanced. So presumably I too have a natural gift for sorcery that I did not suspect. And that gift is what Bron has inherited, although for some reason his powers are far greater than mine.'

'So I saw.' Invan's face was still deeply unhappy. 'I had no idea – was *that* why the Ska'i took him, then, four years ago? They wanted him for his sorcery?'

'They burned the Temple down and killed all the priests to get him,' Kefiri said. 'And when they murdered his foster brother, he killed them all. But even so, he's only a child, Invan – don't forget that. He's not a tool, or a vessel of evil, or a threat – he's a *child*, a thirteen-year-old child.'

'Then what in Tayo's name will he be able to do once he's grown up?'

'I don't know,' Ansaryon told him honestly. 'I haven't probed or tested his capabilities. Remember, he'd suffered a terrible ordeal, and he was deeply frightened and disturbed. For months after the end of the Ska'i, he didn't speak. If he has experienced happiness here, it is due entirely to the love and care of Kefiri. She restored him to normality, and he and I will always be in her debt.'

'But I didn't restore him to normality,' Kefiri pointed out, her small round face very serious. 'Please understand, all of you – Bron will *never* be normal, and he knows it. Oh, one part of him – the greater part at the moment – is just like any other boy. He's adventurous, impulsive, reckless, lively – even affectionate sometimes, when no one else is looking. But he carries his power like a boulder round his neck. He has bad dreams, horrible dreams, nearly every night. He daren't use his magic, for fear of harming people, because he's haunted by what he did to the Ska'i. And yet that power is the only reason for his existence – he knows that because D'thliss told him so, throughout his childhood. I suspect that he also thinks it's the reason he's being taken back to Zithirian. If I have done anything at all, I have managed to convince him that I love and cherish him for *himself*, and not for what he can do.' She stared up at her tall cousin. 'And I hope that you can do the same, or he will suffer greatly, in the years to come.'

'I hope I can.' Like hers, Ansaryon's face was bleak and sombre. 'But he must be taught how to use his powers wisely, or he's as dangerous to himself and others as an avalanche crashing down a mountainside. You do understand that, don't you, Kef? He has to learn how to control his sorcery, or in moments of great fear, or great rage, he will run amok. That is how he slew the Ska'i.'

'And that was what happened today, wasn't it?' said Halthris. 'His terror unlocked his power, so that he could save himself.'

'And if you don't think that he deserves our love, or our care, or our compassion,' Ansaryon added, with a glance at Invan's stony expression, 'take a little time to wonder why he didn't slow his descent until the last possible moment.'

There was a deep, sad silence. Kefiri bent suddenly, hiding her eyes, to brush an imaginary mark off her gown. She said, her voice strained, 'I don't want him to go. He's very dear to me.'

'I don't feel I can handle the responsibility,' Invan said heavily. He put out a hand to touch his bride's, a gesture of clumsy tenderness which made Halthris, noticing it, feel unjustly irritated. Once, before she had become Queen of Zithirian and therefore above his reach, Invan had been in love with her, and she had rejected him, well aware that the qualities that made him such a loyal and valuable general would also make him quite unsuited to marriage with a wild barbarian. And she could not, in all honesty, see that Kefiri, used to her independence, accustomed to making her own decisions, would be very happy within the inevitable restrictions of marriage to such a man.

But Kefiri seemed to want it, and she was very determined, so Halthris had swallowed her doubts and wished her well.

'The responsibility for Bron is mine,' Ansaryon said. 'I will teach him everything I know of sorcery – and when he is ready, perhaps I will bring others who are more knowledgeable than I am, to lead him where I cannot.'

'And what will the citizens say?' Invan demanded, frowning. 'You've managed to keep the boy well out of the way here – I certainly had no idea what he was. But it'll be very different in Zithirian. He'll be the object of fear, curiosity, revulsion. You can't surely be thinking of bringing him to live with you at the Palace?'

'Where else can he go?' Halthris pointed out sharply. 'He's dangerous, we know that already – but he'll be safest in his father's care. And don't forget that the Ska'i wanted him. They wiped out virtually the entire priesthood of Tayo to get him. If we can't keep his powers a secret any more, at least we can ensure that he's safe from abduction by those who would like to use him for their own ends.'

'If they can. If anyone can.' Ansaryon's voice was heavy. 'He discovered his own strength four years ago. I suspect I'll find that he has a remarkably powerful will of his own, quite apart from his other abilities. He'll need very careful handling, I think.'

'If he did destroy the Ska'i, he certainly will.' Invan paused, as if nerving himself to confront something extremely alarming. 'Could he do that again, do you think?'

'We have to make sure that he never does,' said Kefiri, her eyes brilliant with unshed tears. 'Somehow, he has to be taught, guided, led – and so carefully and gently that he does not rebel. He is terrified by what he did – he never speaks of it, except in his nightmares. And we also have to make sure that the people of Zithirian don't regard him as some kind of monster. How can you do that, Ansary?'

'By telling them the truth,' said her cousin. And as they looked at him in surprise, he added, 'They deserve no less. I am King because they wished it. And the truth will undoubtedly be less frightening than the wild stories that will be circulating in every tavern and kuldi-house in the city. When we return, I'll summon a full session of the Council, and make a formal announcement. They won't like it – they're still deeply suspicious of sorcery, which is why I've hardly used my powers since I won the throne. But they do trust me, and I hope that they will accept Bron, for my sake if not for his.'

It didn't seem very likely to Halthris, but she knew that her husband's judgement was seldom wrong. He had taken the king-ship of Zithirian on a wave of passionate popular acclaim, wel-comed as a saviour by people who had endured terrible privation during the year of the usurper Tsenit's rule, and so far their adulation had not faltered. After the dismal reign of Ansaryon's incompetent father, followed by the brutal repression of Tsenit and the Ska'i, even the most ordinarily capable monarch would have seemed a model of good government, and Ansaryon was certainly not ordinary. In four years he had overturned many antiquated, hidebound and unpopular traditions and begun a programme of much-needed reform. All the citizens of Zithirian, from craftsmen and women to the wealthiest courtier, now had a voice in government, much to the horror of those few members

of the aristocracy who had survived the Ska'i. To them, it was
unthinkable that anyone not descended from the Divine Ancestor Tayo or his original followers – the First Hundred – could be
allowed such privileges, and most had shown their displeasure at
the new order by retiring to sulk on their country estates.

But it was not their enmity that might threaten Bron. Many
young aristocrats had flirted with forbidden magic, becoming
members of the Mazath, the secret society of sorcerers, amongst
whom was Ansaryon himself. No, it was the ordinary citizens,
mistrustful of authority, hostile to the priests of Tayo and their
powers, who might turn against the boy. And since Ansaryon was
essentially king by their consent, he would have to take their
views into account. For everyone's sake, Halthris hoped that he
enjoyed enough popular good will and esteem to be able to convince them that Bron was not dangerous.

But of course he always would be, however good his training.
And none knew that better than his father, who had never forgot-
ten the horror of the slaughter that Bron had inflicted on the
Ska'i.

Below, in his half-round chamber, Bron slept with the aid of a
potion administered by the citadel's Healer. Unaware of the
voices discussing his fate, he dreamed. He dreamed of D'thliss,
High Priestess of Tayo, who had reared him in her dank lair
beneath the Temple, and instilled in him both terror and hunger
for the power he possessed. He dreamed of Lelya, her grandson
and his foster-brother, some three or four years older than he
was, who had been his only friend: a dark, sturdy, pleasant boy,
who had cherished the humble ambition to be a potter. And he
dreamed of Lelya's death under a Ska'i axe, at the brutal whim of
their chief, Quenait, and of Quenait's shaman, Br'nnayak, unimaginably old, unimaginably evil, who had wanted Bron for his
own creature, to destroy all civilization in the bloodstained name
of Ayak, the Devourer of Souls, the Wolf of Death.

And at last, as always, the Wolf himself appeared, hideous,
menacing, his snarling muzzle and huge fangs dripping scarlet, his
red eyes compelling obedience. Always, his message was the
same. *You are mine. Come to me. Do as I bid you, and I will never
call you, as I call all other mortals. Everyone comes to me in the
end – save you. If you give me the blood I crave, I will grant you*

*eternal life. You are mine already – after all, you bear my name,
and you gave me the Ska'i. Admit the truth, boy – you are mine,
mine, MINE!*

He woke with a wild scream of denial that echoed round the
stone walls of his chamber, and at once someone bent over him,
whispering comfortingly. 'All right, Bron – it's all right. Just one
of your dreams.'

She wouldn't say that if she knew what lived in them, the boy
thought despairingly. It was dark, and he could see her only as a
dim shape, outlined by the soft, familiar lamplight behind her, but
she was not the one he wanted. 'Kefiri?' he said, in a voice that, to
his shame, was almost a sob.

'Don't worry, I'll fetch her for you right away.' She turned and
hurried out.

Alone, he stared at the lamp. Its presence was meant to be
reassuring, but the shadows it cast were black and impenetrable:
outside the bowl of dim yellow light, anything could be lurking.
Easier to forget that, forget the creatures that were not born of
his imagination, if he looked intently at the steady golden flame.
But it did not banish the memory: the memory of falling, of his
acceptance of inevitable death, and the fear – or was it Ayak's
insistence? – that had forced him to save himself just in time. He
was still alive. The burden still weighed down his soul. And so did
the Wolf within his heart.

'Bron?'

Kefiri came into the room. She was still wearing the gown in
which she had greeted Invan, and the close-fitting jewelled silk
bodice, the sunshine yellow of skirt and sleeves, suited her very
well. She smelt of summer flowers, as she always did, and the
exuberance of her dark curly hair was inadequately contained by
a net cap, seeded with drops of amber and gold, pinned to the
back of her head. She was beautiful and kind, and Bron loved her
as he had loved no one else in his brief and unhappy life, not
even Lelya, his foster-brother. To Kefiri, he could confide almost
anything.

He smiled wanly up at her. 'Hallo, Kef.'

'Sevrani said you'd had another dream. Was it a bad one?'

'Not very much worse than usual.' Already, the vivid horror
of it was fading from his mind.

'Oh, Bron.' Kefiri sat down on the bed in a soft sweet rustle of
silk, and took his hand. In daylight, amongst the other boys with

whom he played and learned, he would have snatched it away, but here, alone with her in the bleak hour before midnight, there was no one to see, and her warm touch was very comforting. She smiled at him, but he sensed her sadness. Then she said quietly, 'I have been talking to your father and stepmother, about your future.'

Bron looked down at their joined hands: his, thin and brown with bitten nails and a trail of scabs across the knuckle; hers small, pale, delicate, with Invan's huge emerald and gold betrothal ring disfiguring the slenderness of her middle finger. He couldn't think of anything to say, but he swallowed miserably.

'What happened today, up on the tower?'

It wasn't the question he had expected. He glanced up, startled into the truth. 'I was hiding.'

'Hiding? From me, or from your father?'

Bron's gaze dropped again. 'From both of you.'

'Why? Because you don't want to leave Sar D'yenyi?'

Slowly, the bent fair head nodded.

Kefiri ignored the stream of awkward questions her curiosity was demanding to ask. She said gently, 'You have to leave, Bron. I don't want you to go, either. But your father wants to teach you how to understand your powers, and to use them properly and wisely.'

'I don't want to use them.' The voice, flat, sulky, was that of a much younger child.

'But sometimes you don't have any choice in the matter, do you? Like today, for instance.' She paused, and then said tentatively, 'On the tower – did you just lose your balance?'

He nodded again. She couldn't see his face, or the dark, impenetrable eyes that some people found so unnerving. Then he said, very softly, 'The Wolf was there. Outside my dreams. I saw him.'

Kefiri's free hand made the sign against evil. 'And then you fell?'

'Yes,' Bron whispered.

'It can't go on like this,' she said at last. 'You need help, and teaching. I can't do it – I've got no power, and no knowledge of sorcery. All I can give you is love, and comfort, and support. And you need more than that now, don't you see? You must learn how to defeat the Wolf, or he will destroy you.'

And everyone around you. She had not spoken the words

aloud, but she knew he had heard her thought. His face lifted, and his fingers clenched on hers. 'I do know,' he whispered. 'Oh, Kef, what can I do? Where can I go? How can I live with this?'

Weeping, she hugged him as if he were still the small half-starved child whom she had first befriended here in Sar D'yenyi, more than four years ago. Rocking him in her arms, she said fiercely, 'You have to, Bron – you have to, because you have no other choice. You can't change yourself into an ordinary child, any more than you can change the colour of your eyes, or your hair – it's *you*, part of you, always and for ever. And for your sake, you have to face up to it. I know it will be hard – very, very hard. But you can't stay here now, much as you'd like to, much as *I'd* like you to. And your father loves you, he'll be kind to you, so will Halthris, and there will be your little half-brothers too. I know it seems as though your world has ended. But there's another one, a better one, waiting for you in Zithirian.' She tried to smile at him. 'By Sundim, you'll almost have forgotten us here at Sar D'yenyi.'

'I shan't ever forget,' Bron whispered passionately. 'Never, ever, *ever*!'

And because Kefiri loved him as though he were the child she had not yet borne, she prayed silently that he would not.

CHAPTER
TWO

Bron had last seen Zithirian, the Silver City, the city of towers, when he was nine years old. Until then it had been his home. With Lelya he had run wild in the streets, barefoot, uneducated, glad of the opportunity to forget his other, secret life in the underground chambers beneath the Temple. There the High Priestess D'thliss had used his power to augment her own, and initiated him into her foul and bloody rites. That lair, with the Wolf's head set about with votive candles, the deep shadows and thick, stale, rancid air, had been destroyed when the Ska'i sacked and burned the Temple to seize him, but it still haunted his dreams.

He was very quiet as the cavalcade rode down from the mountain pass that led to Sar D'yenyi and its lake. At first they followed the course of the River D'yenn, swift and shallow, and then, once clear of the mountains, struck south to the causeway at Margayan where the Kefirinn could be crossed in safety.

They passed farms and settlements, many still ruined and abandoned after the depredations of the Ska'i, the blackened walls gradually collapsing under the subsequent onslaughts of wind and weather, a few others rebuilt and thriving. Bron remembered Kefiri telling him that the Ska'i had probably slain more than ten thousand people in the countryside. Some had died under the barbarian double axes, others, fleeing from their homes, had perished miserably in the winter mountains from cold, hunger or disease. In Zithirian, the toll was more exact: eight thousand, three hundred and forty-one men, women and children, a fifth of the city's population, had owed their deaths during that terrible year directly or indirectly to the Ska'i. Many had been soldiers, aristocrats and courtiers, or priests; not one of the men and women vowed to the worship of Tayo had survived the destruction of their Temple.

And the absence of that Temple was the first thing to strike Bron's eyes as they rode under the huge double towers of the

Sunset Gate. He remembered it all too well, the white Annako stone, the nine gilded and spired towers and the air of menacing beauty. But in its place lay a broad green mound, clothed in plants and young shrubs – the Zithiriani were famous for their love of gardens. A flight of curved steps swept gracefully up to a low, circular building, with a wide entrance arch facing the tree-lined avenue of Sunset Street.

Halthris, riding beside him, smiled. 'Of course, you won't have seen the new Council Hall. Your father had the remains of the Temple razed, and built it on top of the rubble. There have been a lot of other changes here, in the last few years. The Palace, for instance, has been altered completely.'

'I never went inside the Palace,' Bron said, rather stiffly. He liked Halthris, who was down-to-earth and blisteringly honest, for he knew that she possessed a sensitive heart that mixed strangely with her barbarian pragmatism. And he knew, too, although he had never been told, that once she had wanted to kill him, to end the threat he posed both to his father and to the people of Zithirian.

But she had changed her mind a long time ago, and although he would never love her as he loved Kefiri, he was usually at ease in her company. Now, however, entering the city that he had never wanted to see again, he couldn't forget what lay before him in the next few days, and months, and years.

Cheering people crowded Sunset Street, clustering between the slender young trees growing in stone tubs, which had replaced those dead from the effects of winter and neglect during the Time of the Usurper, four years ago. Behind them, the handsome stone buildings housed a variety of respectable inns and taverns. There were kuldi-houses too, selling the hot aromatic beverage of that name, which had once been notorious centres of gossip, subversion and political dissent. But there was no malice now in these smiling faces welcoming Ansaryon and his Queen back to their city. With apprehension, Bron wondered whether they would look quite so happy when they learned the truth about their King's eldest son.

Halthris glanced at his pale, set face and felt a surge of sympathy. It would not be easy for any boy to cope with this situation: how much worse must it be for a child so conscious of the burden he carried, and the threat he posed? For there would be many citizens who would immediately assume that he was dangerous.

And she wondered if he knew the truth about his parentage, a secret so dark and terrible that Ansaryon had only ever divulged it to one person: the barbarian woman who was his Queen.

She suspected that Bron was aware of it, for his powers were such that he seemed to absorb information without being told, as a dry towel soaks up water. And once more Halthris contemplated the contradictions within her stepson, for he seemed to be two people at the same time: the child who was in some ways rather young for his age, who was afraid of the dark, who craved love and reassurance; and the sorcerer, master of powers so immense and awesome that even Ansaryon, himself a trained and skilful mage, had no real idea of the full extent of the boy's capabilities.

And he was determined to reveal all this to the Council tomorrow. After that, the whole of Bron's life, every gesture, every word, every look, would be watched by all those around him, terrified that in a moment of childish rage or fear he would destroy Zithirian as he had destroyed the Ska'i.

The Council would want reassurances, and Halthris knew that Ansaryon could not possibly give them: for Bron, untrained and confused, was hardly in a position to control his powers. She had tried to persuade her husband that such a public announcement about Bron was not in the child's best interests, nor his own. He had smiled, and reminded her that for a Tanathi, famously honest, to advocate deception was, to say the least, a little inconsistent.

'It wouldn't be a deception,' Halthris had pointed out. 'You would still be telling the truth – that he is your son, and that you are training him to be a Mazath. You just wouldn't happen to mention how much power he already has.'

'Hard not to, when half the Court and the Council saw him fall from the tower at Sar D'yenyi, and survive unscathed. Hal, I can't keep this a secret, because it isn't a secret any longer. Better the truth now, whatever the cost, than lies and rumours later. Because he is not a danger to Zithirian and never will be.'

She knew why he hated the thought of Bron being the subject of malicious gossip. His younger brother Tsenit and his accomplice, the High Priestess D'thliss, had spread hideous stories about Ansaryon during the years before the Ska'i attack, so that most of Zithirian had assumed that he was an evil necromancer, consorting with foul demons and sacrificing virgins and babies in his tower at the Palace. In contrast, Tsenit, courageous and popular and apparently uninfected by court corruption, had been the darling of the citizens. Too late, they had realized that their hero was as wholesome as a ripe, glowing and maggot-rotten peach, while the hated Ansaryon was the victim of unjust-ified slander.

The procession passed the Council House, symbol of a new, more just and democratic Zithirian, and continued up the Cere-monial Way to the Palace, built on an outcrop of rock jutting above the River Kefirinn, opposite its junction with the D'yenn. And here, too, the change was so disorientating that Bron blinked in amazement. The huge intimidating Palace Gate, through which the Ska'i warriors had poured to slaughter the Royal Family and the Court, had gone. So had the high walls separating the ruler of Zithirian from his subjects. The great cen-tral tower, heart of the city-state, was still standing, and the King's banner, the sky-flower, flapped briskly from the top of the spire. But the buildings below it, a rather rambling collection of royal apartments, servants' quarters, administrative offices, stables and barracks, lay exposed to the curious gaze of the people, and looked distinctly shabby and unimposing.

'Your father had the walls and towers demolished three years ago,' Halthris said, seeing Bron's astonished expression. 'The stone has been used to build adequate defences all along the river. I know what's left isn't much to look at – there's so much to be done, and not enough masons in all Zithirian to work on everything at once. The Council Hall was the first priority, then the new walls, and the reconstruction of the Palace a rather poor third. He has plans, of course, and I think it will one day be very beautiful. But not for a few years yet.'

Bron said nothing, but his dark eyes stared blankly ahead, as if seeing something other than this undistinguished huddle of buildings. Halthris wondered suddenly if he could look into the future. Not even the most adept scryer was able to gaze at the silver bowl of ink, or blood, and see what was yet to come, but Bron had already done much that was supposed to be beyond the reach of any ordinary sorcerer.

One thing, though, was clear. Her stepson's attitude to his terrifying gift was so confused, so riddled with fear and hostility, that he was unlikely to admit, even to know, the true extent of his powers.

*

By the time the forty members of Zithirian's Council assembled,
the morning after their King's return to the city, those who had
not witnessed Bron's spectacular evasion of certain death at Sar
D'yenyi had been given every detail of the event by those who
had. The curved Council Hall, with its huge circular table constructed on the spot by a team of craftsmen from Lelyent, the
City in the Pines, was packed and noisy with the exchange of
rumour, innuendo and feverish speculation.

Ansaryon's entrance brought an instant halt to the fervent
buzz filling the room. As always, the only sign of his rank was
the slim silver band around his pale head; the stiff, ridiculous
traditional court dress had been discarded by royal decree, along
with much else, four years ago, and the King wore a thigh-length
belted tunic and trousers, overlaid by a long sleeveless robe, all in
dark blue silk exquisitely embroidered with silver and turquoise
birds around the hem. The same pattern of dress, in rather less
expensive materials, was worn by every man in the hall, and in
Zithirian too. His position, his looks and the indefinable aura of
strangeness about him would always set Ansaryon apart from
his people, but since seizing the throne he had done everything
possible to close the gulf that his father's stupidity and his
brother's treachery had opened up between Palace and City.

The Council itself was the most dramatic evidence of the
King's genuine desire to change the rigid and hierarchical
government of Zithirian. His father, Varathand IV, had relied
on a small clique of favourites, cronies and toadies, all wealthy
aristocrats who wanted to continue tradition and to feather their
own nests. The Ska'i had wiped most of them out, so even if
Ansaryon had had no desire to reform the city's constitution, he
would have been forced to use men of the merchant class in his
new administration. But he had gone much further, taking as
his model the city of Minassa to the south. Like Zithirian, it
possessed a King, Temiltan, Ansaryon's uncle. Unlike Zithirian,
however, Minassa was ruled in a spirit of co-operation and consent, with none of the priest-led repression of dissident voices
that had characterized the twenty unimpressive years of King
Varathand's reign.

The people of Zithirian had been astonished, and some dis-
mayed, to learn that the deliberations of their new King's Council
were not to take place behind locked doors in the Palace, but in
the new Hall built on the ruins of the hated Temple of Tayo. Even

more amazing, or terrifying, was the news that every man and woman in the city who had undergone the coming-of-age ceremony known as Entering, at twenty, would be eligible to vote for a member of the Council. Each of the four Quarters of the city – Potters', Embroiderers', Merchants', Goldsmiths' – would choose five representatives, five would be elected by those living and working in the Palace, and three by each of the small provinces – Raiyis, Margayan, D'yenn, Enzeth and Hailyan – stretching for nearly three hundred miles along the valley of the Kefirinn, between the steppe and the mountains, from Lake Raiyis in the north to Hailyan, on the border with Minassa, to the south.

The first elections had been held in the spring following Ansaryon's crowning, and now, more than three years later, the Zithiriani were becoming used to the idea that they had a voice in the way their country was run. They did not have absolute power, of course – Ansaryon, as King, made the final decisions – but they could express opinions, discuss issues, and make suggestions. And at the back of each councillor's mind was one unspoken thought. The citizens' support had tempted Tsenit to take the throne. Later, after learning the truth, they had turned against him, and helped Ansaryon to bring him down. The coronation rites in Zithirian had always been in two parts: the Crowning itself was preceded by the Choosing, in which the new monarch was publicly presented to his people for their approval. Once, this part of the ceremony had been an empty formality, but now the citizens were beginning to realize the extent of their power. They had made, and broken, one king; in his place, they had made another. And if he displeased them enough, they could break him, too.

It was certainly in Ansaryon's mind as he confronted them. Forty familiar faces, thirty-four men and six women, stared back at him, their expressions filled with varying degrees of curiosity mixed with some disappointment. But if they thought that he would willingly show off his young son as if he were a deformed freak paraded at the Gathering Fair, they were very much mistaken.

The councillors made the sign of respect which was all the King would now permit in his presence, hands clasped to breast with a brief bow of the head. Then, rather more promptly than usual, they took their places around the table, and stared expectantly at their monarch.

Ansaryon remained standing for a few heartbeats longer, and

then sat down in his beautifully carved and gilded chair. Like the
Council table, it had been a wedding present from another uncle,
Belerith of Lelyent – a magnanimous gesture in view of the fact
that Ansaryon had declined to take one of the Prince's seven
daughters for his bride. He glanced round, and said quietly, 'I
have something of great importance to tell you all, so that you
may pass on the truth in place of the wild rumours that are
undoubtedly already seething in every tavern and kuldi-house in
Zithirian.'

He paused, his eye catching that of one of the few women on
the Council, Kaydi Gandar's Widow, a representative of the
Embroiderers' Quarter. She had played a leading part in the resistance to Tsenit's rule, and was one of the new King's staunchest
supporters. Her son, Herris, had been friendly with Bron and
Lelya during the Time of the Usurper, and Ansaryon wondered
just how much she already knew, or guessed, about the boy.

'I have brought my son, Bron, back from Sar D'yenyi, where
he has been living under the guardianship of the Lady Kefiri for
nearly four years. I want first to make it quite clear that he is my
bastard son, and that he is not and never will be my heir. That
honour belongs to the elder son of myself and Queen Halthris,
Prince Tayma – and if he should die without children of his own,
to his brother Prince Homan, and after him to any other children
that we may have. Even if I leave no living descendants at the
time of my death, I do not intend that Bron should ever inherit
the Kingdom of Zithirian.'

'Why not, sir?'

It was Kaydi, as blunt as a Tulyet battering ram, her arms
folded on the table, her thick grey eyebrows raised. Ansaryon
said, 'I'm coming to that. Have patience, Gandar's Widow.'

Several people smiled. Kaydi was notoriously hasty in everything not connected with embroidery, a painstaking and con-
templative craft in which, astonishingly, she excelled. She gave
her King a penetrating stare – Kaydi was no respecter of rank for
its own sake – and then nodded. 'Go on, then.'

'By now,' Ansaryon said, 'you will have heard some version of
what occurred at Sar D'yenyi seven days ago. In order to correct
erroneous rumours, I'll tell you exactly what happened. My son
Bron had climbed on to a ledge around the central tower of the
citadel, which is at least ten times the height of a tall man. It was
just a boy's prank, although a very foolish and dangerous one. He

overbalanced and fell. Of course, such a drop would normally be fatal. However, he escaped unharmed, although he was considerably shocked and upset.' He glanced at Kaydi. 'And before you ask, no, he did not sprout wings.'

No one smiled. The silence was heavy with uneasy expectation. With a slight frown between his fair brows, Ansaryon continued.

'Bron is possessed of magical powers. He doesn't owe them to any drug – he was born with them, although no one yet understands why. Such a possibility is not discussed in any of the books I have read, or recognized by any sorcerer in the known world. I have reason to believe, however, that he is not unique, and that it is surprisingly common for ordinary people to have some magical ability, to a greater or lesser degree, without being aware of it. But Bron's power is exceptional. He is only thirteen years old, but he has the potential to become the greatest sorcerer who has ever lived.'

This time it was Umeth, a Hailyan councillor, who spoke. 'To what end, sir? Good – or evil?'

'He is not evil,' Ansaryon said. 'He was used by the High Priestess D'thliss, who was certainly evil – but he himself is not evil. He is a *child*. He is afraid of his own strength – he does not use sorcery except in moments of great peril. He used it to save himself from death in that fall.'

'And did he also use it to destroy the Ska'i?'

That was Kaydi again, her hazel eyes sharp and suspicious. Ansaryon had come here to tell them the truth, and he nodded. 'Yes. I don't know exactly what happened, because Bron was too distraught to speak at all, for months afterwards. But the Lady Kefiri told me that the Ska'i killed Bron's foster-brother, Lelya, and so in revenge he slew them.'

'Well, we all know what terrible tempers some children have,' Kaydi said. 'The question is, will he incinerate anyone who tells him off?'

Her apparent lack of respect obviously alarmed some of the other councillors, but it had never worried Ansaryon, who was well aware of her underlying loyalty. He said calmly, 'I don't think so. Remember, he was a prisoner in the Ska'i camp, terrified as well as enraged. Similarly, when he fell from the tower he only used his magical powers at the last possible moment, as fear took over. For the first nine years of his life, he was treated very cruelly, because of his gift. The Ska'i seized him, because of his gift. It took the Lady Kefiri a very long time to convince him that *I* wasn't going to exploit his sorcery as well. Nor shall I. I have brought him here so that I can teach him to use his powers wisely and well, rather than as a blind and instinctive response to rage or terror. And I have called you here to tell you the truth, so that you can relay it to the people you represent, both in the city and in the countryside.' He paused, looking round at the eyes, blue, brown, grey, green, watching him intently.

'As for Bron himself, he will live in the Palace. He will attend lessons with the other children, in the school I set up to replace the Temple. He will be treated just like any other pupil. He is not to be pestered or questioned in any way – he is to be left to continue his studies in peace. And he will live as part of my household, alongside my other sons.'

'Is that not somewhat dangerous, sir?' It was a representative of the Goldsmiths' Quarter who spoke, in the precise and elaborate tones of aristocratic Zithiriani.

'Why should it be? Bron is not dangerous. He is a thirteen-year-old boy, with the normal characteristics and interests of a child his age. He likes to play Pella in winter. He is good at running and climbing. He enjoys stories about Zithirian's history, and traditional tales – Foolish Gan is his favourite. He is learning to play the Sith, and he is a fair shot with the bow. He also happens to possess abnormal powers of sorcery, but those are now my concern, and I will teach him. He is not a monster, nor a demon. He will not destroy us, nor harm us in any way. Indeed, he seems to loathe his gift so much that I suspect it will be some time before I can even persuade him to accept that he is a sorcerer, let alone use his powers to create the smallest Illusion.' Ansaryon paused, feeling the suspicion still thick in the charged air. 'I know that you are all very dubious. I can understand why, and I don't blame you. But I think you trust me. Will you trust me, too, to do what is best for you, and for the city, and also for my son?'

For a long, tense moment no one spoke. Ansaryon was tempted to close his eyes and open his senses to the seething hotchpotch of misgiving, fear and confusion churning inside every councillor's mind. But now was not the time to practise sorcery, and he knew that their trust and respect were still granted cautiously. Presenting them with the truth about Bron, and asking them to accept him, would stretch their loyalty almost to the breaking point.

Yet he had been right to do so, or rumour would soon have branded his tormented, innocent son a monster of evil. At least now, none of them could accuse him of hiding the boy away, or lying about his powers.

'I trust you.' It was Kaydi, of course. 'Hegeden knows why, but I do. You've been honest with us, and I hope we all appreciate it.' She glanced pointedly round at her fellow councillors. 'Well? What do you say? Not that there's much we can do about it, of course. But if any of you have a contrary opinion, I should air it now.'

No one admitted to any doubts, though Ansaryon knew that everyone must harbour them. But few members of the Council possessed Kaydi's robust candour, or were willing to express their dissenting views to the King's face. The memory of Varathand's repressive and absolute rule still lingered, and it would be a long time before all her colleagues were as open as Gandar's Widow.

He thanked them for their understanding, and left the hall, knowing that as soon as the door shut behind him a huge and clamorous discussion would break out. But at least there had been no spoken disagreement, and Kaydi, the unofficial leader of the representatives, had publicly stated her support.

Well, that ordeal was over. But he knew, with considerable foreboding, that telling the Council about Bron had been his first, and easiest task. Now, he must begin the slow, difficult and perhaps dangerous process of winning the trust and affection of his son.

By tradition, sorcerers were supposed to inhabit towers. Since Zithirian was full of them – indeed, 'City of Towers' was a common poetic epithet for the place – it should have been easy for Ansaryon to occupy a suitably sinister turret somewhere. Indeed, before the Ska'i invasion he had kept his magical books, and the apparatus necessary for a Mazath, in the topmost chamber of his tower in the Palace. But it had been destroyed, along with most of the royal apartments, in the inferno that had accompanied the barbarian attack, and the resulting heap of blackened stones had been carted away to help build the new river defences. He had managed to obtain some more books in

Toktel'yi, where sorcery was a respected and useful art: every village possessed its own magician, there was a Guild which regulated practitioners of the craft and ran several schools for aspiring wizards, and Al'Kalyek, the Court Sorcerer, wielded almost as much power and influence as the Emperor himself.

Long ago, Al'Kalyek had advised Ansaryon about Bron, when the child had still been under the baleful influence of D'thliss. The Toktel'yan's interest in the boy seemed benevolent enough: he saw him as a vital key to his research into the origins, extent and potential of sorcery. But Ansaryon did not trust any inhabitant of the Empire, particularly one who had the Emperor's ear. A hundred and fifty years ago, Imperial soldiers had invaded Zithirian, seeking to conquer the city for the sake of its secret gold and silver mines in the Northern Mountains. Many citizens still regarded Toktel'yi as their traditional enemy, despite the valuable help which the present Emperor Djamal had given Ansaryon in his successful attempt to seize the throne from Tsenit: help which, as had been pointed out at the time, put him under a considerable obligation to Djamal, who was also his cousin.

But there was little danger from this Emperor, a dissolute and idle man whose chief passion was his famous retinue of concubines. His young son, Ba'alekkt, however, was a very different matter. Ansaryon could easily imagine that vigorous, devious, aggressive boy, grown to manhood and eager to prove himself, claiming the Silver City for his own because his grandmother had been a Zithiriani princess, and because of the debt owed to the Empire by Ansaryon. Not that Ba'alekkt was the kind to need excuses, and the gold and silver mines would always be a potent lure. And if it were widely known that Bron possessed enormous magical powers, that might tempt the Toktel'yans to seize the child before he fulfilled his potential as a weapon against them. Once adult, of course, his presence in Zithirian might prove a considerable deterrent to Imperial pretensions, but to the Emperor and his ministers, a boy of thirteen was still a tool, to be captured and used – or broken.

And Bron knew it. Brought by his father to a small, dimly lit room in his apartments, hastily repaired after the Ska'i attack and in sore need of rebuilding altogether, he looked round at the books and other paraphernalia piled on shelves and tables, the distinctive musty aroma of old leather bindings and older parchment and charsh paper, and said sullenly, 'I know what you want me to do. And I won't.'

Ansaryon stared at the son he hardly knew. Small and slight for his age, his fair hair bright in the gloom and his dark eyes unknowable, Bron stared back, hostility prickling around him. He cried vehemently, 'I don't *want* to be a sorcerer – I *don't*!'

'But you are,' Ansaryon reminded him quietly. 'Whether you like it or not, your powers lie within you, and you can't deny them, any more than you can deny your sight, or your hearing, or your ability to walk. I know that you are frightened by what you can do – I know that you are afraid of sorcery. And that's quite understandable, given what's happened to you in the past. But D'thliss is dead – and so are the Ska'i. There is no one now who wants to use you for their own ends.'

'Isn't there?' the boy demanded swiftly. 'Why do *you* want to teach me? Don't you want to use me for your own purposes too? Everyone else always has – except for Kefiri.'

The bitterness in his voice appalled Ansaryon. He shook his head in desperate denial. 'No, Bron – *no*! That isn't true. You're my son, and I want to help you.'

'If you really want to help me, leave me alone – let me go back to Sar D'yenyi!'

'You know that's impossible. Invan and Kefiri should be able to start their married life in peace.' Ansaryon paused, fighting the urge to let his mind reach out to Bron, without deception, and reveal the depth of his love for his first son, whom he had so greatly wronged. But it would be pointless even to try: he could sense the strength of the defences the boy had instinctively constructed against any invasion of his thoughts.

Gently, he continued aloud. 'Please, Bron – at least do me the courtesy of listening. I can't force you to learn the art of sorcery. I know you are still a child, but you will be a man before long, and your powers will be correspondingly greater. If you do not like and cannot accept what you have done in the past, that is fair enough. But now you must face up to your responsibilities. Do you *really* want to go through your life terrified of your power, because you have never learned to control it? It isn't like an old coin, easy to lose and forget. It isn't trivial. Rage and grief made you kill six thousand Ska'i. If you don't want it to happen again, you need to be taught and guided – you need to learn what you can do, and how to keep your powers in check. Do you understand me, Bron?'

'But I don't want it!' His son's voice had shed its previous tone of resentful anger, and was high with desperation. 'I don't *want* to be a sorcerer! If there's no place for me here, I want to be a musician, to play the Sith or the flute – that's all I've ever wanted! Why can't I do that? Why can't I forget what I am?'

'Because too many people know.' Ansaryon's tone was gentle, but emphatic. 'Most of my Court saw you fall from the tower at Sar D'yenyi, and saw you save yourself. They know you have extraordinary gifts and they are frightened of you. This morning, I told the Council the truth about you. I also told them that you were not dangerous, and that I would teach you to harness your powers. I hope I reassured them, but I suspect that some of them are still afraid that you will immolate anyone who stands in your way, just as you obliterated the Ska'i. That fear won't go away – and if they see that you are refusing my instruction, it will grow. Then perhaps one day the people will turn on you.'

'Then I'll go where no one knows who I am,' Bron said. There were tears in his eyes, and his face was twisted with anguish. 'Please, father, please – let me go. I'll never ever use magic again – I promise I won't!'

'But you could not keep such a promise,' Ansaryon reminded him. 'Could you have avoided using sorcery to save yourself at Sar D'yenyi? Could you have let the Ska'i escape unscathed, after they had killed Lelya so brutally? It wasn't possible, was it?'

Slowly, reluctantly, the boy shook his head.

'If you don't want any more deaths on your conscience, then you *must* lean how to use your powers wisely. If I sound harsh, it is because your situation is harsh, and the remedy is harsh too. It won't be easy for you. But the hardest part will be accepting that you need help.' He smiled briefly. 'It took me a long time to learn that lesson. But life is a lonely furrow to plough alone. I found Halthris, and having her at my side has made everything worth while. One day, perhaps, you will find someone to share your heart and your mind.'

'I don't think I will,' Bron said.

There was no self-pity in his voice: it was a simple statement of the truth. And Ansaryon found a sudden, extraordinarily vivid image in his mind, of his son wandering in a hostile landscape under vast and menacing skies, his small figure bleak, indomitable, and unutterably alone.

It tore his heart, for he knew that this was how Bron saw himself. And yet it need not be, if the boy would only accept his destiny rather than run away from it.

But he could not be forced, only persuaded. And perhaps with his world so thoroughly disrupted and altered, it was too soon even for gentle guidance.

Ansaryon came to a decision. He said softly, 'It's early days yet. I'll say no more about sorcery for a while. There's so much else for you to learn – the history and songs and poetry of Zithirian, the geography of the known world, the languages and literature of Toktel'yi and Kerenth and the Archipelago – everything that the other children at the Palace School will study. Do you want to join them?'

At last, Bron nodded.

'Good. Make friends, settle down, do the things all boys like to do. The other children will soon forget you're my son – they did at Sar D'yenyi, didn't they? Play games, enjoy your music – and perhaps in a little time you'll realize that what I have said to you today is the truth. Or perhaps you won't. But I will never force you, Bron – I love you too much for that.'

His son looked up and saw the expression on the King's face, telling him what he had already known, but rejected. He whispered, 'Thank you. Can – can I go to my room now?'

Ansaryon smiled at him. 'Of course you can.'

And silently, without an answering smile or even a gesture of farewell, the boy turned and went out.

Alone, his father sat down by the cluttered table, and closed his eyes. He had not won, but neither had he been defeated. He had given Bron time and space to change his mind. But he knew, with apprehension, that the child's chances of winning acceptance by his peers were small indeed.

Once, before the Ska'i, the colonnades all around the wide courtyard at the heart of the King's apartments had been festooned with exotic plants and tubs of flowers, and the elaborate central fountain had enlivened the summer air with the endless splash and trickle of water. The barbarians had destroyed everything they could not understand, and now the stone bowls were shattered and silent, and the ubiquitous trumpet vine, fast-growing and sweet-scented, had sprawled all along the roofs above the walkway in its usual rampant profusion. Bron ducked under a trailing stand, and entered the room he had been allotted.

It was small, barely four paces square, but his own. There was

a low, narrow bed, covered with brightly coloured blankets from
Lelyent, the City in the Pines, almost as famous for its soft warm
wool and skilful weavers as for its woodcarvers. A table, with a
pile of thick charsh paper, a reed pen, rather chewed, a pot of
ink, a few textbooks in Zithiriani and a Toktel'yan grammar. A
wooden chair, with a discarded tunic thrown over it. A clothes
chest, of carved Lelyentan pine. The only indication that this
was not a room in some humble potter's house was the mural
decorating the walls: running stags, leaping lions and soaring
eagles, with a pattern of stars on the ceiling.

Bron ignored them, although last night he had watched their
shapes moving in the uncertain lamplight as though they were
alive, until his eyes closed in sleep. He opened the clothes chest
and rummaged inside. Then he quickly removed the garments he
was wearing, the embroidery proclaiming his rank for all to see,
and put on an old plain grey summer tunic, short-sleeved and
with absolutely no embellishments, and a pair of torn faded
trousers underneath. A rather scuffed and elderly pair of sandals
replaced the new ones, with embossed straps and silver buckles,
that he had worn all day.

Thus attired, he slipped out of the door, across the empty
courtyard and through the Palace. Few people seemed to notice
him as he hurried along, and no one stopped him when he walked
out of the main entrance and across the huge, bare, rubble-strewn
area where once the two double towers of the Palace Gate had
glowered menacingly down at the people of Zithirian.

He turned aside immediately from the Ceremonial Way,
which ran down to the Council Hall. Once out of sight of it, he
was in streets still so familiar that he could follow every turn and
corner with closed eyes. The man running that kuldi-house had
always given him and Lelya cakes; in the house almost opposite,
an old half-mad widow had shouted at them when they stole
bunches of grapes drooping from the untended vine rampaging
across her roof. Down this street they had been chased by a bad-
tempered dog, until Bron had turned and stopped it with the
power of his mind . . .

He shied away from the memory of a time when he had used
his powers as naturally and unthinkingly as another boy might
shout and sing. He had been a young child then, ignorant of what
he could do, and what he was. Now he knew, and the knowledge
terrified him.

He had come to the docks. Zithirian had been built at the

highest navigable point on the Kefirinn, and every year, once the ice had thawed, the beautiful riverboats made the slow journey up against the current from Toktel'yi, trading with the towns and cities along the river. They brought silks from Kerenth, charsh paper, cotton and oil from the Empire, hundreds of miles to the south, scented woods, drugs and spices and exotic animals from the diverse and wonderful islands of the K'tali Archipelago, iron ingots and fabulous jewels from the mountains of Tulyet. In return, their captains received tiny phials of the intense and glorious perfumes of Tamat; Minassan pottery, exquisite and fragile; casks of smooth, delicious Hailyan wine; and from Zithirian, embroidered silks and the gold and silver, cast into flat triangular blocks, that had made the city so desirable.

There were six vessels tied up along the quayside, with a bustle of men loading and unloading. Unnoticed amongst the throng, Bron loitered, waching them. Most of the riverboats were Toktel'yan, and so were many of their crews: short stocky men with curling dark hair and every shade of skin from light tan to black, wearing brief tunics and shouting in their own clattering tongue, full of consonants and sharp vowels. All well-born Zithiriani children learned the language, for although the Empire was their traditional enemy, its culture and civilization were still much admired, and imitated, in the cities of the north. In his lessons at Sar D'yenyi, Bron had not found Toktel'yan particularly difficult, but he could not understand what these men were saying, they spoke so fast and idiomatically. He caught a few words here and there – 'gekken' was a ship, and 'karmick' a rope – but most of it was incomprehensible.

If you allowed yourself, you could understand them.

The voice inside had been silent since his fall from the tower. To hear it now, here, in this busy and very ordinary place, was as shocking as if he had actually seen the Wolf, crouching over by the warehouse that lined the docks. For a moment fear rushed through Bron, urging him to run, to hide from the enemy.

But since the Wolf lay within his heart, where could he go? There was only one defence, though he hated to use it. He closed his eyes and focused his mind, erecting the barriers again. The Wolf snarled in anger once, and then was quiet.

He would be back, sooner or later, but for the moment Bron was free, thanks to the power he loathed, the power that fed the Wolf, and which he could never escape.

'Mind out of the way!'

Someone bumped into him. He opened his eyes and saw a young man struggling under a huge bale of cotton. Hastily, Bron stepped sideways just as the other lost his balance and dropped his load, uttering a stream of imaginative curses in Zithiriani.

The deep voice was not familiar, but he knew the face. Narrow, thin, with an unattractive scattering of adolescent spots, and framed by unkempt, sweat-soaked hair, he remembered it very well. He turned away, but too late: the sharp hazel eyes had recognized him. '*Bron?*' said Herris Gandar's son, on a note of wary disbelief.

Four years ago, Herris had been, briefly, his friend and Lelya's. They had played in the streets of the occupied city, dodging the Ska'i and Tsenit's soldiers, sliding on the frozen river, playing impromptu games of Pella with sticks and flat stones. Or rather, Lelya had been his friend. Bron remembered hovering on the edge of their games, tagging along and watching rather than taking part. But he had been four years younger than the other two; and besides, his mind had been in turmoil as he struggled to find the power to resist D'thliss.

'It *is* you, isn't it?' Herris said. He wiped a dirty hand across his damp forehead and stared down at the boy he had once played with. Lelya had been straightforward, uncomplicated and, to put it bluntly, not clever. Bron, with his rather menacing air of mystery and his weird powers, had disturbed Herris considerably.

'Yes,' said Bron. The older boy had grown, grown up in fact: his voice had broken, his arms were sinewy with well-used muscle, and his nose, never small, had become extremely prominent.

'What are you doing here?' Herris gestured round at the docks, the labouring sailors, the piles of goods. 'I thought – well, I heard you were back – but aren't you living up at the Palace?'

'Yes,' said Bron again.

A Toktel'yan pushed past them, carrying another bale, and barked an order. Herris grimaced at his retreating back. 'Surly sod – but he's the Captain's bedmate. I'm working a passage down to Minassa, and they'll take me on for the rest of the summer with any luck. Look, can't talk now – will you meet me in the tavern on the other side of the docks? You can see it from here – it's called the Flower of Hope.' He bent, and with some difficulty – even adult, Herris was neither tall nor stocky – heaved the bale back on to his shoulders. 'See you there in an hour or so.'

He paused, and then added, 'I heard about what happened to you, but nothing about Lelya.'

'He's dead,' Bron said briefly.

Herris's eyes showed no surprise. 'I thought he must be. See you in the Flower, then. Coming – *staklen k'te suskil*!' And he staggered away in obedience to the Toktel'yan's angry shouts.

When Herris arrived at the tavern rather more than an hour later, he was not seriously expecting to see Bron there. Why would a Prince – for that was what he was, even if no-one knew the identity of his mother – want to renew a rather uncertain friendship with the likes of Herris, his Ma's despair and the butt of the Toktel'yans' harsh words and casual blows?

But one day it would be different, and his life would change just as the life of Bron, underfed, abused and neglected child of the Temple, had changed so astonishingly for the better. But not through an accident of birth, or someone else's generosity. Herris planned to succeed through his own efforts.

The Flower of Hope was owned by a Minassan woman called Skathis, who had a distinctly dubious past that her present respectability could not conceal. A wide variety of rumours speculated about the source of her wealth, the cause of the thin scar across one plump rouged cheek, and the whereabouts of the husband she always referred to as 'Poor dear Enmay'. One tale had her running a Toktel'yan brothel, and Herris could well believe it. Certainly, Skathis's famously elaborate gowns, the tight bodices enhancing her generous figure, did nothing to deny such an assertion: although if she had tried to carry on such a trade in Zithirian, the officials of the Merchants' Quarter would soon have closed the tavern down.

She greeted him warmly, with a smile and a waft of flowery Tamat perfume. 'Herris, dear boy! Your usual?'

'Of course,' he said, putting one of the small silver coins called chells down on the counter. In return, he was given a huge thirst-quenching mug of inferior wine mixed with citrus juice, a concoction of Toktel'yan origin popularly known to Skathis's customers as 'Emperor's Piss'. It swept gloriously down his parched, aching throat: he ordered another, and then looked round for Bron.

He was there, in a secluded and shady corner of the court-yard. Herris walked over and sat down on the bench opposite. 'Hello. I didn't think you'd be here. Won't they miss you, up at the Palace?'

Bron shrugged. 'I don't care if they do. What are you doing? Working your passage, you said?'

'Yes.' Herris paused, looking at the impenetrable dark eyes that had once made him shiver, and which now seemed almost ordinary. He went on, rather against his better judgement. 'I signed on the first ship after the thaw this spring. Working on the docks here and in Minassa, and going back and forth between them. I've done three trips so far, and earned quite a bit. It's hard work, but it gives me a chance to learn about boats and the river.' He grinned. 'Ma doesn't like it – she's a councillor now, thinks having her dear and only son and heir working as a docker for Toktel'yans is an affront to her dignity. But it's the best way to get what I want.'

'Which is?'

'A ship of my own. Oh, I know there aren't any Zithiriani shipowners. I know that I can't keep one here over the winter. But the river never freezes at Minassa, the trade from there down to Toktel'yi goes on all year round. Everyone has a hundred objections,' Herris said, his eyes gleaming at the challenge. 'But I'll show 'em all – and Ma, too!'

'How long will it take, to earn enough to buy a ship?'

'Oh, several years – and if I keep spending my money on this stuff, even longer.' Herris drained his mug for the second time and exhaled with satisfaction. 'That was good. Hegeden's wings, was I thirsty! So you were at Sar D'yenyi, were you? How's Kef – I mean the Lady Kefiri?'

The Lady Kefiri had spent some months in hiding at his mother's house, during the Time of the Usurper. Bron said, 'She's well – and happy, I think.'

'I never thought Invan was right for her,' Herris said. 'A good man, but what a bore!' He gave the younger boy a rather sheepish grin. 'Still, I suppose I'm just jealous. I was rather keen on her once. Now I haven't got time for girls – it's work, work, work, all day long!'

There seemed nothing that Bron could say to this, so he took a sip of his kuldi – Skathis, being Minassan, made it hearteningly strong and fragrant – and wished that he could be like Herris, strong, adult, confident, and without a care in the world beyond his distant dream. He said at last, 'What will you call your ship, when you get her?'

'I'm glad you said "when",' Herris told him. 'The Aiyan, the

Flower of Hope – after the King's own device, of course, as well as this tavern. It's a good name, don't you think?'

For a short while, they talked – or rather, Herris talked and Bron listened, while the tavern courtyard filled with mid-day customers, many of them Toktel'yan. One was the man who had shouted at Herris earlier, and he called to him over the intervening hubbub in his execrable Zithiriani. 'You! No time for talk! Leave your fancy boy and get back to work!'

'Fancy boy!' said Herris, turning a bright shade of pink that suddenly made him seem very young. 'Sorry about that, Bron. Just because most of them seem to prefer boys, there's no need for them to assume that we do too. I'll set him straight as soon as I can – it'll save you a lot of embarrassment when you come down here again.'

He seemed to think that Bron would be a regular visitor to the docks, and the younger boy saw no reason to tell him otherwise. In any case, this area of Zithirian, bustling and tinged with vivid glimpses of the exotic, the foreign, the strange, had its own powers of fascination. The Toktel'yans with their brusque manners and outlandish tongue, the graceful lines and brightly coloured sails of their ships, the bales of cottons and silks woven in distant lands, the aroma of fabulous spices, were a potent reminder that outside the domain of the Silver City lay many other worlds, to which, one day, he might escape.

If the Wolf would allow him.

CHAPTER
THREE

The citizens of Zithirian celebrated the turning of the year with the winter festival of Sundim. It was a time of bitter cold, and the people needed to look forward with hope to the coming spring and summer. At this, the darkest season, it was not easy to remember that soon the days would lengthen, the air would grow warmer, and the ice and snow that had already lain over the city for months would soon, they hoped, begin to thaw.

This was only the fifth winter festival where open homage to the ancient and almost universal deities, Hegeden and Sarraliss, could take place in Zithirian. Until Ansaryon's accession no mention of them, let alone worship, had been allowed: the city's official god was Tayo, self-styled Founder of the city and the Divine Ancestor of its Kings. The Temple dedicated to him had dominated the lives of the citizens, and its priests had used their officially exclusive powers of sorcery to overawe and oppress the people. Now the Temple was gone, the priests were all dead, and those who wished could venerate Hegeden the Eagle, Lord of the Air, and Sarraliss, Lady of the Earth and of Horses, in the traditional way, without pomp or ceremony or priest, wherever and whenever they wished.

To the small remaining number of aristocrats this was yet another example of the new King's hated reforms that seemed to be sweeping away all their cherished ideals and beliefs. To the citizens, most of whom were not descended from Tayo or his First Hundred, it was one more reason to feel gratitude and loyalty towards the man whom their support had placed on the throne, and who, almost uniquely amongst all the Kings and Queens of Zithirian, seemed willing to take notice of their needs and aspirations.

So virtually every family had an image of a mare or an eagle, or both, somewhere amongst the pine-boughs, ivy branches and corn-sheaves that festooned their houses, and many of the younger citizens, gladly embracing the new order, wore some image of the golden feather of Hegeden, or the wheat-ear of Sarraliss.

Queen Halthris, being a barbarian of the nomadic Tanathi tribe, was also a worshipper of the old gods, and it was widely believed that the religious reforms were due to her influence. Certainly, her new gown was richly embroidered with galloping horses, and her coppery hair was interwoven with ribbons in gold and silver, the respective colours of Hegeden and Zithirian. She presided over the festivities – dancing, eating, drinking and winter games were the traditional ways of celebrating Sundim – with her customary friendliness, so that even those who had muttered darkly about this woman from an alien culture had been disarmed by her manner. Moreover, she had already produced two fine sons, Tayma and Homan, and the people, who remembered how she had slain the tyrant and usurper Tsenit, loved her as dearly as her husband. He was a sorcerer, she a barbarian, and once they would have been horrified at the prospect of such a couple ruling their city. But things had changed in Zithirian, and the citizens were well aware of the debt they owed to Ansaryon and Halthris. Without them, the Silver City would probably now be a heap of deserted rubble, littered with its people's bones.

As well as the indoor celebrations, there were always games out on the frozen ice of the Kefirinn, or on the snow-covered fields. Whole sheep or even oxen were roasted over huge fires, and the citizens watched their sons, and some of their bolder daughters, race each other on horse-drawn sledges, on foot or on ice-sliders, play wild matches of Pella that lasted for most of the day, or simply parade about in their winter finery.

Bron was good at Pella. It was the only reason he was a member of the Palace team: there were many others, far less skilful than he was, who had been asked to take part because they were someone's friend. But in the four months since coming to Zithirian, he had acquired no friends at all, except possibly for Herris. The children whose lessons he shared were suspicious, wary and sometimes downright hostile. Many of them had parents or other relatives on the Council, and they all knew that Bron supposedly possessed extraordinary powers of sorcery.

At first they had spent much of their time trying to persuade him, by fair means or foul, to demonstrate them. Bron, gnawed by an inner despair which haunted his dreams and his days, had refused to oblige. He had been coaxed, tempted, taunted, abused and threatened: finally, an older boy with a reputation for aggression had tried to push him into the river. Fortunately, one of their tutors had seen the incident, and intervened. The culprit had been sent back to his family's home near Hailyan in disgrace, and the open bullying stopped. But his fellow pupils still did not make any overtures of friendship: instead, they ignored him in his presence, and sneered at him behind his back.

At Sar D'yenyi, he had made friends, for few there had known about his terrible gift. So this rejection was a new and horrible experience for Bron, and only increased his burgeoning sense of isolation. His father and stepmother had spent much of the autumn on an extended visit to Lelyent, where Prince Belerith's wife Tesi, Ansaryon's aunt, was dying, and in any case Bron was reluctant to confide his despair to them. He was miserably aware that the least Illusion, the easiest movement of some small object, would have bought him the respect, perhaps even the friendship, of many of the other children. But he refused to give in to their blandishments, for the Wolf within him spoke the same words, night after night in his dreams. Instead, as the days shrank towards the depths of winter, he turned for comfort to the lovely, impersonal sound of his Sith.

No one had asked him if he could play Pella, but one of the tutors, a brisk and hearty young man called Omreth, had noticed him standing on the edge of the ice, one very cold day half a month before Sundim, watching a hectic game on the frozen river below the Palace Rock. 'Not playing, lad?'

Bron answered in the polite, uninflected tone he had learned to use long ago, and which gave absolutely nothing away. 'No, sir.'

'But you want to, don't you?'

As the boy's startled face swung round, Omreth added, 'I've seen you watching several times, but you never join in. Why don't you have a go? You're small and quick, you should be good at it.'

'I don't want to,' Bron said woodenly.

'Yes, you do,' Omreth told him. 'Don't deny it, lad, your face tells a different story. What's stopping you? Never played before? It does look a bit rough if you're a novice – '

An exultant shout erupted. One of the Palace teams, distinguished by their blue scarves, had knocked the slider into their own circle, painted on the ice with a long brush dipped in wet soot: there were four such circles marked out, one at each of the corners of the huge irregular oblong, almost the width of the river, that delineated the playing area. The successful player could hardly be seen amidst his seven delighted team-mates. There was no official limit to the size of the four teams in a match: as long as they were numerically more or less equal, there could be any quantity of players from two to forty or more in each, depending on the type of game. This one was an informal contest between three groups of Palace schoolchildren and one of apprentices from the Embroiderers' Quarter, and the apprentices were winning, just, with four scores so far.

'I have played before,' Bron said, thinking of those impromptu games long ago on the ice of the Kefirinn, with Lelya and Herris and other boys. And later at Sar D'yenyi, the spiky blue shadows of the citadel's towers creeping across the frozen lake, and everyone joining in, men and women, even the Lady Kefiri, laughing, her breath like smoke in the cold crystal air, striking the slider home with a gleeful whoop of triumph . . .

There would be no more games of Pella for Kefiri now that she was married to Invan: and none for Lelya, either. With angry shame, Bron felt his eyes fill with tears of grief and homesickness.

'Iyen seems to have taken a bad fall,' the tutor observed. 'Looks like he's hurt – take over, will you, Bron?' And he briskly propelled the boy out on to the ice.

It was obvious that Iyen's team, the Greens, only accepted him because of Omreth's presence, and because they would otherwise be a player short. But Bron didn't care: once he had strapped the bone ice sliders on to his boots, and felt the weight of the broad striker in his hand, he forgot their hostility, and concentrated on the game. With only eight in each team there was a lot of space, and rather less scrimmaging than usual. Bron, small, fast, agile, managed to score twice, and by dusk, when the match ended, the other Greens were letting him take possession of the slider rather than trying to miss him out, or knocking it away from him.

It was not friendship: it was not even really true acceptance. But it was a beginning.

By Sundim he had won himself a place on the Palace team that would compete in the grand tournament always held as part of the festival. He was the smallest and youngest of the twenty men and boys chosen, and although he said nothing of it to anyone, his success was a source of considerable inward pride. And there were signs of increasing warmth amongst the other children at the school. A few of them had even talked to him.

The games were watched by the King and Queen and virtually everyone else in Zithirian: they lined both banks of the river in their thousands, to cheer on friends and relatives. In the opening games, the Palace team, attired in new blue tunics, did well, and Bron scored five times. Glowing from the exertion, and from the sincere and hearty congratulations of his allies, he realized that his efforts had won them a place in the final match.

They were pitted against a team from the Potters' Quarter, who had won last year, and two from the Embroiderers', in one of which was Herris. It would be a close contest, and Bron had no real hopes that they would win, but he was determined that at least they wouldn't get the losers' prize.

The members of each team stood waiting in their circles, ready for the trumpet blast that signalled the start. The smooth stone slider, painted brilliant red to stand out against the dead white ice, had been positioned in the exact centre of the pitch. Bron tensed, gripping his striker. One of the other boys caught his eye, and gave him an encouraging grin. He smiled back, and a small glow of happiness settled somewhere inside his ribs. Whether they won or lost, for the next hour at least he was a valued and valuable part of the team.

And then the trumpet bellowed, and everything was forgotten in the rush for the slider.

It was a hard game. Herris's team, the Whites, scored first, swiftly followed by the Potters. Bron, dodging in and out of the jostling, scurrying players, made up in speed and dexterity what he lacked in physique. And in his excitement and determination to excel in front of those of his team-mates who had publicly disapproved of his inclusion, he abandoned fear and entered that higher level of concentration where nothing mattered, nothing at all, save the game he played.

He scored twice in quick succession, and the Palace team were leading, with half the match already gone. But amid the cheers of the others, he saw at least one sour face. Gorseth was older, stronger, and apart from Bron probably the best player in the team. And over the noise, his contemptuous words came clearly to the younger boy. 'Well, you can't expect anything else from a sorcerer. He's so puny, he must have used magic to score.'

From the looks on the faces of the other players, they didn't agree, and Bron, exalted by success, took no notice. The game restarted, and for a while, with every team making frantic efforts to knock the slider into their ring, there was deadlock, eighty men and boys frantically tussling in the central part of the pitch. Then Bron, hovering on the outside of the heaving mass of players, saw the scarlet flash of the slider whizzing past him. He gave chase, and found another pursuer beside him just as they closed on the stone. With angry surprise, he realized that it was Gorseth.

'Leave it!' Bron yelled. His striker was already raised and the Palace circle lay open and inviting only twenty strides away. In another few heartbeats, someone from one of the other teams would block him, and the chance would be lost.

'Mine, I think,' said Gorseth, and deliberately cannoned into him.

They were both moving at speed, and it was a very heavy fall. Bron put out his hands to save himself, and heard bone cracking on the stone-hard ice. As he lay gasping with the searing pain in his arm, Gorseth, with a shout of derisive laughter, made the winning score that should rightfully have gone to his rival.

Injuries were common in games of Pella – indeed, it was not unknown for players to be killed. Intentional harm to one's own team-mate, however, was forbidden, and the cheers quickly changed to whistles and hoots of disapproval. As Bron, dazed and hurt, was carried off the ice, Gorseth, scarlet with rage, was told that his score had been disallowed.

The Palace Healer, a man of many years and much experience, was summoned in haste to examine the King's eldest son. He had many superficial, though painful, bruises and abrasions from his violent contact with the ice, but the worst damage was to his right arm, which had taken the full force of the fall, and was broken in several places.

Bron lay on the bed, fighting the agony that threatened to overwhelm his mind, and tried to make sense of what the Healer was telling his father. The prognosis was not good. Even if the shattered bones could be induced to heal, they could not be set straight, and the muscles were torn and weakened. He would probably be crippled for life.

The knowledge lay like a boulder of ice about his heart as the Healer administered a sedative potion and set about splinting the injured limb with practised, gentle hands. Despite the drug, the process was extremely painful and exhausting. He was glad when the old man had finally finished, and left him to sleep.

Alone at last, his damaged arm aching savagely, Bron closed his eyes and tried not to weep: not from the pain, but because he knew that he would never play Pella again, or his beloved, beautiful Sith.

And then he felt the power beginning to rise within him. It was very slight at first: just a tingle in the blood, a sense of exultation. Even as he fought it down, he realized that the Wolf was silent, for this had nothing to do with evil, or destruction.

The effects of the sedative were still swirling in his mind, making him curiously light-headed, but they could not destroy the stark clarity of the choice before him. He could resist the magic, and his shattered arm would remain imperfect, slow to move, useless when he tried to execute the delicate, complicated patterns of the Sith. Or he could embrace at last the sorcery he had loathed and rejected, and use his power to heal himself. For he knew now that the music and the magic were inextricably linked in his soul: the boy whose touch on the Sith, whose breath in the flute was so light and exact and fluent, was also the boy whose other, darker gifts were now impossible to ignore or deny.

He sent his mind running down sinew and bone, examining the damage. The Healer was right: his forearm was broken in three places, and without help would never mend properly. He gathered his strength, feeling the tingling power threatening to burst from his fingertips. Instead, he poured it into his injured limb, willing, persuading, forcing the bones to realign themselves, and weld together as straight and strong as they had been only an hour ago.

It hurt. He had not expected that, and whimpered with the savagery of the pain. But he had no choice now. Ignoring it, he let his powers do their work, and the sweat trickled down his face with the effort of keeping agony at bay while he completed his task.

Nearly there . . . just a little more . . .

The door opened. Lost within his body, all his concentration focused on the mending of his arm, Bron failed to notice his father standing there, staring at him. Then the Healer uttered a cry of dismay and pushed past the King to the bed.

One last effort. '*No!*' Bron gasped in desperation. The Healer grabbed hold of his sound arm. Power surged, and the old man yelped and leapt back. Then white-hot screaming agony seared through the boy's smashed bones, finally fusing them together.

It was over, the pain vanished, the relief absolute. Exhausted, soaked in sweat, Bron lay as still as death, his eyes closed, while the Healer gibbered about his hurt hand.

As if he had viewed the scene from above, he saw his father usher the old man out, ignoring his protests. The door shut behind him, and Ansaryon said, 'What have you done?'

For a long while, fighting faintness and weariness and the blissful freedom from agony, Bron didn't answer him. When he did speak at last, it was in a whisper. 'I've mended my arm.'

It was taken up in gentle hands. There was no pain at all. Ansaryon unwrapped the bandages and removed the splints, and Bron felt the air cool on his overheated skin. After a brief silence, his father said drily, 'So you have.'

'I had to,' Bron said, trying to justify his actions to himself. 'The Healer said it would never mend properly.'

'I know. I was wondering whether it would be wise to try and persuade you to do what you've just done.'

'Well, I did it.' Bron opened his eyes and stared up at the King. Ansaryon still looked surprised, but also pleased, as if his son had done something unexpected, and quite remarkable. Then he smiled, and a sense of his warm approval flooded through the boy's mind.

'I had to,' he said again. 'I had to – I want to go on playing the Sith, and the flute, as well as Pella – I couldn't face the thought of giving up music.' His eyes began to fill with tears as shock and reaction replaced the initial euphoria of success and freedom from pain. 'But I didn't want to use sorcery – not at first.'

'And now?' Ansaryon sat down on the bed, holding his hand.

'I *still* don't want to – but I can't avoid it, can I?' Bron wiped his eyes miserably. 'I've used it now, so there's no reason not to use it again.'

'Listen to me – *listen* to me, Bron. What you did just now is supposed to be impossible. Sorcerers in Toktel'yi can Heal themselves and others, but only minor illnesses and injuries – headaches, fevers, cuts, that sort of thing. They certainly can't mend broken bones. If you wanted, you could become a Healer – if you can employ your powers to treat other people, you will be famous, and loved, throughout the known world.'

'I don't know if I *can* Heal other people,' said Bron. He had started to shiver. 'I'm not even sure if I could do it again to me. I just don't *know*!'

Ansaryon waited until his son was calmer. Then he said softly,
'If you let me, I could help you.'

Bron closed his eyes. He knew, as he knew such things, that
the long defiance was over. His destiny lay before him, the road
clearly marked, without diverging paths. He could no longer
ignore it, or deny it existed. Nor could he refuse to take it.

One and the other: the magic and the music both. They were
linked in his soul, indissolubly. And he saw now that while denying his powers, he had used them unconsciously, intuitively, as he
played his instruments. And realizing that, he also knew that
there was no point in further resistance.

'Yes,' he whispered at last. 'Please, help me.'

It was not easy. Ansaryon had warned him that this journey
would be long and hard, and he knew already that major acts of
sorcery, such as healing his arm, required enormous and concentrated effort, especially if they were not aided by a rush of emotion, whether rage or panic. In cold blood, it was at first very
difficult. But Ansaryon began by teaching him the techniques of
concentration and control, so essential to all less gifted sorcerers
who had to conserve and care for their limited, drug-induced
powers. He knew that he was taking a substantial risk, for once
Bron had acquired such skills, his abilities would be considerably
enhanced. But without them, he was blundering, ignorant and
inexperienced, in the dark.

Bron found that these lessons had an effect that his father
could not have anticipated. And he did not tell him that he had
used the new techniques to help him in his long battle against the
Wolf. He discovered that he could keep his enemy locked away
so deep within his soul that for days, months at a time the Devourer lay dormant, a menace no longer. The nightmares diminished in frequency and intensity, and then stopped altogether. For
the first time in his life, Bron began to feel that his power was
indeed a gift, rather than a burden.

At the same time, the King introduced him to the formal
history and theory of magic. Bron learned how the First Sorcerer,
the revered Ai-Mayak of Jo'ami, discovered by chance the extraordinary properties of the drug Annatal, named after the island
in the K'tali Archipelago where he had found it: how its use
gradually spread through the scattered islands, chiefly to control

the sea and the weather, and direct schools of fish into nets; how it was eagerly taken up by the Toktel'yans, who with their love of order and regulation immediately organized Schools of Magic, with a Guild to govern all aspects of sorcery; and how the Empire's need to control the supply of Annatal, without which all of its mages would die, had led to the conquest of that island and all the others in the Archipelago. Only Jo'ami still remained free, for it was too isolated, mysterious and frightening even for the methodically aggressive Toktel'yans, to whom sorcery was now the highest of all the Great Arts, superior to music, painting, writing and sculpture.

And with the history of magic he learned the Four Rules laid down by Ai-Mayak, more than a thousand years ago. Sorcery should be used unselfishly, for the benefit of many; it was forbidden to harm any living thing, or to damage or destroy; the sorcerer must employ forethought and restraint; and he should accept full responsibility for the consequences if any of the first three rules were broken.

'As I have broken them, several times,' Ansaryon said to his son. 'Did you know that?'

'You killed the Ska'i who attacked Sar D'yenyi,' Bron said. 'Kefiri told me.'

'So you know that I too have many deaths on my conscience,' said the King of Zithirian. 'And other crimes as well . . . You are aware that yours is a terrible gift. I think you learned that lesson four years ago. Now, you must try to balance yourself – to weigh the need and the power. Have you ever made an Illusion?'

Bron nodded.

'Can you show me one now?'

This was a skill that looked easy, but was in fact rather more difficult than it appeared. To construct an image in the mind, and project it so that it seemed real to those watching, required considerable powers of concentration, as well as a strong visual memory. Imaginative flights of fancy were much simpler.

Tentatively, the boy shaped an outline with his hands. Between them stepped a mountain deer, of the kind that proliferated on the slopes of Estray, above Sar D'yenyi. Graceful, with delicate, four-pronged antlers, it glanced round nervously, licking its lips, and then bent to graze unseen plants.

'Very good,' Ansaryon began, and then paused, for in the corner of the room he saw another creature, spotted, sinuous, with gleaming eyes and wicked claws: a beast suddenly and sharply familiar, so that he whispered, 'Fess?'

The hunting cat turned its gaze on him and growled softly. The deer flung up its head and barked a warning. Bron gestured, and both images vanished as abruptly as they had sprung into exact and vivid life.

To make one Illusion took care and skill and power. To make two, interacting . . .

Ansaryon drew in his breath sharply. He said, 'Was that Fess?'

'My stepmother's hunting cat? Yes, it was. I saw her several times, at Sar D'yenyi.'

'And in Minassa,' said Ansaryon, remembering the riverside terrace, and a man lighting coloured lanterns at dusk, and the small fair-haired boy who had accompanied him. And Fess, every hackle bristling, growling as she always did when faced with sorcery: like most animals, she loathed it.

He looked at his son, not a great deal taller now, nearly five years later, and smiled. 'I don't think I can teach you very much about making Illusions.'

There was not much he could teach Bron either about moving objects with sorcery: or scrying, or any of the other skills that had taken the young Ansaryon several years to acquire from the elderly Mazath who had instructed him in secret. His son had presumably learned it all from D'thliss, his evil mentor. Ansaryon did not wish to delve too obviously into Bron's horrible childhood: some of those memories must be hideous in the extreme. Besides, he sensed a block in the boy's mind, a bulwark erected against the prying of others. He had no idea that it was there not only to keep invaders out, but to keep the Wolf in.

Thoughtlink was a major part of any sorcerer's repertoire, one of the most valuable skills, and also the one most open to misuse. For it could also be employed for other, darker purposes: coercion, spying, eavesdropping. Used wisely, it could cement a close affinity between two adepts: Ansaryon's bond with Halthris had begun when they had opened their minds to each other. To have no need of spoken words was a rare and wonderful thing, even if, now, they used the skill mainly to exchange silent ideas and opinions at Council meetings, and on other occasions where such thoughts uttered aloud would be inappropriate. Ansaryon did not know if Bron would prove as gifted in this field as in all the other branches of sorcery which he had studied, but there was only one way to find out.

By now, his son was fourteen, and had been his pupil for more than a year. He was growing, too, although Ansaryon suspected that D'thliss's early neglect meant that he would never be as tall as his father. His face was still a child's, but behind the dark eyes a mind of considerable intelligence and power was coming to maturity. So far, he had shown astonishing aptitude for sorcery: and his studies in more mundane subjects were, so his tutors reported, well in advance of his age. The glowing accounts of his quickness and understanding, his fluency of thought and expression, the ease with which he had learned several languages and above all his glorious talent for music, expressed both in singing and playing, might have been dismissed as flattery: but Ansaryon knew them to be true. Certainly Bron worked hard, so hard that he had little time for play. Most of the other children had come to respect him, but he seemed to have no close friends. His magic was drawing him further apart from his fellow pupils, and Ansaryon, who also knew what it was like to be separated from ordinary people by the burden of sorcery, could offer no remedy. He could only observe the child's self-contained, reluctant isolation, and pity him. For even thoughtlink, necessarily restricted by a forest of rules and precepts, could never prove to be a bridge between Bron and the rest of the world.

He learned it, nevertheless, with the same almost unconscious ease with which he now absorbed all of his father's lessons, so that sometimes Ansaryon had the distinct impression that he was teaching the boy something which he already knew. Certainly, Bron could already defend his mind against unwanted invasion. It was rather more difficult to acquire the ability to open his senses to the chaos of thoughts, emotions and sensations given off by others. Bron was above all reluctant to make himself so vulnerable. And he found, too, that the impressions and facts which he had assimilated so easily that he had never been able to say how he had come to know them, only that he did, were very much more difficult to acquire using conscious effort.

It took another two years of study, for Ansaryon, well aware of the dangers involved, constructed the lessons step by step, reinforcing at every point the inviolable rules of thoughtlink. Any unauthorized entry into another's mind was, of course, utterly forbidden. In any case, most people who were not naturally gifted could not be invaded, although it was easy to obtain a general impression of their current emotions. Sorcerers learned to build adequate defences against such attack: the rule was essential, though, to protect those who were unguarded through illness, stupidity or naïvety – or those who were unaware, as Halthris once had been, of their latent powers.

The rule banning coercion was even stronger, and Bron knew the need for it from his own experience. D'thliss had forced him to do her will, and for a long time, unaware that there was any alternative, he had obeyed her. Then he had discovered that he could defy her, and do it so subtly that she did not realize that he was the culprit. It was rumoured that the Ska'i shamans had known how to make mindslaves, turning people into gibbering husks of humanity who could be ordered to maim or even kill themselves. And one of his most terrible memories was of the day when D'thliss, realizing at last that he was beginning to break free from her domination, had attempted to Bind him to her will, for ever.

The Ska'i, wanting him and his powers for themselves, had rescued him, killed D'thliss and burned the Temple to the ground with all the priests of Tayo inside it. He supposed he ought to be grateful to them, but irony was not yet a quality that he was ready to acquire.

And always, at every lesson, the message was hammered into his brain, over and over again. *You possess enormous power. You have learned how to use it for a wide variety of purposes. You have a responsibility to everyone else, to act with care, and restraint, and forethought. You cannot have power without wisdom – balance is everything. If you employ sorcery foolishly, or recklessly, or maliciously, then you do not deserve to use it, and you will not be allowed to.*

Bron, growing at last, the bones strengthening under the soft child's face, the voice deepening, on the brink of adulthood, listened and absorbed. And the Wolf in his heart, locked away now for so long that sometimes he could almost forget he had ever existed, lay silent, acquiescent, and did not ask who, in all the known world, would have the ability to make him limit or cease his sorcery, if he did not wish it.

He grew until he was eighteen, and then stopped. By then, he was the same height as Queen Halthris, but a handspan or more shorter than Ansaryon. Like his father, though, he was lightly built, agile and quick, and undoubtedly the best player of Pella in the Palace, when he had time for a game in the winter. But he still had no real friends, although there were plenty of girls who would have liked to be more familiar with him. His looks were striking, the fair hair contrasting with the deep, dark, enigmatic eyes, and the gift which set him apart from the other young men of his age also made him extraordinarily attractive to some of their more impressionable sisters. But Bron, deep in study, fascinated by his Art, exhilarated by power, as yet took little notice of them.

Herris pointed it out, at one of their infrequent meetings at the Flower of Hope. He was still labouring towards his heart's desire, his own ship, spending each summer working for Toktel'yans, and much of every winter in Minassa, helping at a ship-building yard. Now that Bron had grown up, the four-year gap between them had diminished in significance, and although their busy lives ensured that they seldom met, in some strange way their friendship had strengthened. They made an odd pair, the ruffianly dock hand and the well-dressed Prince, but Skathis liked handsome young men, and made sure that they always had a quiet table and unwatered wine.

One of the serving girls was also, obviously, attracted. She was new, very young, and boldly pretty. Herris, who fancied himself as Hegeden's gift to women, had been after her for weeks, without success. But, as he ruefully observed, as soon as Bron entered the tavern she was at their table, trying to eat out of his hand.

'Was she? I can't say I noticed.' The younger boy's tone was one of almost comical uninterest.

Herris threw up his hands in mock despair. 'Come on – you can't be serious! All my other friends would give a week's wages for a kiss and a kind word from Djendri – and she's all over you before you sit down!'

'She did take my order very quickly,' Bron said, without a flicker of a smile.

Herris looked at him closely, and then grinned in triumph. 'Liar! You *did* notice her! Well, I suppose that's the way the dice always falls – those who want can't have, those who can have don't want!'

Bron smiled back, his eyes gleaming with the teasing, mischievous humour that only those closest to him ever saw. 'I have better things to do with my time – and my money. In a year or two, I might be interested. For now, I have my studies to finish.'

'Yes. Them.' Herris, who distrusted magic and had in any case abandoned conventional lessons at a rather early age, took refuge in a generous swig of spiced gellin, a popular winter drink made of fermented honey. He swallowed, and glanced round at the other customers in the hot, smoky room. Two months after Sundim, the river was still frozen, so there were no Toktel'yan sailors, but he could see the usual mix of labourers and potters, a few less discriminating merchants, and a group of wealthy students laughing very loudly and displaying their daring at entering this supposedly notorious tavern. As he watched them with some derision, one called out. 'Hey, Bron! Didn't expect to see you here!'

The Prince raised a cool hand in acknowledgement. It wasn't enough for the student: he got up, mug in hand, and swaggered over to their table. Herris, suddenly wary, watched him approach. His fair hair, fine clothes, and consciously affected aristocratic tones represented a great many things that ordinary Zithiriani disliked. Herris knew that he'd seen him before, and suddenly remembered when, and where. This was the boy who had pushed Bron over on the ice at the Pella tournament, five years ago.

'Who's your brawny friend, eh?' said the young man to Bron. He had obviously made a serious impression on the gellin, and was having difficulty speaking clearly. 'You kept him very quiet.'

'Herris Gandar's Son,' Bron said. His calm voice and still face gave nothing away: not for the first time, Herris had no idea of what he might be thinking – or, more worryingly, what he might be about to do. 'Gorseth Mydan's son. We play Pella together, sometimes. I've played it with Herris, too.'

'But I don't make a habit of knocking my team-mates over,' Herris said.

Gorseth appeared not to notice the jibe. His eyebrows rose. 'Is Pella *all* you two play together?'

It wasn't the first time someone had made that insinuation. Herris could understand why – Bron, with his pale hair and austerely beautiful face, drinking in a low tavern with a burly docker – but the other's sneering tone infuriated him. He opened his mouth to say something pungently rude to the jumped-up little toad, but Gorseth forestalled him. 'Don't worry, I won't tell anyone – I'll just leave you two lovebirds to get on with it.' And he turned and pushed his way back to his table, where the laughter of his friends told of their amusement at Herris's and Bron's expense.

'Hegeden's wings, I'll kill him!'

'Don't.' Bron's face was still remarkably impassive, but Herris saw, with considerable alarm, that his eyes had gone opaquely dark in a way that was suddenly and horribly familiar. 'He isn't worth the bother. I should just make sure that if they come in here again, you're necking with one of the girls.'

'What about you? Don't you mind?' To Herris, the accusation struck deep, and he found it hard to understand Bron's lack of reaction.

'I can't mind.' The younger man stared back at him, his eyes still dense. 'If I did, I might do something I'd regret.'

The hairs rose on the back of Herris's neck. For an instant, he had a vast and terrifying glimpse of the immeasurable power that Bron was keeping in check. He said jokingly, trying to make light of it, 'Can't you just scorch his hand or something? Teach him a lesson?'

The disturbing eyes closed. Bron recited in a soft monotone, 'The Four Rules of Sorcery, as laid down by Ai-Mayak, of the Island of Jo'ami in the Reign of the Emperor Tark'yel, fifteen hundred years ago. The sorcerer acts with restraint. The sorcerer does not do harm. The sorcerer uses his powers unselfishly. And if any of the first three Rules are broken, the sorcerer must accept full responsibility for the consequences.'

'Oh,' said Herris, nonplussed. 'I didn't realize – I thought you could do what you liked.'

'I can.' Bron's eyes opened again, and there was a peculiar expression in them which his friend could not interpret. 'But I have to face my responsibilities. If I do break any of those rules, it will be over something really important – not that silly fool with the brains of a marsh vole and the manners of a Ska'i axeman.'

His voice fell into a momentary lull. The raucous laughter at the students' table stopped abruptly. With a sudden sinking feeling at the pit of his stomach, Herris saw Gorseth get up, his overbred aristocratic face scarlet with fury. He said urgently, 'You've done it now! How are you going to stop him and his mates beating us to a pulp?'

'I'm not. You are.' Bron grinned, suddenly and disarmingly. 'By the look of him, a light touch should send him crashing to the floor. I bet you won't even work up a sweat.'

Herris stared at him. For a brief wild moment, he didn't know whether to laugh at the cheek of it, or hit him. Then a loud crash and a howl of pain distracted him. Gorseth had tripped, fallen heavily and cracked his head on a table. He sat in an undignified sprawl, blood trickling down the side of his face, while his friends roared with unkind and inebriated laughter.

Herris opened his mouth to comment on the narrowness of their escape, and was struck by an awful thought. He hissed to his companion, 'Did you do that?'

Bron's face was a bland mask of innocence. 'I told you,' he said mildly. 'A sorcerer acts with restraint. A sorcerer does no harm to others.'

'That's what you *said*.' Herris, quite skilled in the arts of deception himself, knew how to discern the signs of similar subterfuge in others, and he eyed Bron with considerable suspicion. 'I suppose I ought to be grateful to you.'

'No need,' the younger man pointed out. 'His quarrel was with me, after all. He's never liked me, ever since that Sundim game of Pella.'

A dazed Gorseth was being hauled to his feet by the other students, watched by Skathis, her fists on her hips and an ominous scowl on her handsomely painted face. Clearly, the group had overstepped even her rather wide boundaries of good behaviour. Herris tried not to look too triumphant as they staggered to the street door, supporting Gorseth between them, and shouting incoherent threats and insults over their shoulders at their former hostess.

'Good riddance,' Skathis said, dusting her hands briskly as the door was shut behind them by one of the intimidatingly muscular serving men she always took care to employ. 'I run an orderly house here, and I don't mind if you're a king or a peasant – if you cause no trouble and drink your gellin like good boys and girls, I'm always happy to take your money.'

Amid shouts of laughter and approval, she walked back between the tables towards her inner room, with its unobtrusive spyhole, which those who were not numbered amongst her cronies called the Dragon's Den. Herris, a regular customer, tactfully hid his face in his mug. Out of the corner of his eye, he saw that she was pausing by their table. Her bodice, straining to confine her surplus flesh, was loaded with jewels, and some of them looked as though they might even be real. The embroidery on the crimson silk of her gown – the finest weave, one of the most expensive dyes – was of exquisite quality, perhaps even his own mother's work.

'Herris Gandar's Son.'

Reluctantly, he put down the mug and looked up.

'You're a good customer, and I won't chuck you out – this time. But who's this? I've seen him in here with you occasionally. If he's a troublemaker – '

Bron smiled. With his long-lashed dark eyes, his pale hair and fine-featured face, and his slight physique, he seemed a deceptively ethereal creature, and Herris suspected that most middle-aged women would want to mother him.

Not Skathis, however: a less maternal female never breathed. She surveyed him closely for a moment or two, and then said softly, 'You're the Prince, aren't you? The sorcerer?'

'Yes,' said Bron.

'Thought so. I can smell it, you know – I didn't spend all my time in Toktel'yi on my back, and I wasn't born yesterday either. Use it in here again and you're out for good – understand?'

The blond boy nodded.

'Good. Glad that's sorted. Don't get me wrong – I've reason to be grateful to your kind. But not in my tavern, all right? I want to keep my customers, not have them turned into frogs or snakes.'

'Shape-changing,' said Bron, as if quoting from a textbook, 'is not thought to be possible in the current state of the knowledge and practice of sorcery. But if you want an entertaining Illusion, I'd be happy to oblige.'

'No!' Skathis said, too sharply – several heads turned. 'Save that for Toktel'yi, if you ever go there. You should – it's full of sorcerers.'

'I might.' Bron gazed meltingly up at her, his expression completely and deceptively innocent. 'And if I need advice on the best taverns – and other places – I know where to come.'

Skathis laughed, and patted him on the shoulder. 'And with that face, my boy, you'll need to be careful. You'll have women – and men – round you like bees round a honey-jar.'

'Good thing I know how to fend them off, isn't it?'

The tavern-keeper threw up her hands in mock resignation, and continued on her stately progress back to her den. The level of talk around them rose again, but Herris was conscious of the covert scrutiny of many pairs of eyes. He drained his mug and stood up. 'I'd better be going. I'm riding down to Minassa tomorrow at first light, to do some work in the yard, and I won't be back for a month or two – on the first ship after the thaw, hopefully. So see you soon, all right?'

Bron rose as well. They were similar in height, but the older man was far broader and more muscular than the young Prince. He said, 'Skathis has a point. I ought to go to Toktel'yi, one day.'

'I'm hoping to make a trip this year,' Herris told him. 'You can be the first passenger on the *Flower of Hope*, when I build her. Can you do weather work yet? Or control currents and tides?'

'It's part of this winter's curriculum.'

'Then you can travel free of charge.' Herris stopped in the street doorway, his hands extended in the universal gesture of friendship. 'Well, goodbye. And be careful. Is Gorseth the only troublemaker up at the Palace, or are there any others?'

'After that Pella game, I thought he'd learned his lesson – he hasn't been much trouble until today. He's just made no secret of the fact he disliked me. I don't care – the feeling's mutual. Don't worry about me, Herris Gandar's Son – I can look after myself.'

'I know you can,' said his friend. 'That's what worries me. Goodbye, Bron – see you in the spring!'

The Prince watched him swagger away down the street, until his stocky figure was lost amongst the crowds. Then, aware of a sharp pang of envy, he turned towards the Palace. Herris could go anywhere, do anything, be anything: his unquenchable optimism and the bright lure of his dream would carry him onwards to lands and sights and experiences more marvellous and exotic than most Zithiriani would ever know. And he, Bron, was doomed to the necessary constrictions of his position and his power. A King's son, even a bastard, could not work his passage on ships or earn money heaving bales of silk or barrels of wine. And he knew enough about the complex and dangerous relationship between Zithirian and the Empire to know that he would never be able to travel openly to Toktel'yi.

For the Empire would always covet the Silver City, its wealth and its gold. Its spies undoubtedly knew of the extraordinary powers claimed for Ansaryon's eldest son: powers that could be used in defence of Zithirian, or in attack. And if he ever fell into the hands of the Toktel'yans, they would not waste such an opportunity. King's son or not, they would kill him.

CHAPTER
FOUR

'Do it again! *Please*, Bron, do it again!'

The three children jumped up and down, fizzing with excitement. Their elder half-brother gave them a brief, quelling glance. 'Not until you sit down again. All of you. Yes, you too, Zathti.'

The smallest, who was four, dropped with a sigh on to the stool between her brothers. '*Please*, Bron,' she said wheedlingly, her blue eyes imploring. 'I do so want to see it again.'

'Shut up,' hissed Tayma, who was on her left. 'Or he won't do it. Remember last time?'

Zathti gave a last rebellious, impatient wriggle, and sat still. On either side of her, Homan and Tayma were rigid with tense expectation, their gaze fixed intently on the young man who stood in the centre of the nursery chamber which the three children shared.

Bron let his face assume the solemnity thought proper to the performance of the magic arts. He needed no such ritualistic trappings for this, but they liked to see such mumbo-jumbo: it added to their sense of awe and mystery. And Zathti, in particular, had to be put firmly in her place.

Muttering an impressively elaborate stream of gibberish, he stretched out his hands. Between them, the air began to glow softly. His fingers sketched a shape, and fire flowed round it. As the flames faded, a tiny winged horse grew solid in their place, golden, gleaming, as perfect, lovely and transient as a bubble.

Their eyes were gratifyingly distended with wonder and amazement. He made the horse stamp above his palm, and neigh shrilly. Then it leapt upwards and flew round their heads on swift, graceful wings.

Of course, it was Zathti who touched it. As the two boys yelled indignantly, the winged horse faded like a rainbow without sun, until not even the air shimmered where it had been.

'Oh, *Zathti*!' cried Homan. He was seven, a sturdy boy with freckles and his mother's red-gold hair, and a regrettably hot temper. 'Why don't you *ever* listen? Now look what you've done. We'll lock you in the clothes chest next time Bron comes, so we can have some peace.'

'No, you won't!' The ferocity of Zathti's expression contrasted alarmingly with the sweet innocence of her blue eyes and golden hair. 'I'll scream and scream and M'yani will come and then you'll be in real trouble, so there!'

'Quiet, you two,' said Tayma. He was the heir to the throne of Zithirian, and even at the age of nine took his position seriously. His diplomatic skills were already well honed by the necessity of keeping the peace between his two turbulent younger siblings. 'I'm sorry, Bron. Could you make another Illusion for us? Please?'

After a nerve-racking pause, his half-brother smiled. 'Very well. But touch this one, Zathti, and there'll be no more for a month. Understand?'

The little girl nodded, her round face very solemn beneath the unbrushed shock of thick fair hair. 'Yes, Bron.'

Zathti's promises were always sincere, at the time of making them, but her brothers had scant faith in her ability to keep this one. Over her tangled head, Homan's blue eyes met Tayma's grey ones. Silently, as if on a prearranged signal, each boy pinioned the child's arms, Tayma on her left, Homan on her right. Zathti gave an indignant squeak of protest, but a glance from Bron subdued her. United for once in an expectant silence, the three children sat and watched as the most powerful sorcerer, probably, in all the known world constructed another Illusion for their exclusive entertainment.

The thought that such a trivial use of his powers might be beneath his dignity had never crossed Bron's mind. He would be nineteen at High Summer, two months away, and had grown very fond of his father's other children during the five and a half years he had lived in the Palace. In return, their flattering admiration for his powers had played a considerable part in his growing acceptance of his gift. He loved to see their faces in the yellow glow of witchfire, rapt and enchanted. It did not entirely compensate for Gorseth's open dislike, or the wary respect of the other students at the Palace school. But in the children's company, he could forget the distance between himself and the rest of the world, ironically by employing the sorcery which had originally created that gulf.

On the new tiled floor in front of the children, a city began to spread, tower by tower, in the looping bend of a rushing river of swift brown water. Tayma recognized it first. 'Look, it's Zithirian! There's the Kefirinn, and the docks – the Sunset Gate – '

'The new walls,' Homan added, as the river bulwark grew from air with an ease which would have made its builders, who had taken three years to complete it, deeply envious. 'And the Council Hall, look, there, at the end of Sunset Street.'

'I can't see,' Zathti complained, struggling in her brothers' firm grasp, but they ignored her and continued to point out each feature of their city as it grew before them. Now, ten years after the invasion of the Ska'i, the rebuilding of the Palace was almost complete. The Central Tower, the only survivor of the destruction, rose slender and graceful from the middle of a spacious group of stone buildings, each two or three storeys high, set around a dozen courtyards. Everywhere, the harsh regular lines of the new work were softened by plants. Trumpet vines, with their sweet smelling white and yellow flowers, clung to walls and scrambled energetically over the red tiled roofs, sometimes growing the length of a man's arm in a day in good weather. The courtyard of every house, however small, boasted a patch of green herbs, a vine pendulous with tiny grapes, and a huge variety of pots, tubs and containers full of colourful blooms.

'It's like looking down at a map,' Homan whispered, his freckled face rapt.

'It's what a bird would see,' Tayma said. 'Oh, look, Homan, look at the river!'

A tiny boat, no longer than his fingernail, set out across the current, heading for the cemetery on the bank opposite the docks. They stared as the minute oarsman battled against the powerful flow of the Kefirinn in spring, swollen by melted snow from the mountains. When he made a perfect landfall against the jetty on the other side, and folded his oars, the children applauded.

Smiling, Bron gestured with his left hand. The area on the eastern side of the river, where the dead of Zithirian were buried and the living liked to stroll in summer amid the monuments and the gardens, had been just a greenish blur. Now the details sharpened: trees, gravel paths, the stone statues commemorating the wealthy and the famous, the simpler slabs laid over the graves of ordinary people, all suddenly became distinct, as though the children had blinked away tears. Two minuscule passengers climbed from the boat on to the jetty, and walked away along the path towards the green shady heart of the cemetery, hand in hand.

For a while longer Bron kept the Illusion before them, every detail of the city perfect. Zathti longed to stroke the tiny animals in the fields close to the Sunset Gate, to pick up the diminutive citizens hurrying about their business, to touch the crowds in the market, the ships in the dock, the banners flying from the towers along the walls, each one bearing the blue Aiyan, flower of hope. But her brothers still held her arms in their firm grip, and so she had to be content with watching, and wishing that she had a miniature city to play with. She wanted a real one, though, solid and tangible as this, despite its vivid appearance, was not.

At last Bron relaxed his concentration, and the image on the floor gradually faded. The periphery disappeared first, then the outer walls, and finally the rest of the city. Last to go was the Central Tower of the Palace, and the children stayed quite still, gazing at the spot on the floor where it had stood, until not a vestige of it remained.

'Oh, Bron, that was wonderful!' Tayma let out his breath in a big gusty sigh. 'That's the best one yet! I *wish* I could do that.'

'You can't,' said Zathti. 'You're not a sorcerer.'

'You could be,' Bron told him. 'You use thoughtlink with Homan, don't you?'

The two boys stared at him, comically surprised. Tayma recovered his poise first. 'How do you know?'

'He's a sorcerer, of course,' Homan said. 'He's bound to know. Mages always know when power is being used, don't they, Bron?'

'Not always – but usually.' His half-brother, more wearied by the effort of creating such an elaborate illusion than he cared to reveal, sat down on Zathti's bed. 'But you do make it rather obvious. I've often noticed it before.'

'Oh.' Homan exchanged glances with his elder brother. 'We thought it was our secret.'

'Does Father know?' Tayma enquired anxiously.

'Yes, he does. He hasn't discussed it with me, don't worry, but from one or two things he's said, I'm sure he knows. Anyway, it wouldn't be very surprising. Magical powers can be inherited – passed from parent to child like fair hair or blue eyes. And since your father and mother both have natural abilities, the chances are that you possess them too.'

'Me? What about me? Can I do magic?' Zathti cried, bouncing up and down on her stool.

'I don't know. When you're bigger, perhaps.' Bron's dark eyes studied her, and his little sister gave a sudden squirm and went very still, her face pink. 'Yes,' he added. 'When you're grown up.'

'I can't wait till then – I want to do it *now*!'

'Imagine what she'd be like,' Tayma groaned. 'She'd pinch all the food – '

' – make poor M'yani disappear – '

' – probably try and get rid of us, too – '

'I want to fly,' Zathti said. 'I'd rather do that than *anything*.'

'Well, maybe one day you'll have your wish.' Bron smiled at her. 'For the moment, though, you're much too young. I didn't start my training till I was thirteen.'

'Oh.' Zathti looked completely downcast.

Homan patted her kindly on the back. 'Never you mind, Zath. We'll look after you until you grow up – if you ever do!'

'Of course I will.'

'You might not,' Tayma told her solemnly. 'You might be so naughty that Bron puts a spell on you so you'll be a child for ever and ever, so you'll *never* be able to do magic!'

Zathti looked so woebegone at this that Bron took pity on her. 'That's enough teasing. Zathti, you can use sorcery for many things, but not to stop people growing. It just isn't possible, so don't worry.'

'Really?' The little girl looked at him with vast eyes. 'So I could be a sorcerer too one day, if I wanted?'

'No, you couldn't,' Homan said brusquely. 'Whoever heard of a girl sorcerer?'

'There have been women who use magic,' Bron said, and an unwelcome and chilling memory slunk into his mind of D'thliss, her shrivelled body prematurely aged by her use of the drug Annatal, her eyes bright with evil. He repressed the image immediately, but Tayma's face had suddenly whitened, and he knew that the boy had glimpsed it too. Untrained natural ability was dangerous: his brothers would need to be taught to use thoughtlink properly, or there might be all kinds of trouble ahead.

Of course, he himself had desperately resisted instruction for years, but his reasons had been unique. He didn't think Tayma and Homan would lack enthusiasm.

'Bron?' The elder boy was suspiciously eager to change the subject. 'Bron, are you going to enter the Bridal Race this year?'

'He can't,' said Homan. 'He isn't twenty yet.'

The Bridal Race was run each year in spring, and was due to take place in a few days' time. Every young man who had undergone the coming-of-age ceremony known as Entering was eligible, and several hundred usually took part. Most ran only once, but others, keen to show off their physical prowess, took part year after year until they married or decided that it was too risky. Contestants had to make a complete circuit of the city walls, a distance of some three or four Toktel'yan miles from the south side of the docks to the north, and finish by swimming across the Kefirinn to the cemetery, where the King and Queen would present the successful with silver medals. Usually, about three quarters of the field completed the course, some very much more slowly than others. Many collapsed exhausted towards the end of the run, or had to be rescued from the river by one of the boats. Those who failed were objects of pity or ridicule. And almost every year, someone drowned.

Ansaryon, as a young man, had pointedly refused to compete at all, and had been despised for his supposed cowardice at the time, although now his popularity was such that few remembered he had once been thought an effeminate weakling. Bron said, 'Homan's right. I'm not supposed to enter officially, but there'll be so many people that I could join in and no one would know until I'd finished. Herris did that.'

The children had never met Herris, but they had often heard Bron speak of him. Homan said curiously, 'Would you use sorcery? If you found it too difficult?'

'I don't honestly know.' Bron's face was thoughtful. 'I think I'd try *not* to use it. I'd be cheating if I did, after all – I'd have to make sure no one noticed, or I'd be a laughing-stock. But if I was in danger of drowning – yes, I suppose I would. Sorcerers can levitate themselves, so I should be able to walk over the river if I wanted!'

'Oh, please be careful, Bron,' Zathti said anxiously.

Homan laughed. 'Don't be so silly, Zath – he isn't going to run it till next year!'

'Don't worry,' Bron told her kindly: he was very fond of his little half-sister. 'I'll make quite sure I'm safe, even if I have to fly over the river rather than swim it.'

He had not thought about entering the Bridal Race early, but now that Tayma had planted the idea in his head, he found that he wanted to run it this year. He had no fear that he would fail: he had played a lot of Pella over the winter, despite all the other claims on his time, and he was still quite fit. And like all young men in Zithirian, he could swim well. Even the Kefirinn, more than two hundred paces in width and fast-flowing with ice-cold melted snow, would not present a problem unless he was very unlucky.

He remembered that Gorseth, a year older than he was, would certainly be taking part. The thought of his face when he saw Bron completing the course, even though he was officially too young, was very tempting. And Herris had done it a year early, too, to impress some girl.

There were no girls whose eye Bron wished to catch, but there was still a deep-rooted hunger in him for success, admiration, approval. And running the Bridal Race when still only eighteen (though he would be nineteen in High Summer) would certainly increase his status amongst the other young people whose lessons he shared at the Palace school.

But failure was unthinkable: he had no intention of competing unless he was sure he could succeed. He got up very early the next morning, put on an old tunic and trousers, and slipped out of the Palace while even the servants were mostly still asleep. It was too risky to try the official course round the walls: someone would be sure to see him and know why he was doing it, and then his father would probably forbid him to join the race. So he walked out of the Sunset Gate as soon as it was opened at dawn, and ran along the road that followed the Kefirinn, winding down the river valley between farms and settlements until it reached Hailyan, ninety miles away on the border with Minassa.

And, further south, the places that Herris had mentioned, their names hauntingly and enticingly evocative of alien and exotic lands. Tamat; Sabrek; Toktel-yi, where he could never safely go.

It was four miles to the village of Marveth, and he reached it just before sunrise, breathless but not exhausted. He would have plenty of energy to spare for swimming the river. He bought a breakfast of bread and cheese and hot, refreshing kuldi from a surprised and curious farmer's wife, and walked back at a rather more leisurely pace, knowing that he would not be missed until lessons began, two hours after dawn.

The towers of Zithirian shimmered brightly in the clear, brilliant morning light. The sky was the cloudless, limpid blue of spring, and above him summer swifts, just arrived from the warmer lands of the south, swooped and chattered, scooping up myriad insects in their beaks as they flew. The grass was green and sweet, the new-leaved trees seemed to glow with the surge of fresh growth within them, and young animals frolicked in the fields along the road.

Bron took deep breaths of the fragrant air, savouring its scents, letting his senses open, as his father had taught him, to the whole world around him, sight, touch, smell, taste, hearing. He felt that he, like the plants around him, had sprung from the dark fertile soil of Zithirian, a part of this land as if the earth itself had nourished him. He saw the river with the eyes of a grey otter, sleek and shining and playful, cleaving the swift water in search of fish. He soared with the birds, and looked down at the wide valley with its neat patterns of fields and roads and houses; the wild grass of the steppe to the west, kept at bay by wall and ditch; the distant northern mountains sharp as spears, their shoulders still white with the remains of the winter snow; and the towers of his city, built in emulation, piercingly beautiful, demanding his loyalty and his love.

He did love it. But not as he had loved Sar D'yenyi, where he had learned how to be human again with the help of Kefiri's patient, devoted kindness. Some part of him would always linger in the citadel on the lake, a small, waif-like child wandering the stairs and rooms and corridors, safe and happy.

He didn't want to go back, though. Kefiri had made her life there with Invan, and they had two small daughters now. No, he was content to let Sar D'yenyi live in his memory, as clear and sharp and glorious as the Illusion of Zithirian he had created for the children. If he returned, he would find it smaller, shabbier, diminished, and the image in his mind would be for ever tarnished.

But some memories could not always be kept pristine. Every time Kefiri visited Zithirian – which was not often, for she hated to leave Sar D'yenyi, and pregnancy and motherhood were a good excuse to stay – Bron wished that she hadn't. He wanted to remember her as the young, lively, laughing girl who had restored him to life. He hated to see the look of hurt bewilderment in her eyes, as if she could not understand the reasons for her own unhappiness.

So it was with some dismay that he had heard that she and Invan would be coming to the city for the Bridal Race. As it was one of the four great annual festivals celebrated by the city, there was usually an important guest of honour in attendance. Last time, it had been Cathallon, Heir of Minassa, and his young bride, the Emperor's elder daughter K'djelk: before them, Alayni, the ruling Princess of Lelyent since a virulent fever epidemic had killed both her father, Prince Belerith, and her only brother. Bron hadn't met Kefiri for more than two years, although they corresponded regularly, and he did not think he could bear to see her again.

But of course he must. She and Invan arrived two days before the Race, riding down in state from the mountains and entering the city through the Sunset Gate. As usual, they were given a delighted welcome by the citizens, who would always love Kefiri for the part she had played in freeing them from the Usurper Tsenit and the Ska'i.

In two years, she had changed: she was plumper, and her abundant dark hair was speckled liberally with premature grey. Beneath the ceremonial circlet of spring flowers, her blue eyes were at once worried and wary. Her smile, though, as she greeted Ansaryon and Halthris at the new entrance to the Palace, was the old Kefiri, sparkling with pleasure. Invan stood just behind her, beaming with solid self-satisfaction.

He doesn't have the imagination to see how unhappy she is, Bron thought miserably. He hung back, letting his father and stepmother do all the talking, allowing the three younger children to rush forward with their own shrieks of delight: Homan and Tayma had spent a couple of months last summer at Sar D'yenyi, and adored their cousin. He didn't think that Kefiri had noticed his reluctance, but later, when the formal welcome was over, she came to find him.

Since the rebuilding of the Palace, the King and his family had occupied the rooms around the courtyard in the centre of the complex, graced by an intricate stone fountain of Ansaryon's own design. The endless gentle splash and spray of the water was a cooling counterpoint to the vigorous heat of summer in Zithirian: in winter, the streams froze into fabulous and fantastic shapes, a glittering sculpture in ice. Tall flowering trees grew in huge tubs set around it, and there were stone benches where people could sit in the shade on a scorching day, with petals drifting down from the branches above, soothed by the sound of the fountain and the busy endless hum of bees moving from blossom to blossom.

Bron often came here to practise his music. He loved to play in the courtyard, partly because it was such a pleasant place, and partly because, if he were honest, he liked an audience. For years he had shut himself away in his room, and in the days when his fingers had still been his mind's stiff and reluctant partners, he had hated anyone save his tutor to overhear his efforts. But as his confidence had grown, so had his need for approval and praise. Now almost every day the soft, intricate sounds of the Sith, or the pure liquid notes of his flute, could be heard in the courtyard, woven into the water and the bees and the harsher chatter of the brown and gold Zithiriani sparrows.

Kefiri listened, and smiled. He had certainly become extraordinarily accomplished over the last few years. She remembered his first hesitant efforts on her old Sith very clearly. She had never had much aptitude for music, but she loved to hear a good player, and it had seemed to be one way into the heart of the withdrawn, desolate child whom she had promised to heal, to repair the terrible damage done to him by D'thliss and the Ska'i. To her surprise – for she had by then almost given up hope of reaching Bron – the music had proved to be a turning point. The silent little boy began to open up, very hesitantly at first, like a spring flower too frightened of frost to offer its petals to the new warmth of the sun. But she had persevered, and at last he had responded fully to the love and affection which she had always given him, and which he had been too terrified and unhappy to accept.

And now, hearing that cascading pattern of notes, followed by the lovely sorrowful tune of a Zithiriani song called 'Enmayith's Lament', Kefiri felt a surge of pride in his achievement. She had never liked or understood the sorcery, dark and repressed within him during his years at Sar D'yenyi. But this was something in which everyone could find delight. And he was so good, far better than most of the professional singers and players who spent the summer months wandering up and down the towns and villages along the Kefirinn, and all winter as the guest of some rich aristocrat if they were talented and lucky, playing from tavern to tavern in Zithirian or Hailyan or Minassa if they were not.

'You could make a living doing that,' she said, as the final sad, delicate notes died away.

Bron showed no surprise at her presence. He put the instrument gently down on the bench beside him. It looked new: the bowl-shaped soundbox was inlaid with ivory and ebony pieces in a complex abstract geometrical pattern, and the sixteen paired strings, of fine silver wire, glittered untarnished in the dappled shade. 'Unfortunately, I don't need to make a living,' he said.

'Unfortunately?' Kefiri sat down, trying not to look too relieved. She was in the fourth month of pregnancy, a fact which she did not want him to know just yet, and standing still, even for a short while, made her very tired.

'Well, sometimes I think it might be pleasant to be ... nobody.' Bron looked down at the Sith, and drew the fingers of his left hand softly across the strings, so that the air around them shivered melodically for a heartbeat or two. 'Don't you ever feel like that?'

'No.' Kefiri paused. She wanted to tell him that her dearest wish was to be *somebody* again, to be the Lady of Sar D'yenyi, with valuable work to do, trusted, respected, loved. Invan had taken over that role: he had actually told her, soon after their marriage, that she had no need to worry her pretty little head now about such exhausting and unsuitable matters, for he was in control. And for six years she had been his wife, she had given birth to their two daughters, Amali and Tesi, and sometimes, wandering aimlessly through her beloved, beautiful citadel, she seemed like a ghost, unnoticed, unwanted, superfluous.

Yet she had a husband, a good kind man even if he was so unimaginative and very old fashioned about the role of women in his family. She had two delightful children, and above all she had what she had always wanted, a home at Sar D'yenyi. And so she had always felt guilty about her unhappiness, as if she were a spoilt child, crying for the stars when she already held the moon in her hand.

But Bron wouldn't understand. He was young and inexperienced, and although only nine years her junior, she sensed that a great and unbridgeable gulf had opened up between them as he grew up.

'Why are you so unhappy?'

Astonished, Kefiri jerked round to face him. His eyes, very dark beneath the level fair brows, stared seriously back, and she was reminded, suddenly and chillingly, of the Bron who had come witch-led to Sar D'yenyi to spy on her, and who had seemed to change from child to sorcerer in the space of a single heartbeat.

'Of course I'm not unhappy,' she said, hearing in her over-vehement denial the signs of her lie. 'Why should I be? I have everything I want.'

'But do you want everything you have?'

Kefiri took a deep breath. *I shall* not *cry*, she told herself fiercely. *I faced Tsenit and I defeated him – just because Bron has cut to the heart of it, I shall* not *break down like a little girl who's been naughty and can't face the consequences.*

'Yes,' she said, with spurious resolution.

Bron's gaze was unwavering. 'Liar,' he said softly.

With a shock, Kefiri realized that in two years he had grown up. This was not a child talking, not a self-centred boy, but an adult who had recognized her plight, and was willing to discuss it with her on equal terms. And then, she noticed that other things had changed. The sparse, hard-edged beauty of his face; the strength obvious in the set of his mouth, the width of his shoulders, the wiry body only lightly concealed by his thin summer tunic and trousers; the power to make magic and music asleep in his slender fingers; the scattering of fine silver hairs along his bare arms.

Sarraliss help me, Kefiri thought in panic, and averted her gaze. Her own undistinguished hands, the nails bitten down to the quick, lay folded in her lap. She concentrated on them, trying in vain to prevent a revealing blush from sweeping across her face. *This isn't right*, she thought in horror. *He's like a little brother, or a son – I am married, a mother*, old – *nine years older –*

'Kef? Are you all right?'

She nodded fiercely, still too frightened of her own feelings to look at him.

'I want to help,' Bron said, his voice low and urgent. 'There must be something you'd like to do – something you don't feel you ought – not with the baby.'

Startled, she looked up, and wished she hadn't. 'How did you know about that? I've only told one or two people.'

'I know.'

He had said this so often as a child, seeming to absorb impossible knowledge through the pores of his skin. Shaken, Kefiri found she could not look away. She said, 'There's nothing you can do. I have to take care of myself. It took me four days to persuade Invan to let me come. He wants a son very badly, and he's so afraid something will go wrong this time.'

'It won't.'

'How can you be sure? I've felt so sick and tired – ' She paused, seeing the intensity in his eyes. *Why am I sitting here,* she thought in bewilderment, *discussing my pregnancy with an eighteen-year-old boy, and wondering at the same time what it would be like to kiss him?*

'It won't,' Bron repeated. He put his hand over hers, where it lay in her lap. His touch was warm, and friendly, and astonishingly comforting. 'Kef – please – I want more than anything to see you happy again. Do you still play Pella?'

She laughed in surprise. 'No, of course not – and besides, if we tried now we'd sink.'

For the first time, Bron smiled. 'I don't think even my powers are strong enough to prevent that. But you see what I mean, don't you? You don't play Pella any more. You don't run Sar D'yenyi any more. You're treated like a priceless Minassan vase, and you're gathering dust.' His fingers touched her greying hair. 'You're not old, Kef. Come with me tomorrow – somewhere, anywhere – just be free for a day, and remember how to have fun.'

He hadn't mentioned Invan by name, but his image, too solid, too kind, too well-meaning, hovered between them so clearly he was almost tangible. She shook her head. 'No – I can't.'

For a long, long while they stared at each other. Above, in the blossom-laden tree, a flower disintegrated, and dropped its tiny cloud-white petals in a soft shower over them both. Then Bron picked up his Sith again, tucked it into his chest, and stroked a gentle hand over the strings. Her eyes suddenly prickling with tears, Kefiri recognized the light, cheerful notes of a tune called 'Rowing Down the River'.

'I'm sorry,' she said, and rose to her feet. Bron did the same. He was not tall, but even so she hardly came up to his chin. 'I want to – some part of me wants to – but if would be too dangerous. Please understand, Bron – there's nothing you can do.'

'No danger,' he said, smiling, his voice quite light. 'I'd rescue you if the boat capsized.'

But it was not that sort of danger she had meant: and both of them knew it.

The whole of Zithirian always turned out to watch the Bridal Race. Those who could afford it – the ferrymen always charged exorbitant prices on the day – were rowed over to the east bank of the Kefirinn, to watch the finish at the cemetery in the company of the King and Queen. Ansaryon and Halthris had chairs to sit on, an awning to shade them from the sun, and attendants to serve food and wine to them and their courtiers. Less exalted people balanced on tombs and monuments, or lined the banks and the jetty, eager to cheer on the swimmers. Over the river, spectators crowded every vantage point from dock to dock, held back by officials from each of the four quarters of the city.

At sunrise, the first competitors were already beginning to gather in the garden beneath the southern tower guarding the entrance to the docks. Most were obviously the customary age, twenty, but there was a sprinkling of swaggering, well-muscled older men, and one or two who, like Herris four years previously, might well be officially too young. As usual, there were flocks of women in attendance, anxious mothers and bright-eyed, teasing girls.

It had been comparatively easy for Bron to avoid joining the royal party: he had pleaded tiredness, and told his father that he would arrive later, just before the race was due to begin. Then he had changed into his oldest tunic, left the Palace by the servants' entrance, and made his way along back streets to the southern side of the docks. There were two or three ships tied up, including one that had arrived the previous evening. He looked for Herris amongst the labouring sailors and dockers, but in vain.

By now, there were two or three hundred people, half of them runners, milling about in the tower garden, and a handful of officials from the Merchants' Quarter were trying to instil some order into the confusion. Bron slipped into the middle ranks of the contestants as they were herded into some sort of column, the eager at the front, the unfit and the reluctant at the back. He had already spotted Gorseth in the first row, but took good care not to be seen. Once the starting trumpet blew, no one could drop out for any reason save exhaustion, collapse or death, until they crawled out of the river and up the cemetery bank.

The Headman of the Quarter, a lean and reputedly greedy merchant called Rethen, climbed up on to the top of the tower. Seeing him raise the trumpet to his lips, the seething crowds below fell silent. The runners stood ready, faces fierce with eagerness or concealed terror, fists clenched. Bron closed his eyes and concentrated his mind, as he had been taught. The race round the walls should be easy, but the swimming would be more difficult with the river so swift and full at this time of year. But he had no real worries, save being found out in these last moments before the start.

The trumpet sounded, a high shrill note. A great shout of enthusiasm burst from the crowd. Girls leapt up and down, shrieking encouragement to the young men as they jogged past them, up the steps alongside the tower, and began the long run around the ramparts.

At first the runners in the middle and at the rear could only walk, but as those in front sprinted off along the walls, the pace behind them increased. Determined to catch up with Gorseth, Bron began to thread his way through the other competitors. It made people notice him, and he was aware of being recognized, but it didn't matter. No one could stop him now.

By the time he approached the Sunset Gate, he could see his rival, in a red tunic with green braid, not very far ahead. This was not a real race, for everyone who completed the course was regarded as a winner, but considerable prestige attached to those who finished amongst the first dozen or so, and Bron was confident that he would be one of them. He jumped the last few steps leading down from the walls to Sunset Street, raced across the gateway, and up to the ramparts on the next section of wall. The sun was rising higher now, and later it would be uncomfortably warm, but at present it was perfect running weather, the air still spring-sharp and cool, with a gentle breeze blowing down from the western steppe.

He was nearly up with Gorseth before the other knew it. One of his companions glanced round, saw Bron, and gasped out something between strides. The older boy looked back, his face red with angry astonishment. Then he lowered his head and increased his pace.

Bron matched his rival's speed, feeling the sweat soaking his tunic, his heart pounding, his legs driving him tirelessly onward. It was as if he could run for ever at this rate. They were more than half way now, on the new section of the ramparts on the northern side of the city. To his right, below, lay the narrow close-ranked streets of the Embroiderers' Quarter, where Herris's mother Kaydi lived in a modest house on Snowbringer Street. Beyond, he could see the salubrious mansions and broad avenues of the Goldsmiths' Quarter, homes of the richest and most noble Zithiriani. The new ramparts continued right round the Palace, and he looked down as he ran. The gardens were crowded with servants shouting and waving as the runners passed. He thought he heard his name, although it was almost lost in the cheering.

And now the last stretch. Breathing was becoming more painful, and his legs felt heavy, but he had kept up with Gorseth, and there were only seven or eight competitors in front of them. Behind, more than a hundred runners straggled almost back to the Sunset Gate.

The wall running from Palace to dock was also new, and below it the river sped swiftly past, augmented by the chilly waters of the D'yenn, and churning brown and white in its haste. Ansaryon had been considering building a bridge across here: because of the depth and breadth of the Kefirinn at this point, not to mention the swiftness of its flow, it had always been thought impossible. And what would happen to the Bridal race, Bron wondered as he put a last urgent effort into his running, if everyone could walk across the river?

He drew level with Gorseth just as they came to the end of the wall. Steps swept down past the tower to the north side of the docks. As they started the descent, Gorseth glanced round, his face twisted with exertion and fury, and then jabbed his elbow into Bron's side.

The younger boy dodged, suddenly angry. In a race where the only aim was to finish, such behaviour was considered reprehensible. 'Out of my way!' Gorseth gasped savagely, and flung himself down the steps, with Bron in furious pursuit.

Ahead of them, more officials stood by the edge of the dock, beckoning them on. To stop, or even hesitate, was foolish – better to plunge straight in. Already the leading runner, a veteran of several races, was well out into the stream, and several more were toiling in his wake.

Bron reached the edge side by side with his rival. He saw the startled stare of the official as the man realized who he was, he heard someone shouting his name, and then, without giving himself time to think, leapt into the cold and murky water of the dock.

The shock took his breath away. He shot up to the surface, gasping. In front of him Gorseth, almost unrecognizable with his thick fair hair dark and streaming, was striking out for the river. Determined not to be beaten, Bron followed him, clawing through the water.

Swimming in the comparative calm of the docks was easy. Once out in the current, it was a very different matter, and the cold, fierce and insidious, could rob a man of his strength before he realized it. Bron knew that it would be foolhardy to make directly for the opposite bank. Far better to let the river take him with it for a little way. It didn't matter where he crossed, as long as he reached the far side.

Gorseth obviously believed that the shortest route was best, but he was having trouble keeping to it. Bron felt his arms and legs growing increasingly heavy, and realized that he had been stupid to make such efforts to catch his rival. At his age, completing the course would be honour enough. And he didn't want to be forced to use his power to save himself.

There were boats on the river, and ropes strung low across the water to help those in difficulties. Bron ducked under one of them, spurning it. He saw that he was already half-way out into the stream, and he kicked out with renewed vigour, confident now of success.

He had been aware, without taking much notice, of the noise of the crowd on both banks, cheering on the swimmers. Now suddenly the note changed from encouragement to alarm. Bron glanced upstream and saw the people on the jetty pointing, mouths open, screaming a warning. The current dragged against him, and he swam onwards, trying to see what was happening. Ahead of him, Gorseth seemed to be moving frantically without making much progress.

And then Bron saw it. A log, a tree-trunk, long and dark and rolling over and over in the heaving water. It was heading straight for Gorseth, but he didn't seem to have noticed it: he was too intent on defeating the river. Bron tried to shout, got a mouthful of water, spluttered coughing, and tried again. But there was no chance of being heard above the rush of the water and the cries of those watching.

In desperation, he sent his mind battering against his rival's. *Gorseth! Watch out! There's a log bearing down on you* – STOP SWIMMING!

The older boy turned his head. Bron saw his snarl of defiance, and knew that Gorseth thought he was trying to use sorcery against him. Frantically, he tried to send his warning again.

Gorseth's defences were too strong: Gorseth's hatred beat him back. In one last effort, Bron thrust his face clear of the river and screamed. 'Log – look out for the *log*!'

Then it struck, and he saw the other boy's head disappear as the tree-trunk rolled right over him.

It was coming straight for him, but unlike Gorseth, he had the power to deflect its course. A silent sháft of sorcery sent it spinning safely past, almost within his reach. It was three or four strides long, and its jagged broken branches looked capable of sinking a boat if it hit hard enough.

There was no sign of Gorseth in its turbulent wake, but Bron knew where he was. He took a huge gulp of air, and dived.

No point in opening his eyes, he wouldn't be able to see his hands in front of him. He could sense the other boy's body, swept along behind the log. *Concentrate the mind* – CONCENTRATE!

Power flowed from him, but the inexorable current of the Kefirinn was as strong. Under the water, blind, deaf, he yet had no need of air, no need of anything save the abnormal senses that told him where Gorseth was, and told him also that with just one more effort, he could reach him . . .

He never even realized that there was another log until it smashed into him.

CHAPTER
FIVE

On the banks of the Kefirinn, the people had cried their warnings in vain. Ansaryon, sitting with his family in the prime position just above the jetty, saw it all. The two heads in the water: the logs, perhaps the broken halves of a single tree, tumbling inexorably down towards them; the first boy struck, the other diving to rescue him; and the second trunk rolling over them both.

The ropes and the boats were useless. A great howl of anguish burst from the people. Kings were supposed to be aloof from the wild emotions of the crowd, but Ansaryon had never possessed the traditional coldness of Zithiriani monarchs. He leapt up with the rest to watch as the rescuers in their fragile craft rowed frantically over to where the two competitors had last been seen, their hooked grappling poles at the ready. Every ferryman had at some time performed the sad task of fishing for the drowned, and not only in the Bridal Race: there were many graves in the cemetery of those children, and adults, who had thought the Kefirinn was a harmless friend, and who had discovered too late its wayward currents, its life-sapping cold or its grasping weeds.

And then Homan, his face so white that every freckle stood out as sharp as if it had been painted on him, clutched at Ansaryon's hand, screaming. 'It's Bron – Father, it's *Bron*!'

The King stared at his youngest son in horror and disbelief. 'No – no, it can't be – he's not allowed to run until next year!'

'It *is*!' Homan hiccuped noisily, tears pouring down his face. 'It *is*, it *is* – he was trying to save Gorseth and then the log hit him and they're looking in the wrong *place*, Father, they're looking in the wrong *place*!'

He was hysterical now, his fists beating frantically against Ansaryon's chest. The King sent his mind instantly into the child's, heedless of the damage it might do to an untrained adept. *Where? Where is he?*

And Homan, wild with terror, nevertheless gave the answer

immediately. *Downstream, by the willows, in the middle of the weeds!*

Ansaryon tore himself free of the boy's clutching hands and pushed his way through the crowds. *Don't panic*, he told himself, calming the terrible fear, the voice which kept asking how long Bron could survive under water. He stopped on the very edge of the bank, here a miniature cliff of rocky earth about the height of a tall man, and cupped his hands to hail the boats. 'Not there! Downstream!'

One of them heard him, and gestured to the man keeping position with deep strong strokes while the others prodded their hooked poles below the surface. The rower shipped his oars and let the current take the boat downstream. Ansaryon ran beside it until he came to the grove of willows marking the present southern boundary of the cemetery.

There was nothing to see out in the middle of the river except the brown seething water, but Homan had been so certain, and thoughtlink could not lie . . .

He was there. Suddenly Ansaryon could sense him, could imagine his son's lifeless body, caught and held in a hideous tangle of long-fingered weeds, rolling and streaming with them in the current. He yelled, and pointed. The first boat came to the place and turned, the oarsman struggling to keep it more or less stationary while his two companions searched beneath the water.

A shout of triumph. The King of Zithirian watched in desperate silence with his people as something heavy was brought to the surface. One man held it close to the boat with his pole, while the other reached down, grabbed a fistful of cloth and heaved it on board. It could have been anyone, but Ansaryon did not need sorcery to tell him that this was Bron.

The other rescue boats passed, searching for Gorseth, but it was a task without hope, and everyone knew it. Some stayed to watch, or ran down along the banks to see if his body had been washed ashore, although frequently no trace was ever found of those whom the Kefirinn had taken. The rest turned and hurried back to the jetty, where the successful boat would land its sad cargo, and where, away from all the drama downstream, the race was still in progress.

The competitors were struggling across, many of them making shameless use of the ropes. After what had just happened, few citizens would blame them. Soon, Ansaryon would have to welcome them, distribute the medals and speak a few quiet words of congratulation to each successful runner. He would do it because he had to, because he was the King. But now he was just a father, grieving for his drowned son.

He found Halthris suddenly at his side, her face as white as Homan's. Her hand grasped his so tightly that it hurt. Then Kefiri came up, looking as if she might faint. She said wildly, 'Tayma told me it was Bron – but it can't be, he's too young!'

'It is Bron,' Ansaryon said, with the bleak finality of despair.

The rescue boat touched the jetty, and at once there were a dozen eager hands grabbing ropes. The narrow wooden walkway was packed with people, but they made way for their King and his wife and his cousin.

There was no sign of life at all in the limp, dripping body as it was pulled up out of the boat and dumped on the jetty. The boatmen obviously had no idea who he was: nor, to judge by their faces, had most of those watching. But as Ansaryon walked up to where Bron lay, he heard his son's name whispered, the shocked gasps of horror and grief.

'I'm sorry, sir.' One of the men who had found the boy had evidently just realized: his face was aghast. 'He died bravely – he did his best to save the other lad – I'm so sorry, I should have reached him in time – '

'It's all right, Hanmeth,' said Ansaryon gently. He felt dazed, bewildered. Was it only for this end, all that sorrow, all that striving, all that love? A gift so great, so unique, to be extinguished in a few heartbeats of terror?

He knelt beside his dead son, and took up his hand. It felt cold and wet. There was weed in his streaming hair, his skin was grey, his eyes closed.

'Father! Father!'

It was Tayma, fighting his way through the crowd. He arrived panting at Ansaryon's side. 'Father – Homan says – Homan says he isn't dead!'

Around them, the people gasped as one. Ansaryon ignored them, though he could see the swift surreptitious movements as those who were superstitious, or just mistrustful of sorcery, made the sign against evil. He closed his eyes and sent his mind, and his heart, in search of his eldest son's.

There was horror and pain, fear and grief, but not death. No absence. He found a last defiant unquenched spark of life: and then he realized what had inspired that defiance.

In the dark depths of Bron's soul, buried so far down that he had lurked long unseen and unsuspected, the Wolf snarled.

Ansaryon recoiled in revulsion. He could not help it. Once, Ayak had tried to claim him, through the long terrible hours of a winter's night in Sar D'yenyi, and only Halthris had kept him anchored to the world. He crouched, sick and shaking, amidst his anxious people, while the Devourer's voice echoed mockingly in his mind. *Fool! Did you think he was dead? He is my child, not yours – and I and I alone shall decide when and how to take him. He is mine, do you hear me? Mine!*

Ansaryon stood up at last. He stared down at the drowned boy as if he were a stranger. Halthris was still beside him, but he did not notice. Sounding cold and remote to his own ears, he said, 'He is not dead. Take him back to the Palace, and tend him. He will live.'

Ansary? His Queen's mind probed gently, almost tentatively, although Halthris had never been hesitant in her life. *Ansary, what is wrong? Is he alive?*

I can't answer you here, he told her, and with sudden and desperate finality shut her out.

Someone had brought blankets, and Bron was wrapped in them and gently carried away, still unconscious. Ansaryon forced himself to ignore his wife's shocked, stricken face, Tayma's sobs, the bewildered stares of the men and women and children around him. He said calmly, 'He is alive, and in good hands, and other contestants are waiting for their reward. My lady Halthris, let us return to our place, and to our duty.'

The jetty seemed to be full of dripping, shivering swimmers, and still more were clambering ashore. One or two officials were trying to sort out the confusion, and a group of women were distributing blankets, for the breeze was still cold despite the sun's burgeoning warmth. Kefiri watched in angry astonishment as Ansaryon turned and led his Queen back to their station on the bank. She could not understand why he had been so desperately concerned for Bron, and then a heartbeat later so offhand that he might have been talking about a bitter enemy, rather than his beloved son.

She had no gift for thoughtlink, but she knew when it had been used. She also knew that now, perhaps more than ever before, Bron needed a friend. She glanced once at Ansaryon's unyielding back, and then hurried down to the end of the jetty.

They had lowered Bron into one of the long, slender craft

used to ferry corpses and mourners across the river from city to cemetery. He looked very slight, laid out along the board in the centre of the boat where coffins were placed. She called to one of the four oarsmen. 'Wait! I'll come with you!'

Invan wouldn't approve, but Invan was probably somewhere along the river bank, directing the search for the other boy. Kefiri was helped down into the vessel, the bowman pushed off, and the boat's prow swung out into the current. There were many other craft on the river, helping those in difficulties: this Bridal Race would go down in the Annals of Zithirian as one of the most hazardous ever to take place.

She reached over and took Bron's hand in hers. There was a feeble, fluttering pulse under her fingers. Ignorant of Ayak's boast, she thought he might still die, and spoke urgently to the rowers. 'Hurry! Please, hurry!'

They obeyed her, working with impressive strength and exact timing. The long sleek boat cut through the treacherous waters as if there was no power in the current at all, and made a perfect landfall against the stone wharf of the northern docks.

More people, more cries of astonishment and horror, for no one here had realized the identity of the rescued competitor. Willing hands held the boat, helped Kefiri up on to dry land, and lifted Bron to safety. Miraculously a litter appeared, some idle nobleman's, with four muscular bearers and thick silk curtains in blue and gold. Bron was laid inside and transported with all speed up to the Palace, Kefiri riding behind on one of the mules used to haul heavy loads on the quayside.

A face appeared beside her as she urged it forward: a sharp, clever face that was somehow familiar. 'Lady Kefiri!'

She stared in sudden recognition. 'Herris!'

'What's happened? Was that Bron?'

He had been an unruly, wayward, reckless boy, whose eager irresponsibility had made him then, at thirteen, seem very young to Kefiri, four years older. To see him now a man was confusing to say the least, when she remembered him so clearly as a child. She tried to give him a sensible answer. 'There was an accident in the river. Someone else drowned, I think – Bron tried to save him.'

'Was he running in the Race?'

She nodded. The mule broke into a swift trot, and Herris ran beside it, his face distressed. 'Hegeden's wings, that was *my* fault!

I put him up to it – I told him that I'd run it a year early. Is he all right?'

'I don't know yet.' Kefiri wanted to weep, but not in front of Herris, who had once idolized her. 'He's alive – that's all.'

'Can I do anything to help?'

She shook her head. 'No – yes – perhaps later. I'll send word –'

'Ma's house will find me!' he called, as the mule quickened its pace again. 'Snowbringer Street – remember?'

Kefiri had only lived there for two or three months, but how could she ever forget?

She had sent someone ahead, so that when they arrived at the Palace, Bron's room was ready, with two braziers lit and Ansaryon's own Healer in anxious attendance. The old Kefiri took charge, the girl who had fed and organized several thousand refugees and soldiers and held Sar D'yenyi against the Ska'i. Bron was unwrapped, undressed, and laid in his bed. The new bruises covering most of his body were anointed with soothing unguents, and the bloody gash on the back of his head carefully cleaned and stitched up. Then the Healer, who had once told Bron that his broken arm would never mend properly, stepped back with an air of relief, his task completed before the patient returned to consciousness. 'He will wake up sooner or later, Lady. I can do no more for him until then. There may be other damage within, particularly to the brain, but I cannot yet tell what that might be.'

'You may leave us for now,' Kefiri said, and the Healer scuttled eagerly out.

So when Bron woke at last, it was to find her alone by his bedside. She was gazing abstractedly at the painted walls, and in repose her face, once so pretty, had lost every vestige of liveliness and looked drawn, sad, old. He studied her for a while, and then said quietly, 'Kef?'

She gasped, and her eyes filled with sudden tears. As he watched, appalled, she began to sob as if her heart was broken.

Bron waited, with the patience taught him by suffering and sorcery. He had no need of thoughtlink to tell him why she wept, and he knew that in some ways her burden was greater than his.

At last she wiped her eyes and turned to him with a rather watery smile. 'Oh, Bron, I'm sorry. That was very stupid of me – after all, you're alive.'

'Just,' he said drily. Every bone, every joint, every sinew in his body seemed to ache, his head throbbed, his throat was raw from coughing up river water. Lying here in his soft, comfortable bed, it was difficult to imagine ever moving again. He added, though he knew the answer, 'Did they find Gorseth?'

'Gorseth? Was he the one you were trying to save?' She shook her head. 'I don't know. I came back with you while they were still searching. They wouldn't have found you if it hadn't been for Homan.'

'*Homan?* What did he do?'

'He knew where you were – he told them where to look.' Kefiri gripped her hands together so hard that they hurt. 'Is he – is he like you?'

'Homan? Yes, he has some natural ability. He and Tayma have used thoughtlink together for a long time – I suspect since they were old enough to talk. But neither of them have my level of power.'

'A dynasty of sorcerer kings,' Kefiri said, half to herself. 'Some people in Zithirian would find that prospect terrifying.'

'And elsewhere, too. I can't see the Empire relishing the prospect.' He looked up at her, a wry smile twisting his bruised mouth. 'Kef, I have to leave. I can't stay here. But where can I go?'

'Why can't you stay?' she cried, hearing and hating the panic in her voice.

'For several reasons. For a start, how can I look Gorseth's family and Gorseth's friends in the face, when I failed to save him? They'll blame me for his death – and they'll be right.'

'That isn't true! You did your best – '

'Gorseth and I have been enemies for years – ever since he knocked me over in a game of Pella, and I broke my arm. We had another quarrel only a couple of months back. I took part in the race today, partly because Herris ran it early too, and I wanted to emulate him – and partly because I wanted to get the better of Gorseth. I used up almost all my strength trying to catch up with him round the walls – I didn't have enough left to save him.' He smiled bitterly. 'And I could have done. I turned the log aside from myself. I could have made it avoid him too, but I didn't.'

'Why not?'

'Because I was too intent on trying to warn him,' Bron told her. 'And so he died. If I'd deflected the log instead, he'd still be alive. *Now* do you see why I want to go?'

'You can't run away from it,' Kefiri said. 'You told me that yourself, a long time ago, before you left Sar D'yenyi.'

'I know. But I need time – time to think, time to come to terms with – with what happened today.'

'The children worship you. They'll be heartbroken if you leave Zithirian.'

'They'll forget. Children do. Tayma is the same age as I was when I came to Sar D'yenyi. The years before then have almost disappeared from my mind.'

'Have they left your dreams, though?' Kefiri asked softly.

Bron glanced up. His face was still very pale, and marked by deep scratches and purple bruises on one side, where the log had struck him. Her heart contracted for love of him: but what kind of love was it?

'My dreams are beyond my control,' he told her. 'But if it's any comfort to you, most of them now are quite pleasant.'

There were voices outside, and someone knocked at the door. Bron looked at Kefiri. She saw several things in his face: wry resignation, gratitude, even a touch of foreboding. Then he smiled, and his fingers brushed her arm. 'Don't worry,' he whispered. 'I'm not a child any more. I may not be able to master my dreams, but I don't need looking after. I can do that myself now.'

Kefiri opened her mouth to inform him that she was well aware of it, and was forestalled by another knock. 'Come in!' Bron called, and gave her another quick smile.

It was entirely friendly, but even so, she felt rebuffed.

The Healer appeared, his lined face at once anxious and relieved. 'So you are awake, Lord Bron. If the Lady Kefiri will allow me, I will examine you now. There could be deeper hurts that I have not yet discovered. My lady?'

Reluctantly, Kefiri rose and left the room. She felt raw, lost, grief-stricken, and could not understand it. He was alive: they were still friends. Why then did she feel as if he had slipped from her grasp for ever, as though the river had indeed possessed him?

In the courtyard, the sun shone brilliantly, and the warmth was astonishing. She realized that it was afternoon: she must have sat by Bron's bed for several hours. She sank down on a bench beneath a gracefully arched tree laden with heavy pale pink blossoms, and tried to calm herself.

He had not said anything, but he must surely know, as he always knew such things, that the nature of her feelings towards him had drastically changed. And she knew, too, what he must think: that she, imprisoned in an unhappy marriage, had fastened upon him as a means of escape.

And perhaps that was indeed so. But it didn't make her treacherous emotions any less real, or painful, or true. And she was certain that her altered love was one reason why he wanted to leave Zithirian.

And go where? Certainly not to Toktel'yi. That would be more dangerous than walking into the lair of a mountain tiger. Only Minassa or Lelyent would welcome him. And wherever he went, whatever he did, he would be recognized. People would fear him, or hate him, or try to use him, because of the powers he possessed.

Now she understood why he had wanted to be nobody.

'Kefiri?'

It was Ansaryon. He was wearing the splendid red garments he had put on for the Bridal Race that morning, but above the richly embroidered cloth his face was drawn with anxiety and distress. Beside him, in the long Zithiriani gown that always looked so incongruous on her, stood Halthris, her coppery hair dishevelled, and her freckles as prominent as her son Homan's had been. There was no sign of the children.

'How is he?' the Queen demanded.

With something of a shock, Kefiri realized that she was angry rather than upset. 'He woke a little while ago,' she told her cousin's wife. 'He's tired, of course, and rather bruised and battered, but I think he'll be all right.'

'How did he seem?' Ansaryon's eyes were haunted, and Kefiri remembered that strange moment on the jetty, when he had turned away so abruptly from his unconscious son. 'Did he – is he himself?'

'Very much so.' Kefiri thought of the cool voice, the impression she had received of a boy – no, a man – who was completely in control of himself and his own destiny. He had decided what he wanted, she was certain of it, and he would not allow anyone, or anything, to deflect him from his chosen path.

'Please,' Halthris said to her husband. She glanced round the courtyard, where several servants and courtiers were hovering under the arcade, and lowered her voice, but her anger was still apparent. 'What happened on the jetty? Why did you turn away from him? Ansary, what in the name of the Mother is going on?'

He stared at her, and made no answer aloud, though Kefiri

saw her face change and knew that he had spoken to her mind to mind.

The Wolf possesses him. The Wolf would not let him die. That's why he survived – because Ayak claims him for his own.

I don't understand. Halthris shook her head in bewilderment. *Ayak? What has Ayak to do with Bron?*

D'thliss dedicated him to the Devourer at his birth. His life so far has been a struggle between the Wolf of evil, and the good that lies in his own nature. I thought he had won – but now it seems Ayak has defeated him.

Kefiri, her fists clenched, stared up at her cousin and his barbarian wife. She said heatedly, 'I don't know what you're saying, but I would very much like to be included.'

Halthris looked at her as if she had never seen her before, although they had been friends for ten years. She said with some difficulty, 'I'm sorry, Kef. I – we forgot.'

'Yes. I'm sorry too.' Ansaryon looked suddenly tired, and much older than his thirty-eight years. 'Kefiri – has Bron ever spoken to you about the Wolf?'

His cousin stared at him in surprise and alarm. 'Yes – yes, a long time ago, at Sar D'yenyi. He didn't want me to tell anyone else. He said something about the Wolf in his heart, trying to dominate him. He wanted to resist him, but he was very frightened – terrified he wouldn't have the strength to do it.' She thought with pity and grief of that child, his guilt and desperation. 'He used to dream of Ayak. And he told me that when he fell off the tower, he was trying to escape from him.'

Ansaryon ran his hand through his hair, a gesture of tiredness that both women recognized only too well. 'I wish you'd told me before.'

'He wanted it to be a secret, between him and me. And he seemed so happy here,' Kefiri said, hating the defensiveness in her voice. 'He said his nightmares had almost vanished. I thought the Wolf had, too.'

'He hasn't.' Ansaryon's face was very grim. 'It seems Bron has always belonged to the Devourer. And you say he seemed unharmed. Even after what happened this morning?'

She nodded. 'He's very tired, of course, and bruised and hurt. But he's certainly the same Bron.'

A door closed, and the Healer emerged blinking from under the colonnade around the courtyard. He saw the little group under the trees, and made his way over rather hesitantly. Ansaryon turned to him at once. 'Well? How is my son?'

The Healer was a skilled and experienced man, but rather too anxious to please. 'Quite well, sir. Indeed, remarkably well, considering what has happened to him. How he managed to survive for so long under water – '

'I asked you how he is,' Ansaryon interrupted him sharply.

The old man gave the King of Zithirian a frightened glance, and added hastily, 'As I said, sir, he is well. He has been very painfully bruised over much of his body, and his head was gashed open by the tree, but there is nothing broken, and no internal damage.'

'And the injury to his head? Has that affected him?'

'No, sir. He is remarkably calm and lucid.'

'Good.' Ansaryon gave him a smile, although it was obviously an effort. 'Is there anyone with him now?'

'No, sir. Although I told him that it was not very wise, after such a blow on the head, he asked me most particularly to leave him alone.'

The King glanced at him shrewdly, well aware of the tone Bron had probably used. 'Did he? I'm sure he won't mind if I look in on him for a moment or two. Excuse me, ladies.'

He strode away. The Healer looked after him, shrugged helplessly and scuttled off in the opposite direction.

Left alone, the two women stared at each other for a few heartbeats. Then Halthris gave a wry, despairing grimace. 'So that was it. I wondered why he seemed suddenly so cold.' She glanced round, but the Healer was already out of earshot. Even so, she lowered her voice to a whisper. 'Ever since – since that first night in Sar D'yenyi, long ago – do you remember? Ever since then, he has loathed the Devourer. Far more even than most men do. To find the Wolf in Bron, when he thought the boy was healed, and safe . . .'

'I understand now.' Kefiri felt sick, and apprehensive. 'But what will he do to Bron?'

'Nothing. Ansary loves him too much even for this to affect his feelings. But I'm frightened, Kef. What about the children? Tayma and Homan use thoughtlink. Zathti may be an adept too. And the new baby . . .'

She paused, and looked significantly at her husband's cousin. 'You're pregnant too, aren't you? When is it due?'

'Two months before Sundim.'

'Mine should be born at Sundim itself. I've only been sure of it for a few days.' Halthris's hand stroked her body gently. 'You said that Bron was his usual self. Is that true?'

Kefiri nodded. 'But you were talking as if you feared he would harm the children. He wouldn't, Halthris – I *know* he wouldn't!'

'How can you know? How can anyone know? We thought the damage D'thliss did to him had been mended. We thought he would be safe – that once Ansary had trained him, he would be able to use his powers for everyone's benefit. And I suspect that we were very naïve and foolish to believe it.'

'*I* believe it! He isn't evil, Halthris – he *isn't*. He has fought the Wolf before, and defeated him. I'm certain he will do it again, if he has to.'

'Are you?' The Queen's voice was bleak. 'But your children are safe in Sar D'yenyi. Mine are here, and they worship him, they want to be sorcerers just like him. What if Ayak wants to possess them as well? What if Bron can no longer resist him?' She put a hand on Kefiri's arm. 'I know you love him dearly. But you must face the truth. He only survived today because Ayak desired it. Ayak lives within him – I don't know how, but he does. And that makes him dangerous, Kef – dangerous to all of us, and especially to the children.'

'He wants to leave Zithirian,' Kefiri said. She had wept a river of tears today, but more were rising to the surface. 'I didn't realize – perhaps that's why.'

'I don't know if that's the reason.' Halthris's blue eyes were implacable. 'But you must understand this – as I think Ansary understands it. Perhaps it would be the best thing possible for all of us – including Bron – if he did go.'

In Bron's room, father and son sat looking at each other.

No spoken words were necessary: thoughtlink said everything. The boy's hands gripped the edge of the quilt that covered him, and his face was almost as white as the bandage around his head.

Can you defeat him?

I thought I had. He doesn't control me – I control me.

I know that. Ansaryon's silent voice was dry, almost amused. *It's probably the most terrifying thing about you. But would you know if you obeyed Ayak rather than your own wishes?*

Of course I would!

The certainty of youth . . . Do you know what I'm going to ask of you?

Yes. You want me to leave, because the children are at risk. Don't worry. I want to go too, but not for that reason alone.

Ansaryon waited, but there was no further explanation. And, conscious, Bron's defences were awesome: no point whatsoever in trying to probe. He said at last, *I think you are ready. I have taught you almost everything I can. You will be nineteen at High Summer – you are nearly grown up. But I don't want you to feel cast out, or rejected. Wherever you go, whatever you do, we will always love you.*

Whatever I do? Bron's tone was drily ironic. *Yes, I do know that. But I don't know where I can go.*

I've thought of that. In a few months' time, Halthris's people will bring their horses to Zithirian for the Gathering Fair. Her brother Abreth is Chief of their Clan now. He has always said that if any of our children wished to live with the Tanathi for a season or two, he would gladly welcome them. If you want time to think, to be away from us and all the pressures on you –

Yes, I do. But do they know about me? About my powers?

There might be rumours. I don't know. But you will still be alone, even amongst the Tanathi. Can you bear that?

Of course I can. His son paused, his eyes desolate. Then he said aloud, very softly, 'Abreth will welcome me. But will you and Halthris, ever again?'

It was a question which Ansaryon found, with anguish, that he could not answer.

The Gathering Fair was months away, at the end of summer. Bron knew he could not wait so long to escape. The city, his home for six years, seemed suddenly to have become a prison, and he was desperate to be gone.

And for many reasons, he did not want anyone to know where he went. No one trusted him, not even his father, and the hurt of that was bitter: but he knew the justice of it. The Wolf still lurked deep within him, hidden so well that he had thought himself free.

But if he had been free, he would have died with Gorseth,

drowned in the Kefirinn. The Wolf had saved him – and so it must
have been the Wolf who had told Homan where to find him.

The thought that Ayak could enter the untouched mind of his
seven-year-old half-brother was peculiarly horrible. He recalled
D'thliss, the sense of evil, the terror and the despair. He would
rather disappear now from the children's lives, to be remembered
afterwards with nostalgic and wistful regret, than to risk being the
agent of their destruction.

It was all too easy to imagine Ayak using them to force him to
obedience. It had happened to him before, when the Ska'i
shaman Br'nnayak had threatened to kill his foster-brother Lelya
if he, Bron, did not help him to destroy Ansaryon and his army.
And, desperate to save Lelya, he had agreed.

But Quenait, the Ska'i chief, had ignored the shaman and
commanded Lelya's death anyway. And in a paroxysm of grief
and rage, Bron had destroyed the Ska'i army instead. Every warrior in that camp, more than six thousand of them, had perished
horribly. And Ayak had laughed, for he was the Devourer of
men's souls, and all deaths were pleasing to him, even of those
who had worshipped him and brought him innumerable corpses.

Yes, Bron was vulnerable. Ayak had seen how the threat to
Lelya had forced him into acquiescence. He could not risk the
same thing happening to Tayma, or Homan, or Zathti. Somehow
he must defeat the Wolf within, finally and for ever. And in the
long battle ahead, he could not allow himself to become assail-
able again. His father, his stepmother, the children, Kefiri, he
loved them all, and nothing could alter that. He could not bear it
if any evil were to befall them. And only by leaving Zithirian
could he ensure their safety.

So he lay in bed for several days, making plans. He asked for
books, and amongst the stories and histories and poems, made
sure that he received a copy of Mydreth's *Geography* – complete
with maps of the known world.

Three days after the race, his father told him, reluctantly, that
Gorseth's body had been found. It was ten miles downstream,
and recognizable only by a ring still on its finger, engraved with
his family's device. And as Ansaryon's spare, quiet voice gave
him the sad details, somewhere Bron seemed to hear the echo of
a Wolf, howling with glee.

And that afternoon, Herris came to see him.

It was raining hard outside, probably one of the last downpours before the usual dry heat of summer arrived. Bron did not have a personal servant, by choice, and so his visitor knocked on the door and walked in unannounced.

He was up, and dressed, and sitting at his table poring over a book. His face lit up with pleasure at his friend's arrival, and he jumped to his feet. 'Wonderful! Kefiri told me you were back, but I hadn't expected a visit.'

'Only the one, I'm afraid – the ship sails at dawn.' Herris surveyed Bron with some concern. 'That log made quite a mess of you, didn't it!'

'I was lucky. Gorseth wasn't,' Bron pointed out, and there was a hard, bitter edge to his voice that Herris had never heard before. 'Don't waste your sympathy on me – I was a fool, and I got what I deserved. Gorseth didn't. I know he was an arrogant bully, but that's not a capital offence.'

'No,' said Herris, although in fact he could hardly have cared less about Bron's adversary, or his unfortunate fate. Such tragedies happened almost every year in the Bridal Race. It was sad, of course, for the families and friends of the victim, but life moved inexorably on, and he had no intention of squandering any grief on a young man whom he hardly knew, and to whom he had taken an instant and virulent dislike.

There was an awkward pause. Bron dropped his gaze to the book laid open on the table. Herris saw that he was looking at a coloured map, beautifully drawn across the width of two pages. He said jokingly, trying to lighten the atmosphere, 'You're not thinking of leaving Zithirian, are you?'

Bron swung round. Staring at his impenetrable dark eyes, Herris had a sudden and disturbing sense of unease.

'Yes,' the younger man said softly. 'Yes, as a matter of fact I am.'

'Why? When we talked a couple of months ago, you said you had a year or more of studying to come – and you couldn't leave anyway. What's changed? Why do you want to go? It's not because of Gorseth, is it?'

Bron's expression altered slightly at the incredulity in Herris's voice. He said slowly, 'Yes, believe it or not. Part of the reason, anyway. There are others, but I don't want to discuss them.'

'Some girl?' his friend enquired hopefully.

It was several paces wide of the mark, but it was plausible. Bron allowed himself the hint of a smile. 'Perhaps.'

'Good. Now maybe people will stop thinking you're my fancy boy. When are you going? And where? Does the King know?'

'I don't know exactly where I want to go. But if your ship's sailing tomorrow morning, is there any chance I could have a passage on it?'

Herris stared at him in astonishment. '*Tomorrow?* Are you serious?'

'I've never been more serious in my life. I'll work for it, of course.'

'*Work?* You? A Prince of Zithirian?'

'Why not? It's about time I stopped living in pampered idleness and earned my keep. Is it a Toktel'yan ship?'

'Yes, of course it is – only about half a dozen Minassans are trading at present, and I'm still a few hundred silver bars short of what I need to build my own.'

'Will they know who I really am if I don't tell them?'

Herris regarded him thoughtfully, chewing a fingernail. 'Probably not. You know what the Toktel'yans are like – if it doesn't concern them directly, they're not interested. You'd only be recognized if you'd been pointed out to one of them, I should think. And you never dress like a prince when you come down to the docks, anyway.'

'They mustn't know who I am – that's very important. I'll have to call myself something else. Who was that boy you used to go around with years ago? The one with bright red hair and a wheezy chest?'

'Kenmet Rigan's Son. He's working in a kuldi-house now, the Night Owl on Sunset Street. I hardly ever see him, and the Toktel'yans won't know him. I see his sister a lot, though,' he added with a grin. 'Remember Djumi, the very pretty one with the sneer? She's a lot more friendly to me now than she was ten years ago, I can tell you.'

'Your mind only runs on one path,' Bron said, without rancour.

'No – two. Women, and ships. So you'll call yourself Kenmet? I don't see why not. But what if the Captain won't let you sail? Old Katez, he's a mean old skinflint. You'll need to pay him a fortune, or he'll make you work all the skin off those fine hands of yours.'

'Does he like music?'

'I suppose so,' said Herris with some surprise. 'All Toktel'yans seem to. But why – oh, I see, of course. You play the Sith.'

'And the flute. Well enough to satisfy most ears, I hope. D'you think he'll take me?'

'He might – if you slip him several silver bars as well. And where will you find that kind of money before dawn tomorrow?'

'I'll find it.' Bron's face had acquired a thoughtful look. 'Anyway, I only want to go as far as Minassa. Visiting Toktel'yi might be a little unwise.'

Herris didn't need to ask why. He walked over to his friend's side, and looked down at the map.

Mydreth, who had died only a few years ago at a very advanced age, had been a master cartographer, with a reputation that had travelled, as he had, to the furthest edges of the known world. These two pages, coloured as vividly and exactly as jewels, represented the culmination of his art and his knowledge. Down the middle, winding from the spiky mountains at the top to the expanse of wavy blue ocean at the bottom, ran the River Kefir-inn, with the great cities strung along its banks like diamonds on a necklace: Zithirian, Minassa, Tamat, Sabrek, Toktel'yi. The boundaries and provinces of the Empire were marked in red, stretching from the nominally independent princedom of Tulyet, a rocky peninsula jutting out into the Southern Sea west of the K'tali Archipelago, to Tatht in the east, neighbour of the fabulous Queendom of Kerenth, land of women. The thousands of islands were intricately drawn, with here and there a spouting fire-mountain, or a friendly looking dolphin smiling out of the waves. Only the biggest were named: Balki, Tekkt, Onnak, Annatal, original home of the sorcery drug, and, largest and richest of all, Penya the Great, close to Kerenth in space and in spirit, and only conquered by Imperial troops within the last fifteen years.

And far, far to the south, sketched in lightly as if even Mydreth had been unsure of its position, perhaps even of its existence, Jo'ami, island of wizards, rumoured to be guarded by demons who moved it through the warm azure seas like a vast boat, whenever danger threatened.

If, if even half the stories told about Jo'ami were true, it was there that Bron must seek the answers to the questions that had haunted him for so long. *Why? Why me? What can I do? What are my limits? And my purpose, my destiny? And above all, how can I be rid of the Wolf within my heart?*

But he could not reach Jo'ami from Toktel'yi. It was the

only island in all the Archipelago that was still free of Imperial domination. Bron seemed to remember that some Emperors had tried to seize it, but all had failed: ships had sunk in unexpected storms, crews had mutinied, acquisitive rulers had suddenly died . . .

All things which a very powerful sorcerer could have arranged.

No, he could not risk going to Toktel'yi, and anyway the wizards of Jo'ami would never let an Imperial vessel anywhere near their precious island. But there were other lands bordering the Southern Sea, other ports, other ships. And he had time. He was eighteen, nearly nineteen. He had a skill that would buy him food and shelter, and a restless longing to see the marvels of the world. And though he wanted answers, he had patience. He could wait. There was all the known world, as brilliant and enticing as Mydreth's map, to be explored. And after the Bridal Race, he had no fear of premature death. The Wolf would not allow him to escape his destiny – whatever it was – so easily.

'There's Minassa,' Herris said, pointing to the centre of the map. He could read, but not very fluently: there was no need of such a skill on board a river ship, and he was out of practice. 'And that big blotch down there by the river delta must be Toktel'yi.'

'It is. Where the Emperor Djamal would probably love to imprison me, if I gave him the chance.'

'I doubt it. Word is, he was very ill during the winter. I expect his fifty concubines have worn him out.'

Bron thought it unlikely. Djamal was still only in his forties, but his son, now twenty-four, was a very different character from his idle, dissolute father. 'Or Ba-alekkt has something to do with it,' he said. 'I expect he's getting impatient.'

'I don't know.' Herris saw his friend's raised eyebrows and added, 'I try not to listen to the gossip. You know what Toktel'yans are like – they're addicted to intrigue and plotting. Talk can be very dangerous, and so can inconvenient information. People have been known to fall overboard, and if they thought I was a spy . . .'

Bron couldn't blame him. In any case, Herris was single-minded in pursuit of his ambition. He wouldn't want to entangle himself in anything that might endanger his chances of living long enough to build his own ship. And Toktel'yans, born conspirators to a man, not unnaturally saw other conspirators everywhere, even when they didn't actually exist.

'Don't worry,' he said. 'All I want is a quick and easy passage to Minassa, incognito and without any fuss. We ought to be able to manage that between us, I'd have thought.'

'No trouble to a rascal like me,' Herris said, grinning.

He left soon afterwards, and Bron sat down again at the table, staring at the map. He had gazed at it so often over the past few days that its outlines were engraved indelibly in his mind. Once more, the names of remote lands, distant cities and exotic places jostled enticingly in his head. Lelyent . . . Minassa . . . Kerenth . . . Penya. Lying there beyond the walls of Zithirian, waiting for him.

It was best this way, best to make a swift and sudden break. They wanted him to leave, and he would not have the agony of a prolonged parting from those he loved. He regretted that he wouldn't have the chance to ride with the Tanathi: he had always loved Halthris's stories of their wild, free life on the limitless steppes. But despite his father's reassurances, he knew that if he joined Abreth's clan, sooner or later some shaman would realize what he was. And he would still be too close to Zithirian, within easy reach of his family.

And Tayma, Homan and Zathti would be within easy reach of him.

The further he went from them, the better it would be for everyone. And however tempting the thought of riding with the Tanathi, roaming the steppe would not bring him nearer to Jo'ami, and the answers he sought.

He gathered essentials in an old canvas bag. A few clothes; a dagger, ornamental but sharp, necessary for eating and for emergencies; and, most important of all, his instruments.

The flute was far too good for the wandering player he would claim to be, but it came apart in three smaller sections that could be carried unseen. There would be no hiding his Sith, however. A gift from his father, it had been made by the finest craftsman in Lelyent, city of wondrous workers in wood. It would always attract attention, and people would look at him with suspicion and mistrust. At the very least, they'd think he had stolen it.

So instead, he packed the instrument on which he had learned to play. It was simply made, but he restrung it with the silver wires from the other Sith. No competent professional player would skimp on the strings, anyway. And although it was plain and unembellished, the old one had a fine, mellow, resonant tone.

Finally, he put twenty small silver bars, good currency throughout the known world, and a handful of the tiny silver

Zithiriani coins called chells, into the pouch sewn to his best belt.
Even if he planned to earn his keep as a singer, the money would
buy his passage to Minassa, with plenty left over for emergencies.

Kefiri came to see him that evening. He wanted to tell her his
plan, but resisted the temptation. She would only try to make him
stay: she might even weep. And he hated to make her unhappy.
Best for all of them if her feelings for him remained undeclared,
unspoken, so that one day she could look back on her inappropriate infatuation without too much embarrassment, knowing that it
existed only in her mind. He loved her dearly, for she had
restored him to life. But not in the way she now wanted, for he
had known her too long.

He asked after the children, who had visited him just once
since the accident, in the company of their parents. He suspected
that they had only been allowed to see him because they were
convinced he was dead. Halthris now wore an aura of fierce
maternal protectiveness that seemed, to his sharpened senses, as
prickly as a needle-hog. He remembered that once, long ago, she
had wanted to kill him rather than allow his power to be used,
through D'thliss or the Ska'i shaman, to destroy Ansaryon. And
although his stepmother had always treated him very kindly,
there was far more warmth and affection between him and Kefiri.

Kefiri told him now that Tayma and Homan were well, but
asking after him constantly. They had obviously realized that they
were being kept away from him, but could not understand why.
And Ansaryon had started to teach them the basic principles of
thoughtlink: something which, Bron knew, he should have begun
some time ago, as soon as it became obvious that the children
were blessed, or cursed, with the gift of sorcery.

His parting with Kefiri, when she said good night, was
unusually distant, and there was a look of hurt bewilderment on
her face as she left. Perhaps tomorrow she would realize that he
had seemed so cold because he had not dared to disclose his true
feelings, his grief and guilt, in case he broke down or, worse,
changed his mind.

He slept a little, woke before dawn, dressed and left his room
without a backward glance. The Palace was dark and empty,
everyone else still asleep. He walked through the maze of corridors and courtyards swiftly and silently. Even if he did encounter
an early riser, they would only see a dark, moving shadow,
unrecognizable in the gloom. It was not a skill he had ever been

taught, or often employed, but it might prove very useful at some point in his uncertain future.

He slipped out of a side gate, past the oblivious guards. Once out of sight of the Palace he shed his shadow-guise with relief – it was very tiring to keep up for any length of time – and walked quickly down to the docks. There, tied up at the northern wharf, her white masts and furled sails and shipped oars a glimmering network of geometry in the burgeoning light, lay the *Rose of Sabrek*. And waiting for him by the boarding plank was Herris, his face inflamed with the boyish enthusiasm for adventure which had never left him.

It was even easier than he had expected. He paid over five silver bars to the Captain, a burly middle-aged Toktel'yan, taller and fairer than most of his breed, and was shown his space under the deck awning: only the Captain and First Mate had cabins, and the rest of the ship was filled with cargo. He was given his first task, and duly played a rhythmic working chant on his elderly Sith while the *Rose of Sabrek* left Zithirian at sunrise under oar and sail, sliding gracefully with the current along the swift dark waters of the Kefirinn, her slender prow pointed south.

He looked back once. The Silver City, the city of gardens, the city of towers, lay already diminished by distance, and the rising sun sparkled dazzlingly on the gold pennants flying stiffly from the summit of every spire. It was so beautiful, and his heart ached: but he did not belong there any more.

With sadness, but also with eager expectation, Bron turned his face to the warm lands of the south, and the destiny that awaited him there.

PART TWO

KERENTH

CHAPTER
SIX

Like Zithirian, Minassa was famous throughout the known world. Not for its own beauty, though: unlike the Silver City, this was a bustling, unassuming place that gave itself no airs. Squatting astride the banks of the Kefirinn and its tributary, the Ger, on which Lelyent stood two hundred and fifty miles to the east, Minassa, its houses built of oven-baked brick, or wood floated down from the Lelyentan forests, had a distinctly workmanlike and grimy appearance.

Its people, though, were fiercely proud of their city, and what it made. Most Minassans were potters, or the parents, children, relatives or friends of potters, and their skill and reputation were such that almost every house throughout the known world, from Zithirian to Onnak, from Fabriz to the remote desert land of Ma'alkwen, could boast at least one carefully hoarded piece of Minassan ware. The wealthiest families had whole sets: bowls, plates, jugs, dishes, mugs, goblets. The craftsmen of Minassa did not stoop to producing utilitarian pieces: they left that to humbler potters in Zithirian or Toktel'yi, churning out the cheap coarse red earthenware used and broken every day in ordinary houses or taverns. Minassan pots were graceful and delicate, with painted decoration and wonderfully coloured glazes whose exact composition was a jealously guarded secret. Certain patterns – the fish, the grapes, the windflowers – were regarded as the traditional property of individual families, passed down from one generation of artists to the next. And Temiltan III, King of Minassa for almost forty years, was a noted craftsman himself, an enthusiastic creator of new glazing recipes and the inventor of a coloured glass that was now used in palaces and noble houses all over the known world.

Temiltan was Ansaryon's uncle and knew all his family well. Although Bron had never been to Minassa before he was likely to be recognized. Zithirian was a prime market for Minassan ware, and many potters travelled north with their consignments every year. But once he had disembarked from the *Rose of Sabrek*, Bron knew he would be in no danger. This city was a friendly place, and the people were too busy about their own affairs to bother much about one stray bastard Prince. Eventually, news of him would probably filter back to his father in Zithirian, but by then he would be beyond anyone's reach.

He had sung and played for the Captain and crew during the brief two days of the voyage, swept along by the speed of the Kefirinn's spring current. They seemed to accept him as Kenmet Rigan's Son, friend of their comrade Herris. He did not disclose how well he spoke Toktel'yan: ordinary Zithiriani children were usually taught no more than the rudiments of the language, whereas the sons and daughters of the wealthy were normally fluent. Certainly, the real Kenmet would not be expected to know much more than how to ask the way.

At least the ship didn't carry a sorcerer: on the Kefirinn, hazards of weather and water were few. According to Herris, though, every seagoing vessel in the Archipelago, where sudden storms, treacherous currents and uncharted rocks were commonplace, had its own worker of magic to detect and if necessary change the direction of winds and currents. It was why sorcery had first flourished there amongst the scattered islands.

Minassa shared with Zithirian a mistrust of mages, but for different reasons. The potters were a practical people who had little time for what they called the Invisible Arts of magic and music. One sorcerer would always recognize another, but in Minassa, Bron had no fear of detection.

The *Rose of Sabrek* tied up at the East Wharf, just downstream from the Kefirinn's confluence with the Ger. Here the water was wide, but comparatively shallow and sluggish compared to the deep, fast, dangerous river, swollen with melted snow, that sped past Zithirian. The Minassans had built three bridges, one above the Ger, one below it, and one across it. They were plain but graceful structures in Annako stone, with a lifting wooden span in the centre of each, to allow the riverboats to pass through.

Bron had never seen such things before, but he had no intention of gaping too obviously at the first bridge as the *Rose of Sabrek* drifted gently through it, watched by a crowd of citizens on either side who were waiting to cross over the Kefirinn. Presumably Minassa, like Zithirian and any other large town or city, had its share of thieves and pickpockets, and Bron did not want to attract anyone's attention by appearing to be too much the country bumpkin, ripe for robbery.

The quayside was lined with craft. The lovely Kefirinn ships, with their graceful lines and bright sails, contrasted favourably with the lumbering barges, little more than rafts, which plied up and down the shallow Ger between Minassa and Lelyent. Bron looked at these with covert interest. He had not brought Mydreth's map with him, but he had committed every detail of it to his memory and had already decided where to go once he reached Minassa.

He could not travel through Toktel'yi or any of its provinces or dependencies. If he wished to reach Jo'ami, which according to the map lay almost a thousand miles due south of Minassa, he must now turn either west or east to avoid the Empire.

To the west and south lay the steppe, desolate hills and plateaux thinly populated with bands of fierce nomads very different from the Tanathi – and they might include the remnants of the Ska'i, worshippers of Ayak, whose warriors he had slain as a child. Beyond them lay the marshland city of Gulkesh of which he knew very little. Mydreth had described it as a damp and unhealthy place, full of surly and uncouth fishermen, and even more surly and uncouth robbers. There he might find a ship which would take him to Jo'ami, but it was unlikely: the sea south of Gulkesh was infested by pirates from Fabriz, which lay on its western shore, and any voyage in those waters would be very hazardous. He had no wish to be captured and sold as a galley slave to some fierce Fabrizian pirate with red hair and a nose-ring, or transported into the unknown lands further west, chained to a hundred other unfortunates.

So he would have to go east. East lay Lelyent, where his cousin Alayni now reigned as its Princess. He had been there once with his father a few years ago, so they would know him. But at least he would be able to pause there and gather his strength, and his nerve, for the next part of his journey.

As the ship was made fast and the boarding-plank run out, he picked up his bundle and made his way over to Herris, who was standing with the rest of the crew by the deck hatches, waiting to unload.

'So you're off, then.' His friend gave him a wide, encouraging grin that was also tinged with relief. Bron knew that he had feared his passenger's real identity would be discovered, and his own position on the *Rose* therefore put in jeopardy. 'Well, goodbye, and good luck, wherever you're going.'

'Thank you. Thank you for all you've done – it was a great help.' Bron hesitated, his hand fingering the small piece of paper which he had brought with him from Zithirian.

By now, Ansaryon's first shock and grief at his son's sudden disappearance might have diminished: by now, he should be recognizing that this way, after all, was best. Bron was sure he would not be pursued, but even so he wanted to offer some explanation to those he had deserted.

He came to a decision, and held out the letter to Herris. 'When you finally get back to Zithirian, can you make sure my father gets this?'

The older man gave him a startled glance. 'What is it?'

'An apology, and a farewell.' Bron pushed it into Herris's hand before he could object. 'There's nothing incriminating in it – nothing to say who I am. You're not even mentioned. You could send it back to Zithirian by pigeon if you wanted.'

'Too expensive,' Herris said, his face at once puzzled and relieved. 'I'll hang on to it.'

'Goodbye, then, and my thanks. And I hope you do get to build your own boat one day. You deserve it.'

And with a final, casual wave, he turned and walked to the boarding-plank.

The Toktel'yan Captain was standing there, his arms folded, his narrow brown eyes staring suspiciously at Bron as he approached. He said curtly, in passable Zithiriani, 'Wait. Not yet.'

'This is Minassa, isn't it?' Bron's voice was calm, though his heart had begun to beat the pulse of danger. 'I told you I was leaving at Minassa.'

'You've only paid as far as Hailyan.'

'I have not. I paid the agreed price to Minassa – five bars. And I sang and played for you, free of charge.'

'There's been a mistake, boy. The price has gone up. Another two bars, or you don't get off. We could use another oarsman.'

Bron stared up into the big man's face. There was greed there, brutality, a leering enjoyment of his victim's predicament, but no hint that he knew the true identity of the young man in front of him. He said, sweetly reasonable, 'You'd have the bother and expense of feeding me. And I'd make a lousy rower. My hands are too soft – and if I wore them to the bones on your oars, I wouldn't be able to play the Sith, either.'

For a moment longer, the Captain's expression remained intimidating. Then he laughed briefly and stepped aside. 'Nothing meant, boy – just my little joke. Be on your way before I change my mind.'

Bron walked past him and down the plank, waiting for the shout, the heavy hand on his shoulder. He did not look back, but in his mind's eye he saw the Captain standing on the deck, a sneering bully who took pleasure in the pain or discomfiture of others. With a small inward smile, he yielded to temptation and employed a brief spasm of power. It made certain rearrangements within Katez's ample belly, and ensured that he would shortly be laid low with an acute attack of bilious diarrhoea.

The East Wharf extended several hundred paces upstream on the River Ger, and most of the Lelyent boats were tied up here. Bron walked right up to the end, where rafts of tree-trunks, lashed together, were moored until hauled ashore or towed on down the Kefirinn to the Empire, which was acutely short of good timber. He counted nine craft, none of which looked either safe or comfortable. And they would be struggling up to Lelyent against the current, a slow and difficult voyage. He came to a decision, and left the docks in search of a convenient inn.

His pale hair and good looks attracted some attention, but his self-contained manner discouraged closer contact, although the serving girl who showed him into a small private room above the bar was doing her best to make him notice her. He paid for one night – it was not as cheap as the communal sleeping hall downstairs, but he wanted privacy – and for an evening meal and breakfast. Then, alone at last, for the first time since leaving Zithirian, he lay down on the bed and closed his eyes, the better to concentrate his mind on what lay ahead.

Horses, like most animals, were disturbed by Bron's presence, and refused to carry him on their backs, unless they had been trained to tolerate the stench of sorcery. The inn had several for sale or hire, and they watched him apprehensively as he entered the stable with the head groom, their eyes rolling with alarm.

The groom, a stocky dark man with a cheerful expression and hair cropped short in the practical Minassan style, did not seem to notice his charges' unease. He described each one in glowing terms, praising them for qualities that were just what Bron didn't want: fire, spirit, speed. He could see one at the end, though, that seemed more suitable to his needs. It was solidly built, and marked in a bizarre pattern of black and white. And unlike the others, it took absolutely no notice of him at all. It didn't even raise its head from the manger.

'I'll take that one,' he said, interrupting the groom in mid flow.

The Minassan stared at him in surprise. 'That one? The piebald mare? But that's hardly a quality riding horse.'

'Is she saddle-broken?'

'Yes, sir, but—'

'Then I'll take her, if she's sound. How much?'

The groom obviously thought his giftday had come early. 'Well, she's a good reliable mount – trot all day without tiring, never lame in her life, nice-tempered – to you, sir, six silver bars.'

'The finest Tanathi racehorse doesn't fetch more than eight. I'll give you three bars for her, take it or leave it.'

His air of certainty defeated the groom. He shrugged, well aware that no one else would want to pay more than two bars for such an ugly beast. 'Done. And the tack, sir?'

'I'd assumed that was included,' Bron said, his eyebrows raised. 'If it isn't, I'll make do with a rope and a blanket.'

The groom assured him that the necessary saddle and bridle were indeed part of the deal. Bron walked over to the horse, who would carry him all the way to the shores of the Southern Sea if she were indeed as reliable as the man claimed. She turned her head and surveyed him with calm interest, and he wondered why, alone of the dozen or so animals in the stable, she showed no fear in his presence. Had she perhaps encountered sorcerers before?

'What's her history?' he asked, rubbing the striped nose gently. It was possible to use thoughtlink with some animals, for that was how Halthris had communicated with her hunting cat Fess, but he had no idea whether it could be done with horses.

The groom told him that the pied mare was about ten years old, and had previously belonged to a man from Tamat, once an independent city-state like Minassa, now an outpost of Empire. So she probably did have some experience of sorcerers: enough at least to know that they need not be a threat.

He paid over the three silver bars and rode out of Minassa the next morning. In his shabby grey tunic and trousers, with a bat-

tered old felt hat to shield him from the sun, no-one gave him a
second glance, although several people looked askance at his
oddly-marked horse. One bag, strapped to the comfortable old
Tanathi-style saddle, contained his few possessions, and another,
bought from the inn's cook, was filled with the usual supplies for
a long journey: dried meat, twice-baked bread, raisins, and a box
full of kuldi leaves. He had also purchased a leather water-bottle,
and a simple bow, with a quiver of twenty arrows, for hunting. He
had learned to shoot at Sar D'yenyi, and had often practised with
his fellow pupils at the Palace. He probably wouldn't need to use
it on the way to Lelyent, for farms, inns and villages were scattered all along the valley of the River Ger. But after that he
would be travelling south-east across the Empty Lands between
the mountains and pine-forests to the north, and the Toktel'yan
Empire and Kerenth to the south. And even Mydreth's beautiful
and detailed map was singularly uninformative about that vast
area. He had no idea what rivers, what animals, what people – if
there *were* any people – he might encounter.

The prospect of travelling through country unknown even
to the greatest geographer in Zithirian's history was undeniably
exciting and intriguing, but Bron knew that he should not forget
that his eventual destination was Jo'ami, even though it didn't
really matter whether it took him a year, or five years, or ten, to
reach the island. As long as he could still keep the Wolf at bay.

Minassa stood behind him, smoking busily with the stoked
fires of a thousand hard-working pottery kilns. On his left lay the
fertile meadows and fields of the flood plain, green with new
crops, the apple trees in blossom and the warm scented air filled
with the sound of birdsong. The Ger swept by, bustling down to
its junction with the Kefirinn, and he passed a raft toiling
upstream and was glad he had chosen to ride.

Bron took a deep breath and sighed with sudden happiness.
Now, for the first time in his life, he was truly alone. He had no
friend, no companion save the pied mare, no one to talk to,
no one to pry, no one to make demands on him, and he was
beginning to realize that he preferred it like that. He could do,
and go, and be exactly as he chose. And after nearly nineteen
years of a life under the control of others, whether loathed or
beloved, at last he was free.

The miles to Lelyent were slow but pleasant. He spent the
nights at inns or farms, paying for his bed and food with songs

and dances. In a village by the shores of Lake Ger a spring festival was in progress. He played the Sith for them that evening, and found that in the atmosphere of celebration and revelry, the temptation offered by one of the girls crowding round him was impossible to resist. It was the first time for him, but not for her, and he learned a great deal in the darkness of the stable after the dancing had ended: not least the fact that there is one sensation more powerful even than sorcery.

It was a very pleasurable, uninhibited and light-hearted encounter, and Bron said goodbye to her the next morning with true gratitude, and a friendly kiss. Now at last he understood Herris's enthusiastic pursuit of women.

She was his first lover, but not the last. In the small settlements where he stopped each night, strangers were an exciting novelty, and girls flocked eagerly around the young musician, lured by his striking looks and his sure, sensitive touch on the Sith.

In three villages, his favoured partner was young, pretty and unattached. In the fourth, he made the wrong choice.

She was as tall as he was, with hair the colour of autumn trees and a fierce, hungry face. As soon as he met her eyes across the inn's taproom, he knew that he could have her. She thrust her way through the crowd and stood beside him, claiming him for the night as plainly as if she had written it on his forehead. And Bron saw the curves that even her shapeless peasant tunic and skirt could not conceal, but failed to notice the looks on the faces of the other women around him, the covert whispers, the significant glances, the smothered giggles.

She came to his room after the inn was quiet for the night. He never found out her name, but she was an enthusiastic and skilful lover and that was all that mattered.

And then the door was hurled open, and light spilled all about them. It shone on the girl's face, which showed neither shock nor surprise, but a wild and delighted defiance, as though she had expected this to happen, and welcomed it. A young man plunged into the room, while others held lanterns high and sniggered at the couple on the bed. He yelled something in the swift Lelyentan dialect, yanked Bron to his feet, and punched him full in the face with what felt like the force of a battering ram.

Bron crashed back across the bed. Pain and humiliation overwhelmed him, and ignited his rage. Through a haze of blood, he saw the young man pull the girl up by her hair, and strike her too. And in that moment he forgot everything that Ansaryon had taught him, and the power within him exploded furiously, seeking revenge.

One of the lanterns fell. The glass broke, and fire lapped eagerly at the ancient dry wood of the door. Someone yelled, in pain or alarm, and the blaze sprang up suddenly in a great roaring sheet of devouring flame.

Bron rolled off the bed. His packs lay on the floor by the window. He snatched them up, hurled them through the unglazed opening, and leapt after them.

His room was on the upper storey, and he forgot to slow his descent. He landed on the innkeeper's herb garden with a thud that jarred his legs and knocked most of the breath from his body. Above him, someone yelled angrily, and a missile flew down and smacked into the foliage beside him. A strong smell of bruised mint attacked his senses, along with the urge to escape.

Bron scrambled to his feet. He could only see out of one eye, and the moon wasn't up yet, but he located his bags, picked them up and ran unsteadily along the side of the building until he reached the stables. Behind him, there was pandemonium: the fire had taken hold, and people were screaming and shouting in panic. He found his horse, saddled her with the aid of sorcery, and rode away from the burning inn as if demons were after him.

It was only later, when the mare slowed to an exhausted halt deep in the forest, that he realized that he had no clothes on.

Rather weakly, he began to laugh, but stopped because his face hurt too much. He looked back, but he could see only the darkness between the silent, crowding trees, and there was no sound of pursuit. He had escaped a potentially lethal situation with his person, if not his dignity, largely intact. But as the cold shock of reaction set in, he recognized how stupid he had been. The girl had evidently only been using him to teach her jealous lover a lesson. He had ignored the obvious signs of danger, and when discovered he had used indiscriminate sorcery to extricate himself.

He closed his eyes, and reluctantly sent his spirit back down his trail to the village. He could see the blazing building, the flames leaping greedily into the night amid a shower of sparks as the roof fell in. He saw, as the people around it could not, the bodies of those trapped beneath the burning wreckage: two serving men, the innkeeper's baby son, and the girl who had so briefly shared his bed.

They were all dead because of him. His thoughtless folly, his uncontrolled rage, had killed them as surely as if he had stabbed them to the heart, and a good deal more horribly.

His spirit fled the terrible scene, back to the haven of his body. Sick and shaking, Bron slid down from his horse and buried his head in his hands. The night air drifted cold on his bare skin, but he did not care. Nothing mattered now except the consequences of his sorcery.

The black and white mare turned her head and whinnied anxiously. He ignored her, for his mind was filled with dreadful images of destruction and death, and despair overwhelmed him.

And deep within his soul, he knew that the Wolf was laughing.

After a very long time, something blew warm over his back, and the mare's soft muzzle nudged him gently. He spoke to her mind, not really expecting any reply. *Don't waste your sympathy on me. I have only myself to blame.*

The response came as a sensation of comfort, followed by a rather distorted image of a naked man, lying curled on the ground. For a moment, Bron did not understand; then he realized that he was seeing what she wanted for him through her eyes.

'I can't sleep,' he said aloud. 'Not yet. I have to think.'

But now that she had roused him from his stupor, he found that his face was throbbing with pain too savage to ignore. Wincing, he used his mind and his hands to explore the damage. His right eye was swollen shut, and bleeding profusely. His nose was certainly broken – he could move it with a finger – and also bleeding. His ankle hurt too, where he had sprained it jumping to safety.

He had a choice. He could use his power to mend the damage. Or he could deliberately neglect it, so that the pain and the misshapen nose would remind him of the harm his arrogance and thoughtlessness had done to innocent people. He was guiltily aware that this could hardly be called suffering, compared with the death and destruction he had wreaked that night. But he would not avoid the cost to himself. And he vowed, with silent resolution, never again to use sorcery, however beneficial it might seem, where others were involved. Until he reached Jo'ami, he would keep his powers under the control of all the mind-locks he could devise.

He constructed them then and there, blocking out the pain and discomfort in his face and the fits of shivering that shook his body. It took a long while, and the sky was beginning to lighten and the birds to sing by the time he had finished. But at least now he felt that he could restrain himself from any automatic, unthinking use of sorcery; and the Wolf was mercifully silent.

The mare whickered again, reminding him of his other, physical needs. He fumbled in his pack, found tunic and trousers, and put them on. His riding boots had been left behind at the inn, but he had an old pair of sandals. He wrapped himself in his cloak and sat down with his back against a tree, trying to think about what to do next.

He could not go on to Lelyent now. It was only a day's ride away, and those who had survived the fire might come looking for the man who had caused it. And in all the villages and farms and settlements along the valley of the Ger there could be no one else answering to his description, so it would be easy to find him.

No. He would forsake the dubious comforts of inns, people, and over-eager girls. The next time he lay with a woman, he would make very sure that she had no jealous lover, or family, lurking in the background.

At last, as the mare had wanted, he curled up on the soft dry earth and slept for an hour or so. Then he ate a little hard bread, drank the stale water in his bottle, and rode away, deeper into the forest.

Long, long ago, these lands had not been empty: for Toktel'yi was not the first Empire the world had known.

When there was no more than a huddle of mud huts at the wide mouth of the Kefirinn, ruled over by a savage who called himself Akkatanat, King of Toktel'yi, there had been a great city between the steppes and the eastern ranges of the Northern Mountains. It lay where two rivers joined, and it was famous for its beauty, but it was not Zithirian: that place then did not even exist.

Its history lay so far back in time that none now remembered how it had been founded, by three brothers who had come down from the mountains. Legend spoke of them as shape-changers, who on moonlit nights roamed the forests in the guise of a stag, a bear and a mountain tiger.

Under their leadership, and the rule of their descendants, the city grew and prospered. There was wealth under the mountains:

gold, silver, copper, iron, stone. For a thousand years the city of Tyr, governed by the Triple Kings, traded its riches for the luxuries offered by the warmer lands of the south: Terebis, Djebb, Mynak, and Kerenth and Katho in the full glory of their power. Its merchants sailed down the Estris and the Kefirinn to Toktel'yi, beginning to expand its dominions under Akkatanat's descendants, and by now rather more than a collection of mud huts.

As Toktel'yi rose, so Tyr declined. Many of its mountain mines were worked out. Its people grew idle and apathetic. Fewer children were born, and the highlands, once terraced, irrigated and cultivated, reverted to barren steppe, where herds of feral cattle roamed aimlessly. Visitors spoke of the sadness, even despair, that settled over the beautiful city like a shroud. Weeds grew in the side-streets, and the Triple Kingship dwindled to a single monarch. There was supposed to be a curse on the land, invoked by a past Queen of Kerenth who had demanded one of the Triple Kings for her Consort, and had suffered humiliating rejection. Certainly the Queens of the Goddess's sacred land had a reputation for effective malediction. And if the strength of a curse is measured by the number of believers then Queen Eyona's imprecation was extremely potent.

Then one winter something happened, for no boats came trading gold and silver down the River Estris in the spring. The camel caravans, laden with silk and jewels and exotic spices, that travelled northwards across the steppes never returned. It was as if a vast hole had opened up in the earth and swallowed the city of Tyr, with its five gracefully arched bridges, its palace, its temple dedicated to the mountain firegod Urgan, its tall houses built of yellow stone and its fifty thousand people, as if they had never existed.

And such was the length of the memory of the world that within a hundred years the name of Tyr had trickled like sand from the minds of men, for something so terrible had happened there that no-one wanted to speak of it. And so for many generations the lands around it had lain empty, and no curious traveller had ventured east of Lelyent, or up the stately meanderings of the River Estris, to discover what might be left of the fabulous city of Tyr.

Until Bron, who had not even intended to come this way, but had been guided by chance, or fate, or the half-remembered stories and a name sketched on a map.

Bron's route should have lain to the south-east, across the steppes to Sarquaina, northernmost city of Kerenth, a land steeped in ancient magic and ancient beliefs, where if anywhere he would find a ship to take him to Jo'ami. And instead the pied mare's gentle steps had transported him through the forest, heading towards the sunrise, as if she and he had been pulled by an invisible rope.

In all that journey, he saw no one. There was water in the plentiful streams pouring down from the mountains, and an abundance of game in the forest clearings: deer, rabbits, boar. His face mended, although his nose had set crooked, marring his good looks and reminding him, every time he glanced at his reflection in the clear water of pool or stream, of how dangerous he was. And the sun was warm, the wind gentle, the rain sparse and soft. He let the mare guide him onwards, content to enjoy this beautiful, uninhabited country. There were wolves and bears in the forest, perhaps even mountain tigers, but they avoided him. He knew that he had nothing to fear from ordinary animals.

He came upon Tyr quite unexpectedly. It was almost a month since he had fled the burning inn, and the wounds on his face were nearly healed. With no opportunity to shave, the young and haphazard growth of his beard only added to his villainous appearance. He sang to himself and his Sith and the magpie mare each night, letting his voice flow like melting honey into the silky dark depths of the forest. He had renounced sorcery, and the Wolf was in hiding. And despite the deaths and the destruction he had caused, he had never in all his life been happier.

Then he rode suddenly out of the trees, and stood blinking on the summit of a rocky ridge, staring down at what lay below him.

The broad glint of the Estris wound through the valley. It was joined by another, similar stream, and the two waters rolled on united towards the south-west, eventually to flow into the Kefir-inn on the borders of the Empire, five hundred miles away as the eagle flew. And on the long narrow island where the two streams met, had once stood the great city of Tyr. He knew what it must be, even without recourse to his mind-map. Its name, its history and the catastrophe that had destroyed it seeped into his brain as he breathed. *This is Tyr, mighty, loved, admired, feared, hated. So shall end all cities and all empires, no matter how great they be.*

He urged the mare downhill. She was reluctant to pick her way between the tumbled rocks, but he encouraged her softly. At the foot of the ridge there was a tangle of trees, but he could make out the tottering shapes of broken masonry, almost hidden amongst the leaves. A flight of crows launched into the air, clattering in alarm, and wheeled above him. He wondered if they had ever seen a man before. But they were not his concern: it was Tyr that drew him on.

There was a path of some sort, running through the trees so straight that only humans could have made it. And when Bron looked down, he saw, half-hidden beneath the encroaching vegetation, the smooth close-packed stones of a paved highway. To left and right there were tumbledown walls covered in undergrowth, following the line of the road. If they formed its boundary, then it had been at least fifty paces across.

They came to the river's edge so suddenly that the piebald mare reared, startled, and came back to all fours with a snort of alarm. Bron soothed her with his hand and voice and mind, letting her know that there was nothing to fear. When she was calmer, he looked up, and saw what lay before them.

The island on which the city of Tyr had once stood was at least a mile long, perhaps half that width. But with no room to sprawl, its people had built upwards. Although Zithirian was called the City of Towers, this place deserved the epithet far more. Even now, hundreds of years after its fall, many were still standing, though none was complete. Their jagged shapes spiked the sky like a forest of giant broken spears, in tragic echo of the distant mountains in the north.

Five stone bridges had joined island to mainland. The remains of one stretched in front of him, perhaps thirty strides out into the slow broad stream of the Estris. Some cataclysmic force had shattered it in mid-span. He could see a long gap in the centre of the river, then another, briefer length reaching the island. All along the remaining fragments of balustrade stood plinths, where presumably statues had been placed. One had fallen to the ground not far away from him and lay in several pieces. He dismounted and knelt beside it, drawing aside the clinging ivy with a touch as gentle as if the stone had been living flesh.

He had not expected to see a woman's face. Strange and exotic, she was nevertheless very beautiful, with a remote, almost severe loveliness. He thought that the Goddess Sarraliss might appear like this, save that this woman's tilted eyes and curved mouth were entirely human. Had she been made in the image of the people of Tyr?

Bron closed his eyes and opened his mind, knowing there would be no danger. His spirit slid reluctantly from his body and drifted upwards. If he looked down he could see himself, kneeling beside the broken statue, the pied mare standing patiently by, and the Estris pouring slowly, inexorably, heedlessly, through the ruined bridge.

He saw the island on which Tyr had stood, shaped like a rocky boat just south of the place where the rivers joined and pushed around it. The other four bridges had also been destroyed, in a remarkably similar manner, as if a giant child, bored and delinquent, had kicked at its toys. And the towers looked as though a huge scythe had sliced them off to roughly the same height. A horrible suspicion awoke in Bron's mind. Had this city been devastated deliberately? And, if so, who, or what, could possess the power to wreak such terrible destruction?

The people had never returned, but other denizens of this wilderness now inhabited the ruins. Birds and bats roosted in shattered towers; mice, rats and feral cats slunk along the remains of imposing avenues, finer than any in Zithirian. There was a flourishing colony of rock-rabbits, and another, even more remarkably, of small horned and hoofed animals, either sheep or goats. He saw them browsing on the vegetation sprawling over the ancient stones, and wondered how they'd managed to reach the island, with all the bridges broken. But of course the rivers would freeze over in winter. They had probably just walked across the ice, and had been marooned by the spring thaw. Certainly they were safe from predators now.

He looked closer, and saw the traces, pathetic, mute, yet eloquent, of those who had lived here. A shattered skull by a doorway. A tangle of bones, sticking out from under a heap of fallen masonry. The fifty thousand people of Tyr lay where they had perished, with no friends left alive to bury them.

But had they all died?

Bron reached out, for the first time seeking sensations that could not be heard, or touched, or seen. He felt the first unease, the disturbance in the air. And then with terrifying suddenness they were there, fifty thousand souls, screaming, panicking, weeping. Buildings fell, the earth roared and shook, and the pale winter sun disappeared behind a great erupting cloud of dust. People five hundred years dead clutched his hands, begging him to save them. A child Zathti's age stood bewildered, her mouth a huge wailing circle of shock and terror, and even as he tried to snatch her up, the stone building behind her quivered and broke, smashing her down in a torrent of rubble.

He could not bear it. He fled from them, their frantic voices and grasping hands. And as his spirit burst from the falling city and soared above it, he knew what had caused this destruction. The people of Tyr had somehow angered the god they worshipped, Urgan, the Earth-shaker: and in revenge he had obliterated their city, and every man, woman and child within it.

Like a pigeon seeking its home, Bron plunged back into the empty shell of his body, and slammed his mind shut against the screaming souls of the dead.

For a long, long time he lay by the broken statue, shivering with fear and relief, his hands crossed over his head as if by doing so he could ward off his assailants. They gibbered in the air all around him, pleading for salvation, and he cowered away from them, helpless and terrified behind his mental defences.

At last they faded from his consciousness, and it was quiet both inside and outside his head. Something nudged him gently, and he gasped and started like a frightened deer, before he realized that it was the mare, wondering why he hadn't moved for so long.

Stiffly, Bron uncurled himself and stood up. His legs tingled and his fingers felt numb. When he rubbed his hands together, the restored flow of blood was surprisingly painful. The ordinary, prosaic physical sensations helped his return to reality. Yes, he was in Tyr, but now, in Zithirian Year 296. Those people had been dry bones for five centuries, but so dreadful and catastrophic had been their end that his unnatural power, his abnormal sensitivity to the spirits of this place, had attracted their ghosts and forced him to witness their city's destruction. But their terror was long over, and they were at peace now. They had no existence outside his mind.

The sun was setting, far away behind the ridge down which he had ridden only a few hours earlier. It would soon be dark, and he must find somewhere sheltered to spend the night. Clouds were gathering over the Northern Mountains, and the air smelt of rain.

The people of Tyr had frightened him with their desperate need, but he knew they had no power to harm him. He would be safe here, with only their ghosts to walk in the ruins of what had once been the mightiest and most beautiful city in the known world. And he felt a faint but growing sense of kinship with them. For over and over again they had screamed in anguish, 'Why? Why is this happening to us? What have we done? How have we offended?'

They did not know. He did not know either. But Urgan was a capricious, fickle god, destruction lurking in the heart of the smallest, most friendly seeming fire. On a whim, perhaps, he had moved the earth and annihilated Tyr. So all the people had died, guilty and innocent, young and old, good and bad. And the injustice of it tore at Bron's heart.

For he too had slain like that, in a moment of blind rage, and the Ska'i had perished. A month ago, four people had died in the fire at the inn. And the idea woke in his mind, that one day, he might make reparation. To recreate, here, what Urgan had destroyed. To comfort the ghosts, and make Tyr rise again.

It was a dream even less realistic than his planned voyage to Jo'ami. But when he sat close to his own friendly fire that night, in a dry grove of trees by the hidden road, listening to the rain and the wind in the branches, he played the notes on his Sith of an old Tanathi song that his stepmother had taught him. It spoke of the Harpers of the Four Winds, and their wonderful, magical, mythical gifts:

The Harper of the West is made
Of twilight and of hope:
He takes our dreams and with his harp
Spins them into a rope.
Singing birds and summer rain and fire in the sky,
The Harper of the West strolls by.

CHAPTER
SEVEN

The city of Sarquaina had only one reason for its existence, and celebrated the fact every year with a festival that was famous throughout the known world for its wild excesses. After Harvest, when the moon rose full and blood-red over the sleek inland waters of the Kerentan Sea, women from all over Kerenth left their children and their men and came to Sarquaina to give thanks to Sarraliss, Lady of Earth, Lady of Ripeness, Lady of Fertility, for the year of abundance past, and to ask for many years of plenty in the future. And because Sarraliss loved fruitfulness, and generosity, and exuberance, for the twelve days of the Revels the women who took part, from adolescents to grandmothers, from the Queen of Kerenth to the humblest tiller of earth, were free to forget the men who shared their lives, and lie with anyone they fancied.

Not unnaturally, the sacred Priestess prostitutes at the Temple of Sarraliss regarded this annual invasion of enthusiastic amateurs with mixed feelings. Since all of them were chosen for their looks, and retired at the age of forty, they would always find some customers, usually rich ancients from Toktel'yi who couldn't persuade any of the revellers to oblige, and were forced to pay for their pleasure. And the Priestesses were careful to emphasize that a night spent in their company brought good luck and long life. Business did decline at Harvest time, but they were not kept idle.

The Revels also attracted enormous numbers of men. The Kerentans, usually tied to the home and the demands of their women and children, welcomed this chance to let their hair down, and their wives let them go with cheerfully ribald comments on their inability to attract anyone other than the most desperate. Like dogs let off the string, the men flung themselves into an orgy of abandoned indulgence in wine, song and above all women. And the Toktel'yans, pouring over the border in search of pleasure, were taken aback at their first encounter with the straightforward, bold and uninhibited females of Kerenth, so very different from the fragile, cosseted and secluded wives, daughters and concubines they had left behind.

Sarquaina was built above the River Aïthana, that rushed down from the steppe to the Kerentan Sea. From the Temple of Sarraliss, a large but simple building on the summit of the hill with a wide market square in front of it, a narrow, confusing maze of streets jostled steeply down to the quayside. From the roof of the Temple, open to anyone who made an offering to the Goddess, you could see over the whole of Sarquaina, the huddle of small houses and the larger weavers' sheds, where the beautiful silk cloth was produced that made Kerenth famous. And all about the town lay the groves of mulberry trees where the silkworms fed and grew fat and spun their delicate, valuable cocoons.

For many, many years, Kerenth had kept the secret of how silk was made. Even now, with mulberry farms flourishing in Terebis, the province of the Empire with the most suitable climate, the finest and most exquisite cloth was still made by Kerentan women, working at their special looms in the huge, well-lit sheds. Those who did not have the weaver's gift, or inclination, tilled the land. Since the Earth belonged to Sarraliss, and was sacred to her, the Kerentans believed that only women could tend it. Men, barred from the fields by religious taboo and from the looms by their big, clumsy hands, did rough construction and menial work, looked after the children and the household, and spent any time left over drinking and gossiping with their friends. The women did not mind: they ruled in Kerenth, their labours brought wealth, plenty and prestige, and men were notoriously only good for one thing – and that wasn't always as satisfactory as it might be. So the women of Kerenth converged on Sarquaina for the Harvest Revels, for fun and freedom and a welcome change from the tedium of their usual bedmates.

Inrai'a had been Queen of Kerenth for six years. It was a hereditary monarchy: her mother, Oranna, had had three daughters by her two Consorts, and according to the custom had chosen her successor from amongst them. Inrai'a was the youngest, but possessed a strong and dominant personality and had bullied her elder brother and sisters from the cradle. She would not be easily led, or frightened, or persuaded. And in these uncertain times, with the Toktel'yan Empire, in which women were enslaved, glowering across the border, Kerenth needed a strong ruler more than ever before.

Unfortunately, Oranna had died quite young, while her chosen heir was only twenty. True, Inrai'a had been groomed for the throne since the age of ten, but she was still a young, untried girl, and her elder sisters had tried to overturn her claim even before their mother's funeral. With commendable skill and ruthlessness the young Queen had outwitted them, and her advisors accepted her unanimously as their monarch. Inrai'a was used to getting her own way, by charm and persuasion if possible, by threats and force of character if not. And she was quite capable of more devious methods. Her eldest sister found herself elected High Priestess of Sarraliss in Sarquaina, a post so prestigious that it would have been unthinkable to refuse it, and was thus excluded from contention. The other, who had always been rather foolish and gullible, was persuaded to fall in love with a handsome Toktel'yan, soon unmasked as a spy. The resulting scandal ensured her retirement in disgrace to one of the royal villas in a remote spot on the shores of the Kerentan Sea, and she took no further part in politics.

So Inrai'a now reigned supreme. She was beautiful, arrogant and domineering, an awesome combination. Because she was also intelligent, her advisors were prepared to put up with her high-handed ways. And the people of Kerenth were just happy to go on with their lives as they had always done, in peace and prosperity with the blessing of Sarraliss.

There was only one thing Inrai'a lacked, and that was a Consort. She had been searching for someone suitable for years, and so far no one had managed to live up to her very exacting standards. It was also widely believed – though not by Inrai'a – that most men were intimidated by her manner and her reputation. Kerentan men would do almost anything for a quiet life. Undoubtedly, marriage to Inrai'a would ensure the opposite.

Of course, she didn't need a *man*, just a father for her unconceived children. But she didn't want them to be ugly, or stupid, or ill-tempered. And unattached, intelligent, good-looking and charming men seemed to be very thin on the ground in Kerenth – or at any rate they were when Inrai'a was looking for them.

He didn't have to be Kerentan, though. He could come from any island in the Archipelago, or Gulkesh, or Katho, or the hot, savage desert land of Ma'alkwen. He could even be Toktel'yan, although after the scandal of her sister's affair that might be a little unwise. And because Inrai'a had the usual needs and desires of a healthy young woman, and because she firmly believed that one day soon she would find her ideal Consort, she went to Sarquaina for the Revels with a feeling of hopeful anticipation. And with her went her thirty waiting women, her priestesses, her horse-mistress, her laundry staff, her seamstresses, and all the other women, and a few men, who made up the travelling entourage of the Queen of Kerenth, to the number of a hundred and fifty.

Sarquaina was overflowing. Every dwelling had turned itself into a lodging-house, and every inn was full, the wealthy in private rooms, the poorer or less fussy bedded down in communal sleeping halls or even in the stables, their horses led off to rented fields along the river to cavort in idleness for the twelve days of the Revels.

Inrai'a, of course, had been here many times before. Sarquaina was the sacred place of pilgrimage, and she had often visited the birthplace of Sarraliss, in the Hidden Valley high on the great mountain called Skathak that reared up to the southwest of the town. But this was the first time she had attended the Revels as Queen and also as participant. Her yellow dress was packed carefully in her baggage, layered between drifts of special, gossamer-light paper and sprinkled with scented waters from Tamat, guaranteed to inflame men's passions. And once wearing the traditional colour, her hair loose and her feet bare, she would be able to join the crowds looking for adventure, excitement and a handsome lover for the night. And she would be unrestrained and anonymous, a woman rather than a Queen.

It was a vain hope, of course. Everyone in Sarquaina knew those proud, imperious features, and her waist-length mass of curling, rich brown hair was famous. Her personal maid, brushing it loose in the privacy of her bedchamber, shaking out the corn-yellow silk that was creased despite all her efforts, might insist that no one would recognize her. In her heart, Inrai'a knew better, and perversely took some pleasure from the fact.

Still, it was fun to pretend otherwise, and she was young enough to relish the thought of shedding her status and her responsibilities for a while. She put on the yellow dress and turned this way and that before the polished silver mirror, admiring the effect. Then, with a silent prayer to Sarraliss, she collected the members of her entourage who wished to join the Revels. In a laughing, excited group, they left the luxurious villa

just outside the town, that had been graciously lent to her for the
Revels by a local dignitary, and walked along the dusty road
above the river to Sarquaina.

It was dusk and the sun had set in a flare of crimson and gold,
scarlet and turquoise and amber. Inrai'a saw the fireflies glowing
in the orange trees above her head, heard the crickets rasping
rhythmically amongst the grass and bushes, smelt the fragrances
of lavender and rosemary, felt the soft earth under her bare feet
and the gentle touch of the warm air against her skin. Around
her, the other women giggled and chattered, their voices rich with
anticipation. And between the branches of the trees, the evening
stars glinted like chips of new minted silver, promising a fine
night.

Near to the town they joined other revellers, in groups of two
or three, or a dozen or more. Many women carried the traditional
round lanterns on poles, with painted paper shades, and similar
lamps hung outside every house, so that the road into Sarquaina
seemed to be a river of bobbing lights in a myriad glowing
colours.

By custom, the taverns and inns served their wines half-price
for the nights of Revel. Such was the quantity consumed that the
vendors still made a handsome profit. At the heart of the town
lay the great Temple Square, a hundred paces on each side, and
here all the musicians, entertainers and sellers had congregated.
A girl from one of the southern islands, her dark skin shiny with
sweat, danced to the swift notes of her partner's flute. An ancient
in blue robes, perhaps from Ma'alkwen, had trained his two monkeys, dressed in miniature Toktel'yan tunics, to turn somersaults
and run through the crowds with their paws outstretched for
money. A blind woman, with white-clouded eyes and grey hair
straggling from under the fringe of thin square gold coins sewn to
her head-cloth, told long and intricate stories to an enchanted
audience of both children and adults. A team of half-naked acrobats, five girls and a token man, formed a tottering pyramid to
wholehearted cheers, which changed to derision when they collapsed into a hot, swearing, undignified heap on the ground.
Another group were juggling, sending balls, fruit, breadsticks and
even a couple of flaming torches spinning accurately between
them with dazzling speed.

Around the edge of the square the food vendors had set
up their stalls. You could buy sweet oranges, bread, skewers of

chopped meat and vegetables roasted over glowing braziers, sizzling spiced fish with brown shrivelled skins and hot fragrant flesh, nameless fried parcels that might contain anything, meat, oranges, peaches, peas, prawns, fish, alike only in the mouth-watering intensity of their flavours. There were middle-aged women selling flagons of strong rough wine, or the dark earthenware jars, the shape of a very large pear, that contained the sweet, fiery and potent spirit distilled from honey and peaches, and known as Summer Sap.

And everywhere there were Revellers: women in dresses of every shade of yellow from cream to gold to deepest ochre, men in the long loose hooded robes, in cotton or silk, that were ubiquitous along the eastern shores of the Southern Sea. This early in the evening, few people had paired off, and most were still in single-sex groups, the women sizing up the opportunities available with bold, discriminating eyes. There was no doubt who did the choosing in the land of the Goddess.

Inrai'a watched the monkeys dance and applauded the jugglers. She and her women ate grilled fish and sweet juicy peaches, and passed jugs of wine and spirits from hand to hand. Their group was smaller already: Shlaaran had gone off with a young man in white, and Sumis had stayed to watch the acrobats. The Queen's warm brown eyes searched the shifting, noisy crowds, endlessly seeking a man who didn't pretend that he hadn't seen her, a man with the courage to return her gaze. Her mood of joyful celebration began to trickle away in resentment. What did the fools think she'd do to them, turn them into snakes? All she wanted were twelve nights of fun, no cares, no obligations, no inhibitions. It was as she had secretly feared: the feeble men of Kerenth were too frightened to Revel with their Queen.

She met one pair of eyes that didn't slide away, but they belonged to a Toktel'yan: he had that hateful look of masculine arrogance common to citizens of the Empire. She wasn't that desperate, yet, and ignored him. More wine went round: she was feeling increasingly reckless, wanting to shed her royal skin, to do something wild and unconventional even for the Revels.

In the centre of the square, a group of musicians had set up their instruments and were playing the slow, tuneful notes of the Ring Dance. A circle of men, hands linked, stepped and turned and paraded: in the centre, the women rotated in a closer ring, waiting for the moment when the music suddenly speeded up, and the two sets would join and weave in and out, faster and faster, in a pattern at once simple to perform and impossibly intricate to watch.

Laughing, her remaining women dodged through the ring of men to take their places in the centre. Left behind, Inrai'a stood watching them for a moment, the jar of Summer Sap in her hand. She drained it, and then turned away, pushing through the crowds, glad to be alone.

In the furthest corner of the square, by the Rose Tavern, a single musician was playing. Inrai'a stopped at a wine-seller nearby to refill her jar, and stayed to listen, attracted by the unusual sound of his instrument. It was some sort of lyre, but much sweeter and more mellow in tone than those of Kerenth, which were usually made from a tortoise's shell. The air was vibrating with the confused music from a dozen different sources, overlaid by the increasingly frenetic rhythm of the Ring Dance, but his soft notes, separately and together, pierced through the louder discordance around him.

And then the musician began to sing, and her heart was ensnared.

He had a voice like molten amber, a sound as pure and liquid as a flute. And he sang in a language she did not know, of things that she understood only too well. Love and heartbreak, loneliness and grief poured from his throat, and she stood bereft, the Summer Sap forgotten, tears streaming down her face as she wept for a life she had never had, and never known she wanted until now.

Other people had crowded in front of her, blocking her view. Inrai'a pushed through them, wiping her eyes on her sleeve.

He wasn't from Kerenth, that was certain: not from Toktel'yi, or the Archipelago. The pale hair indicated that he was a North-erner, but if so, he was a very long way from home. And Inrai'a, educated to the highest royal standards, fluent in every one of the five languages spoken around the Southern Sea, had no idea what he was singing.

The song ceased, to appreciative applause: the crowd around him was small, but rapidly growing. The musician turned the tuning pegs on his instrument, and looked up, and into Inrai'a's eyes.

His were very dark, set deep and wide under straight fair brows. She saw his strong, sensitive face, its beauty at once marred and made more interesting and attractive by the crooked nose. Suddenly he smiled at her, and her heart leapt. This was the one: this man she would have.

His gaze lingered on her, and she knew he understood. No one, not even the newest stranger, could fail to comprehend what happened in Sarquaina at Harvest Revel. Then he bent his head to his instrument, the silver strings shimmered, and he sang.

This time, it was a Toktel'yan tune that everyone must know, written in celebration of the composer's concubine. And as he employed that wonderful, effortless voice, he looked again at Inrai'a, standing at the front of the crowd in her corn-gold dress, and she knew that she too had been chosen.

When the song had ended, he laid down his instrument, and the people threw him coins, mostly square Kerentan money in copper and silver, along with some semi-circular half-Imperials bearing a rising sun on one side and a hawk's wings on the other. He gathered them up with a smile, and thanked his audience in strongly-accented Kerentan, and rather better Toktel'yan. As the crowd began to drift away in search of other entertainments, Inrai'a walked up to him.

He was young, she realized with surprise: those eyes had seemed as ageless as the sea. Young, but not inexperienced, he wore an air of reserve, of self-possession, that was at once enigmatic and attractive. But there was nothing ambiguous about the look he gave her, and she realized, with a sudden wild sense of liberation, that he had no idea who she was.

They didn't talk much: words were unnecessary. They shared the Summer Sap, and Inrai'a failed to notice that she drank almost all of it. They danced in the Ring Dance, and bought sweet honey cakes to nibble, licking the crumbs from each other's fingers, every touch of his lips like fire on her skin, a promise of delights to come. They joined a line of energetic Revellers snaking along the main street that led down from the Temple Square to the river, and watched some women, refugees from Penya, doing the Flame Dance on the quayside. There were taverns there, more music, harsher and less tuneful than the songs the man beside her had played, wine, food, heat, more dancing. Her head whirling, every pore of her skin open to sensation, Inrai'a danced and drank and sang, and for the first time in her life forgot her royal status.

It was very late when she found herself, without quite knowing how she had come there, in a meadow by the river. Distantly, the songs and voices rose from the town beyond, where the celebrations on this first night would last until dawn. Her head reeled, her senses were curiously distorted, as though only a few things still existed outside the wild, glorious chaos within her head. She turned to the man beside her, and under the huge misty gaze of the yellow harvest moon, pressed her body greedily against his.

The ground was soft, but she never noticed it, nor the curious, light-stepping horses who came to see what they were doing and wandered away again, leaving the man and woman to their own concerns amid the long grass by the river.

She had had plenty of lovers before, but not like this. Drunk with wine and Summer Sap, with freedom and intoxicating passion, Inrai'a shed every fragment of restraint, aware of nothing but the man whose name she did not even know, and whose body had ignited such overwhelming and insatiable desire.

At last, as the birds began to sing, she slept exhausted in the grass. Golden poppies, their fragile petals like the bright shivering silk of her crushed, torn dress, whispered above her in the dawn breeze, and her long hair, tangled with flowers and grass-stems, spread over her bare breasts and across her pale, lovely, sleeping face.

And when she awoke, he was gone.

'I don't care how long it takes – find him!'

The women winced at the imperious tone of their Queen's voice. Everyone in the room had an aching head except, it seemed, Inrai'a. And, unfairly, she was the one who most deserved to suffer a hangover. Sumis, who had indulged in a particularly inventive and athletic night with the male acrobat, said hesitantly, 'There must be twenty thousand people in Sarquaina, madam. It'll take days.'

'He shouldn't be very hard to locate,' Inrai'a said forcefully. 'There can't be too many blond Northern musicians here. And I want him found – today, if possible.'

The women exchanged glances. They knew their Queen too well. In this mood, she brooked no opposition, and if they failed her anger would be terrifying. None of them wanted to be dismissed: positions in the royal household were pleasant, prestigious and lucrative, and there would be a queue of eager applicants to replace them if they were thrown out.

Shlaaran, who had been with their mistress for ten years, said at last, 'We will do everything possible to find him, madam. But what if he doesn't want to be found?'

Inrai'a's gaze was fiercely indignant. 'Of course he does. I'm the Queen.'

'But will he know that, if he's a Northerner?' Sumis pointed out.

Their mistress's face revealed a sudden and very rare uncertainty. She said slowly, 'Perhaps . . . perhaps he didn't realize who I am.'

'He's bound to be still here,' Tiana said, with cheerful confidence. 'No man ever leaves Sarquaina during the Revels. You might as well ask a child to walk away from a sweet stall.'

But all morning the ladies of Inrai'a's household scoured the city, enquiring at inns, taverns and houses. At last, Sumis found her acrobat, and learned from him that the fair-haired musician had been staying at the Rose in Temple Square. The landlady showed her his room, but it was empty. 'Paid first thing this morning and gone,' she said, her plump face bursting with curiosity. 'Been a naughty boy, has he?'

Sumis, wishing she had done something about her headache, was in no mood for a gossip. 'No,' she said shortly. 'Any idea where he's gone?'

'I can't say as I have.' The landlady gave her a knowing wink. 'Things are so busy here at Revel time, and my memory isn't what it was—'

With a sigh, Sumis fumbled in the money-belt at her waist. 'Will this help you?'

The landlady snatched the square silver coin and curled her fist triumphantly over it. 'Strange how well my mind works now. I thought it was odd when he said he was leaving. Didn't say where he was going, though. Isn't like a man to run away from Sarquaina at Revel time. Usually you have to kick 'em out when the twelve days are up.'

'You mean, he was leaving the town?' Sumis asked, with a sinking heart.

'Reckon so. You'd better find out which gate he used – that'd give you some idea where he was going. Handsome boy like that – and a voice like sweet honey – yes, if I were your age I'd be after him myself.'

But Sumis had already left.

As Inrai'a had earlier pointed out, blond Northerners were almost as rare as snake's legs in Sarquaina, but none of the gate-keepers had seen him. *So that means he must still be in the town after all*, Sumis thought. *Unless . . .*

She hurried down to the waterfront. The Aïthana was quite narrow here, but broadened out a mile or so below the town, becoming a wide estuary which flowed between rocky cliffs into the Kerentan sea. Below the Town Bridge, small stone wharves edged the river on both sides, and here the smaller boats tied up: larger, seagoing vessels anchored downstream and unloaded their cargoes into shallow barges that were rowed or poled up to Sarquaina when the tide was favourable. There was a road to Kerenth, hugging the coastline, but many pilgrims and Revel-lers came to Sarquaina in the fast galleys that were common on this comparatively sheltered inland sea.

It was unlikely that the Northerner would have found a ship to take him away from Sarquaina after only one night of Revel, but Sumis had to cover every possibility before she organized a more thorough search of the town. And with a peculiarly mingled sense of relief and dread, she discovered from one of the dock workers, a brawny man in a leather kilt and bronze arm-rings, that a man answering Inrai'a's brief and hectic description had indeed hired one of the small coastal sailing-boats, and left Sar-quaina that morning.

'And I don't know where he was going, lady, but Exe'an took him, and he's been wanting to go down to Kerenth to see his sister. He'd only leave Sarquaina at Revel if he had a very good reason. I reckon your man's paid him to ferry him to Kerenth.'

Inrai'a didn't take the news very well. She ranted, she stamped her feet, she dismissed all thirty of her women and then, weeping, reinstated them an hour later (Shlaaran, who knew her best, had advised the others only to pretend to pack). Finally, she calmed herself and sent the long-suffering Sumis back to the quayside.

Following strict and detailed instructions, she hired a galley. It took ten gold coins, more money than most Kerentans saw in a lifetime, to persuade Captain Trahay and her crew to leave Sarquaina, even for their Queen. But before the afternoon was over, Sumis was being rowed down the estuary in pursuit of a small fishing boat with two patched yellow sails.

The Captain didn't think they would catch up with their quarry at least until sunrise the next morning, and after the day's frenetic activity, Sumis was glad of some rest and peace. She leaned over the galley's painted wooden rail, admiring the swift even strokes of the oars as the vessel swept through the gentle blue water. Toktel'yan galleys were rowed by slaves, but these were free men, and some stalwart women, attracted by high wages, the chance of a more interesting life than their stay-at-home fellows would enjoy, and the prestige of belonging to the crew of one of the crack galleys that raced in the Narrows off Katho every year at High Summer. In addition, the women of Kerenth much admired muscular men, and rowers were popular visitors in the towns and villages around the coast of the Kerentan Sea.

After her night with the lithe acrobat, strapping arms and legs like tree-trunks were not at present to Sumis's taste. She wondered what this Northern musician was like. A more than competent lover, if Inrai'a's reaction to his unexpected departure was any guide. More than that, and the fact that he was a master of his art, she could not guess.

The galley, *Lady of Corn*, emerged from the estuary, set her sails and stood out to sea, helped by a steady offshore breeze. The Captain was anxious to negotiate the two islands known as the Whale and the Dolphin, lying just off the Aïthana's mouth, before it grew dark. Their low humped shapes lay to the galley's left: ahead, jutting out into the water, was the great rocky peninsula called Little Skathak, a paltry imitation of the huge sacred mountain, one of the highest in the known world, rearing up into the clouds behind it. Once clear of these cluttered waters, the *Lady of Corn* would sail on all night, steering by the stars and the lodestone under the Captain's awning in the stern. With the wind behind them, the rowers could rest, and their lone passenger had one of the tiny but comfortable cabins packed below decks forward and aft.

Sumis had never been able to sleep well afloat: she found the constant motion of the ship, the creak of timbers and shouted orders and the muffled voices of the crew, singing or chanting, very difficult to ignore. She was up before dawn, well wrapped in a warm cloak for protection against the cool maritime winds, and climbed the ladder to the deck.

The *Lady of Corn* plunged on through the dark sea, her

breaking bow wave glimmering white. Across the water to the
east, the sky was beginning to glow with the promise of sunrise.
Nothing showed above the flat horizon, but Sumis knew that
hundreds of miles away, on the far side of the sea, mountains and
forests tumbled down to a rocky, inhospitable shore, inhabited by
primitive savages. Many years ago daring explorers from Kerenth
and Katho had briefly mapped that distant coast, and left in a
hurry, pursued by stone-tipped arrows and barbed fishing spears.
They had never returned there, for Kerenth had all the land she
needed. Unlike her aggressive Imperial neighbour she was not
interested in conquest for its own sake.

Sumis used the sidewalk to reach the bow. Below her, the
rowers had resumed their labours, and the First Mate beat time
on a deerskin drum. None glanced up as she walked past them:
they were too intent on earning their bonus. She had promised
them five silver coins each if they could bring their quarry back to
Sarquaina by nightfall today.

The bow curved up sharply, but there was a viewing platform
jutting out in front of it, reached by a narrow and precarious
catwalk made of rope and wood. With a brief prayer to Sarraliss,
who had no dominion over the ocean, Sumis tucked her skirts
into her belt and negotiated the swaying structure with considerable trepidation.

The Captain's small daughter was there already, her fierce
gaze intent on the lightening sea ahead. She glanced at Sumis
with some curiosity, and shook her head. 'Can't see them yet,
lady.'

'I just hope we haven't passed them in the night.' Sumis
crouched down beside the child, wrapping her skirt and cloak
around her legs. Spray struck up from the plunging bow, and the
girl laughed. One day, if she survived winter storms and
uncharted rocks, she would inherit this beautiful ship. Sumis,
whose childhood had been spent on her mother's luxurious farm
just outside Kerenth, did not envy her at all.

'There!' The child pointed, and Sumis peered through the
spray, her lips tingling with salt. As the *Lady of Corn* crested a
wave, she caught a glimpse of a sail, quite close. A second sighting
confirmed it: a small fat fishing boat, with a triangular patched
yellow sail on each of her two stubby masts, bouncing in leisurely
fashion through the choppy morning sea.

As the sun rose above the eastern horizon the galley came
within hailing distance of her prize. The fishing boat put about

and drifted into the bigger ship's lee, her gunwale crowded with curious heads.

Sumis had returned to her cabin to change her soaked clothes. She stood on the stern deck, proud and imposing in her best gown, with the silver pendant of the royal household, shaped like a crescent moon, gleaming on her breast. The galley's crew put out grappling hooks, drew the fishing boat alongside, and made her fast.

It was the right one. There, amongst the dark heads of the Kerentan fishermen, was one startlingly pale. With a heartfelt sigh of relief, Sumis walked to the rail and pointed to him. 'You! I have orders to take you back to Sarquaina.'

His face, turned up to hers, was a politely negative blank. 'I do not wish to return to Sarquaina, lady.'

At least he spoke Kerentan, albeit with a strong accent. Sumis said, in a passable imitation of Inrai'a's imperious manner, 'I am afraid you have no choice. The Queen commands it.'

'The Queen? The Queen of Kerenth? Why does she want me?'

'She told me to say to you – because of the poppies.'

Suddenly, obviously, his bewilderment cleared. He said, 'Was she – is she the *Queen*?'

The entire crews of both vessels were listening avidly. Sumis said patiently, 'Yes. And she commands you to return.'

'And if I don't want to? What if I refuse?'

Captain Trahay sucked in her breath with a whistle. Sumis said, 'I regret that refusal isn't an option. I am ordered to bring you back with me, by force if necessary.'

For a moment there was silence, broken by the slap of the waves on the hulls of both boats, and the creak of their planking rubbing together. Sumis stared down at the Northerner. His eyes were as dark as a native of Onnak's, a strange contrast to the flaxen hair, and she felt a sudden tingle of unease, as if the advantage lay secretly on his side and not hers.

Then he smiled suddenly, and shrugged. 'I don't want anyone hurt. I'll come with you.'

A few moments later he was climbing up the rope ladder slung over the galley's side, two packs on his shoulder. Close to, he was surprisingly slight, and also, she saw, very young. She said formally, 'I am Sumis, Lady of the Household of Queen Inrai'a. And you are?'

There was a slight pause before his answer. 'Kenmet, lady.'

Sumis was sure he was lying, and it increased her misgivings. But she must follow Inrai'a's orders, and so she said, 'Very well, Kenmet. Will you come with me below? I wish to talk to you in private.'

As the fishing boat cast off, and the galley began to make the sweeping turn that would point her once more in the direction of Sarquaina, she ushered him into the cabin next to hers, and indicated that he sit down on the narrow bunk. She herself remained standing: foreigners did not always understand the dominance of women in Kerenth, and it was prudent to remind him of her authority.

He was looking at her with a curious expression on his face, though his eyes were so dark as to be impenetrable. She avoided them, and said briskly, 'I apologize for this heavy-handedness, Kenmet, but when the Queen commands in Kerenth, she must be obeyed. I can assure you, though, that you are in no danger whatsoever.'

'I know that,' he said, still studying her rather as if she were a fine Katho statue, the work of some famous and ancient master. 'Was one night not enough for her, then?'

He spoke as a Kerentan man would, with a complete absence of pride or bravado: indeed, with some surprise. Sumis said carefully, 'It appears not. Tell me – why did you go, when there were eleven more days of Revel left?'

'I wanted to go to Kerenth. The opportunity presented itself, so I took it.'

Once more Sumis sensed he was lying, though no evidence of it showed on his face. She said, 'You've made a considerable impression on the Queen. I should warn you, I think she expects rather more from you than a few nights together.'

For the first time, a shadow of disquiet furrowed his face. 'Does she?'

Sumis gave him the truth. 'She wants you to be her Consort.'

There was a stunned silence. Then, to the woman's indignation, the musician began to laugh with apparently genuine mirth.

'What's so funny?' she demanded. 'It is a very serious proposition. Haven't you heard of the Consorts of Kerenth?'

'Of course I have – the whole of the known world has.' He grinned up at her, and for the first time she saw why Inrai'a had been so desperate to have him back. 'I just don't think I'm . . .

Consort material, somehow. And besides, I had no idea she was the Queen.'

Sumis sighed. She said cautiously, 'How long have you been in Kerenth?'

'Oh, about six days, I should think.'

'And before that?'

'I was travelling through the Empty Lands . . . Tell me, Lady Sumis, have you ever heard of a great city in the north, called Tyr?'

'I'm afraid I haven't. Is that where you come from?'

'No – but you look a little like the people there. They also have – had – dark hair and golden skin and slanting eyes.'

'My mother is Kerentan,' Sumis said rather stiffly. It was considered impolite to comment on someone's personal appearance to their face.

'I'm sorry. I didn't mean to offend you.'

'It doesn't matter.' Sumis stared at him with growing apprehension. He obviously had no knowledge – how could he, a virtual stranger to her country? – of the nuances of acceptable behaviour. True, Queens had taken foreign Consorts before, but not in the memory of anyone now living. Sumis had never had much interest in Kerentan history, but she was sure that such practices had led to trouble in the past.

However, the Queen alone was entitled to choose her Consort, so the final decision must be Inrai'a's. And her position in the hearts of the people was as secure as Mount Skathak. They wouldn't quibble if she took an Onnak ape to bed, though they'd gossip about it endlessly. And an itinerant musician who was, by the look of him, barely out of his teens was, although unusual, not an impossible choice. Inrai'a's own father, her mother's second Consort, had been a groom in the royal household. Since he was forbidden to take part in politics, it didn't really matter who, or what, he was: his entire purpose was to please the Queen, in bed and out of it, and father her children. Sometimes there was genuine long-lasting love between ruler and Consort, matches which endured happily for many years. Other Queens, more capricious or less easily satisfied, got through dozens. Amath, who had reigned four hundred years ago, held the record with fifty-two, the last when she was over seventy. Sumis, knowing Inrai'a as she did, strongly suspected that this young man would be the first of many.

She said carefully, 'How much do you know of our customs?'

'A little. That your land is sacred to Sarraliss, and ruled by women. That the silk you weave is the finest in the world, and that you have known peace and stability for many thousands of years.'

'Is that all?' Sumis sighed, and sat down on the bunk opposite. 'With any luck, we'll reach Sarquaina before nightfall – so I'll only have a few hours to teach you – '

'Does the Queen think I need teaching?'

His eyebrows were raised, his tone gently teasing. Sumis said irritably, 'I wasn't thinking about that part. Of course she doesn't. As far as she's concerned, you're the gold in the stream. No, I mean other things. Our customs, our ways. If she does make you Consort, there are certain matters you must understand. And foreigners, particularly men, often find it difficult.'

'Try me,' he said, a challenge in his voice. And with another prayer to the Goddess, Sumis plunged into her explanation.

She talked all morning. Food and drink were brought, and she asked for fruit juice rather than wine. Kenmet drank it as well. Either he too had over-indulged last night, or he was a sparing imbiber. She told him about the duties of the Consort: that they were purely ceremonial, that he could wield no real power save by influencing the Queen, that she could divorce him without warning or explanation, with only the words 'I renounce you', in front of three witnesses. Any children he might father were regarded as hers, and he had no rights over them nor any say in their upbringing and education. And unless formally divorced, he could not desert his wife on pain of death: nor could he lie with anyone else. These strictures only applied to the Consort: other Kerentan men were much more loosely attached to their women, for since inheritance was passed down the indubitable female line, in law it didn't much matter what the men got up to.

'But the Queen's dignity is sacred,' Sumis told him. 'After all, she is the mortal representative and embodiment of the Goddess. And although she may take lovers, she is permitted only to do so when she does not have a current Consort. So it isn't all to her advantage.'

'I should hope not,' said the musician.

Sumis glared at him. 'Now why do I think you aren't taking this very seriously? The Consort is a very important and prestigious position, you know. And the Queen is very choosy – she's searched for the right man for six years.'

'And now she's picked on me.' He began to laugh again. 'I can't think why.'

'Can't you? Look in a mirror. Better still, look at her when we get back to Sarquaina. Do you always persuade women to fall in love with you after one night?'

The mirth drained away from his face like water. He gazed at her, his eyes suddenly very bleak. 'No. It was not my intention. But I don't think I can be the Consort, whatever your Queen wants. There are . . . difficulties.'

'What difficulties? You're young, fit, attractive, obviously of sound mind – and if you've any unsavoury perversions, you hide them well. If you've a wife back home, that doesn't matter – Kerentan law only recognizes Kerentan marriages. I admit it's unusual to choose a foreigner, but it's happened several times before. And it's unthinkable for you to refuse. Inrai'a won't allow it.'

He looked as if he was about to say something, and then changed his mind. 'I'll have to talk to her,' he said at last. 'There are things she should know.'

He would say no more, and Sumis eventually gave up pressing him. She had no idea what his problem might be, but one thing was certain: Inrai'a would not take no for her answer. Like it or not, the musician would be escorted up to the Temple, tomorrow or the day after, garlanded with flowers, made to recite the solemn vows required of a Consort, and ceremonially linked in blood with the Queen of Kerenth.

The rowers worked their hands to shreds against a strong head-wind, and the *Lady of Corn* reached the estuary just as the sun was setting. Knowing that her mistress must be waiting with fretting impatience at the villa, Sumis hurried her captive over the side and into the small shallow boat, rowed by a dozen men, that would take them upriver to Sarquaina. The tide was flowing, and bore them swiftly along: and before dark had fallen, they reached the quayside.

Someone must have been watching for the galley's return, for word had evidently got about. A thousand lanterns, blue, red, yellow, green, purple, orange, glowed along the waterfront, carried by the joyful people of Sarquaina. Sumis glanced at Kenmet's face. As usual, it was impassive, revealing no emotion. She had no idea what he was thinking, and it unsettled her. Kerentans were accustomed to sharing thoughts and feelings: they were a warm, outgoing, friendly people. This young man gave very little of himself away.

And yet he must have some passions, or Inrai'a would not have fallen in love with him after just one night.

They were singing, men and women together, as Kenmet and Sumis climbed up on to the quayside. At the appearance of the distinctive Northerner, everyone began to cheer. As he stood at her side, a shower of petals drifted down over his head, the traditional windflowers, red as blood, and poppies, golden as ripe corn. Another man might have seemed bemused by this unexpected welcome, but already Sumis knew that he was observing everything closely.

The High Priestess appeared in her robes of yellow and green and brown, the colours of earth, and her sacred staff, tipped with a golden ear of wheat, carried high in her hand. Nerana was Inrai'a's eldest sister, and had once considered the throne to be rightfully hers. Now, six years later, she appeared to accept her present exalted position and certainly, after the Queen, the High Priestess of Sarquaina, mouthpiece of the Goddess, was the most important lady in the land.

But Sumis saw the lines of bitterness around Nerana's eyes and mouth, and knew that her defeat still rankled. Even now, she suspected that the Priestess might try to avenge it.

Nerana's smile, though, was apparently genuine, and her voice rang out confidently over the massed, joyful crowd. 'Women and men of Sarquaina – behold, the Consort of Kerenth!'

And amid the crash of applause and a new cascade of red and gold flowers, Kenmet's face was as still as a stone mask.

CHAPTER
EIGHT

Inrai'a had been waiting at the Villa of the Mulberry Tree all day, in a frenzy of anxiety and impatience. She had no faith in the ability of Sumis or the galley to catch up with her lover, although she was certain that once he learned why he was being pursued, he was sure to return to her. After that magical, glorious night, which melted her body just remembering it, he could not fail to come back – as long as he knew.

She made her remaining women miserable with her fretfulness and bad temper. Finally, at sunset, she sent them out of her room with a few choice words, and told them not to return unless they brought the Northerner with them.

Alone at last, she paced the room like a prowling tiger: stared obsessively out of the southern window, from which a tiny glimpse of the estuary was visible: viewed herself in the mirror, discarded her dress, put on another, changed her mind again and chose the watered blue silk. Its weave was so soft and fine that it fell from a jewelled clasp on each shoulder to the floor, clinging to all the perfect curves of her body as if it were liquid. She strung gold bracelets up her slender bare arms, and let her hair hang loose down her back, confined only by the slim golden crown, with its curved spikes and engraved horses and wheat ears, that the Queens of Kerenth had worn for thousands of years.

She studied her reflection for a long time, fighting a new and most unwelcome lack of confidence. Never before had she been so enamoured of a man that she was uncertain of her own attractions: never before had a lover's opinion meant so much.

Despite her fears, she saw no fault in the scented, beautiful, seductive figure before her. She lit lamps and lanterns, filling her bedroom with warm, glowing light. And as she hung the last one on the wall above the bed, she heard the cheering in the distance.

After what seemed to be an unbearably long interval, there came a knock on her door. Inrai'a turned away from the window overlooking the courtyard, now crowded with curious and euphoric members of her household, and spoke in her usual imperious voice. 'Enter!'

First, of course, came her sister Nerana, clad in her priestly robes and hung about with an aura of jealousy that was almost tangible. Then Sumis, with a quite justifiable look of triumph on her face. The rest of her waiting women, Shlaaran at their head. And finally, his face calm and self-possessed, the Northern musician.

He stood before her, the soft lamplight gleaming on his pale hair. He wore a tunic and trousers, as he had the previous night; they were worn and rather shabby. Over his shoulder he carried two packs, one of which must contain the slumbering instrument from which he could coax such beauty. She realized how little be possessed, and how great her own wealth and status must seem to him.

'Highest lady of all the ladies of Kerenth,' said Nerana formally, a bite of bitterness in her voice. 'I bring to you and present to you the man known as Kenmet, whom you have chosen to be the Consort of Kerenth. Seeing him now, do you approve your choice?'

Inrai'a stared at the man she had last seen gazing down at her, intent and alight with passion. His eyes were even darker than she remembered. She ached to feel his touch, his kiss, his body filling hers. Her avid hunger must have shown on her face, for she saw, briefly, an answering desire on his.

'I approve it.' Her voice hardly shook at all. 'I confirm that I, Inrai'a, daughter of Oranna, descendant of two hundred and five Queens of Kerenth, do choose this man as my Consort, to be the warmth in my bed and the father of my children. I pray that Sarraliss, Lady of Earth and Corn and Harvest, and Guardian of this, her own sacred land, will bless our union and make it joyous and fruitful.'

'Do you accept?' Nerana had turned to the musician, standing alone in the centre of the room.

For a nerve-wracking moment, he did not answer. A rustle of whispers rose from the eager huddle of women. Inrai'a's face began to acquire a desperate, almost pleading look. Sumis wished that she had told Kenmet that those who refused to be Consort would be sacrificed to the Goddess then and there. It wasn't true, of course, but a foreigner couldn't be expected to know that.

His voice came suddenly and strongly, with none of the sweetness it carried when he sang. 'Yes. I accept.'

Thirty women let out a collective sigh of relief. Joy sprang into the Queen's face, as if someone had lit a lamp behind her eyes. She walked forward and took his hands in hers. 'Most beloved Consort, I bid you welcome,' she said, and kissed him on the mouth.

Shlaaran, who knew her best, was already gesturing to the other women. In a soft, giggling rush they left the chamber, glancing back again and again at the man and woman who stood entwined in the centre of the room, utterly absorbed in each other. Nerana was the last: with a deep line between her fierce brows, she swept through the chattering ladies and strode away across the courtyard, her iron-tipped staff striking sparks from the cobbled stones beneath it, and her acolytes scurrying after her.

Sumis had thought that the formal ceremony would take place the next morning, but Inrai'a had locked her door, and did not emerge until a night, a day and another night had passed. There was still time to change her mind, but one look at her knotted, dishevelled hair, bruised lips and sated expression convinced Sumis that her Queen's choice was fixed, and nothing could alter it. There would be no chance to confide her own doubts about her Consort: and even if she did, she knew that Inrai'a would not listen.

She did not consider the musician's feelings. His destiny was not of his choosing, but that was usual for the men of Kerenth, and for women all over the known world outside the borders of the Goddess's own land. He had willingly accepted his fate, after all: and if he now had regrets, that still face gave nothing away.

And indeed one half of Bron, now calling himself Kenmet, delighted in this new and quite unexpected twist in his fortunes. Since leaving Tyr he had wandered for months south across the Empty Lands with only the pied mare for company, seeing no humans, only vast herds of grazing animals and their predators. After so long alone, the bustling, bawdy, joyful life crowding into Sarquaina came as a considerable shock. He had never heard of the Revels until now, and at first kept to his room, enjoying the luxury of good food and a comfortable bed with a roof above it. Persuaded to play in the tavern, the reaction of the other guests had been so favourable that he had found himself a place in the square outside to sing for his supper and his bed, on the first night of the festival.

And, if he were honest with himself, to attract a woman. The

gossipy landlady had told him all about the customs of the
Revels, and he knew that any lover he took would come with no
strings, no jealous admirer attached. And the relationship would
be guaranteed to end in twelve days. No one could be harmed or
hurt by such a brief passion.

He had seen many eyeing him with interest as he sang: and
then there had been only one.

That night had brought delights undreamed. In her arms,
Bron had forgotten the darkness and desolation in his heart, and
existed only for the next moment of glorious pleasure. And as she
slept, amid the poppies, the colour of new flame and symbol of
overwhelming passion, he had known that he must desert her
now. For how could he inflict on this beautiful woman, hungry
and fierce and utterly desirable, the terrible weight of his sorcery
and his secrets?

So he had left her sleeping in the meadow, and found a boat
which would take him to the city of Kerenth, although at the cost
of almost every piece of silver he still possessed. And if the
woman had not been Inrai'a, Queen of Kerenth, he would have
evaded the consequences.

He had returned to Sarquaina because he had no other
option. But he knew that he could have refused to accept her
choice of him as Consort: could have told her the truth, about his
name and his burden. Afterwards, though, as they made love, and
slept, and woke to make love again, voraciously all through the
night and the day and the night that followed it, he forgot, or
ignored, the perils of his situation. But the menace remained,
curling below the surface of his mind like some mythical monster
of the sea.

And still he said nothing, wilfully letting his body and its
needs and desires rule his mind. None of those girls in the villages
along the Ger had prepared him for the all-consuming passion, or
lust – he could not call it love – that overwhelmed him now.
Inrai'a had set out to enchant him, and he was caught fast in her
web. And he did not want to destroy this magnificent pleasure by
struggling.

In justification he told himself that it would not last for ever.
Sooner or later – in six months, a year, two years – they would tire
of each other. He would be free to leave Kerenth, and voyage at
last to Jo'ami. The Island of Sorcerers had been there for over a
thousand years. It wouldn't go away. It could wait until he had

exhausted every delight that this imperious, arrogant, infuriating, intoxicating, fascinating woman could offer him.

On the second morning after his return to Sarquaina they lay in each other's arms, drowsily watching the yellow slabs of dawn sunlight moving down the wall opposite the bed. He kissed her lazily, but she did not respond: she freed her lips, brushed away a lock of tangled dark hair, and said softly, 'I know so little about you. You are called Kenmet, which is not a name I know in any language around the shores of the Southern Sea; you are a musician; and you are a Northerner. Where do you come from? What land made you? Are you unique, or are there any more of you?'

He had already planned what he would say to her if she asked. He smiled, and his hand stroked the strong planes of her face. 'I come from Minassa.'

'Minassa? Ah, I know – the city where pots are made.'

'The same.' He indicated the vine-patterned goblets on a table beside the bed. 'Including those.' He hoped that she knew nothing about the place in detail: that those practical people had never produced any musicians, despite all their other virtues.

'Minassa.' Inrai'a's voice was dreamy. 'On the Kefirinn, many miles upstream from Toktel'yi. I must confess, I've never been very interested in those cold northern lands.'

'Not so cold in Minassa, lady – snow is rare there, and the river never freezes. We grow vines, and even olives in the south near Tamat.'

'You need not call me "lady" here,' said the Queen. 'In private, you may call me Inrai'a.'

'And you may call me Bron – which is my personal name. According to the customs of my city, only very close friends are allowed to know or to use it.' He did not dare use his real name openly, so close to Toktel'yi, when spies might discover his presence. The Emperor would probably have him killed or abducted, and he didn't want to risk it. But neither did it seem right to have his lover call him by someone else's name. If she could be relied upon to address him as Kenmet in public and Bron in private, that would solve the problem neatly.

'Bron,' she said, her voice caressing the brief syllable. 'I like it. I like you – very much.'

'Do you?' he enquired, grinning at her wickedly. 'I'd never have guessed.'

Inrai'a did not return his smile, and Bron realized that she'd probably never been teased in all of her spoilt, pampered life. She said, as if she were interviewing him for a household post, 'So who was your mother? And your father?'

With elaborate invention, Bron described a fictitious family who had tried to force him to become a potter when his only love was music. 'So I left Minassa to see the world. I knew that with a skill like mine, I'd always find food and shelter.'

'With a gift like yours, I'm surprised all the known world has not heard of you.' Inrai'a surveyed him curiously. 'Have you been in Kerenth long?'

'I came to Sarquaina six – no, eight days ago, lady – Inrai'a.'

'You speak our language very well – though your accent is strong. What tongue do they use in Minassa?'

'A form of Zithiriani. It's spoken all over the Northern Lands.'

'What were you singing in the Temple Square that night? Sing it again for me now,' Inrai'a said, and in her face, though softened by love, was the firmness of command.

So he played for her the song of Hathenas, beloved of Varathand, son and heir of Tayo the God-King, founder of Zithirian, who died tragically young and was universally mourned: and the Queen of Kerenth, her soul in her eyes, wept for a beauty and sorrow she did not understand.

Then Tiana came knocking on the door, with breakfast, and the inquisition was over. Bron had no compunction about lying when the truth would be so unpalatable. He could not tell her that he was the bastard son of the King of Zithirian and – something that Bron had never been told, but had always known – his twin sister. How could he reveal his sorcery, so dangerous to everyone around him that he had vowed never to use it in the presence of others, until he reached Jo'ami? And above all, how could he tell her of the Wolf lying, silent, waiting, watchful, in his heart?

So he went up to the Temple, wearing the formal white silk robes of the Consort, which flapped annoyingly round his ankles. Inrai'a, in rich green, had never looked happier or more beautiful. And Nerana, her sister, performed the ceremony with a frown clamped to her brows, and seemed positively to enjoy the moment when the silver knife cut the wrists of Queen and Consort so that their blood could mingle together.

Bron ignored Nerana's hostile stare. Sumis had told him why

she was so bitter, and he knew that the Queen had treated her very generously in the circumstances. His own father's younger brother Tsenit had stolen the throne of Zithirian and been killed for it. Few other rulers would be so magnanimous to such an enemy, even an enemy so close within the family. A hundred years ago, an Emperor had ordered all his relations killed – brothers, sisters, uncles, aunts, cousins, even his own mother and two of his wives – because he suspected them of plotting to assassinate him. Kerenth was a softer, kinder place, it seemed, than elsewhere in the known world. It had no army, no soldiers, no fortresses, no defences save the guardianship of the Goddess. And yet this rich and vulnerable land had remained free and peaceful for thousands of years.

In the days that followed their formal union, he and Inrai'a made many public appearances. They inspected and tasted the first fruits of the grape harvest: they were rowed up river in a ceremonial barge, with a flotilla of lesser craft jostling behind them. They attended the ordinary Temple rituals, although Bron, being a man, was not allowed within the Sanctum to be blessed with the sacred earth of Sarraliss. He found these ceremonies strange, for in his homeland the Goddess, and Her counterpart Hegeden, Lord of the Air, were worshipped and invoked in private, without priest or temple. But this was Sarraliss's own country, and they were entitled to do things differently here. And on the last day of the Revel, they made the pilgrimage to Skathak.

The sacred mountain, birthplace of the Goddess, loomed above Sarquaina. In the eighteen days since Bron had arrived in the town its summit had been veiled in cloud, despite the blue skies around it. But as the cavalcade of horses climbed the long, well-used road up through the foothills, the mists parted, the sun shone, and the perfect symmetry of the snow-covered peak lay revealed, sharp against the azure sky.

Bron drew in his breath, surprised by the sudden yearning that had filled him at the sight. He hadn't seen a mountain so close since leaving Sar D'yenyi. And Skathak was even higher than Annako, Estray and Sargenn, the three lofty peaks that guarded the citadel and its lake. Its shape, though, was quite different: a perfect cone, with gently concave sides. And from its slightly flattened summit drifted a lazy wisp of cloud that must be smoke.

He had never seen a fire-mountain before. And it seemed

strange to him that Skathak was sacred to Sarraliss. In the north, She governed the fertile surface of the earth, its fruits and animals, not its dark, secret interior. He remembered the people of Tyr, who had worshipped Urgan. Had the capricious, earth-shaking firegod once ruled here too?

Then they reached the Hidden Valley, and he understood. This perfect elliptical bowl, lush and green, cupped in a fold of the mountain, was overflowing with life. The priestesses here tilled the land and grew orchards of plums and apricots, mulberries and peaches and almonds. Vines dripped ripe grapes along the southern slopes, and the Pilgrim's Inn was almost invisible beneath the riotous foliage of a dozen different climbing plants, all with dazzling flowers in every colour. There was no sign of a temple, though, and when he asked Inrai'a, she looked at him with surprise. 'Here? The valley all around us – *that* is Her temple. On Skathak, the Goddess is everywhere.'

He hadn't known it, although he had allowed his senses to open, just a little, to the rich beauties around him. It seemed that whatever else he was, he did not belong to Sarraliss: the Goddess did not speak to him. But then, of course, he was a man. And, he realized when they dismounted, the only man here. He hadn't thought it odd that Inrai'a had only brought her women with her: the few men in her entourage were mostly menials, hired for their brute strength. The priestesses had children, of course, and half of them were presumably boys, but there were no grown men.

In the privacy of their luxurious apartments – fur rugs on the tiled floors, soft cushions on the bed, exquisite murals and a huge marble bath with a stream of miraculously warm water perpetually running through it – he asked the Queen why.

She stared at him. 'Because this is the place of the Goddess, of course. Men are forbidden to come here except during the twelve days of Revel, when they may make the pilgrimage to ask Her blessing. As this is the last day, the men have all gone now. We passed a group of them going down the mountain on our way here, don't you remember?'

Bron did. He said after a while, 'So – is the Consort privileged to stay longer?'

'If the Goddess accepts you, yes. If not, then you must leave the valley immediately, on pain of death.' Inrai'a smiled at him reassuringly. 'But She is very forgiving. The last man to be rejected by her turned out to have murdered his wife. And that was fifty years ago, when my grandmother was Queen.' Her smile broadened. 'That journey has made me so hot and dusty.'

Bron knew what she wanted, and reached out to undo the nearest of her shoulder-clasps. 'Then why not wash it off?' he suggested slyly.

Inrai'a's great brown eyes darkened with anticipation. 'Bring me a jug of water, and I will.'

'I have a better idea.' He got up and pulled her with him towards the bath. She realized his intention and began to struggle, but he was holding her too tightly. With a scream and a splash, he dropped her into the steaming, fragrant water, and sprang in after her.

Inrai'a sat in the bath, her hair soaked, her gown moulded to her body above the water and flowing free below, her face flushed and indignant. 'How dare you! This is my best silk – look at it!'

'I'm looking.' Bron grabbed her as she struggled furiously to her feet, and pulled her back into the water. They grappled together for a moment, until Inrai'a's screams of protest suddenly changed their note. Astonished and delighted, Bron realized that she was laughing. Gently, with real affection, he bent and kissed her.

They made love there and then in the bath, while the expensive indigo dye in the Queen's dress bled blue feathery clouds into the silky water, and the warm stream poured in regardless until it overflowed on to the floor with every impassioned, violent movement of their coupled bodies.

She lay afterwards in the lapping water, still inadequately clothed in the ruined gown, her eyes, her face, her skin glowing. And Bron said softly, 'I have never heard you laugh before.'

'Haven't you? I used to laugh all the time – before my mother died. But even in Kerenth, Queens are not supposed to be light-hearted.' She pulled herself upright and shed the blue dress, leaving it lying in the bath like a huge crumpled leaf. 'It's getting dark. We must hurry up and get ready for the Blessing. Didn't I tell you? It takes place at midnight. You must enter the Womb of the Goddess, and no man is allowed to know where it is.'

When Sumis came for them, they were ready. Inrai'a, in a trailing ceremonial gown of gleaming amber silk, with gold and emerald clasps at her shoulders and the crown on her head, looked magnificent. Beside her, Bron wore the traditional bleached white cotton of the male supplicant. He could not get used to Kerentan clothes: the long loose hooded robes seemed so impractical to a man used to an active life, and it was difficult to ride in them.

It was a long walk to the Womb of the Goddess. They were guided and guarded by priestesses, shepherding them through the darkness, and led by Nerana, with her sacred staff and her long, brisk stride. After an hour, Bron began to suspect that they were being led in circles: they had gone uphill and then down again, twice. But the path lay through a thick wood, although he could not remember seeing any mass of trees in the valley, and the stars were not visible, nor the first sliver of the new moon.

At last they came to a halt. Bron, standing beside Inrai'a, cautiously reached out his mind. There was a cleft here in the mountainside, almost hidden between folds of stone. He probed no further. Here, of all places, he would not employ his abnormal senses to feel his way. He was a sorcerer, after all, and such powers were abhorrent to the older, deeper, more mysterious magic soaked into the earthy flesh and rocky bones of Kerenth, and shared by her women. He had no fear of Sarraliss, but he respected Her, and his stepmother paid homage to Her. So did most of the people of Zithirian and the other northern cities, men and women alike, for She had given life to all of them.

The blackness was impenetrable to his unaided eyes. He stumbled blindly through the rocks, with Inrai'a stepping sure-footed beside him, and the soft sounds of the six priestesses and Nerana, in front and behind them. He could feel the weight of the mountain above, as heavy as if he alone were carrying it upon his shoulders.

'Light!' Nerana cried suddenly, and torches burst into dazzling brilliance.

Bron blinked in the glare. They stood, eight women and one man, in the centre of a huge cave. Above, the roof stretched up and was lost in shadow. Ahead, too, the torches could not reach into the darkness. But where their light struck the nearest walls of the cavern, the rock sparkled and glittered as if it were a facet of some vast, rough-cut jewel.

'Behold the Womb of the Goddess!' Nerana's voice echoed eerily around them. 'Most sacred Heart of the Land of Kerenth. Here our Holy Mother came to life, and this place will we venerate for as long as women inhabit this country. Now, stranger, *man*, kneel.'

Obediently, Bron knelt on the uneven floor. It was quite dry and the air was surprisingly warm. Somewhere within this mountain were the rivers of white-hot fire that would burst up from the fractured rocks during an eruption. He could feel the ground beneath him trembling almost imperceptibly, as if it were alive.

'Lady! Lady, here within Your most precious hidden Womb, I, Nerana, Your High Priestess of Sarquaina, offer this man for Your blessing. His name is Kenmet, and he is beloved of Inrai'a, Queen of Kerenth, who has chosen him for her Consort. I ask for Your approval of their union. May You grant that it will be long, and fruitful, and happy, according to Your desire. Lady, he is here, and kneels humbly in Your presence, as should all men. And on his behalf I crave Your acceptance of his homage.'

Her last words, multiplied by the walls of the cavern, gradually died away. Bron glanced up at Inrai'a. Her eyes were closed, her face as rapt and ecstatic as if she were making love. Her lips moved in a pattern he could not read, and her body swayed gently. The other women were similarly entranced. Perhaps the Goddess was speaking to them, but if She was, he couldn't hear her. Only Nerana, as regal as her sister in her robes of office, seemed to be alert.

Then another sound mingled with the echoes and grew in volume as they faded. A soft hissing, like a summer wind amongst leaves, save that here there were no trees. It grew, filling all the vast underground hall. Nerana lifted up her arms in welcome. Bron, staring at her, saw her eyes close, and her mouth opened, but no words emerged. And although the air was quite still, and she did not move, her robes stirred as if disturbed by a gentle breeze.

Then he felt the rocks beneath him shiver and tilt. He fell forward on to his hands and knees. A violent convulsion shook the earth, followed by a cataclysmic roar of sound, and all the torches went out.

Bron crouched in the heaving blackness, feeling the mountain shift and then return to its sleep. A falling rock crashed beside him, and shards and splinters of stone peppered his skin painfully. The Goddess had not spoken to him, but he knew her decision.

One of the priestesses whimpered, and was hushed by Nerana's sharp voice. Then for a long, long while, no one spoke, and the silence grew as heavy and oppressive as the mountain above them.

'Lights!' Nerana cried suddenly. There was the sound of fumbling, and then one of the torches flickered into hesitant life, as if afraid of what it might illuminate.

Bron looked around. The vastness all about them seemed quite undisturbed, save for the fallen rocks and stones now littering the floor. Blood was running down the face of the youngest priestess, and everyone's robes were scattered with dust and tiny crystalline slivers of rock, but no one seemed badly hurt.

Nerana's gaze was fixed on him. Drawn up to her full and impressive height, her face stern and hostile, she was an awe-inspiring figure. She said loudly, 'Lady – we have received Your answer. This man is repugnant to You. Your blessing is denied to him. We therefore cast him out from this, Your Holy Womb, and from Your sacred mountain. As he is the chosen Consort of Inrai'a, Queen of Kerenth, she must decide whether or not to repudiate him. I trust that she will heed Your voice, for she cannot love a Consort who is abhorrent to You, our most gracious Lady, fountain of all life.' She flung out her arm, gesturing to Bron. 'Man of evil – go!'

He wanted to protest, but he knew it was pointless. You could hardly argue with a Goddess, or try to hide the Wolf from Her. She had seen through his defences to the dark, hideous place where Ayak lurked in his heart, and denounced him.

Chilled, shaking, he scrambled to his feet. Inrai'a's face was pale with shock and disbelief, but she said nothing. Without a word, without a smile, he turned and walked away in the direction of Nerana's pointing finger. Somehow, his feet remembered the way he had come. After what seemed an eternity, he found himself gulping huge breaths of fresh air and coughing the dust out of his lungs. It was still dark, and he had no idea which way to go. Behind him, deep in the cavern, there was utter silence, as though it was empty of life.

With something close to despair, Bron stumbled down the mountainside. He didn't want to anger the Goddess further by using his powers. The rock which had fallen so close could have killed him. Perhaps it was a warning: perhaps She had been merciful. Next time, he probably wouldn't be so lucky.

So he blundered against unseen obstacles in the dark. Once he fell and cut his hands and knees on the rocks, but the sharpness of the pain was almost welcome. It was another reminder that he was, after all, much less than a Goddess.

As dawn began to seep into the sky, he emerged at last from the trees and saw the sacred valley below him, wreathed in mist. He thought of Inrai'a, who loved him, and who must now banish him from her land: and of Nerana, who hated them both.

Nerana. Had she *arranged* that rockfall? He remembered the foul D'thliss, who had manipulated the other priests of Tayo with impressive demonstrations of the Divine Ancestor's pleasure or hostility that she, a more skilful sorceress than any of them, had blasphemously created herself. Sarraliss had not spoken to him here. Was that truly because he was an abomination? Or had Nerana somehow prevented any contact?

All the legends and stories of Kerenth spoke of the sorcery in this land, but it was not a kind he recognized, or that seemed to recognize him. Perhaps Nerana had used it to drive him out by persuading him that the Goddess had denied him her blessing. It was certainly possible, but he knew that the other, more unpalatable alternative was more likely. After all, the Lady of Life must loathe the Wolf of Death. And how could Nerana have known about the presence of Ayak within him, when he kept it so closely hidden?

Those whom the Goddess had repudiated had to leave the Hidden Valley immediately, on pain of death, but he was not going to forsake his Sith, nor the piebald mare who had carried him so faithfully on his wanderings. In his haste to leave Inrai'a after that first night, he had decided, with some guilt and regret, to abandon her. Once installed as Consort, he had reclaimed her from her lush meadow, with silent apologies for his callousness. For she had no name, she was no more than a beast of burden, but through the long days of summer in the wilderness she had been his only friend and companion, and a deep and affectionate bond had grown up between them.

The Pilgrim's Inn stood silent in the half-light. There was no-one about: perhaps in Nerana's absence the remaining priestesses were enjoying a lie-in. The room he had shared with Inrai'a was exactly as they had left it, her blue gown still leaking dye like blood into the bath, puddles on the floor, the bed in disarray. And suddenly a sense of loss, utterly unexpected, rent his heart. He did not love her – no, he knew he did not. But oh, how he loved what they did together.

It lasted only a moment. He found his Sith, still in the worn leather bag which had protected it all the way from Zithirian.

With relief, he shed the white robe, now torn, dirty and blood-stained, and put on his old shabby tunic and trousers. He tucked the knife into his belt, and bathed his grazed and bruised face and hands. Then he went to the stables.

There was a small boy there, filling water buckets and distri-buting hay. He stared at Bron in horrified astonishment, made the sign against evil, and fled.

The piebald mare's head came out of her stall, and she blew a welcome through soft pink and black nostrils. Bron leaned against her, feeling suddenly faint from hunger, shock and fa-tigue. He wanted to lie down in the prickly straw, and sleep, but if he did, Nerana or one of her acolytes would probably kill him before he woke. He was beginning to understand that beneath the gentleness, the sunlight and the beauty, Kerenth was a much sterner land than he had thought.

So he saddled and bridled the mare, and led her out into the empty courtyard. The sun had risen, and the valley, which lay on the eastern side of Skathak, was bathed in glorious light. But there was something wrong, he thought as he mounted. As the mare walked out of the courtyard he realized what it was: no birds were singing. But as he sent her trotting up the road that led out of the valley, he heard their joyful chorus break out behind them.

It was then that Bron knew, fully and finally, that his rejection was the command of Sarraliss Herself, and not Nerana's doing.

As the mare cantered up towards the rim of the valley, with the rising sun on their right, he noticed a figure running through the fields ahead, towards the road. He saw flying dark hair and a yellow gown, and his heart began to hammer. He yanked on the bridle and the mare halted in a cloud of dust. She eyed the lush grass at the edge of the road with interest, and began to graze. He let the reins go slack, and waited.

Inrai'a burst out of the almond orchard just ahead of them and stopped in the middle of the road, some twenty strides away. Her crown was missing, her skirts were hitched up in her belt to reveal bare, scratched, filthy legs, her hair was tangled with twigs and leaves and damp with sweat. When she saw the man on the piebald mare, she stood quite still for a moment, breathing hard. Then she began to walk toward him.

She had never looked less like a queen, or more beautiful. In spite of himself, Bron felt the first, familiar stirrings of desire, and ruthlessly repressed them. He did not move, but braced himself, gathering his defences for what must come.

'You lied to me,' Inrai'a said abruptly. She came to a halt by the mare's mottled head, her eyes brilliant with grief, and rage, and the agony of betrayal. 'You're not just a wandering musician, are you? Bron, Kenmet, what are you?'

He said nothing, because even now he did not want to tell her the truth.

Like a child, Inrai'a screamed with frustration, and stamped her foot. 'Answer me! *What are you?*'

'A wandering musician is all I have ever wanted to be,' he said.

She shook her head furiously, the long brown hair whipping over her shoulders. 'No! *Tell me!* Are you a sorcerer?'

Still, around them, no birds sang. And Bron knew that he had been foolish not to confide in her from the start. For she had trusted in him, and in her mind transformed him into something which he was not. And now, her illusions brutally shattered, her anger, and her vengeance, would be bitter indeed.

'Yes,' he said at last, so quietly that his voice was barely audible.

All the life, the fight, the rage seemed to drain out of Inrai'a's face, leaving only the husk of defeat and despair. She said, almost in a whimper, 'Why? Why didn't you tell me?'

This time, he did not lie. 'Because I was afraid. And because my power is not of my choosing. I was born with it, and it is a burden I have never wished to carry. If I could, I would lay it down.'

'But sorcerers are not born,' Inrai'a said, her voice shaking. 'Even here in Kerenth, the power is given by the Goddess to Her servants, when they are dedicated to the priesthood. No one is born with power – not here, not in Toktel'yi, nor on any of the islands. Even in Jo'ami, they take drugs.'

'But *I* was born with it,' Bron said, and the desolation in his soul was plain in his voice.

Inrai'a's beautiful eyes began to spill tears. '*Why?* Why you?'

And he gave her the bitter truth that he had always known. 'I was bred for it. Like a prize race-horse, or a hunting dog, or a good cow, I was bred for my power. I did not ask to be like this, but I thought I had learned to accept it.'

'Until now.' Inrai'a smeared tears and dirt across her

scratched face with an impatient hand. 'Nerana thinks you are evil. Is she right?'

Bron shook his head wearily. 'I don't know.' He wanted to tell her about the Wolf, but something, perhaps Ayak himself, held him back. 'I have evil in me, but so do all men and women. I don't *intend* to do evil.'

'She hates you even more than she hates me,' said the Queen, as if she had just realized it. 'I think she is jealous. Priestesses can't choose husbands or Consorts – it is their sacred duty to be generous and welcoming to all men, and to bear children to the honour of the Goddess. She wishes she was in my place, and had you all to herself.' Her voice became suddenly and strongly defiant. 'I knew you would go – so I ran away from them and came to stop you. I won't let you leave, Bron – I won't!'

He stared down at her in amazement. 'But the Goddess – '

'Sarraliss has denied you her blessing. That's what Nerana says. But what if she's lying?'

Bron shook his head. 'No – no, lady, she is not.'

'How can you know? The Goddess doesn't speak to you – you're only a man! I feel it *here*!' Inrai'a thumped her breast vehemently. 'The High Priestesses have great power, here in the Valley – power enough to move the rocks of Skathak, if they wish. That's what Nerana must have done. She wanted to make it look as if the blessing was denied.'

'But how would she know that there was a *reason* for the Goddess to reject me? My magic and hers are different. There doesn't seem to be any link between them.'

'Women's magic is more powerful, and speaks only to women – but I'm sure that Nerana could detect that you were a sorcerer.' Inrai'a reached out her hand to grasp his. 'Bron, there is no need for you to go. I am Queen of Kerenth, and outside the Valley my power is greater than Nerana's. If I wish you to be my Consort still, that is *my* choice and *my* decision – not hers.'

'And do you wish it?' Bron felt suddenly sick and dizzy with exhaustion. Inrai'a's pale, determined face seemed to slide in and out of focus. He dug his nails savagely into his palms, and forced his weary brain to concentrate.

'I do wish it.' The Queen's grip tightened suddenly on his other hand. 'I don't care if you are a sorcerer or not, nor how you came to be so. I love you – *you*, not your power. I *know* you are not evil, I can feel it. I wanted – I wanted to hear your answer to

Nerana's accusations. And I know now that I want you to be my Consort, for as long as there is love between us.' Her voice trembled suddenly with the force of her emotions. 'But if you still wish to go – if you wish to leave me, and Kerenth – then I will not prevent you. I will understand, and my love will go with you always.'

Her hand slid from his. She stood back from the pied mare, her mouth set, and dread in her eyes. And Bron knew suddenly that she was expecting him to leave her.

And he couldn't. Given a second chance, he couldn't do it. Even now, he was certain that he didn't love her. But the sight of her tall, splendid figure, her brave though not quite perfect concealment of her grief, struck a deep chord within him, as sad and as true as the notes of his Sith.

'It's all right,' he said softly, and smiled at her. 'If you will have me, I will stay with you.'

And as he swung her up on to the back of the piebald mare, and rode on out of the Hidden Valley, he heard rising behind them the sweet, rippling sound of the birds, singing out their hearts for joy at his leaving.

CHAPTER
NINE

Spring in Kerenth always came early, after a winter that was hardly cold at all. In this verdant, lavish land, the fruit and almond trees were nourished by the warmth of the sun and the soft gentle rain that would fall almost every night until banished by the heat of summer. As a result, every orchard was thick with blossom in the second month of the year, promising an abundant harvest.

But not this year, the seventh of Inrai'a's reign. As all Kerenth now knew, she had defied the Goddess, and kept her chosen Consort, the foreign musician known as Kenmet. The winter following her wilful act of disobedience was almost dry, and unusually cold. Snow fell in Sarquaina for the first time in living memory, and Skathak retreated behind a thick curtain of menacing cloud. Even in the city of Kerenth, warmed by the waters of the Southern Sea, the winds blew chill and sharp and the sun hardly ever shone.

All through the second month, and the third, they waited for the rain. It did not come, and the gloomy, overcast sky never changed. No sun, no rain, only the endless dry winds blowing down from the bleak hills of the Empty Lands to the north. The blossom shrivelled and died, and so did the bees, bereft of nectar. The women of Kerenth, tilling their fields and sowing their seeds, wondered with growing alarm whether their labours would bear fruit that summer, if summer ever came. And every night they prayed to She who watched over them, to strike some sense into their rebellious Queen's heart, so that she would divorce her wicked Consort and lift the curse of the Goddess that surely lay over their land.

But Inrai'a remained infatuated. She ignored the whispers, the sullen, accusing sky, the hostile silence which greeted her whenever she appeared in public with her Consort. Blinded by love, she was certain that Nerana was to blame. She had defeated her jealous sister before, and she could do so again.

And then the news came: news so momentous that for a few days Kerentans forgot the miserable yellowing crops standing sparsely in the fields, the barren fruit trees, the sickly cattle and withered vines. The Emperor of Toktel'yi was dead.

The Imperial Ambassador, giving the Queen the sad news in her audience chamber at her Palace in Kerenth City, was clad in formal mourning grey and seemed genuinely grieved. Inrai'a, who though young was well versed in the ways of the old enemy, knew that appearances were deceptive. The Emperor Djamal was not yet fifty, but his undistinguished reign had lasted for twenty-eight almost entirely idle years, characterized chiefly by his determined pursuit of pleasure. While he lived, the Empire would remain stagnant, as deeply sunk in venal corruption as its master. Even Djamal's solitary attempt at military glory, the attack on Penya, had been bogged down for years in a vicious guerilla war until his energetic son took a hand. Few of his people would regret his passing.

'There has been, of course, a smooth transition of power to the Emperor-in-Waiting,' said the Ambassador. 'His Imperial Majesty Ba'alekkt, son of Djamal, bids me inform you, Gracious Lady, of his sincere feelings of friendship towards your honoured and ancient land, and asks me to convey his hopes that the long and peaceful relationship between our two nations will continue unaltered into the future.'

Which is about as likely, thought Inrai'a, her face expressing polite interest, *as a Priestess of Sarraliss vowing celibacy*. Toktel'yi had not become an Empire by being friendly and peaceful towards its neighbours. Djamal's inertia had given some respite to the lands on its borders. But now Ba'alekkt's accession to the Onyx Throne would surely mean an ominous change in policy. He was young, able and aggressive: his father had put him in charge of the war in Penya, and he had pursued a policy of repression with brutal and successful vigour. Even now, with rebellion almost entirely crushed, the once beautiful island could be located by the pall of smoke that hung above it day and night as its towns and villages burned.

Inrai'a had asked for details of Djamal's end, and was given an account that only increased her conviction that he had been helped into the after-life, probably by his impatient only son and heir. It was nothing unusual: perhaps no more than one Emperor in five died a natural death. She expressed her sympathy with the deceased's sorrowing family, echoed the Ambassador's hopes for peaceful relations between the two countries, and watched him leave with feelings of profound distrust and dislike.

For more than two thousand years the women of Kerenth had witnessed the relentless progress of the aggressive, man-ruled Toktel'yans along the coast of the Southern Sea towards their sacred land. One by one the city-states between them had fallen to the greed of Emperors and their inexorable armies, whose soldiers were the finest in the known world. Mynak, Djebb, Terebis, even Tatht, like Kerenth governed by a line of queens, had succumbed to the Empire, their women enslaved and the hallowed earth tilled by brutal, ignorant men. And the islands of the Archipelago, too, had been conquered one by one as the Toktel'yans sought to control the spice trade, and above all the supply of the sorcerer's drug Annatal. Within the last three years, Penya the Great, once also dedicated to the Goddess, had finally yielded to Ba'alekkt's ruthless slaughter.

Even Kerenth had been invaded, less than a hundred years ago, by a huge Imperial army. They had expected little resistance, for the sacred land was ruled by despised females. Its towns had no walls, its people carried no weapons, its Queen possessed no army.

But this was the Goddess's own soil, and its rape invoked Her wrath. The Queen, Sumis, cursed the invaders in the name of Sarraliss with all the power and malevolence at her command. Disease swept through the invading soldiers, killing so many, so horribly, that their resolve faltered. The agonizing death of the Emperor provided the final blow. Cowed, exhausted, terrified, the survivors streamed back over the border in abject disarray, leaving behind the festering corpses of nearly ten thousand of their comrades. The earth must not be tainted by the decomposing flesh of its mortal enemies, so the women and men of Kerenth burned the bodies on huge stinking pyres, gathered the ashes and threw them into the Southern Sea, so that no trace remained of their violation of the land of Sarraliss.

After that, the Emperors had, not surprisingly, left Kerenth well alone, and since the invasion the country had returned to its usual state of peace and prosperity.

But now, perhaps, Kerenth's tranquil millennia were almost at an end. Refugees from Penya had told Inrai'a a great deal about Ba'alekkt. He was unlikely to be deterred by a curse nearly a century old. A year or so previously he had publicly stated his intention, once he became Emperor, of expanding his dominions to what he called their 'natural boundaries'. And the obvious natural boundary to the east was undoubtedly the Kerentan Sea.

An unpleasant feeling of apprehension filled Inrai'a's mind. She dismissed her attendants, and went in search of her Consort.

The city of Kerenth was built on the south-facing cliff-tops surrounding a perfect natural harbour to the west of the Narrows of Katho, which led to the Kerentan Sea. The Palace perched on the highest point of the cliffs, a compact and beautiful building of white-painted stone. Every window, every balcony was placed to catch the sea breezes, the warmth of the sun, and the spectacular view over this sheltered inlet of the Southern Sea. The Queen's suite occupied much of the upper floor, and from its broad balcony on a clear day you could see right across the mainland peninsula to Penya seventy miles away.

As she had expected, Bron was sitting on one of the stone benches placed along the balcony, in what would have been the shade if the sun had been shining. The sea, once a glorious and perfect sapphire, was now sullenly grey, with a low heavy swell that broke into white only when it reached the feet of the rocky cliffs below. For the first time, a serpent of doubt awoke in the Queen's mind, and showed its wicked fangs. What if Nerana was right after all? If Sarraliss had indeed withdrawn Her blessing from Kerenth, then there would be no obstacle to any invasion, and no way of defending the land from the Imperial troops.

She stood at the entrance to the balcony, listening to Bron play. He did not appear to have noticed her, but she knew that he probably wanted to finish the song.

As if this were the first time that ever she beheld him, or the last, Inrai'a studied her Consort. The fall of pale, straight hair over intent dark eyes; the narrow, precise lines of his face, marred and yet enhanced by the broken nose; the sureness of his slender musician's hands, rousing sweet sounds from the silver strings of his Sith, just as he roused other, even sweeter sensations from her body; his deceptively slight, agile build; the aura of stillness, of calm around him which also gave the impression of contained power. And although he had admitted to her in the Sacred Valley that he was a sorcerer, she had never, in all their months together, seen him reveal or demonstrate his skill. Whatever his abnormal abilities were, he kept them very deep, under mind-lock and soul-key. If he had not told her, or if Nerana – or the Goddess – had not known, she would never had guessed.

But she could not give him up – she could *not*. Like a greedy child, she wanted to devour all he had to offer, until their passion was exhausted. She loved his strangeness, his calm, his music, the teasing smile that was so unexpected, the laughter that he concealed from the world, his mysterious and enigmatic personality, a labyrinth whose extent and complexity she had barely begun to explore. And besides, in eight long months of dedicated and enthusiastic lovemaking, she still had not conceived a child.

Inrai'a's soul grew suddenly very still and cold. She remembered the words of the Priestesses who had examined her before her mother announced her as the Heir. She had submitted to their gentle but thorough probing with eagerness, because all potential Queens must undergo this procedure, to ensure that they were blessed with the fertility of the Goddess. And Nerana's predecessor, D'mina, had pronounced her to be healthy and fruitful. 'She will bear many children, for the glory of Sarraliss and the royal line of Kerenth.'

She was twenty-seven years old, in her prime. Bron was seven years younger, a virile and apparently potent lover. And yet she had not conceived. Like the ruined orchards and withered vines of Kerenth, she was barren.

Inrai'a closed her eyes, feeling the hot tears behind her lids. Sickened, despairing, she knew that Nerana must be right. Or by now she would surely be nourishing Bron's daughter or son within her womb.

But she could not admit to anyone, save herself, that her sister's hatred of Bron was not entirely based on jealousy and spite, but sprang from the truth. One day, soon, she would have to choose between her realm and her Consort. And for Kerenth's sake, she knew what she must do. She had no choice.

But not yet: not yet.

She walked along the balcony and sat down beside him. His hands did not falter, and the tune, a lovely lilting folk-song from Sarquaina, danced brightly on. Like warm honey, he was singing it softly as he played.

And far below them the sea, relentless, oblivious, menacing, battered dourly at the cliffs of Kerenth.

Five hundred miles to the west, in another very different palace on the shores of the Southern Sea, the ninety-ninth Emperor of Toktel'yi, Ba'alekkt son of Djamal, sat in council with his father's ministers.

There were thirty of them: Sekkenet, General-in-Chief of the Army, and his deputy; the Court Sorcerer, Al'Kalyek, a mage of enormous power and prestige and also, paradoxically, one of the very few honest men employed by the late Emperor; the assorted Governors of the Nine Provinces, Jaiya, Lai'is, Ukkan, Sabrek, Tamat, Mynak, Terebis, Djebb and Tatht, and of the five largest islands in the Archipelago, Balki, Tekkt, Annatal, Onnak and Penya; the Prince of Tulyet, who was Ba'alekkt's cousin; the Captain of Ships; the respective Archpriests of Toktel'yi's official deities, the twins Kaylo, Lord of Life, and Olyak, Master of Death; and the ministers in charge of finances, trade, roads, spies, lawkeepers, prisons, all the essentials that made some Toktel'yans rich and prosperous, and others poor and oppressed.

They sat there, the most powerful men in the Empire, in their fine silk robes and a thick layer of sweat which not even the most fastidious could avoid on this sultry, humid day in early summer. And Ba'alekkt, the youngest there by twenty years at least, looked round at all the familiar faces, some respected, others despised, and knew with profound satisfaction that he had unchallenged mastery over all of them. With a snap of his fingers, he could have them tortured or killed, imprisoned or sent into ignominious obscurity. And he saw in their eyes that they knew it too, and were afraid of him.

He listened to the usual briefings on the state of each councillor's preserve. The accession of the new Emperor had apparently been welcomed throughout his dominions, and celebrated everywhere with feasting and jubilation. People looked to Ba'alekkt to provide the new beginning, the fresh taste of glory which had faded from their lives. The young man smiled, knowing that their confidence in him would not be misplaced.

There were more glowing reports. The new Governor of Penya spoke of the total elimination of one of the last pockets of resistance on the island, after many years of war. The Trade Minister produced a wad of charsh paper, covered with figures, to demonstrate the healthy condition of commerce throughout the Empire, and particularly along the River Kefirinn. A frown appeared on Ba'alekkt's face as the elderly Prince of Tulyet complained querulously of the need for more soldiers to put down the bandits infesting the interior of his country. It faded when

Sekkenet read a detailed description of the two hundred and fifty thousand men under his overall command, their weapons and training and general readiness for any action, and finished with a recommendation that they be given a rise in pay to mark the Emperor's accession.

Ba'alekkt smiled. 'They won't need it. I have a job in mind for them – and by the time it's finished, they'll be so awash with plunder they won't notice if their pay is cut by half.'

Sekkenet's thin, lined face stiffened with eagerness, like a hound sighting its quarry. After the long and frustrating years of Djamal's reign, he scented real fighting. 'Yes, Imperial Majesty? What have you in mind?'

Ba'alekkt's smile widened, but it was not particularly pleasant. He said softly, 'A land of peace and prosperity. A land of softness and luxury, of feeble men and beautiful women. The land of Kerenth, my friends, undefended and ripe for conquest.'

There was a brief, taut silence. Then Sekkenet said slowly, 'Then – then Your Imperial Majesty has no plans to move against the northern cities?'

'Oh yes, I have.' Ba'alekkt's smile became broader still. 'But not yet, honoured General. Zithirian and Minassa have walls, towers, defences. They have trained men who can fight. By conquering Kerenth, we will demonstrate our eagerness to bring the whole of the known world into the shelter of our Empire. Free cities will hear of our victory, and tremble. They will know that the new Emperor fears nothing and nobody – particularly not some hag of a goddess and a Queen mouthing empty curses.'

The Governor of Tatht, whose province bordered Kerenth, put up his hand to speak. 'Imperial Majesty, I have some interesting news concerning Kerenth.'

'I've heard it already,' said Ba'alekkt, grinning. 'Sarraliss doesn't like the Queen's new Consort, and has turned Her back on Her own country. The sun hasn't shone since last year, the rains haven't fallen, the crops will fail. The land will be defenceless. If we march in, we'll be doing those poor women a favour, and the Goddess won't lift a finger to stop us.'

The sorcerer Al'Kalyek coughed pointedly. Ba'alekkt glanced at him. 'If you've something to say, I should say it.'

The mage's dark, frowning face stared back. The Emperor noted, without surprise, the total lack of fear in his eyes. Of all the gaggle of toadies, time-servers and incompetents his father had picked for his Council, only this man, along with Sekkenet and one or two others, had the potential to earn his respect.

'Imperial Majesty, I am well versed in magic, the kind which we all know. It has few mysteries and few secrets. Our craft is as familiar as a carpenter's, or a wheelwright's. But ours is not the only sort in the world. There are other, more ancient types of sorcery. And one of them lies buried deep within the soil and the blood of the women of Kerenth. I advise you not to despise them, or to ignore their power. There are things in that country which I cannot hope to understand: and when the wise man does not understand, he is cautious and careful. Please, Imperial Majesty, do not assume that because the Goddess appears to have deserted Kerenth, you will be able to invade it with impunity.'

'I'm not afraid of Her.' Ba'alekkt's face was full of the supremely confident arrogance produced by absolute youth and absolute power. 'The women worship Her in the Empire, of course, but only as a handmaiden of Kaylo, Lord of Life, shining face of the sun. She is no more than the pale and variable moon, waning into insignificance beside His dazzling splendour. In any case, I have no belief in that old tale about the curse. It was just an epidemic of camp fever, or tainted meat, and very lucky for Kerenth that it happened when it did.' He leaned forward, his hazel eyes, surprisingly light in his brown face, intense and avaricious. 'We have all the Archipelago under our sway. From the eastern shores of the Gulf of Fabriz, to the city of Tatht, all the lands on the coast of the Southern Sea pay homage to me. Soon, Kerenth will fall to us as easily as a rotting peach. Then we can turn our attention to the north. Minassa is rich, Zithirian is richer by far. Is it right that one city, out of all those in the known world, should have a monopoly on the supply of gold and silver? We should persuade them to be more generous.'

The Governor of Tamat sniggered. Sekkenet said, 'There is the small matter of the King's son. Not his legitimate offspring, but his bastard. There have been some very peculiar stories about him.'

'They were true.' Al'Kalyek's deep voice intruded. 'The boy – man, he is now – was born with enormous power. He destroyed the Ska'i when still a child.'

'I saw the results,' said Sekkenet, with an expression of revulsion. 'He could be extremely dangerous to us, if we were to attempt an invasion.'

'Indeed he could,' said the Court Sorcerer. 'And I'm sure that King Ansaryon, who is, as you know, Imperial Majesty, a sorcerer of some skill himself, will have given his son a very thorough training.'

'You have no need to fear him, Imperial Majesty.' It was the sweet, deceptively pleasant voice of the Spymaster, Olkanno. 'The boy is no longer in Zithirian.'

'Oh?' Ba'alekkt's gaze sharpened. 'Why have you not informed me of this, Olkanno?'

'I told your late and much lamented father, Imperial Majesty. He did not seem to think it was important. You are obviously of a different mind, and so I have taken care to let you know now, at your first Council.'

'Very well.' Ba'alekkt eyed the Spymaster with interest. 'Tell me what has happened to this boy.'

'Nobody knows, Imperial Majesty, but he appears to have run away. Unsurprisingly, news of his departure was not trumpeted from the Sunset Gate – instead, it was given out that he was visiting Sar D'yenyi and Lelyent. It was only recently that my spy learnt that in fact he had vanished from the city about this time last year. Apparently no one, not even his father, knows where he is. He was traced to Minassa, and then seems to have disappeared into nowhere.'

'I hope he's not here,' the Minister for Foreigners muttered, looking anxiously at the Emperor.

'Well, I hope he is,' said Ba'alekkt, with an unpleasant smile. 'And if he is, you'll find him for me, won't you, Al'Kalyek? And then I shall have him eliminated – in secret, of course, I wouldn't want to upset his father just yet. We're cousins, after all, as well as past allies. But such a dangerous person cannot be allowed to wander around my Empire unhindered.'

'I should warn you, Imperial Majesty,' said the sorcerer, 'that I would not necessarily know if he was here in the city. True, such power as this boy possesses is blatantly obvious to any mage, even the greenest novice – but only if it is used. If it is not, then such an adept may be able to conceal himself from everyone else. The greater the power, the greater his ability to hide or defend it. But I can give you a brief description of him – he is twenty years old, he has blond hair like his father, and he is called Bron – a Ska'i name meaning servant, or slave. It should not be too diffi-cult to locate him, if he is here in the city. I doubt it very much,

though, for I suspect that he is intelligent enough to realize that
this is the one place in all the world where he is most in peril.'

'Olkanno.' Ba'alekkt's thick finger stabbed at the Spymaster.
'You may instigate a search. Discreetly, of course. Our honoured
sorcerer is probably right, but if the boy has been foolish enough
to come to Toktel'yi, then we must not let him slip through our
fingers. And if you do find him, ensure that he is unaware of it
until the moment you seize him. Or your precious agents will be
fried in witchfire, and he'll escape.'

'Of course, Imperial Majesty. As always, you may rely on me.'
Olkanno was a small, plump, olive-skinned man with a fringe of
curling black hair around a face apparently as chubby and good-
natured as a baby's. But in certain parts of the Empire, the mention of his name made women tremble, and children weep with
terror.

Ba'alekkt had already put the Spymaster on his brief list
of those councillors he planned to keep. Such a reputation was
invaluable, even if much of it stemmed from Olkanno's ability to
employ men of utter subtlety and absolute ruthlessness. He
looked round the circle of faces, and smiled very pleasantly.
'Then we are all in agreement? We invade Kerenth, in a month's
time.'

Sekkenet's mouth opened to protest at the insane brevity of
notice. Ba'alekkt nodded to him. 'You have nearly a quarter of a
million men at your command, General. You shouldn't need
more than a twentieth of that number to subjugate a country with
no army whatsoever. Indeed, I suspect that the garrison of Tatht
by itself will be quite adequate for the purpose. But you may
collect, say, five thousand soldiers each from Mynak, Djebb and
Terebis on your way east. With five thousand from Toktel'yi,
that should be ample. Speed and surprise will be your greatest
weapons, so I suggest you embark at Terebis, and invade by sea.
They will not be expecting it, and you will be able to strike at the
heart of Kerenth before they even know our plans.' He looked at
the Commander of the Navy. 'Are you in agreement with this
plan, Klemenek?'

The sailor, his face at once astonished and delighted, nodded
eagerly.

'Good. We will discuss the details later. In the meantime,
I have ordered refreshments in celebration of our momentous
decision.' Ba'alekkt snapped his fingers. At once, a procession of

slaves hurried in, bearing trays of refreshing drinks. When each of his thirty councillors had been served with a cup of iced fruit juice, he lifted up his own goblet, of finest Minassan ware. 'My friends, I ask you to salute the successful conquest of Kerenth!'

As one, the men around the low table swallowed their drinks. Ba'alekkt sipped his own and gazed at them, a small satisfied smile on his face.

The Governor of Djebb coughed suddenly. The spasm turned to a choking gasp. His face empurpled and his eyes horribly distended, he clutched at his throat: then he fell backwards on to the cushions.

Ba'alekkt laughed. The sound was drowned by another uncontrollable fit of coughing, on his left. This time, it was the Governor of Tekkt. Then another, and another, and another. The Minister for Foreigners was the last to die, clawing frantically at his mouth until he collapsed, gurgling and twitching, across the table.

There was a sudden, profound silence. The ninety-ninth Emperor of Toktel'yi surveyed his Council table. The polished black ironwood was marred by puddles of vomit and spilt juice, overturned goblets, sprawled bodies. Of his thirty councillors, only Al'Kalyek, Sekkenet, Olkanno and Klemenek were left. Their eyes, dark, tense, fearful, stared back.

'Don't worry,' Ba'alekkt said, grinning. 'Your drinks were quite untainted. They're not worth bothering about – fools, the lot of them, and a few traitors as well. I hope you've learned a valuable lesson today, and I'm sure I don't have to spell it out.'

'Indeed not, Imperial Majesty,' said the sorcerer, his deep voice quiet and calm. 'And I am honoured that you saw fit to spare me this rather abrupt and wholesale, er, resignation from your service.'

Ba'alekkt laughed again. 'My father's judgement was appallingly deficient, but at least he managed to pick four good men alongside the scum. Once this mess has been cleared up, my friends, we can concentrate on the real business of the day – planning the invasion of Kerenth, down to the last detail.'

At High Summer, the clouds over Kerenth dissolved at last, and the sun shone. At first the people and their Queen rejoiced, seeing the signs of the Goddess's returning favour. But as the days crept by in the pitiless, withering heat, they realized that they had been mistaken. With no rain, the fertile soil was baked so hard that neither hoe nor spade nor plough could pierce it. The green leaves in the orchards grew limp, turned yellow, shrivelled and died. Now they lay in drifts under the naked branches, and small children, heedless and ignorant, played with them until their mothers screamed at them to come away.

And every evening Inrai'a went to bed with her lover, her Consort, and prayed that tonight the rains would come. And every morning she woke, sated with love, sick with hope and dread, to find that Sarraliss had not answered her.

Here in the city, they were protected from the disturbing scenes in the countryside. Water still flowed through pipes and conduits, and spilled over from the mountains. There was plenty of food stockpiled in the store-caverns burrowed through the rock below the Palace, and Inrai'a's women and servants attended her dutifully. They did not dare to express their doubts and fears to her face, even if they talked incessantly behind her back.

And Bron, being a mere Consort, was kept away from the mechanics of government. He did not receive the reports of ruined crops and dried-up lakes and rivers. He did not hear the hostile talk, the whispers that reminded those who had forgotten how, that Sarraliss could be appeased, if only their Queen could find the courage. He had sworn not to use the sorcery that would have told him these things, but he could feel, as anyone with ordinary eyes and ears and senses could feel, that the wrath of the Goddess lay heavy on the land.

He spent all day in the lovely airy suite at the top of the Palace, playing his Sith, or singing, or watching the azure, infinite sea. He seemed content, but Inrai'a remembered the bird she had owned as a child. It had sung happily in its cage, and fed from her hand, as tame as any cat or dog. But the instant she had opened the cage door, knowing that the creature loved her and would stay, it had snatched its moment and soared away to freedom without a backward glance. For days after, she had wept for its betrayal, although the treachery had only existed in her own mind, fruit of her illusion.

And so each night they coupled with increasing frenzy, as if she were denying the inexorable reality outside the room, as if he were repudiating the distant vision of Jo'ami that glimmered beyond the far horizon, reminding him that his destiny did not lie with this land or this woman.

A month after High Summer, Nerana came to the Palace.

She did not arrive alone. Behind her, milling round the main entrance, were thousands upon thousands of people, caught up in the High Priestess's wake as she travelled the road from Skathak: men and women in rags, who had sold all they possessed to buy food; children too weak and sick to cry, with distended stomachs and hair like faded straw and limbs as thin and knobbly as old sticks; people more fortunate than these, but who were terrified that they, too, would soon starve; people who were desperate enough to turn on their beloved Queen, if that was the only way to save their land and their children.

Nerana swept up to her sister's apartments. She had never been plump, and even in the voluminous earth-coloured robes of her office, she looked more gaunt and intimidating than ever. She demanded an immediate interview with the Queen, and when Sumis tried to bar her way, pushed her aside with an angry word and a blow from her staff.

Inrai'a was in bed, alone. Her astonished, furious face appeared beneath a tangle of dark hair: then she sprang up, and flung a gauze robe over her naked body. Kerentan women were never shy, but in the heat of Nerana's rage she felt at a considerable disadvantage.

And it was worse for knowing in her bones that the High Priestess was right, and that her own intransigent selfishness and her personal dislike of her sister had led her to betray her people.

'Where is he?' Nerana demanded fiercely. 'What have you done with him?'

'I am here,' said the Consort, at the entrance to the balcony.

He did not look like a man of evil. He was as wiry, self-possessed and watchful as a cat, and even in his long Kerentan robes he looked alien and exotic. Nerana made a dismissive, contemptuous gesture with one hand, and turned back to the Queen. 'Do you know, sister, why I have come?'

Inrai'a drew herself up proudly, and looked the High Priestess in the eye. 'No, sister, I do not.'

'Then you are extraordinarily blind and obtuse. Look out of the window above the gate, then. You will see that your people need you. They trusted you, and you have betrayed them. For the sake of a foreigner, a man so evil that the Goddess denies him, you have let your citizens starve.'

Inrai'a said, 'They are not starving yet.'

'Are they not? I beg to differ. Go now and look at them, if you have the courage. Listen to their cries and their entreaties. And then come back and tell me that you intend to cling to this – this *nothing* of a Consort.'

'He is not a nothing!' Inrai'a cried. 'Nor is he evil. And I *love* him!'

'Love?' Nerana bit on the word and hurled it back at her. 'That isn't love, you silly child. Love has no place in the lives of Queens. Lust, yes, infatuation, yes, passion, yes – even friendship. But not love. Not for a man like this. You don't even know where he comes from.'

'I do,' Inrai'a said. 'He is a Minassan.'

'So he says. He'd tell you the sun rose in the west and you'd believe him, you little fool. And so you hide in here with him while your land and your people despair and perish. I wish our mother had died birthing you, rather than watch you now, destroying everything we love. Your love is not meant to be given to *men*, Inrai'a – love is for the Goddess, and for Kerenth.'

'Are they dying?'

The male voice seemed extraordinarily deep after the high, angry tones of the two sisters. Nerana whipped round, her dark arched brows snapping together. 'Yes, foreigner, they are dying. Sarraliss has withdrawn Her love and Her blessing from Kerenth. The fields are barren and the people are starving.'

'Then I will go.'

'No!'

The two women cried out simultaneously. Nerana's stronger voice prevailed. 'No. It must be her decision, not yours. And there is another matter to be considered. Did you know, sister, that the Emperor of Toktel'yi is at this moment sailing to Kerenth at the head of a fleet of fifty warships? And I doubt very much that he comes with peaceful and friendly intentions.'

There was a terrible silence. For a moment Inrai'a crumpled under the impact of the news: her shoulders sagged, her knees trembled, her mouth slackened. Then her courage and her pride flooded back. She took a deep breath and looked her sister in the eye. 'Is this true, Nerana?'

'It is. The crystal has shown me. He will be here in two days. And without the power of the Goddess, this land and its people will be as dust beneath his feet.' The High Priestess walked forward until she was within touching distance of Inrai'a. Together, the likeness between the sisters was sharply apparent: both tall, dark-haired, dark-eyed, beautiful. But at this moment Nerana possessed an edge, the ruthlessness born of being right, that the younger woman temporarily lacked.

'Bron.' Inrai'a turned her face away from her sister's relentless gaze. 'Bron – Kenmet – I love you. I will always love you. But – but I have no choice now.'

'I know,' he said softly. 'Say what you must, and I will go.'

'It will not be enough.' Nerana's voice was menacing. 'The Goddess has spoken to me. In reparation for your disobedience, she demands a life.'

The bright angry colour drained slowly away from Inrai'a's face, leaving her eyes huge, aghast. 'No,' she whispered. 'No. Not that.'

'Yes. The Goddess has spoken. Would you defy Her in this too? You have deeply offended Her by continuing to harbour this man. Long, long ago, in harsher times, the Consort was killed every seven years. Then the Goddess decreed, in Her wisdom and mercy, that such a gift was not necessary. She is the Creator, the Life-giver, after all. But as a punishment, Inrai'a, She now demands the highest penalty. Your chosen Consort is evil, defiled. Great darkness lurks in his heart. He is a bringer of death, a devourer of souls. Knowing this, will you still persist in defending him?'

'He is *not* evil!' Inrai'a screamed. 'You're jealous – you hate me – that is why you are lying to me now!'

'She is not lying.'

A curious smile, compounded of triumph and respect, suffused Nerana's fierce face. 'No, Kenmet, or Bron, or whatever you call yourself – no, I am not. Will you tell her, so that she may learn from your own lips who you really are? There are no secrets from the Goddess, whatever you in your arrogance may have thought. As a man, you can know nothing of Her magic – but She knows every detail of your puny powers.'

'I thought She did.' Bron came to stand next to Nerana. His face was very pale, but his dark eyes were steady and unfathomable. 'Inrai'a – Nerana is right. At my birth, I was dedicated to Ayak, the Devourer. I have never been called Kenmet, save by myself. I am the bastard son of Ansaryon, King of Zithirian, and my real name is Bronnayak, which in the language of the Ska'i means the slave or servant of Death. I was created by evil, for evil.'

The Queen's skin was greenish white with shock. She took a step backwards, shaking her head. 'No – no! It's not true!'

'It is.' His voice was still soft and remorseless, deliberately severing the bond between them. 'I am an abomination. I should never have been born – I should not be alive. And knowing that, would you not be glad to see me dead?'

Inrai'a stared at the man she loved, with whom she had shared so many nights of ardent pleasure. She said hoarsely, 'You told me – you told me you were not evil.'

'I lied.' His gaze did not waver. 'But I spoke the truth when I told you that my powers were a burden I could not lay down, even though I longed to. Inrai'a, it is the Goddess's wish. And I respect that. I have grown to love Kerenth and its people. And if I can be the means of saving them, whether from starvation or from Toktel'yi, then I will.'

Her face was still distorted with horror. 'Even though you must die?'

'I am not afraid. And the Wolf will welcome my soul.'

Even Nerana seemed appalled by his calm words. She said sharply, 'You accept your fate very willingly.'

Dark eyes met dark. The High Priestess said at last, very softly, 'You are right. It is better this way. For you, for her, for Kerenth, for all the known world. And so you will redeem yourself by the manner of your death. Perhaps there will be a place for you in the fields of Sarraliss, after all. Do you wish to know what will be done to you?'

Inrai'a, who knew very well, turned away with a sob of despair and ran out on to the balcony.

'Yes,' said her Consort, his eyes never leaving Nerana's face.

'There is a chasm, a cleft in the cliffs to the west of the city of Kerenth. No one knows how deep it is – but it is the most sacred place of all in our land, after the Womb of the Goddess in Skathak. Since before recorded time, the Sacrifice has been made there. In front of the people, you will leap into the embrace of the Goddess. It is a good death. For the last heartbeats of your life, you will soar as the eagle does – and the end will be swift.'

'I understand.' He smiled, rather bitterly. 'It's strange – I always assumed that Kerenth was only a resting place on my journey. And now I have come to journey's end here.'

'It is not such a bad fate,' Nerana said softly. 'Of all lands, this is now the most blessed, the most lovely, the most favoured and

fertile. You will save it from starvation, and from the horror that
has destroyed Penya. And make no mistake, if you had never
crossed our borders, Ba'alekkt would still have come. True, we
would not have suffered the Goddess's curse, but to defeat such
an invader requires the deepest and strongest magic of all. And
to seal its power, there must be a life sacrificed – a life that is
young, strong, potent, and valuable, or there is no Sacrifice.
Better you, servant of Death, than one of our own people, lacking
your special abilities.'

'When? I would rather not wait,' said Bron. And he glanced
significantly at the balcony, where the Queen of Kerenth stood
with her back to them, the sea wind pulling at her hair and the
thin transparent silk of her robe.

'It can be done now,' Nerana said. 'The ritual is not long, or
complicated, but it must be performed in full sight of the people.'

'Then make it now.' The Consort took a deep, steadying
breath, the first sign of apprehension that Nerana had seen in
him. 'For her sake, and Kerenth's, if not for mine.'

The citizens stood outside the Palace and cheered the Consort as they had never cheered him before. Clad in the greens and
browns and yellows of the Goddess, for he belonged to Her now,
he walked through them and they fell back before him, awe and
hope and wonder in their gaunt faces. Never in living memory
had a Consort offered himself to Sarraliss: and now, one foreigner's death seemed to promise them deliverance not only from
starvation, but from the brutal Toktel'yan invaders as well.

Like all days since High Summer, the sun glared down from a
harshly metallic blue sky. As the procession, with Nerana and her
acolytes at its head, wound up the track out of the city towards
the sacred chasm, the wind dropped and the heat became fiercer
still. Out to sea, Penya had disappeared behind its own sinister
cloud, and there was a brazen, oppressive shimmer along the
horizon. The High Priestess and her followers toiled on, sweat
soaking their robes, and the undernourished, sickly people
struggled in their wake, some collapsing with exhaustion in the
thick, menacing air. Along the far edge of hearing, something
grumbled long and low, as if the sky itself were complaining of
the heat. Of all the thousands who came to watch the Sacrifice
that momentous morning, only the Consort seemed unaffected
by the blistering air all around them.

A mile to the west of the city's edge the line of the cliff was
broken by the huge scar of the chasm, as if some unimaginably

vast giant had slashed down through the rock with a sword half a mile long. The sides of the cleft were sheer, the few rough, narrow ledges the haunt of gulls and sea eagles. As the straggling procession approached, one soared lazily into the air with a high, keening cry, and circled far above them.

Nerana came to the edge of the void, and looked down. Far, far below, the sea rippled impotently against a great pile of stones. Behind it, the chasm narrowed, its depths concealed by boulders and the sparse vegetation clinging to the rockface. But a narrow dark crack could just be discerned by those who knew it was there.

Nerana knew. If the Sacrifice's body remained visible, then the Goddess had rejected his offering. If he was swallowed up into the fathomless deeps of the earth, it indicated that She had embraced and accepted him. Silently, she urged the man beside her to leap vigorously from the clifftop, so that he would be lost in the abyss.

The High Priestess turned and surveyed those around her. The people, breathless, expectant, silent in this holy and perilous place. Her acolytes, perspiring, their red faces shining with awe. Her sister Inrai'a, her skin as white as chalk despite the heat, a look of disbelief in her eyes as if, even now, she did not expect her lover to be forced to pay this last, terrible price. *Fool*, Nerana thought, with angry contempt. *He has offered himself – his Sacrifice has been demanded. It is him, or Kerenth – she should not even hesitate.*

She raised her hands and in the still, menace-laden air began the Ritual of Sacrifice. These words had not been spoken here for nearly a hundred years, but all High Priestesses knew them: they were engraved into blood and flesh and bone, to be used only when the Goddess's sacred land lay in darkest peril.

Under the glowering sky, the colour of Tulyet steel, even Nerana's strong voice seemed puny and impotent, like the squeaking of a mouse before the cat pounces. The language she spoke was very old, an archaic and expanded form of the liquid, beautiful Kerentan tongue, and no one else there would be able to understand it.

But the Consort knew what she was saying. She could see it in his eyes, and despite the molten heat a chill shivered through her, as she realized anew just how strange, how unknown, how mysterious this man was.

Well, it did not matter now. In a few moments he would be

dead, all his evil and his alien, monstrous powers made safe and impotent within the embrace of the Goddess.

She finished the last words of the Prayer of Sacrifice, and gestured to her acolytes. They had been standing in a tight semi-circle, shoulder to shoulder, between Nerana and the edge of the chasm. Now they broke apart and the nine women, four on one side and five on the other, formed two lines. And the empty strip of ground between them led to the edge of the abyss.

Behind Nerana, the people tensed. She could feel their emotions, their hope, their desperation, held like hounds on a rope, waiting for the moment of release. In the silence, someone gave a little sigh, almost a sob. It must be Inrai'a, and her sister frowned. She swung round to face the man standing next to her, robed, as no man ever was save as a Sacrifice, in yellow and green and brown. 'Lady!' she cried, her strong voice cutting through the dense air. 'Most gracious and glorious Lady of Life, Creator of all women and all men and all plants and creatures of the earth – accept this, our Sacrifice! Save us from the enemy, and return Your sacred blessings to Your beloved land of Kerenth!'

For one brief, unexpected moment, she met the Consort's eyes, as deep and unknowable as the chasm below. Suddenly and shockingly, he smiled, and for the first time, with a stab of regret, Nerana saw why her sister had almost destroyed Kerenth for love of him.

And then he turned, and started to run.

He ran between the acolytes, his pale hair flying, his robes swirling round his ankles. He came to the edge of the chasm, and did not hesitate. As joyously as if he were about to take wing, he leapt out into the infinite air.

Inrai'a's raw, terrible scream of grief would have been the last thing he ever heard.

And then, as its echoes died away, the rain began to fall.

PART THREE
TOKTEL'YI

CHAPTER
TEN

For longer than man could count, or books relate, the city of Toktel'yi had squatted in the centre of the delta formed by the River Kefirinn as it reached the low marshy shores of the Southern Sea. At first no more than a collection of squalid huts built of the mud and reeds all around, it had expanded over the centuries in line with the ambitions of its rulers. Akkatanat, the first and most vigorous of its warrior kings, had transformed his city and his people into the most feared and well-organized nation bordering the Southern Sea, and his descendants had consolidated and built on his reputation and his success. Their calendar was dated from the first year of Akkatanat's reign: now, two thousand, three hundred and fifteen years later, Toktel'yi was the centre of an empire comprising nine provinces, all of which had once been independent states, the nominally separate Princedom of Tulyet, mountainous land of iron and steel, and every island in the scattered K'tali Archipelago save one. Only Jo'ami, the wizards' isle, remained free, so distant and mythical that the Emperors had been able to pretend that it did not actually exist.

The present incumbent of the Onyx Throne, Ba'alekkt, son of Djamal, had ruled for three years now, and had impressed his subjects with his vigour and ruthlessness, qualities much admired in Toktel'yan Emperors, and sadly lacking in his corrupt and indolent father. The mass poisoning of twenty-six members of his Council was approved by everyone who had cause to regret the venal, stupid and corrupt ministers and governors whom Djamal had appointed during his reign. Ba'alekkt's replacements were men like himself, young, energetic, and determined to work not only for their own reward – that went without saying – but for the greater good and glory of the Empire.

Unfortunately, the Emperor's boldest strategy, the invasion of Kerenth in the first summer of his reign, had ended in disaster. The Imperial Navy had been wrecked, sunk or scattered by an unexpected and terrible storm which had hurled them on to the

rocky northern shores of Penya, only a day's sail from the land
they had intended to conquer with ease. By a miracle, attributed
to the intervention of Kaylo, Lord of Life, Ba'alekkt himself had
escaped the fate of fifteen thousand of his troops and all but a
handful of his ships. But he had learned his lesson. Most Toktel'yans attributed the fatal storm to the agency of the Goddess,
defending Her sacred country. Ba'alekkt, who had the scorn of a
practical man for anything outside his comprehension, nevertheless accepted this view. After all, the Empire's own sorcerers
were competent weather-workers (though they had dismally
failed to predict the destruction of the fleet), and it was perfectly
possible that the Priestesses of Sarraliss had raised the storm,
even if their deity had nothing to do with it. True, their magic was
only women's power, and surely inferior to the male version
practised in the Empire, but even the misogynist Toktel'yans,
who kept their wives and concubines secluded in harems purely
for the pleasure and procreation of men, had considerable
respect for the ancient mysteries of this apparently defenceless
land. After all, it had now successfully repelled two invasions, in
overwhelming force, by the greatest Empire the world had ever
seen.

So Ba'alekkt, reluctant but realistic, had turned his attentions
from Kerenth and spent the next three years on less ambitious
activities. There had been a serious outbreak of banditry in
Tulyet, where the new Prince, brother to the one slain at the
Council of Poison, had proved even more ineffective than the
man he'd replaced. Stamping it out had taken considerable but
necessary effort. Tulyet, a huge, mountainous and arid peninsula
curving like a Ma'alkwen sword round the south-western islands
of the Archipelago, was rich in iron and other minerals as well as
precious stones, and could not be allowed to slide into lawless-
ness. It was a nuisance, and it meant that Ba'alekkt could not
proceed, yet, with his next plan of conquest. But Sekkenet was
confident that the bandits would soon be eliminated, and the
Emperor had considerable respect for his General's abilities. The
northern cities would not go away. Let them relax in the false
belief that he intended them no harm. It would make his attack,
when it came, even more effective.

In Toktel'yi itself, only the favoured and wealthy knew much,
or cared, about Ba'alekkt's cherished strategy. The majority of
the half a million people inadequately contained within its

sprawling suburbs and slums pursued their traditional struggle against squalor, hunger, poverty, disease and the ravages of a ruthless, desperate underworld of destitute criminals who must steal, harm and kill to survive.

In the heart of Toktel'yi lay the Old City. Until two hundred years ago, the Emperors had lived here, in an ancient, splendid but decaying Palace constructed, like everything else around it, of baked mud brick. Then the new Palace had been built, in pure white Annako stone, close to the clean sea and as far away as possible from the filth and stink of the delta waterways and canals. The aristocracy and the rich had hastily followed in the Emperor's wake, and their beautiful villas now occupied the drained and reclaimed marshes between the Old City and the sea. Like a spring tide, the poor were sucked out of the ancient slums to the north of Toktel'yi, and flooded in to fill the vacuum. They took over the deserted homes of their betters, sometimes two or three families to a room, so that a single four-storey building might contain several hundred people from a dozen different cities or provinces, speaking twenty different dialects or languages, and all scrabbling for a tiny share of the huge wealth of Toktel'yi.

In such an environment, death, from accident, murder or disease, was commonplace. Children swarmed everywhere, even though at least a quarter of them died before they could walk. The poorest of all did not sleep in the streets, for save in the Old City, built on a large flat island at the heart of the delta, there were no streets. Water-lanes, channels, canals and ditches served as highways amongst the rotting slums, and those who could find no place in the rickety buildings tottering above the water made their homes in boats or on rafts if they were lucky, or on the foetid mud of the banks if they were not.

In the Old City there were shops, markets, stalls, hucksters, pedlars, street-sellers; taverns and kuldi-houses and cook-shops; music dens, pleasure rooms and brothels catering for every taste, pocket and perversion. In daylight, as long as you kept hold of your money-belt, this part of Toktel'yi was comparatively safe, and sightseers flocked here, gawping at the attractively dilapidated buildings and the astonishing variety of goods and services on offer. After dark, however, the City Guard retreated to their barracks down by the West Dock, and left the maze of lanes, alleys, small squares and backstreets to the creatures of the night.

People from the slums to the north and east of the city came to
beg, to steal, or to spend their few chips of copper or silver on a
night's entertainment to keep desperation at bay. And the
wealthy came in from their handsome, spacious stone villas to
sample the assorted delights that those not so fortunate as themselves were offering.

Some places, like the Lotus Tavern down by the South Bridge,
had an evil reputation: you would be really stupid, or foolhardy,
to enter it without a friend at your back and a knife in your belt.
But young men with more money and bravado than sense
trooped through its doors in swaggering gangs, eager to taste the
famous and potent brew, concocted by the proprietor in huge
copper vats in his ground-floor still-room, and misleadingly
known as Mother's Milk. The tavern proper, like most buildings
in the flood-prone heart of the city, was reached up a flight of
stairs. To enjoy the attentions of the Lotus's girls, if they were still
capable after a jar of Mother's Milk or a jug of spiked Balki wine,
customers had to stagger right up to the flat roof where pallets
were laid out in rows. There were other places, even more dubious than the Lotus, mostly down by the Teldjek Cut near the
docks, where strangers were regularly robbed, or disappeared
only to surface again, naked and knifed, in the noisome waters of
the Kefirinn or one of the other canals and channels webbing the
city of Toktel'yi.

In some establishments, clustered around the more salubrious
parts of the Old City near the former Palace, you could eat, or
drink, or listen to music, or watch pretty dancing girls, without
fear of being robbed, but you paid heavily for the privilege. The
women were clean, skilled and expensive, the music delightful,
the food excellent and unlikely to give you gut-rot, and the wine –
no Mother's Milk here – of the highest quality, good Hailyan or
the sweet, potent vintage produced around Djebb. The best and
most exclusive of all was K'mek's, named after its proprietor,
where two huge muscular gatekeepers from Onnak stood at the
door to turn away those customers who didn't measure up to
their master's exacting standards. But several other places, large
and small, aspired to such excellence: and one of them was called
the Golden Djarlek, run by a woman called Mallaso.

The building itself had once been part of a city dwelling
belonging to a wealthy family, and even in decline bore several
indications of its more splendid past. Although made of kiln-

baked mud brick, like all the Old City, it had a band of intricately carved stone around the walls at first-floor height, and the window frames were black ironwood from Onnak. Upstairs, the main room was decorated with faded frescoes, depicting a riotous feast complete with half-naked dancing girls, musicians, and lounging sensualists swallowing wine and dipping into bowls overflowing with exotic fruits.

Over the years, customers who fancied themselves as artists had added their own embellishments here and there. One day, when there was money to spare, Mallaso would have it all repainted with something more tasteful. Too many of her clients looked at the scenes on the walls and decided to imitate them, and she was tired of explaining to belligerent young men that this place was an eating house and music room, but not a brothel.

Most people knew little about Mallaso beyond a handful of essential facts, of the kind that few, in this land of busy bureaucrats and nosy officials, could keep secret for long. She was twenty-five years old, a freed slave, and a native of Penya who had been captured and brought to Toktel'yi at the age of ten. Her staff, and some of her more intimate customers, knew that she had a small daughter who was living with foster parents on Tekkt, the nearest island of the Archipelago, to save her from the dangerous, violent and unhealthy squalor of the city. Most of the profits of the Golden Djarlek went to keep little Grayna in happiness and comfort. Mallaso had never revealed the identity of the child's father, but almost everyone assumed that he was the wealthy merchant who had bought Mallaso in the slave markets, a terrified child fresh from the horrific slaughter on Penya. As was the custom, she had been freed at his death nine years later, shortly after her daughter's birth.

If anyone knew the truth, it was Metru, her cook, who had been a slave in the same household. But Metru, who came from Gulkesh and had arrived in Toktel'yi as part of the cargo of a Fabrizi pirate, was totally loyal to the woman who employed her. She was famously garrulous, but if anyone asked her curious questions about Mallaso, she kept her mouth shut, her small light eyes fixed with hostility and her scrawny arms firmly folded. Metru was the exception to the Toktel'yan proverb, 'Never eat at a thin cook's table': her food was exquisite, and people came from all over the city to sample her fish baked in Hailyan wine, her spiced fruit jellies, and her ten different ways of serving rice.

To get into the Golden Djarlek, the customer had first to negotiate Umai, the doorman. Rumour asserted that he had been trained in the esoteric fighting arts of Ma'alkwen, where they could maim with one small squeeze of the fingers, and kill with two. Whatever the truth of it, Umai was so big, and so impressive in his pleated soft leather tunic, that few people had ever crossed him. Those gangs of young hotheads who were only interested in getting drunk and picking fights avoided the Golden Djarlek. It catered for people who enjoyed good food and wine, pleasant surroundings, a relaxed atmosphere and high-class entertainment. The girls who served the customers were pretty, and Mallaso did not mind if they made their own arrangements for the night, so long as the tryst was elsewhere. As she pointed out to one indignant pair of lovers discovered on the back balcony, she'd spent a year trying to get away from a brothel, and she had no intention of starting one herself.

Some men remembered her from the Blue Hyacinth, and made the mistake of assuming that she could still be bought. Mallaso swiftly corrected them, and Umai was there to enforce the point, if necessary. It usually wasn't, for she had a very cutting tongue, and could trade insults in five languages, without repeating herself, for one level of the water-clock.

Most people called Mallaso handsome, magnificent, spectacular: 'beautiful' was too soft and feminine a word to describe her, although it might have suited her if her life had not been filled with hardship, suffering, bereavement and despair. She was tall, and dark-skinned like most Penyans, with a smooth, proud, sculptured face and high cheekbones. Her slightly slanted eyes gave her an exotic, alluring air that had attracted many men over the years. She cut her crinkly hair very short, like a man's: it emphasized the elegant shape of her head, and did not detract from her features. In repose, her full mouth drooped slightly, making her expression rather wistful. Well aware of this – she had a polished silver mirror in her bedroom – Mallaso had cultivated a hard, confident smile for the customers. In Toktel'yi, where wealthy women lived in pampered seclusion and almost all the rest depended on serving men for survival, it was dangerous to reveal any hint of vulnerability. Umai had taught her what to do if attacked, but she knew that her position was precarious. A woman alone, without the conventional protection of father, brother, husband or owner, was a prime target for any slum crime chief who wanted to add her establishment to his empire.

This evening, Mallaso had decided that she would dance. She rarely did so, and if word got round the place was always packed, for she had a gift that was greatly admired in Toktel'yi. Once, though, every woman on Penya had danced like her, gracefully, joyfully, with movements that could be slow and languorous, or swift and athletic. Her mother, long dead, had taught her the basics, and she had clung to her skill fiercely, desperately, through the long dreadful years of slavery and exploitation. She had danced to celebrate the birth of her daughter, to rejoice in her freedom, and for the only man whom once, briefly, she had loved. Tonight, she would dance because she enjoyed it, and had not performed in public for too long: and, more prosaically, because the leader of her usual troupe had twisted her ankle falling down the outside steps after too many cups of wine.

It was a mistake Mallaso had never made. Too much of her life had been ruled by others. Now at last she had complete control, and she intended to keep it that way.

A pretty box of inlaid wood lay on her table: she opened it and studied the jewels within, before making a careful selection. Earrings of tangled discs and chains and loops, each the length of her hand, the beaten gold as light and thin as paper. A pair of traditional Penyan ring-bracelets, one thin chain encircling the wrist, five more branching off it to join rings on thumb and fingers. These again were gold, mountain-mined from the fabled Silver City, far to the north. It had cost her a month's rent to buy them from the bazaar in Old Palace Square, but they were almost certainly the work of Fallairo, famous jewelsmith of Penya, who had been her mother's great-aunt. Such plunder from her native island turned up regularly in shops and bazaars and on market stalls all over the Empire, sold by the soldiers who had looted Penya of its riches over nearly twenty years of bitter warfare.

Last, she chose the dress. As befitted a woman in her position, with appearances to keep up, she had two dozen hanging from the rail in the alcove opposite her bed. Gowns in Kerentan silk, simple and stately, for formal occasions: ordinary cotton for every day, with matching headscarf and veil to conceal her face when she went out in public. Mallaso despised Toktel'yan conventions and Toktel'yan attitudes to women, but any adult female, even in the more respectable areas, had to go veiled, or risk assault and worse. She fingered her traditional Penyan dress, two huge pieces of gossamer silk in gorgeous, brilliant colours, falling from jew-elled shoulder-clasps and tied with an embroidered sash at the hip. Lovely as it was, she would not wear it tonight. A slight frown between her strong arched brows, she contemplated her collection of special dancing costumes. Then she picked one out and made herself ready.

Down in the main room, people were beginning to arrive. Long, low boards ran round three sides of the rectangular space, leaving a large open area in the centre for entertainers. Luxurious feather-filled cushions were heaped beside the tables, and several men were already seated, drinking from Minassan goblets and sampling Metru's appetizers – bowls of salted olives, assorted nuts, segments of fruit, chips of flat bread dipped in tangy or spicy sauces, fiery scraps of grilled fish or chicken. There were no female customers: respectable men did not allow their wives and daughters to patronize a place like this. Any woman loose in Toktel'yi at night was there only for one purpose.

On the edge of the central space, the musicians were playing softly. They were the traditional quartet, one flute, two djarleks, one man on the hand-cymbals. Their leader, a stout bald Mynak-kan in a sweaty blue robe that was rather too tight, had been employed at the eating-house for years, and Mallaso had acquired his services with the lease, because he had useful relations who owned a vineyard and supplied the place with good wine at reduced rates. His colleagues were natives respectively of Balki, Mynak and Toktel'yi itself. They were competent and professional players, uninspired but reliable. Mallaso couldn't afford anyone better – yet. But she had ambitions, and a growing sum deposited with a banker near the Temple of Kaylo.

There was a brief discussion at the entrance, and then Umai made his way across the room to the screens concealing the bal-cony door, moving with surprising agility between the increas-ingly crowded cushions and tables. The balcony, which overlooked Cormorant Channel, was empty and dark, but he heard the distinctive soft clash and chime of glass, and called quietly, 'Madam?'

'What is it, Umai?' Mallaso padded softly along the wooden balcony above, and descended the narrow steps. She was wearing her bead costume, and the newly risen moon glittered on the innumerable strands and spheres, ovals and cylinders, as if the gown were made of diamonds.

'There's a man at the door asking if we want to hire a musician. I told him we probably didn't, but he claims someone said there was a job going here.'

'Who?'

Umai shrugged. 'I don't know, Madam. He doesn't look like he'll give any trouble, but I thought I'd check with you, just in case. Do you want me to send him packing?'

Mallaso's face, sharply delineated by the moonlight, looked like the silver and ebony sculptures produced on Annatal. 'Do you think he might be any good? And, more to the point, cheap?'

Umai laughed. After four years in her employment, he knew the way her mind worked. 'Cheap enough, Madam. But you get what you pay for in this world. Free gifts only come in Kaylo's Halls.'

'You don't need to tell me that. If there's the smallest chance he might be good, I'll see him. We need a new attraction.'

'Fire-swallowers?' Umai suggested, grinning. A troupe of them had recently performed in a tavern nearby, and almost burned the place down.

'Over my dead body,' Mallaso said. 'Where's he from, this music-maker?'

'I don't know, Madam. Not Toktel'yi, that's for sure – he's got a noticeable accent, though he's as fluent as you or me. But how many people do you know who were born here?'

'Rather than brought here as slaves or captives,' Mallaso said. She moved, and all the heavy beads, glass and jet and lapis, clinked and swayed softly. 'Find him a corner and some food and drink. I'll see him when everyone's gone.'

'Done, Madam,' Umai said, with a flash of a smile, and was gone.

Mallaso turned and leaned her arms on the rough splintery rail of the balcony. It was a rickety wooden affair, and several of the girls were convinced that it would collapse at any moment. She had chosen this place, rather than another, slightly more expensive and very much more spacious, that she had been shown near the Temple, because she loved to look out over water. As a child, she had lived in a house above Penya Harbour, and even now, such a view had the power to soothe and entrance. True, Cormorant Channel by day was a murky muddy branch of the Kefirinn, edged with a dirty brown scum and bearing unmentionable horrors within its depths. But at night, with the moon's

reflection glittering in the black velvet water, it was as magical as
a sorcerer's Illusion. She never tired of looking out at the piled
dark shapes of the houses crowding the opposite bank, the lights
from their lamps wavering across the stream, places she knew as
half-derelict slums transformed into beauty by the kindly
darkness.

The costume was heavy, but she would not dream of doing
the Flame Dance in any other. She breathed the stinking air,
wondering how Grayna was, if she had been good, whether she
had learned her letters yet, whether she missed her mother. In a
couple of months or so the rainy season would start, and Mallaso
had her passage already booked for Tekkt, to spend a precious
few days with her beloved daughter before returning to Toktel'yi
to earn more money. And one day she would be able to sell up,
retire to the island and have Grayna to live with her, before the
little girl forgot her mother.

The door from the kitchen opened, draping a slab of warm
yellow light and a stream of hot fragrant air over the narrow
balcony, and Metru appeared with a tray in her hands. 'I thought
you might need this.'

The cook was the only one of her staff who had never, on
Mallaso's insistence, called her 'Madam'. Fifteen years ago,
Penya had been suffering brutal slaughter and destruction simply
because the Emperor Djamal had decided to add it to his
dominions as an easy way of acquiring much-needed prestige.
Mallaso had been wrenched from her secure and loving home,
forced to watch the execution of her entire family – parents,
brothers, aunts, uncles, cousins – and then despatched with thousands of other sobbing, bewildered children to the slave-markets
of Toktel'yi. Metru, a slave for most of her life, had achieved a
grudging acceptance of her condition until a former master had
sold her son to one of Toktel'yi's many male brothels, the all too
frequent fate of handsome boys, whether slaves or not. Perhaps
the terrified, orphaned girl had aroused her maternal sympathy:
certainly, after several years working in her purchaser's kitchens,
Metru had almost taken the place of her real mother, whom she
could only recall with any clarity in her dreams. And even after
their owner, noticing the young Penyan's ripening beauty, had
had her trained as a dancer and concubine, she had turned to the
elderly cook for comfort and companionship.

At the old man's death, all his slaves had been freed, as was the custom. Some favourites, amongst whom was Mallaso, had been given a handsome sum of money to keep them in comfort. Grayna was then only a baby, and the master had adored her. Mallaso, intoxicated by her liberty and also by more money than she had ever dreamed of, had accepted an apparently lucrative offer from the owner of the Blue Hyacinth, one of the Old City's most expensive brothels, in the hopes of earning another fortune. She had quickly realized her mistake, but it had taken more than a year to buy herself out, find foster-parents on Tekkt for Grayna, and take a lease on the Golden Djarlek with what remained of her hoard. She had kept in touch with Metru, who'd been working in a cookshop near the docks, and her old friend had accepted this new and much more pleasant job with alacrity.

Mallaso ate the tender, delicately spiced cubes of chicken and vegetables with enthusiasm, and washed the food down with a goblet of fruit juice. It would have tasted even better cold, but only the extremely wealthy could afford the packed snow brought by fast galley from the mountains of Tulyet to fill the insulated ice-pits dug in the service quarters of many Toktel'yan villas. The air was close and warm, though not yet full of the heavy humidity that made the rainy season so oppressive. Everyone who could afford it tried to escape from Toktel'yi during the winter months, and she longed for just a few days on breezy Tekkt, carefree in the happy company of her daughter.

'Thank you, Metru – that was delicious.' Mallaso handed back the bowl and the goblet, just as one of the serving girls slid round the woven rush screen which hid the balcony door from the customers. 'Madam – it's full. Are you ready?'

Metru disappeared back into the kitchen with a click of her tongue. She had never really approved of Mallaso's way of life. In Gulkesh, apparently, women simply didn't dance for men, even in private, and husbands could only take one wife and were supposed to remain faithful to her, and she to him, until death. The wealthy Toktel'yan man, allowed three wives, unlimited concubines and catamites and the choice of over a thousand brothels offering the services of both sexes, would be appalled.

With a smile, she nodded to the girl. 'Yes, I'm ready. Tell them the Flame Dance, then the Courting Cranes.'

The girl, wearing the plain blue dress of all Mallaso's female staff, ducked back into the main room. The rather mundane music came to a smooth halt, and she heard the Mynakkan's voice. 'These players demand your attention and your applause for – Mallaso!'

She stepped between the screens, tall and stately, and even those who had seen her dance before gasped at her entrance. The bead dress, in a hundred, a thousand different shades of blue and green, poured and shimmered like a waterfall over the slender contours of her body. She wore nothing underneath, and as she moved forward into the centre of the room, the shifting streaming rivers of beads revealed tantalizing glimpses of dark skin. For an instant she stood quite still, waiting for the music, her cropped head and long slim neck growing like an ebony flower from the cascade of beads. And then, with the small flickering gestures of a new flame, a new passion, she began.

More than a hundred men were watching her, but she noticed none of them, so intent was she on the steps of the dance. Once, she had believed that she would love like this: the bright, fragile sparks of initial attraction growing into the full and glorious maturity of the fires once lit on Penya to celebrate the Birthday of Sarraliss.

So she danced for all those lost, unknown women of her native land, for the loves and the lives and the dreams all shattered, for the barbaric destruction of her beloved isle, for all the children, sold into slavery, who would never go home. And the men of Toktel'yi, some of whom had probably served as soldiers on Penya, watched her with lust and longing in their eyes, in complete ignorance of what lay inside her head.

She finished at last, and crouched trembling, the fire dead, sweat pouring down her face and body. Slowly, the reality of the space around her slid back into her mind, and the trance faded. She smelt food, wine, the pungent smoke of khlar, a very fashionable narcotic drug, all mixed with the aroma of hot male bodies and a more distant and much nastier stink from the river outside. Then the applause crashed down on her, hands beating vehemently on tables, urgent shouts for more.

Restored to herself, Mallaso stood up. A glance round the room showed her the faces of her customers, black, brown, golden, their open mouths and waving hands. She smiled coolly, and inclined her head in acknowledgement of their praise, with a nod here and there to old friends. Not all Toktel'yan men were brutal, insensitive or unpleasant, and she had grown very fond of one or two of them.

The man in the corner opposite the door was probably the hopeful musician. She couldn't see very much of him because he was in shadow, but he was pale-skinned, probably from Tamat or even further north. He was studying the quartet, who were tuning their instruments, but as she gathered herself for the next dance, he turned his head, and his eyes met hers. She had a brief and disturbing sense of darkness, and then the flute broke into the lively tune of the Courting Cranes, the djarleks joined in with the skipping beat of the hand-cymbals, and she began.

It was brief, but very energetic, and taxed her powers of mimicry, as well as her leg and arm muscles, to the full. She finished with a whirl and a leap, praying that the beadstrings wouldn't break, and stood awash with perspiration, revelling in the applause. Then she bowed, studiously graceful, and ran lightly from the room, leaving a thunder of acclamation behind her.

Upstairs, she pulled the bead costume over her head and stood naked, enjoying the comparatively cool sensation of the night air against her hot skin. She stepped into the wooden tub and poured two large jugs of cold water over her head, towelled herself vigorously dry, and slipped into a crimson silk dress which set off her dark skin and lithe body to perfection. Then she went back downstairs, as she always did after a performance, to be pleasant to her customers. It was one of the things that made the Golden Djarlek different, that drew them back. Some of them obviously didn't think that a mere woman was capable of doing anything other than pleasing men, let alone of conducting an intelligent conversation. And as long as the talk avoided politics, a very dangerous subject unless you were slavishly devoted to the reigning Emperor, Mallaso was willing to discuss any matter her diverse customers – soldiers, merchants, artists, aristocrats, students, musicians, priests, sorcerers, philosophers, poets, even one or two government officials – might wish.

She sat down next to Sargenay, a sorcerer from Tatht, and perhaps her best and oldest friend, apart from Metru. As befitted his occupation, he was unconventionally dressed in flowing blue robes with an extravagantly large hood, and he affected a neat and rather sinister-looking beard, although it was currently fashionable to be clean-shaven. Sargenay was one of the few men who hadn't tried to lure her into his bed, though as he preferred boys she had probably never been in much danger of seduction. Certainly it was pleasant to talk to a man who wasn't continually trying to undress her with his eyes. She was proud of her body, but she had a mind as well, and Sargenay respected it. Tatht had been dedicated to the Goddess once, before Toktel'yi had tied it to the Empire with blood-stained and brutal chains.

'You were especially splendid tonight,' the sorcerer said, smiling as she sat beside him. 'You should dance for us more often.'

Aware of the other ears listening, Mallaso shook her head. 'No, I shouldn't. It would be much too exhausting. Anyway, you'd all become bored with me very quickly if I performed every night.'

'Not *every* night – perhaps just every other night?' Sargenay proffered a dish of spiced pork mixed with rice and nuts, and she took a handful with thanks, and another firm shake of her head. 'No – definitely not. Which reminds me – have you decided to accept my offer?'

'After long and very deep thought, I will say yes. For just one night, you understand? One solitary night. Any more would be too exhausting, as you put it. Sorcery is not something you can do with a snap of the fingers, you know. More pork? Or will you try some of the skewered chicken?'

Mallaso took the chicken. Dancing always made her ravenously hungry and thirsty. One of the girls brought her the usual goblet of wine mixed with peach juice, and she drank it gratefully.

'I'm only doing it for you,' Sargenay went on. 'K'mek could grovel to me on bended knee, offer me a hundred gold Imperials, and I'd still refuse. But for you, lovely Mallaso, I will gladly walk on fire, venture into Fabriz with a sack of treasure, or prostitute my Art – for one night, and one night only.'

'And I'm very, very grateful to you,' said Mallaso, and gave him one of her rare genuine smiles. Sargenay was young – the ageing effects of Annatal had not yet begun – but he was very talented and had a flair for showmanship that, so far, only his closest friends and lovers had been allowed to see. But she knew very well the intoxicating lure of public performance and praise. If they liked him, and showed their appreciation, he'd soon be asking, in that slyly humorous way, if she could bear to book him for another month.

'A special favour for my favourite lady,' said the sorcerer, and bestowed a light, affectionate kiss on her cheek. 'You're the only woman I've ever wished was a man, did you know that?'

'And you've had too much Hailyan,' Mallaso said, laughing.

She kissed him back, touched his hand lightly in friendship, and rose gracefully to her feet. She ought to speak to other friends as well, and the beautiful grey-eyed boy at his side was looking petulant.

As the quartet played, she moved amongst the diners, always with a brittle smile and a friendly word. Her banker was there, wanting to interest her in another, much larger building actually on Palace Square, the best position in the Old City. She declined, with a rueful shrug. 'Are you trying to put me in debt, K'tyaalin? I'd love to be able to afford it, no question, but I can't. In a year or two, perhaps . . .'

'In a year or two, the opportunity will be gone,' the banker said. He was a very fat, shrewd man with small black eyes almost lost in the smooth heavy flesh of his face. He'd been a good friend of her old master, and he was trustworthy, for a Toktel'yan, as long as she resisted his over-ambitious plans for her business. Mallaso was naturally cautious, and very careful with her pains-takingly accumulated hoard, despite K'tyaalin's urgings. But now, after more than five years of her custom, they had reached an understanding, and this discussion, in various guises, had become an old and familiar game.

'Someone with ready money and no taste will snap it up and turn it into a fancy bordello,' the banker added, with a heavy sigh. 'Obliterate all the wonderful frescoes, divide up those beautiful rooms – '

'It's no good – I'm not interested. Anyway, I know the place you mean, and the roof's cracked. Someone told me they'd spent a fortune covering it up.'

K'tyaalin spent some time protesting that the building was immaculate, fit for an Emperor, and Mallaso listened to him with an indulgent smile that masked her irritation. Much of the time, he was excruciatingly boring, but her continued prosperity depended almost entirely on his good will. She'd taken good care, though, not to let him know that she had nearly fifty gold Imperials hidden under a loose stone in Umai's room, on the ground floor. No one, not even Umai, knew it was there. If K'tyaalin was arrested for some misdemeanour, or spent all his clients' money betting on horse races, or absconded to Tekkt and bought himself a palatial villa, or purchased a bevy of expensive concubines, she wouldn't be left entirely destitute. And apart from the rent on this place, she owed nothing to anyone.

Mallaso extracted herself at last from the banker's wine-flown garrulity, and went over to the hopeful musician. He was sitting a little apart from everyone else, and although his plate was empty, his wine-cup was still full.

He looked up as she sank down on the cushions beside him, and she realized with surprise that he was quite young, no older than herself. 'Hallo,' she said. 'I understand you're looking for work.'

He nodded. 'Anything – one night or several, I'm not fussy.'

She studied him. He was slightly built and only of average height, though he gave the impression of considerable wiry strength under the plain cotton floor-length tunic, worn in some form or other by all men in Toktel'yi who were not slaves or manual labourers. Someone had obviously broken his nose at some time in his past, but he didn't look the type to use his fists very readily. She suspected that he would rather talk his way out of trouble, and certainly his livelihood depended on his hands. His eyes were as dark as hers, but his pale skin and hair marked him out as a Northerner, from Tamat perhaps, or even Minassa.

If he was reliable and good at his craft, she didn't care if he came from Toktel'yi, Minassa or the deserts of Ma'alkwen. She said, 'What instruments do you play?'

He indicated the leather bag beside him. 'Flute, and djarlek. I'm not too bad on the reed-pipes, either.'

He had a good idiomatic command of Toktel'yan, but Umai was right, he wasn't a native. Mallaso said curiously, 'What's your name? Where do you come from?'

'My name is Hanno, and I come from Minassa – but I left four or five years ago.' He smiled ruefully. 'They haven't much time for music there – they're too busy making pots and plates and cups.'

Something didn't quite ring true: something made her think he was lying. But what mattered was the music. Mallaso said, 'Where have you been since then?'

'Most places outside and inside the Empire. Lelyent, Zithirian, Tatht, Terebis, Onnak – '

'Penya?' Mallaso asked, before she could stop herself.

He gave her a quick enquiring glance. 'There's no call for music on Penya any more.'

No, there was not. She let the comment pass. 'And what songs can you play? My customers have open minds, for Toktel'yans, but they like old familiar tunes best, that they can sing along with. They'd be prepared to tolerate one or two from Minassa or Lelyent, but not all night.'

'Don't worry, I have a very extensive repertoire,' said the man called Hanno, and he stroked the bag that contained his instruments with gentle, reflective fingers. 'Would you like me to demonstrate?'

'Now?' said Mallaso, startled. But it was a good idea, as long as the quartet weren't offended. A musician's pure skill was only half his value as an entertainer. If he hadn't learned the trick of pleasing his audience he wasn't much good to her, or anyone else.

Of course, if he'd made a living for four or five years, he must be fairly good, but the Golden Djarlek was a classy establishment with a growing reputation for the high quality of its entertainment. Such was the shortage of really excellent players, however, that he'd only have to be better than competent and she'd hire him straight away.

'Now,' said the musician. 'I always play better with an audience.'

'I'll go and ask Djekkel,' she said, indicating the leader of the quartet. 'He shouldn't mind – it's not as if you're competing with him, after all.'

Djekkel, though, didn't like it. He was an arrogant man, with a very inflated idea of his talent and his importance, and he'd never adjusted very well to being employed by a woman. She phrased it as politely as she could, in her most placatory manner, and received a glare from under thick, scowling eyebrows. 'So you want us to sit and watch while that fancy foreigner takes over our show?'

'Only for a couple of songs, that's all,' Mallaso said. 'And I'm not going to sack you and employ him instead. I need you far more than I need this man – however good he may be. A single djarlek or flute can't play dance music – only a quartet can do that. And you're by far the best quartet in the Old City.'

Even when blatantly untrue, flattery always worked wonders with Djekkel, and he was stupid enough not to be aware of it. Out of the corner of her eye, Mallaso caught the raised eyebrows and exasperated expressions of the other djarlek player and the flautist. The quartet had been together for many years – which explained why their playing was so stale and conventional – but it seemed that Djekkel's partners were at last becoming tired of him.

A few more kind words, and he was almost eating out of her

hand. Mallaso had endured almost a decade of slavery, followed by a year in a brothel and then the freedom and constraints of running her own enterprise, and she was adept at hiding her contempt. Toktel'yan men always thought, however well they tried to conceal it, that it was their right to own and rule the world. She remembered, with sudden, ancient grief, her long-dead father, everyone's equal, everyone's comrade. It was no coincidence that all her closest male friends were not natives of this city, but came from the islands, or Kerenth, or the further provinces of the Empire, where older, kinder attitudes still prevailed despite the oppressive hand of Imperial domination.

The quartet struck up one last tune, and she went back to the musician. He had removed his instruments from their bag, and was tuning his djarlek. It was plainly made, without any of the pretentious fancy silver and ebony inlay that embellished Djekkel's, and looked quite new. Even above the noise, she could hear that it had a rich and beautiful tone.

'That sounds a good instrument,' Mallaso said. 'Have you had it long?'

'A while.' He finished testing the last, highest string and dragged his fingers carefully across each one, listening intently to the pitch. Satisfied, he laid it down.

'What will you sing?' She didn't know why she kept asking him nosy questions which he plainly didn't want to answer. Metru would say that she was naturally perverse.

'I'd decide when I get out there,' said Hanno of Minassa, and turned his attention pointedly to the quartet.

They finished their piece shortly after that, and before Djekkel could strike up again, Mallaso rose to her feet and walked out on to the dancing floor. 'My friends – we have a new singer tonight, eager to display his talents. If you like him, I'll hire him – so show your appreciation, please, for – Hanno of Minassa!'

The musician stepped into the centre of the floor. One of the girls brought out a stool, and he accepted it with a brief smile of thanks. The audience waited expectantly, quiet save for Sargenay, who was whispering to his catamite. She sent a significant glare in the sorcerer's direction, and was rewarded with an arch look, and silence.

The Minassan ran his hand across the strings. A pure bright ripple of notes followed his fingers. There was a brief, intent pause, and then he began.

She hadn't expected the music to touch her soul. That sort of emotion had surely died in Penya, along with all her family. It was an old tune, with a very sad lyric about misunderstandings and unrequited love, and he sang it beautifully, with a voice like a flute's, warm and pure and full of longing. To her embarrassment, she felt her eyes fill with tears. Even the light-hearted, sophisticated Sargenay looked melancholy, and one or two of the more emotional customers, and several serving girls, actually had tears running down their cheeks. As he finished the final verse, there was a brief, rapt silence. Then the applause began, hands smacking tables with genuine appreciation. Only Djekkel looked dissatisfied.

'Now something to lift your spirits,' said Hanno of Minassa, and swept into a rollicking, bawdy song from Balki called 'The Grapepicker's Daughter', full of suggestive innuendo and excruciating puns. It was in the form of a dialogue between the eponymous daughter and her would-be lover, a boy of touching naïvety compared to her extensive experience, and he sang each verse in character, revealing a gift for comic mimicry that had many of Mallaso's customers in tears, this time of laughter. At the end, the cheering and slapping of palms went on for so long that she had to raise her hands for silence, and Djekkel looked as if he was going to be sick.

'I take it you want me to hire him?' she asked, and a hundred enthusiastic voices bayed their assent.

The musician bowed his acknowledgement, and left the dancing floor to the quartet. Mallaso beckoned him out on to the balcony: she preferred to discuss business details in private.

'They liked you,' she said, rather unnecessarily. 'Can you do twelve nights a month?'

'I think so.' He was smiling absently, as if his mind was still on his performance. 'What will you pay?'

'Ten silver half-Imperials a night. I don't mind if you play elsewhere when you're not booked here, but at private parties and exclusive evenings only, please – I don't want you working for any of the other eating-houses or taverns in the Old City. I know them all, and I'd soon hear about it if you did.'

The moonlight was full on his face, but his eyes were still in shadow. Mallaso wondered if he wanted more. 'Is that acceptable, Hanno of Minassa?'

'Oh, yes,' he said. 'Very acceptable.'

'Your first night can be tomorrow – unless you have other plans.'

'No, no other plans.' He paused, and then said, 'Do you know of anywhere I can rent a room? I'm not fussy, so long as it's clean, private and secure.'

Mallaso stared at him in surprise. 'How long have you been in Toktel'yi?'

'Just today. My ship docked from Terebis early this morning.'

'Have you ever been here before?'

Smiling, he slowly shook his head. 'No, never. The provinces, some of the islands, but never the city.'

'Sweet Mother,' said Mallaso, wondering how he had escaped being robbed by the pickpockets and thieves who infested even the more respectable areas of Toktel'yi and preyed on country bumpkins and obvious foreigners. She came to a quick decision. 'I've got a room downstairs. Two, in fact, but Umai, my doorman, has the other. It's only got one small window, so it's rather dark, and it hasn't been used for a while, but you're welcome to it as long as you need it. Metru will feed you if you want, or you can eat out. A dozen half-Imperials a month for rent?'

'That will suit me very well. Thank you.'

'Thank *you*. If you always play like you did tonight, we'll be looking for larger premises soon.' Mallaso gave him her hard, confident smile, and held out her hands. 'Have we a deal, Hanno of Minassa?'

'Certainly,' he said, and they struck palms in the traditional gesture of business successfully completed.

And she remembered the loveliness of his singing, the blemished beauty of his face, and realized, for she knew herself very well, that she wanted him to be more than just another musician.

CHAPTER
ELEVEN

Word travelled fast in Toktel'yi, and on the following night they were queuing up the steps an hour before Umai unlocked the door. The serving girls, coming in up the back stairs to the first-floor balcony, were chattering excitedly, and speculating which one of them would be the first to warm the new musician's bed.

Mallaso, dressing for the evening, heard them and smiled wryly to herself. She couldn't blame them – not when she was taking extra care with her own appearance tonight. He had seen her dance in the bead costume, so she had little of her body left to hide, but she didn't want to make her interest too obvious. She was no longer a concubine, or a whore, and she had hated it when she was. She would only allow a man in her bed now for reasons of mutual love, or desire, or need, and after years of more or less forced submission to male lusts, she was very discriminating. In the four and a half years of her real freedom, since leaving the Blue Hyacinth and taking this place on, she'd only had three lovers, and regretted none of them. And she knew, with the confidence of a beautiful woman practised in the art of pleasing men, that she could have almost anyone she wanted.

Did she want Hanno of Minassa? Now, she wasn't sure. He didn't give very much away, save when he sang, but neither did she, save when she danced. Her last affair, with a Fifty-Commander in the City Guard, had ended when he'd been posted, ironically, to Penya, and that had been six – no, ten months ago, at the end of the last rainy season. She liked a man in her bed, occasionally, but her past experiences had soured her. In fact, she was surprised they hadn't put her off men altogether, like some of the girls in the Blue Hyacinth who always went with other women in their spare time. No one minded: Toktel'yans, in other ways so authoritarian, tolerated every imaginable fetish, quirk and perversion, so long as their own wives and daughters weren't involved. And concubines and whores, by definition, belonged to no one and everyone.

She put on her Penyan dress, which her last lover had found irresistible, and she matched its swirling colours, scarlet and cinnabar, orange and flame, crimson and amber, with huge gold clasps at the shoulders, and a necklace and earrings of red enamel poppies. In the silver mirror, her image stared coolly back, strikingly exotic, intelligent and glamorous. With a smile at her own boldness, Mallaso went downstairs.

Umai had unlocked the doors, and was taking a silver half-Imperial in entrance money from each customer. She caught his eye and raised both her hands, fingers and thumbs outstretched, to indicate that he should let a hundred in before barring entry. From what the girls were saying, there'd be as many left outside as let in. Perhaps K'tyaalin was right – perhaps she did need larger premises. Certainly she would if Hanno could pull in a crowd like this every night he played.

'Mallaso! My dear, this is a triumph!'

It was Sargenay, alone tonight: perhaps he'd quarrelled with his beautiful boyfriend. Despite his cool, sophisticated demeanour, he had a hot temper and often said things he regretted later. Two months ago, he'd entered into an argument with another customer over something very trivial, and had tipped a jug of wine over the man's head from four paces away. Then he'd followed it up with a wickedly funny Illusion, out on the dance floor, depicting his adversary in a series of deeply embarrassing and undignified encounters with a very amorous female ape. The other man hadn't stayed to watch, but everyone else had, and the episode had prompted Mallaso to offer the sorcerer the chance to display his talents officially – though not quite so explicitly. As she had reminded him, she didn't run a brothel.

'I wouldn't call it a triumph,' she pointed out. 'He hasn't even left his room yet.'

'You always were too cautious,' Sargenay said, smiling at her. 'You look magnificent tonight. Who's the lucky man, eh?'

'No one. I am Penyan, after all.'

'Yes.' Sargenay's hooded eyes dropped for an instant. The wounds in Tatht were old – no one now living could remember the bloody years of conquest by Imperial troops – but the scars had never truly healed. She had spent one entire evening, long ago, listening to a drunken Sargenay telling her how his ancestors had fought, and died hideously, in the struggle against Toktel'yi. It made a bond between them that was deeper than mere affection.

'Sit with me,' she said, on a rare impulse. 'I want someone by me who'll keep quiet when I brush the tears away.'

'Do you?' Sargenay's gaze was sharp. 'So he affects even you, does he? A voice like sunshine, and a face to break hearts – and he walks into your eating-house asking for work! You were born lucky, Mallaso.'

'No, I wasn't,' she said softly. 'I was born on Penya.'

Sargenay shook his head. 'No,' he whispered. 'No, dear Mallaso, forget it. We are all Toktel'yans now. There is only danger, bitterness and grief in clinging to the past.'

She wanted to remind him that he hadn't felt like that on a hot dry-season evening three years ago, but kept quiet. He was right, of course – she must try to abandon ancient memories, ignore the horrors which could never be undone, and live her life as most Toktel'yans had learned to do, for the moment, the hour and the day.

So Mallaso took her place at the sorcerer's side, in the centre of the middle table. It was pleasant to be part of an expectant audience, although she and the serving girls were the only women in the room. Already there were scarcely any gaps in the long row of profiles and faces to either side of her, and the air was hot and noisy.

She had told the man called Hanno to come on half-way through the evening. He had kept himself very much to himself during the day, but she had woken at noon to the faint sweet sounds of his flute, and all through the afternoon's business – eating, discussing the evening's food with Metru, counting the previous night's takings before sending Umai off to the banker's house, hiring a couple of additional girls – she had been aware of the music hovering on the edge of her hearing. Finally, as sunset approached, she had gone down to his room.

She had been wearing one of her plain, all-enveloping cotton robes, in a dull shade of dark red, with a scarf wrapped round the back of her head in the style popular with women all over the Archipelago. He had, obviously, not expected her to appear in something so modest. She glanced round the room, noting the small signs of his occupation: a woven rug over the bed, his instruments – djarlek, flute, reed-pipes – laid out on the table, and a pile of small, leather-bound objects which, she realized to her surprise, were books. That was unusual: not many ordinary people in Toktel'yi could read, let alone possess even the Chronicles of Kaylo, the most commonly used religious work. Curious, she opened one. It was in Toktel'yan script, flowing and graceful, but not in a language she knew.

'It's Minassan,' he said, and again she felt uneasy, as if she had strayed on to quicksand. More than ever, she sensed that this man, young as he was, had something terrible in his past, a secret which he did not wish to share with anyone. Paradoxically, it gave her a sense of kinship with him, for she too was forever haunted by what had happened to her.

She had spoken of mundane matters, told him when he was expected to sing, asked if he would like one of the girls to knock on his door when the time came. He had answered briefly, and she had sensed that she was irritating him, though his face and voice gave no indication of it. So she had bid him good afternoon rather curtly, and left, smiling ruefully at herself and her idle thoughts. He obviously had no interest in her: perhaps she ought to introduce him to Sargenay, who was obviously very taken with him.

The room was now full to bursting. Umai had barred the door, but there were still people hammering on it, trying to get in. Sooner or later, some of them would remember the stairs round the back, but Mallaso had anticipated that dodge. Metru's neighbour had an attack-dog, one of the huge Onnak breed, with fangs as long as a finger-joint and as sharp as a razor, and a temperament that made a marsh tiger seem friendly. Umai had gone round to collect him earlier in the day, paid over a prearranged fee (this was not the first time they had borrowed Demon), and brought him back, complete with spiked collar and thick chain. Now he was tied to a hook just inside the back entrance, and any stranger trying to pass him risked mutilation, or worse. Mallaso hadn't gone too close, though Metru assured her that the beast was as soft as a kitten with those he knew. She liked her smooth skin and slender fingers and long graceful throat whole and unmarked.

She ate the prawns in coconut milk and fried vegetables, which were particularly good tonight, and drank sweet wine from Djebb, taking care to have it well watered. Two of the girls who'd been trained as acrobats did a tumbling routine: their oiled, half-naked bodies always pleased the customers. And when they had finished, and the faces around her were beginning to look flushed, hot and impatient, Mallaso beckoned the senior girl, Temek, over to her and told her to fetch the musician.

He appeared from behind the screen, and those who had heard him the previous night were vociferous in their applause. The rest, true Toktel'yans, roared and beat their palms in eager anticipation. He sat down on the stool, laying the flute and pipes on the floor beside him, and took up the djarlek. His dark eyes swept round the room, and rested briefly on Mallaso's face. She thought she saw him smile. And then, into a sudden expectant hush, he struck the first notes of the first tune.

Afterwards, Mallaso tried to remember what he'd played. Some songs were in another language, presumably Minassan. There were romantic ballads from Terebis, dances from Tatht, songs of lost love from Djebb, even a working tune sung by woodsmen on Onnak, with the staccato rhythm of the axe chopped out with his foot on the floor. His voice was clear and flexible, able to croon soft sounds of love or to shout out the beat of a sailor's chant sung, though never so tunefully, every day down on the dockside in Toktel'yi. He was skilled, professional, and he seemed to pour his soul into his playing.

Beside Mallaso, Sargenay was enchanted. 'A bit too old for me,' he said, sighing, in her ear, but he looked hopeful, all the same.

'You're as young as your heart,' Mallaso whispered back, and the sorcerer smiled sadly.

'Youth and beauty, dearest lady – youth and beauty, soon gone!'

She made the serving girl who brought the wine water his as well, when he wasn't looking. She didn't like it when he got maudlin.

Hanno of Minassa picked up the reed pipes and rose to his feet. One of the girls moved the stool out of the way, and he blew the first bars of a lively Tekktish jig called 'The Grasshopper'. Within a few moments the floor was crowded with those quicker and luckier men who'd managed to grab a serving girl for their partner.

Mallaso stared in astonishment. She couldn't remember this happening before: usually, when Djekkel's quartet played, she had to persuade people on to the floor by getting up to dance herself. It was just as well the Mynakkan wasn't here tonight, or he'd be murderously jealous. She made a mental note to warn Hanno: the sly knife in the back in the dark was a common way of solving personal disputes, even here in the comparative safety and respectability of the Old City.

'I thought you said only a quartet could play good dance music,' said Sargenay mischievously. He got up and stretched out his hand to her. 'Will you be my partner, dearest Mallaso?'

Laughing, protesting, she allowed herself to be pulled to her feet. 'But it's my night off – if you make me strain a muscle, you'll be barred for life, Sargenay of Tatht.'

'I don't intend to make you exert yourself too much,' said the sorcerer, and swept her merrily into the dance. Her floaty gossamer silk swirled round her ankles, and the heavy enamel earrings pulled on her lobes with every step, while the reed pipes capered and leapt like the grasshopper in the song.

The musician finished just the right side of exhaustion, and Mallaso made Sargenay escort her back to her seat. It was just as well, for the next tune was slow and sensual, and those couples still on the floor were taking full advantage of the opportunity. One of the girls who didn't have a partner came down to the table with a fresh jug of wine, and another brought bowls of fruit. Mallaso sat on the cushions, cross-legged and straight-backed, eating a peach with neat precision and making a point of letting the girls on the floor know that she was watching them. She didn't take a cut of their earnings, or anything like that – they were free to make their own arrangements with interested customers, and over the years several had been installed in the households of wealthy men as concubines, with all the advantages and disadvantages that position entailed. But she didn't want them enticed off to some squalid brothel down by the docks, where they'd probably be dead in a few years, either of disease or at the hands of a client. She had experienced the edge of that life herself, and none of her girls would go down that road if she could help it.

'Do you know everyone here?' asked Sargenay, his mouth close to her ear.

Mallaso shook her head. 'No, I don't. About half are regulars, some I've seen occasionally, the rest have never been here before. Why?'

'There's another sorcerer here. I don't know who or where he is, but I can just sense him. A tingle on the skin, no more.'

'That's the breeze from the windows,' said Mallaso, laughing at him. Sorcery was the one thing that Sargenay took seriously: even his parade of beautiful catamites seemed only to touch the fringes of his emotions. She enjoyed chaffing him about his powers, just as she had once taunted her elder brothers about their girlfriends. If you couldn't tease your closest friends, who could you tease?

As always, Sargenay rose to the bait. 'I tell you, my senses never lie in these matters. There is another sorcerer here, I can feel his presence.'

'I'll ask who it is – then you can arrange a Battle of Illusions.'

'No!' Sargenay said hastily. 'No – no – that would be altogether impossible. I'm not one of your performing monkeys, my dear – if I do agree to Prostitute My Art, it is only for your sake.'

Mallaso was saved from having to think of a suitably rude reply by the musician. He had finished the slow tune, and his voice cut loudly across the hush. 'I have almost finished. I have one last song to sing, though, and I dedicate it to the lady of this place – Mallaso of Penya.'

And even as she was wondering how he knew, he began to sing, to the soft notes of the djarlek. And the tune was one she had not heard for more than fifteen years, since the men of Toktel'yi began their dreadful rape of her island home.

> I have travelled many miles
> Along many dusty roads,
> Amongst a thousand scattered isles
> I have sailed with the wind.
> But my heart still lies in Penya,
> My heart still longs for Penya,
> The blue waters of the harbour
> And the breezes sweet and kind.

> I dream of her at sunset
> When the darkness folds me round,
> And all the people I have met
> Come flocking to my mind.
> For my heart still lies in Penya,
> My heart still longs for Penya,
> The mountains and the valleys
> And the pure and golden wine.

> I can never now return,
> I roam this world bereft.
> I cannot watch her people burn,
> Or hear her children's cry.

But in my heart lies Penya,
Inside my heart lives Penya,
And as long as I can still draw breath
She cannot truly die.

Sometime during the last verse, whose words she had never heard before, Sargenay took her hand and squeezed it so tightly that it hurt. It was that which anchored her to reality, to sanity, amid the wild wave of grief overwhelming her heart. Those who knew her history must be looking at her, and her long training kept her back straight and her face still. A woman, unprotected in Toktel'yi, could not afford the dangerous luxury of tears, even when reminded of her own tragedy, just one amongst so many thousands.

So when he had finished she smiled blindly in the musician's direction and smacked her palms on the table with the rest. She didn't see him leave the floor, she was too busy trying to force that terrible sense of loss back into the locked compartment of her mind where she had kept it, more or less successfully, for all her adult life. And then the comments around her changed their note, and she looked up and saw him standing on the other side of the table, the djarlek in one hand and the reed-pipes and flute tucked under his other arm. There was a curious expression on his face, almost of apology, as if he knew how much his song had moved her, and regretted causing her such pain.

But of course that was impossible. Mallaso gave him her usual smile, and saw his eyes become blank as he recognized her defensive skills. 'That was truly splendid, Hanno,' she said. 'You can consider your booking confirmed – for an indefinite run.'

'Thank you,' he said, as if he'd expected nothing less.

Mallaso smiled graciously, and indicated the space on her left. 'Will you sit with me for a while?'

On the other side, she felt Sargenay's appreciation warming her like the sun, and smiled inwardly. There was no harm in him trying, but she didn't think he'd get very far. There was something about Hanno of Minassa that repelled hopeful boarders as effectively as a spiked chain round the gunwales of a Fabrizi pirate ship.

'I thank you, Madam, but I regret I must decline,' said the musician. 'I am very tired after my performance, and I fear I would be poor company. Please forgive me. I'll be more sociable tomorrow, after a good night's sleep.'

'The cheek! The effrontery!' said Sargenay, as Hanno made his way through an admiring throng in the direction of the balcony. 'I should sack him, Mallaso – men have been beheaded for less.'

'But only by Emperors,' she said, without thinking of who might be listening.

The sorcerer frowned warningly, and launched at once into an absurdly exaggerated tirade concerning the contrast between the musician's talents and his manners. Mallaso knew why he was doing it, but all the same she couldn't help feeling irritated by his pose. She herself found it very difficult to descend from the pinnacle of emotion on which her dancing left her, so she understood only too well why Hanno of Minassa, perhaps a less experienced performer, didn't want to face a barrage of enthusiastic praise and sycophantic flattery after that heartbreaking last song.

'My heart still longs for Penya . . .'

How had he known? For it was true, of course. Like a traveller long lost in the hostile sands of the Ma'alkwen desert, she yearned for the cool turquoise waters of her home. And she did not even possess a true picture of what she had lost, for her memories, filtered through a child's eyes, were distorted and incomplete. And there would be no going back, never, never, never . . .

The night wore on. She talked to Sargenay, to another friend, Islan the famous artist, and to Metru, who had come in, as was her habit, for the last hour or two. The water-clock, freshly filled every evening, dripped away softly on the wall until the lower chamber was almost full. The air grew thick and hot with sweat, body odour, stale perfume and the all-pervasive reek of khlar, so strong it was beginning to invade her mind at second hand. Gradually the room began to empty, until at last only she and a few die-hards – Sargenay, Islan and a couple of his friends, and K'tyaalin – were left.

The serving girls were clearing the tables, and the eastern sky outside the balcony windows was beginning to pale. The water-clock trilled suddenly, indicating that the upper chamber was empty, and Mallaso stood up, stretching her long slender body with a dancer's grace. 'That's it,' she said to her five remaining customers. 'Time for you to go. I need my beauty sleep.'

'Nothing could make you more beautiful,' said Islan, rising to his feet. He was a native of Tulyet, and looked like one of the

notorious bandits infesting that mountainous country, with rings
in both ears and a wickedly handsome face under an exuberant
mop of curly dark hair. Like Sargenay and his robes and unconventional beard, his appearance was deliberately intended to
confirm and enhance his reputation. He had two long-suffering
wives and a string of concubines, and had been Mallaso's first
lover after she left the Blue Hyacinth. She hadn't regretted his
reminder that love could be made for reasons of friendship and
affection as well as for pure lust or mercenary gain, but Islan was
as rampant as a tomcat and she'd never liked the idea of being
one of such a vast number. Once, he'd even had the cheek to list,
in her bed, all the women he'd had in the past five days. He
certainly meant more to her as a friend than as a lover, and he
had been so understanding when she explained her reasons for
ending the affair that she knew she had made the right decision.

One man who had once been her lover, one who wanted to
be, and one who never would. She bid them good-night, and saw
Sargenay's swift, significant glance. He made sure he was the last
to leave, and lingered close to her as the others went out. 'A word
in your ear, dearest Mallaso.'

'Make it quick,' she said, suppressing a yawn, though she
knew he wouldn't be offended.

'I know who the sorcerer is.'

If he'd expected her to be agog, he was doomed to disappointment: it was too late at night, or early in the morning, to rouse
much interest. 'Yes?' Mallaso enquired.

'Perhaps I won't say anything. Perhaps I'll let you find out for
yourself. I'll tell you one thing, though – he doesn't want it
known. He's got it under bar and lock and key – nine out of ten
wouldn't even have sensed him, and it took me all night to locate
him. I have a special talent in that direction,' said Sargenay, with
a look of arch pride.

'There's no need to preen yourself. What does it matter to
me? As long as my customers pay their money and behave themselves on my premises, I don't care if they're sorcerers or
murderers or two-headed demons in disguise. Anyway, there's no
harm in sorcery.'

'That's where you're wrong, lovely Mallaso.' Sargenay looked
very solemn, and she was so tired that she almost laughed.
'There's a great deal of harm in sorcery. It's not all weather-
working and love-spells and making Illusions and finding lost

property, I can assure you. You ought to know that, being a
Penyan.'

'I was taken when I was ten years old. I was too young to have
been initiated into the Mysteries. *You* know that.'

He obviously heard the abrasive note in her voice, for he
smiled in apology and touched her arm. 'I had forgotten. Forgive
me, lovely Mallaso – I understand how you must feel tonight.'

'I don't feel anything except exhausted,' she told him. It
wasn't true – she was tense, touchy, her nerves stretched and
scraped bare by the unaccustomed friction of raw emotion. 'Go
on, Sargenay, please tell me. Who's the sorcerer? That huge man
from Balki with rings on every finger?'

And Sargenay said softly, 'Oh, no, my dear. Hanno of Minassa is the sorcerer.'

There was a small, plummeting silence. Mallaso stared at him,
and her pet mage stared back. Finally she said, 'Are you sure?'

'I'm sure. I knew for certain when he came over to our table.
And he knew that I knew. That's why he wouldn't sit down with
us.'

'I don't understand.' She pushed her fingers into the sides of
her forehead, where a dull ache had begun, the legacy of a long
night and too much noise and wine and khlar smoke. 'What's
wrong with being a sorcerer? I know at least half a dozen.
They're everywhere in Toktel'yi. It's not like Kerenth, where it's
restricted to women, or in those northern cities . . .' Her voice
trailed off.

'Exactly. Those northern cities where it's fôrbidden. Though
apparently the King of Zithirian is a sorcerer. This man's from
Minassa, isn't he? That's why, then. He's probably had to keep it
hidden.' Sargenay's eyes gleamed speculatively. 'I could show him
that sorcery is the most respected branch of the Five Arts.'

'Don't you ever give up? That young man is surely only
interested in his music. Go home, Illusion-maker, and leave me in
peace.'

'I will.' The sorcerer's manner became suddenly and
uncharacteristically earnest. 'But dearest Mallaso – if you are
ever worried, or frightened – if you ever need help – you know
who to ask, don't you? I will always come.'

'Oh, Sargenay.' She smiled at him, unable to feel annoyed. 'It
will never happen, I hope, but – thank you. You're my truest
friend.'

'Truer than any other,' he said, and kissed her cheek lightly as he left.

The girls had gone. Umai locked the door behind the sorcerer, and went off to his room. Usually he escorted Metru home, but as she was taking Demon back to his owner, his presence wasn't necessary. The attack-dog was a far more effective deterrent to robbers even than a burly Onnakan built like an ironwood tree. Mallaso bid them good-night, or good-morning, and stood still for a moment in the centre of the dancing floor, trying to force herself to relax. If she didn't, she knew she would never get to sleep.

It was impossible. Images jostled in her head: Sargenay's serious eyes and voice, warning her of the dangers of sorcery; the floor filling with dancers; and the face of Hanno of Minassa, pale hair, black eyes, letting her see that he had perceived her pain.

She turned and walked out to the balcony. The sun was almost up, and the sky behind the huddle of slums across Cormorant Channel was a pale and luminous yellow. Overhead, the last and brightest stars were fading fast. This hour was always the coolest, and a breeze blew refreshingly up from the sea. Mallaso leaned on the rail, enjoying the wind's touch through the thin gauzy material of her dress.

'Madam?'

She whipped round, startled, though she should have remembered she wasn't alone in the house. The musician stood at the further end of the balcony, by the steps. He walked towards her, and stopped just a couple of strides away. Under the lank strands of pale hair, his face showed concern. 'You don't feel well. Can I help?'

Mallaso thought of asking how he knew she was here, how he knew of her headache, but of course if Sargenay was right, such questions were unnecessary. She said forbiddingly, 'I don't think so, thank you.'

'Your head hurts. I would like to help.'

He'd repelled her previous friendly overtures so firmly that this offer astonished her. She asked bluntly, 'Why?'

His dark gaze didn't waver. 'Because I can. And because by doing so, I can repay some of the debt.'

Mallaso didn't ask what he meant. She said at last, 'Can you do it here?'

'Of course. It's cooler out here, anyway.' He paused, and then came close. He was exactly the same height as she was, and above the loose cream cotton robe, his skin was flushed with sunburn. She wondered again what had happened to him, and such was the exhausted disarray of her mind that she nearly asked him, but stopped herself in time.

'You can begin,' she said, and braced herself, knowing what was coming. Sargenay had sometimes cured her headaches this way.

The touch of his fingers on her forehead was cool and impersonal. She closed her eyes, feeling the breeze on her hot skin, waiting for the flaring intensity of pain that would be its last defence before dying.

It didn't come. Instead, the tension and the sharp throbbing ache drained away quite suddenly, and were gone. Mallaso gave a deep sigh of relief. Despite the long, fraught night, she felt suddenly very relaxed, and absurdly light-hearted.

'Has it gone?'

She nodded, smiling. 'Yes, thank you. I'm very grateful. I should be able to sleep now.'

'I'm glad of that,' he said, and smiled back. For the first time, other than when he played, she could see genuine emotion in his face. And it was a very attractive smile.

'Sargenay told me that you were a sorcerer,' she said, shedding her usual caution.

'Did he? I thought he might. Do you mind?'

'Of course not. I don't care if you've got two heads or breathe fire, if you play like you did tonight then all our fortunes are made. I don't know how they treat sorcerers in Minassa,' said Mallaso, wondering why she was suddenly talking to him as if he were an old friend. 'But here in Toktel'yi, magic is an ancient and honoured profession. If you ask Sargenay nicely, he might get you enrolled with the Guild – then you'd be able to practise legally. You'd do very well – you can Heal much more gently than anyone else I've tried.'

He shook his head slightly. 'No. I – I have renounced sorcery. I am a musician, pure and simple.'

Mallaso stared at him in bewilderment. 'But I thought – but you still must take Annatal?'

The impersonal look slid back over his face. 'Yes,' he said curtly.

'And you offered to Heal my headache. You knew I had it –

that must have taken a degree of sorcery. And you knew how – how I felt about that last song. Once you become a sorcerer, you can't just cast it aside like an old cloak.'

'Perhaps not,' said Hanno of Minassa. 'But I am a musician now. And I would be grateful if you could keep my other talents to yourself.' And without any other courtesy, he turned and walked back along the balcony, the sound of his bare feet hardly audible even in the comparative quiet of dawn.

Mallaso turned and stared out over the sliding brown water of Cormorant Channel, lit by the first blinding brilliance of sunrise. It was not this familiar, squalidly picturesque scene that filled her eyes, though, but another view entirely. Water deep and still, the marvellous pure blue of a peacock's breast; small, graceful boats riding at anchor, or drifting into harbour, their bright red and yellow sails drooping in the hot, dreamy air; white-painted houses, with rough-cast walls and flat roofs covered with the luxuriant growth of climbing plants, fruits and flowers; the incessant harping of the crickets and the sudden, piercing song of a blue-wing serenading his mate; the laughter of children at school in a courtyard, under the shade of an ancient, convoluted tentellen tree, with its big yellow flowers and sweet scent; the chanting of the old songs, the old rhymes and stories by which the lore and legends of Penya were transmitted from one generation to the next; the haunting tremulous sound of the battered three-stringed enedo, which her mother used to play when she thought no one could hear her.

With a sob, Mallaso wrenched herself free from her memories, and ran upstairs to her room.

'Of course we have a claim on them.' The Emperor glared round at his Council. Sometimes, he wondered why he didn't get rid of this lot as he had the last. But although some of them had a habit of making idiotic suggestions, and others had to be bullied into opening their mouths, he was usually satisfied with his choice. And of course, the memory of what had befallen their predecessors would be a very compelling reminder of their duties. They had every incentive to crush dissent in the provinces, to collect every last silver chip of taxes due, and to ensure that his huge Empire continued to function with the smooth efficiency that had glued this vast, diverse and unwieldy collection of states and peoples together for more than two thousand years.

'The heir to the Minassan throne is married to my sister,' Ba'alekkt went on. 'Their baby son is my nephew. My grandmother was a Zithiriani princess, and the present King of Zithirian is my cousin. In the wider sense, both Temiltan and Ansaryon are members of my family. And at my bidding, my father helped them to drive out the Ska'i, fifteen years ago. They have never repaid the debt. And now, I think it is time to call it in.'

He obviously relished the prospect. Further round the table, General Sekkenet looked like an attack-dog scenting prey at last. The other men – governors of provinces, ministers in various state departments – did their best to imitate him. Only the dark face of Al'Kalyek, the Court Sorcerer, showed any doubts.

'Imperial Majesty, have you considered the reputation of King Ansaryon? His powers of sorcery helped to defeat the Ska'i, after all.'

'With the aid of his bastard son, who was Sacrificed in Kerenth more than three years ago. The best day's work that Queen ever did, in my opinion. No, he is now in Olyak's lowest halls, and can trouble us no longer.'

'His father's powers are still considerable,' Al'Kalyek pointed out gently. 'And although he is the only sorcerer of any great skill in Zithirian, his other children share his abilities. It will not be long before they, too, will become adept – I believe the eldest is now thirteen.'

'Then if you are going to strike, Imperial Majesty,' said the Spymaster, Olkanno, 'it must be soon. And your priority must be the extinction of the entire Royal Family of Zithirian. No one, not even the baby, must be spared.'

'And in Minassa?'

'King Temiltan and his son will die too. And as you have just pointed out, your beloved sister K'djelk is married to Prince Cathallon. It would seem most convenient to install her young son as King of both cities – he is of the Royal line of Tayo, after all, so he would be acceptable to the population. Then your sister can act as Regent, or you can appoint a suitable governor.'

'Really, Olkanno, I might almost believe you were a sorcerer – you have stated my own plans exactly.' Ba'alekkt looked round the table, grinning. 'We tried to conquer those lands nearly two centuries ago, and failed. This time we will not fail. Tulyet is under control now, and Penya has been subdued at last. The hour has come for us to add to the glory of the Empire. Next year, as soon as the rainy season ends, we will gather our armies on the borders. I rely upon you, Sekkenet, to prepare your men for the onslaught. You may have as many as you require, and all the supplies and equipment you need, regardless of expense. In a year's time, we will have Zithirian's mines under our control, and money spent now will be recouped a thousandfold later. Do you understand me?'

Sekkenet nodded, his small eyes gleaming. 'I do indeed, Imperial Majesty – and I am most grateful for your trust in me.'

'Good. I know I can leave it all in your competent hands.' Ba'alekkt leaned back, an avaricious smile on his handsome face. 'We will discuss our strategy in more detail at our next meeting. And although I will make no formal declaration of war, I do not propose to keep this plan a secret.'

There was a brief, shocked silence. Around the table, the councillors looked at each other, wondering whether anyone would dare to utter the necessary words of reason and common sense.

At last, Sekkenet spoke, his voice quiet and persuasive. 'Perhaps, Imperial Majesty, you might think again, and reconsider that decision? If the Kings of Zithirian and Minassa are made aware of our plans, they will be given ample time to prepare their defences.'

Ba'alekkt stared at him. 'I did not think you so foolhardy, General, as to question my judgement. I am Emperor, after all – had you forgotten that?'

'No, Imperial Majesty. Your command, of course, must be obeyed. But I have many years experience in this field, and I understand the value of surprise.'

'You should know, General, none better, that our strength is overwhelming. My armies are the finest in the known world, now and in all the ages of the past. The King of Zithirian himself told me, many years ago, that one Toktel'yan soldier is worth ten of any other. They are armed with steel spears and double-edged swords, they are protected with armour and shields, they are trained to march and fight and kill without mercy. And what can Minassa and Zithirian produce in their defence? Only a huddle of civilians armed with blunt spears and warped arrows, led by two kings who have never experienced true warfare. If you imagine that they could even persuade their subjects to the field of battle, let alone mount an effective opposition, then you are flattering them and deluding yourself. Do I make myself clear, General? After all, anyone foolish enough to believe that such a rabble could trouble my superb fighting machine, must be dangerously close to treachery.'

His eyes glittered malevolently, inviting further conflict. Beside Sekkenet, Al'Kalyek nudged him warningly under the table with his foot.

At last the General, defeated, lowered his gaze submissively. There would be no shortage of others to take his place if Ba'alekkt had him executed for dissent: but none of those others could match his competence and ability to command. Let the foolish boy trumpet his plans all over the Empire and beyond, if he wanted. At least if he, Sekkenet, remained in command of the army, there was an excellent chance that he could retrieve any advantage that Ba'alekkt's lunatic vanity and over-confidence would lose them.

'I am your very obedient servant, Imperial Majesty,' he said, concealing his anger and humiliation with the skill of long practice.

'Good. Just make sure you remember it. I have given this matter a great deal of thought, and it is by far the best strategy. With winter already upon them, they will be unable to prepare for our invasion until the spring. Rumours will abound, playing on their fears, sapping their morale. Our ambassadors will deny everything, of course, but in such a way that they will not be universally believed. If the populations of Minassa and Zithirian can be induced to panic, so much the better. It will make your work, my friend, Sekkenet, so much easier.' He yawned, and smiled menacingly at his councillors. 'Does anyone else have any . . . suggestions to make? Excellent. I knew you would agree. And now, I will dismiss you. I have the most delightful new concubine, skilled in all the sweetest arts, and she kept me awake all night. I really must rest. Good day to you all, and we will meet again tomorrow, at the usual time.'

One by one his thirty councillors filed out. Ba'alekkt watched them go, his eyes narrowed, seeking any further signs of reluctance or dissent. There were none. He had indeed chosen well.

He rose to his feet, and snapped his fingers to summon his personal slaves. With the business of government concluded, the rest of the long hot day stretched ahead of him. And where better to spend it than in the cool shade of the latticed pavilion in the garden of his Imperial suite, sampling the lazy pleasures offered by one, or some, or many of his seventy concubines?

CHAPTER
TWELVE

The last day of the last month of the year was marked in Toktel'yi by a festival in commemoration of Akkatanat, the first King, or Emperor, who had supposedly been born at this time. The Toktel'yans were a people dedicated to the joint pursuits of wealth and pleasure, and this had always been encouraged by successive Emperors and the priests of Kaylo and Olyak, the official deities. Those who resented Imperial rule were savagely crushed. Those who resigned themselves to it were rewarded with prosperity (for some), peace, and all the other benefits and disadvantages of a well-organized and bureaucratic government. Included amongst the former were the arenas built in every major town and city, accommodating horse-races, exhibition fights between troops of slaves, theatrical and musical performances, and other crowd-pleasing spectacles. In provincial capitals such as Mynak, Terebis or Sabrek, you could go to a different public entertainment every night, and wind up the evening at one of the numerous brothels that were known as Little Temples, because, like those of Kaylo and Olyak, they were exempt from tax.

But Toktel'yi had been built on mud-flats and reclaimed marshes, and had no suitable site for a grandiose arena of the sort provincial residents took for granted. Plays and performances on a small scale were held in the Palace Square, in the Old City. And once a month, horse-racing took place on the broad sweeping strand along the sea-shore, close to the new Palace. All the meetings were popular, but the biggest crowds attended the races held on Akkatanat's Giftday, at the turn of the year, just before the start of the rainy season. They came to watch the horses, bet on the results, and patronize the side-shows, drinking-booths, kuldi-sellers, khlar vendors, snake-trancers, whores of both sexes, and all the other services and goods that Toktel'yans considered essential to sweeten their path through life.

Every year, Mallaso said she wouldn't go: every year, she was

swept off by her friends, half-heartedly protesting, and trying to
pretend that she wasn't really enjoying herself. This time, her fifth
as proprietor of the Golden Djarlek, was no exception. When the
rest of Toktel'yi was decking itself out in its finery, counting its
coins and looking forward with eager anticipation to the holiday,
Temek was trying to persuade her to wear something more exotic
than a plain green gown, scarf and veil.

Mallaso had no intention of flaunting herself in something
exotic. A woman wearing anything other than the all-enveloping
dress expected of Toktel'yan females in public would be assumed
to be selling herself. As she always did in the end, she compro-
mised, putting on a thin cotton gown with narrow braid at neck,
hem and sleeve, with a matching scarf and veil for her head. No
jewellery: she didn't want to encourage the army of thieves and
pickpockets who infested any gathering, and especially Akkatanat's Races.

They didn't start until two hours before sunset, when the
noon heat had had a chance to cool. And she had her own private
ceremony to perform now, as she had on this day for fifteen years.

She gathered up what she needed and went out on to the
balcony. The heat struck her like a wall through the loose cotton
dress, but she ignored it, and the rancid stink wafting up from the
festering channel below. She went quickly down the back stairs,
and at their foot encountered Hanno of Minassa.

He had been part of her household for nearly two months
now, and she still knew little more about him than what she'd
discovered on his first day. He kept his part of the bargain, and
played like an inhabitant of Kaylo's Paradise on his allotted
nights: she'd had to turn so many away that she had increased his
bookings, much to Djekkel's disgust. By now, he must have a fair
sum stowed away in his room, for he hadn't spent any of it. He
seldom went out, he didn't buy clothes, and he didn't seem to
have any expensive habits like khlar, or dancing girls, or drink.
His Annatal must cost something, but she supposed he still had a
good supply with him. Certainly he didn't take it in public, unlike
Sargenay, who got Metru to mix it into a special batch of her
sweet sticky cakes. Mallaso was still interested in him, curious
about the secrets lurking behind his enigmatic face, but she no
longer expected to attract him, much though she would have
liked to.

'Hallo,' she said, with her usual empty smile. 'Are you coming to the Races later on? Sargenay has hired a boat, and there's room for you.'

His dark eyes looked blankly at her. 'I might,' said the musician, his voice flatly non-committal.

'You should,' Mallaso said briskly. 'You spend far too much time in your room. This is supposed to be the most wonderful city in the known world, and I don't suppose you've been out in it more than half a dozen times since you've been here.'

'I've no particular desire to be robbed,' he said gravely, but with an unexpected flare of mischief in his eyes.

'With Umai in our party, who's going to dare?' Mallaso said, mildly exasperated. 'Anyway, you're a – '

'That's my affair,' he said sharply. 'As we agreed.'

'Yes.' Mallaso surveyed him with more than a touch of impatience, and then suddenly held out her hands. 'I don't like this. I don't like feeling there's a stranger in my house. The people I hire are my friends – except for Djekkel, and he and his quartet came with the premises. I want you to come with us later, and see the Races, and enjoy yourself.'

'And if I don't?'

'I can't *force* you to be my friend!' Mallaso cried. She dropped her hands and glared at him. 'You have a soul. I've heard it in your singing. Why can't you let a little of yourself go?'

No answer, save for that blank stare. Mallaso gave a snort of annoyance, and brushed past him. Furious with him and with herself, she stalked into the street outside, draping her veil over her head, and heard running steps behind her.

'Wait!' said Hanno of Minassa. He caught up with her and stood in front of her, blocking her way. 'I'm sorry. I didn't realize how you felt.'

'Didn't you? You seem to know a lot else about me. And I know almost nothing about you. I don't even know if Hanno is your real name.'

It isn't.

The thought dropped into her mind, and rang with truth. He said, 'I owe you a great deal, and I've been more than a little rude and ungrateful. I'll gladly come with you this afternoon – if you'll let me come with you now.'

'No!' Mallaso said in angry astonishment. 'This is private, for me alone.'

'This is Akkatanat's Giftday, the last day of the year. It's also the Penyan Day of the Dead, isn't it? Did you think you were the only one with memories to mourn?'

Never, never had she had a companion. Even as a slave, lighting hoarded stubs of tapers and launching them into the fountain pool of her owner's house, she had managed to avoid detection. For this day had been a solemn festival on Penya, when each family remembered those they had loved and lost, and sent tiny candle-boats out into the night sea to commemorate the departed. It was one of her clearest memories, seeing her mother launch the light that represented her grandmother's soul, and the host of tiny valiant flames dotting the dark waters of the harbour.

'No,' she said at last. 'But you are not from Penya.'

'I have been there, though.'

Mallaso's heart contracted. She longed to ask him how it was, how it looked, and yet she was terrified of the answer. Finally, she said softly, 'So you know what I am going to do?'

'Yes – but why during the day?'

'Because here it would not be safe in the dark. I would need protection.'

'And now you have me, even if it is broad daylight.'

At last, Mallaso nodded in assent, and gestured for him to escort her. She did not trust herself to speak, and for a while they walked side by side through the busy streets in silence.

Behind the Old Palace, at the apex of the triangular island on which the Old City stood, lay a neglected garden. The Toktel'yan officials who occupied the building now had no interest in it, and the land was gradually sinking back into the swamp from which it had been made. Mallaso led her musician along uneven, muddy paths, past overgrown shrubs and bronze statues blurred green with verdigris and draped with rampant foliage. Birds as bright as flowers flew from branch to branch above their heads, shrieking and whooping. The bustle and noise of the Old City lay only a hundred strides away, but this place resembled a jewelled fragment of some tropical forest on one of the southernmost islands of the Archipelago. Onnak, perhaps, or Jo'ami . . .

'The Toktel'yans are not lovers of wild nature,' Mallaso said. 'They like to tame it, and set it into gardens. No-one comes here now – it's too chaotic and uncivilized. Sooner or later someone will hack it all down and dump bargefuls of stone in the mud, and build on it, and never notice what they've destroyed in the process.'

They had come nearly to the water's edge. Reeds and rushes grew here, and a grove of low, flat-topped swamp trees with their roots twined deep in the mud. Dragonflies, iridescent blue and green, buzzed to and fro in the sun, preying on the countless midges swarming above the reeds. In front of them lay a circular lagoon, one side lapping gently at Mallaso's feet, the other opening on to the river beyond, where the main stream of the Kefirinn flowed left to the docks, to the right down Cormorant Channel.

The woman from Penya knelt in the soft, bitter mud. From the bag on her shoulder, she took out four small boat-shaped pieces of wood, each one concave at the top. Into the hollows she placed a brief length of cotton string, neatly cut and trimmed. Then she picked up two tiny glass vials, removed the stoppers and poured a few drops from both on to each wick.

The musician stood, looking down at her. He watched as she removed scarf and veil, leaving her close-cropped hair exposed to the dappled shade under the trees. She bowed her head, her arms crossed in an attitude of prayer, or deepest sorrow. Then she placed a small taper on the ground in a patch of sunlight, and withdrew a convex circle of glass from the bag. She held it above the taper so that the sun's rays, passing through, concentrated on the cotton wick below in a tiny fierce core of light.

The taper began to smoulder, then to burn. Mallaso put the glass back in the bag and picked up the length of waxed cord. Her soft chant was in Penyan, which was closely related to the language spoken in Kerenth, but the man beside her gave no sign that he understood.

'For your soul, Tipeya my mother, I light this flame. For your soul, Saaray my father, I light this flame. For your souls, Tarrenett and Elkar my brothers, I light these flames. May you shine for ever in the face of the darkness of death, and may Sarraliss the Mother of us all take you to Her breast. I, Mallaso, your daughter and sister, remember you with love.'

One by one, the chips of wood were launched into the lagoon, each topped with a small and steadfast flame. Mallaso watched them, her hands still crossed over her breast. A breeze caught them and spun them round in the centre of the pool, out in the dazzling sunlight. For a moment longer she knelt there, watching until the flames died, and then rose to her feet and turned back to her companion.

'I have finished – they are remembered,' she said softly,

hoping that he would not notice, in this dim shade, that her eyes were full of tears. 'Shall we go home?'

'If that is what you want.'

She nodded, and glanced ruefully down at her muddy dress. 'I have to change, and Sargenay will come for us soon. If I'm not back, he'll send out a search-party, and our lives won't be worth living.'

'Is he your lover?'

'*Sargenay?*' Mallaso laughed suddenly. 'Hardly. He's only interested in boys, the more beautiful the better. He fancies you – or hadn't you noticed?'

Hanno of Minassa gave her a rather wry grin. 'Yes, I had, but I assumed he faced both ways.'

'Most do, but not Sargenay. It's one of the reasons why he's such a good friend. There is nothing else to come between us.'

'Would you like there to be?'

Mallaso had begun walking back towards the Old City, life, reality. She stopped and turned to face him. 'No,' she said slowly. 'No, I wouldn't. I tried to have Islan both as a friend and a lover, and it didn't work. We argued too much, and I didn't like being one of many. Now, we don't share a bed, not even occasionally, and we get on much better.'

'So you have no lover at the moment?'

'I'm as celibate as one of Olyak's monks,' Mallaso said lightly, although her heart had begun to quicken. 'But not vowed to it.'

'I'm glad. It would be a waste.'

The message in his eyes was unmistakable. She smiled at him, letting him know her own feelings, and touched him gently on the hand. 'Thank you. But we should go back now, or Sargenay will be tearing his beard out.'

The sorcerer was indeed waiting for her in the empty dining hall, his smoothly handsome brow thunderously furrowed. 'Mallaso! Thank Kaylo – where have you been?'

'Where I always go on this day,' she said. Hanno had already returned to his room, so Sargenay wouldn't realize that he had accompanied her. And somehow, she didn't want to admit that she had shared her private moments of grief with a man she hardly knew, in preference to her dearest friend.

Leaving him scowling his disapproval, she hurried upstairs to change into another dress, dyed a rich mixture of opalescent greens and blues. The deep, vivid colours set off her dark skin and enhanced her slender grace, and she had no need of any other adornment. She draped a loose gauzy veil round her head and face, leaving only her eyes exposed to public view, and ran back down to Sargenay with a degree of anticipation that she had never felt before on Akkatanat's Giftday.

The boat was big, and needed to be. As well as herself, Sargenay, Metru, Temek, Umai and Hanno, the party included Islan and his friend Bereth, a sculptor from Ukkan, along with Islan's current bed-mate, a dancing girl who worked at a dubious tavern down by South Bridge, and Bereth's favourite concubine, a pert red-head of Fabrizi origins and appropriately uncouth manners. Four water-men manned the oars, and once their passengers were safely aboard, propelled the boat out into Cormorant Channel and upstream, with the incoming tide, under the North Bridge and round the tip of the Old City's island, to join the stream of craft, large and small, rowing down to the strand where the races were to be held.

Mallaso sat amidships, between Sargenay and Hanno. The Tatht sorcerer had recovered his good humour, and talked about the certainty in the third race, on which he had wagered a fair amount of money. Bereth, a loud and opinionated man whom Mallaso didn't particularly like, disagreed with his choice, and a voluble discussion developed, in which the four women, and the musician, took no part.

Instead, Mallaso watched the crowded docks slide past, a familiar sight transformed by this different viewpoint, and thought of Penya: How many of those ships were bound for the island she still called her home? How easy would it be to sell the lease on the tavern, pack her few possessions, abandon her friends and journey back into her past?

She wouldn't ever do it, of course, for she was terrified of what she would find. The song was right: let her memories of Penya as it once had been remain untainted by the island's terrible fate.

'Do you ever bet?'

It was the musician. She turned away from contemplation of the ships, and smiled. 'No. It's not one of my vices. Sargenay doesn't either, except on special occasions, but to hear him you'd think he was a seasoned gambler.'

'Then why do you go to the races?'

'For the same reason as everyone else. To watch the spectacle, to enjoy a day off, to forget my problems – '

'Have you any problems?'

'One or two,' said Mallaso. 'The chief one being that I've booked a passage in three days' time, to see my daughter on Tekkt. And now I'm not sure I can go.'

'Metru told me you had a daughter. How old is she?'

'Six.' Mallaso smiled, thinking of Grayna, her beautiful smile, her carefree laughter. One day . . .

'I have a little sister . . .' Hanno's voice stopped abruptly, as if he had revealed more than he had intended.

Mallaso decided to probe. 'Have you? What's her name?'

'Zathti. She's slightly older than your daughter, she'd be about eight now, I think.'

'What's she like? Is she naughty, or good?'

'Good?' He grinned reminiscently. 'No. Good at being a nuisance, good at mischief, good at annoying her brothers – but not *good*. Is your daughter?'

'Grayna is like most children – she wants her own way, but she can be so loving, so sweet . . .' She glanced at him. 'If I go to Tekkt, will you come with me?'

That did surprise him. 'Why? Why me?'

'Because I can't travel alone. Sargenay usually escorts me, but he's having trouble with his boyfriend, and I think he's afraid he'll lose him if he leaves the city, even for ten days. Umai has to look after the eating-house, and Islan's second wife is expecting a baby any moment, and he hopes it'll be a son this time – he's got five daughters.' She lowered her voice. 'I don't want to ask Bereth. He can be quite entertaining company, when he wants, but I don't like him – or trust him.'

'And you trust me?'

'Oh, yes,' said Mallaso softly. 'I know next to nothing about you, but in the things that matter, I trust you. Will you come?'

'I should be delighted to accept, Madam,' he said with mock formality, and smiled.

Their boat tied up at the wharves below the New Palace. These were low, wooden structures designed to take smaller craft, unlike the stone-built docks lining the river upstream. Sargenay paid the oarsmen to wait for them, and they disembarked one by one and joined the crowds of people, thousands of them, pouring through the palms and sand-dunes to the shore where the races were held.

Of course, with such numbers present, a good vantage point was at a premium, and the dunes nearest the finishing flag had been roped off by some enterprising individuals, who were charging exorbitant sums for admission. Sargenay ushered his party into the most expensive of all, dropping a shower of silver half-Imperials into the doorman's hand with a casual air that didn't deceive Mallaso, who knew that he'd spent a lot of money to keep his temperamental catamite sweet. She resolved to pay him over the odds when he performed his public Illusion, so that his pride wouldn't be hurt.

They sat beneath parasols made of loosely woven rushes, waving palm-frond fans, drinking the warm wine and tepid chicken on offer in the enclosure. Mallaso glanced at the others in their party. Sargenay was entertaining Islan and Bereth by using his sorcery to interfere with the clothing of an aristocratic lady sitting ten strides away. Every so often a breeze would arrive from nowhere and tug at her loosely wrapped veil, disclosing glimpses of her remarkably fine features. To vary it, he let the wind pull her dress, moulding the light cloth revealingly against her body. Mallaso watched with a feeling of irritation. *Children's games*, she thought, as Bereth sniggered like an overgrown schoolboy at the sight of an outlined breast. *To achieve his power, he takes a drug that'll age that handsome face long before its time and then preserve it like a shrivelled insect in amber for far longer than is natural – and then despite all his high words about his Art, he uses sorcery for purposes so negligible and frivolous that most people would be ashamed of it.*

'We're not all like that, you know.'

It was Hanno. His face was serious, and she couldn't tell if he'd used ordinary perception, or sorcery, to read her thoughts. She turned away from the other men, and gave him her full attention. 'No, I know you're not. Nor is Sargenay, usually. It's just that when he's with Islan and Bereth, he seems to need to be one of the lads. A lot of Toktel'yan men are like that. On their own, they can be charming, courteous, thoughtful, friendly. Throw them together, and they're about as sensitive as a pack of unleashed Onnak hounds.'

'I'm not from Toktel'yi.'

'I know that,' Mallaso said. 'But are you from Minassa?'

His dark eyes held hers. 'Yes,' said the man who called himself Hanno, and she knew he was lying.

The trumpets blew for the arrival of the Emperor, down on the shore. He rode in a gilded, canopied palanquin borne by six huge slaves, and followed by several dozen more, carrying his most important ministers and officials, his favourite concubines, his young unmarried sister Djeneb, and the Archpriest of Kaylo, robed in sunshine yellow, and his counterpart of Olyak, clad in gloomy grey. The litters took up the plum position by the winning post, thus blocking many people's view, and with another blast of the ceremonial bronze trumpets, the Emperor declared his ancestor's Giftday Races under way.

Mallaso didn't have much interest in horses, but she liked the ones who were raced in Toktel'yi. They were a different breed entirely from the narrow-chested, scrawny nags that were common in less waterlogged parts of the Empire. These were sturdy, compact beasts with well-muscled quarters and gracefully arched necks. They paraded first, garlanded with flowers, prancing and scuffing through the soft hot sand, the boy riders on their backs waving to the cheering throng.

'That's mine,' said Sargenay, abandoning his sport with the unknown lady. 'That grey, there, see, with the red garland and the rider in blue. S'k'gann owns him, you know, the Minister of Roads. He bought that one in Zithirian last summer, paid a fortune for it.'

'Did he?' Bereth's rather loud voice carried clearly to Mallaso. 'He should have waited. This time next year, he'll have the pick of thousands of prime horses from Zithirian, and he won't have to pay a copper for them.'

'What do you mean?' asked Islan, who was playing footsie with the giggling dancing girl.

'Haven't you heard? I got it from K'tyaalin this morning. The Emperor, may Kaylo bless his days and give him long life, is planning an attack on the northern cities. It's no secret – I expect he wants them shitting themselves before the army even marches. And then Minassa and Zithirian will be part of our glorious Empire, and all their gold and silver and horses will be anyone's for the taking.'

Beside Mallaso, Hanno had become very still. She thought of the flames above Penya, the slaughter and the destruction, the suffering and grief, and felt sick. Bereth came from Ukkan, which had been part of the Empire for more than a thousand years: he could have no idea of the terrible reality lurking behind his cheerfully casual words.

Sargenay was frowning, but in this very public place it was

more than anyone's life was worth to express disapproval of their aggressive, greedy and all-powerful Emperor. Mallaso looked down at the soft, shady sand under her fingers, gold beneath black, and curled her hand into a tight fist of impotent rage and hatred.

'You're from Minassa, aren't you?' Bereth said to Hanno suddenly, as if he'd only just remembered it.

The musician's taut body jerked as if pulled by a string. As Mallaso stared at him, he lifted his eyes to the sculptor's, and the bleak darkness in them raised the hairs on her neck. 'Yes,' he said, in the curt voice that gave nothing away.

'Well, you'd better send a message home. Tell them that it's their duty to welcome the Imperial armies – they can look forward to a glorious future, as part of the greatest Empire the world has ever known!'

Hanno of Minassa went quite white under the sunburn, and the look on his f e made Mallaso shiver, as if a cold wind had brushed against her skin.'No,' he said softly. 'No – I would tell them to send the women and children and old men into the hills, and then stand and fight – for their homes, their lives, and above all for their freedom from tyranny and evil.'

Mallaso, suddenly afraid, touched the musician warningly on the shoulder. Bereth raised his eyebrows. 'That kind of talk is treason, you know,' he said, with sneering contempt. 'Much greater men than you, little djarlek player, have died in agony for words much less.'

Hanno of Minassa sprang to his feet. 'Treason, is it? To speak the truth? To desire life and freedom, not slavery and death? Your precious bloody Emperor has half the world grovelling at his feet, and still he's greedy for more – more deaths, more torture, more destruction, more misery – '

Mallaso jumped up too, and grabbed his arm. 'Come on,' she hissed urgently. 'Come on, let's leave now, before you say anything else you don't mean – '

'I mean every single word,' said the musician venomously. He was rigid with fury, and his dark eyes, fixed on Bereth, were menacingly intense.

Sargenay rose abruptly and took hold of Hanno's other arm. 'You heard the lady,' he said forcefully. 'Get out of here, quickly – come on, let's go.'

Between them, the woman and the sorcerer hustled Hanno out of the enclosure, leaving forty or fifty shocked and horrified faces staring after them. Despite his initial resistance, the musician came with them quite calmly, but his eyes were still wild with rage, and Mallaso could feel the muscles of his arm tingling under her fingers.

At the foot of the next sand dune, out of sight of the race, the sea and the people they had left behind, they stopped in the orange glare of the westering sun. Sargenay drew a shaking breath and wiped the sweat from his face. 'Sweet Kaylo, if you ever do that again, just make sure I'm well out of range, will you?'

'Do what?' Mallaso stared at her friend. The musician made no reply: he had closed his eyes, and seemed to be trying to control his fury.

'He was going to fry him,' Sargenay said, in a voice that only the three of them could hear. 'I felt it – that's why I told you to get him away, before he cooked Bereth in his own juices. By Olyak's bones, man, where did you get that kind of power?'

Hanno did not answer: he looked as if he had entered another world, deep within himself.

'He was going to *kill* Bereth?' Mallaso stared at Sargenay in bewilderment. 'How? With sorcery?'

'Of course with sorcery – that's why I knew. And any other mage within ten miles will know too – that level of power just can't be hidden. Al'Kalyek is with the Emperor – if he's got even half his wits about him, he'll be sending soldiers to look for the source of it, right now.'

'But *why*? I don't understand – '

'Because, lovely Mallaso, this man here, young and innocent though he looks, has more power in his little finger than I have in my whole body. You're not supposed to be able to kill with sorcery – but *he* can. What are you, Hanno of Minassa – if that's your real name? And how did you come by such power? Are you a demon?'

The flesh beneath Mallaso's fingers seemed real and human enough. The man shook his head. 'No,' he said, his voice sounding very remote. 'No, I'm not a demon.'

'Aren't you? Well, my advice to you is to get out of here – now, before the Emperor's soldiers find you. Your sort of power breaks all the natural laws of sorcery – at the very least, they'll want to find out how you do it. And I wouldn't wish a session with Olkanno's torturers on my worst enemy. Go on, quick, before they catch up with you. And if I were you, Mallaso, I'd tell him to return to his room, get his things and *go* – anywhere in the known world, so long as it's not near us. You're trouble, Hanno of Minassa, deep and dangerous trouble, and we don't want you.'

Abruptly, the fair-haired man pulled himself free from their grasp, and without another word walked away. Appalled, Mallaso stared at his retreating back as he strode towards the belt of palm trees that fringed the dunes. Then she turned to Sargenay. 'We can't – we can't let him go just like that!'

'You'd better, or we'll regret it. That man isn't human – he *can't* be. He doesn't take Annatal, I've never smelt it on him, but he's a sorcerer even so, and the most powerful one I've ever known. Stay away from him, dearest Mallaso, I beg you – he'll bring you nothing but grief.'

She knew Sargenay was talking sense, she knew he was only thinking of her safety, but she couldn't let the musician go – not like this, not with rage and despair in his heart, and the condemnation of those he had thought his friends echoing in his ears. 'I'll be back in a moment,' she said, and ran after him.

He was walking faster than she had realized, and she only caught up with him by the palm trees. She wasn't used to running in such heat, and the sweat was pouring off her skin, sticking her thin dress to her back and soaking her veil. 'Hanno!' she cried, and when he didn't turn round, she shouted again. 'Hanno – *please*, wait!'

He stopped then. Under the fronded palms, the shade was dappled over the loose sand and sparse scrub. A lizard, mottled gold and brown, scuttled away into the undergrowth. Behind them, distant cheering indicated that the first race had begun. But there was no one near: within the trees, they were quite alone.

'Was it true?' Mallaso demanded. 'Was it true, what Sargenay said?'

There was a very slight pause before Hanno nodded. 'Yes. He was right. I should go now, before they come looking for me. Once I'm back in the city, I can hide myself. I don't want to put you in danger – I'm too much in your debt. I wouldn't hurt you – I would never hurt you, not deliberately. But somehow I always seem to bring harm to everyone around me. I should forget you ever knew me. It's safer. I'll be all right, they'll never find me in the city. And I'll be leaving soon, anyway.'

'Yes,' Mallaso said softly. 'Aren't you escorting me to Tekkt?'

His eyes flew to hers, then he shook his head again. 'No – I can't.'

'Why not? No one else knows I've asked you. If you hide for a few days, you can join me on the ship. I'll tell Sargenay I've hired someone, for form's sake. And no one will think of looking for you on Tekkt.'

'They might follow you.'

'They might – but we won't meet till the ship sails.' She dropped her voice. 'It's your decision. I'll leave it open. The *Leaping Dolphin* leaves East Dock in three days' time, on the morning tide. I've booked two berths, and I'll hire a guard anyway – I know a reliable man, I've used him before. If you're on the ship, I'll send him home. If not – well, goodbye, Hanno of Minassa.'

He smiled then, and she added, 'I should go now. Get your things from your room and rent a place somewhere else. There's a lodging-house just the other side of the North Bridge – they'll ask no questions, and it's cheap. If I see you on the ship, I shall be glad. If I don't, may the Goddess smile on you always. But if what Sargenay said is true, then I should leave Toktel'yi very soon. You aren't exactly inconspicuous, and you certainly frightened the wits out of Bereth and everyone else. There's bound to be talk.'

'I frightened myself,' said Hanno of Minassa softly. 'I was a fool – I let the . . . anger rule me. I'm sorry.'

'You're not a fool.' Mallaso took a deep breath, her rich brown eyes staring at him above the blue and green veil. 'I understand why you got angry. I know how it feels. It's like a fire-mountain inside me – trying to control all the rage, and hatred, and grief, trying to live like everyone else, pretending it didn't happen, pretending that my life is here, now, pretending that I'm happy – and then a few thoughtless words and it all boils up and spills over. I wish we could do something to stop it – I wish beyond anything that there was a way to make your city and your family safe. But there's nothing anyone can do. When you leave Toktel'yi, you should go home, and try to help.'

'I can't,' he said. 'I can't ever go home. But thank you, Mallaso of Penya – thank you for your kindness and your help. I hope I haven't put you in danger. Goodbye.'

He gave her the two hands of friendship, briefly, and then with a final wave of farewell turned and walked out of the palms, back towards the river, the wharves, the city. For a moment, Mallaso stood and watched him go, and in her heart was a sudden grief, surprisingly sharp. For she knew that she could not expect to see him again.

CHAPTER
THIRTEEN

The *Leaping Dolphin* made the run to Tekkt, the nearest of the thousands of islands in the K'tali Archipelago, perhaps fifty times a year. She was an old ship, small by modern standards, but soundly constructed of Onnak ironwood, painted above the waterline in rich blue, with a long pale eye on either side of the bow to ward off sea-snakes and other mythical monsters and evil spirits.

She was mainly a cargo ship, ferrying supplies such as paper, cloth, oils and other luxury goods from the mainland, and carrying back the limited produce of Tekkt: dried fruit and nuts, sugar, peach wine, citrus fruits, and cages of the pretty blue and green parrots which were bred on the island. But at the start of the winter rainy season, when the wealthy of Toktel'yi left their unbearably hot, humid and disease-ridden city in droves, the *Leaping Dolphin*'s hold was turned into cabins with the aid of temporary wooden screens fastened to the deck beams above, and transported whole families, with their children, pets, slaves and luggage, to villas on the breezy, beautiful hillsides of Tekkt.

Mallaso owned no slaves, and no pets, and her belongings were limited, on this voyage, to a bundle of clothes and another bag full of gifts for Grayna, collected over the six months since she had last seen her daughter. Ten days was the most she could allow herself this time, and she meant to enjoy the little girl's company to the full.

She had sailed on the *Leaping Dolphin* several times previously, and arrived on the quayside about an hour before the ship was due to depart. She'd arranged to meet her guard, Grimek, a freed slave like herself, by the boarding-plank. If Hanno turned up, she would send her escort home: if not, he would accompany her to Tekkt and back. Grimek wouldn't blab, whatever happened. He was from Penya too, and although he was only an acquaintance, his loyalty to her was unquestionable and absolute.

Mallaso had expected some repercussions from that all too public argument between Bereth and Hanno, and found, to her considerable surprise and utter relief, that nobody mentioned it. Nor did any soldiers come looking for a sorcerer with too much power, either there on the strand or later, back at the eating-house.

Hanno had gone, leaving his room utterly empty, as if it had never been inhabited at all. Several customers, over the next three days, asked her about the musician with the golden voice, and she told them, as she told everyone, that he'd had an offer he couldn't refuse, and had gone off to play in Djebb to avoid the rainy season. It was so plausible that she almost believed it herself. She informed Sargenay, when he raised the subject the night before she was due to leave, that Hanno had gone for good. She knew he would disapprove of her asking the musician to escort her to Tekkt, but she was beginning to feel that the sorcerer's alarming forebodings had been greatly exaggerated. Perhaps, after they returned from Tekkt – *if* he was on the ship – Hanno might come back to sing again at Mallaso's, as if nothing had happened.

She arrived in a hired boat, less than an hour before the *Leaping Dolphin* was due to sail. The morning sun blazed pitilessly down on the dockworkers toiling up the boarding-plank, their backs bowed beneath bales of cotton cloth, jars of oil, packs of spices. The oarsman tied up at the quay just above the ship, and handed up her bags. She paid him, and looked round for Grimek. There was no sign of him, so she walked over to the ship, threading her way between the perspiring workers and ignoring their muttered abuse. Women alone in Toktel'yi, even veiled and clad, as she was, in unthreatening and unalluring grey from head to foot, were usually at the mercy of any man, but Mallaso had learned to ignore them. Nothing, after all, could be worse than what she had already suffered in her life.

She knew the Captain, L'ktek, quite well. He was elderly, his hair grizzled and his skin turned to the colour and texture of well-cured leather by the sun and wind of forty years at sea. Like so many sailors, he was a native of the Archipelago, some little island in the Scatterlings between Balki and Penya, so he didn't share conventional Toktel'yan attitudes to women. Still, she hoped that Grimek would turn up soon. Even L'ktek would think twice before allowing her to travel alone on his ship.

He was telling the labourers where to put the cargo in the *Leaping Dolphin*'s hold, and she had to cough loudly before he noticed her. 'Ah, Mallaso! Your usual cabin is ready for you, and your escort is already here, and waiting for you below. Forgive me, but I don't have time to talk now – we can't miss the tide. I'll see you later.'

She left him with a smile, and walked aft. In common with most seagoing ships of this type, the passenger accommodation was in the stern, and comprised four tiny cabins, two each side of a central ladder leading down from the deck above. The Captain had the rearmost compartment, and his sailors slept under awnings on deck, cool but lacking in privacy.

Mallaso dropped her bundle of clothes down the companionway, and climbed carefully after them down the ladder, the bag of presents in one hand. She'd bought Grayna a pottery horse, not Minassan, but nicely made by some craftsman in Sabrek. It was just what the little girl liked, and it would be all too easy to break it. She set her burden down by the first door on the left, and opened it with a determined shove: the wood always stuck.

There was a man sitting on the narrow mattress. Not Grimek, big and dark-skinned: and Grimek wouldn't know one end of a djarlek from the other, whereas she had surprised this man in the act of playing it.

'Hallo,' said Hanno of Minassa.

Mallaso stared at him in delighted astonishment. Then she hauled her bags in and shut the door behind her. 'You came! I thought you wouldn't.'

'Did you really?' He gave her a wide, teasing grin. 'I'll go if you like.'

'No – no, don't.' Mallaso was acutely aware that she was breathing as hard as if she'd just run round the Old City. 'I assumed you'd left Toktel'yi – that's what I told everyone, that you'd had an offer to play in Djebb for the rainy season.'

'And Sargenay?'

'He doesn't know I asked you to come to Tekkt – he thinks you're safely out of my life.'

'He guards you almost as jealously as a husband.'

'He's my old and dear friend, and he's taken it upon himself to act as my protector, since I'm lacking one.' Mallaso took several deep, steadying breaths, and found herself wishing she'd put on something just a little less dowdy than this all-concealing grey dress. And, being thicker than those she usually wore, it was very hot.

'I'll have the other cabin,' she said, and picked up her bags again.

He rose to his feet and put out a hand to detain her. 'Will you – will you stay here?'

Their eyes met. She saw that he was still holding back, as if unsure of her feelings. *Not a very good sorcerer*, she thought wryly: *my attraction must be obvious to all but the blind.*

But still she hesitated, knowing that once she surrendered, her life would become infinitely more complicated. Of all the men she could choose, why pick on a mysterious musician who said he was from Minassa, and apparently possessed powers of sorcery that should be impossible? She'd be better off with Bereth.

No. Not Bereth. Bereth was loud, insensitive and had a very high opinion of himself: the very opposite of this quiet, reserved, enigmatic young man. But her natural caution was asserting itself now. She withdrew her hand, still unwilling to commit herself. 'I might,' she said softly. 'But as you're supposed to be just my escort, I think we'd better have separate cabins, for appearances' sake. L'ktek has known me for a long time.'

'Don't tell me,' he said, with a rueful grin. 'He wants to be your protector too. You don't *look* that vulnerable.'

'I'm not,' Mallaso snapped, with a return to her usual acerbic manner. 'But a woman in Toktel'yi is supposed to have some guardian, husband, father, son or brother – or owner. My father and brothers are dead, I have no husband or son, and my master freed me at his death. Ironic, isn't it? The women who have most freedom under Imperial custom and law are those who were once enslaved. Even widows are supposed to be subject to their surviving male relatives.'

'There's a Kerentan proverb, isn't there? "All men long to live in Toktel'yi, and all women wish to leave it".' He smiled bleakly. 'Do you want to leave?'

'Of course I do – I don't intend to stay in that filthy rat-hole for the rest of my life,' Mallaso told him. 'One day soon, I'll buy a villa on Tekkt, and grow peaches and figs and oranges, and watch my daughter grow up in health and freedom.'

'And Penya?'

'Penya is dead,' said Mallaso, and turned and went out.

She put her baggage in the other cabin and hurried back up on deck. The cargo had all been stowed, and the last of the dockers were filing back down the boarding-plank, their pay clutched in their hands. The twenty-oared barge which was to tow the ship the two miles downriver to the open sea was already tied to the *Leaping Dolphin*'s bow, and L'ktek was issuing last-minute orders. Mallaso searched the crowded quayside, and caught sight of her other escort, making his way towards the ship. 'Hey! Grimek!'

He saw her, and waved. She ran to the gunwale, and waited until he was close enough for a spoken conversation. 'Grimek – I'm sorry – '

'That's all right,' he told her cheerfully. 'So your friend's turned up, has he? Well, have a good voyage!'

She threw down a bag of half-Imperials. It was a very generous sum, considering that she had no need of him after all, but he was Penyan too, although quite untainted by the bitterness and anger which still lurked within her soul. Besides, he needed all the money he could raise to move out of the slums, where two of his children had already died of a fever.

He felt the weight of it, and his dark face lit up with surprise and delight. 'Thank you, Mallaso! May the Goddess bring you joy!'

'And to you,' she said, lifting a hand in farewell. 'I'll see you when I get back, Grimek. Give my best wishes to T'nemm and the children.'

She stayed, leaning on the rail, to watch his broad back disappearing through the crowds. There were always idlers on the docks, whores, workmen, or sightseers passing the time watching the ships. There were no soldiers, though, coming to snatch a man who might be the possessor of superhuman power.

She wondered why he had vowed not to use his magic. He had said something about always harming his friends. Perhaps that was why he had it under such iron control, for most of the time. Until Bereth's stupid, callous remarks had made him lose his temper.

There were so many questions she wanted to ask him, but the month or so that she'd known him had taught her that the man calling himself Hanno of Minassa wasn't going to answer them very eagerly.

The sailors were casting off, and the team of dockers raised their poles to push the *Leaping Dolphin* away from the quay. She listened to the melodic chant as the fore and aft hawsers were wound in, a tune that had been sung, very recently and very differently, in her own dining hall. She consigned the musician firmly to the recesses of her mind, and concentrated on watching the docks as the vessel got under way behind the tow-barge.

There were hundreds of ships tied up, and she, from a seafaring island, knew their origins and purposes as well as any sailor. Bluff-bowed cargo vessels from the western coastal cities, Jaiya, Lai'is and Ukkan, with a single big square sail of sewn leather, and a workmanlike air. Kefirinn riverboats, slender, shallow-draughted, with two steering oars, one or two masts, and brightly coloured triangular sails. Graceful seagoing craft, bigger versions of the *Leaping Dolphin*, distinguished by the rudder hung from the sternpost, the high sides and sweeping prow. She could tell which island they came from by the colours of their hulls: blue from Balki, red from Tekkt, green from Annatal, black from Onnak, yellow or white from Penya.

There were only two Penyan boats, amongst all those moored between the *Leaping Dolphin*'s berth and the open sea. *No*, Mallaso told herself sternly, as the sails were hoisted, casting her into sudden shadow, while the men chanted and the sea air touched her hot head with blessedly cool tendrils. *No, no, no. Penya is in my past, and there it belongs. Look forward – even if it's no further than tomorrow, when I see Grayna again.*

The *Leaping Dolphin*, freed from the tow barge, gathered way. The blue and white striped sails filled with wind, and she slid gracefully between the two tall stone beacons that marked the main mouth of the Kefirinn, into the open sea. She tossed like a restive horse as the waves struck her, and then her bow bit firmly into the water, and turned south-east, to where the low ridged backbone of Tekkt showed dim and distant on the horizon. The nearest part of the island, which was shaped like an irregular arrowhead pointing at the mainland, was only about thirty miles away, but Tekkt Harbour lay almost at its southern extremity, and the ship was not expected to reach land much before sunset on the following day.

Mallaso walked up to the bow and stayed there for a while, watching the waves, revelling in the comparative cool of the breeze at her back, enjoying the white foam and spray as the ship sliced through deep dark water. L'ktek came up to talk to her: she asked after his wife and children, and he asked her how business was doing. He didn't enquire about the identity of her friend, still below in the cabin, much to her relief. And she was glad that his ship, unlike most seagoing vessels, didn't carry a weather-working sorcerer: on the brief, safe run to Tekkt, it was an unnecessary expense. So Hanno's secret was secure at least for the duration of the voyage.

She had hoped he might come on deck: it must be stiflingly hot down in those tiny, airless cabins with only one small porthole that couldn't be opened. But the afternoon wore on, Tekkt and the cloud sitting above it came slowly nearer, and the flat shores of the Kefirinn delta receded into a low grey line on the edge of the world. The wind was blowing, as it often did at this time of year, from the south-west, and the *Leaping Dolphin* had to tack before it, slowing progress. But the sun shone, and the sea was comparatively calm.

They passed a flotilla of about a dozen naval galleys, long and low and sleek, the huge bronze rams projecting underwater from their bows revealed in every trough of the waves, and an unmistakable air of menace about them. Ships like these, with their three masts and double banks of slave-driven oars, had carried the invasion force into Penya Harbour. They were certainly beautiful, but they were also cruel and deadly, and Mallaso could not admire them. Instead, she walked aft, nodded to L'ktek, who was consulting his chart and lodestone, and climbed down to the cabins.

The Captain had told her that the two on the right were occupied by an elderly couple who were prey to seasickness. She ignored their muffled groans, and knocked on Hanno's door.

There was a brief pause, and then his voice. Obediently, Mallaso entered.

He was lying on the mattress, hands behind his head. The djarlek hung by its strap from a hook on the partition, and three bags were heaped in the only free corner. It wasn't much for a lifetime's possessions. Mallaso shut the door, and said softly, 'Are you going to stay in here for the whole voyage? There isn't a sorcerer on board, you know.'

'I do know. Sit down?'

He gestured at the edge of the mattress. Mallaso knelt with her usual careful grace, and unwound her veil. Even in this dark stuffy hole, the absence of cloth between her mouth and the hot air was a considerable relief.

He studied her, his dark eyes shadowed. Finally, he said, 'I'll go on deck later, but I don't want to be too conspicuous.'

'You make yourself conspicuous just lurking in here – unless you're seasick, of course?'

Hanno grinned, suddenly and startlingly boyish from someone whose manner was so reserved. She'd already seen flashes of the mischievous, humorous man he seemed to take such pains to hide, but was unprepared for the shock of her reaction to it, almost like a blow to the pit of her stomach. Suddenly throwing all her caution to the wind, she said abruptly, 'This is stupid. We both know what we feel. Why waste time pretending we don't want each other?'

The smile vanished, and his eyes became dark, impenetrable, secret. And with a feeling that she was about to leap into very deep and uncharted waters, Mallaso leaned forward, and kissed him on the mouth.

For one heartbeat, two, he did not move. And then she felt his arms surround her, and his lips responding, and knew that her instincts had not lied.

She had been trained as a concubine, and had earned good money in a brothel: the accepted moves came easily to her, and she could counterfeit a convincing display of passion. But this time there was no need to pretend, for the pleasure they gave to each other was real, and spectacular. And he was good, a lover at once urgent and considerate, taking delight in her fulfilment before his own.

No regrets, Mallaso thought, lying dreamily beside him, her head still reeling from the last climactic burst of sensual satisfaction. *In fact, I wish I'd asked him sooner.*

'I'm glad you enjoyed it.'

Her eyes flew open. Startled, she said, 'Do you know what I'm thinking?'

'It's considered very bad manners to pry.' He grinned at her teasingly. 'But sometimes the – the *aura* is so strong, I can't help knowing. You don't have to be a sorcerer to see what you're feeling now, for instance.'

'No,' Mallaso agreed. His arm lay across her breasts, pale skin against dark, and she wondered what they looked like from above, two sprawled, abandoned carvings, one in ivory, one of deepest ebony . . .

'Thank you,' she added, rather belatedly, and saw his grin become wider. 'My pleasure. I hope I've helped to relieve some of the tedium of the voyage?'

'I think you have.' She studied the thin contours of his face, and said curiously, 'How old are you?'

'Twenty-three. Two years younger than you. Temek told me your age – she's a terrible gossip, and you're her favourite subject.'

'I know. But she wouldn't get much out of you, would she? Like your real name, for instance.'

He lay very still, and his face had lost its smile. 'My name is Hanno.'

'That's what you call yourself – but it isn't your *name*. And I don't think you come from Minassa, either.'

'That's my business.' His voice was curt and hard, giving nothing away, as if she were a banker querying the source of his funds, and Mallaso wished she had never begun to question him. She would only antagonize him, and the prospect of sharing the voyage with a man whom she desired but who didn't want to speak to her was not very pleasant.

But she *had* started, and she wanted to end this mystery, one way or the other. Obeying a rogue impulse, she disentangled herself and sat up. The musician still lay flat beside her, his wiry body slick with sweat, the blond hair soaked against the pillow. She stared down into his watchful, wary eyes and said forcefully, 'Listen to me. It's my business too. I know next to nothing about you, but you're my lover now, and I don't particularly want to give you up.'

'Don't you?'

'Of course I don't,' Mallaso said honestly. 'You're too good. I'm not going to let a find like you slink off into the undergrowth without a struggle. But I do want to know more about you. Sweet Mother, it's natural! I'd like to know if I'm sharing my bed with an ordinary sorcerer, or something more. I'd like to know if I'm in danger of being fried every time I annoy you. And I'd like to know if you've been telling me the truth – because I don't like lovers who lie to me.'

Silence. Above and around them were all the myriad, rhythmical noises and movements of a ship at sea, the creak of rope and timber, the slap of water on wood, the endless pitch and toss of the waves. He had turned his head away, so that she could see only part of his face, the sharp line of his cheekbone, the irregular shape of his nose.

'I didn't want to lie to you.' His voice was barely audible. 'But it was necessary.'

'Is it necessary now?'

'I don't know.'

'I can keep a secret, if that's what you mean,' said Mallaso acidly. 'At the moment, I only know what I've been told – or what I can guess. Your name *isn't* Hanno, and you *don't* come from Minassa. *Do* you have a little sister called Zathti?'

'Yes. That was quite true. Almost the only thing that was.'

'Then you haven't been to Penya?'

He turned his head and looked at her. The wraith of a smile hovered at the ends of his mouth. 'That was true.'

Mallaso stared at him in rising exasperation. 'This is like getting water out of a stone! Listen, whatever you've done, whatever you are, that doesn't change anything – it doesn't damage what's just happened, or alter what – the friendship we have.'

'You haven't heard me yet.'

She folded her arms across her breasts and glared at him. 'I'm not some shy and sheltered little Toktel'yan virgin, you know. I've seen a great deal of suffering, and grief, and horror. I am an adult, not a child. I think I can also trust my own instincts about you. Despite what Sargenay implied, I know you're not evil, or a demon. I may not be a sorcerer, but I'm a good judge of people. And I'm not afraid. Whatever secret you're hiding from me, I can accept it, and still be your friend, and your lover too. So please, *tell* me. Apart from anything else, I can't call you Hanno if it isn't your real name. What *is* your real name?'

At last, when she was on the point of getting up, gathering her clothes and marching off to her own cabin in a huff, he spoke. 'My real name is Bron. And I come from Zithirian, not Minassa.'

Mallaso released her pent-up breath in a sigh of relief. Then she saw his face, as pale as if something vital had been wrenched out of him, and the words of ironic congratulation died in her throat. Her hand touched his, and she said softly, 'Please – go on.'

'My father is Ansaryon – the King of Zithirian. I am his bastard son.'

Suddenly all the randomly jumbled pieces of information, rumour and gossip coalesced in her mind. She said, 'I think I've heard about you. Weren't you supposed to have astonishing powers of sorcery?'

He nodded wryly. 'Yes, I have. So you see, Sargenay was right. He was nearly right about something else, too. I am not a demon – not yet. But I could become one.'

'Demons don't exist,' Mallaso said firmly. 'My father told me that they are the product of ignorant and superstitious imaginations.'

'Perhaps. But imagine this. Imagine a man with powers that are almost unlimited – save by his own conscience. Now imagine that same man dedicated to the Death-God, the Wolf that lives in his heart, and will not let him die – who urges him constantly to take life, to spill blood, to feed the Devourer with the souls he craves. Isn't that a demon?'

Despite the heat in the tiny cabin, Mallaso shivered convulsively. She whispered, 'Is that what you are?'

'No,' said Bron. 'Not yet. I have the power. I have already used it to kill, before my father taught me how to harness and control it. And I also have the Wolf within my heart. But I have learned how to resist him, and suppress him. Sometimes, though, I fail, and he escapes.'

'When you lose your temper. When Bereth taunted you.'

'Yes. Which is why I usually walk away from trouble. And why I have tried to reject my powers, because I know my potential for evil. When I was a child, nine years old, my uncontrolled sorcery slew more than six thousand people. The horror of it has haunted me ever since. It's why I have fought the Wolf, rather than obeyed him. But he bides his time, waiting for the moment when I lose hold of my anger, and give him what he wants. At the moment, I am stronger than he is – but he is patient. He will wait for ever, if necessary.'

'You said – you said he will not let you die,' Mallaso said. There was a great coldness round her heart, constricting it. The horrors she had expected were petty and trivial, compared to this.

He went on, his voice quiet and appallingly matter-of-fact. 'That is true. Once, I nearly drowned, but Ayak saved me. He spoke to my young half-brother, and told him where I was, trapped under the water, so that the rescuers would find me in time. That was when my father realized that the children might be corrupted by Ayak, through my agency, even if I did not intend it. They possess power too, you see. So I could not stay in Zithirian. Then – then other things happened later, and I decided to abandon sorcery. My power is inborn, I have never taken Annatal, so I thought it would be possible. But it isn't. It's like a seeing man trying to become blind. And there is only one place in the known world where I might find help.'

'Jo'ami.'

'Yes, Jo'ami. So I made my way to Kerenth – I thought I might find a ship to take me there. But something happened in Kerenth, to delay me.'

Mallaso waited. It was getting dark outside, early and swift as always this far south, and she could no longer see his face with any clarity.

At last, he said bleakly, 'I was the Consort of Kerenth – and the Sacrifice.'

She gave a small involuntary whimper of fear. 'Then – then you are dead.'

For the first time, a thread of dry humour invaded his voice. 'Was my performance just now so bad? No, I am not. The Wolf would not let me die. I jumped off a cliff half a mile high, and survived.'

'Did you – did you *know* that you would live?'

'I thought there was a good chance of it. I had been able to save myself before, when I was a child, and fell from a tower. And if I couldn't – if I did die – it would be worth it, to save Kerenth. The people were starving, because the Goddess had rejected me and withdrawn Her blessing. The Emperor's invasion fleet was approaching. My life was demanded as the price for Sarraliss's intervention. I took the chance willingly, knowing that whatever happened to me, it was better than the obliteration of Kerenth.'

Mallaso was silent for a while, remembering the stories that had been rife in Toktel'yi, three years ago, and the joy she had felt at the failure of Ba'alekkt's invasion. Of course, most people at the time had ascribed the fatal storm to bad luck. In the Empire, it was not wise to attribute too much power to a mere Goddess. Those bred in Tatht, or Penya, knew better.

'I don't understand,' she said at last. 'You say the Goddess demanded your life. You did not give it to her – you did not die. And yet the Imperial fleet was destroyed, and the rains came, so Kerenth was saved.'

'I know. I don't understand it either. Unless the High Priestess was wrong, and it was not my blood which Sarraliss wanted, but only my departure from the land.' He smiled rather grimly. 'Do you know much of affairs in Kerenth?'

'We hear stories, but we never know how much is true. I do know that the Queen is young, and beautiful, and apparently very headstrong.'

'That's certainly true,' he said drily. 'She insisted on taking me for her Consort, and even after the Goddess rejected me, she would not let me go. She nearly destroyed Kerenth for my sake. Also, she has a sister, Nerana, who is the High Priestess and thinks she should have been Queen instead of Inrai'a. It was Nerana who told her that the Goddess demanded a Sacrifice: and I suspect, looking back, that Nerana may have exaggerated the Goddess's demands a little. After all, Sarraliss is the Creator of Life. She is worshipped in Zithirian, too, and I have never heard of Her wanting human sacrifice before. I know it was done regularly in Kerenth in ancient times, but not for many hundreds of years, except to repel the last invasion. And priests have been known to misinterpret the messages they receive from the gods, whether wilfully or unintentionally. That is one reason why people in the north worship in private, without temple or priest.'

'There were no priests on Penya, either,' said Mallaso softly. 'Bron – what happened to you after you jumped from the cliff?'

He was silent for a while, and she saw in his face the memory of terrible fear. He said at last, 'I thought I would die. The air rushed past me, and I heard Inrai'a screaming my name. I knew I could not survive it – and for a moment I did not *want* to survive it. And then the fear – and the Wolf – took control. I slowed my descent, just as I did when I fell from the tower at Sar D'yenyi, when I was twelve. I landed awkwardly, I hurt my leg, but I was alive. And I heard the Wolf's voice, telling me that he had saved my life three times, and demanding that the debt be repaid.'

She waited, silent in the dark.

'I knew they would look over the edge of the cliff, so I crawled under some bushes and hid. I was exhausted from the effort of saving myself, but when darkness came, I made my way down to the sea, and stole a boat. The rain meant that the Goddess had returned to the land, but I knew I couldn't stay in Kerenth. If they found I was still alive, then Nerana would probably have killed me with her own hands.'

Mallaso had already moved ahead to the next part of his story. 'The storm that destroyed the invasion fleet – did *you* make it happen?'

'No, I didn't – I was still determined not to use sorcery. The storm seemed to pass me by – I think it was intended for the fleet, and no one else. Which makes it very likely that Sarraliss did raise it, to save Kerenth. And I'm glad she did. Of all lands in the known world, it least deserves to be part of the Empire.'

'What happened, after the storm?'

'The boat was washed up on Penya. On the eastern coast, where the cliffs fall sheer into the sea – do you know it?'

Mallaso nodded, though he couldn't have seen her. 'I know it. I sailed round the island once, with my father – he was a fisherman. I remember the cliffs, and the sea birds in white rows all along the ledges. It was called The Hammer, from its shape on the map.'

'It still is. There are people living there, in caves inside the cliffs. Native Penyans, in hiding. They survive by fishing, and scavenging whatever the sea brings – driftwood, cargo that's been washed overboard, wrecked ships, beached whales. They found me, more dead than alive from exhaustion and thirst, and gave me shelter. They saved my life.'

'Who were they?' Questions burst from Mallaso, as if an ancient wall had been breached. 'What were their names? What villages did they come from?'

'I can tell you some of their names, but that's all. Ondax, he was the one who found me: his wife was called Sulayan. There was a man called Astrellen, he was their leader – '

'Astrellen! I remember that name! What did he look like? Was he young, old?'

He answered her patiently, despite her eagerness. 'He was my father's age, forty or so. Tall, lean, a rather long face, hair already going grey.'

'No.' Mallaso gripped her hands so tightly together that she thought the bones would crack. 'I remember now – one of my brother's friends was called Astrellen. It's quite a common name, on Penya.' She drew a shaky breath. 'I'm sorry – it's just that after all these years, to meet someone who has been to Penya, who can tell me about it . . . it's given me hope.'

'There isn't much hope left,' he told her gently. 'They told me that after the invasion, there were many groups like theirs, hiding in various parts of the island – the central mountains in particular. They managed to survive for quite a long time, raiding Imperial forts and stealing food and weapons to carry on the struggle – until Ba'alekkt came to Penya, a few years before I did. In a few months he managed to do what no one else had done in fifteen years – he wiped out almost all resistance left. Astrellen told me that he only knew of five other bands of Penyans, barely surviving and living in constant fear that they would be found by Imperial soldiers. And if the Empire doesn't kill them, hunger and disease eventually will. Once, there were over a hundred in Astrellen's group. When I left them, there were just twenty-eight. And all the babies had died.'

'Oh, Penya,' Mallaso whispered. She was glad that he could not see the river of tears, pouring down her face in the dark. 'What did we ever do, to deserve such a terrible fate?'

'You did nothing,' said Bron bitterly. 'You were there – you were there, and peaceful, and defenceless. Just as Kerenth was there to be taken, until Sarraliss raised the storm. Just as Minassa and Zithirian are there, the next peaches to be harvested. And as long as there is an Emperor like Ba'alekkt on the Onyx throne, there will never, ever be peace in our world, until all the lands between Fabriz and Ma'alkwen, Sar D'yenyi and Jo'ami, are ground into dust beneath the Empire's heel.'

'To save Zithirian, and all the others – would you kill the Emperor?'

There was a long, terrible silence. At last, Bron said quietly, 'I have made a vow. I have enough deaths on my conscience, and their cries still haunt my dreams. Oh, Ayak would love to have Ba'alekkt's blood – and I can feel him stirring now, at the thought of it. But I must deny him. And besides, have you thought what would happen, if the Emperor were killed? He has no direct heir yet. One of his sisters is married to Cathallon of Minassa, and the other is still unwed. I suppose the nearest male heir would be K'djelk's baby son – and that would be an irony indeed, for a Prince of Minassa to inherit the Empire. But there are many other claimants. Djamal had several brothers, sisters, cousins – '

'Including the Prince of Tulyet. Apparently there's a chance he'll marry the Emperor's other sister, Djeneb.'

'Thus putting himself in the front rank of heirs, as I'm sure he's realized. Do you see, Mallaso? It would not stop at one death. If Ba'alekkt were killed, many more would die in the struggle for power. Toktel'yans aren't content to eliminate one or two rivals – whole families would be wiped out. Do you really want that?'

'Do you want Zithirian and Minassa to suffer the same fate as Penya?'

'No,' he said at last. 'No, I don't. But there is nothing I can do. I will not use my powers to do murder. And without sorcery, I would never get near enough to Ba'alekkt to kill him. But if I can drive the Wolf out of my heart, I will go back to Zithirian and help my father against the Empire. I dare not do anything while the Devourer is still within me – if I tried to take part in any fighting, He might . . . take control of me.'

'How will you drive him out?'

'I will do what I should have done years ago – I will go to Jo'ami. They will surely help me. And then at last I will be free, and my powers will not seem like a burden any more.'

She found his hand in the dark, and held it tightly, trying both to give and to receive comfort. At last, she said softly, 'Can you tell me more about Penya?'

'Do you really want to know? I was there for over a year, I saw a great deal . . . I saw too much.'

'Tell me,' Mallaso said steadily. 'Tell me. However terrible, however sad – tell me. I need to know.'

So he told her, in a soft, dispassionate voice that did nothing to disguise the horror that had befallen the island of her birth. The pretty houses around the Harbour, wrecked and burned. The rich groves of nut and fruit trees hacked down, the fertile earth salted and barren. The terraced vineyards ruined and overgrown. The few who had made peace with their conquerors, eking out a squalid existence in shattered homes, on the verge of starvation, despised by invaders and resistance fighters alike. And those who had pledged to carry on the struggle, living like animals in caves at the sea's edge or in the central mountains, killing a few soldiers here, setting fire to stores and barracks there, growing fewer and fewer in number. With most of the adults dead and their children taken into slavery, there would soon be no one left to remember the golden days of peace and plenty: or to fly the banner of Penya, yellow crescent moon against a deep blue evening sky, with one brave star of hope.

His tale ended, he touched her cheek. 'Oh, Mallaso, brave Mallaso – I did not know you could weep.'

'I am not weeping,' she said, with the tears pouring from her eyes. And then he took her into his arms, and she sobbed against his shoulder like a child, for all that had vanished, and for the pain of wounds so deep that no joy in all the world could heal them.

At an hour before sunset on the following day, the *Leaping Dol-*

phin entered the broad shallow bay at Tekkt Harbour, and dropped anchor amidst a swarm of smaller craft, eager to unload her
cargo and ferry it ashore.

Mallaso loved Tekkt. It reminded her a little of Penya, as
she remembered it, although there the harbour had been much
deeper, with a stone jetty against which quite big ships could
moor, and steep-sided hills rising above the turquoise water. The
southern end of Tekkt was comparatively flat, and the houses in
the principal town were laid out in straight streets, rather than
perched on convenient plateaux of rock.

The elderly couple and their two slaves were lowered down
into one of the small rowing boats, the woman heavily veiled and
calling upon Kaylo to preserve her, and her husband looking
rather embarrassed by all the fuss. Then it was the turn of Mallaso and Bron, with their few bags.

She hardly looked at the boat below, but climbed down the
rope ladder with her usual agility and sat in the stern, her eyes
fixed on the town. Somewhere beyond it, hidden by the trees on the
low hill rising behind the houses, was the farm where Grayna was
fostered, with a kindly family who treated her like one of their
own. The child could not remember Toktel'yi, her home for the first
two years of her life: she had grown up happy and healthy in
the pure sea air of Tekkt, with food and freedom in abundance,
far from the disease-ridden slums of the Empire's capital city.

The boat beached on the broad sandy shore, and they paid
the rowers and waded to land through the warm, gentle waves.

The universal beast of burden here was the donkey, a sturdy,
placid breed much in demand throughout the Archipelago and
beyond. A dozen or so stood waiting patiently in the shade of a
clump of palms on the sand's edge, and Mallaso selected two
strong-looking animals, paid over two half-Imperials for their
hire, and climbed on to the smaller one's back while its owner
tied her bags to the padded felt saddle.

The other donkey refused to carry Bron. It moved sideways,
ears laid back and an expression of frightened obstinacy in its
eyes. Mallaso suddenly remembered Sargenay telling her that
most animals didn't like sorcery – although, with patient training,
most of them could be persuaded to co-operate sooner or later.
But Bron was no ordinary sorcerer, and the donkey, panicked out
of its usual stolid obedience, was terrified of him.

'It's all right,' he said to the handler, and held out his palm for
the return of one of the coins. 'I'll walk.'

With a mixture of reluctance and relief, the donkey's owner handed the money back, and they set off through Tekkt town. Bron took care to keep well away from Mallaso's beast, who was eyeing him suspiciously.

At this late hour, shops and stalls were being shut up, and people were strolling home for their evening meal. No one ever hurried on Tekkt: it was one of the charms of the place, so different from the noisy bustle of Toktel'yi. Even during the winter months, when the island's population was almost doubled by wealthy visitors from the mainland, fleeing the sticky heat and humidity and disease of the rainy season, Tekkt was still peaceful and spacious.

Mallaso had taken off her veil, for Tekktish people ignored the stifling conventionality of the Empire. They had been part of it for several hundred years, by assimilation rather than conquest, but observed their own customs with a quiet yet determined independence. Most of the aristocratic female visitors remained immured in their husbands' villas, observing the strict rules of Toktel'yan society for respectable wives and daughters, while Tekktish women walked the streets with their faces uncovered and their arms bare. Some of the younger Toktel'yan men assumed that they were therefore fair game, and every year there was trouble, but on the whole the visitors respected the customs of their holiday island, and the Tekktish people smiled warmly and accepted their money with eager hands. Prices always doubled during the winter, which was one reason why Mallaso preferred to visit her daughter outside the rainy season.

The brown donkey climbed willingly up the narrow track which led to the Villa of the White Doves. By now, the sun had set behind the trees in the orchards to their left, their rounded black shapes masking the brilliant colours of the western sky. Crickets called from the bushes, and a Nightsinger, deep within the grove of peach trees, began to pour its sweet liquid song into the evening air.

The villa was like all others on Tekkt, and most of the Archipelago. Built of whitewashed, plastered stone, the house hid behind high walls surrounding a paved courtyard. Farm buildings, barns and byres, lay in a cluster off to their right, and the track led up to a tall arched gateway, with two flaming torches thrust into iron brackets on either side of the entrance.

At a nod from Mallaso, Bron walked forward and hammered

twice, hard, on the wood. The hollow sound echoed around them. They heard footsteps crossing the courtyard on the other side, the creak of the opening door, and then a man's head, balding and fringed with long greying hair, appeared around it. He stared at Bron, and said curtly, 'Have you business here, young man?'

'Hello, Gekkul.' Mallaso urged her donkey forward and dismounted, smiling. 'I'm sorry we've arrived so late, but the ship only dropped anchor an hour ago. Where's Grayna? Is she in bed?'

The man stared at her. Abruptly, his head disappeared, and she heard him calling his wife, a note of panic in his voice. 'Anmit! Anmit, where are you? Mallaso's here!'

Under the thin layer of her grey cotton dress, her heart began to beat the quickening pulse of dread. Normally the gate would be flung open, and she and her escort would be welcomed with joyful cries, and Grayna would run laughing into her arms. Something was wrong, terribly wrong.

The gate creaked again, and Anmit appeared, a small, slender middle-aged woman as dark as Mallaso. Her usually cheerful face was lined with sorrow, and there were tears on her cheeks.

'What's happened?' Mallaso whispered. 'It's Grayna, isn't it? Oh, tell me, Anmit – what's happened?'

'Oh, my dear – ' Anmit's voice cracked. 'Oh, I'm so sorry – there wasn't time to send word – she took a sudden fever, poor little mite, and there was nothing we or the Healer could do for her, nothing at all – she died three days ago – oh, Mallaso, Grayna's dead.'

CHAPTER
FOURTEEN

Afterwards, Mallaso was to remember Anmit's words as the moment when ice entered her soul. Her beloved, joyous, laughing daughter was dead. And now, the future had no meaning.

A numb, frozen weight surrounded her heart. She stared at Anmit, and shook her head in denial. 'This isn't happening. It can't be true – she can't be dead – I sent her here to *live*, not to die!'

'Come inside, dear.' Anmit, tears spilling down her face, was in the throes of grief herself, for both she and Gekkul had loved the little girl dearly. 'What a terrible shock – come inside, do, Gekkul will find you something – '

With Bron on one side and Grayna's foster-mother on the other, Mallaso allowed herself to be led through the gate and into the courtyard. For a heartbeat, she seemed to see her daughter, skipping merrily over the flagstones to greet her, heard her high, happy voice and her excited laughter as she received the bag of gifts. And then the vision faded, and Mallaso was utterly alone.

The villa's kitchen, where the family spent most of their time, was cluttered with people: farmworkers, servants, Anmit and Gekkul's three half-grown children. She was guided to a high-backed wooden settle, well away from the cooking-fire, and a cup of fiery peach spirit pressed into her hand. 'Go on, dear,' Anmit begged her. 'Please drink it – it'll help.'

She drank, coughing as the raw liquor seared her throat. It warmed her stomach, but nothing, nothing, could thaw the ice. She wiped her streaming eyes, and said, 'Can I see her?'

Anmit shook her head compassionately. 'Oh, no, dear – no, we put her on her pyre the morning after she died.'

Of course, funerals must be conducted quickly in this hot climate. Mallaso closed her eyes, and conjured up the image of Grayna. Her curly dark hair, tortured into a dozen braids and bright with red ribbons: her huge brown eyes: her wide smile, revealing the gap where one of her milk teeth had fallen out: her lively, sparkling grace. Gone, dead, vanished for ever beyond her touch and her love. And all she had now of her daughter were memories that would fade too soon, and a handful of gritty ash to sprinkle on the sea. And on the last day of the year, another candle to be lit, representing her child's soul.

'Tell me,' she said hoarsely. 'Tell me what happened – *exactly* what happened. Don't try to spare me the details. I want to know everything.'

She saw Anmit exchange glances with Bron, and his almost imperceptible nod. Automatically she took another sip of the spirits, and listened to the older woman's soft, hesitant, sympathetic voice describing the swift and devastating progress of the fever. One day, Grayna had been in perfect health and lively spirits: the next morning she had been lethargic, complaining of a headache: by that evening, in the grip of raging delirium. The Town Healer could do nothing to help: there had been several similar cases in the district recently, all young children, and none had survived. By midnight, Grayna was in a coma, and by dawn she was dead.

'She didn't suffer,' Anmit whispered. 'She didn't have time to suffer, poor lamb. And now she is in Olyak's sunniest halls, with all the other innocents, and she will never know pain again.'

'But she isn't *alive*,' Mallaso said bleakly. 'Only the living know pain.'

'Cry if you want to,' Anmit said, squeezing her hand. 'Come on, dear, cry – it'll do you good.'

But she could not. Last night, in happy ignorance of the tragedy that had already befallen her daughter, she had wept for Penya, so brutally destroyed. Now, she could summon no tears for the child who had lit up her life, who had given her days purpose. For Grayna's sake, she had endured the brothel: for Grayna, she had worked so hard to make the Golden Djarlek a success. And always, bright and beckoning before her, the image of her future here on Tekkt, living with Grayna in safety and freedom, tending the peach trees, keeping goats and chickens, watching her beloved daughter grow up.

A dream which had ended three days ago, on a funeral pyre outside the black marble Temple of Olyak, on the hill above the eastern edge of the town.

And she hadn't known. Nothing had prepared her for this. No hint of her child's death had entered her mind from across seventy miles of island and ocean. Her future was destroyed, and she hadn't even been aware of it.

'What purpose is there now to my life?'

She hadn't realized she had spoken aloud until she saw Anmit's shocked face. 'Oh, my dear, you shouldn't think like that. You're young, you have everything to live for – you'll have other children.'

Others, to carry her hopes and then die? She shook her head. 'No – I only want Grayna.'

Anmit whispered something to Gekkul, who was standing beside her. He went away, and she turned back to Mallaso. 'I'll give you something to make you sleep tonight. Your young man will look after you. What's his name?'

'Hanno,' she said, remembering his alias just in time. He was sitting beside her on the settle, his arm around her. *I expect he wishes he'd never come*, she thought. *Most men are frightened of grief – and they can't possibly understand how it feels, for a mother to lose her child.*

Her own mother had been forced to watch as her sons and her husband were tortured to death, before her own execution. And beside that fate, Grayna's end had been kind and gentle.

The cup was taken away, and another given to her, with a smell at once sweet and bitter. Mallaso said flatly, 'I don't want it.'

'Go on, dear.' Anmit's voice was very gentle. 'Drink it. Sleep will do you good.'

'It won't bring her back, will it?' The bitterness of her tone surprised even her.

'No, it won't,' Bron said, speaking for the first time. 'Nothing will. But it will help. And tomorrow, you can begin to be strong.'

Mallaso looked down at the cup. It was Minassan, of course, a rich yellow glaze with blue flowers in a linked design around the outside rim. The liquid within it was a cloudy brown colour, with bits floating in it. Kuldi, mostly, with poppy juice added. And suddenly she realized that she did want to sleep: to sleep, and forget, to sleep, and never wake up to the terrible pain that would surely soon overwhelm her.

She lifted it to her lips, and drank.

Bron stood by the bed, looking down at the woman who lay on it. She still wore the grey cotton dress that had shrouded her throughout the voyage. In sleep, the beauty of her face was starkly apparent, but lacking, as yet, the marks of her grief.

He had felt her pain: he could not defend himself against such acute anguish. Only last night, she had made love to him with unrestrained passion, exulting in the union of their bodies. And all the time, *this* had been lying in wait for her.

The two bags lay in a corner, one filled with the presents that Grayna would never receive. It could have been pathetic, save that nothing about Mallaso was pathetic. She was strong, she had endured so much, and risen triumphantly above it. Eventually, he knew, she would even recover from this.

But for now, she needed him, even though she slept. He knew what grief was. Long ago, he had watched as a boy called Lelya was casually and brutally slain, and he had killed thousands of men in revenge. And Kefiri, with love and compassion and understanding patience, had brought him through his torment of guilt and sorrow and fear, and restored him to life.

Mallaso's anguish was different, but he knew what she needed. Gently, so as not to wake her, although she was heavily sedated, he lay down beside her, and took her hands, and entered her dreams.

The Villa of the White Doves lay half-way up the low hill above Tekkt harbour, perhaps a mile from the town. Through the peach and orange groves around it, you could catch glimpses of the sea, sharply and startlingly blue. To get a better view, it was necessary to climb up to the summit of the hill, where goats had grazed it bare, down to the pale, hot rocks thrusting out through the thin soil.

It was worth the effort. From here, looking southwards, the town of Tekkt, colourwashed houses and red-tiled roofs, crowded around the broad sweep of the bay. To the south-west, a long low promontory sprawled out into the ocean, pointing at Balki, just visible on the horizon some twenty or thirty miles away. Turn due south, and there was only blue water: the Scatterlings, thousands of islands large and small, flat and rocky, inhabited and empty, lay beyond the rim of the sea.

Mallaso sat on the highest rock, in the full glare of the noon-day sun. She wore her thinnest white dress, and an old straw hat of Anmit's. The heat never had much effect on her, and there was a brisk breeze up here to liven the air and sift through her clothes.

It was three days since her arrival on Tekkt, to receive the terrible news of Grayna's death, and this was the first time she had felt any desire to leave the dim and private sanctuary of her room. At first, she had taken refuge in sleep, with the help of Anmit's poppy juice, and her dreams had been beautiful. She had seen Grayna, had taken her hand, had walked with her through the high white halls of Olyak's upper realm, amongst the other dead children. Her daughter had gone, but her end had been merciful, and her spirit was happy.

The thought comforted her, and she clung to it through the long grim hours when sleep evaded her, and her mind trod obsessively down the same paths, blaming herself for leaving Grayna here, for not coming in time, for letting her die alone. It was all futile nonsense, of course, but she could not help it.

Something rustled in the scrub below the rocks, but it was only a couple of the bony, agile goats that were everywhere on Tekkt, usually tended by a small boy. Two triangular caprine heads, one brown, one black with a white stripe down its nose, emerged from the undergrowth, surveyed her with curious yellow eyes, and returned to their browsing.

Anmit had told Mallaso that Grayna had often come up here to pet the goats, and chat to the boy who herded them, and play among the rocks. It had been her favourite place. And so, drawn by pointless, stupid hope, she had followed her child to this sunny, arid, beautiful hilltop, in case the little girl's spirit lingered here still.

But there were only the goats, and the crickets, and a bright green lizard with a frilled neck that scuttled away into a crevice as soon as she appeared. She was not a sorceress, nor a necromancer: despite her dreams, she had no power over the souls of the dead. And now she sat here alone in the fierce sun, knowing that soon she must say farewell to Anmit and her family, and leave Tekkt, this time perhaps for ever. For how could she bear to return, when Grayna would not be here to welcome her?

It would not be easy either, to leave this still, clean, lovely place, and return to the grim life of Toktel'yi. At last, she had almost begun, reluctantly, to accept the reality of Grayna's death. Here, where her daughter had lived most of her brief, happy life, people understood her pain. But her mind shied away from the inevitable explanations her sophisticated Toktel'yan friends would demand, and their sympathy, quickly tainted with boredom. City children died so frequently, why all this fuss about one small girl?

'Mallaso?'

It was Bron. He stood just below the rocks, rashly bareheaded in the sun, wearing the brief tunic of working men on Tekkt. He had not forced his company on her during the last three days: he had helped Gekkul and his sons on the farm, and in the evening and at night he had left her alone, as she wished, to endure her sorrow. Wishing he had not disturbed her now, she said, 'Doesn't Gekkul need you?'

'Not for a while. And I'd like to talk to you.' He held out his hand. 'You'll roast your head, sitting in the sun like that. Come into the shade.'

Reluctantly, she got up and scrambled down, her leather sandals protecting the soles of her feet from the hot rocks. He took her hand to help her jump down from the lowest boulders, and led her round the side of the hill. A tall tree, too big for the goats to molest, sprouted out of the bushes and scrub, and in its shade there was a small open patch of grass.

The comparative cool beneath its branches made Mallaso realize just how hot it had been, out on the rocks. She sat down with her back against the ridged trunk of the tree, and pulled her hat off to fan herself with it.

'Have one of these.' Bron handed her a peach, golden, furry and sunflushed. Gratefully, she bit into the sweet flesh, feeling the juice run down her chin. All too soon there was nothing left but the stone. She tossed it into the bushes and wiped her mouth. 'Thank you, that was very welcome.'

'Do you feel better?'

She met his gaze, knowing what he meant, and slowly shook her head. 'No. I feel more calm, and I have accepted now that I will never see her again. But I feel so – so *empty*. I know I can survive this. I know I have to exist without her. I have lost others I loved, after all, though never my child before now. I want to blame someone, myself, I feel so guilty – '

'Why? It wasn't your fault. You did all you could to protect her. But no one can predict when such a fever will strike. You could have fostered her in any household, on any island, or in Ukkan or Sabrek, and the same thing might have happened.'

'I know.' She took a deep breath, and stared at him. 'Tell me honestly. Tell me the truth. If we had arrived before she died, could you have saved her?'

The long pause, the haunted look in his eyes, told her a great deal. At last he said, 'I don't know. I *can't* know. I do have more than an ordinary sorcerer's power of Healing, but I have no idea whether I could have cured the fever or not.' He reached forward and took her hands. 'Mallaso – don't torment yourself with such thoughts. No one, not even the gods, can alter the past. She is gone for ever, until you meet in Olyak's kingdom. Surely she is happy there, and waiting for you. The Lord of the Dead is kind to children.'

She nodded mutely.

'You are alive, and you are young. You have to go on living, for her. She'll always inhabit your memories, but that's all they are – memories, and dreams. And whatever you want, I will do for you.'

'I know.' Mallaso gently withdrew her hands. He knelt before her, the pale hair glimmering even in this deep shade, and suddenly she knew what must be done: for Zithirian, for Minassa, for Penya and all the children dead, or lost, or sold into slavery.

But she could not ask for Bron's help. He had vowed not to kill, and she could not demand that he feed the alien and terrible creature who inhabited his soul. She would say nothing of what she intended, for he would surely try to prevent her, for her own safety.

Now, she did not care whether she lived or died. If she died, she would be reunited with her daughter. And the sacrifice would be worth it, to rid the world of the danger it faced.

Bron had said that it would not stop at one death. She knew that: she had seen Toktel'yan repression and Toktel'yan justice at first hand. But the only life that really mattered to her was Grayna's: and Grayna was beyond the reach of Imperial vengeance.

She knew how it could be done, too: the whole plan lay in her head, as clear and bright and convincing as the little pictures they painted in Balki, on pebbles. The audacity of it terrified her, but it did not affect her resolve. She would avenge Penya, and prevent the bloody conquest of Zithirian and Minassa, with one blow. She would kill Ba'alekkt.

'What are you thinking?'

Startled, Mallaso looked up. Bron was staring at her with a strange expression on his face. She wondered, with sudden alarm, whether his abnormal powers had perceived her intention. She said hastily, 'I was thinking . . . I don't really want to stay at the villa for much longer. Anmit and Gekkul have been very kind, but . . . there are too many memories there.'

'I understand. Do you want to go back to Toktel'yi then?'

Mallaso opened her mouth to say yes, and remembered something. Soon, perhaps even in a few days' time, the rainy season would begin on the mainland, and everyone with the opportunity to leave would come to Tekkt to escape the humidity and discomfort.

Including the Emperor. Ba'alekkt had a Palace on Tekkt, built by his great-grandfather. It was small compared to the vast structure he inhabited in Toktel'yi, and in the relaxed atmosphere prevailing on the island, it would certainly be less well guarded. Her task would surely be very much easier if she made the attempt here.

All her love for her dead daughter was now being channelled and twisted into this new, deadly purpose. She had a sudden vision of the Emperor's face as she plunged a knife into his body, and the intensity of her hatred frightened her. Aware of Bron's evident concern, she thrust the image away, and answered his question. 'No – not yet. There are several very good inns, down by the harbour. I want to stay here for a while, before – before I tell her father.'

'Then she wasn't your owner's daughter.'

'No, she wasn't. He thought she was, that's why he gave me such a generous settlement in his will. He wanted to provide for the child of his old age. But her true father was his eldest son, Kumenek. And Kumenek knows it. He's the only person who does – apart from Metru. And you now, of course.'

'I won't tell anyone.'

'I know you won't. Kumenek only has one wife, and she is very jealous. She would make his life a misery if she found out. Woman do have some power in Toktel'yi, even if it is only the power to make happiness or sorrow. And I don't want him to be poisoned – he's a nice man, he doesn't deserve it.'

'Would she do that?'

'Oh, yes. There are ways of obtaining such things, and administering them, even if you never stir out of the female quarters. That's why I turned him down when he offered to make me his concubine. I knew Djaakin would get rid of me, sooner rather than later, and in such a way that no suspicion would ever fall on her.' Mallaso looked at his face, and smiled, glad that she had so successfully diverted his attention. 'Do Toktel'yan domestic arrangements shock you?'

'Just a bit,' said Bron, looking rather dazed. 'What else goes on behind the walls of those luxurious villas down by the sea?'

She gave him the juiciest nuggets of gossip she had heard over the past few years, and kept her mind successfully away from betraying images of assassination. But she had no doubts, no second thoughts. If Ba'alekkt was killed, the Empire would be plunged into turmoil by the struggle over the succession to the Onyx Throne, and the northern cities would be safe for the foreseeable future. And whatever happened to her, whether she survived, or died swiftly, or slowly, she would have no regrets.

The rains arrived in Toktel'yi at exactly the time when they were expected, and with them all the inevitable effects of torrential downpours on a waterlogged, tropical city. The thick, humid air, like a damp veil over the face; the floods in low-lying slums; the sudden increase in disease, especially the marsh-fever endemic in the Kefirinn Delta; and the inconvenience of living under a sky which seemed to be perpetually pouring water.

So the wealthy closed up their households, leaving a few trusted slaves in charge, and fled to their villas on Tekkt, or in the more temperate northern provinces of the Empire. Others took refuge with family or friends living in drier, healthier places like Djebb, or Sabrek. Those tied to Toktel'yi because of duty or poverty often took a perverse enjoyment from the uncrowded streets and waterways, and thieves seized the opportunity to plunder those unoccupied houses whose owners had left them inadequately secured. Even the docks, the lifeblood of the city, were quiet: the trade with the north had ended for the winter, and many of the riverboats were laid up for repairs in yards up and down the delta, while the seagoing ships ferried passengers across the short stretch of ocean to Tekkt.

The Emperor, of course, had his own vessel, the *Glory of Toktel'yi*. It was new this year, and glittered with fresh paint and gold leaf. Within its cabins, cramped and dark save for the Imperial suite in the stern, were packed all those personnel without whom Ba'alekkt could not survive two months on sleepy

Tekkt: household officials, cooks, courtiers, dancers, musicians, personal slaves, and every one of his seventy concubines. A rotund cargo ship, labouring in its wake, carried supplies, exotic foods, spices, drugs, furnishings, bedding, clothes and other luxuries and essentials. No one with any sense set sail for the island at the same time as the Imperial boats, for Ba-alekkt's household would commandeer every last donkey, litter or cart on Tekkt to carry the baggage, and the concubines, up to the Palace.

By this time, Bron and Mallaso had left Anmit's house, and moved down to a tavern called the Pelican, in the heart of the town not far from the harbour. Their rooms were light and airy, and comfortably furnished. They were also expensive, but Mallaso had plenty of money with her, brought to pay for Grayna's future fostering. She gave the landlord half a month's rent in advance, and hid the rest beneath the heavy wooden chest in the corner. Bron helped her to lift it, and pushed the bag of silver and gold Imperials underneath. With luck, no casual thief would think of looking there, and moving it would make a lot of noise.

In the evenings, Bron played in the tavern, still calling himself Hanno of Minassa. Performers of his calibre were rare on Tekkt, even in this busy season, and both he and the landlord did very well out of it. Mallaso could not bring herself to join him, for with Grayna so recently dead, she had no heart for it. Nor could she endure to have Bron in her bed: grief had robbed her of desire, indeed of every emotion save hatred. And yet she could not grieve as most women did, washing away some of her anguish in tears.

The rains fell relentlessly on Toktel'yi, and the ships streamed into Tekkt Harbour, as many as a dozen a day. Boatmen and donkey-handlers made a fortune, and the fifty or sixty inns and taverns in the town rapidly filled up with customers who weren't sufficiently rich to have their own villa, or lucky enough to share with friends or relatives.

And then the Emperor came.

His two ships arrived in the harbour in the morning, an hour or so before noon. Word had already been sent by fast galley, and Tekkt was ready. The Governor of the island stood on the beach in his finery to greet the most powerful man in the known world, and a fleet of canopied palanquins lay waiting in the shade of the palms. There were three trumpeters, and an escort of the most senior soldiers of the island's tiny garrison (there had never been any whiff of rebellion or disturbance on drowsy Tekkt), their bronze armour polished to a blinding brilliance. And almost every man, woman and child who could walk or hobble had come down to the harbour to cheer their Emperor, and gawp at the unrestrained splendour of his retinue.

Bron knew that Al'Kalyek was almost certainly part of Ba'a-lekkt's entourage. For whatever reason, he seemed to have escaped detection at Akkatanat's Races, but he was still vulnerable: Sargenay had scented his power, despite all his efforts to conceal it. And the Court Sorcerer undoubtedly possessed far more skill and ability than Mallaso's friend. So he stayed in his room and constructed an invasion-proof bulwark around his mind, far stronger than his usual defences. On a small island like Tekkt, it would be easy to locate him: and extremely difficult to escape.

He was also very concerned about Mallaso. She ate, she slept, she spoke and moved and even occasionally smiled, but he sensed her emptiness, her bleak and terrible despair. Briefly, they had been lovers, but that transient closeness had vanished with the news of Grayna's death. She was still beautiful, even in grief, and he wanted her very much, but he would not try to overcome her reluctance. Not yet, not until she was ready. He had hoped that she would turn to him for comfort, but instead she seemed to have retreated into herself like a wounded animal taking refuge in its lair. She did not share her thoughts, or her pain, and he did not know how to breach the gulf that now gaped between their souls.

So he sat in his room and played, softly, on the djarlek: and did not realize that Mallaso had left the tavern.

The Emperor rode in his palanquin through the narrow streets of Tekkt, acknowledging the cheers of his people with a smile and a gracious wave of his hand.

He always enjoyed his sojourn on the island. In Toktel'yi, the essential business of government never ceased to intrude into the pleasures of his life. Admittedly, he had always intended to take a greater part in affairs of state than his late and idle father. Djamal had relied on the fact that his Council, and his many other advisers and officials behind the scenes, did almost all the routine work involved in keeping such a vast and disparate

Empire functioning efficiently. Governors saw that the provinces remained quiet, and tax collectors ensured that revenue poured in a smooth, unbroken stream into the Imperial coffers. As long as he had money to spend and women to fondle, Djamal had been happy.

Ba'alekkt had appetites greater even than his notorious father, but he also possessed a greedy lust for power. He enjoyed the knowledge that the lives of millions of his subjects, from the courtiers and officials in his Palace to the lowest slave or prostitute, depended on his whim. If he ordered the entire population of a town to be exterminated, it would be done without question. His rule was absolute, and his commands were instantly obeyed. Everyone remembered what had happened to his first Council, and feared him.

It was what Ba'alekkt wanted. He had always been contemptuous of rulers who courted cheap popularity. He had no desire to be remembered as an Emperor who was greatly beloved by his people: he wanted the reputation of Akkatanat, revered for more than two hundred centuries as a man of war, a man of battle. It was what Toktel'yans admired above all else, and it was why Ba'alekkt took such a keen interest in his Army. The finest in the known world, its soldiers had won the Empire on his ancestors' behalf over the past two thousand years, and now, in garrisons in every town and city and province, on every island, they kept it safe.

The soldiers on Tekkt, however, were not real, battle-hardened warriors, but local boys doing their compulsory five years' service, proud of their splendid bronze armour and gleaming weaponry. Ba'alekkt smiled grimly at his immaculate troops. These fancy boys, tricked out in their finery, had no idea what war meant. He decided to order their transfer to Penya forthwith. Sekkenet had been telling him only a few days ago that the Governor there needed more men, in case fighting flared up again. A year on the island should harden these soft children, and transform them into useful soldiers.

Sekkenet had stayed in Toktel'yi to organize the invasion of the northern cities, and anyway there was no urgency. Ba'alekkt cooled himself with a few waves of his fan, made from the glittering silver tail feathers of a firebird, and eyed the Tekktish women with interest. If anyone looked promising he would tell the Chief Eunuch to have her brought up to the Palace. Last year he'd had

a most delicious girl. She'd been someone's wife, and notably
unwilling to join the Imperial menage, even temporarily, but her
reluctance had only added to the fun, and of course her husband
hadn't dared to object. Indeed, most of his subjects would count
themselves honoured by his interest, and he always ensured that
his transient lovers, or their male protectors, were suitably
rewarded with a hefty bag of gold.

As the slave-borne palanquin passed slowly by, he caught
sight of a woman at the front of the crowd. She was black-skinned,
like many Archipelagians, and stood with the elegant poise of a
dancer. But it was her dress that had attracted his notice. Amongst
the Tekktish women, clad in their traditional and voluminous
dark blue and grey robes, the sunburst colours, yellow, scarlet
and crimson, positively shouted for attention. Like everyone else
here, she was unveiled, and her dark eyes fixed on his with an
interest that was both unmistakable and extremely provocative.

Ba'alekkt had never been one to resist temptation. He
snapped his fingers, and the slaves halted instantly. Ignoring the
sounds of confusion to the rear of the procession, caused by his
unexpected stop, he beckoned to the woman.

Her eyebrows lifted slightly in acknowledgement, and then,
with a smile, she emerged from the crowd. The Emperor watched
her graceful, swaying walk, and licked his lips. She stood beside
the palanquin in the full light of the sun, and Ba'alekkt looked at
her smooth ebony face, her sculpted, sensual mouth, and knew
that he must have her.

'Your Imperial Majesty commands?'

Her voice was low, and rather husky. He imagined it whispering
lewd words into his ear, and his loins hardened at the thought. The
sunburst dress was made of an almost transparent gauze, and her
breasts were clearly visible beneath the splashed, brilliant colours.

'I would like to know your name,' he said, feasting his gaze on
her face and her body, breathing in the musky, enticing aroma
of her perfume. She was probably a whore, but by Kaylo's bones
she looked as if she enjoyed her work. And his seventy concubines had never satisfied his thirst for novelty. This woman probably knew every trick in every pillow book ever written, and a
few of her own invention besides.

'My name is Mallaso, Imperial Majesty. Of Toktel'yi.'

'Ah.' That air of sexual sophistication was hardly native to
Tekkt. Ba'alekkt smiled, slowly and greedily. 'And whose are
you?'

It was the usual question asked of any Toktel'yan woman. The answer would name her father, husband, owner, master or pimp. This Mallaso's response, however, was unexpected. 'I belong to no one, Imperial Majesty. I am a freed woman, and a dancer – one of the best in all your dominions. Would you like me to . . . dance for you, Imperial Majesty?'

'Indeed I would.' Ba'alekkt's surprisingly light, greenish-brown eyes gleamed with lust. 'I look forward to it with considerable anticipation. Tonight? Present yourself at the Palace tonight, and . . . dance for me. I have the finest musicians in the Empire to play for you, Mallaso.'

'I shall be glad to entertain you, Imperial Majesty,' said the woman, and gave him a slow, curved, sensual smile.

The palanquin continued at a snap of his fingers. Mallaso stepped back into the crowd, acutely conscious of the curious looks and whispered comments on her brazen proposition of the Emperor. She found it hard to stop herself shaking. It was done, and there would be no going back now, even if she had wanted to. Tonight, all the dead of Penya, all those thousands of souls, would be avenged at last. And if she succeeded, she did not care if she never saw another dawn.

She walked back to the tavern, her heart thudding, forcing herself to plan what she must take with her, what she must wear, what she must do. And she must somehow behave normally, in case Bron suspected anything. She would leave him a message, so that if it all went wrong he would have a chance of escape. But this was her plan, her vengeance, hers alone.

His door was shut when she returned to her room. She stripped off the sunburst dress and hid it at the bottom of her bag. She had already, on the previous day, bought the clothes she would wear for Ba'alekkt from a stall in the market. The vendor had looked at her curiously – there probably wasn't much call for that sort of thing from Tekktish women. She regretted the bead gown, left at home with all her other dancing costumes, but it wouldn't have been practical for what she planned.

It was now nearly noon, and the heat, even in this comparatively cool, north-facing room, was thick and oppressive. She sponged herself with cold water, and then lay down on the bed, with only a thin cotton sheet to cover her.

Surprisingly, she slept, and was woken by a light double knock.

Mallaso sat up, her heart racing. 'Who is it?'

'Bron. Can I come in?'

She wrapped the sheet round herself and unlocked the door. He stood outside in the colonnade which surrounded the tavern's rear courtyard, now plunged into the shade of early evening. He gave her a brief smile and walked past her, into the room. 'Have you thought any more about dancing tonight?'

She shook her head. 'No. I'm – I'm sorry, Bron, but I still don't feel ready. Tomorrow, perhaps.'

He reached out to touch her shoulder, with a gentle compassion that failed to reach her ice-bound heart. 'It's all right. I understand. But would you like to come and watch me play? You've been shut in here all day, it'd do you good to get out for a little.'

'No,' she said. 'Please, Bron, I have a headache, and I would like to lie down again.'

He looked at her with such concern that she almost felt guilty. 'Are you ill?'

'No – no, I think it's the heat. I'll be better soon.'

'I wish I could Heal you. But I can't, in case Al'Kalyek is on the island.'

'It doesn't matter – it's not very bad. I shall be much better in the morning.'

'Good night, then.' He walked forward and kissed her lightly, affectionately on the cheek. 'Sleep well. I'll see you tomorrow.'

'Good night,' Mallaso said. She watched him leave, shutting the door gently behind him. Her skin tingled where his lips had touched her, but she ignored the sensation.

She did not go back to bed, but locked the door and dressed herself with care in the garments she had bought yesterday, adding every scrap of jewellery in her baggage: neck-strings, brooches, finger-rings, earrings, bracelets, shoulder-clasps, and a set of exquisite jewelled clips, in the shape of tiny birds, to scatter in her hair. She covered all her betraying finery with a voluminous grey Tekktish robe. It enveloped her from scalp to toe, and left only her face exposed, though hidden in the shadow of the bulky hood. Then she opened the wooden window grille, which looked out on to a narrow, deserted alley behind the tavern. She scrambled through, pulling it closed behind her, and walked off towards the centre of the town.

It was almost dark now, and there were few people about. Mallaso strode briskly and purposefully down the empty streets, ignoring one or two hopeful calls from holidaying Toktel'yan youths. She crossed the big central market place and began to climb up the winding road leading to the Winter Palace, perched on its hilltop to the north-west of the town, and designed to make the most of any cooling breeze wafting up from the sea.

Everyone who'd ever been on Tekkt knew where the Palace was: indeed, since its site dominated the harbour, they could hardly ignore it. Like all Toktel'yan villas, it was low and rambling, built round a succession of courtyards and gardens. Mallaso had never set foot inside it, but she could easily guess at its layout. A private and intimate suite of the most luxurious rooms for the Emperor, around the central court; another, more spacious, where the seventy concubines would be installed, to await their master's pleasure; and further quadrangles, diminishing in splendour, size and importance, for guests, officials, and household or menial servants and slaves.

Six guards stood at the entrance, two low squat towers either side of an arched gate, the carved wood heavily embellished with gold and silver paint. It glittered richly in the flickering light of the torches placed in their iron cressets. Moths and other insects blundered about, attracted by the light, and in the honeyflower trees beside the road leading up to the Palace, a myriad fireflies smouldered in miniature rivalry.

They had been told to expect her: when she gave them her name, they opened the gates, with knowing grins and a whispered, 'Enjoy yourself, darling!' She gave them her whore's smile, deliberately provocative, and heard their raucous laughter as she was escorted across the first courtyard by a very fat and over-dressed eunuch, who'd obviously been waiting for her.

He asked her the usual questions, and she answered them patiently, knowing this to be routine with any new girl, whether in brothel or palace. She was twenty-five years old; no, she had had no disease; yes, she had borne one child; yes, she had undergone a concubine's training; yes, she was also a dancer. When he asked her where she'd been born, she told him Onnak: now was not the time to rouse suspicion by saying she came from Penya.

In return, she had some queries of her own concerning the Emperor's expectations of her, beyond of course what was obvious. With some relief, she learned that Ba'alekkt did not usually indulge in any of the more unsavoury perversions. She was unlikely to be tied up, or whipped, or maimed. With his reputation for cruelty, she had expected the worst. She had never anticipated any pleasure for herself in this encounter, but at least she wouldn't be hurt.

Until she killed him.

The central courtyard was dominated by one huge parasol tree, growing out of a circle of earth in the middle of the quadrangle, and so gnarled and ancient that the whole palace had probably been planned around it. The broad horizontal branches spread like a roof over the ground beneath, and sweet-scented creepers twisted up the trunk, filling the air around them with a delicious, lemony fragrance. Lanterns hung from every bough, red and yellow, blue and green and white, and illuminated everything with a rich, seductive glow.

In one corner, near the colonnade that ran round all four sides of the area, there was a great heap of cushions, and on these reclined five or six men, with plates and wine cups on low tables beside them, and expressions of lively anticipation on their faces. Four musicians were stationed under the tree, playing, with exquisite skill, a complicated piece by the Master of the Imperial Music, Yemeck, and in the space between tree and cushions two girls and two boys, hardly more than children, performed an acrobatic routine of considerable daring.

Mallaso waited in the shadows as the eunuch stepped forward to announce her arrival. She was not nervous or afraid: she seemed to have gone beyond such trivial emotions, drawn past them by the fierce intensity of her purpose. She heard the man's high unbroken voice, announcing her. 'Imperial Majesty, the woman named Mallaso is here.'

'Excellent,' Ba'alekkt said, and snapped his fingers. As the tumblers ran off, she walked forward into the pool of light in front of the cushions, and knelt before him in the correct posture of humble subservience.

'You may rise, Mallaso,' said the Emperor. 'Welcome to my Winter Palace. And may this be the beginning of a night that both of us will long remember.'

CHAPTER
FIFTEEN

Mallaso unfastened the cord at the neck of her cloak, and with a graceful twist of her body let the folds of grey cloth slither down to the floor. Beneath it, she wore a gown made up of two lengths of scarlet silk, with gold threads running erratically through the weave. It was fastened in Penyan style with a huge pinned gold brooch at each shoulder, and fell gleaming over the contours of her body to the ground. Tantalizing glimpses of dark skin, anointed with aphrodisiac oils and glittering with gold dust, showed between the edges of the cloth.

Ba'alekkt smiled, and leaned forward. 'You look magnificent, Mallaso of Toktel'yi. Will you dance for us?'

She smiled in assent, and turned to the musicians. At her bidding, they began the slow, stately tune, originally from Tatht, called 'The Parade of Flowers'.

Mallaso danced, as she always did, with perfect grace and skill. She had performed this one so many times, for more men than she could count, but never before had so much depended on her powers of seduction. Not that Ba'alekkt, lolling on the cushions and making lewd comments about her body to his companions, needed much seducing. But the eunuch had told her that he liked to be teased, tantalized, tempted. It was unnecessary when he could take her there and then, without any preliminaries at all, but it was part of his preferred game of love. Perhaps the very fact that he could have any woman in the Empire with a snap of his fingers made the pretence of uncertainty so exciting.

In situations like this, she had always managed to remain detached from herself. It was as if she were watching another woman, one she did not know, performing the erotic rituals of lust. She turned and swayed and stepped with the rhythm of the music, a seductive smile on her lips, and all the while her mind assessed the situation as coldly and logically as if she were planning a battle.

She had recognized one of the Emperor's companions, a

young man called N'kennan who was notorious, even in Tok-tel'yi, for his excesses. He'd been a frequent customer at the Blue Hyacinth, though as he'd always kept to one or two favourite girls, she thought he wouldn't remember her. The others were rather older, stout men full of their own importance and fawning all over Ba'alekkt. With a sudden pang of unease, she wondered if the Emperor liked to do it in front of an audience.

Well, it wouldn't stop her even if he did. She told the musicians to play a different piece, and began a whirling, stamp-ing, leaping dance which ensured that very little of her body remained hidden beneath the flying red silk. Ba'alekkt's eyes gleamed, and the other men stared at her with avid, lustful faces.

She finished with a wild spring into the air, and stood panting, sweat pouring down her back and sticking the cloth to her body. Ba'alekkt smiled lasciviously, and beckoned. 'Come here.'

Mallaso walked towards him. He was undeniably handsome, in a rather florid way, and in a few years he would be fat. Plenty of women had lusted after him, so he had no cause to suspect her. And her long years as a slave and a concubine had taught her to disguise her real feelings behind this smiling, concupiscent mask.

It had deceived almost everyone, and it certainly deceived Ba'alekkt. She slid into his embrace, murmuring encouraging endearments, and his hands fondled her beneath the scarlet silk. He obviously did like to do it in public: she would have to comply, and persuade him afterwards that they would have more fun in private. Of course, he might want to pass her over to his com-panions, but she was certain that, whatever happened, she could ensure they were alone for at least part of the night. Flattering words about his prowess and her need for more should do the trick.

Surprisingly, he was good. If she hadn't hated him, hadn't wanted to kill him, she might almost have enjoyed herself. For a spoiled, arrogant, selfish, brutal man, he was very considerate. But then, of course, his enormous vanity probably relished mani-pulating his women's passions.

Mallaso, well aware that the other men were watching her every move, gave an unrestrained display of lust. If only they had been alone, it would have been so easy . . . but they were not. Cronies, musicians, slaves, probably even the eunuch, were all still present. And although she was prepared to kill him here if necessary, despite the inevitable consequences, she would prefer privacy. Apart from anything else, success would be much more certain.

He finished at last, and disentangled himself, grinning with satisfaction. 'Well, friends, what did you think of that?'

Mallaso rearranged the silk over her body and sat amongst the cushions, listening to the other men complementing Ba'a-lekkt on his extraordinarily fine technique. The irony of it made her smile. She said, into a pause, 'Don't you intend to ask my opinion, Imperial Majesty?'

Ba'alekkt turned to her, surprised. 'Your opinion?'

'I am the one most closely concerned, Imperial Majesty – aren't I best able to judge?'

He stared at her, frowning, and then laughed indulgently. 'Perhaps you are. Well, then, Mallaso, what is your opinion?'

She smiled at him, and leaned over to whisper in his ear. As she had hoped, he was at once delighted and intrigued by her suggestion. 'Later, my girl,' he said, and his hand squeezed her breast lasciviously. 'Later. You've given me a powerful thirst – let's eat and drink now.'

The musicians played on. More food and wine appeared. N'kennan brought out a pipe, filled it with khlar leaves, and lit it. The intoxicating smoke writhed around Mallaso's face, making her want to cough. A troupe of dancing girls ran into the court-yard, and Ba'alekkt, still caressing her, grinned at his com-panions. 'Those are yours, if you want them. I'm keeping this one to myself, tonight.'

She had been tired before coming here: now, her weariness, combined with the fumes of the drug, the rich food and strong wine, had pulled her into a strange, almost trance-like state. Afraid that she might fall asleep, she whispered again into Ba'a-lekkt's ear.

He laughed, and bit her neck. 'You're keen, aren't you! I love it when they can't get enough of me . . . I'll see you later, friends. Don't forget to enjoy yourselves – and the girls.'

By the look of N'kennan and the other men, there was no danger of it. Mallaso followed Ba'alekkt between two pillars of the colonnade, and into the room beyond.

She had never been in an Emperor's bedchamber before, and it was even more luxurious than she'd imagined. The huge bedstead was made of carved and gilded wood, and took up nearly half the space. There was a low, draped couch, a table and chair, a curtained-off alcove for clothes, and an inner room containing a bath, sunk in the tiled floor. Scenes of Kaylo's Paradise, where absolutely nothing pleasurable was forbidden, had been painted on the walls with considerable skill and stunning realism. Mallaso glanced at the innumerable entwined and half-naked figures, and wondered if the artist had done his research in the Blue Hyacinth.

'I had this decorated last year,' Ba'alekkt said, seeing the direction of her gaze. 'Give you any ideas, my lovely?'

'Perhaps,' she said, with a coy smile. He had closed the courtyard door, and the two wide windows opposite, each covered by a pierced wooden grille, probably looked out on to a dark and empty garden. They were alone at last, and beneath the red silk her heart was beginning to beat faster. She took his hand, and smiled. 'How about a bath, Imperial Majesty?'

It was certainly big enough for two, or even four. Steps led down into it, and on one side a statue of a naked girl carrying a ewer spilled endless streams of water into the pool. Mallaso didn't bother to remove her dress: she slid gratefully into the silky, cool liquid, and Ba'alekkt followed her.

And it was easy to sit astride him, simulating ecstasy, her body arched and her head thrown back: and easy, too, to remove the long steel blade fastening her left shoulder-brooch. For Penya, she thought, gripping it tightly in her fist. This is for Penya. And with all her strength, she stabbed down at the unsuspecting man beneath her.

At the last moment, he opened his eyes and saw the knife descending. With a look of horrified astonishment, he twisted aside. She had aimed for the soft, vulnerable place where neck joined body: instead, the point glanced off his collar-bone and scored a deep furrow across the brown, muscular flesh of his shoulder. Wild with fear and hatred, she lifted her hand to strike again, and Ba'alekkt grabbed her wrist. She sank her teeth into his arm, and he let go with a curse. Then, with desperate strength, she drove the blade at his eye.

The Emperor jerked his head away, and his face disappeared beneath the water. She stabbed at him again and again as he struggled, and the water became tinged with red. She knew she was killing him, she knew he would die. A vast insane glory filled her, and she raised her arm for the death-blow.

There was a convulsion below her. Ba'alekkt erupted from

the water, his face and body pouring blood from half a dozen wounds, and flung her backwards. Her head cracked on the side of the bath, and she gasped with pain: then he gripped her arm and brought it down hard on the tiled floor. She screamed in agony, and the shoulder-pin dropped uselessly from her numbed fingers and spun out of reach.

'Kill me, would you?' cried Ba'alekkt, and his hands clenched around her neck, forcing her down, down under the water, despite her frantic struggles. 'I'll give you a taste of your own medicine, you murderous little whore.'

And his face, contorted with rage and pain and shock, was the last thing Mallaso saw before oblivion overwhelmed her.

As usual, Bron had spent the evening playing for the customers at the Pelican tavern. His fame had grown, and the place was packed. Afterwards, the landlord, Tongren, had given him, as arranged, a purse of half-Imperials. He accepted his fee with thanks, and stayed to talk over a cup or two of good golden wine that was surely Hailyan. Tongren was a noted amateur musician, and they spent some time discussing the merits of their respective instruments. Bron didn't mention his Sith, left behind in Kerenth: afterwards, he had acquired the djarlek, common throughout the Empire, and easier but less satisfying to play. Tongren preferred the brannekka, similar to a harp but held horizontally on the knee and played by striking the strings with a padded hammer. Each had its advantages, and both men enjoyed this good-natured argument.

At last, Bron said good-night, picked up the djarlek, the flute and the pipes, and left Tongren to the rest of the wine. Outside in the courtyard, it was quite dark: the moon was only a slim curve of brilliance, high in the southern sky. Fireflies danced around the clump of shrubs in the centre of the broad square space, and the tables and benches, swept and ready for tomorrow's customers, were empty. He wanted to open his mind to the soft warm night, but it was too dangerous. If Al'Kalyek was on the island he would immediately pick up the use of sorcery. Instead, he obeyed a sudden impulse and tapped gently on Mallaso's door.

There was no reply, so she must be asleep. He stifled a yawn, and turned away into his own room next door. Inside a small clay lamp on the table glowed as gently as a firefly, and it was stiflingly hot. He dropped his instruments on the bed and went to the window grille. It was risky, even on law-abiding, sleepy Tekkt, to leave it open all night, but a few moments with the cool breeze streaming uninterrupted into his stuffy room should ensure that he slept well. He lifted the iron bar, swung both halves of the grille carefully inwards, and leaned out.

It was becoming increasingly difficult to repress his power, to keep it locked away inside the deepest recesses of his mind. He longed to let his spirit leave his body and soar free in the air, to join the night creatures in the fields and orchards, to fly with the owls amongst the trees, and swim with the dolphins through the eerie, glowing waters of the Southern Sea. The yearning gnawed at him, the urge to use his magic ever stronger. He had been wrong: he could not restrain it indefinitely. He had felt no qualms about using his skills to Heal: after all, what could be more alien to Ayak than curing illness? But he could not endure much more of this. When Mallaso returned to Toktel'yi, he would try to make his way to Jo'ami. He didn't want to desert her, though he thought she no longer had need of him. But living in this strange limbo, neither ordinary man nor sorcerer, was becoming impossible.

A noise, gentle, insistent, had rubbed away at the edge of his hearing for some while. He peered out into the alley, and saw that Mallaso's window grille was unfastened and creaking softly in the night air.

Suddenly, he remembered the look on her face: set, drawn, yet determined. At the time, he had ascribed it to her headache. But now he wondered if something was wrong. And he thought of her sad, bleak voice, a month ago, speaking of her own death.

With one swift, agile movement, Bron swung himself over the sill, jumped down and ran the few steps to the next window. The alley was low here, worn down by thousands of footsteps over hundreds of years, and he wasn't tall enough to look inside. Aware that he might be making a fool of himself by giving Mallaso the fright of her life, he pushed the two halves of the grille inwards.

There was no scream of alarm. Suddenly sick with foreboding, he grabbed the sill and hauled himself up, over, and into her room.

He'd made quite a lot of noise, but there was still no sound, and he couldn't hear her breathing. Bron found his way to the table where she kept her lamp. It had almost gone out, so he picked the glowing wick out of the oil, and blew gently on it. At once the light brightened. He lifted the lamp up, and turned round, afraid of what he might see.

There was no body on the bed. There was nothing. The room was quite empty. But on the table, next to where the lamp had been, there was a small folded piece of paper.

It had his name on it, in her neat, precise script. He opened it, and scanned the brief lines with the dreadful certainty of disaster.

She had gone to the Palace to kill Ba'alekkt. He lit the message with the lamp and waited, his heart hammering, until its ashes fell smoking to the floor. Then he blew the wick out, put it back on the table, and climbed out through the window. He dropped into the empty alley below, reached up to pull the grilles shut, and then ran.

His feet sounded terrifyingly loud, echoing in the silent streets. A small shadow, perhaps a cat, fled down a passageway, and behind him, making a trail almost as obvious as footsteps in wet sand, dogs began to bark.

But he reached the edge of the town unmolested, and stopped for a moment, fighting to control his breathing and the wild sense of panic that had flooded him as he read Mallaso's note. The peace of the night, broken only by the endless, soothing, rhythmic noise of the crickets, settled back round him like a cloak. No one had seen him, no one was chasing him. There was still a chance.

He would have to use magic soon, he couldn't avoid it. But he still didn't know if Al'Kalyek was with the Emperor. Bron was certain that his own power would be greater than the Court Sorcerer's, but to use it wisely, economically, expending only what was needed, would not be easy. And he was afraid that his emotions might take control, creating a hideous conflagration that would be far worse even than his slaughter of the Ska'i. For they had all been evil beyond redemption, but there was surely no evil anywhere in the pretty Winter Palace – only men who possessed too much power, or not enough.

He caught the sound of voices, and ducked into the thick scrub at the side of the road. A small patrol was coming up from the town: he could hear the distinctive tramp of their nailed boots, and the jingle of armour. They halted a score of paces below him, and he could discern scraps of their conversation.

'Nothing here . . . You're imagining things again . . .'

'The dogs barked, though . . . Must have been something.' And then, more loudly, 'Koulous, go on up to the Palace. Check all's well.'

Grumbling dissent could be heard from the soldier. Discipline on Tekkt must be very lax: elsewhere in the Empire, the penalty for even mildly questioning orders was death. Bron waited until the man had trudged past, muttering imprecations under his breath. Then he turned and slipped deeper into the trees, and began to make his way up the hill, parallel with the road. Somehow, he must enter the Palace without attracting the attention of any guards. And he had no idea of its internal layout, beyond what he could guess.

The undergrowth was thick, and almost impenetrable. The ground here sloped up steeply, and there was a low cliff immediately below the Palace walls. Fortunately, from what he could see of it in the starlight, it looked like an easy climb, and Bron was strong and agile. He paused for a moment at its foot, listening. The sound of music, beautifully played, drifted over the wall above him, but there were no other sounds from within the Palace. He couldn't hear or see any soldiers patrolling the ramparts, and nothing to indicate that the Emperor had been attacked.

The urge to employ sorcery to see inside the building was so strong that he was almost overwhelmed by it. And deep in the darkness of his soul, something was stirring, savouring the imminent prospect of blood.

He could not use magic, not now, when he was still outside the Palace. Trying to ignore the rising clamour within him, Bron began to climb the cliff. He moved slowly and carefully, resisting the temptation to ascend too quickly. Stealth and utter silence would be vital if he were to save Mallaso – or help her.

That was a choice he'd hoped never to make. Even now, with the dilemma almost upon him, he didn't know what he would do.

Suddenly there was a yell from inside the Palace, and the tramp of running feet. Bron froze, cramped to the rock, balanced on a ledge too narrow for comfort or safety, and listened with a thumping heart to the unmistakable sounds of serious disturbance. He had no way of knowing, down here, what was happening, or if Mallaso was involved.

But at this particular moment, any guards were unlikely to be looking over the wall. Bron resumed his climb, his eyes, sharp even in the gloom, assessing handholds and ledges, concentrating on this one vital task, and trying desperately to ignore the uproar above, though his mind boiled with frantic questions. Was the Emperor dead? Was Mallaso dead? What was happening amidst the wild shouting and screaming?

Suddenly, almost before he had expected it, he had reached the top of the cliff. In front of him rose a low bank covered with grass, boulders and a few scrubby plants. None of it offered any concealment whatsoever. And emerging from it, at least twice his height, was a sheer whitewashed wall. There were no convenient cracks or crevices to accommodate toes and fingers, just a flat expanse, glimmering pale in the restricted light of the horned moon.

He would have to use magic after all. He didn't want to reveal himself before managing even to infiltrate the Palace, but without a rope or a tree to climb, he hadn't a chance otherwise. He glanced around and up. Nothing moving on the bank, no-one looking down from the ramparts.

Even if someone had been watching, they would have seen no more than a flicker or a shadow creeping over the wall, between one blink of an eye and the next. But the guards were elsewhere, and the walk along the top of the wall was quite deserted.

Bron crouched in the limited shadow cast by one of the triangular battlements. Below him lay the sloping roof of a colonnade, with a small garden beyond it, lush, tropical and exotic in the preferred Toktel'yan style. On the other side of the tangled greenery he could see another wall, pierced by two low-silled windows. Intricately carved wooden or iron grilles hid most of the room beyond from his view, but he could see enough movement, and hear enough noise, to know that here was the heart of the disturbance.

No more sorcery. If he wanted to find out what was happening, he would have to risk the flimsy-looking roof below him. Glad that he was not a large or heavy man, Bron slipped cautiously over the edge of the wall and crept down the shallow slope. There were no shouts of alarm. He reached the gutter, tested it briefly, swung over and dropped to the ground.

Once in the garden, there was plenty of cover. He dodged between the bushes and hid behind a substantial tree, just a few paces from the windows and as close as he dared to go.

He heard voices, all shouting at once. And another, a man's cutting through the hubbub like a knife. 'At last, Olkanno. Where in Kaylo's name were you?'

'Imperial Majesty, you're hurt! You're bleeding in a dozen places!'

'It's hardly surprising when some mad whore tries to knife me, is it?'

Bron moved slightly to his left so that he could get a better view. The room was obviously the Emperor's bed-chamber. It was full of soldiers, officials and slaves, jostling and crowding round Ba'alekkt. He was clad only in a blue cotton robe, soaking wet and liberally stained with blood. His heart sick, Bron wondered if some of it was Mallaso's.

'Who is she?' It was Olkanno again, his rather high-pitched voice sharp. By craning his neck, Bron could just see him. Small, balding and plump, he was not an impressive sight, but the Spymaster's sinister reputation made him feared throughout the Empire.

'I'd have expected you to tell me that.' Ba'alekkt's tone was ragged, revealing just how greatly the assassination attempt had shocked him. 'It's your job, remember, to inform me when murderers come walking into my Palace.'

'And who invited her?' the Spymaster enquired pointedly. 'Sooner or later, Imperial Majesty, given your habits, this was bound to happen.'

There was a brief, hostile silence. Then Ba'alekkt said, 'Just for tonight, little man, I'll forget you dared to speak to me so insolently.'

'I – I humbly crave your pardon, Imperial Majesty.' Olkanno hastily knelt in a posture of submissive apology, but Bron could sense his angry resentment, simmering beneath his apparent capitulation.

'Granted – for now. Her name is – or was – Mallaso. Of Toktel'yi, she said. Kaylo's rod, she was good – until she tried to skewer me. Did I kill her?'

Another voice spoke, different, deeper, with a resonant timbre that suddenly raised the hairs on Bron's arms. 'No, Imperial Majesty, you did not. She will live long enough for Olkanno to question her. And I should warn you – there is sorcery concerned. I felt it just now, only faintly, but quite unmistakable.'

That must surely be Al'Kalyek. And Mallaso was alive. He

couldn't see her, but he knew she must be present. He should use his power *now* to save her, but still something, the terrible dread of the unknown and the irrevocable, prevented Bron from taking the final and inevitable step towards his fate.

'Send out the guards. Where?'

'The sensation was very brief, and took me by surprise, Imperial Majesty, so I did not have time to ascertain its direction. But I am positive that it was quite close, within the Palace.'

Ba'alekkt turned and snapped his fingers. 'Search – now. Every corner, every possible hiding-place, down to the last mouse-hole. And a bag of gold Imperials to the man who finds any intruder. Go!'

The soldiers ran out. Bron, pressed against the rough trunk of a young palm, knew it wouldn't be long before they found him. And then . . . how powerful was Al'Kalyek? Could he keep the Court Sorcerer at bay while he rescued Mallaso?

'If the woman is still alive, bring her out.'

Two more soldiers appeared from some other room, dragging her between them. Even with the elaborate curls of the grille obstructing his view, Bron could see much more than he wanted to. She was dripping wet, half-naked, the bruises darker against the dark skin of her slender throat, and she hung in the soldiers' ungentle grasp as if her legs could not obey the fierce, desperate pride that suffused her face.

'Mallaso of Toktel'yi. You tried to kill the Emperor, so I understand.' Olkanno's tone was quite mild, but the look on his face, at once menacing and greedy, made Bron shiver.

'Yes.' The woman's voice was hoarse and uncompromising. 'And he deserved it.'

'You lie. But you shall deserve the death awaiting you – though I assure you that it will not come nearly as soon as you might wish. Stand up, bitch, before your Emperor!'

The Spymaster's hand shot out and smashed once, twice across her face. Sickened, Bron clenched his hands and slowly, desperately, repressed the instincts that urged him to leap up and immolate them all.

'He is not my Emperor,' Mallaso said. 'For I am not of Toktel'yi. I am of Penya.'

She spoke the name proudly, with a challenge in her voice, although her nose and mouth were both pouring blood.

'Penya. That explains it,' said Ba'alekkt. 'By Olyak's sword, I should have had that island burnt from end to end, and slaughtered every living creature on it, friendly or not. No, Olkanno, you can have your fun with her soon enough. Tell me, Mallaso of *Penya* – did you act alone? Or do you have an accomplice lurking somewhere?'

'I'm alone. No-one else knows I'm here.'

'She's lying!' Olkanno said contemptuously. 'No woman could plot this without a man's help.'

'You might be wrong,' said Al'Kalyek. 'She is of Penya, remember, and they had very similar customs to Kerenth.'

'Then the sooner they're forced to conform to our ways, the better,' Olkanno said. 'Well, whatever the truth, I'll get it out of her. I have no instruments with me, but it should be easy to improvise.'

'I can obtain all the information you need from her by sorcery,' Al'Kalyek said. 'And the process would be . . . kinder.'

'*Kind?*' Ba'alekkt laughed in disbelief. 'Olyak's bones, man, she did her best to kill me, and she nearly succeeded! Can't you see me bleeding? I don't want anyone to be *kind* to her. You have my full approval, Olkanno, for whatever you wish to do to her. Take as long as you like – enjoy yourself. Employ any technique or mutilation short of actual death. There's a room in one of the towers you can have, out of earshot – I don't want to hear her screaming day and night. When you've wrung her dry, let me know – I'd like to savour it. And then, dear Mallaso of Penya, I'll take great pleasure in watching you die. Slowly, in public, in the market place, so that all Tekkt can see the fate reserved for those who dare to attack their Emperor.' He walked forward, smiling, to face the woman. 'But before you take her away, Olkanno, I intend to have some entertainment in return for what she did.'

Mallaso watched him approach. Half-drowned, battered nearly into unconsciousness by the soldiers, she had understood very little of the discussion, save that it involved her and her death. She had already accepted that. What she regretted, searingly and bitterly, was her failure. She had gambled, and bungled it, and lost. Ba'alekkt, appallingly, was still alive: and standing right in front of her, with the long, wicked blade from her brooch, a little wider than a pin, a little narrower than a dagger, gripped in his hand. His smile broadening, he reached out and stroked the sharp point across her bare breasts.

Blood welled up, but she refused to flinch, although the pain was swift and sharp. Al'Kalyek gave a sudden exclamation of disgust, and strode out of the room, pushing his way between the crowded onlookers.

'I didn't think he'd have the stomach for it,' said the Emperor, and considered his handiwork thoughtfully. 'Now where shall I go? Across again, perhaps? Or lower this time?'

The slender tip carved its way down her belly. She could not control her attempts to twist away from the exquisite agony. The soldiers grasped her more tightly, and pulled her forward, on to the blade. Ba'alekkt laughed again, savagely, and lifted his hand, aiming the blade straight at her face . . .

And stopped. She stared at him stupidly, wondering why he hadn't slit her nose or her cheek, and saw that his eyes were bulging, and sweat was breaking out on his forehead. And then her battered wits struggled at last to the truth. He *couldn't* move.

Neither could anyone else in the room. Mallaso found that she could turn her head, and saw their distended eyes, their frustrated faces, their bodies frozen into immobility. But the two soldiers on either side of her still had her fast in their grip. She tried to wrench herself free, and failed. Then suddenly, their hands relaxed, and she was released so swiftly and unexpectedly that she fell to the floor.

It was sorcery. It must be. She could feel power humming in the room, just below the threshold of sound. And such a power could only come from one person.

With a sob of desperation, and terror, and panic, Mallaso scrambled to her feet and staggered over to the window grille. She pushed it open. Outside, the dim, tangled garden offered no clues, but she knew he was there. She fell rather than climbed over the sill, and landed painfully on her hands and knees. *Al'Kalyek*, she thought frantically – *where is Al'Kalyek?*

'Come on.' It was Bron's voice, warm, real, encouraging. His hand took hers, and pulled her to her feet. 'Quick – I can't keep them still for much longer.'

He propelled her through the bushes. She saw the colonnade at the end of the garden, and the wall above it. 'How – how can we—?'

'Easy.' His grip tightened, and suddenly she felt herself leave the ground. At the same instant, noise exploded behind them. Mallaso looked down, and saw the top of the wall passing a handspan beneath her feet. And then abruptly the ground was coming up to meet them, much too fast, but they just sailed down past it, and she realized that there was a cliff below the wall, and beneath it . . .

Nothing, save a white cloud. They entered it, and she couldn't see any more and didn't want to. This was like a dream, or a nightmare – at any moment, she would surely wake up to the screaming agony of Ba'alekkt's knife, and then Olkanno would drag her off to his lovingly improvised torture chamber . . .

They landed. Weak with pain and fear, her knees gave way and she fell against something hard and prickly. Bron was urging her to get up. Somehow her body obeyed him, and she struggled to her feet. The white cloud still surrounded them, but at least they weren't flying any more, and the ground felt solid and real.

'Come on. I'll help you. They'll never find us in this.' Bron had his arm round her, guiding her down a steep slope. She stumbled again and fell, and this time, her head swimming, she knew she couldn't get up.

'Leave me, *please*!' She stared up at where his face must be, although the fog was so thick she could see nothing at all. 'Oh, Bron, go – leave me and go – I can't—'

Behind and above them, muffled by the mist, people were shouting. 'Leave you?' Bron said. 'After I've gone to all this trouble? You must be joking. I'll carry you.'

'You can't!' She hated the feeble whine in her voice, but she was so exhausted by pain and terror that she couldn't help it. 'I'm as tall as you are, and almost as heavy.'

'Oh, yes, I can.' She heard the wild laughter in his voice, as if it was only this extremity of danger that had finally brought him fully to life. 'Get up. Come *on*, Mallaso, for the Mother's sake get up!'

And somehow, clinging on to the last rags of her courage, she did. He pulled her up across his shoulders as if she weighed nothing, with an easy strength that must come from sorcery, and ran down the hill through the blinding mist as though he could see as well as in daylight.

She must have lost consciousness, for suddenly she was lying on something soft and wet, with no idea of where she was or how she had come to be there. And around them she could hear only the normal, ordinary sounds of Tekkt in darkness, the endless crickets and the solitary, heartbreakingly beautiful song of a Nightsinger.

And waves, washing gently on to a beach.

She moved in sudden fear, and whispered, 'Bron?'

'I'm here. We're nearly safe. Come on, get up – I'll help you – we're going to swim out to the ship.'

Mallaso was beyond asking any more questions. He pulled her to her feet. Dizzily she tried to orientate herself, but it was impossible when they were still tightly wrapped in that thick, impenetrable fog. Bron guided her across what must be sand, for she could feel it squeezing between her toes, and then quite suddenly they were in the water, its warm touch spilling round her legs, the soft waves of the sheltered harbour washing around them. Once it had reached her waist, she sank into it, ignoring the sharp pains as the salt stung her wounds.

Long ago, as a child, she had loved to swim in the turquoise seas around Penya. She lay in the ocean's embrace, her eyes closed, feeling Bron's hand under her back, gripping her body, towing her through the gentle swell. A curious and remote sense of peace settled over her. Surely this was a dream: surely she had not been rescued from certain death and brought here by a man whose powers of sorcery, it seemed, were almost unlimited.

'We're here. Hold on to this.'

His voice jerked her out of her stupor. Mallaso found her hands touching a thick sisal rope. She opened her eyes and realized with alarm that the protective mist had vanished. Around her, the dark, sheltered waters of Tekkt Harbour undulated gently: and above her towered the steep, curving sides of a sizeable ship.

'Don't worry. The mist is still covering the area around the Palace. As long as it's there, they can't see through it – and they'll assume we're within it somewhere.'

'What about Al'Kalyek?'

'He'll work out the truth sooner or later, but we'll be gone long before then. In any case, I suspect he won't try too hard to find us. He loathes Ba'alekkt's little pleasures – didn't you see him walk out?'

'Yes.' She looked up at the wooden wall. 'I don't think I can climb that.'

'Don't worry, there's a ladder, just astern. I'll help you.'

Slowly she made her way along the side of the ship. Save for the whisper of the sea and the inevitable creaks and sighs of a large boat, there was no sound. She wondered bemusedly if it really was as deserted as it seemed, or if all the crew were aboard, but frozen by sorcery. And if so, how could they possibly sail it? She'd been taught to handle a small fishing boat by her father, fifteen years ago on Penya, but this was a two-masted, ocean-going merchantman, and such craft usually carried at least thirty sailors.

There was the ladder. Peering up, Mallaso knew that she could never climb it. Much, much easier to lie back and let the waves take her, out to sea with the tide and the dolphins.

'You can, you know. I'll help you.'

She wanted to shout at him, tell him to go away and leave her alone. Instead her hands came out of the water to grasp the rope. Without any conscious effort on her part, she ascended the ladder, sure-footed and strong. There was a pierced decorative rail running round the side of the ship which she clambered over before collapsing on to the deck, all that brief, unnatural vigour drained out of her.

And suddenly, as she lay there in a growing pool of water, the enormity of what she had done, of what had happened, hit her with the force of a hammer blow. She had tried to kill the Emperor. She had failed, totally and humiliatingly. Bron had put himself in terrible danger to rescue her, though she didn't deserve it. She wanted, *needed* to die – for Grayna was dead.

And then, at last, she wept for her daughter.

She hardly noticed Bron crouching beside her. She did not feel him lift her again in his arms. And she had no knowledge of the moment when he laid her down on a soft, feather-filled mattress in an empty cabin, for by then, mercifully, her exhausted, grief-stricken heart had sought refuge in unconsciousness.

So she did not know when the Balki trader *Silver Swan* raised its anchor, although none of its crew were on board, hoisted its two brightly painted sails to catch the night breeze, and sailed due south out of Tekkt Harbour, leaving no trace behind. Nor did she see the sunrise across a calm, empty sea, or feel the steady sorcerer's wind, gentle and inexorable, that pushed the ship ever southwards, all that day, and the next night and day, and the next. She slept on, deeply and evenly, as her stricken body healed itself, and her mind, lacerated with grief and fear and pain, wandered far away and long ago, in a place and time when happiness was still possible. She did not watch as the *Silver Swan* negotiated the hidden rocks and fickle, treacherous currents between the innumerable islands called the Scatterlings, covering the three hundred miles of sea between Balki and Penya, and then, on the third day, slip between the rocky peninsula of Tulyet, with cliffs a mile high falling sheer into the sea, and Annatal, the lush, green, mountainous island where the sorcerers' drug was produced. She was not even aware of the tropical storm, fierce and malevolent, which swept around the ship and onwards, without disrupting her course or even filling her sails.

But on the afternoon of the fourth day of her strange sleep, on this stranger voyage, Mallaso woke. At first, she had no idea where she was. The cabin was lit by one tiny square window, just under the deck above her, and she stared up at the daylight while her mind struggled to make sense of the gentle motion of the ship.

Then she remembered everything, and her heart raced. How long had she been asleep? Where were they? Where was Bron? All around her, the vessel creaked and sighed softly in rhythm with the waves, but she could hear none of the normal loud, cheerful noises, the bustle as sailors worked at rope and tiller.

Bewildered and curious, she sat up. Beneath the thin sheet, she was naked. She looked down at herself, and saw that her body bore no scars. And yet her clearest and most dreadful memory of that last terrible night was of Ba'alekkt leaning forward, 'r blade in his hands, enjoying her agony as he carved patterns on her skin.

Her mind shied away from all the implications. With some difficulty, for her legs felt weak and rubbery, she struggled to her feet. The cabin was tiny, just a mattress and a small wooden chest. Laid over the top was a clean, short, rather threadbare cotton tunic, such as sailors generally wore, and a broad leather belt with a bronze buckle. She put the tunic on. It didn't cover her knees, and she felt distinctly odd wearing it, but there was nothing else except the sheet – and no sign of her jewellery, or the scarlet silk, slashed and ruined, which she had worn to seduce Ba'alekkt.

She left the cabin, still feeling peculiarly light-headed and remote from reality, as if this were happening to someone else. There was a ladder just outside, leading up to the deck. She climbed it slowly and laboriously, and the heat of the sun struck her bare head as she emerged, dazed and blinking, into the brazen glare of a tropical afternoon.

Above her arched a vast vault of blue sky, unblemished by

clouds: below it, a bluer, empty sea. The ship's deck stretched in front of her, the wood bleached by the sun, dazzlingly white except where the sail's shadow lay sharp and dark across it amidships. Her eyes watering in the brilliance, Mallaso turned to face astern.

Bron stood in the shadow cast by the mizzen sail, his hand resting lightly on the tiller. Mallaso saw that beneath the sunburn and the unshaven stubble around his mouth and jaw, he looked utterly exhausted. But he smiled at her, and his eyes were full of hope.

He pointed forward. 'Look,' he said. 'Look there, ahead.'

She turned again, obediently following the line of his finger. The sea was not empty after all. On the horizon, topped by a cap of fluffy white clouds, lay an island, grey-blue with distance.

'What is it?' she asked, shading her eyes. Bemusedly she wondered if it was Penya – although it didn't look big enough to be Penya.

'It's where I should have gone long ago,' Bron said softly. 'The island of legend and sorcery and myth – the island of Jo'ami.'

PART FOUR
JO'AMI

CHAPTER
SIXTEEN

'A ship. There, Wisest – do you see? And Toktel'yan, if I am not mistaken.'

The High Sorcerer of Jo'ami peered into the scrying bowl. On its dark surface sailed a tiny craft, with the pronounced and graceful sheer of all Archipelagian traders. Her two quadrilateral sails, both painted bright red with broad yellow stripes, were filled with wind, and the white bow-wave curved and flowed around her slender prow.

The High Sorcerer studied the ship for a long, long moment, while the acolytes watched anxiously. Few vessels came to Jo'ami, remote, isolated, hidden by fear and by myth. And a ship from Toktel'yan lands had not been seen for many, many years.

At last, the elderly sorcerer straightened and looked round, smiling, at the watching faces. 'I think the ship is friendly – despite appearances.'

Suddenly, all the tension left the chamber. 'Then they pose no threat,' said Tu Kar-Lyen, grinning with relief. Since Ba'alekkt's accession to the Onyx Throne, there had been very disturbing rumours about the new Emperor's intentions.

'I didn't say that.' The High Sorcerer fixed the chief acolyte with a significant stare. 'On the contrary, one of them at least carries the potential to alter the world. Do you not remember the Prophecies of En Sy-T'lyear? This, my dear friends and colleagues, is the One.'

There was a brief, shocked silence, broken only by the high clamour of the seabirds, wheeling in the sky outside.

Tu Kar-Lyen recited softly, 'A child born of evil, who is not evil, who yet bears evil in his heart. Because of his birth, empires will fall, cities crumble, and the world will change for ever. So spake En Sy-T'lyear, six hundred years ago. And does that ship truly bear the One? Here and now, to Jo'ami?'

'I knew he would come,' said the High Sorcerer. 'If he is aware of what he is, he must seek the answers. And from us, in Jo'ami, he hopes he will find them.'

'And will he?' asked Tu Kar-Lyen. He was much younger than the High Sorcerer, and his hair was still brown, though dusted with flecks of grey.

'If he has any wisdom within him, yes. And he must possess some, or he would not come here.' The High Sorcerer moved to the north-facing window, and looked out. The School of Wizards stood on the summit of the mountain above Jo'ami Haven. Below, the hot, shimmering, tree-cloaked land sloped down steeply to the curving bay, where a few small boats lay beached on the white sands. The only sails in plain view belonged to the island's fishing fleet, but the High Sorcerer's mind could reach much further than the misty line where sea met sky in a sapphire haze.

'Yes, he is there. He will make landfall this evening. I will call him, so that he knows where to come. But he is not to be helped, even though he will need all his strength and all his powers to reach us. He must pass the test.'

'If he is the One, he will succeed with ease.'

'I know. But he is very tired, and he has sailed that boat alone, using his sorcery, all the way from Tekkt. He has not slept for five days. And he has a companion – a woman, heartbroken with grief for her child. They are both in great need of rest, and healing.'

'Has the woman any power?' asked one of the junior acolytes.

'I cannot discern it within her, although she is of Penya, and once the old magic, the Mother's magic, was strong in that island. She may possess some without knowing it. But she does not matter. Beside him and his power, she is nothing.' The High Sorcerer turned away from the window and gave the others a shrewd, lingering stare. 'You are afraid of him. Don't deny it – I can feel your fear. You are right to be frightened, for this man trails danger like a cloak, and carries death within him. But it is the Empire which is in greatest peril, not Jo'ami. He needs us, and we need him and his power. Therefore, if he asks us for help, we will give it.'

The faces of Tu Kar-Lyen and the other acolytes, brown, pale-skinned, black, stared back with considerable apprehension. The High Sorcerer smiled. 'I told you – we have no reason to worry, if we are careful. He will fit our purpose as a blade fits the haft. Indeed, we should celebrate his coming. For he will change the world, and it needs changing – and sorcery, even now the greatest of all the Arts, will become transformed, supreme, all-powerful.'

Then the High Sorcerer dismissed them all, and they left reluctantly, turning to look at the scrying-bowl as if it would reveal the profoundest of secrets. But there was still only the bright little image of the ship sailing busily over the calm surface of the ink, blown by a mage's wind towards Jo'ami.

All day, the island had drawn steadily nearer. Bron stood in the stern, the shadow of the taut red and yellow mizzen sail protecting him from the fierce sun. Here, four hundred miles south of Tekkt, it was directly overhead at midday and the heat was searing.

They were alone on the boat. Bron held the tiller, and his mind provided the wind, and told him where to go. Mallaso had noted his intent, haggard face, taut with effort and lack of sleep, and the torrent of questions pouring up had died on her lips. For it was obvious that sailing the *Silver Swan* required all his powers of concentration, all the time.

So she went below and searched the ship. She found several small casks of water, hot, stale, brackish, but very welcome. There was a substantial store of preserved food in the galley: she carried raisins, wine, olives, flat dried bread and honey up to the deck. She ate ravenously, but Bron hardly touched his, although he drank some of the water, and thanked her with a brief, abstracted smile.

After a time, Mallaso walked forward to the bow. Here, there was no shelter from the sun, but the steady wind, blowing at her back, was cooling and pleasant. She felt the spray in her face and the salt on her lips, and drew a deep shaky breath. She was alive. Despite all that had happened to her, all that she had done, she was still alive. And for the first time since she had learned of Grayna's death, she was glad of it.

She gazed at the distant island. It didn't look like a haunt of demons and evil spirits. True, it shimmered on the horizon, but that was probably caused by the heat. It was hard to tell much detail from this far away, but she thought it was smaller, and higher, than Tekkt. And the symmetrical central peak looked suspiciously like a fire-mountain.

Jo'ami. Like everyone else living in and around the Southern Sea, she had heard the stories, and never paid much attention to them because she'd thought she had as much prospect of sailing to Jo'ami as of riding a camel to the desert city of Ma'alkwen. All the legends agreed that it was the Sorcerers' Island, but some said that it was protected by demons, others by spells. A sailor from Annatal, one of her customers at the Blue Hyacinth, had sworn that it could be moved through the ocean like a ship. It was the only island in the K'tali Archipelago that had not yet been seized by the Empire. And such was its reputation that even Ba'alekkt had never expressed the slightest interest in its conquest.

Why had Bron brought them here? What would they find? The questions seethed in her mind along with others, more mundane. How had he managed to sail the *Silver Swan* without food, water or sleep? And where was the crew?

On her right, the sun was beginning to slide towards the horizon. Mallaso tried to remember the maps she had seen over the years. Somewhere over there lay two rocky peninsulas, Tulyet nearest, then Fabriz. And beyond them . . .

Beyond them, no one knew. As far as the cartographers were concerned, the world ended south of Jo'ami, in an endless amethyst ocean populated by monsters and sea-serpents. A sense of wondering terror crept over Mallaso at the thought. No-one she knew had ever gone so far, sailing out of reality and into a legend. Only ships of Kerenth or Ma'alkwen or Fabriz, cities who were hostile to the Empire, ever reached Jo'ami.

She shivered suddenly, as the island ahead seemed all at once much closer. Several high peaks rose steeply into the sky, furry with lush vegetation, around what appeared to be an enclosed bay. Mallaso rose to her feet and walked back to the stern.

She saw, with concern, that Bron had almost reached the end of his resources, vast though they must be. She said on impulse, 'Please, let me help you.'

He turned his head and smiled at her, with some difficulty. 'No – no, it's all right. There's a natural wind now, which should take us in. All I have to do once we're inside the Haven is drop the anchor and furl the sails.'

'I thought – Sargenay always seems to do his tricks so easily.'

'That's because they're only tricks. I can create Illusions with a flick of my fingers, and so can any self-respecting sorcerer. Working the wind, and steering a ship, take rather more effort.'

She asked the question that had been burning on her tongue since she woke. 'Where are the crew?'

'Still on Tekkt, I should imagine. They'd gone into the town for some fun. There were two men left on guard, so I made them swim ashore.'

There was something rather chilling in his matter-of-fact tones. Mallaso thought of the Emperor and his minions, temporarily turned to statues by the power of this man's mind. And she remembered how he'd given her the strength to climb the rope ladder, despite her exhaustion and despair.

'Did you make me sleep, too?'

'Yes,' said Bron. He picked up one of the water-jugs and poured the contents over his head. 'You needed it. And I needed solitude to do this. I wasn't sure I was capable of it – I've never sailed a ship before, and I didn't have much idea of where I was going at first. I only knew that Jo'ami lay to the south, and far away.'

'But you found it.'

'Yes, I found it. And I should have come here long ago. I left Zithirian certain that if anywhere in the known world held the answers to . . . to what I am, then it was Jo'ami. But I was delayed a little, in Kerenth. And in Toktel'yi, too.' He smiled, rubbed his hand over his wet face, fast drying in the heat, and he touched his crooked nose. 'A jealous lover gave me this. I kept it as a reminder.'

Mallaso looked down at her hands. She thought of their love-making on the voyage to Tekkt, filled with urgency and desire and delight, and of how she had offered herself to Ba'alekkt, like the whore she once had been, inciting his lust so that she would have the opportunity to kill him. Around the Southern Sea, sex was one of the accepted currencies of life, bartered without shame or disapproval unless you happened to be daughter or wife or mother in a wealthy and respectable family. In Toktel'yi, women were subjugated and exploited: in Kerenth, men were the under-dogs. But in Penya, until the invasion, they had been equal. And she did not know what was considered shameful, in those cold northern cities. Would he be angry with her, when she told him what she had done, in order to be alone with Ba'alekkt?

'I am not jealous,' he said softly.

Startled, she looked up. He was smiling at her. 'Did you think I would be?' he added.

'Yes,' Mallaso told him.

'But that doesn't mean I have no feelings for you. I do. We

were lovers once, all too briefly – and when you are ready, if you wish it, I want us to be lovers again.'

Foolishly, tears had come to her eyes, and she turned away to hide them. Jo'ami was so close now that she could see the individual trees on the two headlands encircling the harbour. She said, '*Can* you read my thoughts?'

'I know that a normal sorcerer shouldn't be able to. Thought-link should take place between two consenting individuals. All mages can join their minds, but they are also trained to defend themselves against unwanted invasion. So can ordinary people, for they don't know how to listen. The vulnerable ones are those with some natural but untaught power, like my stepmother. But I can overcome almost anyone's defences, if I want to. My father called it Coercion, and under the Four Rules of Sorcery it is forbidden. But I used it to rescue you from Ba'alekkt at the Palace, and also to force the guards to leave this ship. I don't like doing it, though. Such power can easily be misused, with terrible consequences.'

'You haven't answered my question,' Mallaso said. 'Can you read my thoughts?'

'Yes,' Bron told her. He rubbed his hand over his face again, looking desperately tired. 'I can't help it. I try not to – to eavesdrop. But your emotions, your feelings are so strong, I can't ignore them.'

'Can you speak to my mind, too? Can I hear you?'

He didn't answer her. She opened her mouth to repeat her question, and found his voice inside her head.

I am here. You have the power too. All you need to do is to listen.

It was so strange, so frightening, that she cried out, and put her hands over her ears. At once he said gently, aloud, 'I'm sorry. I didn't mean to alarm you. But it seems you do have some natural ability of your own.'

Mallaso brought her hands down and clenched them hard in her lap. She took several deep breaths, trying to rid her mind of an unpleasant sense of violation. Strange, that she should not mind when her body's privacy was invaded, yet looked on her thoughts as sacrosanct.

'I wish I didn't,' she said at last. 'I don't like it – I'm sorry, but I don't. I've kept my mind to myself for so long, it's been my refuge . . .'

'I feel the same,' Bron said. 'But I have always been able to defend myself. If you want, I will teach you how to do it.'

'I don't know.' Mallaso found she was shaking at the very thought of it. 'I'll think about it.'

'All right.' He smiled at her, and pointed. 'Look – we're almost there.'

The *Silver Swan* was gliding between the two high promontories marking the entrance to Jo'ami Haven. The cliffs plunged raggedly into the sea in a jumble of boulders. To judge from the swirling water and breakers to either side of the ship, the rocks stretched out a considerable way, leaving a fairly narrow channel in the centre. Bron frowned with effort, and his hand was clenched on the tiller. Mallaso turned away, unwilling to disturb his concentration. She was beginning to realize that his magic, apparently such a marvellous gift, was in fact a burden as crippling as if he had been born with a hunched back, or deformed limbs. It seemed that such a high level of sorcery could not be attained without terrible and exhausting effort. And the possession of vast powers inevitably implied heavy responsibilities, if they were not to be used for evil purposes.

She got up and walked back to the bows. The sun was close to the horizon now, and the western headland cast a deep purple shadow over much of the Haven. Ahead, a fleet of perhaps a score of small boats with curved triangular sails and spindly outriggers skimmed over the still water, heading for the white sickle of sandy beach at the end of the bay. She could see thick forests clothing the steep slopes of the island, and a cluster of whitewashed houses near the water's edge. Above, a gaggle of hopeful seagulls called and circled, evidently expecting the *Silver Swan* to be laden with fish. Mallaso watched as they approached the shore, with curiosity and also with apprehension. If this place was indeed full of sorcerers, they would already know about Bron. What sort of welcome would await them, when they reached the island?

It was almost dark when the anchor, untouched by any hand, dropped into the water with a loud splash. The *Silver Swan* glided on for a moment and then stopped. Her bow swung gently round to point out towards the sea, only just visible between the towering cliffs at the entrance to the bay. Mallaso watched as the sails furled themselves without help, and lights flickered in the lanterns at masthead, prow and stern. Over the flat water came the distant sounds of voices, and music. She could just see the shapes of the fishing boats, drawn up on the paler sand, and lights glowed in the houses amongst the palm trees on the western side of the beach.

'Are you coming with me?'

She had been so intent on the land that she hadn't noticed Bron's silent approach. She stared at him, surprised. 'Now? Are you going ashore now? But it's almost dark.'

'I can't wait till morning.'

'You haven't had any sleep for five nights,' Mallaso said. She touched his arm, and realized that he was trembling like an over-wound djarlek string. 'Oh, Bron, you must sleep, or you'll collapse.'

'I must go.' His voice was curiously flat and uncompromising, allowing no dissent. 'I have to. They want me.'

'Who want you? The sorcerers? But – '

'You can come with me, or stay here. It's your decision. But I'm going ashore.' He turned and walked to the side. With horrified astonishment, Mallaso watched as he vaulted on to the rail, balanced for a moment, and dived.

There was hardly any splash. She ran to the gunwale and saw his head break the surface and begin to move towards the shore. With a muttered curse on all sorcerers, she hurried aft to the rope ladder, still slung over the side, clambered down it and struck out in pursuit.

The water was deliciously warm, like silk against her hot skin. She was a good swimmer, but sadly out of practice: her feet touched the bottom just as Bron emerged from the sea and walked up the beach. She called to him to wait, but he did not turn round. Mallaso splashed through the shallows and raced after him, angry and frightened. It was as if some spell had hold of him, reeling him in like a fish on a line. And the sense of danger prickled all around her.

She caught up with him at the edge of the trees, where the palms sprouted, tall, curved and graceful, out of the sand. He had paused, his face tilted up to the highest peak, in an attitude of listening. But apart from the inevitable crickets, and the distant noises from the harbour town away to their right, there was no other sound.

'What's happening?' she demanded urgently.

He ignored her, and she shut her teeth on her anger and

waited. Some overlarge insect blundered between them, and she swatted it away. The sharp movement seemed to rouse Bron from his trance: he said curtly, 'If you want to come with me, keep up. I can't wait for you. And you might be in trouble if you get lost.' And without another word, he turned and strode purposefully into the forest above them.

At least he wasn't running. She followed, surprised by how strong she felt, despite her energetic swim to the shore. It was as if that long, long sleep during the voyage had restored all her old vitality, lost since she learned of Grayna's death.

Bron was following a path that climbed steeply upwards, away from the beach. He walked quickly, looking straight ahead, sure-footed in the gloom. Mallaso, tripping over uneven ground, pushing through encroaching fronds and branches, wondered how he could avoid all the obstacles in the dark.

By sorcery, of course. But as she toiled in his wake, she realized that his path was clear, whereas hers was being obstructed.

And then real fear caught her throat. With a frantic effort, she broke into a run. The ground seemed to grow impossibly steep: she struggled upwards, gasping for breath, creepers lashing her face and sweat soaking her salt-crusted tunic. But Bron's stride was not even broken, and he was drawing further and further away from her.

'Don't leave me!' she cried in desperation, and saw at last the pale shape of his face, turning back to her, and then his hand outstretched. Like a drowning sailor, she reached out in panic, and felt his fingers grasp hers.

And then the creepers coiled tight round them both.

'They are caught fast. Perhaps he is not the One.'

The High Sorcerer's gaze did not waver from the surface of the scrying bowl. 'If he is, he will free himself. He is not afraid of the forest – it is her fear that has attracted the Terror Vines to them. He should not have gone back for her.'

'Surely that is a virtue – to display compassion.'

'He would have done better to leave her there, and go on alone.' The High Sorcerer's face was set like adamant. 'She should never have come here – she will bring us trouble, I can sense it in my bones. It will be hard enough to persuade him to our view, without a woman complicating matters. You do not seem to understand, Tu Kar-Lyen. This is not a mere man, with ordinary, petty, unimportant gifts and feelings. This is the One – a sorcerer who, if he wished, could rule the known world through his power. He should not encumber himself with emotional baggage like that woman. He should be above such trivial things. If he can find the strength to abandon her, then he will pass the test.'

'And if he does? What will happen to her?' Despite his superior's harsh words, Tu Kar-Lyen's concern was evident.

The High Sorcerer's mouth was a thin, inexorable line. 'It does not matter. But it will not take her long to die, in the grip of the Terror Vines.'

Some instinct told Mallaso that struggle was quite futile. She stood very still as the cool impersonal coils of the creepers wound round her, binding her to Bron as close as if they were still lovers, breast to breast, skin to skin. She could breathe, just, and although the tendrils around her back were very taut, pinning her arms to her sides, at least her head and neck were free. She wondered if the wizards were watching, and imagined the two of them pictured in some scrying bowl, trussed up as tightly as a pair of fowls for the market. The absurdity of it struck her, and she laughed rather wildly.

'It isn't funny,' Bron said, but the sudden richness in his voice told her that he, too, could visualize how ridiculous they must look. 'We could die here. And this won't be the worst we have to face, I'm sure of it. The sorcerers of Jo'ami must be well protected. Perhaps these forests are full of the remains of aspiring mages, choked to death because they lacked faith.'

'Faith?' Mallaso was almost sure that the vines had relaxed their grip just a little as she laughed, and it gave her a small brave spark of hope.

'You have to believe in yourself,' Bron told her. 'It's almost the first requirement for sorcery. Power first, then conviction. If you begin to doubt yourself, your strength fades. Long ago, my father was forced to stop taking Annatal. Usually, that means inevitable death, but he didn't die, though he came very close to it – my stepmother saved him by linking her mind with his. After he recovered, he assumed that his power must have left him, that he was no longer a sorcerer. And so it had. But then he began to wonder if perhaps he was wrong. And once his faith returned, so did his sorcery. I believe I can free us from these vines. Do you believe it too?'

'Yes, I do,' Mallaso whispered, and felt another, almost imperceptible slackening of the coils around her, so that she could take a deeper breath. She added softly, 'I think fear makes them stronger. It was my fear that trapped us both, when you touched me. If we go on, we must go *together*, side by side, and face whatever else is up there together – or we are lost.'

For answer, Bron kissed her lightly, and then flexed his arms. She felt the sudden tension in the cords that bound them, and then they loosened. Standing here in the night, amidst the unnatural stillness and silence of this jungle, she suddenly felt an extraordinary sense of her own strength, as if that earlier panic had never been. She extended her arms sideways, and the vines, defeated, slithered suddenly to the ground. They were free.

'Together,' said Bron, and took her hand in his.

They climbed onward, upward. Now that she knew the secret of this enchanted forest, Mallaso was no longer afraid. It fed on fear, and hers had vanished: she trusted in her own strength, and in the power of the man beside her.

She said softly, in the unnatural quiet, 'Do you know where you're going?'

'To the wizards' lair.' Bron glanced at her, and she saw the white flash of his grin. 'I don't know exactly where it is, but it's somewhere up there – at the top of the mountain.' He stopped abruptly, so that she bumped into him, and said urgently, 'Keep still. Keep very, very still.'

And then she heard what he had heard, the only noise that they themselves had not made. A sharp rustling, a few strides away in the undergrowth.

The fear returned. Mallaso, rooted to the ground, could not have moved even if she had wanted to. She peered past his shoulder into the gloom, but there was nothing to see. Under these thick trees, the darkness was almost absolute.

Again the sound, but coming from their left this time, as though something quite large were circling them. Her heart pounding, she tried to control her wild sense of panic. Whatever it was, she knew its intentions must be hostile.

'It's behind us now,' she said, hating the way her voice seemed to emerge as a feeble whimper of terror. 'Oh, Bron, what is it?'

'I don't know.' He turned, keeping himself between her and the unseen creature. Mallaso could hear its breathing, rasping in its throat. What large, predatory animals lived in jungles like this? Leopard? Panther?

The sounds of movement had ceased. Mallaso saw that something was beginning to illuminate the forest around them, with a faint, pale, eerie glow. For a brief moment, she thought it might be sunrise: then she realized that dawn was still many hours away, unless time had no meaning in this mysterious place.

Bron lifted his hand, and light flowed from it. She saw the fronded undergrowth in front of them, the crowding tree-trunks, the small signs of the trail they had made.

And two red eyes, glaring back at them.

As she cried out, it leapt forward and sprang. Mallaso had a brief glimpse of a huge black shape, rushing through the air, and then Bron shouted.

The light coalesced into a blinding flash. There was a roar that seemed to rip the forest apart. She found herself lying on the soft dry ground, her hands over her ears, shuddering with terror.

'Mallaso? Mallaso, are you all right?'

At least she could still hear. She sat up, shaking her head. That roar seemed to be reverberating inside her brain. 'I think so,' she said. 'Has – has it gone?'

'It was never there. It was an Illusion.'

Shocked and astonished, she stared at him. There was still enough light to see his face, and the expression on it didn't make her feel happier. 'An Illusion? Why – how did you know?'

'Animals hate sorcery. Remember the donkey on Tekkt, that refused to carry me? This forest is choked with magic and power. I suspect there isn't a living creature anywhere here, not the smallest fly or beetle. And so I knew that if we did see an animal, it wouldn't be real.'

'It fooled me.' Now that the danger was over, Mallaso was beginning to feel anger. 'Are the sorcerers doing this?'

'I'm certain of it. They're putting me through some kind of test, I think – and probably watching the results from their eyrie up on the summit. We seem to have passed the first two trials successfully – but I should warn you, these things tend to come in threes.'

'I'm delighted to hear it,' Mallaso said sarcastically. 'I'm beginning to wish I'd stayed on the ship.'

'I don't.' He touched her hand gently. 'I need you – I want you here. And besides, as you pointed out, it's easier to face such things with you, than on my own.'

'I know.' She took a deep breath, trying to control her thumping heart. 'I wonder what they'll throw at us next? Lethal creepers and an Illusion that was so real I nearly died of fright – what could be worse?'

'I don't know – but I'm sure they'll think of something. And there's only one way to find out.' He helped her to her feet. In the last remnants of the witchfire, she saw his encouraging grin. 'Are you ready?'

'No, but let's get it over. Apart from anything else, I'm exhausted – and so are you.' She glanced at him, but the darkness had returned, and she could see nothing of his face.

'I'll manage,' Bron said briefly, and walked on through the forest.

For quite a long time, they climbed upwards. Nothing else molested them, and the silence was oppressive and yet somehow comforting. Mallaso concentrated on conserving the dregs of her energy, determined not to let Bron drain himself still more by helping her. He seemed to be tireless, but she remembered his exhausted face on the *Silver Swan*, and his days and nights without sleep, and knew that he could not sustain this forever. Sooner or later, if he didn't rest, he would collapse.

They came quite suddenly to an open space, a narrow plateau in the middle of the steep-sloping forest. Mallaso looked up and saw the stars in their old familiar patterns, and felt an extraordinary sense of relief. She said, 'Is this the end of it?'

'No, I don't think so. There's more to climb – but not as far as we've come already. You can see the summit, just, against the sky. And right on top, hidden behind the trees, is the School of Wizards.'

'School? Do they teach sorcerers here, then?'

'They come from all over the known world – apart from the Empire, of course. Toktel'yi has its own schools. I expect that aspiring apprentices have to negotiate that forest too.'

'If they do,' Mallaso said drily, 'I suspect they don't face quite the same hazards. Shall we go on? If I stand still for very long, I shall want to lie down – and then I shall sleep.'

'We'd better move, then,' Bron said, and walked out from under the trees. With a renewed sense of energy at the thought that they were nearing the end of their journey, Mallaso followed him.

She could just see the ground, which seemed to be covered with thick grass and aromatic flowers: a heady scent rose from the crushed blooms and leaves as they walked across. Her nose tickled, and she sneezed several times. Bron stopped to wait for her. 'I haven't got a handkerchief, I'm afraid.'

'I'll wipe my face on my sleeve, then.' Mallaso paused by him and rubbed her arm across her streaming eyes.

And a woman rose up from the ground in front of them.

She was old, old, and even Mallaso, untrained in the arts of sorcery, could smell the stench of evil which enveloped her like a venomous shroud. She wore blood-red robes, and her lank white hair coiled snake-like around her ravaged face. Within the folds of ash-grey skin, her eyes glittered with an insane, reddish light, and she laughed.

It was another Illusion. It must be. Surely this dreadful apparition was not real. She glanced at Bron, and to her utter horror saw him transfixed, his face as livid as that of the ghastly creature before them.

The old woman laughed again, and lifted her staff. Her voice wild and harsh, she began to chant an incantation. It was in no language that Mallaso knew.

'Bron!' She grabbed his arm and shook him. 'Bron! Who is she? What's she saying?'

He paid her no attention at all, his eyes fixed on the apparition. 'D'thliss,' he whispered in despair and horror. 'No – no, it can't be.' His voice rose suddenly to a great howl of denial. 'No – no – NO!'

The woman cackled gleefully, and swept the ground with her staff. At once, a great flare of fire sprang up in front of her.

The heat from it singed Mallaso's face. She screamed, and instinctively cowered away from it. At once another flame erupted behind them, and another, and another, until she and Bron were encircled by a blazing ring, only a dozen paces across.

This was no Illusion, to be defeated by Bron's innate power. This was real. Mallaso, hiding her face, could feel the heat searing her bare skin, and hear the greedy roar of the flames. If this was another test of his sorcery, then he must pass it, or they would both die, turned to charcoal within the inferno.

The chant went on, remorseless, inexorable, freezing the

muscle to the bone and the blood in the vein. The flames reached out eager fingers, and Bron stood as still as stone, in terrible thrall to that endless, dreadful voice.

But Mallaso was not. Ghastly as that spectre was, it meant nothing to her, it carried no past burden of terror and enslavement. She risked a brief glimpse between her fingers, and saw him standing beside her, brilliantly lit by the leaping, dancing fire. And as the old woman laughed again, there was only defeat and despair in his eyes.

Her arms and legs were burning. She could feel her thin cotton tunic, heavy with sweat, begin to dry in the intense heat. Somehow, she must bring him out of the nightmare into which the old woman's appearance had plunged him. Heedless of the consequences, she took her hands away from her face and grabbed him, shaking his unresponsive body as if it were one of Grayna's dolls. '*Do* something!' she yelled. 'You have the power, of course you can! You can do *anything*, Bron – you can defeat her! Go on, Bron, *make it die*!'

The flames seemed to waver, and then burst up with renewed vigour. It seemed her skin would begin to bubble and blister, so fierce was the heat. 'She's an Illusion!' she cried, willing him to listen to her, to believe her. 'Bron, she's not real, she isn't *there*! And if you think the fire will destroy us, then it will!'

His eyes were dark pits in the glare of the blaze, and as impenetrable as the abyss. Mallaso couldn't bear to look at him. With a sob of impotent terror, she shielded her eyes from the flames, and tried to reach him again. 'Bron! You're strong enough – you have the power – *use it*, for the Mother's sake *use it*, or we'll die!'

'I can't,' he gasped, and she saw that he had begun to shake. 'I can't – she's too strong for me.'

His response tore at her heart. '*Use it!*' she screamed frantically, and her fists beat wildly at his chest and his face, trying to drive him into action.

The flames reared above them, huge, greedy, devouring. She felt their savage intensity, and knew this would be the end. And the irony of it struck her with terrible force. For she did not want to die, not here, not now – even though Grayna was dead.

'No!' Bron cried, but not to her. 'No, you will not – you cannot – go back to Ayak, you loathsome hag, and haunt me no more!'

The witch's mocking, hideous laughter cut through the fire's roar. Suddenly, with a desperate effort, Bron pushed Mallaso away from him, the first time she had ever seen him use violence openly, and flung out his hands.

The laughter faltered, then became a terrifying howl of defeated rage. Abruptly, the flames wavered. The fire seemed to fold in on itself. The roar became a sigh, then a soft, sibilant hiss. As suddenly as it had erupted, the blazing circle shrank, faded and died back into the ground.

A cool breeze fanned her sweltering skin. Mallaso found she was trembling. She stared wildly round her, hardly daring to believe that the witch and the flames had both vanished, as utterly as if they had never existed. Then, sobbing with relief, she turned to Bron.

He was swaying on his feet, his face haggard and drawn with extreme exhaustion. Vanquishing D'thliss and the fire had obviously taken the last of his strength. 'Mallaso,' he said, and reached out towards her. 'Mallaso – help me.'

She caught him just before he fell. He was heavier than she'd expected, and she almost lost her hold. He sagged against her, and she felt the raw heat of his body against hers. Then, as carefully as she could, she lowered him to the ground.

His eyes were already closed, and he lay quite still. Suddenly frightened, she felt for a pulse, and found it beating against her fingers, surprisingly and reassuringly strong. She examined his hands and his face, but they were miraculously unmarked by the terrible heat. His tunic, though, was drenched with sweat, just as hers was.

She realized suddenly that the silence had gone. Tentative at first, but then stronger and more confident, a bird began to call from further up the mountain. Its voice was raucous and unmusical, but to Mallaso as beautiful in its normality as the sweet liquid tones of a Nightsinger. Dawn was approaching, and with its arrival, sorcery had fled the forest.

A great torrent of relief poured over her. She turned back to Bron, and picked up his pale, unresponsive hand. 'Wake up – it's daybreak, Bron, wake up!'

But there was no answer. She tried to rouse him, to no avail. At last she sat back on her heels beside him, fighting fear with the firm inner voice of logic and reason that had sustained her through the many nightmares of her life. *He is not dead. He will*

*come to himself eventually. Until then, you'll just have to wait
beside him and watch over him, until he wakes.*

And after six nights now, without rest, he certainly needed
sleep.

'He is not dead.'

The voice, so utterly unexpected, made Mallaso gasp. She
leapt up in terror and saw a woman standing a few paces away,
leaning on a long, gnarled stick. But this was not the dreadful
witch, returned to destroy Bron while he was defenceless. This
woman was small and unimpressive, with thick grey hair hacked
off raggedly at shoulder-length, and a lined, shrewd, blunt-fea-
tured face. She wore long loose robes of a muddy dark green
colour, rather grubby round the hem, and her eyes, surprisingly
blue against her brown complexion, gazed intently at the man on
the ground.

'I know he isn't dead,' said Mallaso, her alarm diminishing at
the sight of this unimpressive figure. 'He's just asleep. He's very
tired.'

'He is – but that is not why his spirit has left him. Do not
worry – it will return before long.' The woman walked forward,
her long robes trailing through the grass. 'So you are Mallaso.
Why did you come here?'

'I came with him. Together.' Her anger was beginning to rise
at the old woman's obvious hostility, but she kept it under control. 'Are you a sorcerer?'

'Why?'

'Because if you are, and that fire was your doing, then you
nearly killed us both!' Mallaso said forcefully.

'But you are alive, are you not? So what does it matter? He
was put to the test, as he knew he would be, and succeeded. You
should not have doubted him.'

'*I* didn't doubt him – he doubted himself.' Mallaso got to her
feet, and was glad to see that she was nearly half a head taller
than the old woman. It gave her a quite unjustifiable feeling of
superiority. She added, 'It was the sight of that – that other sorcerer that did the damage. If I had not come with him, perhaps he
would have died. Are you a witch as well?'

'Don't look so horrified. As you suspected, D'thliss was an
Illusion. She has long been safely dead – though it seems she still
lives, with all her fear and evil, in his mind. She was Zithiriani,
their High Priestess, and as a child he was her creature, her vessel

of power. If he could vanquish his memories of her, then he has truly come to maturity. But in answer to your question – yes, I am a sorcerer, as are many women in Jo'ami. More women than men, in fact. They make better use of their skills, I find. Men have an unfortunate tendency to show off.'

Mallaso thought of Sargenay, and smiled reluctantly. 'I know. I have a friend, in Toktel'yi—'

'In Toktel'yi. But none in Penya.'

'Do you know *everything* about us?'

Her tone was sharp with anger, but the old woman did not react. She said calmly, 'You keep many secrets from me, Mallaso of Penya, and they will remain so. But your companion's fear of D'thliss cannot be hidden: nor can your own grief for the island of your birth, for it is the mainspring of your life. And so is your thirst for revenge.'

'If I had not tried to kill Ba'alekkt,' Mallaso said wryly, 'we would not be here.'

'So even failure brings some good in its wake. He should have come here years ago – he is in desperate need of our help. The evil that lies within him will not remain dormant for ever. And he would not have died, even if he had let the flames take him. The Wolf would have saved him – but at a price. For the greater his debt to the Devourer, the more likely he is to submit in the end to Ayak's desires. So far, he has managed to resist him.' She walked over to Bron's prone body. 'His spirit will return very soon. For many, many years the prophecies have spoken of the One, the Forbidden Child, the Carrier of Evil. It was foretold that he would come here. It was not foretold how, or when, or from where he would come. I did not expect that he would be a bastard son of the King of Zithirian. Strange that he should have even more reason to kill Ba'alekkt than you did. For you, after all, were acting from revenge. He, however, could have prevented the same terrible fate from befalling his own city and his own family. Yet he did not. Was that at the Wolf's prompting, I wonder?'

'No,' said the man at her feet, so faintly that Mallaso could hardly hear him. 'No, it was not.'

'Ah. You return.' The old woman leaned on her stick and gazed fiercely down at him. 'But I would not trust the Devourer. After all, whatever you do, whatever you do not do, he is assured of his fill of blood. Ironic, is it not? Ba'alekkt, not you, should have been dedicated to him.'

'He did not have six thousand deaths on his conscience, before he was ten years old,' said Bron.

There was a brief silence. The old woman said harshly, 'I hope you are not proud of that feat . . . Bronnayak.'

He pushed himself into a sitting position, his eyes fixed on the sorceress. 'I am not. It will haunt my dreams until Ayak claims me too.'

'If he ever does.' The old woman continued to survey him, and Mallaso had a sudden, terrifying glimpse of her hidden power, like a shaft of sunlight piercing stormclouds. And as the truth burst over her, Bron said softly, 'Tell us, you who are so much more than you seem. What is your name? Who are you?'

The old woman smiled. 'My name is Sé Mo-Tarmé. And I am High Sorcerer of Jo'ami.'

CHAPTER
SEVENTEEN

The School of Wizards was built on the very summit of the conical mountain overlooking Jo'ami Haven. The peak was called Kayan-Ara, which in the language spoken on the island meant *the Giant who sleeps*. Although it had not erupted for more than a thousand years, legends told of the terrible bloodthirsty rites with which the early islanders had propitiated the cruel, serpent-headed god, or demon, whom they believed to inhabit the fiery realms beneath the volcano. But since the First Mage, Ai-Mayak, had founded his school upon the very lip of the mountain's crater, Kayan-Ara had slumbered peacefully, and the people of Jo'ami abandoned their barbaric practices.

Mallaso was given a room overlooking the ancient crater, its rocky sides sloping down to a vivid blue-green lake at the bottom. The School of Wizards was a huge, rambling building, constructed out of stone and wood in a curiously ramshackle and haphazard way, as if a wall here, a window there, had been added without any concern for appearance, let alone an overall plan. And yet this sprawling, creeper-hung edifice, that seemed almost to have sprouted out of the volcanic rock on which it stood, was surprisingly attractive.

She had not seen Bron since their arrival, but the two young women, robed in yellow, who took charge of her were so friendly and sympathetic that for the moment she had no worries. They brought her food, some peculiar-shaped green fruit, and a plate of grilled fish, a flat circular loaf made from a coarse, sweet-smelling flour that certainly wasn't wheat, and a big jug of cool water to drink. There was a choice of garments laid out for her: long, flowing, amber-coloured robes like those of her attendants, or a very large rectangular piece of brightly dyed cloth. She thanked the two apprentice sorcerers and they left, with smiles and kind words in their own language. And although they obviously could not understand a word of Toktel'yan, they had known exactly what she wanted.

Perhaps they could read her mind. The thought was still very disturbing, and for the moment Mallaso preferred to ignore the implications. She ate hungrily, leaving nothing but crumbs, bones and pips, and drank most of the water. Then she removed the ripped, salt-stiffened sailor's tunic, fit only for burning, and flung it in a corner. There was a big stone bath, freshly filled, but she stood beside it, shaking, and knew that she could not enter it yet, not with the memory of her attempt to kill Ba'alekkt still agonizingly clear in her mind. Instead, she washed herself thoroughly, and put on the robes, which looked cool and appropriate. She wondered where Bron was. They had been so close for so long that it seemed very strange to be on her own, not knowing where he was or what was happening to him. She hoped very much, for his sake, that the High Sorcerer had let him sleep.

She went to the window and leaned out. The side of the crater fell away steeply to the lake below. The harsh outlines of the rocks jutted out of rampant tropical greenery, amongst which tiny birds, glowing like winged rubies and emeralds, darted from flower to flower with a flash of iridescent feathers. The air was hot and still, and saturated with a very sweet and heavy scent, perhaps from one of the huge red flowers smouldering amidst the creepers festooning the wall, or the rocks below her. Everywhere was peace, harmony, beauty. And like one of those fragrant blossoms, Mallaso's tormented heart began to open, a little, in response. She was not home: in all the known world, nowhere, not even Penya, was now home. But at least here she might find rest, and friendship, and healing, and she would not turn away anything that was offered.

She took deep breaths of the perfumed air, and thought about the High Sorcerer. The long years of slavery in Toktel'yi had forced her to accept the idea of women's supposedly natural inferiority. It was a shock to be reminded that there were other places in the world where her sex was no bar to respect, or power. In Kerenth, of course, the Queen and the Priestesses of Sarraliss ruled the land. Penya had possessed no royal family, but was governed by an Assembly of Councillors, elected by the people every two years, and more or less equally divided between men and women. And the L'yain, the chosen leader of the Assembly, had often been female. Sé Mo-Tarmé's position should not seem so strange to her: perhaps she had become more Toktel'yan than she knew.

And as if her thoughts had summoned the High Sorcerer, there was a knock on the door, and Sé Mo-Tarmé walked into the room. She was still wearing those sludge-coloured robes, and her lined face and grey hair were those of an old woman, though her upright, sturdy body seemed comparatively youthful. Presumably that was the effect of the Annatal, which aged its addicts, but prolonged their lives.

She said, rather more bluntly than she'd intended, 'Where's Bron?'

'Asleep, I hope.' The High Sorcerer shut the door and sat down on the draped soft couch that seemed to be intended as both chair and bed. 'He is deathly tired. Such power as he commands is not achieved lightly. In some ways, we who take Annatal have the better of it.' Her shrewd glance was an indication of just how much she understood, or knew, or had learned. 'But I have not come here to discuss Bronnayak. Not now, at any rate. I have come to discuss you.'

Mallaso stared at her. She thought of her grandmother, at once respected and terrifying, who had had this effect on her too, and it was very disturbing to be returned to childhood again.

'Don't look so alarmed,' said the High Sorcerer, with a completely unexpected smile. 'Here in Jo'ami we value all people, with or without power. Like your friend, you have been damaged. You have had the strength to overcome what has happened to you. Even your child's death has not destroyed your spirit. But you are in need of healing. And I cannot help you if you do not tell me your story, for much of it I do not know.'

Mallaso went on staring at her. She said at last, 'I don't – I don't know what you mean.'

'There is no shame in being enslaved,' said Sé Mo-Tarmé softly. 'Only those who enslave others should feel remorse for what they have done. You were a child, were you not? You survived when the rest of your family died, and you have felt guilty ever since, though it was hardly your fault. Do not look so surprised. Even here, far from the Empire, we have heard of Penya, once blessed beyond all other lands, now cursed. Believe me, I can see, only too clearly, the evil that has destroyed it. And which will destroy other cities and countries too, unless it is stopped. And with your help, it will be stopped.'

Mallaso realized what she meant, and her heart clenched for a second and then resumed a slow, ominous pounding. She said despairingly, 'I can't. Not again. I can't.'

'No. Not you yourself. You tried, and failed, but it was an honourable failure. No, your task now is to persuade Bronnayak that his vow means nothing when set against the destruction of everything and everyone he used to love. He is the One. It was foretold, hundreds of years ago, that because of him, empires will fall, and cities crumble. Because of him, Toktel'yi will no longer spread its tentacles over the world, crushing all independence, all resistance, all freedom and hope. But no prophecy possesses absolute and inalienable truth. None of this will come to pass without help. And he will need your help, Mallaso of Penya. He has power unlike any who has been born in all the world before, but he is still only a man. A young man, with a young man's weaknesses as well as a young man's strengths. I and my comrades can help him to overcome and defeat the Wolf in his heart, once and for all. Then you must persuade him to kill Ba'alekkt. And we do not have much time. In four months, after the end of the rainy season, the Imperial armies will prepare to march on Minassa and Zithirian.'

'I know,' Mallaso said. She didn't ask how it was known on Jo'ami, five hundred miles to the south and lacking any official contact with the Empire. She added curiously, 'But why are you so concerned? Toktel'yi is no direct threat to you surely. Ba'alekkt has probably never, even in his most lurid dreams, contemplated invading Jo'ami. You can't tell me it's purely a matter of principle.'

Sé Mo-Tarmé laughed rather bitterly. 'Of course, in Toktel'yi everything has a price, and no one does anything save for personal gain. Your memories of Penya, of course, will tell you differently. But you are right, we do have our own reasons to hate the Empire – although we believe passionately in the cause of freedom, and in the right of every land, each town and city, every island, to rule itself fairly and justly, without risking brutal conquest and oppression by an aggressive and greedy neighbour. Take Penya. Your island was attacked not because it had offended Toktel'yi, or taken its trade, or threatened war. It was not even attacked for its wealth – for Penya's riches grew on trees and stalks and in the ground, or walked on its earth or swam in the sea. It had no rare or priceless drug, like Annatal, no spices or ironwood, like Onnak, not even Balki's reserves of tin and copper. It enjoyed only beauty, and tranquillity, and a way of life and government that, of all the lands in the known world, was most fair and just to everyone, men and women alike. But its greatest possession, above all of these, was freedom. And so the late Emperor, seeking easy glory, ordered its conquest because, he told his Council, he wished to add Penya to his collection.'

There was a terrible silence. Outside, a bird, oblivious, sang a sweet, melodious song, and someone somewhere was chanting an incantation.

'And so my parents died, and my brothers, and fifty thousand other people, whose only crime was that they lived on Penya.' Mallaso's face, fine-boned under the taut dark skin, looked as if she had been stretched to the final edge of suffering. 'They had no army, but they took to the hills with makeshift weapons, because they preferred to die fighting the invader rather than tamely wait for execution. They saw their children carried off into slavery and their lands and houses given to immigrants from Toktel'yi. But still they carry on the struggle, those who are still alive.' She looked at the High Sorcerer in anguish. 'There are so few of them left – and soon they will be gone.'

'If nothing changes – yes, they will. But if the world were to change – if Ba'alekkt were killed – perhaps the invaders could be driven off the island. And then there is a chance that, like the firebird, a new and even more glorious Penya might arise from its own ashes. And there, I think, lies your destiny.'

Mallaso stared at her in bewilderment. 'My destiny? On *Penya*? But . . . but I don't want to go back. It would be too – too painful to bear.'

'Even if by going back, you could help to restore the island to its former peace and beauty and prosperity?'

'I don't know.' Mallaso frowned down at her hands, clenched together in front of her. 'If Ba'alekkt was dead, then, yes, perhaps I might. He has no direct heir, and the Empire would be taken up with the struggle for the succession. It's happened several times before, in Toktel'yan history. But Penya – Penya has been utterly destroyed. We could never bring it back, never.'

'Anything would be better than what is there now,' the High Sorcerer observed. 'Well, we will say no more about it for the moment. I merely offer suggestions and advice. Coercion is forbidden to sorcerers. And perhaps you now believe me when I tell you that the liberation of those unwilling parts of the Empire is my chief concern, along with the continued freedom of cities not yet within its clutches.'

'And your more personal reasons for wanting the Emperor

dead?' Mallaso prompted, not without a touch of malice.

The High Sorcerer gave her a sharp glance. 'Well, it's obvious enough. Come and look.'

She rose from the couch and went to one of the two tall, narrow windows looking over the crater. Mallaso stood beside her, staring down at the distant water, fringed with reeds. Two long-legged pink birds were meditating in the shallows, motionless in the morning heat.

'Not down there,' said Sé Mo-Tarmé. 'Along to your right and your left.'

The School of Wizards stretched out on either side of them, fitted so skilfully into the rocks that it seemed to have evolved out of them. For the first time, Mallaso realized its vast size. She began numbering windows, and lost count after fifty. And that was only to one side.

'The School was founded by the First of all sorcerers, Ai-Mayak. He was a fisherman here on Jo'ami, more than a thousand years ago. Then, all the islands in the Archipelago were free: the Toktel'yans called themselves an Empire, though they had only annexed Mynak, on the coast, and Sabrek, on the Kefirinn. The names of Zithirian and Minassa did not exist, and the world was younger, perhaps more savage, and certainly more innocent. People still used stone tools, though in Kerenth they had discovered how to smelt copper, a secret that would soon spread along the coast of the Southern Sea.

'Ai-Mayak, out fishing alone in his boat, was engulfed by a sudden storm. It swept him north, far from Jo'ami. He survived by eating raw fish and drinking rainwater, and used his skills to keep his damaged and waterlogged craft afloat. Eventually, after four or five days, he sighted land, and steered towards it. He knew what it must be, for he was not the first fisherman from Jo'ami to be blown northwards, nor would he be the last. But he was afraid, for few had returned, and those who did spoke of savage and terrible people.

'But to his relief, the shore seemed empty. He beached his boat where a stream ran into the sea, by a grove of tall palm trees. There were fish, and he made a small fire and cooked them. Then he searched for other things to eat. There were hama-nuts, just like those on Jo'ami, and he climbed the tree for them. He found some of what we call bread-roots, which are sweet and sustaining when roasted. And all around him in the forest were bushes he had never seen before, with fronded, fragile leaves and clusters of bright red berries, very tempting.

'Ai-Mayak was suspicious. Often the more delicious a berry appears, the more poison lurks within. And although the trees were full of birds, they did not seem attracted by these delicacies.

'In the end, however, his curiosity overcame his common sense. Telling himself that one small berry could not harm him, he squeezed it very cautiously, letting a few drops of juice trickle on to his tongue. To his surprise and delight, it was sweet and good, with a very pleasant taste, quite unlike any other fruit he had ever eaten. Sure that it would not hurt him, he picked several clusters, took them back to his fire on the beach, and ate them all.'

The High Sorcerer glanced at Mallaso, who was careful to appear properly enthralled. 'Have you heard this story before?'

'No – not in such detail. I had a friend in Toktel'yi who was a sorcerer. He told me something of how his Art was discovered.'

'Did his account differ from mine?'

'I don't know,' said Mallaso, suppressing a smile. 'You haven't even reached the point where he started.'

Sé Mo-Tarmé gave her a swift look. 'I see, as I feared, that much has been lost in Toktel'yi. I will continue.

'Ai-Mayak dozed off beside his fire, his belly full of content. He woke at dusk, to find a group of men standing round him. Their hair was braided with bones and they wore only leaves to cover themselves. Their bodies were painted with wild patterns, and each one carried a sharpened stick for a spear. As soon as they saw that he was awake, they raised their weapons, and Ai-Mayak knew that they were going to kill him.'

She paused for dramatic effect. Mallaso could imagine her telling this story to an audience of breathless young apprentices. She said gently, 'But?'

The High Sorcerer's thick brows drew together slightly. She said, 'Even in his terror, Ai-Mayak had no intention of allowing himself to be slaughtered like a market pig. In desperation, he snatched up a smouldering piece of driftwood from the fire.

'As soon as he touched it, the wood burst into flames. And these were not ordinary flames, but white, blue-white, and searingly bright and hot. To his amazement, the islanders screamed and ran away, throwing down their spears as they fled. Ai-Mayak pursued them for a little while, to make sure that they were truly gone. Then, with his brand still burning, he returned to the fire, wondering why the savages had been so terrified. It could not be his camp fire, for they had stood close to it, and anyway all people, however primitive, are masters of fire: it is one of the things that separates us from beasts. No, they had been frightened of the strange flames that were still pouring from the branch he held.

'Not a little wary himself, Ai-Mayak laid the piece of wood back on the fire. As soon as he let go of it, the flames disappeared. He picked it up again, and immediately the peculiar white blaze flared up once more. Yet the wood itself did not seem to be consumed by it, as you would expect with an ordinary fire.

'Then Ai-Mayak began to realize a strange thing. He *felt* different. He felt immortal, young, exuberant, full of power, as if he could defeat the world with one blow. And although he was a young man, no older than you, he had never experienced such sensations before, not even after too much palm wine. It was as if his humble human blood had been transformed into the marvellous liquid which flows through the veins of the gods.

'Intoxicated by his discovery, and very curious, Ai-Mayak started to experiment. He found that every branch he plucked from the fire would burst into white flame at his touch – but not those which were not already alight. He discovered that he could make those flames die down and regenerate simply with the power of his thought, whether he were touching them or not. He could move things, too, across the beach – stones, shells, driftwood – although he was sitting a dozen paces away from them. And all without breaking into a sweat.

'At last, he slept through what was left of the night, and woke the next morning wondering if it had only been a strange dream. But he could still raise flames from the wood – though not as brightly as before – and still move objects with the strength of his mind alone, though not so far. Plainly the power was waning, and Ai-Mayak wanted it back.

'The source was obvious – the red berries. He returned to the place where he had found them, half afraid that they would have disappeared. But they were still there, in abundance.

'For a month, Ai-Mayak lived on the shore of Annatal's southern coast, consuming the berries, working and thinking. There was no sign of any more islanders, though once or twice he saw distant smoke, or heard far-away talking drums. And several times a fishing canoe, a primitive dug-out type with three or four men inside it, was paddled past his beach, well offshore and out of range of whatever they thought he would do to them.

'The more Ai-Mayak discovered about the effects of the berries, the more determined he became to take a good stock of the plants home with him to Jo'ami. Not just for himself, for he could see that, properly used, they would benefit everyone. He could not possibly sail the half-wrecked, waterlogged fishing boat which has carried him to Annatal. And so, using his own skills, and his new-found power, he began to construct a bigger and better one. For a man who had been reared in a fishing village by the sea, finding the tools was easy – stones, shells, wood, fire: creepers to lash the logs together to make the hull, large leaves sewn into a sail. Normally, building such a boat would take several men two or three moons. On his own, Ai-Mayak completed it in less than half that time. Then he dug up as many of the bushes as he could find, wrapped their earthy roots in wet leaves, and tied them to the boat's mast, where they would be safe from all but the most ferocious storm. And he continued to eat the berries, knowing that if he stopped, so would his power.

'At last, Ai-Mayak launched his vessel into the wide blue water, and set sail for Jo'ami. Normally, at this time of year, the prevailing wind would be blowing north or north-east against him. But by now nothing seemed too daunting for him to attempt. When the breeze blew against him, he turned it round so that it filled his sail, and reached Jo'ami in just three days.

'Of course, he had been given up for dead, so he was welcomed with tears of joy by his wife and children, his aged mother, his brothers and sisters and all the other people in his village. And when they heard about the wonderful red berries, and the extraordinary powers they had given to Ai-Mayak, they were amazed. Some doubted; others were frightened; a few were greedy.

'I need hardly tell you that it did not end happily. Ai-Mayak was a gentle, intelligent, peaceable man. His only faults were a certain rash curiosity, and a rather touching but naïve faith in human nature. He found himself having to fight those he had once called friends for possession of the berry trees. In vain he pleaded for restraint, for common sense, for careful experimentation. It was no use. War broke out on the island. Most of the precious bushes were destroyed in the fighting, and many people were killed, the innocent along with the greedy and the aggressive. In despair, Ai-Mayak took his remaining plants, his wife and his children and those few who supported his views, and fled into the heart of the island.

'And as the war bands pursued his trail through the forest, the serpent demon convulsed in anger, and the same mountain that lies beneath us now burst asunder.'

It did not seem possible, so peaceful were the rocky slopes and the turquoise lake. Mallaso, caught up in the drama of the tale, waited for its end with a racing heart, as if she were a child again, listening to her mother's stories.

'All those in the war bands were killed by the molten rock that poured down the mountainside. And the earth shifted, too, so that those in the villages around the Haven died when their houses collapsed, or when boulders fell on them from the heights above. Many, many souls were lost that day. But Ai-Mayak and all with him – perhaps a hundred people, no more – were spared. The serpent-god had shielded him, or so the survivors thought. At last, at a terrible cost, with thousands dead and their lovely island devastated, they had learned their lesson. They listened to Ai-Mayak. They made him their chief, and today his blood runs in the veins of every child born on Jo'ami. And with their help, and his extraordinary powers, he rebuilt their villages. The precious plants were tended in a garden in the most fertile spot on the island, and cherished like children. And those who wished to do so – and not everyone did – were allowed to take the berries too, on condition that they swore to follow Ai-Mayak's Four Rules of Sorcery.

'Of course, over the years they made many discoveries, some welcome, some unpleasant. Any part of the plant, leaf, root, berry, flower, properly prepared, would yield the potency of the drug. And they were hardy, easily grown, and long-lived. Soon there were groves of Annatal trees, as they were called, all over Jo'ami.

'But there were other, darker revelations too. Once taken, the drug had to be continued. If not, the user died.'

Mallaso thought of Bron's father, who had stopped taking Annatal, and survived, but said nothing.

'Also, it was found that Annatal had ageing properties. After about ten years or so, the men and women taking it would begin to look older than their contemporaries. After fifteen years the difference was marked. A forty-year-old would look sixty – those of sixty appeared to be in their dotage. And yet those taking the drug lived much longer than ordinary people, as much as sixty years longer. The twentieth High Sorcerer died at the age of a hundred and forty-three, and that is the oldest I have ever heard of. But those who do not reach a hundred are rare. If you can resign yourself to living more than half your life as a withered husk – though with mind and faculties as alert as if you were twenty – then there is no difficulty about taking Annatal.' She smiled suddenly. 'Though I have to say, beautiful sorcerers are rare, even as apprentices.'

Mallaso, looking at her, could see that she had never been pretty.

'But you are probably wondering why I have spent so long on this story. Well, I wanted to explain to you why Jo'ami is the cradle and the heart of all sorcery in the known world. In whatever guise or form, from Fabriz to Zithirian, in Kerenth or Toktel'yi or the Scatterlings, it all began here.

'Ai-Mayak realized that he had to pass on what he had learned to his followers, and teach them the Four Rules. You know what they are?'

'Yes,' Mallaso said. 'Sorcery must be used for the benefit of others, not exclusively for oneself: it should not hurt or kill or damage: it should be employed with care and restraint: and he who breaks any of these rules must take full responsibility for the consequences. Sargenay – my friend in Toktel'yi – told me once.'

'I am glad to learn that they are still taught in the Empire,' said Sé Mo-Tarmé drily. 'There will always be men and women, though, who think that rules are made to be broken. Sorcery has been responsible for great evil, alas far outweighing the good that it has done. Weather-working, Illusions, finding lost things or children, scrying, these are trivial uses compared to the destruction of buildings, the coercion, subjection, even the murder of unwilling victims. So you see, the work of this School of Wizards is vital. Once, five hundred years ago, when the Archipelago and Tulyet and other cities on the mainland were still free, we had apprentices from every island and every country. The registers have been kept, so we know the young men and women came from all over the Archipelago, from Kerenth, from Katho, Tulyet, Gulkesh, even Fabriz – which is more civilized than one would think, nose-rings or not. But they did not come from the Empire. Toktel'yi set up its own schools of sorcery, and thought it could do better than Jo'ami. The Four Rules were learned by rote, and then ignored.'

'Not entirely,' said Mallaso, thinking of Sargenay, and Al'Kalyek.

'No. Perhaps I am being unfair. But in Toktel'yi, you must admit that the Art has declined to an entertainment for the idle, a tool for the lazy, and, worst of all, an instrument of government interference and repression. And as the Archipelago was conquered, island by island, its inhabitants were forbidden to make the voyage to Jo'ami. If they wished to be sorcerers, they must train at Toktel'yi, or at one of the other schools on the mainland. And women were forbidden to learn magic at all.'

She gestured at the building around them, crowning the crater. 'There is room here for a thousand students, and a hundred tutors. Now we have only ninety apprentices, and their teachers are growing fewer and fewer. There are only seventeen of us left. And it is our power, joined and focused, which keeps the fire beneath us dormant, and has done so for more than a thousand years. Ba'alekkt has no need to attack Jo'ami. If our decline continues at the present pace, in fifty years we shall all be gone. Then the islanders will be at the mercy of the serpent demon again, and will undoubtedly slip back into savagery – if the mountain does not erupt and kill them all. And the free world – the fringes of the world outside that huge, many-tentacled octopus, the Empire – will no longer have the benefit of our accumulated wisdom and experience. Sorcery will inevitably degenerate until it is used, as the barbarian tribes of the southern steppes use it, to enslave and destroy: as a weapon of evil, rather than a force for good. And I would rather uproot every Annatal bush in the known world than allow that to happen.'

'So that is why you want Bron to kill Ba'alekkt,' Mallaso said softly. 'Because without him, the Empire will disintegrate – or at least, that's what you hope. And with the provinces and the islands free again, they can start sending you apprentices.'

'I hope so,' said Sé Mo-Tarmé. 'Though it might be sensible to send out a ship or two—'

'Touting for business?'

The old woman laughed suddenly and unexpectedly. 'Yes, if you like – touting for business. You have listened well, and with understanding. Have you never desired to be a sorcerer?'

'Never,' said Mallaso flatly. 'I have been a dancer, a concubine, even a whore, but all I ever wanted was to live my own life with my daughter, on Tekkt.'

'And now your child is dead, so you feel your future has been stolen from you. Was that why you took it upon yourself to try and kill Ba'alekkt alone?'

Mallaso looked out into the warm, still, perfect air, and slowly nodded assent.

'You do not lack for courage, Mallaso of Penya. You will certainly need it, in the years to come. You grieve still for your child, and that is only natural. But, little though you wish it now, your life will move on, away from her. You will never forget her, but the agony of her loss will start to heal.'

'I know. I think it has begun.'

'Good. And you are young. Your life may be long. You may have other children, to enjoy and to cherish. Your destiny may lie elsewhere, in other places, with other people.'

Mallaso stared at her. She said at last, 'Can you foretell the future? You said there was a prophecy, concerning Bron.'

'Ah. The future.' Sé Mo-Tarmé's face settled into its usual lines of severity. 'Who does not wish to know what it will bring? And yet I feel that to grope blindly towards it, as we do, is kinder for us than if some benevolent deity shone a brilliant light upon it, illuminating the horrors as well as the delights in store. Of course, we all assume our lives will be golden and peaceful, and that we will die happy at the end of a tranquil and comfortable old age. But how many of us ever attain such bliss? It is certainly pleasant to be sure that it will happen to you. But what would you do if, instead, you were told that you would be dead in agony from some cruel and lingering disease, before the end of the year? The time left to you would be spent in miserable terror, not in happy ignorance. And so Ai-Mayak, who saw the danger, forbade any attempt to foretell the future. Most people assume it is impossible, and do not try. Some, of course, disobey the rule – though not after our training, or under this roof – even at the risk of bringing great unhappiness to themselves, or to those whom they love.

'But there are, I will admit, some who seem naturally gifted – or cursed – with the ability to see near or far into the future. The prophecy concerning Bronnayak came from such a man, whose name was En Sy-T'lyear. He was a sorcerer, but his visions of the future arrived in his dreams. He wrote them down, and after his death they were made into a book. They are ambiguous, and very vague – Bronnayak's parentage was not mentioned, nor his birthplace, nor the age in which he lives – it was not even certain which Empire would crumble. So, many people have decided that the prophecies are false, couched in such general terms as to be certain of approximate truth, some time, somewhere.'

'But you believe them,' Mallaso pointed out.

'Yes.' The High Sorcerer nodded. 'Yes, I do. I believe that Bronnayak will save us all from the Toktel'yans.'

'Even if he dies in the process?'

Sé Mo-Tarmé's light blue eyes considered her for a very long time. At last she said softly, 'Perhaps he would think it a sacrifice worth making, for Zithirian, and Minassa, and all the people who struggle under the Toktel'yan yoke. After all, you did.'

'Well, I should ask him first, before you write him into your books and prophecies,' Mallaso said. 'He might not want to be your noble, self-sacrificing hero. He's already done it once, in Kerenth.'

'Ah, yes. Kerenth. The Queen is a headstrong girl, young and passionate. He should have taken more care. I hear that she has appointed another Consort. Presumably Sarraliss will approve this one.' The High Sorcerer turned away from the window. 'The morning has almost gone – the dinner bell will ring soon. I have enjoyed our talk, Mallaso of Penya. Thank you for your patience, and for your illuminating comments. Is there anything else you wish to know, before I go?'

As she must have been aware, a hundred questions jostled for attention in Mallaso's mind. She seized on the one most important to her at this moment. 'Yes. I would like to know where Bron is, and if he is well.'

'He is asleep, and should not be disturbed.'

'I know that. I don't want to wake him. I just want to know which room he's in.'

'Best for you, at present, not to know, I think. Goodbye, Mallaso of Penya. Tu Ey-Gan and Olnez will come soon, to escort you to dinner. I will see you in the Hall.'

And ignoring the younger woman's indignant protest, the High Sorcerer turned and stalked grandly out of the room.

Mallaso wrestled with her anger, and then strode back to the window. She leaned out, scanning the irregular faces of the building on either side of her, the vast numbers of windows of differing shapes and sizes, the clinging vines. In such a huge place, it would be impossible for anyone not a sorcerer to find a man whom its inhabitants wished to keep hidden.

Was it really for his own good, so that the physical and mental exhaustion afflicting him could be repaired by undisturbed sleep?

Or was he being held prisoner?

CHAPTER
EIGHTEEN

'You have slept enough.'

The voice, quiet but quite uncompromising, aroused Bron at last from sleep. Hovering still on the fringes of oblivion, he wondered how long was enough. When he'd lain down on this comfortable, welcoming bed, a year hadn't seemed sufficient to replenish his exhausted body and depleted mind.

'Three days,' said the voice.

It was adequate, he found, struggling into a sitting position. His body ached, but not with weariness. His brain was shaking itself free of somnolent fogs and rapidly assuming its usual unnatural sharpness and scope. He turned towards the voice, and saw, as he had expected, the deceptively drab and ordinary figure of Sé Mo-Tarmé, sitting on a chair, watching him.

'Where is Mallaso?' he asked, to give himself time.

'She is well, and beginning to stretch out her hands towards happiness. She is very hesitant at the moment, but soon she will know that she can touch it whenever she wishes. She is a woman of remarkable strength.'

'Her steel was forged in a terrible furnace,' Bron said, matching her serious tone. She was not a woman to whom he felt he could make a flippant remark, let alone a joke.

The look the High Sorcerer gave him made him wonder if this judgement was false, but he had no intention of testing her sense of humour, if she had one, just yet. 'Thank you for taking care of her,' he said, with genuine gratitude. 'She needs hope – she needs reasons for joy. If she finds them here, both she and I will be forever in your debt.'

'She will. Her wounds are deep, but she is not the only one to have suffered them. They will heal, given love and care and time, and her own stubborn and indomitable spirit. But I have not come here to discuss Mallaso of Penya. I am here to discuss you, Bronnayak.'

It was hard for him not to flinch at her use of his full name.

Every time the last two syllables were pronounced, something deep in his soul seemed to snarl in reply.

'Before any discussion, though, there are certain facts about you which I must know. Contrary to the rumours circulating amongst the younger apprentices, I am not omnipotent, and I do not know everything.' She smiled briefly, 'If I seem blunt, harsh, even brutal, it is not because I bear you any personal dislike or malice. But I need to learn the truth about you, your origins and your powers, before I can help you cast off the alien presence within you. And truth is not usually discovered by treading delicately and tactfully round the edges of its lair.'

By now, Bron was becoming used to her style of speech. He said briskly, 'I agree. But before we begin, there are certain things I need to do. Eat, for instance. Wash. Dress. Shave.' His hand rubbed the considerable growth of beard on his chin. 'Will you grant me an hour, to make myself comfortable?'

'Of course,' said the High Sorcerer. Do you wish for assistance?'

'No,' Bron said, his face very serious. 'I think I can manage on my own, thank you.'

And with something that was not quite a smile, she rose and left him alone.

Food arrived a few moments later. The man who brought it told him that it was afternoon, though the sun was still high in the southern sky. He could hear music, voices, chanting, laughter, drifting on the warm air through his windows. He ate, wallowed briefly in the luxurious cool bath in the little side room, and put on the rectangle of cloth, brightly dyed in a random splashed pattern of brilliant reds and yellows, which he suspected was the usual garb of Jo'ami men. Wrapped and tied securely round his waist, it came down to mid-thigh and left his chest bare. Indoors it was cool, but if he went outside he would have to wear something much more enveloping, or he would risk severe sunburn. Natives of Jo'ami, like those of all the islands in the Archipelago, had sun-proof skins of brown or black. His pale, northern complexion had never been designed to endure this fierce tropical heat.

He used some of the time left to meditate, ordering his mind and building up his mental defences and reflexes, as Ansaryon had taught him to do, long ago. Here in this place, so far from Zithirian that it had swum on the edges of legend, his life there seemed to have belonged to someone else. But he still cared for those he had left behind: Ansaryon, Halthris, the children, and Kefiri.

And it was their images, bright and sharp and real, that were broken when the High Sorcerer knocked on the door at the hour's end.

He called to her to come in, his mind keen and ready for the fray. She had spoken of helping him, but he knew she must want him to use his powers on her own behalf. Everyone had, always, throughout his life.

Everyone – except for Kefiri, his father, Herris – and Mallaso.

'You look considerably better than when we first met on the mountainside,' said Sé Mo-Tarmé, rather caustically. 'A very personable young man, I see. No wonder you keep having trouble with women.'

Bron stared at her coolly. After a while, she added, 'Very well. I will try not to patronize you. It is difficult not to, when you reach my age, and deal so much with students. They all seem to arrive here these days without two thoughts to rub together in their heads.'

'I'm surprised any arrive at all, if they have to negotiate that forest,' Bron observed drily.

'Most of them succeed. The tests are considerably easier for those who do not possess your special qualities. I needed to be sure that you are indeed the One. But we have already strayed from the point. Let us sit down, and be comfortable, and I shall begin my questions. And I require the truth, please, however unpleasant – no lies or evasions. What was the month and the year of your birth?'

'High Summer, in Zithirian Year 277 – that is, Toktel'yan year 2292.'

'So you are now . . . twenty-three. You will be twenty-four in four months' time.'

'Yes.'

'And your father was Ansaryon, now King of Zithirian – he cannot have been much more than a boy when you were conceived.'

'He was nearly nineteen at my birth.'

'And your mother?'

Something in her posture told Bron that she knew this was very significant, although she was probably unaware of the full,

horrible truth. Well, he could not step daintily round the facts
either. He said bluntly, 'She was the Princess Zathti. My father's
twin sister.'

Whatever Sé Mo-Tarmé had expected, it was not that. Her
body stiffened, and her eyes widened. Then she snapped, 'Tell
me. Everything.'

So he told her, in bare bleak words, the hideous story of his
conception and birth, and the first terrible years of his life as the
tool of the witch D'thliss, who had bred him for the power she
hoped he would carry. He spoke of her plot to murder almost the
entire Royal Family, so that she could rule Zithirian through
Tsenit, Ansaryon's younger brother. He explained how D'thliss
had corrupted Tsenit after Ansaryon, revolted by what she had
forced him to do to his beloved sister, had repudiated her. And
he told of her death, as she was about to Bind Bron to her for
ever, at the hands of the Ska'i, her barbarian accomplices who
had occupied the city, and whose evil shaman wanted Bron for
himself.

'His name?' Sé Mo-Tarmé prompted gently.

'The same as my own. Br'nnayak – the Slave of Death.'

'I see. Go on.'

The tale unfolded, seen through the eyes of the child he once
had been, neglected, frightened, yet already beginning to realize
the extent of his extraordinary powers. And with that knowledge,
came defiance. In the last months before her death, D'thliss had
never suspected how much he kept hidden from her. He could
not always bar her from his mind – he was still very young, and
quite untaught. But when she had discovered that he was no
longer a submissive tool, she had tried to Bind him to her will,
and died in the attempt.

Then the Ska'i, intent only on using him to destroy Zithirian,
Sar D'yenyi, which guarded the gold mines in the northern
mountains, and Ansaryon's army. They had killed his foster-
brother Lelya. And in his grief and rage, he had used sorcery to
slaughter the entire Ska'i host, more than six thousand men.

The rest was more bearable: the years at Sar D'yenyi, at
Zithirian, and in exile. He tried to explain about the Wolf within,
and the restraints he had placed on himself because of that
terrible, alien presence. She listened in silence to his low, anguished words, her face grim, and he did not know if she had truly
understood.

The sun had almost set when he ended. Almost immediately, a knock on the door announced the arrival of cool drinks and more food, a bowl of shredded mixed vegetables, pieces of grilled chicken, nuts, and a heap of fruit with interesting shapes and colours. Bron ate and drank ravenously, and wondered how much of his story had been news to the High Sorcerer. She concealed her thoughts extremely well.

'That is enough for you, on the first day,' she said, as he bit into a sweet yellow star-shaped fruit of spectacular juiciness. 'I expect you are weary of questions. You are not a prisoner here, but I do not think it would be suitable, at present, to have you wandering about. Later, of course, once we have decided what to do, once you have accepted our help, you may treat the place as your home, like any other sorcerer. But do not delude yourself. There is a battle ahead, and it will be difficult – very difficult. I believe you will prevail in the end, but others do not. I feel it is only fair to warn you of this, so that you may prepare yourself. And that is best done alone, using the skills you possess. Until the fight is over, you must not clutter your mind with any extraneous concerns. So you will not visit Mallaso of Penya.'

'And if I refuse to obey, or to fight?'

There was a brief, hostile silence. Sé Mo-Tarmé got up and went to the door. Her eyes were as pitiless as splinters of stone. 'We will discuss that later,' she said. 'But I think, when all the arguments have been deployed, that you will find you have no choice. The consequences of failure are too terrible to contemplate.

'And how can you attain real wisdom, or fulfil your true potential, with *that* lurking inside your heart?'

Night fell over Jo'ami, cloaking the School of Wizards in darkness. The hours between the evening meal and retirement were pleasant ones here: the students played games or music, practised their magical skills, especially of Illusion, or spent the time talking, arguing, studying. But tonight Mallaso wanted to be alone, and with sign-language and much laughter let her escorts know that she wished to go to bed.

They led her back to her chamber. Tu Ey-Gan was Jo'amian, a tall girl with deep, rich brown skin and a mass of curly dark hair that was always escaping from its ribbon. Olnez came from

Fabriz, as was evident from her sleek bright red hair and dark eyes, and her prominently aquiline nose. There was no ring in it, but her ears were pierced from lobe to top with a variety of gold loops and studs. Neither of them spoke Toktel'yan, but they were pleasant, friendly and helpful. Mallaso was fluent in five languages, and had already picked up several words of the sibilant Jo'amian tongue. Surprisingly, Toktel'yan was apparently not taught here, perhaps because it was used by their greatest enemy.

Mallaso bid the two apprentices good-night, and shut the door with relief. Her room was dimly lit – one small lamp on the wall – and quite hot. She leaned out of the window, looking along each length of the great building, curving like wings around the crater to either side of her. In the darkness, it was obvious that most of the place was empty: only a handful of lit windows pierced the night. She wondered where Bron was. They had been here for more than three days now – surely he could not have slept for so long?

But of course he had stayed awake all the way from Tekkt. And perhaps the sorcerers had given him something to help him sleep.

She knew enough now about the layout of the school to be sure that all the private rooms, for wizards, apprentices and guests, looked out over the crater. The classrooms, dining hall, kitchens and other offices faced the other way, down the mountainside towards the Haven, edged with cool colonnades and terraced walks. There were no gardens: with the forest all around them so lush, fertile and exuberantly colourful, why go to the trouble of tending flowers which grew in such profusion naturally?

So one of those windows must surely be Bron's. And she knew how to find him. She hummed the tune softly at first, then more loudly as her confidence grew. There was nothing unusual in this: most apprentices seemed to love music, and the place was full of people singing, often very beautifully.

Her own voice was rather throaty, but she could carry a tune provided it did not range too widely. And she sang the 'Lament for Penya', which Bron had played for her in Toktel'yi.

It seemed so very long ago, but in fact, she realized with a shock, it had been less than four months.

> My heart still lies in Penya
> My heart still longs for Penya,

The blue waters of the harbour,
And the breezes sweet and kind.

She was sure that no one else here would know that tune, save
Bron. But in the soft darkness, no answering voice, pure and
melodic as a flute, joined with hers.

But in my heart lies Penya,
Inside my heart lives Penya,
And long as I can still draw breath
She will never truly die.

The last sad notes floated out into the air, competing with
a multitude of warbling crickets. A huge moth, with patterns
on its wings like an owl's eyes, vast and golden, blundered in
past her and began to circle clumsily around the lamp, scattering dust and making a curious buzzing noise. It took Mallaso
some time to catch it and throw it outside. Then she pulled the
thin muslin curtains across the window to stop any other
unauthorized invaders. The lack of response to her singing didn't
really surprise her, but all the same she felt unjustifiably disappointed.

As she turned away from the window, a movement outside
caught her notice. She peered doubtfully back round the curtain,
wondering if another manic flying creature – a bat, perhaps – was
about to invade the room. And instead, she saw a face, pale in the
moonlight, looking up at her.

It was so unexpected that she gasped and dropped the curtain. A voice whispered on the edge of her hearing, 'Mallaso?'

It couldn't be anyone else, clinging to a rockface with, presumably, only sorcery to prevent him falling. She drew back the
flimsy muslin and said in the same hushed murmur, 'Yes. Come
up.'

He achieved it with rather more grace than the bumbling
moth, and stood in front of her slightly breathless, with that rare
yet familiar look of mischief on his face. Relieved and delighted
by his appearance, Mallaso said, 'Did you hear me singing?'

'Yes. I would have found you without it, but it made me sure
of my welcome.' He grinned at her with conspiratorial friendliness. 'I think Sé Mo-Tarmé wants to keep us apart at the
moment.'

'I don't understand why.' Mallaso indicated the tray of jugs and goblets left on the table. 'Would you like a drink, after your climb?'

She poured them each a cup of the red juice of the dewdrop pear, refreshing and not too sweet, and handed one to him with a wry smile. 'Even here, they have pottery from Minassa. That butterfly pattern is beautiful.'

'I suspect that if I voyaged to the furthest ends of the world, and was offered a ritual drink of bull's blood by a savage chief with a necklace of bones and a coat of skins, it would come in a Minassan cup. Thank you. Climbing is thirsty work.'

'Even when aided by sorcery?'

'I didn't use much. I didn't want to draw attention to myself. Though here, where almost everyone employs magic, it's very difficult to distinguish individuals amongst the deafening background of a hundred people all practising simultaneously.'

'Is that what it's like? A *noise*?'

'No, not a noise . . . more a tingling, a sensation. Like so much to do with sorcery, I can't explain it – I just *know*.' He smiled at her, and they sat down together on the couch, sipping their drinks in a companionable, comfortable silence.

At last, Mallaso said curiously, 'What has happened to you? The High Sorcerer told me you were asleep – but for *three days*?'

'It's quite true, I was. I think there was something in the drink they gave me, which helped – certainly, I was completely oblivious. I could have woken up after sleeping for a century, and been none the wiser.'

Mallaso shivered suddenly, despite the warmth of the night. She put down her empty cup and said bluntly, 'Are they as friendly as they seem?'

Bron pondered, his face thoughtful. 'Possibly,' he said at last. 'They have their own interests to consider, though, more than mine and yours. They will not harm us directly, but I suspect they have some plan to use me.'

'Yes, they do,' Mallaso told him. 'The High Sorcerer wants you to kill Ba'alekkt.'

There was another, longer silence. 'Does she?' said Bron. 'Unfortunately for her, I have sworn never to take life. I told her that plainly enough, only a few hours ago.'

'Could she persuade you to change your mind?'

'I don't – ' He broke off suddenly, and she sensed an unwelcome revelation. 'Ah. Yes. Yes, I think I know what she is planning. Very cunning, to kill two deer with one arrow. If they can help me to drive out the Wolf, then I will attain true wisdom – or so Sé Mo-Tarmé said. And incidentally lose my reason for refusing to kill. If the Devourer is gone, I need no longer fear him taking control of me.'

Mallaso said softly, 'And he will no longer be able to keep you from death, either.'

Bron looked at her. 'Yes. I had thought of that. After all, if I failed to kill Ba'alekkt, it might prove a little awkward for the High Sorcerer, to have her assassin captured but invulnerable.'

She thought of Olkanno's instruments of torture, and shuddered. 'But with your powers, wouldn't you be able to free yourself very easily?'

'I hope so. But I am not the only sorcerer in the world, remember. There is Al'Kalyek to reckon with. And I have no idea how strong he is, or whether he would be able to join his power to that of others so that I could be restrained. I just don't know. But I suspect that he might not want to use sorcery for such a purpose. In all Ba'alekkt's court, he is one of the few sound peaches in a very rotten barrel.'

Mallaso looked down at her slender fingers, laced in her lap, dark against the soft yellow of her borrowed robes. She said, very quietly, 'Will you do as they wish?'

'Such a small favour,' Bron said, a sudden and bitter edge to his voice. ' "We will help you to remove the burden you have carried for so long – we will help you attain wisdom – oh, and by the way, will you do just one little thing for us, and kill the Emperor?" If I could destroy him here and now, with a flick of my finger, then, yes, I would. I loathe Ba'alekkt and all his Empire – for what he did to Penya, for what he did to you, and for what he intends to do to Zithirian and Minassa. The armies must be gathering, and soon it will be too late. But to come face to face with a man, however cruel and wicked he may be, and kill him in cold blood – I don't think I could do it, without the Wolf urging me on.'

'I did,' Mallaso reminded him. 'But I had been driven mad then, by Grayna's death. I was obsessed with Penya. I could never try again – I have lost the courage of insanity. But you are different. Think of what happened to my family, and imagine the same fate befalling yours – your father, your stepmother, your brothers and your little sister. Would you want *her* to endure slavery?'

His eyes were very wide and dark, and full of pain. 'No,' Bron said at last. 'But your hatred springs from the past. And that is surely much stronger than mine.'

'Is it? Remember what he did to me, then.' Mallaso found her anger rising. She hadn't meant to try and persuade him, but he seemed so uncharacteristically reluctant, as if he did not feel that assassination was justified.

'I remember.' Bron's voice was flat with appalled disgust. 'He would have carved you in pieces if – '

'If you hadn't rescued me from the consequences of my own reckless lunacy. I never said thank you for that, did I?' And, obeying a sudden and contrary impulse, Mallaso kissed him, with gratitude and affection, lingeringly on the mouth.

'It's futile to argue,' Bron said, a while later. 'We've always been on the same side, you and I. Two faces of the same coin – two halves of the same whole.' He shivered at the touch of her hand, and added with a laugh, 'I bet that whatever Sé Mo-Tarmé imagines we're doing tonight, it isn't this!'

'She probably thinks it'll sap your strength,' Mallaso told him. She knelt astride him, the yellow robe covering some of her body and most of his, and lowered herself down on him. The last time, the man had been Ba'alekkt – but the difference was so great that she could not possibly relate that dreadful, cold-blooded seduction to the warm desire at present flooding through her.

'She could be right.' Bron's eyes closed, but his teeth were sunk in his lower lip, and as they moved rhythmically together, the pleasure she was giving him was written clearly on his face, like words on a page.

When it was over, he held her close, the sweat-soaked robe tangled round them both, and asked softly, 'Do you remember what you said just now?'

'No.' Mallaso could hardly rouse herself from her state of drowsy, sated languor.

'You said, "Give me a child." ' Bron's dark eyes were suddenly fierce. 'Did you mean that?'

With a mixture of hope and terror, she gazed at him. 'Yes. Yes, I did.'

'A child of mine may carry my burden.'

'No,' Mallaso said defiantly. 'No, it will not. There will be no Wolf, and no torment.'

'How can you possibly be sure?'

'I can't.' She gave a sob, suddenly overwhelmed with emotion at the mere possibility of a baby. 'I only know that it would be my child, and yours – and whatever else it carried, or did not, my love for it would not be shaken, ever.'

'You are weeping,' Bron said. His pale fingers traced the shining track of a tear, glittering against her smooth skin. 'It may not be in my power to give – but I know that it is possible.'

And to her bereft, grieving heart, that was as good as a promise.

He left a long while later, the same way as he had come, clinging to flimsy vines and creepers like one of the little green lizards that scuttled amongst the enveloping leaves. She watched him until he was lost to her sight in the darkness. And then, with a smile still on her face and a secret, delicious warmth glowing within her body, she lay down on the couch where they had once again become lovers, and almost instantly fell soundly asleep.

Bron climbed in through his window, conscious of a rather juvenile sense of smug satisfaction. He had disobeyed and outwitted the High Sorcerer, and spent most of the night with Mallaso. And he hoped, for her sake, that he had indeed made her pregnant. His abnormal senses had told him that the chances were high. And if not this night, then there would be others . . .

'Where have you been?'

It was the High Sorcerer. She stood in the centre of his room, with half a dozen of her acolytes around her, robed in azure, crimson and emerald. Amidst their colourful splendour, her dull green garments ironically emphasized her superior status.

As he stood staring at her stupidly, she repeated her question. 'I asked you once, Bronnayak, and I expect an answer. *Where have you been?*'

Her face was implacably hostile. He said quietly, 'Out.'

'I can see that. With her?'

'Yes.'

'I told you that you were not to see her. Why did you disobey me?'

'Because,' Bron said, with exaggerated patience, 'she is my friend, and I wanted to see her and make sure she was all right. I wasn't aware that your prohibition was so absolute. Nor was

I aware that I was a child again, to be treated as such. Am I then your prisoner?'

'No,' said Sé Mo-Tarmé.

'Then surely I have the right to visit anyone I choose.'

'I told you not to see her!'

'Well, I wanted to,' Bron said. He had no inclination to curb his growing anger. 'I was worried about her.'

'Did you screw her?'

The ugly Toktel'yan expression sounded shockingly discordant on the old woman's lips. Bron said forcefully, 'We made love. Several times. Why is this any business of yours?'

'Anything you do under this roof is our business, Bronnayak.'

'Then neither Mallaso nor I wish to be under your roof any longer.' Bron stared at his adversary, his face white with rage. 'May I leave?'

'No, you may not.'

'I don't think you have any choice in the matter,' Bron said. He walked round her towards the door. 'Farewell, High Sorcerer.'

As he reached for the handle, a flash of something like lightning seared down his arm, and he snatched it back with a gasp of pain.

Sé Mo-Tarmé laughed. Bron whipped round. He raised his unburnt hand, and made a quick circling motion.

Sorcery hummed in the air. Sé Mo-Tarmé brought up her own arms, and blue-green fire flickered along her fingers. 'Come out,' she said softly. 'Come out and let us see you, Devourer of Souls.'

'No!' Bron cried. 'No – I'm not ready – you can't want that!'

'But I do,' said the High Sorcerer. 'You have brought this on yourself by your own foolishness, Bronnayak. I want to see him now, this Wolf you keep locked away in your soul. Alone, in cold blood, you can't defeat him. With our help, you have a chance. Your anger has opened the door – let him free!'

'No. You don't know what you're doing,' Bron said. He was breathing hard, and his dark eyes were like pits below the pale fall of his hair. 'I know him – I *know* him – we've inhabited the same mind for twenty-three years. He will show none of us mercy.'

'And neither shall I be gentle,' said the High Sorcerer. She crossed the index fingers of her right and left hands, and uttered a low, singsong incantation. The acolytes, their faces intent, took it up. The language was not that of Jo'ami, but something much older, alien, primitive, and deeply evil. He had not heard it spoken since he was nine years old, but he knew it was Ska'i. Rage seethed and boiled within him as if he were a fire mountain, concealing a torrent of blazing death. And Ayak, his red eyes glittering, his jaws dripping with anticipation, made ready for the slaughter.

Confront him.

Who had said that? The sorcerers were still chanting.

Fight him. FIGHT him!

And using his fury as a weapon, he looked the Wolf full in the face, as he had never dared to before.

Scarlet, glowing eyes. Yellow, slavering fangs. An insatiable lust for blood and death, terror and misery. One of the acolytes cried out, and he realized with horror that Ayak was standing in the corner of the room, a huge and shadowy shape created by the power of Bron's mind. Then its evil overcame him, and it sprang.

The sorcerer in blue fell screaming below its claws. A red mist seemed to fill Bron's mind. Blood filled his mouth, and he exulted in its hot, rank taste. He looked up from the dead acolyte, and saw the others staring at him, petrified with terror.

What are you waiting for? Kill them all!

Defeat the Wolf! You have the power – cast him out before he conquers you!

The conflicting voices screamed over and over again in his mind. He quailed, his hands over his ears, as they battled for control. Then the Wolf's rage overwhelmed him again, and he turned to seek his next victim.

Sé Mo-Tarmé did not shrink or cower. She stood upright and unafraid in the face of Death, her hands by her sides.

You were made for this! Kill her!

No – for the sake of all who love you, do not let him destroy you!

My servant, my slave – kill, kill, KILL!

Sorcery crackled around him. He felt it join with his own power, limitless and omnipotent. He saw the remaining acolytes, men and women, staring at him aghast. The Devourer howled encouragement.

And with a desperate, valiant effort, he turned all the power inwards, upon his enemy.

In the language of Zithirian, rich and stately, he cursed the

Wolf whose name he bore. Ayak's mouth opened in a snarl of hatred, and his roar of defiance burst into Bron's mind. *I will not go – you are my creature – and if you force me, I shall take you with me!*

The acolytes watched in horrified awe as the Wolf turned with a snarl, his jaws dripping blood, and sprang upon his host.

Bron crashed backwards, the Devourer on top of him. They rolled over and over, wrestling frantically. Sé Mo-Tarmé dodged out of the way, and screamed at the surviving sorcerers. 'He cannot do it alone – help him!'

The Wolf was too strong for Bron. Its fangs rent his mind and his body, and tore at his soul. He had kept the Devourer hidden for so long, that he had imagined that his own power was superior. Now, experiencing at last the true, awesome force of his enemy, he knew he could not defeat him. And what awaited him was not death, but something much, much worse.

'Are you a demon?' Sargenay had asked him once.

No, he was not – not yet. But soon he would be the true slave of Death, and all his vaunted, unique and remarkable power could not prevail against it.

Join with us! cried Sé Mo-Tarmé in his mind. *We are here to help you – join with us NOW, or you are lost for ever!*

He felt their spirits uniting with him, giving his failing heart a burst of prodigious strength. Their combined fires, crimson, gold, blue-white, reared up triumphantly. And then a darker, yet no less powerful flame wrapped around the huge blaze of sorcery, focused it, and flung it like a spear at the ravening Wolf.

GO! someone cried. *Be gone for ever, and inhabit me no more!*

In the wild incandescence of flame, white and blue, red and viridian, Ayak howled and writhed in agony as the fire consumed him.

And then, with a last scream of pain and fury, he was gone, and there was only the empty darkness.

CHAPTER
NINETEEN

'You must come with us.'

Mallaso sat up on the couch, clasping the thin sheet to her chest. The High Sorcerer was standing in the doorway, her familiar stocky shape outlined by the lights carried by acolytes in the corridor behind. With a sick feeling of dread, Mallaso realized that it was still dark.

'What has happened?' Her low voice was hoarse with alarm. 'What have you done?'

'What have *you* done, Mallaso of Penya? And what might the consequences be? I told you not to see him yet. Are you normally so disobedient?'

'Yes,' said Mallaso fiercely. 'After all, I am no longer anyone's slave or whore.'

There was a small, angry silence. 'Get dressed,' Sé Mo-Tarmé said finally, her voice hostile in the extreme. 'And come with us.'

She grabbed the brightly coloured rectangle, which was the first garment that came to hand, and tied it round herself, under the arms. Then she followed the High Sorcerer down the long, curving corridor that formed the backbone of the School of Wizards. On the left lay courts, halls, classrooms, libraries. On the right, innumerable doors, each leading to small individual rooms similar to her own, for guests or sorcerers: or to larger dormitories, intended to contain up to a dozen apprentices in each. They passed no-one, heard nothing, but the short hairs on the back of Mallaso's neck prickled, as if a tentacle of cold air had trailed across it. And they were getting closer to the source.

She knew which was Bron's room before the High Sorcerer stopped in front of the entrance. The acolytes stood, men and women, holding their lamps. One wore white robes, and a spatter of bright red drops, like blood, had splashed across the front. And power, or the memory of it, poured like water around the closed door, and flowed around them.

'Please tell me what has happened,' Mallaso cried urgently. 'Is he dead?'

'No, *he* is not,' said one of the acolytes, a small dark-haired woman with haunted eyes. 'But Tu Kar-Lyen is.'

There was a terrible pause. All kinds of dreadful scenes processed macabrely through Mallaso's mind. She took a deep breath, hoping that nothing could possibly be worse than her imaginings, and opened the door.

There was a great dark red pool on the floor. And beside it sat the man who had left her bed only a few hours ago, cross-legged, his hands lax on his knees. His body was liberally splattered with dried blood, although he seemed to bear no wounds. And his eyes, though open, were perfectly blank.

'What happened?' she cried, for the third time. And at last, the High Sorcerer answered her.

'He drove out the Wolf. In the struggle, Tu Kar-Lyen was slain. And the effort took all his power. He needs you, to bring his spirit back – if it can be brought back. And then he will need our help to restore his power and his faith, and to teach him how to live with the emptiness that the departure of evil has created. Will you succour him?'

'For his sake, yes,' Mallaso told her. She stood tall and straight before the High Sorcerer, with condemnation in her face. 'But not for you. You only want him as your tool, don't you? You want him to kill Ba'alekkt. You've done this to him.' Her voice was shaking, and she steadied it with a furious effort. 'Haven't you ever thought about what *he* wants? Maybe he didn't need the Wolf driven out.'

'You err, Mallaso of Penya. No man could carry that within him and still attain true power and wisdom. It had to be done.'

'Perhaps it did. But he doesn't *mean* anything to you, does he? You're like all the rest of them – you don't see the man, you just see what he can do for you.'

'And you do not?'

'*I* have no ambitions to rule the Empire,' Mallaso said pointedly.

'Perhaps not. But you long for a child, do you not, to replace the one that you lost? His child, perhaps, carrying his power, to be moulded to your own will?'

'No!' she cried, in vehement denial. 'Yes, I do want a child – but I want an *ordinary* child, a *normal* child, to sing and laugh and be happy. I've been close to Bron for months, and I think I can understand, much better than you, what it is like to live with his . . . gifts. And I don't want them for any child of ours.'

'He will find it much easier to live with his power now that the Wolf is gone.'

'Not necessarily. Because people will still fear him . . . any sorcerer will know what he is . . . and because people like you will always want to use him.'

'We want to help him,' said the dark-haired woman. 'Abilities such as his cannot ever be easy to live with, or to understand, or to wield. We would like to know why he has been born thus, when it has taken the rest of us many years and many doses of Annatal to achieve a tiny fraction of his power.'

'Well, you can try to persuade him,' Mallaso said. 'But he is a man, not a child. He is strong, and stubborn, and very difficult to mould. If he does what you want, it will be because *he* wants it too, not because of your arguments. But you say you want me to help him now. If that is so, then leave us.'

'Alone? But we don't know for certain – ' The dark-haired woman broke off and glanced at the High Sorcerer. Mallaso knew they must be using thoughtlink, though no echo of their silent speech brushed her mind.

'Very well,' said Sé Mo-Tarmé at last. 'At your own risk, you understand.'

'I understand,' Mallaso said. She watched as all of them reluctantly filed out. Of course, there was nothing to stop any of them spirit-walking back into the room again later, to spy on them. But at least she wouldn't have to see all those eyes, staring in real or imagined contempt.

The door shut behind the last of them. Mallaso did not look at the man who sat, a living statue, on the floor. She lit all the lamps around the wall, so that the shadows were banished. She dragged the sheets off the bed, and mopped up that dreadful pool of blood as best she could. She closed the muslin curtains, and swatted some of the more annoying insects. Then, with a feeling of helpless dread, she sat down in front of Bron.

He was as still as if carved from marble, and his eyes were dilated and fixed. She waved her hand in front of them, but he did not blink. He was breathing, though very shallowly, and his flesh was still warm under the damp, clammy skin. He did not look like the most powerful sorcerer in the history of the known world: he looked like some hopeless lunatic in the public asylum in Tok-tel'yi, chained up for the amusement of more fortunate citizens.

Real fear kicked at Mallaso's stomach. What could she, utterly lacking in sorcery, do to help him? How was she to restore his spirit? And what would happen if his wits had truly deserted him for ever?

If they had, she would plunge the dagger in his heart herself. Even death was preferable to such a ghastly existence. And she could not bear to think of Bron's quick wits and mischief reduced to this mindless shell.

She touched him again, and talked to him. She stroked his hand, his face. She sang songs. She tried to fling her mind at the bastion of his, but it fell back, defeated by her ignorance and terror. There was no response at all, not a twitch of the mouth, not a flicker in the empty eyes.

Perhaps the Wolf had in some way been essential to him – essential to his sanity and to his power. For so long, so much of his sorcery had been devoted to keeping Ayak repressed deep within his soul. And now the Devourer had been cast out, and half his mind as well.

It was growing light. She had talked to him for hours, and he had not shown the slightest reaction. Outside, a bird began to sing melodiously. Stiff and heartsick, Mallaso struggled painfully to her feet and went to the window.

Bron's room was much further round the eastern side of the crater, and had quite a different view to hers. A tree grew just outside, a sinewy, elegant specimen with long slender roots twining through the rocks, and sprays of heart-shaped, glossy leaves arching down gracefully from its branches. Almost within her grasp, the small golden brown bird called a Kiyu trilled softly, and looked at her with its round, bright eye, as if aware that she would not harm it. Mallaso stayed very still, watching, until every smooth curve, every crisp tawny feather, every line of scaled feet and small convex beak was imprinted on her mind, perhaps for ever. The Kiyu sang on, softly and then growing louder as daylight erupted brilliantly in the east. Its call of welcome was taken up by others in a cacophony of different tunes, topped by the raucous shriek of a yellow and blue parrot which alighted heavily in the top branch of the tree. With a look of resignation, the Kiyu flew off, and Mallaso, tired and despairing, turned back into the room.

He had moved. His hands were gripped together. And as she approached him, her heart suddenly full of mingled hope and terror, he turned to look at her, and smiled.

It was not the smile of a demon, or a lunatic. Overcome with joy and emotion, she dropped to her knees beside him, and wept.

'You have shed too many tears,' Bron said softly, and his hand touched her wet face. 'Shed them no more – and certainly not for my sake.'

'I thought—' She stopped, unwilling to voice the horror of what she had imagined.

'I went away within myself. My father taught me to do it, as a means of regeneration, renewal, restoration. There was no other way for me to heal myself. Ayak was almost too strong for me.' He gave her a wry smile. 'I didn't want Sé Mo-Tarmé's help, but I was forced to take it in the end. So now I am in her debt, as she wanted. And I will kill Ba'alekkt, if I can.'

His words sank into her heart like stones. Mallaso stared at him, shocked and appalled. 'But you said – '

'I know what I said. But that was before I drove out the Wolf. I can still hardly understand what that means – to be able to talk and think and above all to *feel* without fear – to be angry without any danger of killing someone. To be able to look into my soul, without flinching . . . it's too new and too strange to appreciate how it will alter my life. But I have come to a decision. You were right, and so was Sé Mo-Tarmé, though for different reasons. Ba'alekkt must be stopped. And I will kill him not for you, or for Penya, nor for any debt I owe the High Sorcerer, nor to prevent the evil she sees creeping over the world. No – I will do it for Zithirian, and for my father and stepmother, and for Tayma and Homan and Zathti and all the other children, so that they may grow up as you never could, in happiness and love and freedom. And since Sé Mo-Tarmé is watching us now, I will say it again. This will be on *my* terms, by *my* arranging. If I need your help, I will ask for it. If I do not, then I will not ask – and I do not want it. Do you understand, High Sorcerer?'

There was a soft sound that might have been laughter. Bron grinned at Mallaso. 'That's sent her back to her body. I expect she'll be knocking on the door in person, very shortly. Does she frighten you?'

'Not in the least,' Mallaso said, with truth. 'In fact, in a curious way, I could almost feel sorry for her and the other sorcerers.'

'Don't let her know that.' Bron's eyes gleamed with mischief. 'But why?'

'Why do I pity them? Because . . .' Mallaso paused, searching for a moment, and then found her answer. 'Because they are a backwater here, a legend without direct power or influence over the world. Their numbers are declining fast, and they're clinging to the memories of past glories. They've been forced to persaude you to do their dirty work for them. And above all because you are so much stronger than they are – without using Annatal. And they can't understand why.'

'I don't understand why either,' Bron said. He stretched, his muscles taut in his arms and back above the brief cloth kilt which was still his only garment. 'I suppose they want answers – and I'm not really in a position to provide them. In fact, I wanted answers from *them*. Help me up? I'm so stiff I can hardly move.'

Mallaso obliged, and he hobbled, cursing, to the couch and sat down.

'The greatest sorcerer in the known world shouldn't suffer from cramp,' she observed drily.

'I agree.' Bron was rubbing his legs vigorously. 'But unfortunately he does. And I've had enough of using my powers for trivial things. Curing aches and pains is too easy.'

'You cured my headache once, and that didn't seem trivial to me.'

'No, I don't suppose it did.' Bron glanced up at her, his face unsmiling. 'I will Heal others, then, if I can, but not myself. Not when a brisk rub and a walk round the room will cure me. Ah – that must be the High Sorcerer.'

It was. She surveyed Bron and Mallaso, her face devoid of expression, and then said, 'I see you have returned to us.'

'I was never away.'

'Were you not? Well, there is much we have to discuss, and very little time. Leave us, please, Mallaso of Penya.'

Mallaso looked at her lover. His eyes bright, he shook his head. 'No. She stays.'

Tellingly, the High Sorcerer stared at him for a long time, and then nodded reluctantly. 'Very well. But I warn you, it will be a long talk. The matter is now urgent. By High Summer, the Imperial Army will be mustered on the border at Tamat, ready to march on Minassa and Zithirian. We have just four more months to plan and carry out the assassination.'

'If I agree to do it,' Bron said. He stretched again and put his feet up on the couch. 'Do sit down, High Sorcerer – that chair looks comfortable.'

'*If* you agree! But – ' The old woman clamped her mouth shut and stared at him angrily.

'I know. I said I would. But not to you. You weren't in the room. I was under the impression that you thought sorcery shouldn't be used for petty, small-minded matters. Of which eavesdropping is undoubtedly one.'

There was an inimical silence. Mallaso observed Sé Mo-Tarmé's discomfiture and felt a resurgence of sympathy. She had been ruler of her own small world for so long, taking refuge in tales of a great past and hopes for a greater future. It must be hard to be forced to acknowledge the superiority of this young upstart whose power far surpassed hers – and, she suspected, whose vision was greater as well.

For something drove Bron forward, some dream that was far more substantial and encompassing than the High Sorcerer's limited ambitions. She did not know precisely what it was, but she knew it existed – even though he ostensibly had no plans beyond the assassination of the Emperor.

'That is what sorcery has sunk to,' Bron said softly, vehemently. 'Used to spy, to manipulate, to delude. Who can take pride in that? Since the days of Ai-Mayak, it has caused strife and grief and death. Too rarely has it been used to create, to build, to cure, to mend. But some of the Toktel'yan sorcerers whom you so greatly despise have shining reputations as Healers. Is that a discipline you teach here?'

'Yes,' said Sé Mo-Tarmé, but her voice was defensive.

'Think, for a moment, what would happen if Ba'alekkt were killed. I can't foretell the future, but I can use my knowledge and common sense to make a good guess. The Emperor has no wife, yet, and therefore no legitimate heir – in fact, I have not even heard that he has any children by any of his concubines.'

'There are two,' Mallaso said. 'Both girls, both babies.'

'So they cannot be in contention. One of his two sisters is married to the Heir of Minassa, and the other is betrothed to the Prince of Tulyet. He has a dozen half-brothers, all by different mothers, all with some claim to the Onyx throne. In addition, his father had three legitimate brothers, all of whom are living and have adult sons of their own. Beyond that, there is an abundance of cousins, and every one with Imperial blood and as good a claim as each other. Within a day of Ba'alekkt's death they'll be gathering support, wooing governors, ministers, councillors, and above all the army. And the army isn't a single entity either. The Imperial Guard owes its allegiance to the Emperor, but all the other units are recruited in the provinces, and will give their loyalty first to their own regions. Then there are those islands and cities which have not been part of the Empire for very long, and where dreams of freedom are still kept alive. Tamat, for instance: Tatht, Onnak, Annatal, Djebb, Penya. If the Emperor dies heirless, they may seize the opportunity to rebel. Lives saved in Zithirian or Minassa may be lost within the Empire, as some of its people struggle for independence.'

'Do you think I am unaware of this?' the High Sorcerer demanded.

'No. But good may in the end arise from evil, as the firebird is reborn from its own ashes. It will be a long struggle, but I believe that a world without the Empire will be a better place. And if I can survive the assassination of Ba'alekkt, I will do my utmost to ensure that it is.'

'You delude yourself,' said the old woman sharply. 'No one man can manipulate events to such a degree. You over-estimate your power.'

'Do I? But after the expulsion of the Wolf, who knows what I can do? *I* don't know where my limits lie yet,' said Bron sweetly. 'So how can you?'

Sé Mo-Tarmé's face was grim. 'This is foolishness. How can you rule the world with sorcery?'

'I don't intend to. Nor do I want to sit here discussing hypo-theticals with someone who may well become my enemy. At present, my sole aim is to kill Ba'alekkt. And not, as I told your spirit earlier, because *you* want me to – but because *I* want to. I needed your help to drive out the Wolf, and for that I am very grateful. But I will not let you use my obligation to you as a lever to persuade me to do your bidding. For a little while, our paths and our wishes have converged. Not for ever, though. And I no longer need your teaching, or your help.'

'Arrogant man!' Sé Mo-Tarmé cried. 'Of course you need us!'

'I do not. *You* need *me*, so that you can increase your under-standing of sorcery. I've worked out some of it myself, as it hap-pens. Shall I tell you?'

Sé Mo-Tarmé nodded. In the few moments of their dis-cussion, or argument, she seemed to have shrunk, and her face was full of weariness.

'Contrary to what you've always believed, many people are born with magical powers,' Bron said. 'In some it is weak, in others, like my father, it is quite strong. Because sorcery was forbidden in Zithirian, his gifts were unrecognized, even by himself – though perhaps they drew him to become a Mazath, a secret sorcerer, without him knowing why. In the Empire, it's common knowledge that some need to take only a little Annatal to achieve power, whereas others need a huge amount to reach the same level. Perhaps those who only take a little in fact don't need it at all – but because it's assumed that only Annatal will confer the gift of magic, it's never occurred to anyone that it could be unnecessary. I think that my powers are so strong because I inherited them in double measure from both my parents – and because, from my early childhood, the witch D'thliss was using and honing my magic. Instead of encouraging your apprentices to become permanently and damagingly addicted to Annatal, you'd probably be better off searching for *children* with inborn ability, and helping them to achieve their full potential without the aid of drugs.'

The silence following his last words was full of unspoken hostility. Bron's dark eyes bored into the lighter ones of the High Sorcerer. He said quietly, 'Aloud, if you please. Mallaso is not an Adept.'

Sé Mo-Tarmé made a noise that sounded suspiciously like a snort of disgust. She said, 'You are asking us to abandon every principle of our philosophy – fifteen hundred years of wisdom and teaching – for an unproven theory?'

'I'm *suggesting* – not asking – that you open your minds a little, that's all. You want the world to change. Do you think that Jo'ami will be untouched by it? If you wish to preside over a resurgence of sorcery, to confirm its place as the greatest of all the Arts, you will need to adapt and respond to what happens, both within the Empire and outside it. I am not the only one – I *cannot* be the only one with natural powers. My father – my stepmother – my half-brothers and sister – they are all gifted, to a greater or lesser degree. In every town or village, all over the known world, there must be a child, a woman, a man, who has the power and does not know it. For those who already take Annatal it is too late. But I think the future is bright for the children. They can be taught to use their gifts wisely and well – and they won't be slaves to a drug that ages them before their time, and then pickles them for the rest of an unnaturally long life. Think of the implications, High Sorcerer. Al'Kalyek in Toktel'yi has already begun the search for children with power. He can accept change, and he can also accept the unpalatable fact that the drug he must take to stay alive might not be needed by those who follow him. Can you do the same? Or will you deny the truth because of your own selfishness?'

'None of this is proved,' said Sé Mo-Tarmé, her lips white. 'This is all hypothetical, as you yourself admitted.'

'Then prove it. That is your duty – to find the natural sorcerers, and, *if* they themselves wish it, to train and nourish their gifts. The only people who will oppose you will be the growers and suppliers of Annatal. My task, as you've pointed out so forcefully, is to break up the Empire. Allow me to make my own arrangements for that. Apart from anything else, I'd quite like to survive the ensuing cataclysm.'

'What are you implying?' demanded the High Sorcerer, frowning.

'Nothing. I have learned not to rely on other people, that's all. Or to entangle them in my schemes. I work better alone. Now, since I am a guest in your establishment, as you never tire of reminding me, I would like you to leave my room – both in body and in spirit. I know when you are listening – did you think me so ignorant and stupid that you could eavesdrop unnoticed?'

'I apologize,' said Sé Mo-Tarmé, through stiff lips. 'It will not happen again. I give you my word.'

'Good. I'm glad.' Bron gave her his sudden, mischievous grin. 'Perhaps this discussion has clarified certain points. I hope that we both now realize what we're dealing with, and that we'll work together more productively as a result. And I thank you once more for your assistance, last night.'

Frigidly, the High Sorcerer inclined her head in acknowledgement, and left the room with impressive dignity.

'Come for a walk?' Bron suggested as soon as she had gone. 'I'm tired of being cooped up in here, and I'd like some fresh air. And I still don't entirely trust her. In the open, she might find it more difficult to pry.' He looked at Mallaso, and smiled. 'That garment suits you – and even in the heat of the sun, you won't need anything else. I, on the other hand, will be burnt to a crisp if I go out in this. But with stunning thoughtfulness, they've supplied an alternative. Do you think it will fool anyone?'

The long, soft yellow robes of an apprentice sorcerer at least protected his fair skin from the sun, although Bron, acutely conscious of the irony, wore them with a casual arrogance alien to most of the students Mallaso had seen. Together, they walked out of his room and down the long corridor. They passed twinges of sorcery, the smell of cooking and the more pervasive, sickly sweet aroma of Annatal, and stepped out of the main entrance.

Below them, the forest through which they had struggled during that seemingly endless night sloped shimmering down to the blue circle of Jo'ami Havèn. Narrowing her eyes, Mallaso could see the ship which Bron had sailed from Tekkt, a tiny shape riding at anchor in the still waters. Scattered around it, smaller craft, presumably fishing boats, drifted with a deceptive air of idleness.

'Let's walk around the crater,' she suggested. Somehow, the thought of entering that forest again, even in daylight, was not attractive.

A neat path led along terraces below the school buildings, but ended in a gate set in the boundary wall. Bron opened it, and they saw that the way continued along the crater's edge. Mallaso, who had considerable reserves of energy to squander, set off at a brisk pace. Her simple Jo'amian garment, ending just below the knee, was far more practical than Bron's trailing robes, and her thonged sandals protected the soles of her feet from the hot sharp rocks. Soon, she had to wait while he caught up, and she realized that his various exertions last night had exhausted him.

A large brayal tree grew out of the mountainside nearby, offering welcome shade. Mallaso sat down under the spreading branches, and plucked a large frond of some palm-like bush to fan herself. Bron joined her, his robes dark with sweat and his hair hanging in limp rats' tails round his drawn face.

'I'm all right,' he said in response to her anxious concern. 'Nothing a good sleep won't cure.'

'You drive yourself too hard,' Mallaso told him.

'Not hard enough, if I'm to outwit Sé Mo-Tarmé and her minions.' He leaned back against the smooth grey trunk of the tree, his hands crossed behind his head. 'Mallaso, I want you to promise me something.'

She stared at him. His dark eyes, desperately serious, stared back. 'I want you to promise that you won't become involved with my plan to kill Ba'alekkt.'

As she began to protest, he went on, his voice low and earnest. 'It's too risky. They know you. Ba'alekkt, Olkanno, Al'Kalyek, half the Imperial Guard – they'd all recognize you. There is nothing left for you in Toktel'yi. At the very least, your friends will be watched, the Golden Djarlek will have been leased to someone else, your name will be at the top of every informer's list. It would be too dangerous for you even to try and enter the Empire. They'll be looking for you at all the ports, and every tall Penyan woman will be arrested. You know what the Toktel'yans are like. All that bureaucracy has a purpose. No one can hide for long from their officials and spies and agents. In the end, they'll find you.'

She knew that he was right, and her mouth was dry with apprehension. She said, 'Where can I go? Because I certainly don't want to stay here.'

Bron looked at her in surprise, and smiled at her. 'I didn't think you would give in so easily. That isn't the Mallaso I know.'

'I was never one to resist the inevitable. You're right – I would be in danger myself, and put you in peril too.'

'Go to Kerenth,' Bron said softly. 'In Kerenth, you will be safe. In Kerenth, you have a chance of rebuilding your life, and finding happiness – although I strongly advise you to avoid Inrai'a. She might be jealous.'

'Why should she be?'

'Because of what you carry.' His tired smile broke out again, and his hand touched hers. 'Our child.'

'Do you *know* that?'

'That you are pregnant? Yes, I am certain. Don't ask how – I just know. It was why Sé Mo-Tarmé did not want us to meet last night. She suspected a child might result. And she fears it.'

Mallaso remembered the High Sorcerer's voice, condemning her disobedience. She said in bewilderment, 'Why?' Why should she be afraid of it?'

'Because of the prophecy. She told you that I was the One, who would make empires crumble. What she didn't add was the rest of the prediction – that my legacy would destroy Jo'ami. And she chooses to believe that the word "legacy" denotes my child.'

'Is – is she right?'

'I don't know. I can't read the future. Only those who have special gifts can do that. But I don't intend to leave you here in this nest of serpents, in case Sé Mo-Tarmé decides to alter the future in her favour. There is a ship due in from Kerenth tomorrow. When it leaves, I want you to be on it – without the High Sorcerer's knowledge.'

'Do you really believe she would harm me?'

'Is it a chance you want to take? I don't know. She is very strict in her interpretation of the Four Rules – but she might have fewer scruples when it comes to an ordinary knife in the dark. She is devoted to Jo'ami and its traditions. I think she is ruthless enough to kill, if her conscience deserted her. And I don't want to leave you alone with them. While I'm here, they will not dare to harm you. But once I go . . .'

Mallaso crossed her hands over her flat belly, where, perhaps, her seed and his were already united. The thought of a child was so wonderful that she knew that she would sacrifice anything to make it come true.

Anything – even the company and comfort of her lover.

'I will go to Kerenth,' she said at last. 'Will you come to find me one day, when all this is over?'

If you survive. She did not utter the words, but they hovered in the air between them.

'I will come,' Bron said. 'If I can, I will come. For there is a long journey ahead of me, and I do not know how I can endure it without you to sustain me, and help me, and guide me.' He picked up her hand and kissed it, gently. 'For you. For our child. And for all the peoples who long for freedom, and whose prison doors I may be able to break down.

'And if I do not come, then you have the child, to protect and cherish, whether it possesses my gifts or not. And you have also the knowledge that the world was changed because of you.'

'It may not be enough,' Mallaso said. 'But I will make it enough, if I have to.'

He kissed her then, and they embraced in the prickly grass beneath the brayal tree, content for the moment just to lie so close, when all too soon they would be parted. After a little while, his stillness and the soft regularity of his breathing told her that he slept. And she lay in his arms, feeling his warmth and the slow, almost imperceptible pulse of his heart, and wept silently for the unknowable future, that might offer too much, both of joy and of pain, for easy bearing.

After fifty years as a sorcerer, Sé Mo-Tarmé was in a position to recognize evil when it came knocking inside her head. But evil disguised as a logical solution to her dilemma was rather different.

Before his landing on Jo'ami, she had welcomed the prospect of Bron's arrival. 'He will change the world,' she had told poor Tu Kar-Lyen. 'And it needs changing.' She had expected a man possessed of great power, but young enough to be malleable and easily persuaded. Instead, she had been faced with a sorcerer whose ability far outclassed her own, who possessed a sense of purpose she could not shake, and a stubborn will that could not be manipulated. And because of his refusal to submit to her superior years and judgement and experience, because of his insolent defiance, the future of Jo'ami had been put at risk.

In daylight hours, she scolded herself for her folly. Prophecies were notoriously treacherous, and this particular set more ambiguous than most. His 'legacy' might not be a child. A child might not even have been conceived, although the Penyan woman's body had been ripe for it. And once, fifty years ago, she had sworn oaths of the greatest solemnity, in the secret cave of Ai-Mayak beneath the crater, not to use her sorcery to wreak harm or hurt, damage or death.

But sorcery was not the only way to kill. And she thought of Jo-ami, the place of her birth, the cradle of sorcery, her sacred trust for unborn generations of mages, her plans for its future and for the Empire, and anger seethed within her, that one man's defiance, one man's seed, should endanger her beloved home.

The voice whispered in her head at night. So easy, once Bron had left on his fateful mission, to ensure that the Penyan miscarried her conjectural child. A potion slipped in her food would suffice, or an unfortunate fall on the rocks.

But that might not be enough. After all, this was one child, one woman. By his own admission, Bron had had several lovers – not least the Queen of Kerenth – and, if he survived the attack on Ba'alekkt, would probably enjoy many more, out of her reach and her knowledge, and all of them with the potential to bear his child. She closed her eyes against the dark, helpless with impotent rage, while his unborn legacies swam in her mind with bright, merciless eyes, promising the destruction of her world.

She went back to the old books, and read them over and over again. No doubt of it, Bron was the One, the Child of Evil Born, who would cause the end of the Empire. The following verse, though, was more ambiguous.

> A legacy shall promise much
> And good and evil both shall touch
> The southern isle's rule no more
> No hearts nor waves along the shore.

It did not make any sense, save to the half-mad seer who had written it many lifetimes ago: but Sé Mo-Tarmé was sure what it meant.

Another, less unpleasant solution occurred to her. Perhaps the child, once born, could be reared in Jo'ami, under her influence. Then surely the island would be safe.

What to do. How to act. The High Sorcerer knew that prophecies had an inconvenient way of making themselves come true, however great the efforts of mere mortals to prevent it. Everyone knew the old story of the Emperor Kakken't, whose death had been foretold for a particular day, and who spent it in bed, surrounded by the Imperial Guard – only to choke on a fishbone, just before midnight.

Stupid doggerel. Crazy prophet.

But she would make sure Mallaso stayed on Jo'ami. Just in case.

The ship called *Lady of Kerenth* dropped anchor in Jo'ami Haven after a voyage covering nearly eight hundred miles, and lasting almost a month. She had beaten against contrary winds, been blown dangerously close to Ma'alkwen by a fierce tropical storm, and had narrowly avoided a Fabrizian pirate ship as well as a squadron of the Imperial Navy, who were quite capable of sinking a ship which they might regard as belonging to an enemy country, particularly if there were no witnesses and no survivors. Her passengers, all hopeful intending sorcerers, were relieved to reach their destination safely, but her Captain, a wizened and wiry woman with the leathery complexion of all sailors, was more philosophical. Such hazards were quite common on the long run from Kerenth, and if it hadn't been for the weather-working sorcerer – hideously expensive, but well worth the money – that storm would have driven the *Lady of Kerenth* on to the barren, rocky and lethal coast of Ma'alkwen. She looked forward to the days of leisure ahead, once passengers and cargo had been landed, and before their return consignment was loaded. Jo'ami was a very beautiful island, with friendly people, a pleasant climate, hot but not humid, and an abundance of clean water and fresh food.

As usual, she supervised the unloading. Sweating sailors, men and women in brief tunics with cloths wrapped round their heads, clambered out of the *Lady of Kerenth*'s capacious hold with sacks of wheat and rice, barrels of wine, jars of honey and oil, raisins, preserved fruit, and bale upon bale of Toktel'yan cotton and Kerentan silk. Alongside the ship, Jo'ami's boats jostled impatiently, waiting to take on the precious cargo. Go'enna watched her industrious crew with a sharp but benevolent eye. Many of them had been under her command for years, and she knew them better than her own children (five of them, all now adult, reared in Kerenth City by their grandmother).

'Captain! Boat approaching!' Ai'an, her First Mate, came hurrying up. 'Looks like we've got a visit from some of those pesky wizards.'

A look of complete understanding passed between them. Ai'an was still, occasionally, her lover, a relationship which went back nearly thirty years: indeed, he was the father of three of her children. To both of them, magic was an annoyingly necessary complication, an attitude largely formed by their experience of weather-workers. The ship's current sorcerer was a typical example of the breed: an overdressed man from a small Kerentan town, he was altogether too fond of good food and wine, and had a pompously inflated idea of his own importance. If it hadn't been for his undeniable and invaluable skills Go'enna would never have allowed him on board, let alone paid him the three gold bars which were his fee for one return voyage's worth of his services.

She turned to the ship's starboard rail to watch the approach of the boat. It was rowed by a dozen half-naked Jo'amians, and carried half that number of robed sorcerers. She caught a glimpse of muddy green amongst the blue and crimson, and frowned. 'This is serious, old man. That's the High Sorcerer.'

'Is it, indeed?' Ai'an shaded his eyes. 'I wonder what she

wants. She's never deigned to visit in person before – we've only ever seen her up at the school.'

'Well, if she's after any silk, she'll have to buy it in the market – it's all spoken for.' Go'enna glanced round. 'I thought *he'd* soon show his face. Get ready to watch some really spectacular grovelling.'

Tliou, the weather-working sorcerer, was wearing a full-length robe in scarlet, the most expensive of all dyes, with an intricate pattern of spirals, one of the symbols of the Goddess, embroidered in gold thread along neck and hem. His smooth brown face – too young as yet to show any signs of Annatal addiction – was set in a mould of obsequious deference. As the High Sorcerer levitated gracefully aboard, her acolytes behind her, he abased himself in a gesture of extreme submission, kneeling down with his head bowed on to the deck.

The High Sorcerer surveyed him unsmilingly. 'For the Mother's sake, get up, Tliou,' she said testily. 'You should know that we have no such ceremonies here.'

'Forgive me, Most Wise – I was only expressing my deepest admiration and respect.' Tliou scrambled to his feet, his eyes shining. 'May I presume to tell you, Most Wise, what an honour it is for me, a humble graduate of your school, to speak with you again—'

'I'm not here to exchange pleasantries with you. I'm here for a private word with your Captain.' The High Sorcerer gestured at her entourage. 'You may fawn on them, if you like.' She turned to Go'enna. 'Where can we talk alone?'

'On the stern deck, madam,' said the Captain, unperturbed. She had had dealings with Sé Mo-Tarmé many times before, and was not afraid of her irascible manner. The High Sorcerer's character was very much like her own – hard, but fair.

She led the way aft, past the tillers of the twin steering-oars, typical of Kerentan vessels, lying shipped in their rope slings. The stern was the Captain's own domain, by long custom of all seafaring peoples, and they would not be disturbed without warning. All the same, Go'enna glanced down at the smooth, clear blue water beneath the rail. The dark shadows of a shoal of fish darted under the surface, but there were no stray boats lurking, full of possible eavesdroppers.

'Well,' she said, turning to the High Sorcerer. 'What's all this about?'

'I wish to know when you plan to sail – and what cargo and passengers you will be taking back to Kerenth.'

Go'enna stared at her in surprise. 'I'm afraid I don't yet know. We only anchored this morning – and such arrangements are, as you know, always flexible. I'll take anyone or anything that's profitable, and I'll leave when Tliou tells me the weather's set fair.'

'And you can't be more specific?'

'Not to the day, no,' Go'enna said. 'As you are aware, storms can spring up quickly at this time of year, and the worst of them test any sorcerer's skills to the utmost. I'm too old and too shrewd to take risks any more. We'll sail when it's safe, and not otherwise. But if the signs are good, we'll stay perhaps six or seven days. That's ample time to trade and collect any passengers from the rest of the island.'

'I see. Well, there are two passengers I do not wish you to take.'

Go'enna's eyebrows lifted. 'Oh, really? May I remind you, High Sorcerer, that I am an independent Captain, and may carry whom I please.'

'And may I remind *you* that you trade here with my good will. Cross me, and your ship will never anchor in the Haven again.'

There was a short, simmering silence. Go'enna detested anyone who attempted to dictate to her: she had been a Captain for nearly twenty years, and was not accustomed to people telling her what she could or couldn't do. But on the other hand, she did not want to risk losing the lucrative Jo'ami trade.

And of course, Sé Mo-Tarmé was well aware of it.

The two women, similar in age and obstinacy, very dissimilar in appearance, glared at each other. At last, Go'enna said reluctantly, 'Who are these people?'

'They may approach you together, or separately. One is very distinctive – a young man twenty-three years old, slightly built, rather above my height. He is a Northerner, with fair hair and dark eyes. His name is Bron. The other is a woman. She is as tall as the man, black-skinned, with close-cut hair. She comes originally from Penya, and her name is Mallaso. If either or both of them ask you for passage, you must refuse them, understand? You do not have to give reasons, but you can tell them that it is by my orders. If they want explanations, they'll have to get them from me.'

'And if *I* want explanations?'

'You will have none. I think that is all. Thank you for your co-operation, Captain. May our relationship long continue to be profitable for both of us. Good day to you.'

Go'enna watched as the High Sorcerer, with a casual wave of her hand, floated airily over the gunwale and down into her boat, followed by the other sorcerers, their robes fluttering as gracefully as birds' wings.

'Beats clambering up and down a ladder, I suppose,' said Ai'an, appearing at her side. 'What did she want?'

'A favour,' said his Captain. 'And a big one, to judge by the threat she made. Jo'ami needs the Kerenth trade as much as we do – and if she bars us, all the other ships making the run will probably refuse to do it either, in our support.' She frowned at the retreating boat. 'I don't like being told what I can and can't do on my own ship. Who does she think she is, eh?'

'Only the most important sorcerer in the world,' Ai'an said drily. 'So what does she want us to do?'

'She wants us to refuse passage to a man and a woman. She's black, from Penya, name of Mallaso. He's very different, young, from the North Lands, fair-haired. Bron, he's called.'

'Bron? That sounds an echo – I've heard it before, but I can't remember where.'

Ai'an's mind was thorough, but slow, and Go'enna waited impatiently, her thoughts already running on to other, more important matters. She noted that the sailors, thinking she wasn't watching them, had slowed their work considerably, and was about to yell at them when his excited cry brought her attention back. 'That's it – I remember now!' His small, bright eyes stared eagerly at her. 'It happened while you were away on the first Gulkesh voyage, so it was nearly four years ago. You must have heard about it when you got back – people were talking about nothing else for months.'

'About what? For the Goddess's sake get on with it, Ai'an, I haven't got all day.'

'About the Queen's first Consort. She was besotted with him, but the Goddess didn't like him, apparently. The rains failed, anyway, and he was Sacrificed. You *must* remember hearing about it!'

Go'enna nodded slowly. 'Yes, I do. So what?'

'The Consort – the Sacrifice. A Northerner, young, with fair hair. He called himself Kenmet, but apparently his real name was Bron.'

'And you think this could be the same man?'

'It certainly sounds like it – but it can't be.' Ai'an's voice lowered to a dramatic whisper. 'It can't be him – because he's dead!'

'Yes. You don't jump off that cliff and live,' said Go'enna drily. 'It must be half a mile high.'

'Unless he was a sorcerer.'

'No mage I ever heard of had that kind of power.'

'There's something odd going on,' Ai'an said, frowning. 'Best to do what the High Sorcerer says, and ask no questions.'

'I make the decisions round here,' Go'enna reminded him. '*I'll* decide who we shall and shan't carry. Not you – and not the High Sorcerer either, whatever her threats. So if either of those two approach you, say nothing to anyone, d'you understand? Say nothing, and pass 'em on to me.'

'Why?' demanded her First Mate, his weathered face wrinkled in perplexity.

'Why? Because I'm a perverse old woman, that's why. And something else.'

'What?'

Go'enna smiled, her eyes glinting wickedly. 'Very simple, Ai'an. I'm curious.'

CHAPTER
TWENTY

The days crawled by, sunk in the soporific heat of Jo'ami in the hurricane season – although, protected by the sorcerers, no storm had disturbed the island's tall trees and calm waters for over a thousand years. The *Lady of Kerenth* unloaded her cargo and took on a variety of good – fruit, dried fish, and large quantities of Annatal in its various forms. Passengers booked: a couple of recently graduated students going home, a group of Priestesses returning from a year of study, some young people looking for adventure far from their idyllic, unchanging island, but no ill-assorted couple, one black, one white. Tliou consulted his scrying-bowl, increased his intake of Annatal, and announced that they should sail on the eighth day after their arrival.

On the evening before the ship's departure, Go'enna sent out her First Mate and half a dozen old hands to round up the rest of the crew from the taverns of Jo'ami Haven, and came back five sailors short.

The Captain had been expecting that there would be some desertions: Jo'ami's delightful, lush, lazy way of life was a perennial temptation to hard-working mariners. But she'd never had as many as five before. To keep costs down, the *Lady of Kerenth* always carried the minimum complement necessary to work the ship effectively. Five missing out of twenty-eight was quite a blow, although she took care to make light of it to the rest of the crew. And one of the absentees was an experienced steersman, too, a man she could ill afford to lose.

So she sent Ai'an out to the town to try and recruit some replacements. There were always some young men and women in Jo'ami who were eager to see the world, and since many of them had sailed fishing-boats since childhood they would make useful members of the company.

He came back with three – two young men, and a woman. They clambered up over the side and stood grinning hopefully on the stern deck, waiting for the Captain's inspection. The boys looked likely enough: they were brown and muscular, and at the very least they could haul on a rope or furl a sail.

And the woman . . .

Tall. Black. Close-cropped hair. Go'enna gave her a very thorough scrutiny, and then beckoned her over. 'You. What's your name?'

The woman moved with a lithe grace, and stood a handspan higher than the Captain. Undaunted, Go'enna fixed her with a fierce gaze. 'Come on. Your name.'

'Tipeya,' said the black woman, in a low-pitched voice that touched the liquid vowels of Kerenth with a different, singsong tone.

Go'enna continued to study her. 'Tipeya,' she said at last. 'And you wish to sign on as a member of the crew? Have you sailed a ship before?'

'Only small boats. But I'm strong, and I learn fast.'

'Good. You're part of the team.' Go'enna slapped her palm on the other woman's in the traditional informal sealing of a contract. 'You'd best get to work. Kamanya will show you the ropes – she's the one in the green tunic, over there. We sail when the tide turns, within the hour.'

A look that was probably relief came over the handsome face of the woman calling herself Tipeya. 'Thank you very much,' she said, smiling. 'You won't regret hiring me.'

'I hope not,' said Go'enna, and her gaze, shrewd and fierce, was quite unambiguous. 'Go on, woman – look lively there!'

She watched Tipeya run over to Kamanya: a few moments later, she was helping to haul the ship's boat aboard, pulling on the line with a dozen other panting sailors. It was obvious, of course, who she really was, but Go'enna had no doubts. Sé Mo-Tarmé couldn't threaten a Kerentan captain and get away with it, High Sorcerer or not.

And besides, she'd only promised not to carry a woman named Mallaso as a passenger. Nothing whatsoever had been said about a woman calling herself Tipeya, signing on as crew.

With a wicked inward chuckle, Go'enna watched her sailors make ready to weigh anchor. She wasn't afraid of the High Sorcerer, who was only a woman like herself when all was said and done. She didn't know why the Penyan wanted to leave Jo'ami, or why Sé Mo-Tarmé was so eager to prevent her. But on the long voyage back to Kerenth, she would have ample opportunity to find out.

*

On the balcony of one of the empty classrooms, Bron stood and watched the *Lady of Kerenth* raise her two blue and green sails and glide out of Jo'ami Haven on a receding tide and a fair and following wind.

He had planned his lover's escape with great care, using his skills to put her in the right place at the right time, and to hide her absence from Sé Mo-Tarmé. If the High Sorcerer looked in Mallaso's room, whether in spirit or in reality, she would see her asleep in bed. It was an Illusion, prevented from emitting the scent of sorcery by his own defences, webbed tightly around the image of the sleeping woman. As he had said to Sé Mo-Tarmé, he himself had no idea of his limits. He felt like a child who sees the ocean shore for the first time, and longs to run for ever along the firm, endless, glistening sand. The sensation was intoxicating, but he knew that he must not be carried away by it. Sorcery still needed care, forethought and detailed planning. His mind wove patterns and designs, and his powers brought them to reality.

And so Mallaso was gone. If he closed his eyes, he could see her with his mind's eye, dark and agile amongst the sailors, her face free at last of tension and fear. He had said goodbye to her in her room, with quiet, yet hopeful sorrow, for all they had endured together, for the child they shared, and for the different futures which confronted them.

'I will come for you, in Kerenth,' he had said softly. 'Wait for me?'

'I will wait,' Mallaso told him. 'Don't worry about me. There are plenty of refugees from Penya living there. I'll find shelter with them.'

'Don't call yourself Mallaso,' Bron said. 'Use your mother's name.'

'Tipeya? why?'

'Because – because your own may be dangerous, even in Kerenth. And because I shall be looking for a woman called Tipeya, not Mallaso.'

She agreed, though with reluctance. She did not tell him that in Penya, taking on someone's name was believed to be taking on their fate as well.

And Tipeya had watched her husband and her sons tortured and killed, before her own execution.

*

It was evening before the High Sorcerer realized that one of her guests had escaped her. When there was no answer to her knocking, she entered Mallaso's room anyway, suspicions rising, and pulled the covers back from the sleeping figure on the couch.

Like all Illusions, it faded at her touch, and she was left staring at a pile of rumpled sheets, overwhelmed with rage and the stink of sorcery, suddenly revealed. Then she turned and strode furiously out of the empty room.

She found Bron in the dining hall, taking his evening meal with the other sorcerers. He was talking calmly to Gen Lul-Tarmé, her cousin and one of her most gifted acolytes, and looked up with an infuriating air of innocence as the High Sorcerer stood over him, her anger coruscating the air around her with a red haze. 'Good evening, Most Wise,' he said politely. 'Will you sit down and share our wine?'

'I want to speak with you now. In private.' Sé Mo-Tarmé's fingers itched with the desire to hurl him against the nearest wall.

'At least let me finish my meal,' said Bron mildly, and picked up his spoon. 'In your room? I will see you there in a little while.'

A scarlet fog of fury obscured the High Sorcerer's vision. She actually had her hand raised to strike him down when some belated sense of the dignity of her office returned to her. She said through gritted teeth, 'As soon as possible. There is urgent business to discuss, and I do not wish to be kept waiting.'

Bron watched her retreating back, so eloquent of her savage mood, with a thoughtful expression on his face. Then, without haste, he returned to his pork stew and ignored the buzz of curious comment that had broken out among the diners as soon as the High Sorcerer had left the hall.

The stew was delicious, and the rice dumplings so good that he had a second helping. Then he lingered over the fruit which always ended a meal in Jo'ami, sipping cool wine from, of course, a Minassan cup. It was dark before he had finished, and he was one of the last to leave the dining hall. Gen Lul-Tarmé wished him luck, with blatant curiosity on her young, pretty face. He brushed aside her questions with firm courtesy, and bid her good night.

As he had known it would, the High Sorcerer's blazing rage had cooled, a little, to a darker and deeper hostility. She answered his knock with a curt command, and when he entered, she glared at him implacably. 'You took your time. You are an extraordinarily insolent, wilful and disobedient young man – a very dangerous combination of defects for one of your gifts.'

'From your point of view, yes,' Bron said. 'But look at it from mine. Those defects, as you call them, ensure that I am unlikely to be used or exploited by anyone else. And strangely enough, that's what most people want to do – to use my power for their own ends. So I go my own way, Most Wise, regardless of your wishes.'

'A pity. A very great pity.' The High Sorcerer stared at him, the aura around her still the ugly dull red of repressed rage. 'Well, what have you to say for yourself?'

'About what?'

'You know very well. About the woman, Mallaso. She is on her way to Kerenth, in open defiance of my express orders. Why?'

'She did not wish to stay here any longer, so she took the first opportunity to leave.'

'With your connivance, of course.'

'Of course,' said Bron pleasantly.

His calm manner seemed calculated to infuriate Sé Mo-Tarmé still further. She said viciously, 'One day, young man, your arrogance will be your undoing. Anyone who is so convinced of his own righteousness deserves to fall long and hard. Do you possess any humility at all?'

'No less than you, Most Wise. Shall we just agree to differ? After all, I shall soon be gone, and your life will return to its usual tranquillity. And I am doing as you wish, am I not?'

'You were told – the woman should have stayed here!'

'Why? So that you could kill her, or the child, at your leisure?'

There was a brief, horrified silence. Then Sé Mo-Tarmé, white to the lips, said hoarsely, 'How *dare* you. How dare you even *think* that I – that I would stoop to such a despicable act?'

'How can I come to any other conclusion? Over the past few days, I have done some research of my own in your very extensive libraries. The prophecy is ambiguous, true, but it could be persuasively argued that my "legacy" might mean a child – and that the third line depicts Jo'ami's destruction. But that's only one possible interpretation amongst many. So – *were* you intending to kill her? Or just make sure the child didn't live?'

The High Sorcerer looked away. She said at last, her voice low and reluctant, 'I will not deny that I *considered* doing – doing evil. But I rejected the temptation. I hoped that if the woman bore her child here, it could be reared by us – eventually to rule Jo'ami, perhaps, if it inherited your gifts.'

'But it may not. And it is Mallaso's child, as well as mine. She will carry it, and suffer the pain and danger of bearing it. So don't you think she ought to have some say in how it is to be reared?'

'She would always have a place here,' said Sé Mo-Tarmé, defensively.

'But she does not *wish* it. You accuse me of arrogance. Can't you appreciate your own? Mallaso is not a child, nor a half-wit. She is an adult, a highly intelligent and resourceful woman with a great deal of strength and courage. Why should you try to rule her life, or her child's? You can't treat people as if they were counters in a game of tek, taking no notice of their own feelings and desires. Two months ago, Mallaso lost her only daughter, a little girl she loved dearly, and with her death the main purpose of her life vanished too. How dare you even consider taking this baby from her? Or have you never been a mother?'

'I have two children.'

'Then you should understand her feelings. And understand something else, too. Jo'ami doesn't *matter*. If the Emperor is killed it will still only be a little island on the edge of the world, inhabiting neither reality nor legend, and with very inflated ideas of its own importance. You lost the struggle to rule the world's sorcerers long ago. What makes you think that once the Empire breaks up – *if* it does – people will start to flock back to your School?'

'They will,' said Sé Mo-Tarmé. 'I *know* that they will. The true will always defeat the false.'

'But the schools of sorcery in Toktel'yi are not false. Different – but not false. Or they would not have produced Al'Kalyek.' Bron looked at her grim face and spread his hands suddenly in a gesture of appeal. 'This is futile. We have very different views, and neither of us is prepared to compromise. Shall we concentrate on the matter on which we both agree, and forget the rest?'

There was an expression of unwilling respect on the High Sorcerer's lined, frowning face. At last she said reluctantly. 'Very well. The woman is gone, and by myself I cannot bring her back. As you must have realized, the sorcerers of Jo'ami act together when great power is needed. And I do not wish to involve my colleagues in this.'

'I'm aware of that. And there is a chance that I may require your help – the help of all of you – to return to Toktel'yi. As I said, I do not yet know the extent of my power. But if I am to kill Ba'alekkt in time to save Zithirian, I can't risk entering the Empire officially. Someone might remember me, and link me with Mallaso. If the army is mustering at Tamat, then I should go straight there.'

'I see. You plan to Transport yourself.'

'I know it can be done. As a child, I was sent by D'thliss from Zithirian to Toktel'yi. But I'm not certain that I can do it alone. I shall need some time and space to find out.'

'Very well.' The old woman sighed. 'I thought I would welcome you, and the changes which you would bring. Now I know that I am not ready for them – and perhaps never will be ready. And I have many years left of my life, to contemplate the new face of sorcery which you represent. It will be a bitter draught to swallow, Bronnayak.'

'You have my name wrong,' he said softly. 'Since you helped me to drive out the Wolf, I have only been Bron. But I am no one's servant.'

'Bron.' The High Sorcerer, bereft of her usual brisk confidence, seemed somehow ancient, and vulnerable. She held out her hands in the gesture of friendship customary over all the known world. 'I offer my apologies. You are right. We need each other's help, to do what must be done. Beside the ending of the Empire, all else is just petty squabbling. We may never be friends, but at least we may be allies.'

'I hope we shall be,' he said, and accepted her touch. 'If you wish to find me, I shall sometimes be in my room.'

The High Sorcerer's capitulation had been unexpected, but it did not fill him with elation. For Sé Mo-Tarmé was so much more than she appeared to be: and neither was her offer of reconciliation to be taken entirely at face value.

But it would suffice, for the moment.

Far, far to the north, armies moved. They gathered in each of the nine Provinces of the Empire, or on the five principal islands of the Archipelago. Seasoned professionals, experienced conscripts and raw sixteen-year-old recruits just embarking on their five years of compulsory service viewed the prospect of an attack on the wealthy cities of the north with a mixture of eagerness and fear. Apart from the conquest of Penya, and the abortive invasion of Kerenth, the Imperial Army had had nothing to do but build roads and bridges, fight stray barbarians and put down rebellions for more than seventy years, and General Sekkenet was uneasily aware that there was no substitute for actual combat. Still, a bout of hard training never did any harm, and the orders went out to all the regiments, intended to ensure that every man arrived at Tamat honed to a peak of fighting fitness.

Back in his luxurious Palace on the shores of the Southern Sea after the end of the rainy season, Ba'alekkt received the reports from his senior officers with undisguised eagerness. At last, his great strategy, the ambition he had nourished since adolescence, was about to blossom. Soon, the proud cities would kneel to his feet. His favourite sister K'djelk would rule Minassa on behalf of her infant son, after the slaughter of her husband and her father-in-law. And in Zithirian, he planned to put his Spymaster Olkanno in charge. Before next winter, the two cities would be part of the Empire, their remaining populations cowed by the awesome brutality of his soldiers. With most of the inhabitants fled or slain there would be plenty of land available for colonizing Toktel'yans. And the gold-mines under the mountains would be his at last.

He would lead his soldiers himself, of course, but the invasion was not scheduled to begin until Midsummer. Meanwhile, he amused himself with his usual pleasures, and with constructing elaborate punishments for those who had dared to associate with the Penyan woman.

She had so nearly killed him. Even now, three months later and safe behind the high walls of his principal Palace, Ba'alekkt often woke up sweating, after dreaming that she had succeeded. And the bitch had escaped, with the aid of magic so powerful that even Al'Kalyek professed himself bewildered – although the Emperor still suspected that his Court Sorcerer knew a little more than he was prepared to reveal.

But he needed Al'Kalyek and his arcane skills, which had wrapped Ba'alekkt snugly in a cocoon of magical protection ever since that ghastly episode on Tekkt. It was not easy to keep up the spells day and night, and lately Al'Kalyek had been looking decidedly weary, as if his ceaseless efforts were sapping his energy. Ba'alekkt ignored it. Once they had seized Minassa and Zithirian, the danger would be over – and he could get rid of the old wizard, whose high moral stance was far too obvious for his liking.

They had lost the woman, but there were others of whom example could be publicly and brutally made. It hadn't taken long for Olkanno and his hounds to sniff out the tavern-keeper who had sheltered her. Then they found the family who had fostered her child. Everyone over the age of twelve was executed in the market place of Tekkt, according to Toktel'yan law: the couple's youngest son, the only one of the family to escape death, was shipped off to labour in the iron workings of Tulyet. Ba'alekkt was disappointed to learn that the Penyan woman's small daughter had recently died of a fever. If she had been alive, he would have executed her too, whatever the law said. Everyone must witness the penalties which befell those who dared to lay murderous hands on the sacred and noble person of their Emperor.

Al'Kalyek protested quite strongly, which infuriated Ba'alekkt. He hid his anger, and took it out instead on the handful of Tekktish men and women who had presumed to voice their opposition to the executions. They, too, were ceremonially disembowelled and beheaded in the market place. After that, there was no more dissent, and the island of Tekkt sank back into its usual state of unbroken tranquillity.

That year, the rainy season ended early in Toktel'yi, and Ba'alekkt had returned to his capital as soon as it was practical, eager to learn what Olkanno, despatched back to the city with precise orders, had managed to uncover. Unfortunately, several of the Penyan woman's associates had somehow obtained advance warning, and were nowhere to be found. But he still had the satisfaction of watching the Golden Djarlek being razed to the ground, and the execution of her doorman and a couple of her musicians in the Old Palace Square, in front of vast crowds. Unwilling to admit that the aspiring assassin had escaped justice, he ordered his Spymaster to spread the story that she had been caught and executed on Balki. So few people visited that barren island that there was little chance of contradiction. But Olkanno and his minions knew the truth, of course, and would continue to search for her. If, of course, she was still on Imperial soil.

Even if she wasn't, it should make little difference. In the end they would find her, and kill her, and he would have his revenge.

Once back in residence at his Palace, Ba'alekkt had taken his

Spymaster's advice and weeded out all those whose loyalty was in the slightest doubt. Anyone from Penya; anyone whose background couldn't be checked; anyone who had ever displayed anything less than total blind allegiance to the Emperor. The one exception was Al'Kalyek, who refused to use his sorcery to uncover those who might one day betray the Onyx Throne. Again, Ba'alekkt curbed his rage, and sent for the Principal of the Terebis School of Wizards, a man called T'lekko. He had a formidable reputation for ruthlessness and cunning, as well as considerable skill, and the Emperor suspected that he might be persuaded, for a large fee and the certainty of becoming Court Sorcerer once Al'Kalyek had outlived his usefulness, to employ his skills where the more scrupulous mage had demurred.

It was an inspired choice. T'lekko proved an invaluable asset, and personally exposed another twenty or more potential traitors. Ba'alekkt rewarded him with a chest of gold Imperials, promised him more in return for his continued assistance, and sent those he had unmasked off to the iron workings in Tulyet, along with more than two hundred other servants, slaves, officials, concubines, cooks and eunuchs. It was almost as good a punishment as execution: few people lasted more than half a year there.

Well satisfied, the Emperor relaxed while his soldiers prepared for war, amusing himself with those of his concubines who had passed Olkanno's and T'lekko's tests. And if anyone left in the Palace cherished any thoughts of bitterness, or resentment, or fear at the summary retribution unjustly meted out to their less fortunate colleagues, they took very good care not to show it.

In the threatened cities they had known of Ba'alekkt's plans since before Sundim. There were some, both in Minassa and in Zithirian, who had panicked, and packed up their belongings and their families and sent them off into the mountain foothills. Or they had fled up the river Ger to Lelyent, which was surely too small and unimportant to be of interest, yet, to the Imperial Army. But those were very much in a minority, particularly in Zithirian, where memories were still strong of the terrible Ska'i invasion fifteen years before. And this time, they would not be taken unawares, or by treachery.

Some people blamed King Ansaryon, who had asked for Toktel'yan help to drive out the Ska'i. Most, however, were of the opinion that Ba'alekkt needed no excuse for his acts of aggression against peaceful neighbours. He certainly hadn't given any reason for his attack on Kerenth.

That had ended in failure because of the intervention of the Goddess, or so everyone said. Admittedly, Kerenth was Her own sacred land, Her birthplace and Her special care. But worship of Sarraliss increased dramatically in both cities during the long winter months of waiting, and every house had one of Her symbols, a running horse or a crescent moon or an ear of corn, painted by the door to confer the protection of the Lady on the people who lived there.

In Minassa, the Princess K'djelk, confused and very unhappy, watched the preparations for the defence of her adopted city against the armies of her own brother, and wept. She had been married to Prince Cathallon for five years, long enough to grow very fond of him. They had a little son, named Temiltan after his grandfather the King, and she was in the exhausting final stages of her second pregnancy. It didn't help, either, that since the news of the Emperor's invasion plans, her husband had been decidedly cool towards her. He told her nothing about what was happening, and expected her to fill her days looking after little Temil and preparing for the birth.

K'djelk had been reared in the suffocating seclusion of the Imperial household, and had embraced Minassa's comparative freedom and informality with open arms. She had almost forgotten the frustrated unhappiness of being ignored and excluded, and suspected that her father-in-law had something to do with it.

She was quite right. King Temiltan III of Minassa was seventy, and still possessed the energy and intellectual curiosity of a much younger man, although his bald head and wisps of white hair were undeniable signs of his actual age. He had reigned for more than forty years, and being the Empire's neighbour had taught him a great deal about diplomacy, politics, deviousness and human nature. As soon as word arrived of Ba'alekkt's intentions, he had taken his son and heir aside for a private talk. 'Keep a watch on that sweet little wife of yours, lad. She may be a Minassan now, and mother of a future King, but five years here won't eliminate nineteen years in Toktel'yi. And she was always Ba'alekkt's favourite sister.'

'K'djelk wouldn't betray me!' Cathallon had protested indignantly. He was a pleasant, good-natured young man with a worry-

ing tendency, endearing in an ordinary citizen but downright
dangerous in the heir to the throne, to take people at face value.

'No, I'm not suggesting she would. But at the very least she'll
be torn between you and her brother. So take my advice and
keep her in the dark, eh? Just in case.'

'She'll find out anyway – her ladies will tell her what's going
on.'

'But they won't tell her everything, because they won't know.
And don't let her, or any of her people, anywhere near the
pigeons, either. Some of them are Toktel'yan, and if she puts a
message on them, they'll fly straight to the Imperial Palace.'

So Cathallon had reluctantly obeyed his father. And because
he was naturally open, and hated any kind of deception, he
became very awkward and offhand with the young woman who
had shared his life for five years with quiet and unassuming content. And K'djelk, nervous about the coming birth – last time,
both she and the baby had nearly died – felt increasingly miserable and resentful. Why had she been despatched to this hum-
drum, ugly Northern city, when her brother must have known
that sooner or later her loyalty to her new family would conflict
with her allegiance to her homeland? She'd pitied her younger
sister, betrothed last year to the corrupt and elderly Prince of
Tulyet, but now Djeneb's fate seemed infinitely preferable. At
least she'd never have to choose between her husband and her
brother.

But, fortunately for Cathallon, though he was not aware of it,
her anger was directed at Ba'alekkt. He had arranged this marriage, knowing full well what might happen, and sent her north
with falsely soothing words and a hefty dowry. And now he was
planning invasion.

She hardly dared contemplate the awful consequences if he
succeeded, but rumour and speculation were so rife amongst her
ladies that she had a good idea of what might happen to
her husband and his father. And if Ba'alekkt offered her the
chance to rule Minassa through little Temil, she would take
the greatest pleasure in telling him exactly where he could put his
Regency, in language very unbecoming to a Princess.

In Zithirian, too, the King was preparing for war.

The Silver City would be much easier to defend than Minassa.

Its Tayan kings had always been conscious of the fact that they were, historically, unwelcome foreign overlords of the native population, and had built accordingly. Moreover, it was a much richer place than the workmanlike, more egalitarian city of potters to the south. Every speck of gold or silver in all the known world came originally from deep under Mount Sargenn, at the northern end of the lake of Sar D'yenyi. It was why Zithirian was so wealthy: and also why, down the ages, it had always been the object of covetous envy. The great walls and towers surrounding it were not there just for show.

Ansaryon and his uncle, King Temiltan, had spent all winter planning their joint strategy. They recruited and drilled their soldiers, stockpiled weapons, laid in supplies, mended and enhanced their defences and kept up the morale of their people. As soon as the vanguard of the Imperial Army stepped on to the Minassan bank of the River Kefirinn at Tamat, pigeons would carry the news northwards. Non-combatants would be sent to safety in the mountains, and the combined forces of Zithirian and Minassa would make a stand against the invaders, on ground of their Kings' choosing. They would be augmented by Tanathi cavalry from the steppes, light, fast-moving, able to harry Ba'alekkt's troops from a distance. And the knowledge that they were fighting to save their cities from conquest and their children from slavery would strengthen their determination to repel the Imperial soldiers, however greatly they were outnumbered, whatever the cost in Minassan or Zithiriani or Tanathi lives.

Moreover, King Ansaryon was a sorcerer of considerable skill, able to command at least as much power as the Emperor's mage. And his two eldest sons, Tayma and Homan, who were now thirteen and eleven, had inherited his gifts. He had been training them for some time, and if the three joined their power together, they would be able to operate a formidable defence against Imperial attack.

So the two boys would accompany Ansaryon and his army. They were still children, but their mother made no objection. Halthris was a practical and realistic woman, raised in the hard and merciless environment of the steppe. She knew that if her sons' powers could trip the balance against the invaders, they must be used. She was less happy about Ansaryon's plan to send her and their three younger children, Zathti, Hathenas and Charnak, to the safety of Sar D'yenyi. She could understand the logic of the idea, and certainly she didn't want to make it easier, if the worst happened, for Ba'alekkt to eliminate the whole of Ansaryon's family. In the end, she agreed, chiefly for the sake of Charnak, who was less than a year old, and needed her.

But the family was incomplete. If anyone could repel the Imperial Army, it was Bron. But he had died nearly four years ago, in Kerenth. In her heart, Halthris still felt responsible for driving him away from Zithirian, to his death. Sometimes, she wondered if Ansaryon might also blame her, but he had never mentioned it, and the strength of their marriage had not faltered.

So she made contact with her brother Abreth, now High Chief of the Tanathi, and together they organized the recruitment of a fighting force formed from the ten clans of the tribe. It was vital work, and it made her feel useful. Fifteen years as Queen of Zithirian had softened her round the edges, as Abreth teasingly pointed out, but good living had not weakened her strong Tanathi heart.

And she would have to be strong, for this was perhaps the greatest danger that had ever faced Zithirian – greater even than the Ska'i.

In the long winter nights, she dreamed, sometimes, of those terrifying savages, to whom cruel and wholesale slaughter was a way of life. They were all gone now, their warriors wiped out by the terrible witchfire of her stepson Bron, and the rest of the tribe harried and hunted to extinction by the soldiers of the Empire, who had suffered their attacks on their western borders for centuries. But that did not exorcize her fear when she encountered them again in her nightmares, or eliminate the memory of the horror they had brought to the people of Zithirian.

And then one night, when spring had taken hold of the land, she had a different dream.

She was walking in a garden, at sunrise. It was not a Zithiriani garden, seamed with neat walks and flowerbeds and elaborate fountains and statuary, but a place much more wild and lush and verdant. At first, she assumed that she was in Toktel'yi, but then she came to the edge of a terrace, and saw, spread below her, the green forested side of a mountain, sloping into the deep and perfect blue of a tropical sea.

It must be one of the islands in the Archipelago that she had always yearned to visit. It did not feel like a dream: the colours around her were too vivid, and the exotic plants, the flickering butterflies and brilliant, darting birds too fantastic to be a product of her imagination.

'Halthris?'

She heard her name, and turned, startled.

A man stood behind her. His hair fell to his shoulders, thick and straight and blond. The face it framed was young, yet strongly marked by character and experience. The crooked nose was unfamiliar, but the dark, impenetrable eyes were not. She cried in amazement, '*Bron?*'

'Don't be alarmed,' he said softly.

'I am Tanathi,' Halthris reminded him, trying to regain her usual composure. 'Very few things alarm me. Are you real? Is *this* real?'

'You are dreaming,' he said. 'But I am real, and alive, as you are. I have called you here in your dream.'

She stared at him, praying that she would not wake up. She said at last, 'We thought – we heard that you were dead.'

'No, I am not.' He came right up to her. A boy had left Zithirian, five years ago: this was a man, with a man's resolution set in the thin, firm mouth and the stubborn jaw. He added, with a sudden smile, 'Remember what happened at Sar D'yenyi? Jumping off cliffs is not necessarily fatal.'

Halthris remembered it all too clearly. Cold trickles of fear slithered down her spine. She said, 'Are you still . . . His?'

Bron shook his head. 'No, I am not. The Wolf has been driven out for ever.'

'Then come home!' Halthris cried, her voice high with urgency. 'We need you—'

'I know. I have not forgotten you. That is partly why I have entered your dream – to tell you that I am alive, that I know what Ba'alekkt is planning, and that I will help you. No, don't ask questions – that is all I can say, for now.'

'And the other reason?'

'I wanted to test myself. To see whether I could do this. And I can.' His smile was suddenly full of mischief, and reminded her sharply of Homan, her lively second son.

'*Can* you help us?' She tried not to sound too desperate. 'We need you – Ba'alekkt's army is nearly two hundred thousand strong – six times the most we and Minassa can field against him.'

'I know – and I swear to you, in the names of all the gods,

that I will help you.' His image was beginning to fade, and his voice was growing faint. 'Whatever happens – *whatever* – remember my promise.'

He was gone. For an instant longer she stood on the terrace, her hands outstretched, calling to him, and then something touched her, someone spoke her name, and she woke to darkness, and the voice of her husband Ansaryon.

Wrenched from the brilliant world of her dream, she felt confused, disorientated and annoyed. There was so much she had wanted to ask him—

'What is it?' she demanded.

'You were shouting. Did you have a nightmare?' He sounded very concerned.

Halthris sat up, struggling to make sense of what she had seen and heard. She said briefly, 'No. Can you make a light?'

Witchfire, tamed and obedient, left his fingers, formed itself into a neat ball and hovered just above them. In its rather limited radiance, the King's face was starkly delineated by light and shadow, and looked eerily like a skull.

'It wasn't an ordinary dream, was it?' he said softly. 'I can sense sorcery.'

'It was Bron.'

She heard his sharp intake of breath, and then his voice in her mind. *BRON? Are you sure?*

I'm positive. Much changed, grown up, but still Bron. He told me he was alive.

Yes. I suspected he might be.

But you never said –

I wasn't sure. Even though we heard the news of his death, I had no perception of his absence. But he never made contact with me, even in dreams.

I don't think my defences are as good as yours. Halthris glanced at him, sensing his hurt, that the son he had always loved had chosen to call her in preference. She put her hand on his, and said aloud, 'I don't know why he came to me. But he told us he would help us. And he said that the Wolf had been driven out.'

'Driven out? Are you sure?'

She nodded. 'That's what he told me.'

'Did he say where he was?'

'No. But I think he was on an island. And the plants and birds

– they were like nothing I've ever seen before. The colours were so bright, they hurt my eyes.' She opened her mind, and let Ansaryon see the memory within it, and the face and form of his son.

'Jo'ami,' he said at last. 'He is on Jo'ami.'

'How can you tell?'

'He was wearing the robes of an apprentice of the School of Wizards on Jo'ami. In Toktel'yi, that colour is called Students' Yellow. And that explains, too, why he was able to drive out the Wolf. Several sorcerers in concert are always stronger than one.'

'Then he can come home,' Halthris said. 'He said he will help us against Ba'alekkt. He wouldn't tell me how, but he told me to remember his promise – whatever happened.' She stared at Ansaryon, seeing the faint but unmistakable signs of stress on his fine-drawn face. 'Do you think it really was him, or just a dream?'

'It was Bron,' Ansaryon said. 'But if he is on Jo'ami, he doesn't have much time to help us. All the reports suggest that Ba'alekkt plans to cross the Kefirinn at Midsummer – and that is only two months away now. It would take almost a month just to travel from Toktel'yi to Zithirian by riverboat. And Jo'ami is the southernmost island in all the Archipelago. As the eagle flies, it must be nearly twelve hundred miles away.'

The thought of her stepson's sorcery possessing the power to influence her dreams at such a distance made Halthris shiver. She lay back on the pillow, pulling the bedcovers up above her shoulders. 'He promised he would help,' she said, frowning. 'But he didn't say how.'

'Then I hope and pray that he can keep his promise,' said Ansaryon grimly. 'For even with the best that Zithirian and Minassa and the Tanathi can do, we will still need him and his power if we are to have any hope at all of defeating Ba'alekkt.'

CHAPTER
TWENTY-ONE

After their agreed truce, an uneasy peace broke out between the High Sorcerer of Jo'ami and her alarmingly talented guest. As he had asked, she gave him time, and space, to prepare for the assassination of Ba'alekkt. It was very difficult, after so many years of ruling every detail of the daily lives of her acolytes and her students, for Sé Mo-Tarmé to refrain from interfering, especially in a matter as vital as this. But she had promised, albeit unwillingly, and for the moment she must sit on her hands and do nothing.

The whole of the School of Wizards, sorcerers, apprentices and servants, had by now learned much about the fair-haired Northerner in their midst. They knew his name, a surprising amount of his more recent history, and something, too, about his extraordinary powers. On the increasingly rare occasions on which he appeared in the dining hall or on the terrace walks, the bolder students gravitated towards him, encouraged by his friendly, though rather preoccupied manner. They did not ask many questions, but afterwards they trawled their memories of his conversation for the most trivial insights into sorcery, and the precise nature of his power, its origins and extent, was the subject of heated debate over evening cups of kuldi or fruit juice.

To Bron, preparing himself for the greatest test of his life, the other inhabitants of this rambling building were an increasingly remote distraction. Now, in the months after Mallaso's departure, he planned every detail of his strategy during the long, hot, solitary days. Each evening, after supper, he retreated to his room, to spend many hours of the night withdrawn into himself, tuning and strengthening his mental powers. Without leaving his bed, he explored Jo'ami, from its rocky Haven in the north to the gentler slopes of its southern and western shores. Then, he ranged further to the nearest land, the mountainous peninsula of Tulyet, satellite of the Empire, with its barren hills, isolated towers and terrible iron workings.

There was little to interest him there, so he ventured to Anna-tal. Ai-Mayak would not have recognized the place: the island now was no more wild or savage than any other part of the Empire, its jungles burned or felled, its people civilized. Neat plantations of drug-laden bushes grew everywhere, and in each village or town the berries and leaves were laid out on scores of hundreds of flat wooden trays to dry in the hot sun.

Bron's spirit hovered above the island, aware of the irony: for if the world changed as he wanted it, and sorcery with it, then all that industry, all that way of life, would become redundant. It would mean the end of Annatal's easy prosperity: they would be forced to cope with the loss of their main livelihood. But he could not feel guilty. If he was right, the spread of a sorcery that did not need drugs would benefit everyone in the long run – and sor-cerers in particular.

One evening, he sent his mind in search of Mallaso's ship, and found the *Lady of Kerenth* making good progress, just rounding the islands off the south-eastern coast of Onnak. Mallaso herself was sitting on deck, eating under the awning with the other sail-ors. She looked happy and healthy, and the deep sadness had vanished at last from her eyes.

That night, Bron lay down on his bed, closed his eyes, and recited the silent chant that focused his mind and his power. Then he entered the mage's trance, and sought his lover's spirit.

He had never attempted to do this from a distance before, and he didn't even know if it would be possible. But he saw her sleeping, and wove himself into her dreams. They spoke, and she told him that her pregnancy was progressing well. He did not yet possess the power to stay very long, but in her mind he kissed her, and left her with hope in her heart and his.

It was not enough for either of them, he knew, but it would have to suffice until they could meet in reality.

If that would ever be possible.

As his confidence and his mental discipline grew, his spirit roamed wider and wider from Jo'ami. Ordinary sorcerers, satu-rated with Annatal, would only be able to travel a mile or two from their bodies. To look further afield normally required the use of a scrying bowl, notoriously one of the most difficult magi-cal skills to master. Bron was sure that the High Sorcerer would be able to scry at a considerable distance. Certainly, she knew what was happening in Toktel'yi, although she had no direct contact at all with anyone in the city. But he didn't think that she could send her spirit walking further than the shores of Jo'ami. This aspect of his power was his alone.

It wouldn't Transport him to Tamat, though. That was a completely different technique. And despite his confident words to Sé Mo-Tarmé, he was not at all sure that it was possible.

True, D'thliss, long ago, had sent him to Toktel'yi. But to do so, she had joined her own, Annatal-based sorcery to his own raw, childish power. Together, they had surely been stronger than he was on his own. He was adult now, his abilities trained and perfected, his mind immeasurably enhanced by the skills of meditation, concentration and trance which his father had taught him. But he still didn't know if it would be enough. And, worse, he had no idea what would happen if it wasn't.

There was only one way to find out.

Still unwilling, though, to put it to the absolute test, he entered his step-mother's dreams instead. Encouragingly, it proved much easier to do than he had imagined. But she had natural but almost untrained powers, which made her susceptible to invasion. Mallaso was the same, though she was not so sensitive.

Still, to find someone over a thousand miles away, and talk to them, was a considerable feat. It might have made him complacent, but he knew that Transporting his body, rather than just his mind, would require an entirely different level of power and skill.

So he began to practise it. He had never tried Transportation on his own, but he remembered, when he had to, how D'thliss had done it. She had stretched her mind to the place where she wanted him to go, and had flung him after it.

The first time, he found himself, not on the beach of Jo'ami Haven, but twenty paces from the shore. He waded back through the warm dark water, laughing ruefully at his own incompetence, while a warning voice within scolded him for his inaccuracy. The same proportion of error, when aiming for Tamat, might lead to rather more than wet feet.

He sat down amid the palms, their fronds stirring gently in the night breeze, and wrung the water from his robes. Having to do this in the dark didn't help, but it was the only way to avoid unwelcome curiosity. And although the people of Jo'ami were accustomed to sorcerers' tricks, he knew that Transportation was not usually one of them.

Now he'd have to get himself back, or climb up through that forest. It didn't matter that it was not at present enchanted: the memory of that long and dreadful night would stay with him for ever. And besides, he was tired. Most people assumed that sorcery was easy. They had no idea of the extraordinary level of mental and physical effort which was necessary to wield such power.

A dog barked in the town. He closed his mind to trifling distractions and let his spirit free. It soared up the mountainside, above the tangled sleeping trees, until the forest ended just below the School of Wizards. There was a clear strip of moonlight along the empty terrace, and utter silence: a total absence of inquisitive eyes and ears.

He stared at the place, absorbing its essence and location deep in his mind, and then threw himself towards it.

And he was there, on that same patch of moonlight, flagstones under his bare feet, the rough-cast wall of the school a couple of paces to his right. Perfect accuracy.

Bron was careful not to let his triumphant euphoria master the caution which, despite the Wolf's removal, was still an essential part of his character, and enhanced by the need for methodical planning and preparation. Spontaneity and impulsive action could be really dangerous, to himself and others, at such a high level of sorcery.

The following night, he Transported himself to the other side of Jo'ami. He didn't get wet, but he landed some distance from his target. The return, though, was just as accurate as it had been the first time. Perhaps familiarity helped – in which case, it might be better to aim for Toktel'yi, which he knew well, rather than Tamat, which he had never seen.

One thing was perfectly clear to him. Whatever happened, he would never again ask for the High Sorcerer's help. Despite their agreed truce, he still didn't trust her. He was doing what she wanted, but only because he wanted it as well. And he would do it his way, in his own time, or not at all.

By the beginning of the Midsummer month, he had Transported himself to Tulyet: to Annako: and to Balki. That trip had nearly ended in disaster: he had appeared right in the middle of some open-air festival, amongst a crowd of revellers. Fortunately, most of them had been too drunk on the thin sour Balki wine to notice his sudden arrival, and he had managed to extract himself from the frenzied dancers and find a dark corner where he could concentrate on a safe return. Even as he entered his trance, though, he had heard a group of people hunting for their village wizard, to tell him about the strange manifestation in their midst.

It was a salutary lesson. Despite all his power and skill, he was still fallible. He was also still extremely vulnerable, especially in the first moments after Transportation, when he was disorientated and temporarily exhausted by the effort involved. Despite the need for haste, he knew that he could not risk aiming for Tamat. Instead, he would have to go to Toktel'yi, and soon. He had learned from his scrying-bowl that Ba'alekkt was planning to leave the city before very long, to join his forces massing on the border.

So the time was approaching, too fast, when he would have to make the final, irrevocable decision, and commit himself. And he was beginning to realize that he dreaded it. For he did not want to die: he loved life, despite the burden that he carried, and he was not yet twenty-four years old. There was a bright future beckoning now: there was Mallaso, and their child, and also his dream of a new world, a new kind of sorcery, emerging from the old Empire and the old ways.

But unless someone killed Ba'alekkt, nothing would change – except that Zithirian and Minassa would almost certainly be conquered after a bloody and brutal struggle. And although he was frightened of dying, Bron knew that he could not live with the knowledge that the free cities had been destroyed, and his family with them, when he could have prevented it.

So he gathered his courage, slowly, painfully, letting it build with his confidence. The disciplines of sorcery had taught him that almost anything could be achieved with the mind's help. He could no longer overcome death, now that he had cast out the Wolf within, but he could keep the terror of it at bay.

He missed Mallaso more than he had ever imagined he would. She had helped him in the forest: she had shown him that fear was entirely a creature of the mind's weaving. He longed to hear her low, dry voice telling him to embrace his fate with open arms. And so he sought her, sending his spirit across the dark expanse of the Southern Sea, following the invisible track of the *Lady of Kerenth*.

The ship was nowhere to be found. He assumed that she had already reached Kerenth, and hunted amongst the ships in the harbour, but could not distinguish one ship in the midst of so many, in the darkness. And he had no sense of Mallaso, her strength and determination, her grace and independence and sudden, healing laughter.

He came back at last to his body, lying on the narrow couch in his room at the School of Wizards, and told himself sternly that there was no need for alarm. It didn't mean that anything was wrong. He was certain that if she had died, or been hurt, he would have known: her fleeing spirit would have searched for his. Because he couldn't immediately locate her amongst the crowded streets of Kerenth, it didn't mean that disaster had befallen her. The most likely explanation was that she had taken refuge with a Penyan household somewhere outside the city itself. He had found her before by knowing roughly where to look. To search for her all through a sizeable country would take time, and he did not have any time. He had already decided, for various reasons, that he would leave tomorrow night.

All his preparations had been made. He was ready. And for Zithirian's sake, and his father's, he must ruthlessly ignore his fears for Mallaso, he must assume that she had reached Kerenth safely, and forget about her. For the task before him would demand all his power, all his skill, all his concentration. He couldn't afford to let anything distract him now.

He lay awake for a long time, thinking about his plans. And when he slept, it was a shallow, restless, unrefreshing slumber, full of half-glimpsed shadows and uneasy images. There were no nightmares, such as the Wolf had given him: but his dreams were not pleasant.

During the following day, too, sleep eluded him, and he, who had prided himself on his mental discipline, found that he could not force his brain into unconsciousness when he needed it most. A trance was not the same. So much depended on what he did, and he was too tense and nervous to relax and rest.

The hours crawled by. He forced himself to meditate, to attend the communal meals, to make polite conversation to students and acolytes as if it were an ordinary day. He did not know if the High Sorcerer suspected anything, but from her conversation at supper, politely friendly as it had been since their truce, he thought she did not. The tingle of magic had hung around him so strongly, for so long, that perhaps she could not sense that its intensity had suddenly increased.

And then at last the hour was upon him. It was dark, and

would be dark in Toktel'yi too, with a waning moon. He put on the tunic he had worn on Tekkt. It was tattered and dirty and made him look like a docker, or a labourer, but that was what he wanted. He had nothing else – no money, no possessions.

Once, he had carried music with him, wherever he went. But now, there was no room for it inside his head.

Bron stood quite still. He emptied his senses of distractions. The distant sounds of the students' laughter and singing faded, and the room grew very dark around him. He sent his mind across the wide sea, over the dark, rocky islands of the Archipelago, due north to Toktel'yi.

He saw the lights of the city below him at last. It was much further than he had ever Transported himself before. The gulf of such an immense distance, more than five hundred miles, was terrifying. He hadn't slept enough: his mind was exhausted with the effort, and the cumulative effect of so many other nights spent practising this skill.

It was still not too late to change his mind. He could go back, and sleep, and renew the world another day.

He saw the quayside, the lights of taverns, the lanterns on the ships. There were still plenty of people about, as it was well before the midnight curfew. He looked for darkness, privacy, a place where no one would notice his sudden appearance. An alleyway between two buildings, an obscure corner, an empty outhouse.

With all his strength, he concentrated his mind on the place he had chosen. The sensations around it, touched, seen, heard, smelt. The tang of salt, the stench of the city, the noise of off-duty sailors and dockers, the feel of stone beneath his feet.

Come, he said to his body, standing untenanted in his room on Jo'ami, far to the south. *Here is the moment, this is the place – come! NOW!*

Voices intruded, and he heard the High Sorcerer. For an instant longer he hesitated, distracted, and she screamed at him, ordering him not to go.

She should not have said it. He felt the first tentacles of some kind of holding spell, and his sudden rage fuelled his power. With a wild surge of energy, he burst free from the High Sorcerer's fledgling web.

Sé Mo-Tarmé, her hands outstretched to grasp him, found his body vanishing between her fingers.

*

The riverboat called *Flower of Hope* had tied up in Toktel'yi several days previously, at the end of her maiden voyage. Built in Minassa, from Lelyentan pine, she was shiningly, sparklingly new. Her fresh paint still reeked, her rigging ropes were pale and bristly with lack of wear and weather, and her sails, striped deep blue and turquoise, had suffered no wind damage yet. She was a sight to gladden anyone's eye, and particularly that of her proud owner.

He had invested all he had, and put himself into considerable debt besides, to build his beloved ship, the vessel of his dreams. It would therefore seem reckless to the point of lunacy to risk taking her down to Toktel'yi just as war was threatened between the Empire and the northern cities. But Herris Gandar's Son was nothing if not a gambler, and this was the biggest chance he had ever taken.

If it came off, he would be rich beyond his most lurid dreams. And since risk was in Herris's blood, he had not taken his new boat, the boat for which he had worked for his entire adult life, tamely back upstream to Zithirian from the Minassan shipyard where it had taken nearly a year to build her. Instead, he had gathered a scratch crew of Minassans and Zithiriani, and a couple of raftsmen from Lelyent, and had offered them the same gamble as he had offered himself. Win, and a share of the fabulous profits would be theirs. Lose, and they stood to lose everything – life included.

Rather to his surprise, those nineteen men had taken the bait. Carrying, of course, a cargo of pottery, they had sailed south with the Kefirinn, a swift easy voyage on a river running fast and swollen with spring rains and melted snow. Herris had had a couple of anxious moments at Tamat, when he'd thought the *Flower of Hope* might be impounded. But although the Imperial Army was already gathering there, war was not imminent, yet. A hefty bribe of silver bars – most of his emergency store – and some very choice and expensive Minassan vases had ensured that the *Flower of Hope* passed through unmolested.

From then on, the trip had been smooth and uneventful. They had tied up at Toktel'yi with some apprehension, but theirs was one of the first cargoes of the year, and such was the demand for Minassan pottery that it didn't seem to occur to any of the myriad officials who came on board to harass the Captain that the *Flower of Hope* was not in fact owned by a citizen of the Empire.

And even if someone had the bright idea of arresting owner and ship, Herris suspected that it would probably take six days and twenty forms signed and countersigned in triplicate by officials ranging from the Dock Master right up to an Imperial Minister, before any action was taken.

As quickly as possible, he and his crew emptied the *Flower of Hope*'s holds, got a very good price for the pottery by auctioning it off in crates on the quayside, and began collecting the return cargo. There was plenty of choice: the warehouses of Toktel'yi bulged with the produce of its nine provinces and many thousand islands. With haste, Herris filled his boat with goods that would command a high price in Zithirian and Minassa after the outbreak of war. Iron, only mined in Tulyet and on Balki, would be vital for weapons; the heaviest cotton canvas could be made into tents; copper and tin were essential for the forging of bronze armour. He had to pay well over the odds, especially for the iron, but it would be worth the expense. He filled up the limited space left with oil, spices and salt. By now, the *Flower of Hope*'s freeboard was so reduced that the tallest member of her crew could reach through the gunwale rail and touch the water: and Herris's emergency fund had dwindled to one small bag of coins.

His Mate, a young and rather disreputable Minassan called Pendeth, lent him a few Toktel'yan half-Imperials, and they went off to celebrate their last night in the city. There was still a great deal left to go wrong, but Herris had spent five exhausting days unloading, selling, buying and stowing cargo, and he needed to relax before the voyage home began tomorrow.

The evening lasted rather longer than he'd intended. They met an old friend of Pendeth's, who swept them off to another tavern he knew where he could get Hailyan wine cheap, and there were some very obliging girls. They were indeed rather better than the usual run of dockside whores, and Herris, who worked hard and played harder, succumbed to temptation. He paid the third, and prettiest, with one of his gold rings, and reeled out into the night with Pendeth, arms linked and singing an obscene but very funny Toktel'yan drinking song he'd learned during his years as a sailor.

The *Flower of Hope* was at the other end of the docks, at least a mile upstream, and after a while discomfort got the better of the two men. Pendeth stopped at the water's edge, next to a Tekktish cargo ship. Herris chose the shadowed gap between two mudbrick warehouses, twenty paces further on.

That was better. He pulled down his tunic, and turned to leave the alley.

There was someone standing in front of him, blocking his path.

'Hegeden's wings, you startled me, Pendeth,' Herris said with annoyance. 'Get out of the way, will you?'

The figure didn't move. Herris, peering through the darkness and having some trouble focusing, realized belatedly that the man was too short and slight to be Pendeth. He said belligerently in Toktel'yan, 'What d'you want? I've got no money left, if that's what you're after.'

'A word, that's all, Herris.'

The voice was sober, pleasant, quiet, and suddenly and terrifyingly familiar. Also, it had spoken in Zithiriani.

Herris's heart began to pound heavily in his chest, and sweat broke out on his forehead. He said through dry lips, 'Who are you?'

'I'm not dead,' said the other man softly. 'Did you think I was?'

'Bron?' Disbelieving, sobered by fright, Herris drew a deep, rather shaky breath. 'Is that really you?'

Out on the quayside, Pendeth's loud voice rose, demanding his Captain's immediate presence with drunken insistence. The figure moved sideways. 'You'd better go. It *is* me – and very much alive, I'm glad to say. I need a favour from you. Where can we meet?'

'Secret?'

'Yes.'

'Thought so. I'll send Pendeth on ahead. You catch me up.' Herris was too tired and too fuddled to think of anything better. He touched the dark shape briefly. It felt reassuringly warm and alive, and he heard Bron's snort of laughter.

More than anything else, that convinced him that his friend was real. He stumbled out on to the quayside, and saw that Pendeth, growing impatient, was already fifty paces further on and walking fast. Even as Herris looked, he was accosted by a girl dressed in the flimsy garments of a dockside whore. They vanished into the shadows of another warehouse, and he turned back into the alley. 'No need – he's fully occupied for a while. What do you want?'

'Passage on your boat. It *is* your boat?'

Pride made Herris indignant. 'Yes, of course the *Flower of*

Hope is my boat. How do you know – ' He stopped. Even as a child, Bron had always *known* things without being told – he had seemed to absorb information with the air he breathed. It was one of the eeriest things about him, and even now the thought of it had the power to raise gooseflesh on Herris's arms.

'I know,' Bron said simply. 'You sail tomorrow morning? How soon do you reckon to reach Tamat?'

'*Tamat?*' Herris stared at the dark, featureless shape of his former friend. 'Why d'you want to get off at Tamat, for Hegeden's sake?'

'I might not. I just want to know when.'

'You mean you don't *know*?' said Herris. He hadn't sobered up as much as he'd thought, and it came out more nastily than he'd intended.

'I don't. And if you don't want to take me, say so. Or I'll look inside your head and see for myself.'

In five years, Bron had become a man, and a very formidable man at that. Belatedly, Herris realized that he had no desire to antagonize him. Not only was it very foolish to annoy sorcerers, as a well-known Toktel'yan proverb pointed out, but despite everything, he still wanted the younger man's friendship. He said quietly, 'I'm sorry. I've had too much wine, and it always makes me aggressive.'

'Good thing I never drink much, then,' said Bron drily.

The menace had gone from his voice, but Herris knew that he hadn't imagined it. He remembered what this man had done as a mere child, and felt sick. He said, trying to sound normal, 'It should take fifteen or twenty days. We'll be going upstream, after all, and I haven't enough crew to man all the oars.'

'I can get you there quicker.'

Herris stupidly opened his mouth to ask how, and hastily changed his mind. 'That would be very helpful. I need to get across the border before war breaks out.'

'I'm sure you do.' Bron's voice sounded amused, as if he were smiling. 'Taking a big risk, aren't you?'

'If I pull it off, I'll be rich.'

'And if you don't, you'll be destitute – or dead. I'll get you to Tamat before High Summer. They won't move without Ba'alekkt to lead them, and he's still here in Toktel'yi.'

'How—'

'I know these things,' said Bron pleasantly. 'Well, will you take me, or not? I warn you, I haven't a chip of copper to my name.'

'Hegeden's wings, of course I'll take you!'

'I'm glad,' said Bron, and sounded as if he meant it. 'I'd like to get aboard without any of your crew knowing. Is that possible?'

'I should think so. The ship's moored about half a mile upstream from here – if I walk back now, you can follow me, at a distance. Pendeth's busy with the whore, and even drunker than me, so he won't notice, and anyway he's never seen you before. I'll beckon you in from the deck if the coast's clear.'

'I'll make sure I'm not seen,' Bron said. 'Shall we go?'

Herris slipped out of the alleyway, trying not to look too furtive. There weren't many people about: it wasn't long until the midnight curfew, and soon the guards would be patrolling to enforce it. The dock, so vital to Toktel'yan prosperity, was one of the few areas of the city where the rule of law was fairly rigorously imposed. Even so, there were always a few pickpockets and thieves desperate enough to take the chance.

He walked briskly, his head almost clear at last, and did not look behind him. He'd seen enough of Bron's powers at work, over the years, to know that if the younger man wanted to avoid notice, he would succeed. Probably if he did glance over his shoulder, he'd see no more than a flitting shadow on the edge of his vision. Once more, he shivered. Like most Zithiriani, the thought of sorcery made him very uneasy.

He wondered what Bron was doing here, and what had happened to him after his supposed Sacrifice in Kerenth. He'd heard the stories about the fate of Inrai'a's first Consort, and had assumed that his friend was dead. It was four years since he had jumped, or was pushed, off that cliff. Presumably his powers had saved him. But what had happened to him afterwards?

Once, secure in the advantage of his superior age and experience, Herris would have asked him. Now, he knew he would not. Even in that brief meeting in the alleyway, he had realized that Bron was not, now, a man of whom you could ask idle and nosy questions.

Yawning, he reached the *Flower of Hope*. There was no sign of Pendeth, and the crew member who was supposed to be on watch was asleep, sitting against the rail by the boarding-plank with his hand on a bottle of spirits. Herris kicked him awake, gave

him a rich torrent of abuse, and sent him stumbling below to the
crew's communal cabin in the fo'c'sle.

All was quiet. This section of the quayside was empty. A stack
of Onnak ironwood, waiting to be loaded on to a neighbouring
vessel, offered possible cover for Bron. Or the row of warehouses
beyond: or one of the ramshackle cranes with which loads too
heavy for sailors' or dockers' backs were hoisted on or off the
ships. Herris glanced at all the shadows, and saw nothing. There
was a group of drunken sailors watching a punch-up about a
hundred paces downstream, but no one nearer. He beckoned,
briefly and inconspicuously, and then walked aft to his cabin. It
was no more than a stuffy hole below the stern deck, reached by a
precipitous ladder, but it was the Captain's traditional territory,
and private. With a sense of relief, mixed with further apprehension, Herris lit a lamp, poured out two cups of wine, sat down on
his mattress, and waited.

It was only a few moments before he heard a series of very
light sounds, barely audible, and then Bron descended the ladder
and turned towards the light.

'Hegeden's wings!' said Herris, shocked. 'You look like something a dog dug up!'

Bron's dark eyes, alone familiar in his haggard face, stared
back. Then he laughed. 'Do I? Well, I'm not really surprised. I
haven't slept much more than an hour or so at a time for about a
month of nights.'

Forgetting his good intentions, Herris demanded, 'What in
Tayo's name have you been doing?'

'Don't fuss, it doesn't suit you. And it wouldn't be wise to tell
you.' There was another mattress on the floor, and Bron dropped
down on to it, disregarding the tangle of unwashed clothes lying
where Herris had flung them, and closed his eyes for a moment. He
looked desperately tired, and his tunic was as tatty as a vaga-
bond's. 'It's for your own safety. Can you accept that, Herris? It's
best you don't know.'

'All right, I won't ask.' He pushed the second cup over the
fresh, splintery pinewood deck. The whole ship smelt fragrantly
of the Lelyentan forest from which she had been made. 'I know
you said you don't drink much, but have some of this – it'll put
some life into you.'

'I just need to sleep – and now I can.' Bron sipped the wine,
and smiled suddenly. 'Hailyan! You must be coming up in the
world!'

'My mother told me that by the time I was thirty, I'd either be dead, or stinking rich, so I've got more than a year to prove her right, one way or the other.' Herris surveyed his unexpected guest. 'You can sleep safely in here. No one will come down. If you want, I can keep your presence secret till Tamat.' He stared curiously at his friend. 'What d'you want in Tamat? It's packed with Imperial troops, and getting fuller by the day. I don't want to have to stop there, but I'll have to if they raise the chain across the river.'

'I can get ashore just before the city, if it's a problem. Or I can stay on board and break the chain.' Bron grinned at him, a pale shadow of the mischievous boy Herris remembered so well. 'I'm a sorcerer, remember. That should be well within my power.'

'If you can get us through safely, I'd be in your debt for ever,' Herris told him. 'I'd even give you a share of the profits.'

'There's no need to go quite as far as that. All I want is a passage to Tamat. And about two days of uninterrupted sleep.'

'I can arrange that for you easily enough.' Herris gestured at the mattress. 'You can start now, if you like. I've got to go back on deck – someone ought to keep watch, and the cargo's worth a fortune. We sail with the incoming tide, just after dawn. When d'you want me to wake you?'

'When there's trouble,' Bron said. He pushed the dirty clothes into a corner, and gave Herris a weary smile. 'Which, knowing you, won't be too far off.'

'Then you'll sleep for a month,' said his friend. He finished his wine and got clumsily to his feet. 'I'm not the scapegrace urchin you used to know. I'm a very respectable man now.'

'Oh, really?' enquired Bron, and his friendly but gently derisive laughter followed Herris up the ladder to the deck.

It was a clear, warm night, and the moon had just set. Herris sat down by the boarding-plank, looking up at the myriad stars in the soft black arch of the sky. Their patterns were at once familiar and alien, subtly different from those which shone over Zithirian, reminding him that despite all his experience and all his considerable bravado, he was a stranger here, and hideously vulnerable.

Though with possibly the most powerful sorcerer in the known world hidden in his cabin, the *Flower of Hope* was hardly defenceless. And if Bron could indeed prevent any attempt to seize the ship, either at Tamat or before, then Harris could stop worrying.

His fear evaporated, he leaned his head against the rail, clasped his knees, and concentrated on staying awake at least until Pendeth returned.

PART FIVE
TAMAT

CHAPTER
TWENTY-TWO

The Kefirinn, the greatest river in the known world, flowed from Lake Raiyis, far in the north below the mountains, to its delta on the shores of the Southern Sea. As the eagle flew, the distance between them was eight hundred miles, but its meandering course between Hailyan, on the borders of Zithirian and Minassa, and Sabrek, an Imperial city above the delta, added almost half as much again to its total length. Using the road that ran from Sabrek to Tamat was very much quicker than taking a boat, even if travelling south with the current. Battling upstream, especially in early summer when the river was flowing fast, was laborious and sometimes dangerous work.

The *Flower of Hope*, fully laden and undermanned, made less progress even than most, despite all her Captain's efforts. It was nearly three days before they finally left the hot, sweltering marshes of the delta astern, and entered the gently undulating country below Sabrek, green with olive groves and white with cotton fields. But by then, Herris's secret guest had finally woken up.

Rather to Herris's relief, he had slept like the dead since the night before they sailed. He pulled the mattress into the darkest corner and heaped various old clothes around Bron's slumbering body, with a strategically placed wooden chest to hide him from any curious member of the crew who might happen to peer down the ladder. They didn't: the tradition of the Captain's sacrosanct privacy was strong even amongst the egalitarian Minassans. But Herris was taking no chances. If Bron wanted his presence kept secret, the Toktel'yans were probably after him for some reason. And favour or no favour, Herris didn't intend to give them any other excuse to impound his ship.

But having a sorcerer aboard was extremely useful. On the third day out, the wind blew against them, making progress under oar alone painfully slow. But by evening, after Bron had woken, it had backed right round, and Herris ordered the *Flower of Hope*'s twin sails to be hoisted. And with the bright painted canvas swelled by a steady southerly breeze, the vessel seemed to skim effortlessly over the broad shining expanse of water.

There was quite a lot of other traffic, most of it heading for Toktel'yi with cargoes from the two Imperial provinces along the river, or small local craft fishing or ferrying. No one made any attempt to stop them. Toktel'yan prosperity was founded on trade, and while there was still formally peace, it was likely that ordinary officials would let them by out of habit. Tamat, where riverboats were routinely stopped and their cargoes and passengers checked in or out of the Empire, would be the point of greatest danger. Until then, Herris felt that he could afford to relax a little, despite the need for haste.

He couldn't spend much time in his cabin without arousing curiosity amongst the crew. He wasn't the sort of Captain who idled below while his men did all the work, as the fresh raw calluses on his hands proved. But once the *Flower of Hope* was safely moored each night for the brief hours of darkness, and the other sailors slept, Herris and his illicit passenger could converse in soft whispers without the risk of discovery.

He learned absolutely nothing about Bron's recent past, or his future intentions. In fact, he found himself doing most of the talking, telling his guest everything he knew about the Emperor and the imminent attack on the northern cities. And he still didn't know why Bron wanted to go to Tamat, or what he would do when he got there. But he was beginning to hope that his friend was planning to use his power to stop the invasion before it had even begun.

If that was true, it certainly explained the need for secrecy and haste. The danger involved made even the reckless gambler in Herris quail with terror. And Bron was quite right: far, far better that he learned nothing whatsoever about it. Just guessing was hair-raising enough.

But if he succeeded . . .

If he succeeded, then Zithirian and Minassa would almost certainly be safe, for a few years at least.

One night, when they were moored a few miles above 'Strek-kell, he said, 'Don't you want to hear about your family?'

Bron looked round, his fair brows raised in mild enquiry. 'Should I?'

'Well, most people would,' Herris pointed out. 'Your father and the Queen have five children now. Hathenas was born a few months after you left, and there's another baby now, about a year old – they've called him Charnak. Is that a Tanathi name?'

'Halthris's father,' Bron said. 'And the Lady Kefiri?'

As a boy, Herris had adored the small slender girl who had secretly shared his mother's home for several months, and plotted with Kaydi and her son to overthrow the usurper Tsenit. In his heart, he still cherished great affection for her, although she was older than him, and married for more than ten years to King Ansaryon's General-in-Chief. He said unhappily, 'She lives in Sar D'yenyi, of course, with her daughters. I believe she's well, though Invan spends most of his time in Zithirian.'

'She should never have married him,' Bron said, with a quick glance at his friend. 'She should have married you.'

'*Me?*' Herris hastily lowered his voice. 'Whatever would the Lady of Sar D'yenyi do, married to a rogue like me? She wouldn't look at me twice, let alone marry me.'

'I know. But at least you'd give her space to be herself, and make her laugh. I owe my life and my sanity to her,' said Bron, his face suddenly bleak. 'And I could never bear to see her unhappy.'

'Was *that* why you left Zithirian?' asked Herris, with sudden insight.

'No, not entirely – but it was one reason why I wasn't sad to go.'

'Well, I don't blame you.' Herris paused, took a deep breath, and said bluntly, 'What shall I tell them, when I get home? Everyone thinks you died in Kerenth.'

'My father and stepmother know I'm alive.'

Herris decided not to ask how. He said, 'Do you – do you want me to talk to anyone? Pass on any message? Or are you coming back to Zithirian too, eventually?'

'No, I'm not coming back.' Bron's face held a grim, stark purpose that made his companion shiver. 'There will be no message. You can tell them about this voyage, if you like. You can say they have often been in my thoughts, since I left them. But there will be no message.'

It was always the same: Herris could probe just so far, and no further. Bron had constructed an impenetrable wall around his mind, and Herris hadn't a hope of getting past his defences.

Later, as he drifted into sleep, he realized suddenly why his friend was shielding himself from all but the minimum human contact.

He was expecting to die in Tamat.

In this, Herris was partly right: but as he had no intimate knowledge of the strange disciplines of sorcery, he could not comprehend the intensity of concentration which was filling Bron's mind.

On Jo'ami, he had decided that he would kill Ba'alekkt in Tamat. In the confusion and bustle of a military camp, the Emperor would be more vulnerable, more inclined to take risks, more absorbed with the fulfilment of his great ambition. In the Royal Palace, he was guarded day and night, and there was now a protective wall of sorcery around him that Bron, investigating from five hundred miles away, had been unable to penetrate. He was certain that Al'Kalyek must be responsible. Once in Toktel'yi, given time, he would have been able to find some way of entering the Palace, but he did not have time. And the most important requirement was success. Whatever happened to him, he must ensure that Ba'alekkt died. And in Tamat, success was more likely, especially if for some reason Al'Kalyek did not accompany his master.

But he could not use his powers close to Ba'alekkt until the last possible moment, for fear of alerting the Court Sorcerer. He knew he was stronger than the older mage, but he could not afford to weaken himself in a prolonged battle of magic. And now he was vulnerable, too, to ordinary physical attack. Once in Tamat, he would have to merge with the crowd of hangers-on who always followed in an army's wake, and use normal everyday means to gather the information he needed. And then he would find an opportunity to use his sorcery to get close to the Emperor, and strike.

And if he died as well as his victim, it would be worth the sacrifice. He had done the same for Kerenth, once, but Ayak, and his own power, had cheated the Goddess of his death. Now, he faced extinction in earnest. And for the free cities of the north, and for the family and friends who had loved him, and whom he still loved, he could do nothing else.

The small riverside towns and villages glided past, the landscape changing subtly. The fields of cotton and olives gave way to vineyards on terraced south-facing hillsides, and the palms were replaced by groves of tall poplars and graceful cypresses. The Kefirinn's course described extravagant loops and curls: it actually swung north, then west, then south again for fifty miles before finally reaching Tamat.

Once, less than two hundred years ago, it had been an independent city, founded by a grandson of the God-King Tayo, first King of Zithirian. Then, Sabrek had formed the northernmost province of the Empire, and the Lords of Tamat had ruled the country as far south as 'Strekkell, where the River Estris flowed into the Kefirinn. But the last Lord, Kindris, had eloped with one of the Emperor's daughters, and had thereby given the Toktel'yans a perfect excuse for attack. The Imperial army had invaded Tamat, killing its Lord and his bride, and their only child, a baby daughter, was taken to Minassa for safety, with her vengeful grandfather in hot pursuit. That city too was overrun, and Zithirian also occupied. The tide was only turned, after a long and bitter struggle, by the strong and resourceful Queen of Zithirian, Zathti the Warrior. With her cousins, Belerith of Lelyent and Cathallon of Minassa, she had driven the Imperial armies back to the borders of Tamat: and before the Emperor could amass reinforcements for a second invasion, he had been assassinated by one of his Ministers. The ensuing struggle for power between his three sons ensured that the cities were saved from further attack. But Tamat still formed the northern border of the Empire, its proud history and former independence all but forgotten in a hundred and seventy years of Imperial rule.

The southern wind which had blown the *Flower of Hope* all the way from Sabrek obligingly swung round to the north as the river changed direction, and pushed the riverboat swiftly along the other side of the loop, south to Tamat. The land within the curve, some twenty miles wide and fifty long, was flat and fertile. Here grew the flowers whose perfume, distilled and concentrated in tiny iridescent glass vials, sweetened the skins of fine ladies all over the Empire and beyond. Lavender, roses, lilies, and more humble plants whose roots or leaves contained hidden and unexpected fragrances, coloured the air with their heavy, sun-warmed scent, and bees and other flying insects buzzed everywhere, laden with pollen. The fields were full of peasants, men in straw hats and veiled women with their babies on their backs, gathering blooms in huge baskets.

Tamat was built on the southern bank of the river. The road which ran from Toktel'yi to the northern cities crossed here, but the Kefirinn was too wide, even several hundred miles from the sea, for the Imperial engineers to bridge. Instead there was a system of ferries which, although slow and inconvenient, made it

very easy for Toktel'yan officials to check on all those entering or
leaving the Empire. Upstream, the river flowed west, forming a
brief section of the border, before swinging north again, meandering through the woods and fields and neatly cultivated orchards of
southern Minassa. And on either side, the flat green floor of its
valley began to slope more steeply up to a bare moorland country.
Beyond that, the vast bleak steppe hills rolled for hundreds of
miles to the west, inhabited by wild animals and wilder nomad
tribesmen. North of the Empire, the Kefirinn was the cord along
which the jewels of civilization were strung together amid the
wilderness.

Tamat itself was an attractive place of painted wood and mudbrick houses, built around courtyards in the manner common to
all the cities on the Kefirinn. The public buildings – the Governor's
residence, the barracks, the twin temples of Olyak and Kaylo, the
City Hall, the Quaymaster's office – were entirely Toktel'yan in
appearance, with much use of carved brick and straight lines; and
all the women in the streets were veiled. Yet less than two hundred
years ago, this had been an independent country, allied to the
Tayan cities of Zithirian and Minassa. And perhaps, given the
chance, these hard-working, apparently docile people would
rejoice in the opportunity of a return to freedom.

But at present the smiths and farmers and merchants of Tamat
were taking full advantage of the presence of the Imperial Army,
camped over several square miles of pasture just to the south of
the city. Nearly two hundred thousand men, and their followers,
needed food, drink and entertainment. They also needed repairs
to armour and equipment, tents, clothing, baggage, wagons and all
the other paraphernalia of war. The location of the camp could be
identified from the cloud of dust and smoke permanently hovering
above it, and the high circling specks of scavenging birds waiting
to descend on the remains of a meal, or to sort through the heaps
of ordure and rubbish that were an inevitable feature of such a
vast gathering.

The low, brown-tiled roofs of Tamat came into view, the skyline
punctuated by the bulky shapes of the larger buildings, the squat,
menacing black marble block of the Temple of Olyak, and the
Temple of Kaylo's characteristic elliptical dome. Now, a natural
breeze swept the riverboat onwards on this clear, sunlit morning,
and the water lapped cheerfully under her bow. A low awning had
been erected on the stern deck, ostensibly for the comfort of

the steersman. And in its darkest shadow, Bron sat cross-legged, wearing a Toktel'yan tunic, his distinctive hair covered by a broad-brimmed straw hat in the manner of local peasants.

The steersman, of course, was aware of his presence, but was under the impression, given by the Captain, that he'd joined the ship the previous night. If any of the other sailors had noticed him, they gave no indication of it. Herris would have preferred him to have stayed below, but as Bron pointed out, the need to conceal his powers meant that he couldn't see anything from the cabin. And it was essential, if they were to pass through Tamat unhindered, that he knew what was happening. He could employ his sorcery only as a last resort, for its use would be picked up by Al'Kalyek or any other mage in the vicinity. And then they'd be after him.

At the village where they had moored the previous night, Herris had learned that the Emperor had just joined his army, escorted by the crack troops of his Guard, and by an entourage that included every member of his Council and six wagon-loads of concubines – not to mention a closed, heavily defended iron-bound vehicle that was rumoured to contain a million gold Imperials to pay the soldiers and finance the purchase of supplies. Ba'alekkt's arrival must mean that the invasion would begin very soon. And it also meant that a ship owned by a man who would shortly become an enemy of the Empire might well be seized.

The river bank at Tamat was low, and sloped very gently up to the small hill on which the Governor's Residence and the Temples stood, dominating the city clustered around them. Usually there were plenty of gaps along the quayside, even during the peak of riverboat activity in summer. Tamat's importance was chiefly as a border post, a bureaucratic centre, rather than as a trading city in its own right. And small bottles of perfume, though valuable, did not take up much room in a ship's hold. Most vessels moored for no longer than a night, or for the six or seven hours it took the Imperial officials to check crew, passengers and cargo. But to ensure that every ship stopped there, a tall stone pillar in the centre of the quayside marked where the chain crossed the river to a similar tower on the northern bank. It was operated by a huge winch turned by a dozen slaves. And as Herris well knew, raising and lowering it took time.

It was raised. He could see it clearly, the huge iron links, draped here and there with trailing hanks of weed, hanging across the river in a gentle curve. In the centre, where the channel was deepest, it was barely half a man's height above the surface.

There were houses and gardens running down to the river before the start of the wharf, with makeshift jetties and landing stages along the bank. People mending nets or fishing from boats stared as the *Flower of Hope* skimmed past them, her sails still unfurled. Several shouted and pointed at the chain, or gestured at the empty space at the quayside, just before the tower. And Herris could see, drawn up beside it, a large body of soldiers, the sun glinting on steel spearheads and bronze armour.

He shouted an order, and ran with his men to the oars, which had been shipped ready along each gunwale. For the presence of the soldiers must mean that the Toktel'yans intended to impound the *Flower of Hope* and her cargo. And the chain had been raised to ensure that she could not escape.

But Bron had thought otherwise. Bron had pointed out that the chain was old, and almost certainly contained several weak and rusty links in its length. 'And a chain is only as strong as its weakest part. If you have to, break it.'

Herris intended to. In swift, frantic harmony, he and his nineteen sailors swept the blades deeply through the rippling water. Shouting erupted from the bank as it became obvious that the ship was not going to stop. An arrow thumped into the rail, an arm's length from Herris's hand: others, less accurate, overshot and dropped harmlessly into the river beyond. The steersman, a middle-aged and reliable man, stood grimly at his post, keeping the vessel on course as the wind and the oars propelled her at increasing speed towards the chain.

Someone on the quayside was bawling 'Halt!' in Toktel'yan. Herris saw archers bending their bows, and braced himself again for an impact. They had the range now, and more arrows smacked into the deck. A rower two benches in front swore and clutched at a shaft protruding from his leg. For a brief instant the tempo of the oarsmen faltered, and then the injured man recovered his rhythm, just averting a possibly disastrous tangle with the other sweeps.

Herris was pouring sweat, his calloused hands bleeding all over the leather grips. He glanced round. The *Flower of Hope*'s prow was no more than half a length from the chain. The yells from the bank rose to a howl of fury, and out of the corner of his eye he saw running figures, and boats full of soldiers putting out from the bank. If the chain held, he'd have a desperate and probably futile fight on his hands. But if it broke . . .

The laden mass of the *Flower of Hope* smashed into the huge links. The force of the impact flung Herris and all his crew sprawling on the deck, the oars kicking wildly above them. The sails lost wind and flapped impotently against the shuddering masts. A shriek of Toktel'yan triumph split the air. Bruised, battered, winded, Herris lay on his back, gasping, and knew that this time, his gamble had failed.

Then he heard the chain break with a loud and reverberating crack, instantly followed by the whine and splash as the two halves whipped through the air and sliced into the water.

Herris struggled to his feet, shouting with the full force of his lungs. '*Row!* Get up and *row*, you good-for-nothing idle sons of whores, while we've still got a chance!'

Those who hadn't had the sense knocked out of them scrambled to obey. There were eight men on one side and six on the other, but it didn't matter. Somehow, they had to escape the boarding boats, laden with heavily armed soldiers, now being rowed at top speed out towards them. The sail above Herris swelled as the wind filled it once more, and his oar dug into the water at the same instant as all the others.

The *Flower of Hope* sprang forwards. One of the little craft, trying to close, was brushed aside by the prow and smashed under the forward oars. The soldiers on board, armoured in heavy bronze plates, disappeared beneath the water like stones. Under way again, her momentum increasing with every stroke, Herris's pride and joy swept through the swarm of Toktel'yan boats, sending several more to the bottom, and surged on upstream, past the quayside, past more houses, and into the open farming country beyond.

As he rowed, he could see the small black shapes of the boarding boats left far behind in her wake, outwitted and outpowered. They had given up the pointless pursuit and were engaged in an equally futile search for survivors.

He had done it. True, there were still some twenty miles more before the southern bank ceased to mark the boundary of the Empire, and it was quite likely that soldiers would be sent out to attempt to intercept the *Flower of Hope*. But they stood little chance of success, for the Kefirinn broadened out again in the stretch upstream from Tamat. If the ship sailed close to the Minassan bank, she would be well out of range of enemy archers, and the boarding boats stood no chance against a swift-moving oared ship. As long as they kept going until all danger had passed, which might mean sailing on after dark, they would escape.

In fact, they reached the stone column marking the end of the Empire's rule, where the river bent northwards again, just as the sun was sinking. Soldiers had appeared on the Toktel'yan bank, brandishing spears and shouting threats, but their furthest arrows fell harmlessly into the river, a long way short. To Herris's secret relief, none had shown themselves on the Minassan side. Perhaps Ba'alekkt did not want to risk jeopardizing his campaign in the pursuit of one fleeing riverboat. In any case, the Imperial army, though magnificently well drilled and equipped, lacked speed and mobility, since it possessed no cavalry (save for a regiment of light auxiliaries posted on the far western borders to repel nomad tribesmen).

The moon was soaring high in the clear, star-flecked heavens when Herris at last judged it safe to drop anchor, out of the main current and close to the right-hand bank, just in case. He congratulated his exhausted but jubilant crew, and distributed food, water, ointment and bandages. Two men had arrow wounds, another had broken an arm when the ship hit the chain, and everyone had raw, bleeding hands. But they were all still alive, and they had escaped from the Empire with their ship and their cargo intact. Against all sensible odds, Herris's gamble had paid off. If they reached Minassa safely, he'd be a very wealthy man.

The dim space under the awning was empty. He realized that he hadn't seen Bron for some time, but then his attention had been entirely given elsewhere. He climbed down the ladder to his cabin, calling the sorcerer's name softly. 'Bron? You can come out now – we're safe.'

There was no reply. He could hear nothing save the soft ripple of water along the vessel's hull, and the tired but excited voices of his crew, discussing the momentous events of the day. Suspicion dawned at last in Herris's weary mind. He found stone and steel, lit a lantern, and raised it high.

The shadows wavered and vanished, leaving no possible hiding place. The cabin was deserted. Bron had gone.

'As you can see, General, I intend to live as my soldiers do. How can I earn their respect if I accept the Governor's offer and sleep in a soft bed in his residence in Tamat? No, I will share their hardships and discomforts alongside them, here in the heart of the camp.'

General Sekkenet stared at his Emperor, hoping that his cynical contempt did not show too plainly on his face. Ba'alekkt was reclining upon a heap of feather-stuffed cushions in the centre of a huge and magnificent pavilion ('tent' was too commonplace a word to describe such a spacious and splendid construction). Half a dozen kneeling slaves proffered sweetmeats, wine, and other tempting delicacies, and three concubines, unveiled and clad in transparent silk, lay beside their master, fondling him and each other so shamelessly that Sekkenet, a hardened and stringy veteran in his late fifties, took care to keep his eyes on the Emperor's face.

'I have made many sacrifices for the duration of the campaign,' Ba'alekkt continued, without a trace of irony. 'For instance, I have left more than half my concubines behind in Toktel'yi, as well as most of my household.'

'Your cooks have come, though, I see,' Sekkenet murmured. Not for Ba'alekkt, obviously, his soldiers' staple diet of hard stale bread, dubious dried meat and suspect broth.

Once, the Emperor would have detected the note of sarcasm. Now, consumed with his dream of glory, he did not seem to notice his General's less than obsequious manner. 'Of course,' he said, with a grandiose wave of his hand. 'Their food is the best in the Empire. And I trust them. None of them will dare use poison now.'

Since the episode on Tekkt, Ba'alekkt had become obsessed with his personal safety – and not before time, in the opinion of both Sekkenet and the Spymaster Olkanno (it was almost the only matter on which they agreed). As a result, his pavilion was surrounded day and night by a score of hand-picked members of the Imperial Guard. Every item of food was publicly tasted by its cook before it passed the Imperial lips, and Al'Kalyek and Ba'alekkt's other sorcerer, T'lekko, had reputedly woven between them such a tight mesh of magic around Ba'alekkt that not even a mosquito would have the chance to suck Imperial blood.

'Anyway,' the Emperor went on, 'I have not called you here to indulge in trivial chit-chat. I have summoned you to discuss the strategy of my coming campaign.'

Inwardly, Sekkenet's heart sank, for this was the moment he had been dreading. Ever since Ba'alekkt's announcement, half a year ago, of the invasion of the northern cities, he had dutifully obeyed the Emperor's instructions. He had spent enormous quantities of Imperial gold and silver on weapons, arms, armour, supplies, training, pay. He had organized the muster at Tamat, overseeing every detail himself, although the logistics of gathering so many men in one place were almost impossible for one man to master. And through it all, he had swallowed his growing doubts about the wisdom of this whole enterprise. The folly of leaving so much of the Empire free of soldiers: the very real danger that even Toktel'yi's vast resources could not meet the huge costs involved: and above all Ba'alekkt's almost insane vanity and arrogance in assuming that Zithirian and Minassa would offer little or no resistance to his invasion.

Sekkenet had known three Emperors very well – he had begun his military service in the Imperial Guard under Ba'alekkt's grandfather. Makkyar and his son, Djamal, had hardly been the most warlike of rulers, but the belligerent nature of this one, his ruthless elimination of his suspected opponents and his brutally efficient eradication of the Penyan rebels, had led the General to hope that he was a true soldier-Emperor in the mould of his revered ancestor Sekkaylo, who more than nine hundred years previously had conducted a series of impeccable campaigns against the cities of Lai'is and Jaiya, annexing them to his Empire. Not for Sekkaylo the fancy food and fawning concubines: he had truly shared the dangers and discomforts suffered by his men, who had in consequence adored him. By comparison Ba'alekkt, for all his flaunted ambition and aggression and energy, was only playing at war.

Sekkenet took a deep, wary breath and coughed with feigned surprise. 'Strategy, Imperial Majesty? I thought we had already agreed on our tactics.'

'Well, I've changed my mind,' said the Emperor, with a smile. 'T'lekko here has had one or two suggestions to make.'

The young sorcerer moved forward, his smooth narrow face full of disdainful contempt as he glanced at the General. 'Indeed, Imperial Majesty. A mere soldier can have no knowledge of the more subtle aspects of a glorious and successful conquest.'

Sekkenet did not care for T'lekko at all. Since his purge of the Palace servants, the young mage had been Ba'alekkt's constant companion, even, so rumour asserted, sharing his concubines and enjoying the sexual favours of the Emperor himself: an indication of their intimacy, for Ba'alekkt, like his father, usually preferred women. It was very obvious that he had his eye on Al'Kalyek's position, and equally obvious that he exploited the vicious streak in Ba'alekkt's own nature. The thought of that sinister and malevolent young man occupying the powerful and influential position of Court Sorcerer chilled Sekkenet's blood.

So he ignored T'lekko's sneer and spoke directly to the Emperor. 'We agreed, Imperial Majesty. Once the bridge of boats has been constructed, the army will be marched across and gathered on the Minassan bank of the Kefirinn. Then we strike first at Minassa itself, ignoring any temptation that the enemy may put in our path. We move swiftly, passing towns and villages by. The city is indefensible, and once it is in our hands, we may subjugate the countryside at our leisure, before moving on to Zithirian.'

'Wrong,' Ba'alekkt said. 'I've changed my mind. T'lekko has pointed out that if we leave settlements intact, their inhabitants may attack our rear. Accordingly, we shall destroy everything we find in our path. *Everything*, General, do you understand? Every town and village, every house and barn and hut. Kill everyone. That way, the people won't have the courage to resist. They'll be running ahead of us to Minassa, begging their pathetic old King to surrender.'

'And if you supervise the executions yourself, Imperial Majesty,' T'lekko said, with a reptilian smile, 'your name will resound triumphantly through all the northern lands, and those upstart barbarians will quake with terror before you. Before winter comes, Minassa and Zithirian will fall like leaves into your grasp, and you will be assured of everlasting glory.'

To Sekkenet's disgust, Ba'alekkt was soaking up the sorcerer's blatant flattery like a sponge. He gestured to his General. 'Exactly. So that is what we'll do. Take our time, and have a little fun along the way. It'll be just like the good old days in Penya, eh, Sekkenet?'

'I was never on Penya, Imperial Majesty.'

'Were you not? Well, you should have been. I enjoyed myself there, I can tell you – and so did my men. Plenty of women for them in Minassa – you can promise them that, it'll put steel into their hearts.'

T'lekko said something softly, and Ba'alekkt laughed lasciviously. 'And that as well. Which reminds me . . .'

He rolled over on top of the nearest concubine and thrust into her with grunts of pleasure. Sekkenet stared at his glorious Emperor with frustrated fury. Was he mad, to overturn his General's carefully considered strategy on the whim of some jumped-up little sorcerer who'd probably never wielded a sword in his life?

But of course he was mad. The realization flooded Sekkenet with a chill like cold water. Mad with vanity, conceit, vainglory – you could call it what you liked, but reason, defeated, had finally left Ba'alekkt's mind, probably expelled by the assassination attempt on Tekkt. The General remembered that since then the Emperor had become dangerously unpredictable, given to bouts of almost insane fury whenever he encountered the slightest hint of opposition. Sekkenet was a valued and invaluable member of the Council, but that wouldn't save his head if he roused Ba'alekkt's temper.

For the sake of his men he must swallow his own rage and do the best he could, under extremely trying circumstances. At least he still had almost total control over the day to day management and organization of the vast army, and if Ba'alekkt didn't interfere with that too, Sekkenet could ensure that, as far as possible, the men were fit, trained, and equipped in readiness for the momentous task ahead. Despite the Emperor's overweening confidence, his General had no illusions concerning the difficulty of the task they were about to undertake. The people of Zithirian and Minassa cherished their independence, and would not surrender them without a long and bitter struggle. And he had seen their two Kings, Ansaryon and Temiltan, on campaign against the Ska'i, fifteen years ago. Despite Ba'alekkt's contemptuous dismissal of their military experience, they were a formidable combination, and he suspected that the Emperor had seriously underestimated their determination and their courage, not to mention the power of Ansaryon's sorcery. At least his mysteriously gifted son was safely dead in Kerenth. If he'd been alive to add his skills to his father's, Sekkenet would have been seriously worried.

Ba'alekkt was still busy with the concubine, her rhythmic gasps of apparent pleasure rivalling his. T'lekko smiled at Sekkenet, openly enjoying his discomfiture. 'You agree with the Emperor's plans, General?'

'As always, His Imperial Majesty's word is to be obeyed,' said Sekkenet, between clenched teeth. 'And now I must take my leave, as I have a great deal to do. Please will you convey my respectful apologies to His Imperial Majesty?'

Ba'alekkt glanced over his shoulder, grinning. 'So keen to go,

General? Why not stay and watch? You might enjoy it.'

'If you wish your army to be in good order when we march,' said Sekkenet, finally losing patience, 'then I suggest you let me carry out my essential duties. Now.'

Ba'alekkt rammed himself into the concubine with sudden and extreme violence, so that she cried out, and his hands twisted into her hair. Unable to leave without permission, Sekkenet had to watch and listen as the Emperor vented his spite on the unfortunate girl. At last the slaves dragged her away, bruised and bleeding, and Ba'alekkt turned his attention back to his General. 'Your men will enjoy her tonight. Well? Have you any comments on our change of plan?'

Sekkenet longed to punch the Emperor's gloating smirk down his throat. Instead, he lowered his eyes and said meekly, 'No, Imperial Majesty. I am in complete agreement with your suggestion.'

'Excellent,' said Ba'alekkt. 'Well, I am sure you have a great deal to do, so I'd better let you go. We will discuss the matter in more detail later. For now, I have something more pleasurable to occupy me.'

As Sekkenet left the pavilion, he glanced back, T'lekko had joined the Emperor on the cushions, and the two men were enthusiastically coupling with the remaining concubines.

It was beyond belief. It was beyond bearing. Sekkenet thought that he would burst with rage. He stood outside, ignoring the curious looks of the soldiers on guard, and fought to restore his composure. Then he went in search of the only man who would understand and share his deep misgivings about the future.

The present Court Sorcerer had his own tent, pitched very close to that of his Imperial master. In comparison with Ba'alekkt's splendid pavilion, it looked small and drab, although the walls were hung with dark blue silk, and it was luxuriously furnished with cushions and couches, and soft carpets underfoot to shield its occupant from the damp hard ground beneath.

A slave removed Sekkenet's shoes, and another brought him a tray of refreshments. There were no women, no other friends: Al'Kalyek preferred to keep people at arm's length, as many sorcerers did. He had a suite in the Palace, in common with other Councillors and exalted officials. Unlike them, however, he kept no household elsewhere. Sekkenet owned a comfortable villa in the best area of Toktel'yi, with two wives, half a dozen concubines and seven assorted children. He was very fond of all of them, and could not imagine a life so inwardly austere as Al'Kalyek's. How could the man relax properly when his duties were finished, with only impersonal slaves for company? No wonder he looked so haggard and exhausted.

The menials retreated into a curtained-off part of the tent, leaving Sekkenet and the sorcerer ostensibly alone. The General, however, had not reached the pinnacle of his profession without learning a great deal about the need for absolute caution and discretion. There were too many people, from slaves to Imperial Councillors, who would be only too pleased to inform on him or on Al'Kalyek: and even more people eager to listen. The naïve, the gullible, the imprudent and the indiscreet did not survive long in Toktel'yan public life. So he could say nothing openly, but their conversation could be conducted on two levels. One was spoken aloud, for the benefit of the listening slaves, and the other employed a complex and subtle language of signs, eye-movements and body positions, communicating the real meaning of their words.

'Greetings to you, Al'Kalyek,' said Sekkenet, sipping the iced wine. 'I trust I find you well?'

To an unenlightened onlooker, nothing else was said, but the sorcerer's dark eyes had noticed the position of the General's hands, linked loosely together in his lap. It was the customary signal for a hidden discussion. Briefly, Al'Kalyek's fingers joined in imitation, before his expansive gesture of welcome. 'I am delighted to see you, old friend. I am well enough, though very tired. I have much to do.'

His fingers pointed downwards, an indication of his dislike of the situation.

'I'm sorry to hear it,' Sekkenet said pleasantly. 'But your presence here is absolutely vital, as you know. Hopefully, once the northern cities have been defeated, you will be able to lower your guard a little.'

'Once the world has witnessed the mighty invincibility of our great Emperor, none will ever dare lift a finger against him,' said Al'Kalyek. He leaned back in his padded folding chair and rested his hands on his knees, palms upwards, indicating profound disagreement with the words he had just spoken.

Until quite recently, the two men had never been particular friends, but they had both survived the infamous Council of Poison. That in itself drew them close, along with their shared loathing of another surviving Councillor, Olkanno, the cruel and devious Spymaster. They also respected each other, as men of integrity and honour inhabiting a very corrupt and dangerous environment. When the wolves are prowling, those who may be their victims naturally gather together for protection.

'And does this sacred burden rest on your shoulders alone?' Sekkenet enquired, while his fingers rapped soundless words on his knees. *I am your friend, remember*, they told the sorcerer. *I may be able to help you.*

'Fortunately, it does not. The Principal of the Terebis School is a young man of considerable power, and possesses a skill far beyond his years. He has already done His Imperial Majesty great service by detecting traitors within his household.' Al'Kalyek's hands pointed disapprovingly to the floor. 'Now he assists me in my work of protection. Without him, I would long ago have succumbed to exhaustion. He is with the Emperor now, while he inspects the camp.'

Do you trust T'lekko? Sekkenet's fingers asked, while his voice uttered inane pleasantries.

No, said Al'Kalyek's firmly flattened hand, held against his body. And aloud, he began to speak of a mutual acquaintance with whom, he said, he had recently embarked on a business partnership. 'But now, I am bitterly regretting it. I fear he may be planning to oust me while I am away.'

Sekkenet, well aware that the acquaintance was not the man being discussed, shook his head. 'Oh, surely not! I don't know Ma'ako very well, but I thought he was an upright and honourable man.'

'Unfortunately, I think that your judgement may be flawed.' Al'Kalyek's tense posture indicated considerable anxiety. 'I've always had my suspicions about him, but his conduct persuaded me that he had acquired some steadiness and probity at last. But now I have heard from my brother that he plans to take over our business. And my dear brother, instead of opposing him on my behalf, actually approves it!'

It was not his brother, a lifelong resident of the isle of Onnak, who was being discussed, either. Sekkenet stared at the Court Sorcerer. 'He *approves*? Why in the name of the Life-Giver would he do that?'

'He thinks the business could do with a younger man in charge. Basically, he doesn't think I'll be capable of managing it much

longer. And they obviously feel free to hatch their schemes behind
my back with impunity.'

'Can you do anything about it?'

'Not at present – and nor would I wish to. My bounden and
sacred duty to the Emperor must come before everything else.
But once His Imperial Majesty is safe, I intend to fight for my
rights. Otherwise, I fear that they will take over my business and
perhaps squander money or good will in reckless speculation. And
I am determined not to let that happen.'

And Sekkenet, studying his dark uncompromising face, was
only partially reassured. At least Al'Kalyek knew what was afoot,
and would not let his rival supplant him without a struggle. He
sipped his drink, and rapped out with his fingers a necessarily
curtailed account of his latest interview with Ba'alekkt. The sorcerer's expression revealed his sympathetic understanding of the
General's predicament, but his own hands, silently gesturing,
offered no solution. His vows bound him: he could do nothing.

But as Sekkenet let the conversation drift to more innocuous
matters, he thought with deep foreboding of one possible future,
in which Ba'alekkt, encouraged in his vicious cruelty by T'lekko
and Olkanno, would begin a wave of terror in Toktel'yi such as
had not been seen since the dreadful reign of Kekken the Mad,
four hundred years ago. And because he loved the Empire, whatever the faults of its customs and its Emperor, he found the
prospect both appalling and deeply upsetting.

Al'Kalyek was not labouring under any illusions either. He
said goodbye to his guest, giving him the two hands of friendship.
Then he dismissed his slaves from their duties and retired to the
second inner room within the tent, where he kept the precious
tools of his Art.

He stood for a long time, just looking at them. The ancient
books of sorcery, concealing within their crackling pages and
archaic script the spells and knowledge that all mages must learn,
from the humblest village wizard or ship's weatherworker to the
most powerful in the land. The silver scrying bowl, ready filled
with black ink, that would show him whatever he wished to see,
save what he most needed and wanted to know – the future.
The ceremonial robes which he wore when in attendance on the
Emperor, of heavy Kerentan silk, lavishly embroidered with silver
thread. And, most important of all, his supply of Annatal, safe
within a locked silver box, and the ancient engraved cup from

which he drank it. Most sorcerers preferred to smoke the dried leaves, but Al'Kalyek came from Onnak, where it was the custom to infuse the dried berries in hot water, and drink the resulting brew when it had cooled. They had tried to persuade him to use a pipe at the Toktel'yi School of Wizards, where he had trained, and where his Archipelagian habits were considered uncouth. But Al'Kalyek had staunchly stayed true to his native island, and in the end they had allowed him to be different. He fingered the worn pattern on the cup – it was silver, very old, very valuable, and said to be of Jo'amian workmanship – and came to the conclusion that he had always been different, taking a pride in his stubborn integrity. The position of Court Sorcerer, long coveted, and held for the past twenty-five years, had required some compromise with his scruples, but somehow his conscience had managed to remain quiescent.

Now, it was not. Now, Sekkenet's visit, and their secret conversation, had forced him to confront the unpalatable truth. There had always been a strong vein of violence and viciousness in Ba'alekkt, running just beneath the Emperor's apparently jovial and pleasant exterior. Sometimes – on Penya, or at that Council meeting where he had poisoned almost all his Ministers, or a sickening occasion when a foolishly impertinent concubine had been slowly tortured and killed with Olkanno's enthusiastic assistance – the pleasure in causing pain and suffering surfaced, and Ba'alekkt revealed his true, terrible nature to those unfortunate enough to endure or witness it. Al'Kalyek had tried to tell himself that this somehow made his master a better Emperor. Certainly, he was feared and obeyed, whereas his indolent father had been largely irrelevant to the government of the Empire. And the blatant decadence and corruption inherited from Djamal's reign was at last giving way to this eager pursuit of glory, which would expand the boundaries of his dominions, and make the name of Ba'alekkt famous through the admiring ages to come.

But Al'Kalyek had never approved of his plan to attack the northern cities. He had met King Ansaryon several times, liked him as a man and respected him as a sorcerer. He hated the thought of facing him in some faceless combat of mages: and hated too, if he were honest with himself, the idea of that free, independent people forced under the yoke of the Empire. And all for the sake of one spoilt, cruel young man's lust for gold and glory.

The old sorcerer sighed, and sat down on the couch. The little sanctum seemed suddenly very bare, although the practice of magic, being largely the result of extreme mental discipline and concentration, needed few tools. It was possible to judge the status of a mage by his use of props, ceremony and obscure apparatus. Only the most powerful could afford to use the minimum. A village wizard, out to impress his peasant clients, would surround himself with a mass of irrelevant paraphernalia and mumbojumbo.

Al'Kalyek thought with deep and nostalgic regret of his childhood home on Onnak, and particularly of his grandfather, a disreputable old sorcerer whose mix of genuine power and outrageous posturing had fascinated him as a boy. After completing his training, he might have returned to his native island, to spend the rest of his life finding lost children, diverting tropical storms, Healing minor injuries and illnesses. He'd had the chance, and spurned it for his own dreams of glory. And now it was very unlikely that he would ever see Onnak or his brother again. For T'lekko and Ba'alekkt couldn't allow him to retreat into retirement, however obscure and distant from Toktel'yi. He knew too much, and could do too much. When Ba'alekkt no longer needed him, he would have him killed.

It was a common fate for superfluous Ministers and officials, but Al'Kalyek had never thought that it might happen to him. Now, his arrogant confidence evaporating, he tried to consider the prospect calmly, and found that he did not in the least wish to go to Olyak's Halls just yet. He was seventy-two, though of course he looked older, but Annatal would probably prolong his life for another forty or fifty years. Years that could be spent on Onnak, employing his power humbly but usefully, getting to know his brother's family, his nephews and nieces and their children. He had looked forward to his retirement, however unrealistically, and he strongly resented the thought of being denied it.

Of course, if he'd always obeyed Ba'alekkt without question, he would not now be in danger. But his dormant conscience had been roused by the thought of feeding innocent lives to the Emperor's obsession with treachery. He had known, of course, that Ba'alekkt would find someone else to do it in his stead, and he had accepted that.

But his rival was T'lekko, with his smooth silky manner and

sneering mouth and eyes like chips of adamant: and Ba'alekkt saw that the young sorcerer was a kindred spirit, also prepared to do anything to satisfy his greed for power.

He became aware of a subdued but urgent bustle in the outer part of the tent. One of his slaves coughed delicately just outside the dividing curtain. 'Most Wise, His Imperial Majesty commands an interview.'

Al'Kalyek silently cursed Ba'alekkt, and rose to his feet. He adjusted his ancient face into lines of subservient wisdom, and drew aside the draped blue silk.

Ba'alekkt stood in the centre of the space, filling the restricted area with the powerful and arrogant aura of his presence. Not tall, but strongly built, his black curling hair and brown skin were pure Toktel'yan. The hazel eyes, bright as a boy's, were the only indication of his strand of northern ancestry: his grandmother, Penyathi, had been a Zithiriani princess.

And by his side, in ceremonial robes that glittered everywhere with ostentatious silver thread, stood T'lekko.

Al'Kalyek made the sign of obeisance to his Emperor, and stood with an air of interested enquiry. The light from the lanterns round the walls of the tent struck a dazzle of sparks from Ba'alekkt's polished steel armour, which had cost ten thousand gold Imperials to make in Mynak, the city of metal-workers. He looked impressively magnificent, and his eyes gleamed with malice. 'Good morning, Al'Kalyek. Were you resting?'

'I was passing the time before I resume my duties in quiet contemplation, Imperial Majesty.'

'That's what I said – resting.' Ba'alekkt grinned contemptuously, showing a lot of very white teeth. 'Well, I'm sorry to disturb you, old man, but T'lekko has some very unwelcome news for you.'

'Indeed,' said Al'Kalyek, glancing at the younger mage. He was taller and much thinner than Ba'alekkt, and his cropped hair was straight, but in his narrow face and full, downturned mouth lurked the same echo of cruelty. 'What has happened?'

'The chain across the river at Tamat was broken not half an hour ago, allowing a riverboat to pass through in defiance of our laws and our soldiers,' said T'lekko softly. 'And it was severed by sorcery.'

There was a small silence. Al'Kalyek said at last, 'I felt nothing.'

T'lekko and Ba'alekkt exchanged glances, as if the old man's words confirmed their suspicions. 'It must have been a very noticeable burst of power,' said the young sorcerer. 'Yet you say you felt nothing?'

'No,' said Al'Kalyek bluntly. 'Did you?'

The pale grey eyes, sinister in that tanned face, did not blink. 'Naturally I did,' said T'lekko. 'At the time, of course, I was not aware of the reason. But when the news about the chain was brought to His Imperial Majesty, I knew at once what it must be. There was a sorcerer of great power on that ship, or on the quayside in Tamat, and he must be found.'

'If that is so, then you are right – we should act at once,' said Al'Kalyek. T'lekko's obvious lies only confirmed his hatred of his rival, but beneath his feeling of disgust he felt considerable unease. For if the chain had indeed been severed by sorcery, and neither he nor T'lekko, despite his assertion to the contrary, had felt the considerable force necessary to break it, then the unknown mage was not only possessed of enormous power, but also the ability to conceal it.

In all his long life, he had heard of only one man with the potential strength and skill to do such a thing.

And that man had died in Kerenth, four years ago.

CHAPTER
TWENTY-THREE

Bron knew that he had taken a huge risk by using his sorcery to break the chain, but there had been no alternative. He had hidden that brief, furious spear of magic as best he could, but the reek of it would linger for days around the chain itself, even if the explosion of power had somehow remained undetected by any sensitive in Tamat.

It couldn't have been helped, he told himself. The *Flower of Hope* had proved unable to force her way through unaided. If he hadn't used magic, she would by now be impounded, and all her crew captured, or dead. He was still very unhappy about the danger, though. If his presence were discovered here, before he'd had time to act, then all the intense planning and preparation of the last few months would be wasted.

Of course, he did have another option, if killing Ba'alekkt became impossible. He could Transport himself to Zithirian or Minassa, and help the two Kings to defend their cities and their people against the Imperial invader.

But that path would inevitably involve many casualties on both sides, and he had slain more than enough people in his lifetime. The presence of Ayak within him had unbalanced him. In his fear and loathing of the Wolf, he had vowed never to kill again. Now, thinking with an untainted mind for the first time in his life, he could see the necessity, even the justice, of what he planned. And unlike Mallaso, and Sé Mo-Tarmé, he would end Ba'alekkt's life not from revenge, nor from selfish fear, but to save the free people of the north from a terrible fate. At least, if he managed to assassinate the Emperor here in Tamat, he would only be directly responsible for one death, and perhaps also his own.

He had slipped below, on the *Flower of Hope*, while Herris and his crew were still frantically rowing the riverboat away from Tamat. He had already marked a secluded place, where a copse of poplars and willows crowded down to the water's edge, about a mile upstream from the outskirts of the city. He dressed quickly in the unremarkable clothes of a travelling peasant: the belted, knee-length cotton tunic, with an old shapeless leather bag to carry some food, and a hooded woollen cloak for protection against any light summer rain. He stepped outside himself – a very useful skill, when there were no mirrors available – to view the result. His hair was a problem, but liberal handfuls of dust and dirt should dull it to an undistinguished colour, and the frayed straw hat would help to conceal it. And after the months on Jo'ami, he was as sunburnt as any farm labourer.

Satisfied that his appearance was safely inconspicuous, he slipped back into his body and began to gather his power. Above him, he could hear Herris's voice shouting the rhythm, and he could feel the judder and sweep of the oars, moving together. Gently, his mind rose up, above the deck of the *Flower of Hope*, and glanced astern. They were in open country, and the houses and buildings of Tamat had receded to a distant blur of reds and browns amongst the fresh green trees along the river. No boats were pursuing them. He saw Herris, strong and muscular, his hands clenched on the oars, and regretted that he couldn't say goodbye to his friend. Then he swept back along the ship's wake, and found his chosen place.

Of course, the process was not as debilitating as the leap from Jo'ami to Toktel'yi: that had exhausted him, both in mind and body, for days. But even so, he was content just to lie for a space under the sheltering willows, while his pounding heart grew quieter and the shaking stopped.

A small bird, vividly green and orange and blue, eyed him from a branch near the river. It obviously decided that he presented no danger, for it turned its attention to the water below. Suddenly, it plunged downwards: there was a brief splash and then it flew up again in a shower of drops, a small silver fish squirming in its beak. A swift gulp, and its prey disappeared. Then, as Bron moved slightly, it leapt up again with a flash of brilliant colour, and was gone.

He realized belatedly that it would soon be sunset. Tamat had walls and gates, which were certain to be locked at dusk. If he didn't want to spend the night out in the fields, he would have to get up and walk.

For a few moments longer he lay motionless, once more gathering around him the defences that would make his power undetectable until he used it. Then he rose reluctantly to his feet and emerged cautiously from the copse.

At this late hour, the sun behind him had almost reached the distant steppe rumpling the western horizon, and there were very few people still about. All along this stretch of the river-bank, the fields were full of grains and vegetables and fruit, grown to feed the city. Most of the crops were still two or three months away from harvesting. A track meandered between the rows of beans and growing corn and neat fruit trees, and ahead he saw the houses of Tamat huddled over its low hill.

No-one took much notice of him, although he saw one or two labourers glance up as he walked along. A man on a stout mule, a prosperous farmer by the look of him, trotted briskly past as he approached the city, paying him no attention whatsoever, although his mount's ears flickered nervously. There were soldiers at the gate, and the usual nosy officials, but Bron had already spotted an ox-cart lumbering along, laden with new hay. It was easy for a light, agile man to swing himself aboard without being noticed by the tired driver, and to hide amongst the sweet-smelling sheaves.

As he had hoped, the slow-witted oxen were too dull and bovine to notice the sorcerer hidden behind them, and did not change their ponderous pace. The cart rumbled up to the gate, and the driver, obviously well-known to the men on duty, was allowed through after the most cursory inspection. Apparently its destination was an inn called the Vine-Branch, so Bron stayed where he was, breathing softly through the tickling grass stems. In the comparative gloom and privacy of a typical inn courtyard, it should be easy to get off without being seen.

There was suddenly a lot of shouting in the distance. The ox-cart halted, and he heard the driver muttering curses. The sounds came closer. Bron resisted the temptation to move in search of a better view, and so risk revealing his hiding place. He repressed his impatient curiosity, and forced himself to stay still, with only a tiny glimpse of the street visible between the hanks of hay.

There seemed to be a lot of people milling about, and the driver had evidently spotted someone he knew. 'Well met, Lewenn! What's going on?'

'Haven't you heard? A riverboat broke the chain this morning, and got clean away. Now the Emperor's ordered all the soldiers on duty on the quay when it happened to be executed – those that weren't drowned trying to board her. They're stringing up half of them on the dockside, and the other half in the camp, as an example. They say the Emperor himself is supervising the executions there.'

'Well, His Imperial Majesty must punish failure with proper severity,' said the driver loudly. Despite his own defences, Bron could sense both the man's disapproval, and his fear and frustration at being unable to voice his true opinion. He was sure that many other people in Tamat must feel the same.

Eventually the uproar diminished, and the ox-cart moved slowly forward again. By now it was almost dark, and the driver kept his beasts to the centre of the street, to avoid any danger from the lanterns hung outside each door to light the way. Hungry and weary, Bron wondered how long it would take to reach the inn, and whether it would admit a humble peasant. He didn't relish the thought of wandering around Tamat at night, looking for a meal and a bed.

At last the cart turned in under an archway, and creaked to a halt. He heard voices greeting the driver, asking why he was so late, and giving news in more detail. Apparently fifty soldiers had been disembowelled, beheaded and hung on poles down at the dock, and the same number had suffered a similar fate outside the vast camp to the south of the city. He could tell that the men were angry and frightened, but their actual words spoke only of their praise and approval for the Emperor's ruthless brand of justice.

Very carefully, he parted a few hanks of hay to get a better view. Night had fallen, and the courtyard was patched with light from torches and lanterns, leaving deep shadows. He heard the men moving away, and the driver announcing in heartfelt tones that he needed a drink before unloading.

Bron waited until everything was quiet, save for the distant sounds from inside the inn. Then he cautiously pushed his head between the two sheaves in front of him. He could see no-one, and this side of the cart was in shadow. Quick as the fisher bird, he slid on to the ground, brushed off as much of the hay as he could, and slunk unobtrusively out through the gate and into the cobbled street.

There were still plenty of people around, so the curfew must start later, after the taverns and brothels and kuldi-houses had finished their evening business. The Vine-Branch looked like an expensive and respectable establishment, and Bron decided to try his luck elsewhere.

As he'd hoped, he seemed no different from most of the other people in the streets, and no one gave him a second glance. This thoroughfare was full of comfortable buildings, either the houses of the wealthy or inns very similar to the one he'd just left. On an impulse, he took the first turning that led down the hill, towards the river. A tavern catering for sailors and dockers would be much more suitable.

He'd forgotten the executions. There were kites everywhere, even after nightfall, and the stench of fresh blood filled the air. According to the gruesome Toktel'yan custom, poles had been erected along the quay, with a severed head and mutilated body dangling from each one.

They claim to be the most civilized nation in the world, Bron thought, repelled and sickened by the savagery. *And in fact they're hardly better than the Ska'i.*

He had a sudden terrible vision of the barbarians who had seized the child Bron, wanting to exploit his power. Their trophy lances had stood outside each tent, festooned with decomposing heads. And again, as in his childhood nightmares, and more recently and hideously on Jo'ami, he saw the witch D'thliss, High Priestess of Tayo: her shrivelled skin, the greedy glitter of evil in her eyes, the sneering, malevolent mouth.

Abruptly, his stomach revolted, and he was violently sick in the gutter. Passers-by hardly looked at him: they presumably thought he was drunk. And indeed, for the first time in his life Bron felt a longing for the freedom, the loss of control, and above all the oblivion, that an excess of wine or ral would bestow.

He found a tavern nearby, out of sight of the horrors on the quayside. It had a communal dormitory on one side of the courtyard, and a couple of private rooms opposite, next to the entrance. Bron had taken some of Herris's few remaining coins, concealing them inside the lining of his belt. Two of them paid for a room, a jug of well-watered wine, and a simple but filling meal of bread, cheese and fruit. No one asked awkward questions: they were all too busy discussing the day's events. He ate the food and drank the wine undisturbed and retired to his tiny room, which had space only for two mattresses pushed together and a battered table with an oil-dish on top. He blew out the feeble flame, lay down on one of the mattresses, and tried to find sleep.

On Jo'ami, and in Herris's stuffy cabin, he had tried in vain to forget Mallaso: her grace, her courage, the smoothness of her night-dark skin and her sudden, joyous smile. They had been lovers, yet they had never talked of love. And now she carried his child, and with it all that remained of his future.

He found that he still missed her acutely. The space next to him spoke bleakly and eloquently of her absence. And he would probably never see her again, for there was a good chance that he would die tomorrow.

Footsteps lurched outside in the courtyard, accompanied by drunken singing. It died away, and soon he heard the gates being shut and barred. Not long afterwards, the tramp of a military patrol drove the last revellers into silence. The profound stillness of fear settled over Tamat like a winter fog.

Sleep must have claimed him eventually, for he dreamed. And in his dreams, he found a stranger.

He stood in a tent, hot and airless, with draped silk walls that seemed to crowd in on him. And a voice, very deep, very quiet, said, 'Have no fear, Bron, son of Ansaryon. I know who you are, and I am not your enemy.'

He turned, and saw a tall man, black-skinned, white-haired, sitting on a folding chair, regarding him with grave interest. And although he was plainly dressed in a long, unadorned Toktel'yan tunic, although Bron had never seen him before, he knew that this was his greatest adversary: Al'Kalyek, Court Sorcerer to the Emperor Ba'alekkt.

'I am not your enemy,' the old man repeated, and smiled. 'I will not betray you. I have been searching for you over many years, since I first heard your father speak of you. And now I have found you.'

'Why?' Bron asked. His mouth felt dry, and his heart was beating fast.

'Because you are unique. Because, unlike my counterpart on Jo'ami, I welcome the future you portend. Because I wish to know more about you, partly, I do confess, from pure curiosity. And now, too, because I wish to help you.'

'I don't need your help,' Bron said.

'Oh, but you do – even if, in the natural confidence of youth, you cannot admit it. I know why you are here, and what you plan to do.'

'How do you know?'

'Your defences are not so strong, in sleep. You are vulnerable then. There is another searching for you, but I alone knew who must have broken the river chain of Tamat, and I alone as yet have the power to find you. You did not die in Kerenth, did you?'

'No, I don't think I did,' Bron said.

'Very few survive the fall from that cliff,' said Al'Kalyek, matching the younger man's dry tone. 'In fact, I suspect no one else has ever done so. I will not ask you how you managed it, but your power obviously far exceeds that of any other sorcerer who has ever lived – and without the aid of Annatal, too. Have you taken it at any time?'

'No.'

'Were it not for the undesirable consequences, it would be interesting to see what would happen if you tried it. However, I did not seek you out to discuss fanciful theories. I am here in your dream to tell you about Ba'alekkt – and to warn you.'

Bron stared at the dark, serious face. The old mage smiled. 'I repeat – I am not your enemy. But I am Ba'alekkt's Sorcerer, for the present. At his command, I have constructed a mesh of protective magic around him. No-one will be able to breach it, and besides, the Imperial Guard now surround the Emperor night and day.'

'It must take an enormous amount of power, to keep such a defence in place.'

'It does. That is why Ba'alekkt has employed another, younger sorcerer to help me. This man is called T'lekko, and he is the Principal of the School of Wizards in Terebis. He has great ambition, and he is a cruel, ruthless man who will do anything to please the Emperor.'

'And he has his eye on your shoes?'

'He can hardly wait to step into them,' said Al'Kalyek. 'Indeed, I suspect that Ba'alekkt means to replace me as soon as his campaign against the northern cities is over. Until then, he needs me and my power. Since Tekkt, he has been obsessed with the – terror, I would call it if he were not the Emperor – of assassination. Did you have a hand in that incident?'

'I rescued her.'

'I thought so. Even then, I suspected that you might have survived Kerenth. What did you do, in the years between?'

'I wandered. In the western provinces and the Archipelago, mainly – learning songs, playing music, doing a little Healing here and there. Onnak is beautiful.'

'I know,' said Al'Kalyek, and on his lined face appeared the shadow of real grief and regret. 'Once, I hoped to return there, to live out my last years in peace and happiness with my brother and his family. Now the Emperor has removed that hope – unless . . .'

'Unless I kill him,' said Bron. 'But why have you not considered doing it yourself? It would be very easy for you.'

'It would – but I have adhered to the Four Rules of Sorcery since I was a student. I do not wish to break them, for I would find it very difficult to live with my conscience if I did. And moreover, if I were to kill the Emperor, my soul would be dismissed to Olyak's darkest, deepest Halls until the end of time.'

'With a master like Ba'alekkt,' Bron said drily, 'you are certain to be asked to break your vows, sooner or later.'

'I know. Yet I would rather die too soon, by the Emperor's order, and be certain of greeting those I love in Paradise. But you are a Northerner – perhaps you do not understand such beliefs.'

'I do,' Bron said, thinking of Mallaso, and her desperate desire to join her beloved daughter after death. 'And I respect your integrity. At least you are true to yourself, and your Art.'

'Not as much as I would like,' said Al'Kalyek, with a sigh. 'But I have always tried to be. And so I am a hypocrite, for I want you to do for me what I with my tender conscience will not, and take the risk that my cowardly soul is reluctant to venture. Do you understand me?'

Bron's dark eyes were steady. 'Yes, I do. But surely, this conversation alone will bring harm to Ba'alekkt, if no-one else.'

'I agree. But I have only vowed not to use my magic to kill or hurt directly. The Emperor, however, is a cruel and depraved young man who has already tortured or murdered countless innocent people. If he is not stopped, there will be many more deaths. That is how I have justified my position to myself – by thinking of the vast numbers of lives that his assassination will save. I admit that I am a hypocrite and a coward. I want to see Onnak again, and enjoy my old age. And although you are young, your power is so much greater than mine, or T'lekko's, that you are certain of success.'

'I'm glad you think so,' Bron said. He stared at the old man, wondering whether or not to trust him. Was this an elaborate trap, woven to entice him into suicidal folly? Or did Al'Kalyek really wish his master dead?

'I speak the truth,' said the old man, his voice heavy with sadness. 'And if you do not believe me, enter my mind and see for yourself.'

A glimpse, no more, was necessary. Bron sensed confusion, guilt, unhappiness, fear – but no deceit, no treachery. Reassured, he withdrew, letting the other sorcerer know of his respect for his honesty.

'T'lekko has no conscience at all,' Al'Kalyek commented. 'Vows are just words to be mouthed to order, and forgotten when convenient. But although he possesses some ability, he is still young, and his power is much less than mine. He has also, as I am sure you will appreciate, the usual arrogance of youth, and I fear that he has drastically overestimated his competence. Certainly, he has led the Emperor to believe that he is already eminently qualified to take my place.'

'And is he?'

'Hardly.' Al'Kalyek coughed in disapproval. 'His protective sorcery is so weak that you will have little difficulty in overpowering it, and him. Moreover, if it so happens that he can be blamed for any lapse in vigilance, then the world will be a better place without him. I will tell you no more, save that we are on duty, turn and turn about, for half a day each. I take the twelve hours of the afternoon and evening until midnight, while T'lekko rests – then he is by the Emperor's side from that time until noon. Does that help you?'

'Yes, it does – and I thank you.'

'And I thank you, son of Ansaryon. And so will all the people of the world, free and unfree, in the years to come. Alone, Ba'alekkt is dangerous enough. With T'lekko and Olkanno to encourage him, I tremble for the future. We will speak no more, but may luck smile on you, and may the Twin Gods of Toktel'yi grant you their blessings, according to their nature.'

His voice faded, the image vanished, and so did sleep. Bron found himself gazing, not at Al'Kalyek's wise, gentle and resolute face, but into the thick hot darkness of his inadequately ventilated little room.

This day, he would do it. This day, Ba'alekkt would die.

The ninety-ninth Emperor of Toktel'yi woke at sunrise, after a sound and refreshing slumber. The concubine whose arts had induced it was not by his side: since Tekkt, Ba'alekkt had always slept alone. True, the women he bedded were now all absolutely trustworthy, selected by the Head Eunuch, who had been in

Imperial service for fifty years, and vetted not only by Olkanno and his network of spies, but by T'lekko. Some of his favourite girls had had to be shipped off to Tulyet, but he did not regret them at all.

The attempted assassination had forcibly reminded him that his life was fragile, precious and uniquely valuable, not only to himself but to the Empire and its glorious future. Until he took a wife and begot an heir, he could be in danger from any one of a legion of relatives, all of whom had a greater or lesser claim to the Onyx Throne, should he die without issue. One of them must have paid the Penyan woman to kill him. He couldn't believe that she had acted alone. Females were simply not capable of such planning and forethought.

Breakfast was served by his own cooks, each of whom must taste his dishes before proffering them for the Emperor's delectation. It was an excellent way to ensure he wasn't poisoned. Replete with fine soft wheaten bread, smoked fish and new summer fruit, Ba'alekkt allowed his personal slaves to array him in his finest garment. It was a long scarlet tunic, the neck and hem worked in heavy gold thread, with a belt of jewel-encrusted silk, fringed with bullion. Because Tamat, even at High Summer, was not as hot as Toktel'yi in the same season, he ordered them to drape a light length of matching cloth elegantly over one shoulder. Even if this splendid attire had not indicated his supreme rank, the Imperial Pectoral, in gold inlaid with rubies, emeralds and other precious stones, spread across his broad chest like a hawk's wings, and a thin gold band, worn by the Emperors of Toktel'yi for two thousand years, circled his head between the mass of gleaming black curls.

Ba'alekkt surveyed his image in the polished steel mirror his slave held out for him, and smiled with satisfaction. Today was Summerday, one of the principal feasts of Kaylo the Lifegiver, the most popular of the Empire's assortment of greater and lesser deities, to whom laughter, pleasure, peace and happiness were sacred, and who abhorred war and death, the provinces of his twin god Olyak. It would not be proper at any time to enter Kaylo's Temple clanking in full armour, let alone on this important festival. Admittedly, the Lord of Life, unlike Olyak, was not malevolent, but he conferred good fortune on his mortal worshippers, and was perfectly capable of removing luck from anyone, even an Emperor, who insulted him.

But of course, Ba'alekkt would not enter Tamat's undoubtedly cramped and provincial little Temple in the company of a few eunuchs and officials. The Imperial Guard had been drawn up in front of his tent, and the morning sun shone dazzlingly bright on the massed ranks of their weapons and armour. T'lekko stood outside the entrance, his lean face full of watchful concentration, a deep frown between his thin dark brows. Ba'alekkt was not in the least sensitive to sorcery, so he could not feel the protective web around him, but the sight of the Terebis mage was deeply reassuring.

Toktel'yans had not fought in chariots for hundreds of years, but they were still used for ceremonial purposes. This one was known as the 'Makkyar', after Ba'alekkt's grandfather, who had ordered it to be built. The body of the vehicle was made of Onnak ironwood, sheathed in beaten and engraved gold, and it was pulled by four matched white Tanathi horses, caparisoned in the Imperial colours of azure and scarlet.

Ba'alekkt acknowledged the salutes of his guard, and climbed aboard the chariot. His Head Eunuch unfurled a silk parasol, fringed with red and gold tassels, which would shade his master's head from the heat of the sun. The driver, a veteran of the Palace stables, waited until T'lekko, too, had taken his place by the Emperor's side. Then the procession moved off, to the shrill blare of the ceremonial trumpets.

All of Tamat, it seemed, had turned out to cheer Ba'alekkt. They lined the approach to the Temple of Kaylo six and seven deep, and the way before the chariot was thickly strewn with flowers, like a gloriously colourful tapestry. The horses halted while a troupe of young girls, unveiled in the traditional and unflattering local costume of dark heavy cotton, performed an elaborate and interminable dance of welcome which involved a great deal of solemn bowing and circling to the sound of very slow music.

The sun was now near its zenith, and Ba'alekkt diplomatically suppressed a yawn. The parasol's shade excluded T'lekko, and beads of sweat were trickling down his bony cheeks. Around the chariot, the sounds of shuffling and subdued chinking of armour indicated that the men of the Imperial Guard were just as bored as their Emperor, and rather less restrained about showing it. In contrast, the people of Tamat stood in a rapt, hushed silence, broken only by the fretful wails of fractious infants.

At last the dancers came to a rather ragged conclusion. The youngest of them, who couldn't have been more than twelve years old, ran up with a garland of blue and scarlet flowers. At once, the two nearest guardsmen crossed their spears in front of her, while a third forcibly removed the wreath from her grasp. As he roughly examined it, scattering petals like blood and sky from his brisk fingers, the child burst into disappointed tears. Still weeping, she was led away by her friends as Ba'alekkt, with a gracious and patronizing smile, took the garland, by now distinctly battered, and placed it carefully over one of the decorative spikes at the front of the chariot.

Now the priests of Kaylo were filing out from the portals of their Temple, singing with every appearance of warmth and sincerity. There were a lot of them, for every younger son of a large family aspired to serve the Lord of Life, in whose name no pleasure could be refused. In their multicoloured robes and gilded smiling masks, they were a splendid sight, and Ba'alekkt looked on them with genuine appreciation. If he had not been born to such high office, he himself would have liked to have been one of them, enjoying a life of ease and idleness on the copious handouts of worshippers eager for good luck and a place in Paradise. The Priests of Kaylo lived like Emperors, awash with food and drink, bedded by devoted female acolytes, waited on hand and foot by teams of slaves. But they suffered neither the burdens of Imperial responsibility, nor the risk of a violent and premature death, for killing one of them would bring certain and life-long bad luck to the perpetrator.

The lesser priests formed up in two lines in front of the Temple, singing one of the Hymns of Summerday. Their leader, known as the Kaylo'enn, moved forward to the chariot, followed by half a dozen of his subordinates, and made deep and reverent obeisance. 'Oh, most mighty Emperor, Master of us all, we the humble servants of Kaylo the Lord of Life give you joyful welcome to this our Temple, at the most favoured time of fest . . .'

He stopped in the middle of the word, frozen as if turned to ice, mouth open and eyes staring. Ba'alekkt tried to tell him to get on with it, and found that he too could neither speak nor move.

It had happened before, on Tekkt. And as the fear began to flood like water through his immobilized body, the Emperor saw a man burst out of the crowd and run straight towards him.

He could do nothing. He could only stand and watch impotently as his death rushed up to him with terrible, unstoppable speed. He wanted to scream at T'lekko, tell him to break the spell that bound them, but the sorcerer was also transfixed by a power far greater than his own.

Ba'alekkt could not turn his head away: he was forced to look at the man who would kill him. He was young, fair-haired, dressed in a shabby tunic – a native, probably, of one of the northern cities which the Emperor had planned to destroy. He saw the narrowed, intent dark eyes, devoid of mercy or pity, and the flash of sunlight on the steel blade of the knife he carried, raised high to strike. And behind him, the priests, the dancing girls, and the people of Tamat, all fixed in almost comical attitudes of astonishment and horror.

Vainly, frantically, the Emperor struggled against the iron bars of sorcery that imprisoned him. Sweat trickled down his face, and his eyes bulged. Not a muscle moved in obedience to his desperate need. The assassin brushed past the frozen Kaylo'enn, and grasped the edge of the chariot. Ba'alekkt saw the knife descend in a fierce, powerful arc –

Frantic neighs shattered the air. The chariot jerked, wrenched forward by the horses yoked to it, who, maddened by the terrifying presence of power, tried to plunge away from the source of their panic. The vehicle behind them lurched wildly, and the four men inside it, unable to move and save themselves, were hurled backwards on to the ground.

It was a heavy and undignified fall. Ba'alekkt was nearest to the open rear of the chariot, and landed first. The others tumbled painfully on top of him. He waited for the blow that would kill him, and heard cries and screams.

Screams. Someone was moaning, almost in his ear. There were the sounds of a scuffle, and shouts of anger. Slowly, the Emperor, still dazed and shocked, realized that the spell must have been broken. He tried to move, and found that his muscles once more obeyed him.

But the assassin might not have been captured yet. Ba'alekkt waited, in considerable discomfort, for death or rescue. The man above him was groaning like a half-killed pig, and, to judge by his almost unbearable weight, must be the Head Eunuch, who was enormously fat.

'Imperial Majesty, are you badly hurt?'

It was Sekkenet. The suffocating bulk above Ba'alekkt was

unceremoniously heaved aside. Gulping air with huge relief, he saw his General's sharp, rat-like face hovering anxiously above him. He said, grasping, 'Have you got him? Is it safe?'

'The assassin? Yes, Imperial Majesty, I am happy to say that he has been struck down. Are you hurt? May I assist you to your feet?'

It was quite unlike Sekkenet to make such a fuss, and indicated how alarmingly close the unknown attacker had come to success. Ba'alekkt found that his head ached, he could feel blood on his face and his ribs were bruised and sore. But he was alive. He spurned the General's proffered hand of assistance, and struggled up unaided.

The crowds had been pushed right back, and the Imperial Guard kept them at bay with linked spears. From the sounds of panic, it had been done with brutal efficiency. Even the priests of Kaylo had been herded away from the chariot, and stood huddled and bleating like sheep in the entrance to their Temple.

'Everything is fully under control, Imperial Majesty,' said Sekkenet, with a brisk air that entirely concealed his nervousness. This attempt, like the last, had so nearly succeeded. But the plunging hooves of the terrified, panic-stricken animals had flung the assassin to the ground and broken the spell, allowing one of the Guard to knock the man unconscious. If it hadn't been for the horses, Ba'alekkt would now be dead.

The General ruthlessly suppressed an improper twinge of regret. No blame could possibly attach to him. Soldiers had never been immune to sorcery – though that hadn't saved the hundred men on duty at the docks yesterday from Ba'alekkt's fury. He knew who must be held responsible for the fact that the assassination had almost succeeded, and he intended to draw the Emperor's attention to it as soon as the opportunity arose.

'Where is he?' demanded Ba'alekkt, looking round.

The chariot stood some ten paces away, the horses, their glossy white coats dark with sweat, stamping nervously in the firm grasp of their driver and three soldiers. The parasol lay wrecked and dusty on the ground beside the prone, corpulent and groaning figure of the Head Eunuch. No one paid any attention to him: instead, one knot of guardsmen were clustered protectively round the Emperor. Another group, of perhaps a dozen men, stood over something sprawled near the chariot.

'Is that him?' Ba'alekkt ignored the pains in his head and chest, shook Sekkenet aside and strode over, his sandalled feet kicking aside the bruised flowers. Like anxious hens round a precious chick, the Guardsmen scurried after him, brandishing their spears as if they feared another assassin might spring out of nowhere, armed to the teeth.

His attacker lay face down in the dust, a soldier's boot placed firmly between his shoulder-blades, and a spear-point resting against the back of his neck.

The Emperor saw that the pale, dirty hair was matted and blotched with a quantity of fresh blood. 'Is he dead?'

'No, Imperial Majesty,' said the Guardsman with the spear. A Hundred-Commander with an excellent reputation, he was the most senior of the men around the assassin. 'But if Your Imperial Majesty desires – '

He pushed on the spear slightly, drawing more blood. The man below it did not move.

'No!' Ba'alekkt said sharply. 'I wish him to answer for his crimes, painfully and publicly, as an example to any others who might be tempted. Is his wound serious?'

'One of the horses struck him down, Imperial Majesty, and the spell was immediately broken. Before he could recover, Duakkan here showed great initiative and clubbed him over the head.'

The soldier concerned was a short, burly man with muscles bulging beneath the brief sleeves of his armoured tunic. He saluted, his dark face glowing with self-satisfaction.

'I hope for your sake that you haven't shattered his skull,' said Ba'alekkt. As the smug expression drained from Duakkan's face, he swung round to Sekkenet. 'Take a look at him, General. I want him kept alive.'

Sekkenet didn't need to ask why. He knelt beside the unconscious man, and probed the site of Duakkan's over-enthusiastic blow. There was a lot of blood, and a sizeable lump, but the bone beneath his fingers felt solid enough. For the assassin's sake, he thought grimly, it would be better by far if he never woke.

He stood up, sending Duakkan a reassuring glance that Ba'alekkt couldn't see, and turned back to the Emperor. 'His skull is intact, Imperial Majesty. Of course, I am no Healer, and such injuries do sometimes lead to death, but most eventually recover.'

'Good,' said Ba'alekkt. 'I want him to know what is happening to him.'

'But if he is a sorcerer—' Sekkenet broke off, and stared at his master in some disquiet. '*Is* he?'

'How should I know? Someone used power to stop us moving.

But not being a sorcerer myself,' said Ba'alekkt with heavy sarcasm, 'I have no idea whether it was this man, or an accomplice.'

'It must have been him, or we would still be under that spell,' Sekkenet pointed out.

And you would now be dead. The words lingered unspoken in the air. The Emperor's olive-skinned face suffused suddenly with rage. 'A sorcerer attacks me, nearly kills me, and no thanks to the man who should have protected me! T'lekko!'

The mage from Terebis moved reluctantly forward. His fine purple robes were torn and covered with dust, and a large graze disfigured the side of his face. 'Yes, Imperial Majesty?'

'Explain yourself. Explain how, despite your all-embracing *protection*, that – that *scum* was able to come within a whisker of murdering me.'

'Imperial Majesty – ' T'lekko's skin was grey under the blood and dirt, and he licked his lips like a frightened dog.

'I'm waiting – and I'm not famous for my patience.'

'Imperial Majesty, believe me, I had no chance, no chance at all of withstanding such power! It burst over me like a tidal wave, I could do nothing, I was helpless – '

'You led me to believe that you were the greatest mage in all my Empire. You boasted that you would be able to detect *any* sorcery. Yet you had no warning of this?'

'No – yes, yes, I did, Imperial Majesty, but such vast power could not be withstood – that man is unique, Imperial Majesty, I have never heard of such a thing, unless . . .'

T'lekko's urgent voice trailed off into silence. He stared at the man lying on the ground, and then shook his head. 'No. No, it can't be possible. He is dead.'

'*Who* is dead?' Ba'alekkt shouted. 'Do you know who this man is?'

And T'lekko, his fingers curled into the sign which warded off evil, said hesitantly, 'The only sorcerer I have ever heard of, who possessed such power, was the son of the King of Zithirian.'

There was a short, horrified silence. T'lekko, well aware that he had no friends and many enemies, glanced around and tried to calm himself. He added, with more confidence, 'But it cannot be him, Imperial Majesty. That man is certainly dead. He was, as we have all heard, the Sacrificed Consort of Kerenth. And no-one can survive a fall from cliffs half a mile high.'

'If he is indeed such a powerful sorcerer, perhaps he did,' said

Ba'alekkt grimly. 'And I seem to remember some tale about him falling off a tower and saving himself, while he was still a boy. Well, perhaps this is him. At least, thanks to Duakkan here, he has been made safe for the moment. How do you propose we keep him harmless, until his execution?'

T'lekko was beginning to look more relaxed. Sekkenet, who had known Ba'alekkt all his life, smiled to himself as the mage pondered with ostentatious earnestness. Finally, T'lekko said, 'If he is indeed the son of the King of Zithirian, and if all the stories about him are true, then he cannot be confined except by superior sorcery. And there are no sorcerers his equal, let alone his superior.'

Ba'alekkt smiled with deceptive friendliness. 'Is that so?'

'He is safe at present, Imperial Majesty.'

'Are you a half-wit?' The Emperor stalked forward until his jutting nose was within a hand's breadth of the sorcerer's face. T'lekko quailed, and stepped back. Sekkenet made an unobtrusive gesture, and four guardsmen placed themselves just behind him, blocking any attempt to escape.

'Imperial Majesty – please – that man will only be harmless if he is asleep, or unconscious, or dead.'

'I don't want him asleep or unconscious. Nor do I want him dead – yet. I repeat – how can he be made safe?'

T'lekko's mouth opened and closed foolishly. More than one person watched his agony of fear with considerable satisfaction, not least Sekkenet. The General judged it time to step forward, clearing his throat. 'Imperial Majesty? Leaving aside the possibility that T'lekko is in some way concerned in the attack – which, as you must acknowledge, is not unlikely – it is quite clear that this – this vainglorious loud-mouthed buffoon has no idea. Perhaps the venerable Al'Kalyek, whose skill, wisdom, loyalty and honesty are unquestioned, can provide an answer.'

'Of course he can't!' T'lekko cried. 'He's a stupid old windbag – he's past it, I told you, he's past it!'

'I'll be the judge of that.' Ba'alekkt's voice was as smooth as satin, as deceptively sweet as a poisoned fruit. 'But I'm sick of you and your posturing, T'lekko. You've failed, and there's only one reward for failure. Sekkenet?'

In disbelief, the mage dropped to his knees, screeching for mercy, his hands plucking frantically at the Emperor's tunic. Ba'a-lekkt kicked him viciously in the ribs, and he fell backwards, still sobbing incoherently. With a mixture of contempt, satisfaction and relief, Sekkenet beckoned. A guardsman came running, his sword at the ready, while others grabbed the sorcerer by the hair and yanked his head back. One brutal sweep of the blade, and the screaming rose to a wild pitch of agony: with the second, some moments later, the hideous noise was abruptly cut off.

'Throw it on to the rubbish heap,' said Ba'alekkt, into the sudden, welcome silence. He had stepped well back, but a liberal spray of T'lekko's blood had splattered the dirty scarlet silk of his tunic. The drops were almost invisible, red on red, but he looked down with disgust, and gestured to the Head Eunuch, who had at last recovered some of his self-control. 'It is not fitting that I enter the Life-Giver's Temple thus defiled. I will return to the camp, to consult with Al'Kalyek. Have the assassin brought to us bound with strong cords, and under heavy guard – and if he shows any signs of life, Duakkan, you know what to do.'

And once more ensconced in his gilded chariot, unharmed and coruscating with malevolent rage, the Emperor of Toktel'yi was driven back to his camp, the soldiers of his Imperial Guard gathered protectively close around him. And along the route, his cowed, bewildered subjects stared between the grim lines of soldiers, and wondered in terror whether the Emperor's savage and unpredictable vengeance would next embrace the people of Tamat.

CHAPTER
TWENTY-FOUR

'So T'lekko is dead?'

Not by one twitch, one fraction of movement did Al'Kalyek betray his delight. He gazed at Ba'alekkt with his usual grave dignity, noting the raging red of the Emperor's aura, so hot and furious that a child could have detected it.

'Dead as meat,' said Ba'alekkt, with gloating satisfaction. 'You should have heard him scream when his guts were spilled – lying, boastful, treacherous little marsh-snake! He was probably in league with the other one. I don't believe that anyone could possibly possess the power that man's supposed to have – there must have been two of them, acting together.'

'Which man, Imperial Majesty?'

'I mean the son of Ansaryon – Bron, or whatever his name was. Yes, I know we've all heard he died in Kerenth, but T'lekko, may Olyak curse him for ever, seemed to think it was him.'

'If it is,' said Al'Kalyek thoughtfully, 'then we must be exceedingly careful. Where is he now? And what does he look like?'

Precisely and forcefully, Ba'alekkt described the exact details of the assassin's present condition and appearance.

'It certainly sounds as if it might be Ansaryon's son,' said the Court Sorcerer, while a watchful inner voice urged extreme caution. 'And if so, then he is best kept unconscious.'

'That's what T'lekko said,' Ba'alekkt told him furiously. 'But I don't intend to allow him an easy death. And I want information out of him as well. There's sure to be others concerned in this – and what about the attempt on Tekkt? He must have had a hand in that too – perhaps he knows where the Penyan bitch is now.'

'There might be a way . . .' Al'Kalyek paused, his thoughts running fast. His own position, made much stronger by his rival's death, would hardly be improved if Bron was tortured into revealing how the Court Sorcerer had betrayed his master.

And yet . . .

And yet, he did not want Bron killed now, with all the questions about his mysterious powers unanswered. Besides, he had liked the young man, despite his enviable abilities and his arrogant assurance.

He could see a solution to his dilemma, although it would only be temporary at best. He said carefully, 'There is a drug, khlar. You know it, of course?'

'Of course,' said Ba'alekkt, with a dismissive air.

'It is a potent narcotic when smoked, as you are well aware. But when its distilled essence is taken in food or drink, its effects are even stronger – strong enough to render the most powerful sorcerer as helpless as a newborn child. He will have no power, and no defences. He will be able to answer any questions without deception.'

Ba'alekkt's eyes glittered with the intoxicating prospect of revenge. He smiled gleefully, and gave the mage a delighted and very painful buffet on one shoulder. 'If it works, old man, I'll give you a chest of gold Imperials. Can you arrange it?'

'Of course, Majesty.'

'Excellent – I'll look forward to the interrogation. Go on, man – go, quickly, before he wakes up and fries us all!'

Al'Kalyek made his obeisances, and left the Imperial pavilion.

Ba'alekkt smiled, and rubbed his hands together. Then he beckoned to one of the waiting slaves. 'Go and find Olkanno. I want him here immediately.'

He was dreaming, but it was not a dream he could control. Dreadful images chased through his mind, the monsters who terrified every little child of the northern lands – frost demons, ice bears, the Ska'i –

The Ska'i. A small boy again, their helpless captive, he trembled and sobbed at the sight of the shaman Br'nnayak, foul and evil beyond all imagining. The wizened, claw-like hand reached out for him, and he screamed and shrank away, but there was no escape . . .

He saw the fires that had immolated Br'nnayak, his chief Quenait and all the tribesmen, thousands of them burned to husks of charcoal by the heat of his own rage and grief. And within him, a Wolf with red eyes and dripping fangs laughed with joy, and devoured their souls.

Despairing, he fled, and the monsters fell far behind. He flew over Zithirian, the city where he had grown up, with its new walls and fine buildings holding the people with whom he had once lived, and knew that he could not inflict on them the burden of his past and his power.

The sunlight vanished: he saw clouds rushing up from the south, dark and menacing. Their jaws opened, and he saw in them the likenesses of ravening wolves, eager to destroy and to devour. And behind them, the sun lurked, the colour of blood.

He fled again. He could not turn and fight: he knew and cursed his own cowardice, but in this dream he was helpless, at the mercy of every emotion. And then suddenly, in the strange way of dreams, he found himself, without seeming to have travelled any distance at all, in the fertile, gentle hills of a southern land.

He had come here before, seeking in vain: and as if he were a voyager in a desert, seeing promise of green trees and pure water, he spoke her name. 'Mallaso!'

In the nearest field, a line of women hoed weeds from around rows of young crops. They were unveiled, and wore the light calf-length cotton garments of Kerenth. One of them stopped and straightened, rubbing her back in the unmistakable gesture of a pregnant woman. She was tall, and black-skinned, and still slender, though under the thin cotton he could see the slight, gentle swell of her belly.

He called her name, but she did not respond. He stood in front of her, and she looked right past him, as if he did not exist, and said something, smiling, to one of the other women. And he saw the glow in her eyes and the subtle relaxation of her face, and knew that at last she had achieved the happiness which had been her birthright, ripped away from her by slavery.

He had no idea if this dream told the truth, or was just another illusion. He hoped desperately that she was indeed in Kerenth, in the company of friends, and looking forward with joy to the birth of her child. It was what he had wanted for her. But in achieving it, he knew too that she no longer had need of him.

There was someone beside him, watching. He turned, and saw the dark, lined face of Al'Kalyek, whom he had only seen in his dreams. It was full of sorrow, and regret. Suddenly aware of the danger to Mallaso, Bron shouted to her to run, to hide, but no sound came from his lips. Her image wavered and faded, and he tried to cling to it, to fix his spirit on her oblivious, beautiful face, but all he could see was Al'Kalyek, and all he could hear was the old sorcerer's voice in his head. 'I am sorry, Bron. This is the best I can do for you now.'

Hands seized his arms and pulled him roughly upright. This was no longer a dream. His head spinning, he tried to struggle, and found something rammed against his lips. He tried to turn his face away, but a hand grasped his jaw and forced it down. Liquid poured into his open mouth: he coughed and spluttered and tried to spit it out, but there was too much, and he could not help swallowing most of it.

It tasted strange, rather tarry, and somehow horribly familiar. He gagged, but already his limbs were beginning to feel heavy and unresponsive. Bron opened his eyes for the first time, and saw the Court Sorcerer's dark, solemn face looking down at him.

It swam slowly out of focus. He blinked stupidly, trying to clear his vision, and failed.

'The drug is taking effect,' said Al'Kalyek. 'You may let him go now – it will be quite safe.'

Abruptly, the arms holding him laid him back. Bron tried to move, and found that his muscles would not obey him. A terrible lethargy was invading his body, rendering him utterly helpless. For a few heartbeats longer, his mind rebelled against the drug seeping into his brain, but he could not reach the level of concentration that sorcery required. For a brief instant the air around him shimmered, and then was still.

'Excellent,' said Al'Kalyek, and smiled. 'You are in captivity, and will shortly pay the full price for your attempt on the life of our glorious Emperor. For a day or two, though, I and others will have the opportunity to question you. The drug has made you powerless – you cannot escape, nor can you use your sorcery. You should feel remote, unreal, detached from the world – am I correct?'

Bron could move his lips, if nothing else. The answer came in a whisper. 'Yes.'

'You have no resistance. Understand? No resistance to our questions. You will not be able to stay silent, or to evade them, or to lie. And if you do, I can rummage through the contents of your head like a thief in a store-room. Like this.'

He heard the silent voice. *There are many things I wish to know, and questions that the Emperor would dearly like to be answered. The Spymaster Olkanno has been summoned. I shall attempt to persuade him that the drug renders his cruder methods unnecessary – but I fear that, like Ba'alekkt, he enjoys inflicting pain for its own sake, and the drug will not prevent you from feeling it.*

Bron could not answer: he lay as motionless as if he slept, save that his eyes were open. But Al'Kalyek, probing gently amid the younger man's useless defences, sensed his horror and fear, and abruptly left his mind.

The Court Sorcerer's own thoughts were far from clear. He stood looking down at the helpless husk of the most powerful mage in the known world, and experienced a curious blend of relief, distress and regret. T'lekko was dead, and so the greatest threat to his own immediate survival was gone. In fact, to judge from Ba'alekkt's manner just now, he could look forward to a considerable period of comfort, basking in the rich warm sunlight of Imperial favour.

But the Emperor's mood could change in an instant, as T'lekko and many others had discovered to their cost. And besides, his precarious safety would be bought at the price of Bron's life. That alone had the power to unsettle his conscience. And when combined with ordinary human compassion, as well as his inconvenient liking for the boy, not to mention his desire for a greater understanding of his extraordinary powers, his regret became acute.

Al'Kalyek knew what he wanted to do, what the teachings of his Art dictated that he must do. But he would thereby almost certainly ensure his own death, and so never exploit or learn from the knowledge he would gain.

The old man turned away from the defenceless sorcerer on the ground, and gestured to the soldiers who guarded him. 'Out!'

They stared at him. All were seasoned members of the Imperial Guard, answerable only to the Emperor. Then the Hundred-Commander, distinguished by the gold and turquoise pectoral over his armour, said curtly, 'Our orders are to stay with the assassin at all times. Even in this drugged state, he is potentially dangerous.'

'He is no more potentially dangerous than a new-born wolf cub,' Al'Kalyek told him, with absolute conviction. 'But I need time to think, to compose myself and to pray for guidance, before I question him. And I am unable to do any of those things while you and your men are crowding round me. You may stand guard outside the tent. After all, he cannot possibly escape.'

The Court Sorcerer was a feared and respected man, and Hundred-Commander Turak had no wish to fall foul of him. He nodded stiffly. 'Very well. We will withdraw. But I warn you, Most Wise, that I shall hold you personally responsible, should anything happen to the prisoner.'

Al'Kalyek's eyes gleamed with satisfaction. 'Have no fear. My methods are gentle, unlike some I could mention, but nevertheless very effective. He will not die at my hands.'

Turak allowed himself a smile in response, and led his six men out of the tent.

It did not seem much more spacious once they had gone. Al'Kalyek listened to them taking up their positions outside, and then sat down on a folding chair next to the prisoner.

This was not his own tent: it was used as a place of detention for soldiers who had committed minor offences, and was not designed to be comfortable. The ground under his feet was ridged and dusty, liberally scattered with the stones of the Tamattan field it had been only a month ago. The walls and conical roof were made of thick grey canvas, and the atmosphere inside was stale and hot, stinking of fresh sweat and old urine. Al'Kalyek breathed in too deeply, thought better of it, and constructed a small, invisible bubble of clean air around his mouth and nostrils. Then, free of distraction at last, he closed his eyes and withdrew into his tangled, painful thoughts.

The clash of arms roused him. He heard Turak hailing the Emperor, and was surprised at his surge of anger. Then, composing his face into lines of welcome, he stood to greet his master.

Ba'alekkt entered without ceremony or grace. He had changed into full armour: evidently there would be no second visit to Kaylo's Temple today. He pushed past the old sorcerer and stood for a moment, staring down at Bron, his full mouth compressed with rage. Then he kicked him.

The dark eyes seemed to flinch, but the prone body was as inert as a bundle of rags. His teeth clamped hard on his disgust, Al'Kalyek watched as Ba'alekkt's booted foot struck his helpless prisoner again and again, venting his rage and fear and spite with each blow.

'If you do that too much, Imperial Majesty,' the sorcerer said, with deceptive mildness, 'the prisoner will not survive until his execution.'

'I'll take good care not to kill him,' said the Emperor. He stood, breathing hard, his eyes glowing with the joy of violence, and smiled down at the man who had tried to murder him. 'Awake, I see. Does he feel pain?'

'Undoubtedly,' said Al'Kalyek, although he knew that the khlar, in the amount he had administered, would dull the edge of the worst agony.

'Good. I have sent for Olkanno. He will make sure that this vermin's sufferings are exquisitely prolonged.' The Emperor stroked his chin, his eyes narrowed greedily. 'I have a mind to assist him. Will you also take part in the interrogations, old man?'

'As I have told you before, Imperial Majesty, my methods are different, though I believe no less effective.' The mage coughed. 'In fact, I have a favour to ask of you, if I may be so bold.'

'A favour? What favour?' Ba'alekkt stared at him suspiciously. 'Be warned – nothing will prevent this scum suffering the extreme penalty of my justice, exactly according to my orders. I will permit no mercy.'

'I am not requesting mercy, Imperial Majesty. I merely ask that I may be allowed to attempt to obtain the answers I seek before Olkanno gets to work. I am more likely to succeed, after all, while his mind is still comparatively clear of pain.'

'Very well,' said the Emperor at last. 'You have until tonight – if I can hold off the Spymaster for that long. The execution has been set for tomorrow, in the market-place of Tamat. And at sunrise the day after, we break camp and begin the invasion. My engineers are at this moment constructing a bridge of boats over the Kefirinn. I will be rowed across in my ceremonial barge, and set first foot on enemy soil. Once the army has crossed, we will follow the road, and come upon our foes before they expect it. I shall be relying on you, Al'Kalyek, to use your scrying bowl to give me the details of their movements and dispositions.'

'I will do my utmost to assist you, Imperial Majesty. Will you still require protection?'

Ba'alekkt looked down at the prisoner, and laughed contemptuously. 'No. Once he is dead, no one else will dare. You may use your skills to detect any malevolent mind that may approach me too closely. But this man and the Penyan bitch were undoubtedly the only dangers.' He glanced up, his face avid. '*Is* he the son of Ansaryon?'

'I do not know for certain, Imperial Majesty,' Al'Kalyek said at last, sure that the Emperor would not know he was lying. 'That is one of the things I wish to discover, before tonight.'

'Then make sure you do find out. If he is, I may keep him alive for a little longer, so that his father may taste the nature of my vengeance.' Ba'alekkt smiled, and his white, pointed canine teeth looked like fangs in the dim light. 'Perhaps he used his son to try to kill me. If that is so, then he will regret that the boy was ever born. I shall parade him, blinded and helpless, below the walls of Zithirian, before I attack.' He laughed softly, and the hair rose on Al'Kalyek's neck. 'I shall enjoy that. Will you, old man?'

'I shall take pleasure in anything that increases the glory of the Empire, Imperial Majesty.' The sorcerer did not betray the revulsion heaving behind his calm, deferential face. Ba'alekkt's vicious pleasure in cruelty had never before seemed so brutally obvious, even during the incident on Tekkt.

'Good,' said Ba'alekkt. 'Don't *you* fail me either, Al'Kalyek. I am relying on you to ensure the success of our glorious campaign against the north. And if anything should go wrong, I intend to hold you personally responsible.'

'I understand, Imperial Majesty.'

'I'm glad to hear it.' Ba'alekkt turned and dropped on one knee beside Bron. He drew his knife from the jewelled scabbard at his belt, and tested the point with his fingers. Then, his face intent, he stroked it lovingly down the length of the other man's arm. A trail of beaded blood bubbled up in its wake. Al'Kalyek found his nails clenched painfully into the palms of his hands, and tried to compose himself.

'Quite harmless now, isn't he,' Ba'alekkt said softly. 'This morning, *vermin*, I was at your mercy for a moment. Now, you are at mine. Do you fear me, vermin?'

The pale, cracked lips at last formed a difficult answer. 'Yes.'

'Good. You are right to fear me. I can cut you, like this, very gently. Or I can carve the Hawk of Empire on your ribs. I can flay the skin from your body, or cut off your manhood, or sever your fingers one by one, if I choose. I can put out your eyes, when I no longer wish you to see me. And you, with all your powers, are helpless, are you not?'

Again, the whispered assent.

'I can inflict agony in ways you have never dreamed, in all your most terrible nightmares. Later, I will come back – and then, I promise, I will make my mark on you. I will make you scream –

except that you will not be able to scream. I shall make you beg for mercy, but no one will hear you. I shall enjoy watching you, *vermin*. So will Olkanno – and beside him, I am only a crude amateur in the art of causing pain. He is already eagerly looking forward to the coming night. He is even now polishing and sharpening his instruments. If I, with my one knife, can do so much, what greater suffering can Olkanno inflict? My only regret is that the Penyan bitch will not be here to share it. No, I do not want to know where she is – yet. You may tell me later, when I ask you. Do you understand me, vermin? Tonight you will endure pain such as you never imagined. And tomorrow, soon, but not soon enough for you, you will die before all the people of Tamat, so that they may see what happens to murderers, and appreciate the awesome power of my Imperial justice. And the day after your death, vermin, my army marches on Minassa and Zithirian. Soon, their pale feeble citizens will be gathered within the shelter of our immortal civilization, to the greater glory and lustre of the Toktel'yan Empire.

'Do you understand me, scum? There is no escape, *no escape*, either for you or for your people.'

'No,' said the faint, frail voice. 'No escape.'

'Then I will see you again, tonight.' Ba'alekkt wiped his blood-stained knife on the prisoner's torn, dirty tunic, and stood, pushing it back in the scabbard. 'Goodbye, old man. I wish you joy of your questions. Do not be too hard on him – leave something for us!'

His mocking, contemptuous laughter indicated his real opinion of the Court Sorcerer. Sick with impotent rage and revulsion, Al'Kalyek watched the heavy tent flap drop behind Ba'alekkt's retreating back, and heard the clash of the guards' salute.

A voice fluttered inside his head, very weak but still stronger than when spoken aloud. *Al'Kalyek?*

Astonished, the old man turned, and saw Bron's dark, desperate eyes staring up at him. Sick and weary with anger and frustration and disgust, he sat down on the folding chair. *I am listening*, he said to the younger man's mind.

You said you were my friend. If you spoke the truth, if you have any spark of compassion within you, kill me now.

I cannot, said Al'Kalyek, with grief. *I have sworn never to take life. You know that.* He retreated a little, afraid of becoming overwhelmed by the terror and despair in Bron's mind. *Why can you still speak to me? The drug should suppress all sorcery.*

Kill me. Please.

Al'Kalyek could not bear to look him in the face. He turned his head away, shaken by the strength of his emotions. *I cannot. I beg of you, do not ask me again.*

For a long while, there was silence. The old sorcerer withdrew into himself, hastily erecting defences against a mind that could still, incredibly, link with his. He thought of the King of Zithirian, who was a man he greatly liked and respected, and who had done nothing to deserve Ba'alekkt's hatred. He remembered, long ago, that man, young, uncrowned, vowing to protect his son from all harm. And he knew, with terrible clarity, that if the Emperor knew the identity of his prisoner for certain, he would indeed carry out his threat to parade the mutilated living corpse of that son before the horrified gaze of his father and his people.

And he knew, too, that he could no longer compromise himself. He could not continue to stand aside, using his vows and his Art as an excuse to do nothing. He would probably die, but Olyak, he was sure, would be merciful to them both, for the Lord of Death, though terrible, was also fair. Did he not, after all, visit everyone in the end? And to this man, waiting helplessly for Ba'alekkt and Olkanno, the touch of the Lord of Death's cool fingers would be a kindness.

But oh, such a *waste*.

And as his mind framed the thought, Al'Kalyek saw how, perhaps, such a waste could be avoided.

It was dangerous, both for him and for Bron. But it was the only chance of survival that the young man would have. And maybe he himself, too, might escape death at Ba'alekkt's hands. That comforting dream of a peaceful retirement on his native island had been a pitiful delusion all along. The Emperor would keep him alive for as long as he needed him, but as soon as another like T'lekko made his appearance, Ba'alekkt would destroy Al' Kalyek as casually as an ordinary man would put down an old dog whose usefulness was past.

His mind made up, he turned and went out of the tent.

To Bron, the passage of time had become frighteningly erratic. Lying staring up at Ba'alekkt's handsome, sneering face, the moments had slithered past with hideous slowness. But when the Court Sorcerer had left him alone, it seemed no more than a few moments before he came back. It must have been much longer than that, because it was by then almost dark.

Darkness. The shroud of fear, of despair, of ugly deeds and nameless horrors. The time when Ba'alekkt had promised to return with Olkanno. And when he heard the guards' salute, with the remote and crystalline clarity of sounds on a winter mountainside, he thought it was the last nightmare, come to herald his death with agony past bearing.

He had wondered why he, the most powerful sorcerer in the known world, could not arrange his own death. Why could he not order his stubborn, oblivious heart to stop beating now?

Perhaps, if he had not been drugged, he might have succeeded. If he possessed the power to Heal himself, then he must also possess the opposing, balancing power of death. But the khlar still held him in thick, unyielding bonds of utter lethargy. As if this were some dreadful dream, he lay unable to move, hardly able to think, save that a small flicker of his self remained buried deep within the narcotic fog shrouding his mind.

His visitor was Al'Kalyek. Past bewilderment, Bron gazed up at him, and wondered hazily why he had returned. Where was Ba'alekkt? The dark was drawing in, and the wolves were gathering. Ayak must be licking his lips in gleeful anticipation.

He could not see the old man's face clearly, but his voice spoke sadly, gently in his mind. *Do not fear. I have something here that will help you.*

And from somewhere, Bron found a last spark of humour. *Nothing lethal, I hope.*

It will bring you oblivion, said Al'Kalyek, with quiet compassion. *Isn't that what you want?*

Yes. If Ba'alekkt intends to carry out his threats, then I want it more than anything. Through the fog, he tried to make sense of the expression on the old man's face, set in lines carved by the wisdom gathered over more than seventy years. *Why did you change your mind?*

Because despite the Four Rules, some things are more cruel than mere death. If I give you this, how can I possibly harm you, when such a terrible fate has been arranged for you? Drink this, Al'Kalyek said to Bron's soul, *and find what you seek.*

He knelt, and gently raised the younger man to a sitting position. Their eyes met, dark and knowing. Bron felt the warmth of the sorcerer's arm against the back of his head, and the touch of a cup against his lips.

Minassan, he said, wryly pointing out the irony. *How many potters will be left in Minassa, when Ba'alekkt has finished with them? He will destroy all that is civilized in the name of civilization, and never know why he is hated. Al'Kalyek?*

Yes? The old man paused in the act of tilting the cup.

If you have the chance, tell my father . . . tell him I tried to save them. Tell him I wished more than anything else that I had succeeded.

I will. The sorcerer smiled sadly. *This will not have been in vain, I promise you.*

I'm glad. Do it now.

The liquid was cool, and bitter. Bron swallowed it gratefully, denying futile regrets. Whatever happened hereafter in the world, his part in it was ended. He had done his best, but it had not been enough. And now, Zithirian and Minassa must stand alone, carrying a single fragile flame against the darkness.

Al'Kalyek saw his eyes close, the shallow breathing become slower and slower. Gently, he laid him back upon the rough hard ground. Then he tucked the empty vial of poison and the small, exquisite cup back into the hidden pocket in his robes, and sat on the chair, watching the still face grow as pale and set as Annako stone.

After a long while, he looked up. He could sense, as never before, the approaching malevolence of his Emperor. And he trembled, sick with fear: for the fate of the world might depend on the turn of the next few moments.

The soldiers saluted with a clash of bronze, and the force of what lay outside buffeted the old mage with shadowed wings. He made his face calm and his body still, and folded his hands, and bowed before Ba'alekkt.

'Well?' demanded the Emperor. 'Have you got your answers yet, old man?'

Behind him, the small rotund figure of Olkanno entered the tent. He was carrying an anonymous black leather bag, which chinked softly.

Al'Kalyek met the young man's eager hazel eyes with a sad and regretful sigh. 'Alas, I have not, Imperial Majesty. For the prisoner is dead.'

CHAPTER
TWENTY-FIVE

'It is true, Imperial Majesty.' Olkanno stood up, his chubby, normally cheerful face suffused with disappointment. 'He is growing cold, and I can feel neither pulse nor breath. I have cut his skin, and there is no blood. The prisoner is certainly dead.'

Ba'alekkt took several huge gulps of air. Al'Kalyek, confronting him, felt the power of his rage as a living thing, and gathered his strength for the breaking storm.

'Are you responsible for this?' demanded the Emperor. His greenish eyes, shadowed by the thick dark brows above them, seemed to contain a reddish glint, like a ravenous beast thirsting for blood. Al'Kalyek remembered the terrible Wolf-god, an aspect of Olyak, worshipped by the steppe tribes and in some of the more primitive and backward provinces of the Empire, and had to clench his fingers to prevent them making the sign against evil.

'I think the prisoner has killed himself,' he said quietly. 'Some sorcerers are supposed to know how to do it, but I did not believe it to be possible. Until today.'

'And you just sat there and watched him die?' Ba'alekkt's voice was dangerously soft. 'Why did you not call me, old man?'

'When I left him two or three hours ago, he was still alive,' said the sorcerer. 'But when I returned, he was dead. It was too late to do anything. My Healing powers are considerable, but I cannot restore life once it has fled. It would have been a waste of time to summon you, and I must admit to feeling considerable disappointment and regret – for he died before he could answer my questions.'

Ba'alekkt looked as if he would have liked to strike the old man. Al'Kalyek tensed, and Olkanno leapt to his feet. Then the Emperor turned abruptly away and kicked the corpse again and again, with furious strength.

'Imperial Majesty,' Olkanno said, with a deprecating cough. 'If I may be so bold, as to remind you of the dignity of your ancestors – '

Ba'alekkt stopped then, the reddish light still glinting in his eyes. Al'Kalyek glanced down at the sprawled, abused body on the ground, and thanked all the gods of Toktel'yi for the potion that had saved Bron from torture, and a terrible and agonizing death.

'Very well,' the Emperor said, his voice reluctant and resentful. 'But he will still hang in the market-place tomorrow, even dead as a dog, so that the world can spit on him, and witness my justice. And I shall order prayers to be said in every one of Olyak's Temples, throughout the Empire, demanding that his soul be immured in the lowest Halls, to endure eternal torment.' He swung round on Al'Kalyek. 'And do not think that I will forget this, old man. You are useful to me now, but soon the time will come when you are not. Then, believe me, you will regret that you ever crossed my path. And in the meantime, I shall be watching you!'

'As your Imperial Majesty wishes,' Al'Kalyek murmured, with deceptive humility, and bowed his white head. When he looked up, Ba'alekkt and Olkanno were gone.

It was over, for the moment. He was still alive, though he knew that it had been a near thing. If Olkanno had not been present to curb Ba'alekkt's rage, the Emperor might well have killed him with his bare hands. He didn't like or trust the Spymaster, whose influence over Ba'alekkt was downright sinister. But tonight, he suspected that he owed the little man his life.

Now that the danger was over, for the moment, he found himself trembling, and his knees felt as weak as a baby's. He sank down beside Bron's body, and arranged the untidy limbs into a more dignified pose. Then, he withdrew into prayer, invoking the gentle face of Olyak's twin, Kaylo the Life-giver, in whose name he had trained as a sorcerer more than fifty years previously, and to whose worship he had always turned in moments of crisis and despair.

At last, his equanimity restored, Al'Kalyek rose to his feet and gathered his robe around him. He felt extraordinarily tired. It must be after midnight: there were few sounds outside, although all around him nearly a hundred thousand men were sleeping.

Before he left the tent, he spared a last glance at the dead man. The dim light from the simple lantern, hanging from a hook on the central pole, lent the pale face a kindly illusion of life. Despite the livid bruises and the dark blotches of dried blood, he almost looked as if he were asleep.

With a last, silent invocation to Kaylo, Al'Kalyek walked out of the tent.

The guards had gone, and the smouldering fire in front of the entrance was the only sign of their previous presence.

The old sorcerer felt a sudden and absurd lightness of heart. He raised his own lantern high in his hand, and strode through the slumbering camp to his bed.

From the muffled screams and sobs emanating from the Imperial pavilion, Ba'alekkt had chosen to turn his anger and frustration on one of his concubines. Al'Kalyek knew better than to intervene, although the unfortunate girl would be lucky to survive the night at all, let alone unscathed. Once more he acknowledged the bitter, unpalatable truth. The Emperor of Tokte-l'yi was a deeply vicious man, depraved and dangerous to the point of madness. And he, Al'Kalyek, Court Sorcerer, lacked the moral courage to confront him.

He lay down on his couch, and tried to block the concubine's wails from his mind. Slowly, carefully, he gathered his strength, and let his spirit rise from his body. He hovered above the camp for a while, and then his mind travelled the short distance that he had just walked in reality, back to the small, unguarded tent where Bron lay.

He, of course, had not moved, though the wick in the oil-dish within the lantern had burned down more than a finger's length. Al'Kalyek surveyed the body for a moment, and then reached out with his power to touch the empty mind.

And the dark eyes opened.

He had hoped for it, but even so, Al'Kalyek could barely control his relief and delight. He looked at Bron's face, seeing the faint but unmistakable flush of life, returning. The dose was so difficult to get exactly right: a difference of one grain, one speck of any of its ingredients would have stopped Bron's heart. Instead, the potion had placed him in a strange state of suspended animation that was closer to death than to life. Like a hibernating animal, he had taken almost imperceptible breaths at very long intervals, and his pulse had slowed to less than a hundred beats in an hour.

The recipe was known to very few sorcerers, and because of its danger was rarely used. Despite this, he had judged it exactly: less, and it would not have worked at all; more, and it would have killed him. But it had served his purpose, making Bron appear dead for

long enough to convince Ba'alekkt and Olkanno. Now, the effect
was beginning to wear off, although the khlar which he had also
administered would take much longer to work through Bron's
system. And there were only a few hours of darkness left.

At this moment, as consciousness returned, Bron would have
no defences. Gently and reassuringly, Al'Kalyek spoke to his
mind.

Do not fear. You are not alone – my spirit is here with you.

He felt the younger man's bewilderment and confusion. *I died.
I know I died – I felt my heart falter – I was dead. Why am I alive
now?*

*I gave you a potion which induces the semblance of death.
Ba'alekkt and Olkanno think you are dead. They have gone.*

But I am not dead. The silent voice was still dazed and disorientated. *How – why – I don't understand. What are you going to do
with me?*

*Nothing. I am not here. Only my spirit is with you. I did not
want you to wake alone, not knowing what had happened to you.*

There was a long pause, while Bron struggled to make sense of
what Al'Kalyek had told him. The old sorcerer waited, outwardly
patient, while behind his defences his own mind screamed the
need for haste. If they found Bron was alive after all . . .

You promised me death, the young man said at last. *You
cheated me, as well as them.*

*No, I have not. I have given you the chance of escape. The
potion has worn off. The effects of the khlar are weakening too. You
should soon be able to move, to stand, to walk. The camp is asleep,
and I will guide you to safety, as far as I can. After that, your life is
in your own hands.*

He withdrew from Bron's mind, and his spirit watched, with a
strange mix of impatience and compassion, as the young man
discovered, by slow degrees, that his muscles could in fact once
more obey the commands of his brain – slowly and imperfectly,
true, but at least he was no longer completely helpless.

Do not make a sound, Al'Kalyek advised him. *The guards have
gone, the camp is silent, but that does not mean there are no ears to
hear you, nor eyes to see you.*

Bron, breathing in gasps, had struggled into a kneeling position. His face was fierce with concentration, a deep line between
his pale brows and his jaw tensed with effort. He grasped the
central pole of the tent and pulled himself upright.

Be careful, Al'Kalyek begged him. *Oh, be very careful. I have not taken all this trouble only to have you killed after all.*

He was rewarded by a brief, almost mischievous smile. *Don't worry, I won't squander your help, or your generosity. I just wish the tent would keep still –*

A voice called sharply outside. Bron froze, clinging to the pole, his eyes suddenly wide with shock.

DO something, Al'Kalyek cried frantically. *Anything –*

It was too late. The entrance flap was abruptly yanked aside and one of Ba'alekkt's slaves pushed into the tent.

For a few short but everlasting heartbeats, the two men stared at one another. Then the slave leapt forward.

Bron pulled the lantern from its hook above him, and hurled it full into the other man's face. As he fell, shouting, in a flare of burning oil, Bron stumbled past him and out into the cool night.

His one thought was to get away. He reeled blindly through the darkness, down the lanes of tents, twisting and turning in obedience to the voice inside his head. *Left here – right now – left again.*

Behind him, he heard screams, and the sudden roar of flames. Within the canvas walls, men were beginning to be woken by the noise. Someone ran past, almost knocking him over, but he struggled on, fear overcoming his weakened limbs and the savage ache in his ribs every time he breathed.

Something dark loomed up in front of him. He tripped over an obstacle and crashed heavily to the ground with a gasp of pain. He could not get up, he could not go on. Exhausted, he lay breathing heavily, while behind him the distant sounds of a considerable disturbance rose and fell in the night.

Get up. I said, GET UP!

I can't. It isn't possible.

If you don't get up, they'll find you. If that slave dies in the fire, they might think it was you. If they find you here, Ba'alekkt and Olkanno will flay you alive and then take you apart, piece by piece, before you die. Do you want that to happen to you? Now get UP.

Somehow, from some unknown source within his soul, Bron found the strength. He had fallen into a ditch marking the boundary of an orchard or a grove of trees. He dragged himself to his feet using a low branch, and stood, swaying, on the edge of freedom.

I can't stay with you much longer, Al'Kalyek warned him. *I*

*don't possess your power. You're almost beyond my range. But
keep moving for as long as you can. On the other side of the
trees there are fields and orchards, and farms, with barns and
outbuildings. The Kefirinn lies beyond them, three miles away to
the north. Hide yourself somewhere, until your power returns. It
will take a day or so – khlar, in the form I gave to you, is a very
potent drug. But at least you can move, you can walk, you can even
run. Now go, GO, before they find you!*

For the rest of his life, whether it might be measured in hours,
or days, or years, Bron would remember this flight, worse than any
nightmare. Behind him, the agonizing death awaiting him if he
was caught alive. Around him, the shrouding darkness, hiding a
wilderness of roots, plants, stones, branches, all blocking his path.
And ahead, the peril of the future.

He came to the other side of the orchard. The field beyond was
sown with young wheat, like grass in the gloom. There was no
moon, only the shivering brilliance of the summer stars. Here they
shone in the figures of the north, remembered from his childhood.
And although they gave him so little light, he found their impersonal familiarity extraordinarily comforting, as though he were
somehow closer to home. He stared up at them for a long, long
moment, conserving what was left of his strength, and then walked
onwards.

Good, said the distant voice of Al'Kalyek inside his skull.
*Don't stop until you can go no further. They do not yet know that
you have escaped, and they do not suspect that I helped you. Just
KEEP WALKING!*

I will, Bron said, although the simple act of putting one foot in
front of the other was now almost more than he could manage. He
could feel the old sorcerer leaving him as he stumbled down the
gently sloping field. *Goodbye*, said Al'Kalyek. *And may the Lord
of Life grant you his blessings.*

Goodbye, Bron answered. *And thank you for helping me.*

He was alone. He glanced back, seeing the dark lumpy shapes
of the trees, black against a faint glow in the sky. In front of him,
many fields distant, was the river, and on the low hill, a couple of
miles away to his right, lay Tamat.

Despite his exhaustion, some sense was beginning to return to
his fuddled mind. *Keep going*, he told himself. *Find somewhere
to hide, somewhere safe, before it gets light.*

In the dark, with his ordinary senses confused and disorien-

tated, and his powers of sorcery completely vanished, that was far
easier said than done. A barking dog alerted him to a cluster of
farm buildings, a few hundred paces ahead. He stumbled across
the fields, falling frequently on the uneven ground, and finding it
increasingly hard to get up again. His mind narrowed to one
obstinate spark of determination. *Keep going. Get as far away
from the camp as you can. And above all, find somewhere to hide
before sunrise.*

To the east, beyond Tamat, the sky was already beginning to
grow pale. Bron realized that he could see what lay in front of him:
another field, bordered by a deep, water-filled ditch that was
simultaneously boundary and irrigation channel. Beyond it lay
an orchard, neatly planted with young trees, perhaps almond
or apricot. And beyond them, glimpsed through the tangle of
branches, the broad deep channel of the Kefirinn.

He waded across the ditch. The water was cold and muddy,
and came up to his waist in the middle. The field stretched away in
front of him, bare, rutted, liberally sprinkled with dung. A pungent
smell assaulted his nostrils, and he saw in the distance a cluster of
squat, pale animals staring at him in alarmed surprise.

There was a small shelter in the far corner of the field, crudely
made out of roughly mortared rubble, with brushwood piled on
top. It wasn't exactly the most salubrious hiding-place, but at this
extremity of need, it was as welcome as a feather bed in a palace.
Bron staggered the last few paces and fell on his knees beside his
unlikely refuge.

A curious snout emerged, grunting. Then the pig squealed in
panic and dived out of the sty, almost knocking him over. Bron
crawled inside. There was plenty of straw, filthy and stinking, but
softer than the hard ground. And surely, in a hundred lifetimes, no
one would ever think of looking for him here.

Almost before relief overwhelmed him, he was asleep.

'No one can say for certain how the fire started, Imperial Majesty.
But it seems most likely that the lantern fell.'

'So you say.' Ba'alekkt stared at the smoking pile of ash which
was all that remained of the tent housing the body of the man who
had tried to kill him. The corpse was still there, hideously charred
beyond all recognition, so intense had been the flames. After
one glance at the blackened, grinning skull, he had turned away,

disgusted by his own unexpected squeamishness. He had thought himself immune to such horrors, and he had certainly enjoyed viewing far worse sights on Penya. But for some bizarre and unfathomable reason, he could not gaze with pleasure on the incinerated remnants of a man whom he had intended to torture to death.

'What shall we do with it, Imperial Majesty?'

'I don't know,' said Ba'alekkt nastily. 'Use it for charcoal?'

Olkanno was quite accustomed to the unpleasant sneer in his Emperor's voice. He said calmly, 'We can hardly hang it up now, in that state.'

'Why not? I want his body displayed to the people. I want everyone to see that he is dead, no matter how he died or what he looks like now. Is the gibbet erected yet?'

'Yes, it is, Imperial Majesty.'

'Then there will be no change in our plans. You hear me? And I shall be there, to see it done.'

'Of course, Imperial Majesty.' Olkanno bowed low as Ba'alekkt turned and strode away, the soldiers of his Guard surrounding him like a protective shell.

Free of the Emperor's unsettling presence, the Spymaster stirred the dry ash with his foot, frowning. Something was not quite right. Certainly the lantern could have fallen of its own accord – after all, loaded hooks or nails were often pulled out or broken off by the weight of their burden. But it was not likely. Not as likely as someone starting the fire deliberately.

But why? Why go to the trouble and risk of burning a corpse beyond recognition?

Beyond recognition. Olkanno's precise, devious, logical mind, the mind that had made him such an excellent Spymaster, began to assess the implications. He walked round the charred tent to get a better view of the body. That horrible, twisted carcass could have been anyone, young or old, male or female, Northerner or Toktel'yan.

Olkanno, who had never felt squeamish in his life, stood for a long time staring intently down at the remains, while his brain worked out various avenues of enquiry. For the moment, it would be best to say nothing of his suspicions until he was absolutely sure. Ba'alekkt's terrifying rage was easily roused at present, and he had no wish to receive the kind of summary punishment that had ended T'lekko's career so abruptly.

He watched as the body was loaded on to a cart and taken away to the gibbet in Tamat. Then he turned, and went in search of his agents.

Voices woke Bron. For a moment, his sleep-clogged brain struggling to wakefulness, he had no idea of where, even who, he was.

And then he remembered.

It took every scrap of his self-control to force himself to lie still, hands clenched in the dirty straw, and listen to the sounds outside.

Snorting pigs. Buckets clanging against something metal. Two people debating, in the almost incomprehensible dialect of Tamat, which of the yearling sows they would sell to old Samien.

So he hadn't been discovered, yet, although he soon would be if the pig-owners decided to clean out their shelter. He waited, tense and apprehensive, until the voices died away into the distance, and he was certain that he was safe, for the moment.

Gingerly, Bron sat up, ducking his head to avoid the low brushwood roof. At least there were no pigs sharing this dubious accommodation. Like most animals, they were probably terrified of the power they sensed within him.

He peered outside, trying to assess the time of day. The sun was high in the south, so it was probably around noon. Inside the shelter, the air was hot and foul, but he turned back into it. There could be more people about, and he had no wish to be discovered. He must wait for darkness before leaving his sanctuary.

He lay back upon the straw, assessing his mental and physical condition with the clear logic which his father had taught him. His mind seemed free at last of the clouding effects of the khlar, and his muscles moved, albeit stiffly and painfully, at his command. Perhaps the hours of sleep had enabled his abused body to expel the remnants of the drug from his system.

But his ribs still hurt with every breath, and there was a deeper, ominous pain within. He probed each bone carefully. Several were indeed broken, there was extensive bruising, and his abdomen felt very tender. In addition, there was a big, crusted lump on the back of his head, and a variety of other cuts, bruises, grazes and scratches acquired during his flight the previous night. None of these were particularly serious, but he must be a terrifying sight.

It was yet another reason to stay here until dark. First, he must plan his strategy: then, he would try to sleep.

Methodically, Bron began to review the various options. He could stay near Tamat, risking discovery, and try once more to kill Ba'alekkt. Or he could abandon that idea altogether, and go north, to help Ansaryon in the struggle to come. He didn't think that he would be able to Transport himself: it required enormous effort, and he knew that the power within him was still weak, and desperately in need of rest and recovery. A few days should be enough, but until then he would have to travel in the conventional manner, like everyone else.

It was a very tempting thought. His heart yearned for the cool, balanced freedoms of Minassa and Zithirian, for winter and summer, ice and sun. There was poverty and injustice in the north, but no slavery and no torture. And he had had enough, and more than enough, of the tainted civilization and corrupt brutality of Toktel'yi.

In his mind, he conjured up an image of the map of the known world which he had studied in Zithirian. He found Tamat, and the red dotted line representing the border of the Empire. Since 'Strekkell, it had followed the Kefirinn, but twenty miles or so west of Tamat the river turned north, and the boundary diverged from it, continuing as a banked ditch striding westward over a hundred miles along the edge of the steppes to Lake Bakkil. He didn't even have to cross the river to leave the Empire. This time tomorrow he could be safe.

He forced his mind to examine the alternatives to that enticing prospect. If he stayed, he risked discovery, and they wouldn't give him a second chance. He would be slaughtered out of hand, Al'Kalyek would probably be executed too, and the Imperial armies would overrun Minassa and Zithirian, burning, killing, destroying. And those who survived it would be assimilated into the gross belly of Toktel'yi, forced to submit to their brutal conquerors and to follow customs and practices that were alien and abhorrent. Tamat, proudly independent less than two hundred years ago, was now just another province of the Empire. He thought of Penya, and Mallaso, and knew that he could not risk his own city, his own family, suffering the same dreadful fate.

Too much hung in the balance. The sanest, safest choice was to go home, and link his sorcery to his father's. Together, they might be able to defeat Ba'alekkt's forces, even if they failed to kill the Emperor himself.

By returning to Zithirian, he would concede the abject failure of his original stratagem. But he was beginning to understand that Sé Mo-Tarmé had been at least partly right. He *was* arrogant, and his pride was dangerous, both to himself and to those around him. Once the Wolf had been driven out, he had thought he would become all-powerful. And now he had been taught a bitter and humiliating lesson. His sorcery was certainly strong, stronger than any other's. But he could be overcome, even by a common soldier wielding a club. He could suffer pain, and grief, and ignominious defeat. He was not immortal. And now, with the fate of his native land depending on his survival, was not the time to take risks.

The decision made, he turned his attention to his injuries. As the hot midsummer sun beat down on the shelter, and the pigs rooted or wallowed outside, he concentrated on trying to Heal the worst of them. Once, as a boy, he had mended his broken arm. Now, he found that mending four fractured ribs, not to mention the more serious internal damage, required a degree of extended effort that he could not sustain.

At last, pouring sweat and gasping with pain and exhaustion, he abandoned the attempt. More than anything else, he needed rest, and Healing would have to wait until he was strong enough to try again. And he must leave the shelter soon, and find water, or he wouldn't be able to move at all.

Much later, the pig-owners returned, disturbing his sleep as they attempted to catch the sow they wanted to sell. Several times, hog and pursuers came close to his refuge, and Bron crouched in the darkest corner, ready to conceal himself with sorcery if he could find the strength, with straw if he could not. At last, however, the animal was trapped in another corner of the field, just out of his line of vision, and amid furious squeals was roped and carried away.

By then, it was almost sunset. The birds in the almond orchard by the river began to settle for the night, with soft calls and sudden outbursts of astonishingly lovely song. Bron waited until all sounds had dwindled into darkness, and then crawled out of the sty.

Its legitimate occupants were busy with a pile of rotting vegetables, dumped at the entrance to the field. His mouth felt as dry as ashes: if anyone spoke to him, he wouldn't be able to respond with more than a croak.

The cool, stagnant water in the boundary ditch did much to
revive him. After several eager mouthfuls, Bron immersed himself
in it, ignoring the pain from his wounds. It was probably filthy, but
at this moment he didn't care. Tonight, if only he could walk far
enough, he would be free.

It was difficult to haul himself out of the ditch, but he managed
it after a struggle on the smooth, slippery bank. Suddenly light-
hearted, and light-headed, he waved farewell to the pigs, now free
of the disturbing presence that had occupied their shelter all day,
and began to make his way through the orchard that lay between
him and the Kefirinn.

He stood for a short time on the bank, looking at the wide
shining stream of water. Beyond lay the dark hills of Minassa, and
freedom, but he knew he would not be able to swim across in his
present state: here, the Kefirinn was at least half a mile wide. He
would have to walk to the border.

There was a crescent moon sailing high in the south-west, and
it gave him enough light to see the track meandering along beside
the river, linking the small farming and fishing settlements surrounding Tamat, each one centred on a rich man's villa. There
would be a dozen or more to pass before he reached safety, with
the risk of capture very high if he were careless.

With so much at stake, he had no intention of being foolhardy.
But he had not gone very far before he realized that his physical
strength was unequal to the task he had set himself. He felt
increasingly light-headed, and his mind was beginning to wander.
Once, he fell into an irrigation ditch, and sat in the water for
several moments, laughing helplessly, with no clear idea of how
he'd come to be there.

Desperately, Bron gripped his wayward mind and shook it into
temporary obedience. At this rate, he wouldn't manage five miles,
let alone twenty. He forced himself upright, and continued his
slow, erratic progress along the track. Ahead of him, the moon
sank towards its horizon on the rim of the distant steppe, and
to his right the Kefirinn, linking the cities together amidst the
wilderness, rolled endlessly down from the northern mountains
nearly five hundred miles away beyond the edge of the world.

A dog barked. Bron realized belatedly that a complex of
buildings lay down a track to his left, only a couple of hundred
paces distant. He saw a sudden light, heard questioning voices,
and stumbled on.

Behind him, he heard the sound of hooves, faint at first but closing with frightening speed. He threw himself into the undergrowth at the side of the road, and lay prone, still, tense. Several horses galloped past, one rider carrying a lantern on a short pole. They must be soldiers, for who else would travel so fast, so late, in this quiet and peaceful extremity of the Empire?

Bron realized that he did not know if the border was guarded. There was no use worrying about it now: time for that when he reached it. If he reached it. And he was too weak and exhausted to carry on much further tonight. He must find another refuge, preferably one more comfortable than the pigsty, and lie up during the day to rest.

But most farm buildings were part of a settlement, unsafe hiding places which would be frequently visited, and haunted by dogs. He couldn't risk it. He went on, toiling through the soft warmth of the midsummer night, watching the moon's descent. When it had set, he would find somewhere.

There was nothing. He'd seen a derelict and isolated barn some way back, when he had still assumed that he would be able to reach the border before daybreak. Since then, the only places he had noticed had been too close to habitation. And if he didn't stop soon, he would collapse.

At the moment when he knew he could go no further, he saw another grove of trees, to his left. There might be some shelter and concealment there. He pushed his way between the trunks, tripped and fell. It seemed futile even to try to get up again. The herbage beneath him was dry, and almost comfortable. He lay exactly as he had fallen, and could not prevent the sudden assault of unconsciousness.

CHAPTER
TWENTY-SIX

The border post at the end of the Empire, eighteen Toktel'yan miles west of Tamat, was not a very busy crossing-point. Most people travelling to and from the northern cities went by river-boat, or used the road that ran more or less straight from Tamat to Minassa, a much shorter route than the lazy meanderings of the Kefirinn through its broad flood-plain. A few of the intrepid merchants who traded with the steppe tribes used this insignificant track, as did the farmers who lived along it. In any other country of the known world no one would have bothered to guard such a place, for sometimes many days went by without a single traveller in either direction. But this was the Toktel'yan Empire, and its rulers liked to keep a check on all the comings and goings of its citizens and visitors, however trivial. So a hut was built, and a small guard installed of four men from the Tamat garrison. They were usually the youngest, the most inexperienced or the most unpopular, and they served there for a month at a time before being relieved.

Olkanno had told no one about his suspicions, save for his few most trusted agents. If the Emperor didn't know of the possibility that his attacker had somehow survived, failure to find the man would not endanger the Spymaster. And if he did manage to recapture the prisoner, then he could present him to Ba'alekkt with a fine flourish, and earn himself even higher approval.

But he would have to hurry. Tomorrow, the army would begin crossing the Kefirinn. The bridge of boats was complete, although the task of the engineers building it had been made very much more difficult by the strict instruction that they were not to set foot on dry land on the Minassan side. To the Emperor alone must fall the supreme honour of making the first step of conquest on foreign soil. Unlike his troops, however, he would not have to scramble across the makeshift and hazardous bridge, risking both his dignity and his safety. The Imperial barge had been brought up from Toktel'yi for the purpose, and he would be rowed over the Kefirinn in state to inaugurate the invasion.

So far, all the preparations had gone smoothly. General Sekkenet had thought of everything, and the two hundred thousand men under his command were well-trained and superbly equipped, brought to a peak of fighting fitness by long hours of drilling, and eager for battle. From what Olkanno's spies had told him, the Minassans had panicked: the small town nearest to Tamat was deserted, its people fled northwards. For the present, the invasion would be unopposed, to Sekkenet's evident disappointment.

Olkanno was not disappointed. He disliked the uncontrollable nature of warfare, but he recognized that it was an unfortunately necessary evil, to be avoided where possible. He much preferred the subtler and more devious methods of spying, informing and torture. He had spent many years patiently building up his web of intelligence agents throughout the Empire and beyond, and he had cultivated Ba'alekkt's favour for many years, while he was still Emperor-in-Waiting. But his master had told him that during the invasion, Sekkenet's scouts would provide the army with essential information. Instead of staying with the Emperor, Olkanno had been ordered to return to Toktel'yi as soon as the army had crossed the Kefirinn, and govern the Empire while Ba'alekkt was on campaign.

It was a great honour, but Olkanno had protested strongly, well aware that in his absence his master might begin to take more notice of Sekkenet and Al'Kalyek. He did not trust either of them, for he sensed their dislike of the Emperor. But Ba'alekkt had insisted, softening his order with flattering words. 'How can the Empire possibly function without you, Olkanno? You know everything about everyone!'

Olkanno was immune to flattery: he was an exact judge of his own worth and abilities. He had agreed to go back to the capital only because he had no choice: if he caught the assassin, though, Ba'alekkt might change his mind. And so, the morning after the fire in the prison tent, the Spymaster had sent out his most trusted men, to make very discreet enquiries in and around the camp.

They returned with news of considerable interest. One of the Emperor's menials had disappeared during the night. There was no way of proving that the horrible remains swinging on a gibbet in Tamat market place were in fact those of the missing slave, but the information crystallized his suspicions into certainty. He told the soldiers guarding the quayside to keep a special watch for anyone trying to cross the river. He sent orders to all the border posts within thirty miles of Tamat, telling them to hold everyone leaving the Empire for questioning. And he instructed his two best agents to lead fast, mounted patrols along the Kefirinn, one upstream and one down.

All this activity was easily concealed from Ba'alekkt, who took little interest in the constant comings and goings in the camp and in Tamat. Olkanno, operating from a wing of the Governor's residence in the city, felt himself safe. The Emperor need never know the possible identity of that charred corpse. He hadn't even missed the slave, one amongst so many. And if the prisoner was found, Olkanno knew where he could most profitably place the blame for his escape.

He sat in the residence, at the centre of his elaborate web, and waited with eager certainty for the confirmation of his suspicions.

The four men on duty at the border post known in official documents as Westernmost Kefirinn, were nearly at the end of their month of duty, and bored rigid by the tedium. When Olkanno's upstream search party arrived, well after dark, the barrier was drawn across the weedy, narrow track beside the river, and its guards were sitting round a table in their hut, engaged in a cut-throat game of dice, and lubricated by an illicit jar of wine purchased from a nearby farm.

They hadn't seen anyone else for days, and Arkun, leader of the patrol, was highly amused by their white, horrified faces and their desperate attempts to hide the evidence that they had been drinking on duty, an offence punishable by death. When they'd calmed down and sobered up, he issued his instructions, and told them to get on with it.

'Now?' quavered the guards' spokesman, a spotty and under-nourished youth who looked marginally less feeble-minded than the other three. 'But it's the middle of the night!'

'Exactly. That's when I'd be on the move, if I didn't want anyone to find me. Now get going, and make sure your search is thorough, or I'll report you to your superior officer. Meet back here after dawn if we don't find him. Got any dogs?'

The boy's pimply jaw dropped even further. '*Dogs?*'

'Yes, dogs. Four legs, long tail, sharp teeth, loud bark. Good at sniffing out vermin. Know where I can find some?'

'They've got half a dozen hounds in the farm just down the road, sir,' said the smallest guard, whose voice had hardly broken.

'Good. I'll go there first. And you do *exactly* as I've ordered, or the Spymaster will personally flay your skin very slowly from your miserable carcasses – *before* you die. Understand?'

They nodded, gulping. Taking good care to hide his smile from them, Arkun strode out, mounted his tired horse, and with his four minions behind him, rode off to the farm with the dogs.

Their owner was not best pleased to be summoned from his bed in the middle of the night, but at the first mention of the Spymaster's name his indignant protests dried up in his throat, and he agreed to the hire of himself, his eldest son and his dogs in the urgent business of the Emperor. His wife watched in bemused terror, clutching a bag of silver half-Imperials, as her husband and son rode away bouncing on the bony back of the plough-mule, with their five hounds, used for hunting deer and other quarry in the steppe foothills over the border, trotting eagerly behind.

As Arkun had hoped, the dogs had been trained to search for any game. The farmer assured him that they would find a hidden man as readily and efficiently as an antelope or a stag, and certainly the ill-assorted hounds, variously coloured and shaped, were questing keenly through the marshy scrub between the road and the river. A big long-tailed bird exploded out of the bushes with a frantic squawk, and Arkun could hear other creatures fleeing through the undergrowth. He said, 'Do they give tongue?'

'Only when they've captured their quarry, sir,' said the farmer hastily. 'We don't want them to warn other game.'

Arkun thought that even silent, the pack's over-enthusiastic methods had probably warned every man, animal and bird for miles around. But Olkanno had told him that the escaped prisoner was likely to be sick or hurt, and unable to move very fast. If he was anywhere along the river, between the border and Tamat, the dogs would surely find him.

They had searched for more than ten miles, and it was nearly sunrise, when a sudden howl from a clump of trees near the road alerted the hunters. The farmer's son, a stout boy almost the age for conscription, gave a tired but jubilant cry. 'They've found something! Over there!'

Arkun drew his sword and dismounted. His companions did the same. The prudent farmer stayed with the horses, holding their reins, while the boy led the patrol towards the excited dogs.

All five of them were standing in a circle, several feet away from something lying beneath a tree. Arkun saw with some unease that each animal's hackles were raised, their tails stiff and their fangs bared. Olkanno had warned him to be careful, as the prisoner might be dangerous, but he had taken little notice. Now, the hounds' reaction forced him to revise his opinion. He moved cautiously forward, his sword at the ready, until he was level with the animals.

The man on the ground was quite still. Arkun assessed his condition rapidly. Bloodstained, filthy, ragged, he did not look dangerous: indeed, he probably wasn't even alive.

'Is he dead, sir?' asked the boy, peering curiously past him.

'I don't know. Get back, just in case,' Arkun said sharply, and pushed him out of the way. Very cautiously, he advanced until he stood over the prone man. There was no movement. He prodded the body gently with the point of his sword. No reaction. He knelt, placed his hand on the fugitive's neck, and felt for a pulse.

It was there, faint and fast, and the skin was fever-hot. 'He's not dead,' Arkun said, sitting back on his heels. 'But he's sick. He'll be no danger.'

Swiftly and efficiently, he issued his orders. One man rode off to Olkanno, ten miles away in Tamat, with the good news. The farmer, his son and hounds were despatched back to their home, with instructions to tell the border guards to call off their search. Arkun and his remaining men bound their prisoner securely with rope brought for the purpose, and commandeered a cart from the nearest farm, for none of the horses would consent to carry the man on their backs.

Well satisfied with his efforts, Arkun began the journey back. By now, the sun had risen above the city on its distant hill, but they should manage to return before the Emperor crossed the river. And then he himself, already high in Olkanno's favour, would rise still further – and come to the notice of His Imperial Majesty as well. For a man of humble origins, with fierce ambitions, it would be a splendid achievement.

The horse between the shafts trotted briskly, trying to escape from the alarming odour of sorcery in the cart behind it. To Arkun's profound relief, the prisoner was still unconscious. Even seriously ill and trussed up as tight as a roasting pig, sorcerers could still be dangerous. He rode close to the cart, keeping a watchful eye on the man, though his own horse kept trying to sidle away from it.

At last they reached the West Gate of the city. The men on guard there knew who Arkun was, and waved him straight through without the usual request for papers and information. And as he emerged from the shadow underneath the archway, one of

Olkanno's lesser messengers ran up to him, and made a quick, furtive sign of obeisance.

It wasn't necessary now, but this man evidently had secrecy sunk into his bones. In a hasty whisper, he informed Arkun that Olkanno was waiting for him down on the quayside, where the Emperor would soon make his ceremonial crossing. Time was exceedingly short.

Unfortunately, everyone in Tamat, from new-born babies to trembling old grandsires, had come out to see the ceremonial launch of the glorious conquest of the northern cities, and Arkun had to force himself, his men and the cart with its precious burden through the seething crowds. They made way reluctantly when he invoked the Emperor's name, and he cursed their slowness loudly, in every language spoken within the Empire. If he could present his captive to Ba'alekkt and Olkanno in this very public situation, then his future was assured. In the fullness of time, he might even become Spymaster himself.

At last, when he feared it was already too late, the thickest throng swallowed them up and then spat them out into the broad open space of the quayside. Soldiers were keeping the spectators well away from the Emperor's sacred person, but Olkanno's messenger had already warned them of Arkun's arrival, and they waved him through. 'His Imperial Majesty is waiting for you – hurry, hurry, he grows impatient!'

And there, across fifty paces of stone-paved dockside, stood the sturdy figure of the Emperor of Toktel'yi. He had evidently just been blessed by the priests of Olyak, god of war and death, for their customary garland of blood-red flowers had been placed around his neck. He wore the fabulously expensive steel armour that only Emperors could afford, polished so brightly that the sun was reflected dazzlingly into Arkun's eyes.

Behind him, the crowd had fallen suddenly silent, aware that something unusual was about to happen. Very conscious of being the centre of attention, the agent led his patrol and the cart up to the Emperor.

Olkanno stood next to Ba'alekkt, a smirk of supreme satisfaction around his full red mouth. But the face of the Court Sorcerer Al'Kalyek, on the Emperor's other side, was set in lines as hard as black marble.

As the cart halted, the prisoner inside it stirred slightly. Arkun saluted uneasily, dismounted and made full ceremonial obeisance to his master, hands and head touching the ground.

'I understand from Olkanno here that you have a surprise gift for me,' said Ba'alekkt. 'You may rise.'

Arkun obeyed. Beneath the tall, plumed conical helmet, the Emperor's face looked as fiercely eager as a hawk's, and his eyes glittered with wild malice. Suppressing a twinge of disquiet, the agent said formally, 'I do indeed, Imperial Majesty. He is in the cart.'

'*He?*' Ba'alekkt stared at him. 'Who is he? Explain.'

'No need for explanation, Imperial Majesty,' said Olkanno smoothly. 'Just a look will suffice.'

The Emperor pushed past Arkun, his plate armour clanking with each vigorous stride. He gave a sharp exclamation and whipped round, his finger stabbing at the Court Sorcerer. 'What is the meaning of this? You lied to me – you told me he was dead!'

Al'Kalyek's face registered only bewilderment. 'Who? Who is it, Imperial Majesty?'

Ba'alekkt marched up to him, his brown face contorted with fury. 'The man who tried to kill me, you old fool! The man you told me was dead! The man who's supposed to be hanging on the gibbet in the market place – and if he isn't, who is? Tell me, traitor, before I rip your heart out with my own hands!'

The sorcerer stared at him in horror. 'But he *was* dead – I examined him myself, on my mother's tomb I would swear he was dead.' He added pointedly, 'Olkanno thought he was dead too.'

'The prisoner is a sorcerer,' said the Spymaster quickly. 'Counterfeiting death must be easy for a man with such power – and easy, too, to deceive those who know nothing of magic. But you, Al'Kalyek, should not have been taken in.'

'He was dead,' the Court Sorcerer repeated calmly. 'He had no breath and no pulse, and he was cold. You saw that for yourself, Olkanno. And I know of no ordinary sorcery that could produce such an effect.'

'But he is no ordinary sorcerer, is he?' The Spymaster glanced at the Emperor's livid face, and added triumphantly, 'He is the son of the King of Zithirian – as you very well know, Al'Kalyek!'

'I had suspected it,' said the old man.

'*Suspected* it!' Ba'alekkt's voice rose to a wild roar of fury. 'You told me you did not know!'

'I did not know for sure. I have no idea how my friend Olkanno can be so certain.'

'I have reliable information from an agent who saw him in Kerenth,' said the Spymaster smugly.

'Is that the truth?' Ba'alekkt demanded.

'Yes, Imperial Majesty, of course it is.'

'Ah.' The Emperor's sudden smile was extremely unpleasant. 'Then I will not have him killed here and now. Put him in my barge.'

'But, Imperial Majesty—' Olkanno began.

'I said, *put him in the barge!* Are you deaf! I want him where I can see him – and I want you at hand too, old man, in case he wakes.'

'I am always ready to be of service to you, Imperial Majesty,' Al'Kalyek murmured deferentially.

'I need you to keep *that* in check.' Ba'alekkt's steel-clad arm gestured savagely at the cart. 'Later – later, I have other plans.'

Arkun saw the murderous expression in his eyes, and had no doubt what those plans would involve. It was unwise, he thought, for the Emperor to make his contempt and hatred for the Court Sorcerer so obvious. It would do nothing to ensure Al'Kalyek's continued loyalty and obedience: indeed, it might well have the opposite effect. And mages made dangerous enemies.

But he was only a humble agent, though a very good one, and so he kept his opinions to himself. Obeying the Emperor's orders, he and his men dragged the prisoner from the cart. His skin was burning hot, and his mouth cracked and dry. Arkun felt a surprising twinge of pity as the sick man was hauled over to the edge of the quay, and dropped unceremoniously into the bottom of the Imperial barge, between the rowers' benches and the heavily fringed and embroidered canopy under which Ba'alekkt and his chief ministers would sit.

The shock of the fall jolted Bron back to full consciousness. He had been vaguely aware of his surroundings for some time, but the sudden pain shooting through his abused body was too sharp to be ignored. He drew several deep, shuddering breaths, trying to make sense of what had happened to him. He remembered a long ride in some vehicle, perhaps a cart. He had heard voices, amongst them Al'Kalyek and Olkanno. And he had recognized, with horror, the unmistakable loud and vicious tones of the Emperor himself.

He had failed to escape. They had found him, and brought him back. He was tied up so tight that he could not move, and fever raged within him, disordering his wits and making any use of sorcery impossible. In vain, he tried to calm his overwhelming feeling of panic and despair.

'Here.' A man spoke suddenly. 'Have a sip of this.'

A hand propped up his head, and water touched his dry, swollen lips and trickled, blissfully cool, down his parched throat.

He drank greedily at first and then more slowly, savouring the taste and sensation, until at last his thirst was satisfied.

'Lord of Life, you needed that,' said his benefactor.

Bron opened his eyes. It was difficult to see clearly against the blazing blue of the sky, but he managed to discern a strong, hawk-nosed face, framed in light red hair like a Fabrizian pirate's. 'I did,' he said, in a hoarse whisper. 'Thank you.'

'Don't thank me – I'm the one who brought you back,' said Arkun brusquely. 'But it's not every day I have the chance to help a King's son.'

'Why?'

'Why did I help you? Unlike my master, I don't like inflicting pain, whatever you've done.'

He rose to his feet, the water-bottle in his hand, and Bron realized that whatever he was lying on was rocking gently. He said, 'Where is this?'

'You're on the Imperial barge. The Emperor himself is taking charge of you – and I wouldn't be in your skin for all the gold in Zithirian,' said the red-haired man. 'Not that you'll keep your skin for very long, I suspect. Farewell, assassin.'

He was gone, and the sun glared down. Bron closed his eyes again, feeling the boat beneath him move as Arkun got off. Then a huge roar of acclaim burst suddenly into the air, interwoven with a shrill brazen fanfare of trumpets.

Ba'alekkt must be coming. He waited, trying to think, to plan, to fight the fogs of pain and fear and fever threatening to engulf him entirely. They knew who he was. And so the Emperor would surely now carry out his threat, and keep him alive until he could be paraded in front of his father, his step-mother, his brothers and sisters, and Kefiri –

And he knew what would be done to him, to emphasize the point.

Sick, terrified, he contemplated torture, mutilation, blinding. He could not let that happen to him, nor allow himself to become a pathetic bargaining counter to satisfy Ba'alekkt's warped and malevolent lust for vengeance. He would rather die.

And then the solution burst into his desperate mind, with all the searing clarity of a lightning bolt.

The boat rocked suddenly, and there was another shrieking fanfare. He heard the clank of armour, and lay quite still, aware that if Ba'alekkt realized he was awake, he would be beaten back into unconsciousness.

'Excellent,' said the familiar voice, very close. 'He looks pretty harmless now, doesn't he? And I shall be relying on you to keep him like that, old man.'

'As indeed I intend to, Imperial Majesty.'

So Al'Kalyek was aboard too. That was a pity, but it couldn't be helped. He considered trying to use thoughtlink to contact the other sorcerer, but rejected it. After all, it was remotely possible that the old man had in fact betrayed him. And even if he had not, it was vital that he remained unaware that Bron was awake.

He listened intently to the sounds around him. The subtle metallic noises as Ba'alekkt, in full armour, seated himself under the awning. The sharp movement as the barge was pushed away from the quayside. The grating of wood against iron as the twenty rowers laboured at their oars, and the water lapping against the boat's gilded hull.

He waited, concentrating his mind and his power, pushing back the feverish mists for one last effort. He could do it, he knew he could. It would not require much strength. Such a little thing to do, to end everything.

He did not want to die, but he knew that death lay within him now, from the damage done by Ba'alekkt's brutality. A deep, bitter shaft of regret pierced him, for what might have been, for all the lands unseen, the seas unsailed, the powers unexplored, and above all for the future with Mallaso that he had promised her, and which he would never live to enjoy.

I love you. He uttered the words in his heart, though he had never spoken them to her aloud. *Think of me, when you cherish our child.*

The barge must be in the middle of the river by now. He heard the brisk beat of swift water against the side of the boat, and the cheering was growing more distant. *Now,* he said to himself. *NOW!*

The craft rocked gently. One of the rowers said something. Bron braced himself for the last, desperate effort of his sick, exhausted mind.

What are you doing?

It was Al'Kalyek's voice in his head. And with the explosion of anger at the unwelcome, uninvited invasion, came the strength he needed.

Power surged within him. Without any warning, sorcery heaved under the barge. It tipped right over, hurling everyone on board it into the cold, deep torrent of the Kefirinn.

The rowers, clad in their brief tunics, could swim. So could Ba'alekkt, but not when he was encased in full, heavy armour. Al'Kalyek, struggling in the current, saw the Emperor's open mouth, gulping his last lungful of air, before the weight of the steel pulled him down beneath the surface of the water. His hands clutched wildly above the waves, and then he was gone.

Somehow, the old man reached the shore. He was an Archipelagian, after all, and every islander could swim, however hampered by extravagant garments of embroidered silk.

He was on the Minassan bank. Gasping, he crawled up through the mud, and turned to look back at the river.

There was no sign of the barge. The water was dotted with the heads of the twenty rowers, making for the quayside of Tamat.

And the ninety-ninth Emperor of Toktel'yi, and the man who had been his enemy, his prisoner and at last his assassin, had vanished for ever, sunk together into the Kefirinn's deadly embrace.

Al'Kalyek sent his mind beneath the waters, in search of that strange, powerful, mischievous intelligence.

There was nothing. No spark, no trace, no life.

The old man stayed for a long time on the bank of the river, his head bowed. He had had so many questions, so few answers. And the waste of such potential, such a spirit, came close to breaking his heart.

Someone called. He looked up, and saw a small boat of four oars, with a man in the bow, hailing him.

The Emperor is dead, Al'Kalyek thought, as if he had only realized it now. *Ba'alekkt is dead, and we can all go home to Toktel'yi. Minassa and Zithirian are safe.*

But he would do one last thing for Bron, as he had promised him. He would tell his father what he had done: and that Ansaryon, and his family, and all the peoples of the north, owed their lives, their homes and their freedom to his courage and his power.

Because of him, the world had changed.

Al'Kalyek clambered slowly and sadly to his feet. There were tears in his eyes, that he had not shed for many years, and his heart was full of pain, and grief, and terrible regret.

But there was also hope now, both for his own future and for Zithirian and Minassa.

Ignoring the boatman's shouts, he turned away from the river and the Empire, and set his face towards the Silver City.